MW01131369

NO TRICK OR TREATS

A NOVEL

HELENA C. FARRELL

authorHOUSE®

AuthorHouse™
1663 Liberty Drive
Bloomington, IN 47403
www.authorhouse.com
Phone: 833-262-8899

© 2020 Helena C. Farrell. All rights reserved.

No part of this book may be reproduced, stored in a retrieval system, or
transmitted by any means without the written permission of the author.

Published by AuthorHouse 10/16/2020

ISBN: 978-1-6655-0442-3 (sc)
ISBN: 978-1-6655-0445-4 (e)

Print information available on the last page.

Any people depicted in stock imagery provided by Getty Images are models,
and such images are being used for illustrative purposes only.
Certain stock imagery © Getty Images.

This book is printed on acid-free paper.

Because of the dynamic nature of the Internet, any web addresses or links contained in
this book may have changed since publication and may no longer be valid. The views
expressed in this work are solely those of the author and do not necessarily reflect the
views of the publisher, and the publisher hereby disclaims any responsibility for them.

This book is dedicated to
My Three Sons
Christopher Gerard, Michael Joseph, and Joseph Anthony Lota

Women are the books, the arts and the academies
that show, contain and nourish all the world.
~Shakespeare

PROLOGUE

Past, present, anywhere, in a state of heightened anxiety, it is a phenomenon mechanism to shut people, places, and memory permanently out. Experts claim, when a victim endures unspeakable memories and avoids unbearable truths, they disengage. They lose track of space, time, and even the continuum of their identity. They transform into someone else with minimal awareness of their surroundings. In order to endure her suppressed secret, Elena must take a circuitous path by burying her secret. Fleeting reality is her only safety hatch.

Elena's story is a voiceless cry that comes from an anguished heart. Her feelings of unworthiness acutely permeate her and cloud her perception of life and reality. It is unrealistic to believe that people can escape from their physical lives, but those who do not have the tools, support, or maturity to face their agonizing reality, escapism and avoidance become their only option. A distorted reality becomes real to them.

To circumvent and to locate a safe space and veracity is Elena's choice. She is incapable of knowing the true basis of her pain and fear; henceforth, she removes herself from the unsolvable situation. She is suffering.

When fear and agonizing thoughts engulf Elena, in order to cope, she experiences a loss of identity. She has no other options but to create multiple realities in different places, periods, and time—this is how she compensates. Elena's fantasies or realities become substitutes for the repulsive truths.

This is Elena Policino's unique story, her transmigration journey. Elena represents all those who hide from and repress their childhood terrors long into adulthood. This shadowy and complicated but empowering story about a young girl/woman who denies her devastating and painful childhood in unfathomable ways is challenging and captivating. Elena takes the punishment herself for the inadequacies of those who should have protected her. Consequently, her adult life is clouded by the past.

Elena copes and deals with her pain and guilt in extraordinary and surreal methods since she fears the truth will hurt and devastate all those around her, especially the ones she loves so dearly. As a young girl, the only way she copes is to hide from it. Eventually, as she gets older, she acknowledges, understands, and recognizes that she can no longer run away from the truth and protect the perpetrator(s). It is a chilling portrayal of the manner in which evil acts create mayhem, distortion, and destruction on unsuspecting innocent young people who eventually grow into dysfunctional adults through no fault of their own. Elena goes on to make survival a grace rather than a grim necessity. *All grand accomplishments and achievements commence in the soul of the imagination* ~ Anonymous.

CHAPTER ONE

Remembrance of Things Past - Marcel Proust
New England, USA
2005

IN A QUAINT New England town on a 120-acre pre-revolutionary estate, at a bucolic gentleman farm, a woman in her mid-sixties is sitting at an antique desk pounding away on her laptop. A black leather-bound photo album, a brownish-red worn diary, and an old history book are stacked next to the laptop. Standing solitary across the other side of the room is a black-ebony baby grand piano. Across the long wide room, a huge, grey stone hearth's fire is casting a shadowy, soft hue across the highly polished hardwood floor. Hanging grandly over the fireplace are two large wooden, black-enamel carved initials of an "A" and a "S." Slightly to the right is a small print of a colorful Braque cubist painting.

The once roaring embers in the fire are slowly reducing to smoldering ashes making the room frighteningly frigid. The preoccupied woman is unaware of the cold. She is intently absorbed in her work. As she is pounding away, a disquieting memory jars and stirs her emotions making her chilled. She is experiencing an unbearable remembrance causing a foreboding panic. Immediately she stops working and closes the laptop. The tense woman pushes away from her chair, rises from the cluttered desk, and slowly walks over to the low-burning, massive stone fireplace. To keep the chill temporarily at bay, and to distract her, she adds more logs to the dying embers.

Outside the earsplitting sound of a grinding, groaning motor backfiring from a dairy truck straining up the steep road unsettles her further. The startled woman quickly turns away from the hearth and saunters over to the panoramic glass window which overlooks a huge, gold-greenish pond.

After all the years, the captivating landscape is still breathtaking to her. An easel with an unfinished watercolor of a replica of the view outside the window stands next to where the woman peers out. *She is in deep thought.*

The waning autumn sun streams through the misty-glass window which creates a rainbow of soft colors. The woman reflectively stares out at the immense, soon to be totally barren trees making them appear skeleton like, eerie and grotesque. Mesmerized she continues to peer out the window as the huge dairy truck makes its laborious trip up the steep hill. Her rich brown eyes lift upward following the bellowing clouds dotting the cerulean blue skies as they leisurely drift along the muted October sky. The shortened fall days cast a somber mood over the entrancing setting. The woman becomes extremely reflective. *The remembrance of things past become overwhelmingly daunting. The long shadows of the past haunt this philosophical woman.*

It is October 31, 2005. The considerable acreage on this gentleman-farm estate is covered with frosted- multicolored fallen leaves. They have infiltrated the soon-to-be frozen pond. As this creative woman views the landscape, she whispers to herself as she turns to look at the painting over the mantle, "It resembles my favorite cubist painting by Braque." Turning she again gazes out at the glistening large fishpond. The woman reflects on years long gone when she frequently looked out this window observing her three active sons playing ice hockey on bitter cold winter days. She blissfully recalls leisurely weekends when she and her husband dressed like *Nanook of the North*, holding their woolen-gloved hands tightly as they skate over their ice-covered pond. Their long, hand-knitted wool scarves whip and flow gracefully behind them. She and her husband rhythmically glide around the solid ice evoking scenes from her much beloved ballet, *Swan Lake*. Their conjoined laughter is evidence of their mutual joy as they absorbed the intoxicating splendors surrounding them. Their frozen taunt yet smiling faces are flushed from the brisk air striking them.

This also brings to mind other bitter cold nights under the New England brilliant, star-studded canopy sky as they vigorously hiked through the snow-covered property. While maintaining her gaze at the night sky, this reflective woman becomes enthralled by the sheer beauty of the unencumbered celestial heavens. The dazzling stars' brilliance gleam out over the mirror-image pond making the long hours of darkness even more breathtakingly surreal. A broad smile spreads across her aging face as she fondly recalls those blissful days of past.

New England seasons each have their own unique charm for her. When winter passes, the vibrant colored crocuses peek out of the earth announcing spring's welcoming arrival soon followed by the daffodils and tulips. She still loves to smell the lush wild lavender lilac bushes which bloom abundantly around their home filling the air with their rich, poignant fragrance. The active pond is always crammed with eggs waiting for early summer to transform them into squiggly tadpoles; eventually into full-grown, croaking, high jumping frogs. The terrain is surrounded by melodious sounds from chirping crickets and the noisy-ceaseless chirring cicadas. Her sons were fascinated by the fleeting dragonflies that flew over the pond. Like Huck Finn and Tom Sawyer, the green-water amphibians kept her inquisitive sons occupied as they enthusiastically tried to catch them only to release them soon after. She smiles as she fondly recalls how her silly sons coined them Jeremiah Bull Frogs. Much to Elena's repulsion, her devilish boys relished finding camouflaged garter snakes under rocks. *She laughs out loud as she thinks of this.* They got a huge kick out of tricking their mother by asking her to guess what was hidden behind their backs in their soiled, muddy hands. They rolled over in laughter hearing her scream watching her jump and run away when they dropped the harmless, squirming snake at her feet.

The entire family relished and was amused with fishing and swimming in the pond. Picking wild blueberries that grew lavishly on their lush property was a summertime given. The motherly woman made huge stacks of fluffy blueberry pancakes which the family lavishly smothered with gooey, sweet tasting maple syrup and fresh turned butter given to them by the dairy farmer up the road. Like starving lumberjacks, her sons and husband gobbled them up in a few mouthfuls. There was also steaming plates of thick, tasty bacon another favorite product from the neighborly farmer and his domestic wife.

One summer the husband surprised the family with a new toy. He purchased a sixteen-foot, bright yellow motorboat. The boys and their dad loved water skiing in the numerous silver-crystal clear lakes in New Hampshire. Not one to be left out, the determined wife/mother eventually got the nerve to try water skiing. Surprisingly she did exceptionally well. She not only amazed her husband but herself. This devoted wife and caring mother never dreamed as a child of flying across the shimmering waters with water-skis on holding tightly onto the line while her husband and sons hooted and hollered from the yellow "Our Chiquita Banana Boat," her husband and sons jokingly named it.

Along with her adventurous husband and sons, the young woman also learned to ride horses from Sue Buffton, the young local equestrian and horse breeder from town. Sue raised and trained Morgan and Arabian horses. Eventually Sue became one of her closest friends. Sue's husband Tom was the town's well-respected veterinarian and his father was the town pharmacist and councilman. Sue taught this hesitant equestrian to ride at her farm on a stately Cordova brown Morgan horse. Thanks to determined and talented Sue, after months of intense riding lessons, she finally put away her fears and learned to feel relaxed and confident on the horse. Noticing her passion for riding, her husband surprised his wife by purchasing a passive, gelding horse. Eventually the entire family learned to ride. They enjoyed cantering and galloping around the huge property. Her industrial husband and handy sons built a corral near one of their barns. Her fearless sons rode like Butch Cassidy and the Sundance Kid in the wild west. Her cautious husband rode gentlemanly like mild-mannered Gene Autry. The woman rode English style, like prim and proper Queen Elizabeth. Their placid gelding handled them all like a true champion.

In time the woman's earlier life in New Hampshire was pleasurably filled with stimulating work at the local college; multiple interesting hobbies; skiing, painting, playing the piano, writing, and horseback riding. She happily participated in all the activities of a New England lifestyle. *Receiving contentment and joy.* Her first love was tending to her endearing immediate family. During this active, earlier period in New Hampshire, making new friends and varied interests left little room for her to ponder on disturbing remembrances *of things past.*

The past thirty years Elena has been living in Walpole, New Hampshire. A quaint, serene New England village nestled among the picturesque Green Mountains of New Hampshire and Vermont. This multi-faceted woman was not an original native New Englander. Elena, her husband, and their three young sons moved there after she was offered a teaching position at Keene State College in New Hampshire as a creative writing instructor. Writing was her passion, along with painting, playing the piano, and listening to old Broadway musical albums. Her husband was in the construction industry. Years earlier he believed it would be wise to move to the New England area. The down-hill ski industry was booming in the early 70s making the construction industry extremely lucrative in that region. This forward thinking, industrious man recognized that there was plenty of money to be made building ski chalets, vacation condominiums, and second-homes for the "Flatlanders," coined by native New Englanders who were threatened by *unknowns* or *unwanted* invaders from the East. These New Englanders, with a long lineage of family in the area, were not pleased with these strangers, who boldly infiltrated their area, changing the once pastoral landscape. While not happy with this *invasion*, reluctant native New Englanders eventually came to the difficult conclusion that economically the floundering region would financially benefit.

The entire family quickly grew to love all the varied seasons in New England. In the winter, Elena's husband and sons appreciated the cold weather. They entertained themselves with down-hill skiing, ice skating and ice hockey. During the warm New England springs and lazy hot summers, they enjoyed horseback riding, water skiing, fishing, and her husband's new passion, golf. The males in the family adjusted quickly to their new environment. Elena loved her teaching position at the nearby college and for recreation painting the beautiful landscape. At nights she would play the piano or listen to her record albums. *Music comforted her!*

The neighbors were cautiously friendly which is exactly what Elena wanted. Her new friend, Sue Buffton, invited Elena to join the local library board and book club. This afforded her the opportunity to meet other women in the area and to learn the history of her new town. This devoted wife, mother, teacher, and neighbor viewed New England as a place to find solace. *A sanctuary of serenity.*

Elena and her husband were both from the East; yet, for some unbeknownst reason, Elena always felt a strong connection there. She believed she belonged in New England. When the family finally agreed to make the move, it was not as easy as they anticipated. Finding the perfect house near the college where Elena would be teaching and close to good schools for their sons was not as simple as they anticipated. Elena could not locate a house that appealed to her even after in-depth research and canvassing the area for months. Summer was fast approaching and the fall semester not far behind. *Time was of the essence.*

Elena and her husband knew they had to settle soon. Fearing she would never find the "perfect home," Elena was blind-sighted when one afternoon while making a last attempt to find a place to live, she saw this run-down, boarded-up, yet charming gentleman-farm house looming high on a secluded hill. It had a massive pond, charming old barns, lush abundant foliage, acres of apple orchards, and syrup-bearing maple trees. Immediately she inquired about it, but the real estate agent vehemently informed her: "It is not for sale!" The female agent explained that Maple Ridge Farm, situated grandly on Watkins Hill Road, has been unoccupied and boarded up for years. For centuries it was originally owned by a well-known and highly respected New England family who migrated from Australia. They were originally sheep farmers from down under and rumor circulated they might have had a hand in bootlegging.

Much to Elena's dismay the realtors explained, after the majority of the family either died or left the area, Mrs. Eleanor Margaret O'Brien-Stevens, the family matriarch and owner who resided in this huge estate was left alone to fend for herself. After many years of neglect, the house, barns, stables, and surrounding property, along with this stubborn, elderly, hermit-like woman, all slowly deteriorated. Charitable church women stopped by weekly to check up on this obstinate, aging 'force-to-be-reckoned with' woman. They faithfully brought her food, necessary provisions and medical assistance as needed. This was the extent of Mrs. O'Brien-Stevens care. In fact, this fiercely independent woman vehemently resented their "interference and charity" and boldly let them know it.

Years later, at the ripe-old- age of 101, she succumbed in the decaying Maple Ridge estate. Gossip and rumors floated around that before Mrs. O'Brien-Stevens died, long-lost relatives, claiming to be the rightful owners of the estate, threatened to have her removed and placed in an asylum. Desperate to take over the estate, the questionable heirs resorted to costly legal representation to no avail. In retaliation, the fearless and fuming Mrs. O'Brien-Stevens warned them that if they did, she ranted, "My angry ghost would come back and haunt you and this house."

After Mrs. O'Brien-Stevens passing, the so-called heirs continued to fight over who were the rightful owners of the 120- acre property and the surrounding structures. The monumental legal costs, along with their hatred for one another, hindered all hope for ever peacefully settling their differences. Over the years, after Mrs. O'Brien-Stevens passing, this further caused Maple Ridge Farm to fall into greater disrepair and dilapidation. The estate was left ruinous and inhabitable. The vacant house was boarded-up indefinitely. The town council even considered tearing it down. The property was covered over with wild-spreading bushes, jungle like grasses as high as towers, and unproductive fruit trees. The house and property were left grossly and ghoulishly unattended. No one ventured to go near it or dared to salvage it. Speculation spread it was from fear of Mrs. O'Brien-Stevens evil warning.

Imaginative young children in the area called it the "haunted house on the hill where a ghastly wicked old witch roamed around haunting anyone who dared to go near it." Ironically, mature, intelligent adults also began to believe this and whispered frequently about "the house on the hill being obsessed by the ghastly ghost of the evil Mrs. O'Brien-Stevens." The legend was: "Before Mrs. O'Brien-Stevens died she swore that she would never let anyone live in the house she put a monstrous, deadly curse on it."

The presumed heirs eventually lost interest due to the exhausting legal burden of fighting over it; the prohibitive financial expense to repair the house and maintain the property; and the well-known *curse* that it was haunted by the witchery of Mrs. O'Brien-Stevens. Warned by Walpole officials that the property would be sold at auction and the proceeds would go to the town, they agreed to put aside their grievances and collectively sell the entire estate, most of the acreage, and equitably divide the money between them when it sold. *If it would sell!*

Unaware of the notorious "Ghost of O'Brien-Stevens Maple Ridge curse," Elena wanted this house desperately! She boldly, locals called her *brave/crazy*, insisted the real-estate agent immediately get in contact with whomever she needed to and make a generous offer. Elena vehemently ordered the agent, "Make sure it is one which will not be refused!" Her skeptical husband was not at all in agreement. Being a professional and seasoned contractor, he knew the house was too big, too old, and from the appearance of the exterior, it would need extensive, if not, unattainable repair. Her apprehensive husband predicted, the damage to the interior from being abandoned for so many years would make it unachievable to make it livable. This frustrated husband/contractor tried to convince his *stubborn, obstinate* wife that the house would *never be habitable.* She pleaded with him and assured him that he could do it. He immediately responded, "Elena, I am not Houdini!" He tried another tactic by alerting her that the isolated property was too far up a torturous hill and miles away from the center of town dangerously alienating them from others. Elena shot back, "I don't care. I want that house!" Slamming his foot down hard he shouts back, "The house should be torn down!"

Loving his wife dearly and seeing the genuine tears rolling down his wife's distraught face and her body shaking uncontrollable he tries to console her by recommending, "Elena, we can tear down this dilapidated chaos of a house and build a contemporary, safe home." Elena adamantly refused. She wanted the existing house to remain. This determined woman's winning manner and firm resolve gave her an advantage during this heated negotiation. This strong-willed woman finally broke her husband's resolve. He promised her that he would consider it; even though he knew it would be the biggest challenge of his professional career. He also feared it would financially ruin them. Even though their family life was structurally strong and intact, he feared this "haunted house" with its weakened, aged foundation and questionable history might shake up their secure and happy life.

Elena's strength of mind, and confidence in her husband, along with an insatiable need to be in that particular home, in that particular town, gave her the force and motivation not to cave into her husband's professional warnings and personal fears. This proud wife had no doubt that her talented husband could fix it; make it comfortably livable; and financially feasible quickly. *This was meant to be her home.*

A week or so later, the real estate agent called and said the owners would be willing to sell the house. After endless discussions and carefully examining their finances, Elena's reluctant but malleable husband finally agreed. This fiercely determined woman never doubted that Maple Ridge Farm would be her future home—*she felt a special kinship to it.* While Elena was thrilled to own this inimitable house, she was also terrified. Her talented and caring husband did not disappoint his spirited wife. *He made it happen!*

Elena and her husband's childhood were far removed from the serene environment of the picturesque snow-covered Vermont and New Hampshire landscape. The immense countryside is surrounded by magnificent mountain ranges. The estate was like paradise abundantly covered with acres of apple orchards, lush wild blueberry bushes, prickly pear trees, and mammoth maple trees. The spacious terrain was heavily dotted with grazing, lazy dairy cows, bleating white and black sheep, and roaming horses. The immense property regally overlooked the meandering Connecticut River. Centuries old, life-sustaining family run dairy farms, handed down from father to son to grandson, have been an intricate part of the unique setting for hundreds of years.

The entire region is populated with passionate patriotic Americans who identify their family linage as far back as the landing of the infamous Mayflower, the religious- zealot Puritans, and hardworking, original New Englanders. Fathers and brothers fought in the Revolutionary War and the Civil War. Even though Elena was passionate about living there, it took her a while to acclimate herself both physically and socially. When the family first settled in at Maple Ridge Farm, the old-stock, local folks and townspeople were not as welcoming as Elena had anticipated. Despite this, it eventually became *a safe haven for her and a joy for her husband and three sons.*

Elena absolutely loved teaching creating writing to enthusiastic students at the nearby college. More so, she adored watching her sons grow into fine young men and thrive in this healthy-natural environment. Their sons were ten, seven, and four years-old when they settled there. The boys adjusted quickly. Their two oldest sons, Christian Gerard and Nicholas Michael immediately became active in downhill snow skiing and ice hockey. They acclimated well at their new school and made friends easily. Four-year old Anthony Joseph couldn't always be with his older brothers, yet he was pleasantly occupied with the family cat and dog and the sweet elderly farm wife up the hill Mrs. Betsy Johnson. She sat for the little guy while his parents were at work. Anthony Joseph loved to bake with her and hear Betsy tell colorful stories about the area. This cute, brown-eyed, black curly haired four-year old was thrilled when Mrs. Johnson took him into her barn to see the dairy cows being milked by machine at the family farm.

In March and April Betsy's husband, farmer Ebenezer, took Anthony and his older brothers into the rickety, old wooden, sweltering Maple Shed where the sap from the surrounding sugar maple trees were poured into ancient vats and boiled down to sweet, sticky, maple syrup. Christian, Nicholas, and Anthony Joseph were amazed to learn that it takes 40 gallons of sap to make each gallon of maple syrup and that the season last 6-8 weeks.

It was one of Elena's sons' favorite events; Maple syrup producing time. The ground was covered with snow in the area through late spring; perfect for syrup flowing from the Maple trees and for the time-honored production of pure maple syrup. Her boys lavishly poured the hot maple syrup on the frosty, pure white snow licking it to their hearts content with Ebenezer looking on proudly. Their tongues were frozen but sweet and their stomachs satisfied. Pro bono, Elena and her husband gave permission to Ebenezer Johnson to allow his dairy cows to graze freely on Maple Ridge's vast property. In appreciation, every year, the grateful dairy farmer and neighbor gave them free maple syrup, along with sweet churned butter, rich heavy cream, and thick cured bacon from his fatted pigs.

Elena and her husband also insisted that Mr. and Mrs. Johnson pick as many bushels of apples from their prolific apple trees. Ebenezer made plentiful delicious apple cider and proudly shared it with Elena and her family. Some of this fine cider became *hard cider* for the thirsty men folks. Ebenezer's resourceful wife Betsy baked fantastic apple pies bursting full of steaming hot apples in a rich buttery flaky crust. The poignant fragrance would travel all the way down to Elena's house. Elena, her husband, and sons waited patiently for Betsy to bring one of her pies hot from her large cast-iron oven to their house. Neighbors sharing with one another is part of New England history. *Bartering was a long tradition in New England and for the diminishing old-timers it was a way of life.*

Mr. and Mrs. Ebenezer Johnson's family have a long history in the area. They lived and worked on Watkins Hill for centuries. Betsy and Ebenezer hoped their only child Daniel would stay in the area and take over the dairy farm when they retired or grew too old to take care of the farm alone. Unfortunate for the Johnsons, when the bright and ambitious Daniel graduated from Dartmouth College, he decided to pursue a career in medicine. While the Johnsons were immensely proud of their "doctor" son, they feared the long history of the Johnson dairy farmers on Watkins Hill would end. Having Elena's family and their sons as neighbors filled the gap after their son Daniel permanently moved to Boston. He established a private medical practice there leaving the Johnsons alone on the dairy farm on Watkins Hill.

Many of the locals called Ebenezer *Scrooge*; if you treated this old-timer right, he would be your loyal and best friend forever. When Ebenezer was convinced that these "flatlanders" were *okay folks*, he confidently introduced Elena's husband to important and influential people in the locale. With Mr. Johnson endorsement, along with Elena's husband's fine character and worthy professional ability, it enhanced and sealed his status in Walpole's close-knit community. Significantly assisting him to ultimately establish a lucrative business in the region. *In a short time, the family settled in nicely.*

While still peering at the pond through the misty-glass window, a haunting trail of recollections flooded the now mature Elena, drowning her in deep thought. Lately, this older, sensitive woman would not only frequently reminiscent about her early years in Walpole but more so, her earlier childhood elsewhere. After recently retiring from her much-adored teaching position, and her husband's decision to give up the construction business since the building boom was fast declining in New England, they decided it was time for them to retire with reservations. To counteract them, Elena and her husband enthusiastically planned on filling their later years indulging in activities they didn't have time to do before. Unfortunately, retirement didn't work out as easily and pleasantly as Elena had hoped for. She had an extremely difficult time! With her sons growing up and moving away, along with retirement, all of this was overwhelmingly challenging for this once very active woman. *She fell into a deep depression.*

Retirement and the "Empty-nest Syndrome" left this formerly preoccupied wife, mother, and professional woman with too much time to reflect. She became despondent. To distract herself, she painted, played the piano, and read extensively for her personal pleasure. She attended the book club at the local library with her best friend Sue Buffton. Unfortunately, even Elena's favorite interests and spending more time with her husband did not fill up the gnawing void inside her. *She was unmoored.*

Elena became exceedingly anxious and remorseful, causing her to sink into a debilitating mental and physical decline. This distressed woman could not sleep, eat properly, or find any serenity. Noticing his wife's rapid decline, concerned, her husband insists she seek professional help. After much coaxing from the *love-of-her-life*, she acquiesced. They located a well-respected psychologist in the area. Elena reluctantly went. After numerous in-depth sessions, and painfully peeling away at the core of her complex problems with the professional, this astute woman realized that only she could resolve her deep-rooted, debilitating issues. In the autumn of her life, Elena decided it was time to come out of the shadows of her past and put to rest the burdening truth. *Writing will be her lifeline and healing catharsis.*

Halloween 2005. As custom dictates, children were preparing to go Trick-or-Treating. In the past, Halloween was an ambiguous time in New England. The appalling historical 17th Century Salem Witch-hunts and ghoulish trials have since been commercialized but the horrific history left an everlasting blemish on Puritan New England's glorious past. Elena, her husband, and their three sons, believed the ghosts- of- the- past were still floating around in their pre-revolutionary house. Intuitively Elena knew it was filled with haunting folklore history and complex memories. Her daring sons capitalized on it thinking it amusing. Those very same spirits or ghosts were profoundly imbedded in Elena's psyche. She believes they are her possessed kindred souls. Life was fleeting she feared. *It was Time for her to address life's past ills.*

❧

Still peering out the window and deeply distracted, Elena's fun-loving husband, holding something in his hand, quietly enters the room where his wife is. With her back to him, he sneaks up behind her and playfully screams out, "Boo!" Startled, Elena quickly turns and impulsively pushes him away. "Oh, it's you!" Composing herself she teases, "It might be Halloween, but you can't scare me." Her adoring husband is carrying a delightfully carved jack-o'-lantern. He places it on the table near the window next to where author Arthur Miller's classic, *The Crucibles* rests next to a printout of a copy of Edgar Allen Poe's poem, *The Black Cat.*

Noticing the precision carved pumpkin, Elena comments, "So that's what you've been doing?" She looks at it lovingly and longingly and praises, "It's lovely." Sighing she mournfully comments, "Wish the boys were here to see it." Her husband states, "If our sons were here this whimsical pumpkin would be gory and scary looking and smashed on some one's head." Laughing, he reminds her, "Remember the ghoulish horror Chris and Nick made one year?" Elena smiles. "It scared their poor little brother Anthony Joseph half to death," her husband adds. Immediately, Elena calls out, "Yes, I remember that vividly."

Hobbling over to her desk, from the bottom drawer, Elena takes out a small wax candle. Walking over to the carved, orange pumpkin she places the candle inside its hollowed interior. She lights it with a large wooden match she retrieves from the fireplace safely placed away from the slow-burning fire. "There, the jack-o'-lantern is lit!" gleefully Elena hollers. She pauses to reflect. "Halloween will never be the same without the boys," she murmurs. Her salt and peppered hair, aging husband gazes at the lighted pumpkin, glances over at his wife's grim face reminding her,

13

"Sweetheart, our sons are all grown; with their own families and doing just fine." Gently reminding his wife, attempting to comfort her he offers, "It's their turn now to carve and light jack-o'-lanterns for their children." With stiff-arthritic knees, Elena struggles over to her husband. She kisses him on the prickly beard growing on his sharp-protruding chin. Pointing at the glowing pumpkin he proudly calls out, "This one's for you dear!"

Elena's devoted husband places his arms around his wife's thickening waist reassuring her, "No Hocus Pocus." Kissing her wrinkling forehead, he whispers, "No more tricks for you, my love. All treats!" With the back of her blue- veined protruding hand, Elena brushes away a tear trickling down her cheek. To avoid becoming melancholy she goes to a cabinet in the nearby dining area. Taking out an amble size bag of miniature chocolate candy bars. Ripping open the cellophane package, Elena empties the entire contents into a large, round, blue chipped ceramic bowl. Alerting her husband, "Honey, the neighborhood children, along with their parents will be coming for Trick or Treats shortly." Elena places the abundantly filled bowl of candy near the front door asking her husband, "Honey, please put the lighted pumpkin in the front window for the children to see."

Smiling while wagging her finger at him, Elena cautions, "Don't eat the candy; remember your diabetes." Teasingly she adds, "You don't want to get pimples." Her husband reassures her that he will not as he sneaks a handful of candy. In jest she tries to grab them from him but to no avail. "Sweetheart, I love sweets; that why you call me "Honey" all these years," he jokes. Knowing it's useless with his insatiable sweet tooth and his charming wit, Elena moves away with a sneaky smile on her face. He further teases her, "Hey, we should dress up and wear our old costumes. Me as Dracula and you in that spooky witch costume. You look sexy in that black satin long cape and that pointed large hat." He runs up to her screaming, "I Vant To Suck your Blood." With a grimace look, Elena pushes her husband away ordering, "Go! Out of here!"

Elena's husband senses his wife is getting testy. He jokes, "Obviously you don't appreciate my humor." She turns and gives him a smirk. "Okay, Sweetheart, I'm going to the barn to check on the horse. I'll leave you be." He stops, throws her a kiss. Informing, "I'll take Atlas with me; he's getting antsy too." Atlas II is their eight-year-old, black Lab. The canine is pacing back and forth near the side door in the kitchen anxious to go out. Still holding onto the candy he sneaked, Elena's childish husband hides the candy in the pocket of his black, puffy winter jacket. Elena hears him whistling loudly. He stops and calls out, "Come on boy; come on Atlas!" He opens the side-kitchen door and walks toward the barn. Faithful Atlas enthusiastically bolts out behind his beloved master.

The kitchen door closes. Elena hears the crunching sounds of her husband walking toward the barn on the dried leaves and Atlas barking at the squirrels; she then returns to the den. The fire is slowly burning. Shaped like a comma, their twelve-year old black cat, Raven, is curled up near the fire, purring. Elena bends over to pat him. Raven raises his furry head as she peers into his deep black glowing eyes. Aloof, the cat stretches his back, then saunters away. "Okay, you spooky soul, I'll leave you alone," she assures Raven.

Near the fireplace, resting on the oval brass table gifted to her by her cousin Blaise from Guam where he was stationed years ago, Elena notices the 20th Century French novelist, Marcel Proust's book, *Remembrances of Things Past*. She recently reread it. Sue Buffton gave it to her the first year she moved to Walpole. Picking up the Proust's book, Elena turns to the page where a bookmark is placed. She reads the quote, *There is no man however wise, who has not at some period in his youth said things, or lived a life, the memory of which is so unpleasant to him that he would gladly expunge it.* Deeply moved, she closes the book and places it back on the table. Limping over to her desk where an old photo album, leather-bound diary and huge history book about the Civil War are stacked near her Mac laptop Elena opens the photo album. She stares at a few of the photos, closes it, and flips through the diary for a while. Atlas's loud barking stirs Elena's out of her deep thought.

Hearing giggles and laughter outside, Elena turns, looks out the window. In creative Halloween costumes excited children are chattering loudly while laboriously climbing up the steep inclined Watkins hill. They are carrying large bags or pillowcases hoping to fill them with lots of sweet treats. Following close by are their watchful parents. "Where did the years go?" Elena moans. It brings back rich memories of she and her husband trick-or-treating with their three sons. Other profound memories haunt her. The distant past returns to spook her. Looking around Elena reflects, "I never dreamed when I was a child that I would ever be participating in this tradition of trick-or- treating; especially in this town and in this house." This reflective woman is now ready to use the *pen* as her sword by writing about and exposing the past and *unsuspecting others*. Assertively, Elena slips down on a chair at her desk; opens her laptop; and proceeds to type: *October 31 is the official day for . . .*

CHAPTER TWO

Samhain: Autumn Equinox and Winter Solstice
All Hallows' Eve
Jersey City, NJ
1955

OCTOBER 31, the official date for Halloween and "Trick-or-Treating." Young children, teenagers, and the young-at-heart happily participate and devotedly observe this special day. It is celebrated in cities and towns across the United States and various countries. Halloween is the extremely popular and fun-filled festival where hordes of gleeful children and good-sport, daring adults prowl the streets wearing spooky or decorative masks and costumes transforming themselves into their favorite heroes or worst-feared enemies: Superman or the scarier witches, gory vampires, and macabre ghoulish-gothic goblins. The infamous Dr. Frankenstein, who created the monster, along with the anti-hero Dracula, have inspired countless Halloween costumes. Scary ghosts and whimsical costumes of Mickey Mouse, Minnie Mouse, Cinderella, and Casper the Friendly Ghost were also favorites. Children dressed in various costumes excitedly ring doorbells and shout out, "Trick or Treat," hoping they will be given special treats such as candy, apples, and pennies. Tricks are never anticipated!

Homes are imaginatively transformed into haunted houses, spooky cemeteries, and\or eerie gothic Transylvania. To this day, the creative, entertaining element of carving gigantic pumpkins into jack-o' lanterns, apple bobbing, and whispering chilling, scary ghost stories are typical activities of this "ancient" yet continuing celebrated holiday.

The ancient Christians' fêted All Hallows' Eve, the day before the Christian feast All Saints Day, which followed after All Souls Day. To this day these religious and non-religious days are still celebrated, revered and honored. On Halloween, chilling creatures, ugly witches and questionable spirits penetrated deeply into the psyche of believers and unbelievers alike.

Natives of Mexico, along with the immigrant population from California, Texas, Arizona, New Mexico, and other parts of the United States, celebrate Día de los Muertos, Day of the Dead honoring their deceased loved ones. The sacred holiday is a blend of pre-Hispanic Indigenous beliefs and Spanish Catholic values. It is a joyous and memorable time filled with honored festivities. They celebrate in their highly decorated homes; churches; street parties; and in ancient family grave sites. Plentiful and varied ethnic food and drink, along with lush decorative flowers and multiple candles are all a part of this Celebration of the Dead. For the Spanish and Mexican population, it is a special and honorable day. A loving ritual, of respect and remembrance of passed loved ones.

Americans love Halloween! Although not all American cities and their citizens participate in Trick-or-Treating. In Jersey City, NJ, from the Depression years through the 50s and 60s, children and adults alike did not take part in the amusing festivities or spooky events of this unique fall holiday. Trick-or-Treating did not exist for them. "Begging for Thanksgiving" was their day to dress as hobos and go "begging" for food and pennies—not for fun but out of necessity. This commenced in the late 1920s during the Great Depression in the United States and continued through the 30s. Employment and food were scarce and people were desperately trying to survive. Sadly, many hopeless people resorted to the unthinkable, jumping out of buildings especially on Wall Street. Clearly there were no *treats* during this bleak period. The *trick* was to find food or earn money to sustain themselves and their families or just to stay alive. On street corners desperate women and men sold apples for mere pennies.

This odd custom of "Begging for Thanksgiving" continued even after the depression years ended and the inhabitants of Jersey City and the nation went back to work improving many lives. This custom of "begging" lasted through the 50s and into the 60s. During this time period, on Thanksgiving morning, children continued to roam the streets ringing doorbells demanding *banshee*. This is the uniqueness or, the unusualness of growing up in Jersey City, NJ after World War II and through the relaxed-hopeful Eisenhower 50s and into the restless and newly challenging 60s.

The 35th President of the United States, John Fitzgerald Kennedy's presidential years, 1961-1963, brought pride to the mostly exclusive democratic-working class inhabitants of Jersey City with their many Catholic parishes and faithful parishioners. Sadly, immediately after the shocking, heart-wrenching, fateful day, November 22, 1963, of the assassination of the young, handsome charismatic, first Irish Catholic US President, John Fitzgerald Kennedy, the hopeful climate changed drastically. American families were glued to their televisions watching JFK's grieving young widow, First Lady Jacqueline Bouvier Kennedy, and her two adorable young children, Caroline and John John live on national TV from coast to coast and around the world as she and her innocent children observed her famous husband and their father's dramatic and historical funeral. *It was devastating!*

After President Kennedy's shocking assassination which echoed President Abraham Lincoln's assassination on April 1865 at the end of the Civil War, the exuberant and optimistic atmosphere in the United States drastically changed to a mournful and anxious period. The turbulent 60s brought other dreadful assassinations. In 1968, Reverend Martin Luther King, Jr., an African American clergyman, human rights activist, humanitarian, and leader in the African American Civil Rights Movement along with United States Senator Robert Kennedy, the late John F. Kennedy's younger brother who was his Attorney General, were also shockingly assassinated.

On April 4, 1968, the thirty-nine-year-old Reverend Martin Luther King, Jr., a revered black man, was shot in Memphis, Tennessee by a crazed racist and died shortly after. A few months later, on June 5, 1968, in Los Angeles, California, after winning the California Democratic Presidential nomination, Robert Kennedy was also shot to death. Once again shocking the nation and stirring the dreadful memory of JFK's assassination. The turbulent 60s instigated dreadful racial riots, massive changes in the once innocent youth, and a malaise of grief while the Vietnam Conflict was slowly looming over the divided country.

Feminism, with shocking bra-burning by young and mature disgruntled women alike, was surfacing. The radical feminist activist Betty Friedan's transformative and ground-breaking 1962 book, *The Feminist Mystique*, was a bible for women who were feeling neglected and needed to be heard. The bold and outspoken New York Congresswoman, Bella Abzug, with her huge trademark hats was a major political icon for the women's movement. The charismatic and beautiful Gloria Steinem was a popular and admired feminist visionary. She was a role model for many young girls and women of all ages and backgrounds. These outspoken champions of women's rights gave a powerful voice to the once silent women and offered them a broad vision to fight for their dreams of equal rights.

Prolific illegal drugs and hippie "flower children" strung out on LSD and other dangerous recreational drugs were rampant during this transformative period. The free-for-all drug scene became notorious. The 1969 legendary Woodstock Festival, a hippie musical movement in NY, where not only drugs were widespread but unbridled sex was open and prolific and new-age music, incurred a huge fanatic following. Their motto was 'peace, love, drugs, and freedom for all.' These *scandalous* yet brave acts and movements were overflowing and extensive. They forced awareness to the American government that the current politic policies of the country must change now.

The American music scene was also altering. The arrival of the British Beatles in the States, Beatle mania, after they appeared on the popular television Ed Sullivan Show in February of 1964, shook up the country making hip-swinging 50s heartthrob, Elvis Presley, the King of Rock, who also had his first TV appearance on the Ed Sullivan Show, seem dated. The 40s and 50s crooners, Frank Sinatra, Tony Bennett, Dean Martin, Patty Paige, and Rosemary Clooney were being upstaged by these young free-spirited musical artists. To this day, crooner Bing Crosby, jazz trumpeter legend, Satchmo, Louis Armstrong, and sensational Frank Sinatra, these 40s and 50s icons are still beloved and popular, along with Elvis and The Beatles.

The tragic Vietnam Conflict created major division, disturbing upheavals, and fierce protests which caused unwarranted deaths in cities and on once peaceful academic campuses around the country dividing US citizens' loyalties–comparable to the American Civil War. The loss of lives was staggering and the young men and women who came home after serving their county bravely were ignored and left alone to deal with the horrors they endured. Up to this point, it was one of the most unpopular war this country has experienced and created great dissention. *The nation was deeply fractured!*

These restless and changing times infiltrated into American households, educational and religious institutions, and the political and military scene creating mistrust, fear, and disillusionment in the previous harmonious Post-World War II. Television's perfect, imaged families, *Ozzie and Harriet, I Love Lucy, and My Three Sons* were typical American -family shows. It was as if the country was abundantly filled with unthinkable tricks with little or no special treats. *Elena's youth lived through most of this.*

CHAPTER THREE

The Falling Leaves and Swaying Trees
Jersey City, NJ
1955

IT WAS A FLAWLESS, windy and extraordinarily blistering cold Halloween day in 1955. The few trees which lined the streets in Jersey City were fast and furiously losing their leaves. They twist and swirl down onto the ground. Elena Rose Policino, a 14-year old school girl, is dizzily spinning in between the large oak leaves as they fall onto the cracked, hard cement pavement. Her black and white scuffed saddle shoes scamper through the carpet of golden leaves making crackling amusing sounds. Elena loves hearing the rustling of the leaves as they crunch beneath her restless *dancing* feet. It is music to her ears - a soothing symphony. She is walking home from school with her classmate and close friend, Ginny Cimino, who lives up the street from Elena. Since the 3rd grade Elena and Ginny have been best friends. When they reach Ginny's two-story, two-family, white aluminum-sided house, they separate. Elena continues alone heading down the street toward her two-family, gunmetal-grey aluminum-sided house; 391 Armstrong Avenue.

Elena is what some might call today a "latch-key kid." This impressionable, artistic young teenager is blessed with thick, curly auburn, shoulder length hair, brown soul-filled eyes, of average height, and boarding on chubby. She usually finds comfort from food due to frustration. Lately she has lost her appetite. Elena is painfully shy, introverted, though, extremely imaginative and creative. Her mother, Tess Adeline, is a spirited, fiery-red head with piercing azure blue eyes. A full-figured woman similar to the 40s popular and glamorous Rita Haywood type. Tess has a sharp-biting tongue. She never minces her words. Tess Adeline is an independent woman, wife, mother, and a college graduate who has a secure position in the Jersey City school system. Elena's dad, Mike Nicholas Policino, is a solidly built, handsome man with slick black hair, dramatically parted down the middle. He has deep-set, jet black, sensual eyes—similar to the 20s silent film star Rudolph Valentino. Mike owns and runs a business in Jersey City which he inherited. Mike is politically active in his "beloved" Jersey City. Due to his connections in the city, Mike was instrumental in obtaining his wife a good position in the school system. His company greatly benefits from his political and other connections. Elena inherited something from both her parents—her father's sensitivity and dramatic looks and her mother's fierce desire for independence and fairness.

* * From Jersey City, New Jersey 1955 to Walpole, New Hampshire 1899 * *

Both Tess and Mike work full time. Elena, an only child, dreads going home to an empty house even though her sweet, caring Aunt Ettie lives downstairs. When life overwhelms Elena, she transports herself to a sprawling, beautiful pre-revolutionary, bluish-gray gentleman's farmhouse in New England in the 1800s. Elena knows it like the back of her hand and frequents it when need dictates. Easily, she navigates around the mammoth maple tree-lined rugged terrain. Lush, beautiful velvet-green fern spreads wildly over the entire periphery of the property. To Elena, they swing to and fro like a delicate oriental fan in a beautiful Geisha girl's graceful hand. This insightful teenager is always mesmerized by the melodious sounds of the trees as they sway in the New England breeze. She happily observes them as they twist and turn in the harsh winds.

It is autumn. Elena flitters through the kaleidoscope of brilliant hues of varied fallen leaves as they pile up on the ground covering the earth with vivid flushed colors. The magnificent rich golden russets and vibrant orange hues spread across a brilliant landscape -Mother Nature' s decorative patched-quilt. The striking beauty of New England's ambiance during the foliage season delights and comforts this emotionally fragile, extremely insightful, and curious teenage girl.

* * Back to 1955 Jersey City * *

A loud noise from a muffler backfiring instantly startles and jolts Elena back to Jersey City, 1955. It is from a gigantic garbage truck. The powerful machine strains as it tries to slow down. The burly bearded man in the truck shouts to this startled young girl, "What are you doing kid? Get home! Your dad will be angry with you." Slowly coming out of a daze, Elena gradually turns and stares at him. She is annoyed and agitated. She wants to stay at the New England farm where she feels safe but she is shocked back to Jersey City and 1955 by the mere command of this surly intruder. When she is back to reality, Elena gives the driver of the truck a snicker and reassures him, "Don't worry, Tony, I'm going right home." Tony is her father's loyal, trusted best worker. Authoritatively, but smiling, he praises her, "Good girl." Tony gears up the powerful engine. Before it picks up momentum, he jokingly blows the powerful horn which makes her jump. He laughs loudly and moves on. Elena knows Tony means business. She heads on home. *Elena is not happy.*

The New England farm, along with her best friend, Ginny Cimino, a tall, athletic, and congenial girl, make Elena feel safe and secure. The other kids don't tease her about being "chubby, gawky, and spacey" when she is with protective Ginny. *Similar to Tony, Ginny watches out for Elena.*

CHAPTER FOUR

Begging for Thanksgiving
Jersey City, New Jersey
1955

IN THE 50s most young people in Jersey City stayed home for Thanksgiving dinner. According to their ethnic and cultural background, some did not partake of the traditional American-bird turkey and fixings of the typical American Thanksgiving dinner. People from varied ethnical backgrounds have sauerbraten, lasagna, Virginia ham, eggplant, kielbasa, tamales, kepi, curry, or hash. Elena's family are proud Italian Americans. Her father Mike's older sister Ettie Policino Cortino and her husband of many years Carlo Cortino live downstairs from Elena. Most of the two-family houses on Armstrong Avenue look identical cookie-cutter style. Elena, her father, and most who have tasted her cooking, insist Ettie makes the best Italian food; especially homemade cheese ravioli. Elena and her father's favorite. Elena loves all her Aunt Ettie's cooking; comfort food.

On Thanksgiving Day, Elena's immediate family indulge in the American traditional turkey and usual fixings - succulent roast turkey, rich brown gravy, savory chestnut stuffing, fluffy sweet potato casserole, bold red cranberry sauce, yellow turnips, and mounds of luscious mashed potatoes. For desert homemade pumpkin pie with mounds of whipped cream and a special pie made from her maternal grandmother's secret recipe which was always ceremonially presented at the end.

Early Thanksgiving mornings, Elena's father Mike faithfully attends the time-honored, traditional high school football game with his best friend Ray Sinnotti between high school archrivals St. Peter's Prep, his

Jesuit preparatory-school alma mater, and the local public high school, Henry Snyder High where Elena and Ginny attend. After the high school football game is over, where St. Peter's always wins, Elena's Dad watches the pro football games on their 12-inch Philco Television set. The TV is located in a decorative mahogany cabinet which includes a radio and a 78-inch record player.

Typical of the 50s, the women do all the cooking, serving, cleaning, while catching up with the family gossip. After the television athletic games are over, and the feast is consumed, numerous and varied delicious desserts, including a cornucopia of fresh fruits, mixed nuts to be shelled, coffee or espresso, and a variety of cordials are served throughout the day into the wintery-dark evening. This National Day of "Giving Thanks" is the kickoff for the hustle and bustle, but joyful and holy Christmas and Hanukkah holiday season.

A week before Thanksgiving, walking home from school, Elena's best friend Ginny excitedly talks about going "begging" on Thanksgiving morning. Casually Elena comments, "I won't be able to go with you." "Why not?" Ginny blurts out. "We're not going to be in Jersey City for Thanksgiving," Elena nonchalantly responds. Surprised and disappointed Ginny questions, "Where are you going?" Before Ginny utters a word, Elena brags, "We're going to my grandmother's house in New Hampshire this year." Perplexed, Ginny disputes, "You're joking! You don't have a grandmother in New Hampshire." Pausing, Ginny questions, "I thought she lives in California?" Elena deliberately ignores her friend's comment. She interjects, "Anyway, we're getting too old to go begging anymore." To avoid further questions, Elena waves goodbye, heads toward home calling out, "See you tomorrow!"

A few neighborhood boys congregate near Ginny messing with her in a playful but annoying way. On the corner of Sterling Avenue and Armstrong Avenue, near Mr. E's Pharmacy/Candy Store, ignoring the teenage boys teasing her, Ginny baffled, watches her friend Elena walking down Armstrong Avenue. Recalling and disturbed by her conversation about not going "Begging for Thanksgiving," Ginny shakes her long, graceful neck back and forth. Not one to get upset for long, Elena's best friend hollers back to her, "Sure enough. See you tomorrow!" The boys annoyingly are cat whistling at Ginny. Infuriated, she raises her powerful fist at them warning, "Hey, Bowery Boys, see this fist? You want a mouth full." Getting her message, the cool, scary cats move along. *Ginny is not a girl to mess with.*

CHAPTER FIVE

Over the Mountain and Through the Woods
Thanksgiving Morning
Jersey City, New Jersey
1955

IT'S A BRIGHT, frosty Thanksgiving morning in 1955 in Jersey City, NJ. Elena stays indoors least Ginny sees she is home. When her mother and father inquire as to why she is not going *begging* for Thanksgiving with her best friend Ginny, she surprises her parents by telling them she wants to stay home and help with the family dinner. Before Elena's parents could question her further, she abruptly leaves the kitchen and heads down to the dark, stifling basement. She rushes over to the oil heater. In a flash, like Superwoman or a Time Traveler, Elena flies *over the mountain and through the woods* back to 1899, returning to the farm in the Granite State, New Hampshire.

1899 Walpole, New Hampshire

Elena levitates and hovers above the barren trees while savoring the moment as she observes the beautiful, idyllic New England landscape below. The late autumn icy- drizzle makes everything sparkle like radiant cut crystal. The gusty, bitter wind forces Elena to find a safe-warm space. She hesitates for a moment. Seeing there is no one around, Elena gently floats down onto the frosted solid ground. She lingers on the large property which overlooks the meandering Connecticut River. In the horizon, through the spaces in the sterile trees, where earlier gorgeous colorful leaves grandly showcased their vivacious beauty, Elena absorbs the majestic snow-capped Green Mountains of Vermont that soar above the Connecticut River dividing New Hampshire and Vermont.

The brilliant bellowing white cumulous, cotton-like fluffy clouds are suspended in the magnificent lavender-blue sky. The half-acre, slightly frozen, glistening pond, soon-to-be solid ice which is great for ice skating, forecasts that winter is fast approaching. The leaves embedded on top of the frozen pond creates an illusion of a Braque cubist painting. Elena is intoxicated by its beauty. *She is under its magical spell.* This impressionable young girl feels secure and solid as the rocks that form the Granite State in this serene environment at this altered time and in this distant place.

Next to the muted-gray painted clapboard farmhouse, Elena glances through the misty glass panes of the kitchen-door window. It triggers an impressionable memory for this susceptible young girl. She observes Anna Lee, a middle-aged, soon to be totally grey-haired, newly wrinkled but lovely face woman, calmly but feverishly cooking in the kitchen. As this hard-working woman has done for many years each Thanksgiving, she is baking fresh pumpkin and apple pies, cooking sweet cranberry sauce, and homemade flaky buttermilk biscuits and hearty corn bread. Elena carefully lifts the door latch and slowly enters through the great, wooden kitchen door. As she quietly approaches Anna Lee, Elena reaches over and gently kisses the woman on her well-earned lined face. Unaware, Anna Lee vigorously does her kitchen duties. *Elena's presence is akin to an unsuspecting spirit.*

Savoring the moment, Elena breathes in the poignant aroma of the enormous fresh-killed bird roasting in the roaring cast-iron hearth. The comingled aromas fill Elena's quivering nostrils with nostalgia. They evoke fond yet complex memories. When recollections don't do the trick, Elena accesses her vivid imagination. The immense heat coming from the massive oven warms her body and soul. Elena's searing saucer shaped espresso-brown eyes methodically scan the room as she wonders where the others are. Elena grabs a large calico apron hanging behind the preserved- food, laden pantry door and proceeds to peel the potatoes sitting in a colorful blue ceramic bowl on the long wooden table. As she skillfully peels potato after potato, and places the bright, newly skinned spuds in the huge ceramic blue bowl, a sense of well-being envelopes her. Elena loves to be in this room; she feels she belongs and has a purpose here. Sadly, this feeling doesn't last!

A burly, ominous-looking figure is lurking near the ghostly-foggy glass panes on the mammoth sturdy oak kitchen door. A terrible inhuman force of nature, with great fists, aggressively pounds on the door. When no one responds, it viciously kicks at the door with a goliath footed boot. This terrifying, enormous creature-like being, with brutal strength, effortlessly shatters the door causing it to violently crash down onto the highly polished wooden planked floor. The great gap in the open kitchen door frame causes the fierce New England wind to gush in like an uncontrollable Nor'easter.

The severe gust of the frigid wind rattles the trees outside and transforms them into unspeakable spooky creatures. The empty space where the door once was becomes an uncontrollable wind tunnel allowing for an avalanche of parched leaves to swarm wildly through the kitchen. The dry crumbled leaves scatter about smothering everything in its path. The bowl of freshly peeled potatoes crashes to the floor making them roll randomly around the floor next to the family heir-loon ceramic bowl which is turned upside down on the kitchen floor.

The warmth of the kitchen suddenly becomes frigid, hostile, and eerily surreal. The cruel powerful gusts make humans and spirits shiver in its path. Petrified, Elena is temporarily paralyzed with fear. When she comes to her senses, she rushes past this creature (who does not see her) and bolts out the open space where the violent winds blew everything from in its path. The farm-house elderly woman Anna Lee stands frozen like the ice pond outside or similar to a statue made from the granite in the mountains of the Granite State of New Hampshire. Suddenly, the *creature -like* human disappears into thin air defying logic.

1955 Jersey City

Elena is blasted back to 1955, in the dark beastly hot corner in her Jersey City basement. A creeping feeling consumes her. Shaken Elena crouches into a fetal position behind the oil burner where once the coal furnace had been. This traumatized young girl is sobbing. She is not only stunned with fright, but she is gravely disappointed with herself for not confronting her most horrific terror. The stream of tears rolling down her flushed face are not just for her alone, they are filled with immense guilt for abandoning Anna Lee, the gentle woman whom she swore to herself that she would protect along with her family. To justify her failings, Elena rationalizes that she had to get away. Her immature reasoning is ambiguous and dubious.

CHAPTER SIX

Feast or Famine
Noon on Thanksgiving
1955 Jersey City, NJ and 1899 Walpole, NH

THERE IS LITTLE time for self pity when Elena hears her mother calling down from upstairs, "Elena, where are you? Come and set the table!" Tess continues, "The children coming to our door begging has kept me from finishing all I have to do. I need your help!" Even though Elena desperately wants to ignore her mother's call, she slowly uncoils from behind the warm oil burner. Since Elena does not respond immediately, her mother screams down, "Elena Rose, come upstairs this minute!" Tess turns to her husband and comments, "She didn't go begging with Ginny this year! You see why I'm so concerned about her?" Mike ignores his wife.

Tess adds, "Elena hasn't been herself for quite some time." "You're exaggerating," Mike responds. Tess exclaims, "No, I'm not! That girl constantly ignores me - it's as if she is somewhere else." Attempting to console his anxious wife, Mike assures her, "She's growing up; she doesn't want to go begging with the little kids anymore." He attempts to console his wife, "As I keep telling you Tess, there's nothing to concern yourself about." Leaning over to kiss her neck he lectures, "She's a teenager. They think their parents are freaks. Even you, her red-hot Momma."

Typical of a 50s male, Mike insensitively jokes, "You know how you women are?" He grabs a butter biscuit in a basket on the table. Before he eats it, thoughtlessly he lectures, "Don't let Elena bother you; ignore her. Do as I do; I ignore you all the time." Mike puts the whole biscuit in his mouth. Angry, Tess retorts back, "Mike, you always avoid a serious conversation. You make a joke about everything." Exasperated, Tess tells him to leave and get the liquor ready to serve their soon-to-arrive guests.

Disillusioned and too busy to argue with her husband, Tess resumes her holiday cooking she prepares for her guests. Grinning at his wife, Mike nonchalantly shakes his head. Before he leaves the kitchen, Mike grabs a Rheingold beer bottle out of the refrigerator. With deliberate force he slams it shut rattling the other bottles on the top shelf. Frustrated, Tess heatedly insists Mike leave the kitchen. Upset, Tess hollers down again for her daughter, "Elena, last call, come up here now!"

Under his breath Mike slyly comments, "I don't blame Elena for not wanting to come." He heads to the living room, turns on the television, and plops down on the sofa. Mike camouflages his uncertainties by ignoring them. The holiday feast is overshadowed by the famine in their current emotional lives. *Clearly this family is starving for attention and understanding.* This becomes even more apparent on this US National Holiday of Thanksgiving.

Hiding in the basement, Elena hearing her mother's continuing screaming threats, she wipes her misty-tearful eyes with the calico apron. Hastily she brushes off the leaves plastered on her new orange-wool sweater. Racing up the two flights of stairs passing Aunt Ettie's hall door on the first level. When she gets to the second floor by their side door, Elena stands frozen in time. Admonishing herself, Elena murmurs, "Will I ever understand?" She agonizingly questions herself, "Will I ever have the courage to face the demons?" Confused and conflicted, Elena reluctantly opens the back door to her home in Jersey City. Young Elena faces her parents but not her devastating uncertainties.

Stoically standing in the kitchen where her mother is busy peeling potatoes, Elena coughs; her mother turns, gazes at her daughter. "Where were you?" Tess lectures, "Look at the new orange sweater I bought you. Don't get it dirty." Frustrated, Tess continues her tirade, "I'm all in a dither here and you didn't even feed the fish you begged me to get you?" Feeling sad she is upsetting her mother, Elena rushes over to a kitchen cabinet and takes out a small box of fish food. She sprinkles a pinch of the delicate flakes into the round glass fishbowl which is sitting on the kitchen counter. Her only pet Goldie the fish is swimming to the top to reach the food.

"Who's coming to dinner?" asks Elena. Banging the bowl full to the brim with the freshly peeled potatoes on the kitchen table Tess looks at her daughter quizzically, "Why are you asking me? You know; the usual, Aunt Mary Grace, Uncle Geoff, your cousins Timothy and Regina Helen. Pausing, Tess adds, "Also the guest your father invited." With a confused look, Elena questions, "Who? Who did Dad invite!" Not having time to answer in detail, her irritated mother balks back, "You'll find out soon enough." Tess grabs a stack of dinner plates and hands them to Elena. Recognizing her antagonizing attitude is spoiling this special day for her daughter, Tess quickly kisses Elena's red rough cheeks. She assures her daughter, "Forgive me sweetie, we're going to have a great Thanksgiving!" She pushes her daughter Elena toward the dining room, smiles ordering, "Now go and set the table!"

Elena places the special dishes and silver flatware on the sturdy, antique mahogany dining room table. It originally belonged to her paternal grandmother, Antonella. Elena never knew her paternal grandmother. Antonella died of cancer in her early fifties before Elena was born leaving her father Mike and her Aunt Ettie to take care of their bereaved father Nicholas, their younger sister Rose, and the Jersey City home. A few years after Ettie and Mike's mother passed away, and soon after his youngest daughter, Rose, unexpectedly died, their bereaved father Nicholas, succumbed due to a "broken heart."

Ettie and Mike believe that their grieving father never got over the premature loss of his beloved wife and his young, beautiful daughter, Rose. Their younger sister Rose died six months after their mother on Christmas day leaving them heartbroken, especially, the elderly heart-broken father. Rose was coined a "pepper pot" by her siblings. Their young sister was lively, entertaining, and the joy of her father Nicholas, older sister Ettie, and brother Mike's lives. Rose was missed terribly. Her premature senseless death left a deep void in their lives. Only after the birth of Elena, a few years after Rose's death, did Ettie and Mike's lives brighten once again.

Languidly setting the dining room table, Elena breathes in the rich aromas surrounding the house, especially the ones drifting up from her Aunt Ettie's kitchen. The soothing aromas temporarily relax Elena. The air in Aunt Ettie's house is always perfumed with incredible fragrances of Italian cooking filled with garlic, basil, oregano, dried sausages, aged cheeses, rich tomato sauces bubbling over in well-used enamel pots. These poignant scents floated upstairs and overwhelmed Elena's mother's bland cooking. Elena and her parents rarely spend holidays with Aunt Ettie and her family. As long as Elena could remember, Aunt Ettie always lived downstairs from them with her two older cousins, Rosaria and Blaise, who no longer live there.

The two-family house on Armstrong Avenue was originally owned by her father's parents, Nicholas and Antonella Policino. After they died, the house was left to their children. Elena's father Michael (Mike), and his oldest sister Ettie, short for Antonella, became the co-owners. Since Elena's mother's younger sister Mary Grace did not live in Jersey City, and Tess didn't get to see her as often as she would like, she insisted on spending most holidays with her. The holidays were the most opportune time to catch up with her only sibling Mary Grace, her husband Geoff, their young daughter Regina Helen, and their oldest child Timothy Daniel.

After Elena finishes setting the table, the front-door bell rings announcing their Thanksgiving guests. Mike is busy getting the drinks ready and Tess is basting the huge turkey sizzling in the conventional oven. In unison, her preoccupied parents call for Elena to go down and open the front door. Elena hurries down; she thought for sure that it was her Aunt Mary Grace, Uncle Geoff, and her 14-year old favorite cousin Regina, and older teenage "annoying" cousin Timothy who constantly taunts her and his young sister. As she approaches the front door, Elena sees a man standing there holding something in his large black-gloved hands. His head is turned aside and the wide-brimmed felt black hat he is wearing covers his eyes concealing most of his face. A creepy feeling overwhelms her. Immediately Elena begins to tremble and experiences a sense of crushing fear and extreme anxiety. Instinctively she feels compelled to flee to another space and time. The farmhouse in New Hampshire was no longer safe, but she knew she could go to the barn and hide there. *Elena must escape!*

* * 1899 New Hampshire * *

In the blink of an eye, she is back in New Hampshire 1899 squatting down behind the golden bales of dry hay which feed the various barn animals. Nonetheless, she continues to hear the doorbell ringing louder and louder back home in Jersey City and her dad's shouts, "Get the door." With her freezing naked hands Elena covers her ears to drown out the insatiable ringing and her father's impatient shouting, "Elena Rose, open the damn door!" The terrified girl buries her head deeper between the bales of hay desperately trying to make her father's angry voice and the intrusive doorbell from back home cease.

CHAPTER SEVEN

Friend and Foe
Thanksgiving Day
Walpole, NH 1899 and Jersey City, NJ 1955

IT IS 1899, the warmth from the breath of the animals in the red-blood colored painted, wooden shingled New Hampshire barn, warms and soothes Elena's shivering body. This special young girl also has the unique gift to communicate with animals. She understands and respects them and they respond in kind. The elderly, coco brown, sway-back gelding, Buck II, saunters over to the squatting Elena. Buck II has a distinct white patch which flows down between his pointed ears, through the middle of his broad head. It is sandwiched between his large brown eyes right to the tip of his flaring nostrils.

Buck II gently nozzles Elena's perky pink ear she is covering with her freezing hands to block out the noise from her Jersey City home. The horse playfully tickles her bringing a smile to her face. Safely sheltered she removes her pressing hands from her ears. The ringing doorbell and her father's booming voice in Jersey City in 1955 ceases. Buck's tail swishes and brushes her arm. Both are happy to be in one another's company once more. *They are friends.*

Grabbing on to Buck's front leg, she pulls herself up, and hugs him around his muscular, pulsing neck which is beating as fast as her racing heart. Elena fusses over Buck II. She feeds him handfuls of hay, making his long tail excitedly swish to and fro. Feeling free and at ease, she looks outside the barn observing the rolling, swirling white smoke coming from the multiple stone chimneys of the expansive gentleman farmhouse. The numerous fireplaces inside the stately old house is all aglow warming and comforting the exceptional family inside. *Elena hope this is so.*

Cautiously looking about, she notices the elderly farm-hand Zeke is not around. Observing things seem safe and protected at the house and barn, Elena decides to head over to the main house. Her purpose is to check on Anna Lee and her family. She once more strokes and pats Buck II. Elena leaves the safety of the barn walking cautiously toward the house. As she reaches the kitchen door at the side of the house, she peeks through the hazy glass panes. Elena is comforted seeing Anna Lee is fine and the house is back in order.

About to enter, Elena hears echoes of her father's booming voice, "Elena Rose, get over here, now!" She ponders by the kitchen door in New Hampshire, but her father's demanding voice raises her unwillingly into the air. Similar to Mary Poppins with her magical umbrella or holding onto a string of an air-born balloon, Elena once again flies over the countrified New England landscape. Over the vast sky she swirls high above the New England rooftops with their massive chimneys' curling, white smoke. The clean, fresh New England chimney smoke is overtaken by the polluted black soot from the industrial plants in Jersey City. Lingering over her Jersey City house Elena hears her father's imposing voice. She closes her eyes and drops down into her Jersey City home back to 1955.

1955 Jersey City

When Mike sees his daughter sneaking around the hallway, exasperated, but not wanting to make a scene, he forcefully motions for her to come to him. Mike instructs his daughter, "Elena, say hello and Happy Thanksgiving to Father Kelly." She looks disdainfully at this intimidating priest with his prominent-sharp cheek bones, deep set, dark-remote, sullen eyes, and his pasty chalky complexion. As customary for a priest, he is dressed all in black. She recognizes and distrusts him. With a sneer on her face, Elena spurts out, "Hello Father Kelly. Why aren't you eating at the rectory?" Embarrassed, Mike reprimands his daughter, "What has gotten into you, Elena! Apologize immediately!" He turns to the priest explaining, "Sorry Father, Elena is not herself today." The unsuspecting priest hands Mike a lovely floral arrangement. Under her breath Elena mutters, "I'm not sorry." To save face for himself and his uncomely, rude daughter,

Mike coyly ignores Elena's surprising cryptic sarcasm. He hands Elena the priest's outer garments. With a warning glare Mike orders, "Here, Elena Rose, hang Father Kelly's coat and accessories in the hall closet." Elena sneers at her father while holding Father Kelly's long black, wool coat and handmade knitted scarf. She is juggling the priest's black felt hat and black leather gloves. With his long-bony cadaver-like hands, Father Kelly pats Elena on her head, and gives her a quirky smile. She quivers.

"How are you, my child?" Since it is Thanksgiving, Father Kelly inquires, "Did you go *begging* today?" He was referring to this Jersey City Thanksgiving ritual of begging. Before Elena can respond, Father Kelly preaches, "It's like the 'Heavenly Beggar' in the bible, Rev.111, 20: 'Behold, I stand at the door and knock. If anyone hears Me calling and opens the door, I will enter his house and have supper with him and he with Me.'" Mike smiles and agrees, "Well said, Father." Elena ignores both of them. She drags the long *Draconian* coat and noose-like scarf on the floor and heads to the hall coat closet. She struggles to hang them in the crowded space. Listening to her father and the priest conversing, with a questionable smirk on her face Elena glares at the lanky-spindly Father Kelly. *Angelic meets devil?*

Mike is clearly thrilled the priest is having dinner with them. He thanks Father Kelly for the beautiful flower arrangement. The priest proudly informs him, "The Rosary Society ladies made these. They were selling them to send the money to the missionaries in Africa." Holding onto the flowers Mike responds, "Thank you. Tess will love them." The two men head upstairs and Mike humbly tells his guest, "Father, we're honored you chose to have dinner with us at our simple home." Hearing this dialogue repulses Elena. *Is she afraid of this holy man? Does he bring tricks or treats?*

The doorbell rings again. This time it is not the ominous man or the *heavenly* children "Begging for Thanksgiving," it is Aunt Mary Grace, Uncle Geoff, her cousins, Regina Helen, and Timothy. Hearing their familiar voices, Elena bounces down the stairs and swings open the door. After hugs and kisses, they all labor up the stairs with their arms filled with food, wine, and other treats. Aunt Mary Grace is holding on tightly to a large covered pie. Elena, without hesitation, grabs it out of her Aunt's hands. "Don't drop that!" Mary Grace nervously orders. Boldly, Elena proudly holds up the lemon meringue pie as if it were the Holy Grail. This pie is Elena's favorite dessert. It is the secret recipe of her maternal grandmother who Elena is named after. Her maternal grandmother is Elena's only living grandparent. She moved permanently to California a few years ago leaving her daughters and their families grudgingly behind.

Introductions to Father Kelly are made to Mary Grace, Geoff and Timothy and Regina Helen. The guests settle in. Calling from the kitchen, Tess welcomes her guests and demands that her sister come directly to the kitchen and *help*. "Mary Grace, there are no moochers in this house," she teases her sister. She calls out, "Of course, not you, Father Kelly." Joking back, Mary Grace defends, "Who you calling a moocher? What kind of word is that?" Adding, "And you call yourself a college graduate and a literature major at that."

Grabbing the precious pie from Elena, Mary Grace heads into the kitchen. She carefully places it on the oval, beige and white Formica kitchen table. The sisters kiss and Tess immediately hands Mary Grace the calico apron Elena had on earlier. Mary Grace looks at the apron, laughs and jokes, "What is this apron? From Laura Ingall's *Little House on the Prairie*?" Tess is too busy getting the food ready to respond. Mary Grace places the apron over her perfectly shaped beehive, blond hairdo. She ties it around her once slim but now age appropriate expanding waist. The sisters work in communion to get the plentiful holiday meal ready.

The festive spirit of Thanksgiving is finally surrounding the house. Having her cousin Regina there makes Elena finally feel happy. She coaxes Regina into her bedroom where she proudly shows off her favorite record albums. The latest oil-by-number painting Elena recently completed of a country scene with a red barn and a lone horse in the paddock is on display. Regina, only three-months younger than Elena, glares at the painting not interested. She is more theatrical than her cousin and dreams of being in the theater or in the movies one day. Regina casually looks at the baseball posters hanging on the walls in the room while sitting on her cousin Elena's bed which is covered with a blue chenille bedspread. While shuffling through the record albums, Regina benignly inquires, "Who's that strange man in the living room?" She makes a scary sound and dramatically screeches, "He looooks like Drac-u-la!"

Elena lightly hits her cousin on her scrawny back. She teases, "You're so dramatic!" Looking in the mirror and trying to puff up her long, straight, light blond hair, Regina again questions, "Well if he isn't Dracula, then who or what is he?" Elena nonchalantly answers, "A so-called friend of my father's." While continuing to brush her long blonde hair Regina resumes her interrogation, "He's never been here before for Thanksgiving; why today?" Grabbing the hair brush out of Regina's hand Elena comments, "Evidently Dracula has nowhere else to go for Thanksgiving." She murmurs, "Probably nobody else wants him." Regina blurts out, "His creepy looking." Elena's cousin smirks saying, "I like that." Pretending to bite Elena's neck Regina growls out, "I Vant to Suck your Blood!" Elena humorously pushes her cousin away. Both fall down on the floor laughing hysterically.

Regina begins to fuss with Elena's paint brushes pretending she is painting. Regina asks her cousin, "You still watching the artist on TV who gives painting lessons?" "Yes," Elena happily answers. "What's his name again?" Regina continues to inquire. Taking the brushes away from Regina she responds, "Jon Nagy." Regina brings the conversation back to the *spooky* man in black and inquires, "Dracula is really a priest, isn't he?" Elena ignores her cousin.

Avoiding further discussion about Father Kelly, Elena chatters about music and her favorite sport, baseball. Elena is a die-hard New York Yankee baseball fan. She has a secret crush on Mickey Mantle, the young, handsome Yankee center fielder. A switch hitter and a popular homerun hero. There are numerous posters of the Yankees and a huge one of her Yankee slugger crush, "The Mick," on her bedroom wall. Elena is back to her age appropriate self again; acting like a *typical* young teenager.

Continuing her playfulness Elena grabs the paint brush from her cousin's thin hand and begins to tickle her with it while calling her *an undernourished bologna sandwich*. Not taking this lightly, Regina pushes her cousin away and calls her *an overstuffed liverwurst sandwich*. Their bantering is infectious. Elena is clearly having fun with her cousin acting like normal 50s 14-year old.

In the living room, Timothy hears Elena and Regina's silly giggling. He calls out to them, "What are you two dumb goof balls doing in there?" No reaction from Elena or Regina; therefore, Tim taunting adds, "You two sound like a fat wobbling, gobbling turkey and a skinny, stinking brainless scarecrow." Tim is not teasing, he is clearly annoyed. Hearing Tim taunting the girls, his father Geoff snidely warns, "Leave them alone, Knucklehead!" Muttering, Tim mockingly retorts back, "Me? What about you, Mr. Wandering Hands!"

In the steaming, sweltering kitchen, Tess and Mary Grace, the two devoted sisters, are ready to bring the food to the beautifully decorated holiday table. The long rectangular mahogany table is covered with Mike's deceased mother's handmade creamed-colored, crocheted-table cloth used only for special occasions. The beautiful 16-year old fine china and long-stemmed crystal that Tess and Mike received for their wedding add a touch of elegance. A vibrant, fresh floral center piece of orange, yellow, and russet mums by Father Kelly graces the center of the dining room table.

In the living room Father Kelly is enjoying an amble glass of fine Irish whiskey. Mike and his brother-in-law Geoff are holding ice-cold bottles of Rheingold Beer. Timothy, bored, is drinking a Coca Cola also right out of the bottle. He makes a face after taking a sip and asks, "Hey, don't you have any Dr. Pepper?" Holding up his coke, he further comments, "This stuff takes paint off of cars." Mike rebuffs, "Be thankful with what you have, wise guy." Tim's father and Father Kelly disregard him. They are preoccupied watching the post-TV reels of the annual Macy's Thanksgiving Day Parade in New York City. The men are biding their time anxious for the pro football games to commence. Geoff turns to the priest and asks, "Hey Father, are you a NY Giants football fan?" "Sure, am!" the priest immediately responds. After taking a short slug of his beer, Geoff comments, "That Frank Gifford is the best Giant player! A great half back, right Father?"

Father John Kelly tells Geoff to call him just *Jack*. Before Geoff acknowledges the priest's request the women are carrying in steaming plates laden with a variety of home-cooked food. They are trailed by Elena and Regina juggling smaller serving plates. Tess requests that everyone come to the table, "Dinner's ready. Please sit down at the dining room table wherever you are comfortable." The men are engrossed in the pre-football TV programs. When they hesitate to adhere to Tess's call, she threatens, to "give the food away to the begging poor." Anxious to finish eating so they can get back to the TV the men hustle over to the dining room table.

Mike insists that Father Kelly sit at the head of the table next to his wife as he proceeds to sit at the other end. Tess graciously thanks Father Kelly for the beautiful floral piece. He smiles back. Once they are all seated, a pithy, moving blessing is given by Father Kelly. Other than Tess who eats hardly anything, the others gluttonously partake in a huge meal while discussing the latest movies; corrupt city and national politics; the recently ended Korean War; the changing religion scene; and, of course, sports. The adults give their diverse thoughts on the R-rated Frank Sinatra movie, *From Here to Eternity,* along with their take on the latest young, heart-throbs Nathalie Wood and James Dean's controversial movie, *Rebel Without a Cause*; the first professional African-American baseball player Jackie Robinson; and Republican President Dwight D. Eisenhower; also enter their conversation. Elena and Regina are bored. Tim listens attentively but does not comment.

Stuffed like the huge bird they just devoured, and restless to return to the football games, the lackadaisical men head back to the living room. Walking back to the living room, to shake them up, Geoff boldly states, "Mickey Mantle will never be as great as Joe DiMaggio and Babe Ruth." Father Kelly agrees. Heatedly they continue to debate Billy Martin, Mickey Mantle's baseball buddy and his negative influence on him. The infamous Yankee coach Casey Stengel is also heatedly discussed. Elena listens attentively but does not comment. Children should be seen and not heard in the 50s. Tess barely contributes to the conversation during the dinner. Clearly, she is elsewhere. Mary Grace observes Tess's aloofness and preoccupation.

Typical of the 50s, the women remove the plates and left-over food. They put the left-over food away. The arduous duty of washing and drying the dishes by hand commences. There are no dishwashers at this time. Elena and Regina are in their mothers' way. Tess and Mary Grace chase them outdoors. Always afraid someone might get sick, Mary Grace insists they wear their coats, hats, and gloves, "You don't want to be sick for Christmas?" Tess argues, "Sure, try and get them to listen." Like racing thoroughbreds, Elena and Regina grab their coats and hustle down the stairs.

Geoff calls to his daughter, "Hey, Reggie, aren't you going to give your Dad a kiss before you head outside?" Regina, who hates being called Reggie, stops in her track. She reluctantly goes over to her father and quickly pecks at his prickly stubble cheek. Regina barely touches her father's rough face. Her father laughs pinches her backside, and jokes, "What a skinny little behind. There's no meat on it." Blushing she moves away from her father yelling, "Stop doing that!" He makes light of it and says, "I'm your father! I can do whatever I like." When the priest and Mike stare him down, Geoff complains, "The kids today have no respect for their elders." Mike and Father Kelly give him a critical look. To defend his actions, Geoff comments, "It's a sign of affection." Trying to seduce his brother-in-law to justify his inappropriate actions he asks, "Right, Mike? All Italian men do it, especially in Italy." Silently, Father Kelly, just Jack, finishes his whiskey.

Standing by the door and hearing her uncle's ludicrous comment, Elena shoots him a killing glare. Taking hold of Regina's delicate hand, as if they were being chased by a monster, they run fast as they can down the stairs to the front door. "Last one out is a rotten loser," Regina shouts. This prompts Elena to push past her cousin to get outside first. The cousins are extremely competitive with one another.

In the living room, placing his head back on the back of the green velvet sofa, Geoff gulps down the rest of his beer. Trying to take the heat off of him for patting his daughter inappropriately, Geoff changes the subject. He asks Mike, "How do you know Father Kelly?" Father Kelly immediately interjects, "Not only are Tess and Mike fine exemplary members of my parish, St. Victors, Mike has been generous enough to collect the parish garbage twice a week gratis. "In fact," he continues, "Even on special days when we have church events. Saving us a lot of money and keeps our property in tip top shape." Before Father Kelly continues, Mike shyly remarks, "That's the least I can do Father for the church." He immediately corrects himself, "Please excuse me, Monsignor. I'm so used to calling you 'Father Kelly' all these years." The holy man reassures his friend, "Mike, please continue to do so; we are like family - Christ's family."

Turning to his brother-in-law Mike shares, "Geoff, did you know that I grew up in his parish." "Yes," Father Kelly reaffirms, "I saw this young boy grow up to be a fine man. Sadly, I partook in the funeral services for his mother, father, and his younger sister Rose." Reflectively Father Kelly mentions, "What a sweet young thing Rose was. Elena looks somewhat like her." The priest makes the Sign of the Cross. He mournfully notes, "Sadly she died too young!"

In a different vein, Father Kelly comments, "Mike, I fear what will happen when the county takes over the garbage collection; not only for the parish but for your business." He pauses; mentions, "Politics in this city is so unpredictable." Intensely listening, Geoff blurts out, "More like corrupt! Hudson County is the worst. It started when Frank Harrigan became mayor years ago and took over this city with his so-called "Political Machine.""

Mike and Father Kelly look aghast. Unfazed, Geoff resumes his criticism, "And I hear it's no better now with Mayor John D. McKenna and his political goons." Geoff murmurs, "The Mafia, the church, the politicians are all in cahoots." Mike warns Geoff to leave Hudson County politics to its own constituents. He cautions him, "You guys from Essex County should stay out of Hudson County politics." Geoff pays no heed to his brother-in-law. He is still surprised by Father Kelly's remark about Mike possibly losing the lucrative city contract.

Geoff ceases to talk about Hudson County's politics. He boldly questions his brother-in-law, "Mike, is that really going to happen? You losing the city garbage contract? Your family's been in the business for years and always had the Jersey City contract." Father remarks, "That's right, Mike's father started the business as far back as the early 1900s with his younger brother. They came from Salerno, Italy." Mike, trying to avoid this conversation, makes light of it and says, "No worries! I never sweat the small stuff."

A huge fan of Mike, Father Kelly brags, "You know Geoff, after Mike graduated from Villanova University, he was heading to New York University Law School. Unfortunately, he was unable to go; Mike had to take over the family business." Geoff adds, "I knew he wanted to be a lawyer; didn't understand why he never pursued it." Frustrated Mike orders, "Enough about me! Let's enjoy Thanksgiving." He walks over to where Father Kelly is sitting saying, "Enough about this nonsense." He takes Father Kelly's empty glass offering, "Let me top that off for you." Geoff and Father Kelly get it! Mike is not willing to continue the conversation. They wisely change the topic back to sports, national politics, and religion.

Mike hands Father Kelly his whiskey; questions him, "How do you like the new young priest who recently came into the parish, Father?" Taking a sip of his Irish whiskey Father Kelly responds, "It's too soon to tell Mike. In time, we'll know." Curious Mike continues, "What's the story about the new young janitor you just hired?" Before Father Kelly can respond, Mike adds his opinion of him, "He seems odd." Father questions, "You mean Juan?" "Yes," Mike responds. The elderly priest explains, "The new priest, Father Arthur Schultz, not only recommended him but brought him with him from Texas. Evidently Juan needed a sponsor and a job." The priest takes another sip of his whiskey. Wiping his mouth with a Thanksgiving cocktail napkin Father Kelly offers, "Juan was originally from Juarez, Mexico. I don't really know much about him, other than Father Schultz met him at his former parish in El Paso, Texas. "What else do you know about him?" Mike inquires. Father Kelly sighs, "I heard the poor young man had no family. Thankfully, like the good Samaritan, Father Schultz took him under his wing." Father Kelly blesses himself praising, "Father Shultz is Juan's guardian angel."

Perplexed by Mike's interest, the priest inquires, "Is there a problem with Juan, Mike?" "Well," Mike reluctantly responds, "I heard from my workers that he is not very cooperative with them. When they go to pick up the garbage, especially on off days and holidays, he gives them a hard time." Mike gulps his beer then continues, "Even my foreman Tony has his reservations about him. He usually gets along with everyone." Surprised,

Father Kelly apologizes, "Sorry to hear this." Mike adds, "So, I went to see the janitor the other day to smooth things over, unfortunately, he was abrupt and evasive with me too." Squinting his eyes in thought, Mike adds, "Strange thing, from a distance, I noticed that the new priest was listening to my conversation with Juan." Disturbed by Mike's observations Father reassures Mike, "I'll look into it right away." "No need to get involved just yet Father," Mike remarks. "Tony will check it out for me. Now let's finish our drinks," Mike assures Father Kelly.

Sensing conflict, Geoff changes the subject. He blurts out, "Did you know Father Kelly that my younger brother was in the Army infantry? He fought on Pork Chop Hill in Korea." Surprised and impressed, Father Kelly comments, "And he made it home in one piece?" He blesses himself and calls out, "Incredible! A miracle!" "Well," Geoff shares, "He might have come home safe, but my poor brother hasn't been the same since. He's a changed man, moody, depressed, and no one seems to know what to do for him." The priest comments, "How sad." Geoff continues, "You're not kidding Father, my brother hardly talks or communicates with anyone. You know, he hasn't worked since he returned. It's as if he lost both his voice and vigor." "What's this brave soldier's name?" Father compassionately inquires. "Danny," Geoff informs. Father reassures Geoff, "I will keep him in my daily prayers." "Thanks Father Jack," reaching for his beer Geoff says and takes a huge gulp. The men avoid any more unpleasant talk and resume their drinking and TV watching. Their collective eyes are getting heavy. Feeling woozy, Father Kelly's head droops on his sunken chest. Mike is preoccupied. Geoff is anxiously looking at his fancy gold Rolex watch to see what time it is. Paying little attention to the men's conversation, Tim is uneasy.

To relieve his boredom Tim plays Solitaire with the cards he brought with him. Avoiding any more talk about his business and noticing that Father Kelly and Geoff are dozing off, Mike suggest to his nephew, "Hey, come on tough guy, what say we go outside and throw a football around." Gesturing Tim to get up Mike insinuates, "Having all these women around must make a strong young man like you frustrated." Tim is taken back by his uncle's suggestion to throw a football with him. Anxious to get out of there, Tim slams the cards down, jumps up shouting, "Sure enough!" Heading to the hall closet Mike takes out his worn-out pig skin football from his treasured prep high school football days. Irritated Mike and his bored nephew head outdoors to cool their heads hoping to release family and life's pressures.

The sisters are in the kitchen performing their 50s *womanly* kitchen duties– all *seems* peaceful. Noticing her sister Tess is not quite right, Mary Grace probes, "What's going on Tess? You're not yourself?" Giving her sister a strange look, Tess sits down on the chrome kitchen chair. She places a dish towel over her mouth. Confused seeing her sister upset, Mary Grace coaxes, "What's wrong, Tess? Talk to me!" Tess removes the towel, glances into the living room, and whispers to her sister, "I'm worried about my marriage and my daughter." "What are you talking about?" Confused Mary Grace remarks, "Even though I'm your younger sister, I can be wiser than you at times. Tell me what's wrong!" Tess pulls Mary Grace down to the chair next to her and shares her concerns, "Mike and I have had no intimacy in more than a year; we no longer communicate, and we fight all the time about Elena."

Mary Grace cautiously mentions, "Tess, ever since you lost the baby prematurely a few years ago you haven't been the same." Tess says nothing. Mary Grace continues, "A miscarriage affects the husband too. Perhaps it upset Mike more than you know." Tess remains mute. Bold, Mary Grace adds, "Even though he adores Elena, Mike desperately wanted a son to take over the business." Shaking her head, Tess protests, "No, Mike is over that, as am I. Now leave my miscarriage out of this. It's Elena I am worried about. Elena has been distant, secretive, and anxious for a while now." Taking a deep breath, Tess further informs, "When I try to tell Mike about my worries, he ignores me. He accuses me of being overbearing and an overly sensitive mother." Mary Grace tries to dissuade Tess from talking negatively about Mike. "Mike is a great guy!" Mary Grace blurts out. Fueling Tess she complains, "Mike's insensitive and clueless regarding his daughter or me!"

Irritated that Mary Grace always takes Mike's side, Tess vomits out, "Mike only thinks about the garbage company, sports, politics, and going to Walsh's Tavern every damn night to drink with his stupid cronies. With her voice rising, Tess rampages on, "He doesn't care one iota about me or Elena. He turns a deaf ear to me saying, "Elena is a normal teenager!" Compassionately rubbing her older sister's trembling hands, Mary Grace reassures her, "Mike is right! Elena's a typical teenager." Reminding her sister, "Remember what I went through with Timmy? He's still acting up and is a constant thorn in my side." She smiles saying, "All men are alike. Geoff calls Tim a moron; that's the only support I get from my husband."

"You always make excuses for Mike, you never take my side Mary Grace!" Tess blurts out. "All men think about is their work, sports, and their beer. They all have vices," trying to make light of the situation, Mary Grace undiplomatically comments. "Mike's a good provider and faithfully pays the bills," Mary Grace carelessly mentions. Tess immediately interrupts, "Are you forgetting Mary Grace that I work too? I pay for a lot of the bills around here." She smirks and sarcastically suggests, "It's even questionable that Mike really goes to Walsh's Tavern on the nights he says he is." Seeing her sister becoming extremely agitated, Mary Grace kisses her sister on the top of her carrot red head and reiterates, "Elena seems fine to me; maybe she's getting ready to get her womanly thing." Tess resents this, "What kind of a mother do you think I am. Elena knows all about that; trust me that is not the problem." Wiping a lone tear dripping out of her eye Tess moans, "She got it last year and is fine with it."

Not convinced her sister trusts her, Mary Grace uses shock treatment, "You shouldn't be so hard on them." Continuing to employ scare tactics, Mary Grace warns, "Tess, if you continue like this, you might lose your family and secure home." Tess exclaims, "Secure home! After we got married Mike promised me we would only live in this forbidden place, filled with ghosts, a short time." She further explains, "Mike reassured me it would only be until his sister Ettie and brother-in-law were financially secure to keep the house independently of us."

Sarcastically Tess tells Mary Grace, "Your so-called good guy Mike promised me we would buy a house near where we grew up, not far from you and Geoff." Raising her arms over her heard and making a huge circle around the kitchen she yells, "Look, it is over 15 years and we are still living in this stifling, doom-filled, gloomy place!" Extremely upset, weeping Tess condemns, "Mike has been playing tricks on my heart and mind for years." Mary Grace reminds Tess, "Sis you have a great job in the city school system, if you move away, you'll lose it. Besides, Ettie watches Elena for you and she truly loves her." "There you go again Mary Grace always defending them and going against me," Tess complains.

Recognizing she is not penetrating her hardheaded sister, Mary Grace cautions, "When you see things slipping through your fingers Tess, you'll recognize what you might lose. You might want to try to do everything to recapture what is precious to you." She warmly reminds Tess, "Remember when you first met Mike on the tennis courts, down the shore, you thought he was 'the Cat's Meow'. You thought living in a city would be great." Tess Adeline brusquely comments, "Passion and fantasies dissipates with disappointments." Annoyed with her sister, Mary Grace accuses, "You're a tiger Tess, always being theatrical and demanding. I know where Regina gets it from." These disparaging comments upset Tess. She jumps up pushing Mary Grace away. She angrily rants, "Stop scolding, threatening, and pacifying me. I've resigned myself to living and working here. That's not my real problem." She again emphasizes, "Elena's behavior is not typical and Mike is a cold-hearted, selfish fool." Deeply worried and with conviction, Tess pleads stressing, "Mary Grace, you must believe me. I know there's something wrong with my daughter!" She moans, "Elena has been so insular and inaccessible for a while now."

Tess discloses, "I've taken Elena to counseling. Mike is not aware." Shocked by this revelation Mary Grace scolds, "You didn't tell him? You went behind Mike's back?" Mary Grace counsels, "Perhaps that's why he is so upset; maybe he surmises and feels left out. Have you forgotten his horrendous reaction when you didn't tell him you were pregnant until after the miscarriage?" Tess raises her voice, "He would never understand! Mike's incapable of it." Fearing the others will hear, Mary Grace insists Tess lower her voice.

Tess whispers, "Mike and his family are from the old school. Their motto is to keep things to yourself; never let anyone know your business; ignore it." Snapping her fingers she shouts, "Poof it will go away." "You're exaggerating," Mary Grace defensively responds. This truly angers Tess. Again she pounds her fist on the Formica table making the newly towel-dried, stacked dishes rattle. "Don't you get it!" she pleads to her sister, "I fear for my daughter; she's despondent and distant most of the time." Mary

Grace, finally concerned, grabs a napkin from the counter and wipes the tears rolling down her sister's anguished face. Truly upset for her sister, Mary Grace hugs Tess tenderly. Tess pauses a moment, then offers, "Elena seems to be someplace else; a distant place." Loudly, Tess reminisces, "Elena was once such a happy child, always smiling and dancing about - I wonder what or who took that smile from her innocent face and the lilt in her step?" Looking toward the living room, Mary Grace again warns her sister, "Lower your voice; you don't want the others to hear." While Father Kelly was sleeping, and Mike and Tim were outside, bored Geoff went towards the kitchen where the sisters are having their heated conversation. Secretly, Geoff hides behind the kitchen door listening to the entire conversation.

Physically and emotionally exhausted, Tess moans, "I wish Mom was here. She raised us with an iron hand but with much tenderness. We never felt alone with her around; she always had the right answers." Choking back her tears, Tess questions, "Why did she have to move to California and leave her family back east?" Mary Grace defends their mother, "Did you want her to retire to a convent? She has a right to go off and start a new life." Compassionately Mary Grace adds, "Once Dad died, she felt a need to be by her only sibling Uncle Albert and he happens to live in California." Tess replies, "Of course, I understand all of that but did she have to turn into "Grandma Hollywood." Mary Grace, realizing that she was not getting anywhere with her sister regarding their mother, decides to let it go.

Hearing Mike and Tim come in Geoff heads back to the living room where Father Kelly is still snoozing; snoring loudly. The drama is broken hearing Mike and Tim laughing loudly, banging doors, coming back in the house. Geoff hustles from behind the kitchen door and rushes back to the living room and plops on the couch. Sweaty Mike and Tim go back into the living room. Sitting on the couch, Geoff coyly asks his son if he had a good "throw" with his uncle. Father Kelly wakes up.

Returning his prized football back in the hall closet, Mike hollers out to Tess, "Hey little woman, bring in more beers for your deserving hubby, thirsty brother-in-law, and a whiskey for the good Father." Thumbs up Mike looks at Tim calling out, "Don't forget a Dr. Pepper for the young man!" Tess screams back, "Come and get them yourself!" Realizing an uncomfortable situation arising, Mary Grace encourages her sister to go to the bathroom to wash her face and gain her composure. She helps shaken Tess up from the kitchen chair. Mary Grace reassures her, "All will be fine Sis. They can't keep the two Rapp sisters (Tess Adeline and Mary Grace) down." Compassionately Mary Grace smooth's Tess's frizzy red hair with her heavily laden hand covered with sparkling rings promising her, "We'll talk later." Traumatized, Tess goes to the bathroom.

Taking two beers from the refrigerator, Mary Grace rushes to bring them to Mike and her husband. Seeing Mary Grace's frown while taking the beer, Mike gives her a perplexed look. To lighten things up, Geoff pats his wife on her well-molded amble buttocks playfully commenting, "Getting a little junk in the trunk these days." Mary Grace quickly pushes her husband's hand away giving him an odious look. Once more, trying to get out of another mess, Geoff remarks, "That's a compliment Mary Grace. You have a better body than Marilyn Monroe." With a half smile and half frown Mary Grace gives Geoff a stern look. Smiling, her son Timothy chimes in, "You mean that sexy Blond Bombshell?" Sensing a confrontation, Father Kelly flashes an uncomfortable and dubious gaze at the young couple. He quickly swallows down the last of his third whiskey. To distract them, the insightful priest humbly and politely requests Mary Grace to pour him *a wee bit more of that fine Irish Whisky* emphasizing, "Hold the ice!"

Humorously Geoff calls out, "Hey, I wonder if Joe DiMaggio had as much trouble with his ex Marilyn Monroe as we do Mike?" Mike responds, "That's why the marriage only lasted a short time." With a nervous laugh, Geoff adds, "I'm sure the Slugger handled that blond bombshell better than we handle the feisty Rapp sisters we married." Mary Grace yells, "You're digging your grave deeper and deeper Geoff. I suggest you drink your beer and keep your mouth shut." With a triumphant smile on his face, Father Kelly applauds.

Timothy pretends not to notice or care what has transpired between his parents. He is flipping through a woman's magazine taking special notice of the young models in bathing suits. Noticing that his mother is frowning at the scantly clothed women he is goggling over in the magazine, Tim shuts it. He slams it down on the coffee table, gets up and sneaks into Elena's bedroom. Seeing the fury in Mary Grace's face, Mike and Geoff ease down deeper into the cushions of the sofa trying to disappear. Father Kelly is sitting erect anxiously waiting for his next libation. All that once seemed like a typical normal Thanksgiving Day evolved into a complicated, unpredictable and uncomfortable holiday.

CHAPTER EIGHT

Confrontation and True Confessions
Thanksgiving, late afternoon
Jersey City, NJ
1955

ELENA AND REGINA are still outdoors. Mike and Tim were throwing the football around. Ginny Cimino, Elena's best friend, comes plowing down the street. When she sees Elena, she sarcastically shouts across the street, "I thought you were at your Grandmother's farm in New Hampshire?" Hearing this, Mike, Tim and Regina are perplexed. Tim throws the ball for Ginny to catch, "Hey, Wonder Woman, catch this." Ginny catches it and throws it back with a hard spin. Mike yells, "Ginny you have a better arm than Tim." He teasingly punches Tim. "Come on Dr. Pepper let's leave these girls alone." Ginny calls out to Tim, "Bet I can throw farther than you." Tim laughs at her. This greatly disturbs Ginny; she responds, "I throw better than my brother Angelo and he's quarterback for Snyder High School." Strutting to the back area with his Uncle Mike who is holding tightly onto his football, Tim cries out, "Snyder High football players? Heck, they're first-class losers! They never win a game and never will." Leaving Elena and Regina in the front, Tim and Mike continue to throw the ball behind the house.

Outside in front, Elena and Regina see a car driving toward them. Driving in a used blue Ford is Robbie Savini. He is best friends with Aunt Ettie's son Blaise. Robbie sees Elena, stops the car and rolls down the window. He calls out, "Excuse me Elena, is your cousin Blaise home for Thanksgiving from the Marines?" Shyly Elena hesitantly walks over to the car and responds, "No, but he'll be here for Christmas." "Good," responds Robbie. "Tell him I want to see him when he's home." Okay, I'll tell him," Elena replies. Getting his nerve up Robbie asks, "Will Rosaria be home too?" "Most likely Rosaria will be here too," Elena shakes her head affirmatively. Robbie rolls up the window, drives away. Regina walks over to her cousin and asks, "Who is that cute guy? Isn't he a little too old for you?" Annoyed Elena replies, "He's my cousin Blaise's best friend."

Meanwhile, Tim deliberately throws the football up front where Ginny is standing. Instinctively, she picks it up. Throws it back at him almost knocking him down when he catches it. Tim hollers at her, "Hey Wonder Woman, are you trying to kill me?" Elena ignores Ginny and Tim's flirtatious banter. Regina is taking this all in. Grabbing hold of Regina's arm Elena attempts to lead her back to the house. Seeing Elena leaving, Ginny intercepts. She goes directly up to Elena and taunts her, "I knew you were only joking with me; you didn't go to New Hampshire." Boasting, Ginny says, "You missed out on *begging* this morning. My brother Angelo came with me." Ginny proudly reports, "I got five dollars." Elena ignore her but Ginny persists, "You won't believe this but old sour puss Mr. Hanrahan, who always screams at us when we play ball in the street, gave us money." Elena doesn't respond. Annoyed, Ginny yells out, "Old four-eyes, Mr. E at the candy store, gave each of us a couple of Hersey Chocolate Bars with almonds and other treats." "Who cares; I hate chocolate!" Elena finally comments. Ginny is taken back. Tit for tat, Elena responds, "Angelo, your show-off brother, is too old. He's almost seventeen; he shouldn't be going begging." Elena adds more insults, "If you eat all that candy Ginny, you'll get pimples like your brother, Mr. Acne Angelo." Realizing she is being mean to her best friend, Elena tries to distance herself from Ginny. The "Begging for Thanksgiving" subject is making her too anxious. Saving Elena from more explaining and embarrassment, Mary Grace hollers from the front window, "Pick and Peck" come upstairs; dessert is ready to be served." Elena shyly turns to Ginny. She attempts to make amends, "I'll see you tomorrow. Okay?" Ginny gives her a reassuring smile, turns and heads up the block to her house.

As Ginny is leaving, her older brother Angelo rides down the street on his black Schwinn bicycle. His rubber wheels screech as he makes a sudden daring stop near Elena and Regina. It makes the girls turn abruptly. Cool Angelo whistles at Regina and Elena. He teases, "Hey, you good-looking chicks, want to share some kisses with me?" They make a face at him. Laughing loudly, he calls back, "I mean Chocolate Kisses; you goof balls." Spinning his bike around Angelo almost runs the girls down as he speeds up the street whistling. Regina's taunting eyes follow him up the hill. She hollers out to Angelo, "Why you couldn't handle a woman like me!" Annoyed, Elena takes hold of her bold cousin's spindly arm pulling her toward the house. Reprimanding, "Stop flirting with him. Angelo's nothing but a tease." Regina winks bragging, "Why I can handle his kind."

Pick and Peck, Elena and Regina, race back to the house. Reaching the front door, Regina inquires, "Elena what's this about a grandmother in New Hampshire? Our grandmother lives in California." Cruelly, Regina chants, "Is this another one of your bizarre fantasies?" Exasperated, Elena ignores her cousin. Regina changes the subject; observes, saying, "Wow, Ginny's brother is getting cute; he used to be a wimpy, skinny kid with bad skin." Elena dismisses the comment; quickly opens the door and dashes up the stairs.

In the house, Elena goes into her bedroom. Seeing her *irritating* cousin Tim sprawled across her bed looking at her personal items, seething, she screams, "What are you doing?" Rushing over to him Elena pushes Tim off her bed shouting, "Get out of my room!" Making tiny circular motions with his finger to the side of his head, Tim calls out, "You're loonier than I thought." Shoving something into his pants pocket, fearing the others might hear, Tim slithers out of Elena's bedroom. Elena goes after him, slamming the door on him. Tim falls down. From the kitchen, Tess and Mary Grace observe this. Both are upset. Not wanting to make matters worse, Mary Grace makes excuses, "Ignore them; teenagers like to tease one another." She takes Tess's hands and says, "Come let's have dessert." Confused, Tess hesitantly follows her sister.

Minus Elena, who has locked herself in her bedroom, the rest of the family and Father Kelly sit down for dessert. They behave as if everything is customary. The thought of the lemon meringue pie activates Elena's yearning taste buds. She finally comes out of her safe haven bedroom and joins the rest after much coaxing from Mary Grace. Regina makes room for her cousin to sit next to her. She pats Elena's knee hoping to comfort her cousin. "Tim's a jerk!" she whispers in Elena's ear. "Ignore him. That's what I do." Elena looks at her cousin and reassures her, "I'm fine." She holds out her plate to her Aunt Mary who is serving the famous lemon meringue pie requesting, "Give me a huge piece Aunt Mary." "Sure Peck and what about you Pick?" Mary Grace coined the girls that when they were babies. Elena loved to eat and Regina had to be forced to eat. Normally, Elena would finish Regina's food whenever they were together. Mary Grace slices a hefty piece, puts in a plate and attempts to give it to her daughter. Regina refuses, "No Mom, I have to watch my figure if I'm going to be in the movies." Tim snickers mocking, "Yeah, sure Regina; you look like a Q-tip, no body and a big head." Coolly Regina smirks at her brother calling him "Jerk!" Geoff their father warns Tim and Regina to stop, "Enough you two; your acting like spoiled brats."

Geoff asks Mary Grace to give him the piece she originally sliced for Regina. "I'll eat that, it looks fantastic." He devours it with gusto. Mocking Geoff says, "Regina, you have no idea what you are missing Miss Drama Queen." Cool and collected Regina retaliates, "You'll eat those words one day, Dad." After the "legendary" lemon meringue pie is devoured by everyone except Tess and Regina, along with hot roasted chestnuts; a medley of fresh fruits, minced meat pie topped with Breyer's hand-dipped French Vanilla ice cream; after-dinner mints; and an array of cordials for the adults, everyone settles down.

Calmly Tess asks Elena to play some Christmas songs for the guests on the piano. "Great idea," responds Uncle Geoff as he begins to sing, "It's beginning to look a lot like Christmas." With a revolting look on her face, Elena glares at her mother. She blatantly refuses, "Not now Mom!" Everyone pleads, especially Father Kelly, "Please do! You must play extremely well. I know you take lessons from Sister Margaret Mary at our parish, correct?" "Yes." Tess explains, "Since first grade." Father Kelly interjects, "Sister Margaret Mary is also an excellent history teacher. Did you know that she is a scholar on the American Civil War?" "Really?" Tess responds. Looking at her daughter Tess asks again, "I am sure Sister Margaret Mary would want you to play for Father Kelly." Elena gives her mother a distained glare. Perturbed, Mike stands up, goes over to his daughter, and puts his arm around Elena. Exerting his parental authority, Mike insists, "You can't disappoint a priest. It's your Christian duty to respect his wishes." Mike resumes, "You like that TV show *Father Knows Best*? Follow what it implies."

Noticing Elena is not budging and she is annoying his wife Tess, Mike reprimands his only child, "You better, young lady. I've spent plenty of money on your piano lessons." Insisting, Mike requests, "Let me hear what my hard-earned money is being spent on." Demanding Elena play, Mike's insensitive manner infuriates Tess. Observing her sister is ready to erupt, Mary Grace rushes to soothe her. She hands Tess a glass of wine. Turning around Mary Grace goes up to Elena. She politely pleads, "Do it for me Elena. I made that pie especially for you." Hearing her aunt, Elena reluctantly saunters over to the piano. She defiantly plops onto the piano bench. Just as she begins to play "Jingle Bells," like a predator Elena eyes Father Kelly, who sits down next to her. The priest's bony hip touching her thigh repulses Elena.

Abruptly Elena recoils from Father Kelly. Her need to flee consumes her. She stops playing, bangs the piano shut, stands up announcing, "I'm giving up piano lessons. I hate going there! Sister Margaret Mary moved the piano to the basement and I don't like it there. I'm never going into that basement again!" Shocked by this outburst, everyone is silenced even the orator Father Kelly. In a flash, Elena runs out of the room. Like mystified zombies, the stunned others remain immobilized. Not wanting to upset the holiday any further or her emotionally sensitive sister, Mary Grace heads to the piano, sits down, and plays a lively version of *Jingle Bells*. She encourages everyone to sing along, "Come on now; let's get some holiday spirit going." Mary Grace, counts, "One, two three…everybody sing loud and clear, *Jingle Bells, Jingle Bells*."

While everyone is singing, Elena's spirit bursts out of the house zooming over the lighted buildings that inhabit the *happy* families enjoying their Thanksgiving holiday. For survival, the frightened inner girl again must escape to a safe haven far away. As Elena is slipping away, in the background the others are singing, *"Jingle Bells, Jingle Bells; Jingle All the Way."*

CHAPTER NINE

Currier and Ives Setting/ The Princess Angel
Thanksgiving Evening
Walpole, New Hampshire
1865

THE MERRY SOUND of jingle bells from a lone horse-drawn sleigh carrying a young family home to their New England farm fills the air with joyous sounds. A multitude of brilliant stars in the vast sky on this frigid Post-Civil War cultural "day of thanksgiving" evening brighten the night. The young woman and little child in the one-horse open sleigh are covered head to toe in luxurious, furry-white hats and hand muffs. The thick, lush wool blanket warms their fragile bodies making them feel protected and cozy against the harsh frigid air. The blanket was made from the wool from their own sheep. The husband-father driving the sleigh is woozy from overindulging the homemade hard apple cider made from his apple orchard and shared with neighbors who just had them over for Thanksgiving dinner.

Austin O'Brien- Stevens drives cautiously knowing that he has his beautiful young wife and precious little girl in the sleigh. The gelding Buck is slipping on the treacherous icy path. Having traversed this route numerous times, the mare handles it guardedly like a pro. When they approach the heavily snowy, circular driveway the driver praises his faithful old buddy, "Good job Buck!" They finally arrive in front of the main house. The young family is pleased to be home safe and sound after a lovely dinner on this day of thanksgiving with fine friends and good neighbors.

While pregnant sized snowflakes fall, they are unaware of a brilliant apparition above. Like the wind unseen but felt, it surrounds the sleigh carrying this loving family. The petite country girl, cuddled in her mother's arms, looks up at the velvety, coal-black sky all aglow with glittering diamond-twinkling stars. The full moon is temporarily hidden behind passing clouds making the sky pitch black spooky. The clouds roll on unveiling the silvery moon. A magical specter appears to the little child. She pictures a "beautiful princess" suspended in the majestic sky. With a child's whimsical imagination, she points cheering, "Look Mama, the princess angel is flying over us." The adoring mother smiles and looks up. Seeing only a starry night sky, she explains to her daughter that's the *Milky Way*. "No!" the determined little girl insists. "It's the wandering angel who comes at night to visit me," she cries out.

The one-horse sleigh pulled by faithful Buck halts when he reaches the front entrance to the house. Well trained, the horse patiently waits for the family to disembark. No longer listening to her daughter's *fairy tale*, the mother Anna Lee hands her daughter Theresa Edith to her husband Austin. Ann Lee guardedly steps down out of the sleigh. Austin lovingly carries his daughter in his powerful arms. Anxious, the three hustle into the warm gentleman farmhouse.

From his small living quarters next to the barn, caretaker Zeke sees the sleigh returning home with the family. Zeke stomps through the heavily encrusted snow toward the horse-drawn sleigh. Through the snowy haze he appears ghost like. Reaching the sleigh Zeke takes hold of the horse's reins guiding Buck and the now empty sleigh to the red painted, aged-worn barn. The father stops at the front door of the house. He calls out, "Thank you Zeke." Zeke waves back. "I hope all is well," Austin asks. Zeke nods his head up and down in a positive manner. Holding the reins of Buck tightly in his large gloved hands, the reclusive farm hand continues to tromp through the deep snow-covered trail leading faithful Buck safely to the barn. You can hear the sound of the sleigh bells as Zeke and Buck move slowly along in knee deep snow. Austin hollers out again to Zeke, "Make sure you give Buck a good rubdown and cover him with a warm blanket. It is a brutally cold night." Zeke reassuringly nods affirmatively to his boss.

Safely in her pre-revolutionary farmhouse, the young mother goes from room to room lighting the lanterns with a long candle holder. Holding a lantern, she guides her husband and child upstairs to their bedrooms on the second floor. The third floor has been permanently closed to the family since the grandfather left to go to Australia years ago. The little girl falls asleep in her father's reassuring arms as he is carrying her up the winding stairs to the second floor. The parents go into their daughter's bedroom with her. The father gently places his daughter on her bed. Austin kisses his precious girl. Leaving the bedroom, he informs his wife he'll be in their sleeping quarters. As Austin is leaving, he instructs his wife, "Call, if you need me."

The mother quietly undresses the sleeping child, puts her in her long winter nightgown and covers her head with a warm cap. Once Anna Lee's daughter is on her goose down mattress she tenderly places a huge patchwork quilt gently over her. Assured that her child is comfortable and snuggled in, Anna Lee gives Theresa Edith a kiss on her flushed, red-apple cheeks and quietly walks away. Reaching the door, the loving mother stops and gives her daughter one more adoring look. She thanks God for the blessing of this beautiful child and for her husband Austin's miraculous safe return from the Civil War. Gently closing the solid maple door, Anna Lee exits her daughter's room.

Little Theresa Edith sighs as she rolls over dreaming of the *princess angel*. In a deep slumber, the "princess angel" swoops down suspending over Theresa Edith. Seeing the sweet little girl sleeping peacefully and all is well, she travels back years ahead to her family in Jersey City.

CHAPTER TEN

I'm Dreaming of a White Christmas
Christmas Eve
Jersey City, NJ
1955

ELENA, TESS, AND MIKE are admiring their natural-blue spruce Christmas tree which is standing majestically in their living room. Elena and her father picked it out themselves a week before Christmas after Mike returned home from work. As father and daughter started out for their "perfect" Christmas tree search, it began to snow enhancing their holiday mood. It is always fun for Elena and her Dad to go together to pick out the "ideal tree." Tess stays home wrapping Christmas gifts. This particular year, father and daughter picked out a tree—larger than any other year. Mike stubbornly haggles with the salesman to give him a "good price." After much discussion, a fair price is decided upon. Mike pays more than he intended but seeing Elena's beaming face when she sees this beautiful tree, money is no object. Getting the tree securely tied onto the top of their automobile is a haggle. Eventually they get the tree securely tied on the roof and head for home. The snow is falling fast and furious making it difficult to keep the car from skidding on the slick icy roads. Their 1952 red and white Chevy Bel-Air sways and slides down Westside Avenue. The wind shield wipers are feverishly fighting the battle against the blinding snow which is building up on the frosted front glass windshield.

Due to the fierce swirling snow, Mike can barely see out the front window. Hearing Elena's joyful singing, *I'm Dreaming of a White Christmas*, Mike perseveres. Hearing his daughter singing makes Mike extremely happy. Under his breath he comments, "There's nothing wrong with my daughter. Listen to her sing." Thankfully father and daughter make it home unscathed. They are thrilled to find a parking space near the house. Leaving the warm car to head out into the cold snow, freezing Mike and Elena struggle removing the huge Blue Spruce tree from the top of the snow- covered auto. With branches laden with heavy-wet snow father and daughter laboriously drag it up the front porch into the hall drenching the carpeted main stairwell. Mike and Elena are so proud of this perfect tree.

Their "ideal Christmas tree" is securely up in its sturdy metal stand. It looks fabulous even undecorated. Mike trims a few inches off the top so the family's special white and gold angel fits perfectly on the top. It is always a joy for father and daughter to decorate it while Tess stands by making futile suggestions. Mike always covers the tree with enormous amounts of silvery tinsel whereas Tess always complains that he puts too much on. This traditional bantering of "too little or too much tinsel" continues Christmas after Christmas. Mike constantly ignores his wife. "It looks beautiful," Elena reassures her Dad. Mike transforms into "Jolly Old Saint Nick" during the holiday season. He loves every minute of it, as does Elena. She is all aglow like the twinkling lights and glittering tinsel on the tree during this blissful season. When the beautiful angel is placed on the top of the tree, Elena stares at it long and hard experiencing a connection to it.

On Christmas Eve, Tess, Mike, and Elena always have dinner with Ettie and Carlo in their place downstairs. Italians usually fast from eating meat on Christmas Eve (La Vigilia). The traditional custom was to eat seafood and no meat. It is called the "Feast of the Seven Fish." The seven fish represent the Seven Christian Sacraments. Every Christmas Eve Ettie makes the seven fish to fulfill the time-honored European tradition. There is baked eel; broiled flounder; fried crisp calamari; rich shrimp scampi; pasta with hot anchovy sauce; fried smelts along with codfish salad known to most Italians as Baccala salad. Ettie always makes plain pasta for her niece Elena since she doesn't like fish.

After dinner, Elena and her parents attend Christmas midnight mass at Saint Victor's Roman Catholic Church. Monsignor John Kelly usually officiates at Midnight Christmas Eve Mass; concelebrated this year with the new priest Father Arthur Schultz. It is the first time Elena attends midnight mass on Christmas Eve. As she enters the church and views all the beautiful candles a glow, the magnificent huge poinsettia plants surrounding the altar, and the life-like Crèche of the Holy Family, she is awestruck. During the mass Elena marvels at the magnificent melodious voices of the huge church choir. Dressed in their long, red-choir robes, the choir performs beautiful Christmas Carols along with traditional religious songs. Elena especially adores the hymns, *Oh Holy Night and Hark the Herald Angels Sing*.

After almost two hours, the beautiful traditional Christmas Eve midnight mass is over. Leaving the church Elena and her parents are greeted by Monsignor Kelly and Father Schultz. They stand at the back of the church wishing all the parishioners, "A Holy and Blessed Christmas." Mike and Tess go up and offers their holiday greeting to them. Sister Margaret Mary is still in the church praising the choir. Seeing Tess and Mike, Sister Margaret Mary smiles and mouths to them "Merry Christmas." Tess assumes Elena is behind them. She isn't. Before her parents realize, Elena rushes out the front door of the church. She waits outside under the beautiful star-studded frosty night on the snow blanketed sidewalk. *The serenity creates a sense of peace and good will toward man.*

In the alley between the St. Victor's church and the rectory, Elena notices janitor Juan shoveling snow. She thinks it strange that on this bitter cold night he is wearing a light jacket and does not have hat or gloves on. Turning around, Juan notices Elena looking at him. In an ambiguous manner he gazes at her causing Elena to feel uncomfortable. The young janitor is not much older than her cousin Tim, Elena notices. She nods to acknowledge him and quietly murmurs, "Feliz Navidad." Acknowledging her, Juan places his lips into a half-moon smile. Elena stands frozen; Juan resumes shoveling the ally.

After wishing Monsignor Kelly and Father Schultz a Merry Christmas, Tess and Mike walk over to Elena. "We're ready to leave," Tess tells her daughter. Elena looks to see if Juan is in the alley still shoveling snow. Down the dark alley Elena is disturbed watching Juan being pulled along by Father Schultz. This upset's Elena! Seeing her daughter sullen, Tess inquires, "What's wrong?" Before Elena could answer, her father, standing next to their car, in a festive mood calls out to his wife and daughter,

"Come on you slow pokes! Santa can't deliver his presents until we are *all snuggled in bed.*"

Mike brushes the snow off the car, warms the engine while Elena and Tess are still poking around. He opens the door for his wife and daughter motioning them to hurry. In the car the Policino family head home. Feeling pleased that they were in church all together on this Holy Night Mike is feeling more positive. Elena was feeling uneasy seeing Juan, but she is determined to block it out of her mind at least for tonight. It especially helps when her father, Old Saint Nick, begins singing loudly, *"Santa Claus is Coming to Town…"*

This sensitive young girl is determined not to upset her parents on this special night. Elena sings along with her Dad. Tess sits content listening to Elena and Mike resoundingly sing out, *You better watch out, you better not cry, you better not pout, I'm telling you why…* The holiday spirit is contagious. Tess joyfully joins in on their rendition of, *Santa Claus is Coming to Town.* Cheerful, Mike says, "Now that's what I call holiday spirit!" Honking the horn, he calls out to the imaginary reindeer, "Now Dasher, now Prancer, now Donner and Blitzen, Dash Away, Dash, Away, Dash Away All."

As soon as they arrived home, Elena goes to her lone hanging Christmas stocking. She always felt disappointed that they did not have a fireplace to hang her huge red and green stocking with her name Elena Rose embroidered in script on it. Her grandmother Elena made it for her when she was a baby. Elena has had this stocking as long as she can remember. Not having a fireplace, Tess improvised by hanging it on a hook near the living room window next to the Christmas tree.

This was another bone-of-contention with Tess. She always dreamed of having a small private house in the suburbs near where she grew up in Monmouth County. Tess visualized it. An amble piece of property for a garden, pets to roam, and a fireplace in the living room—her dream has not become a reality. *No, Tess, there is no Santa Clause,* Tess mimics looking at the lone stocking hanging on a make-shift hook. Putting aside her thoughts, and leaving Elena alone to check out her stocking, Tess goes into the kitchen. Mike heads to the bedroom *for a long winter's nap.*

Sitting on the floor under the glowing lighted tree heavily weighed down with silvery, sparkling tinsel is Elena. A small Crèche with figures of the Holy Family, Mary, Joseph and a crib for the infant Jesus, is placed under the glorious tree. Looking at the clock on the living room wall which showed it was 1:30 a.m. Elena, realizing that it is officially Christmas day, jumps up and calls out to her parents. She heads to the side table drawer where they always keep the miniature figure of the baby Jesus. At midnight, on Christmas, it is their family tradition for Elena to take the tiny baby Jesus figure from the drawer and gently place it in the manger. This family ritual makes it official that the Christ Child is born. Mike hearing Elena jumps up from the bed. He goes into the living room. Walking into the living room, Tess is carrying a tray, with her hot English breakfast tea, a rich, dark-as-midnight espresso for Mike, and her traditional hot chocolate for Elena. Elena and Mike are standing by the Creche. Glancing at Elena, Mike and the Christ Child in the Manger, Tess internally prays hoping for "Peace on Earth and Good Will toward Men" in their home on this special night.

Proud and pleased that she placed the little Babe in its crib, extremely tired, Elena dozes off besides the Christmas tree. Fast asleep Mike carries Elena into her bedroom. It reminds him of when she was just a little child and he would read to her *The Night Before Christmas* as she anticipated the arrival of Santa. He gently places Elena on her bed. When Mike leaves, Tess goes in. Not wanting to wake her daughter, Tess gently places sleeping Elena into her nightgown. She is sleeping soundly like a baby. Tess tucks her in recalling when she did this from the day she was born. Hoping her daughter will be up bright and early to open up her presents in the morning as Tess and her sister Mary Grace had done as young girls. Tess never wants her daughter to lose that sense of "Christmas Wonder" no matter what age. *Both parents adore their daughter.*

Mike and Tess go to bed with a warm feeling, especially knowing that Elena is peacefully fast asleep in her bed. *"It was the night before Christmas and all through the house, not a creature was stirring, not even a mouse."* Outside the snow is falling gently covering the city streets making it look like a Currier and Ives painting. There was a silent hush surrounding the Michael Policino household. *Peace on Earth Good Will Toward Men.*

It is customary for Elena's immediate family to open their presents on Christmas morning. Even though Elena is a teenage, Mike likes to think that Elena still believes in Santa Claus. In the 50s teenagers were not as sophisticated as they are today. Tess wishes the spirit of Christmas will encapsulate her troubled daughter and resolve all of her recent problems. With the spirit of Christmas surrounding her family this "Holy Night," Tess prays all will be right.

After a fairly restful night, finally it is Christmas morning. As in past years, Elena wakes up exceedingly early. In her heart of hearts, she believes a special spirit places the gifts under the Christmas tree even though she is aware there is no real Santa Claus. It was so upsetting the year her "spiteful" cousin Tim told his naïve cousin Elena and his equally naïve sister Regina that their parents are the real Santa Claus. To save face, they lied and told Tim they already knew. At the time, it was devastating for them; especially Elena. The fantasy was broken but this young girl transcended reality. She believes there is an altruistic force beyond comprehension somewhere out there.

CHAPTER ELEVEN

"We Wish You a Merry Christmas"
1955 Christmas Morning
Jersey City, NJ

EARLY CHRISTMAS MORNING Elena jumps out of bed, heads straight to her parents' bedroom door; knocks and begs them to go to the Christmas tree. She is excited for her parents to open the presents she bought for them. Also, she is anxious to see what she receives. Elena is not disappointed. She is thrilled with the record albums of Broadway shows which she wanted. Along with the albums, Elena is thrilled with the standing easel, new oil paints, brushes, and painting instruction books. The white angora sweater with a matching white hat and knit gloves pleased her beyond. Just when Elena thought she had opened all her presents, Tess hands her daughter one more gift to open. "Here, dear, there is one more present for you."

Smiling broadly, Tess holds it toward her daughter. Hesitantly but excitedly Elena takes it. Gazing longingly at the red and gold paper with the large velvet red bow on it, she looks at her mother who gives a reassuring nod. Elena rips the gorgeous wrapping paper off. She quickly removes the cover off the box, unfolds the tissue paper, and peeks inside. A broad smile spreads across her beaming face. Tears well up in her eyes. "Well, aren't you going to take them out?" her mother excitedly asks. Mike is anxious also; he has no idea what it is. Slowly, Elena removes one gorgeous black velvet slipper covered with brilliant, multicolored-glass jeweled stones all over it. She takes out the other and stares with amazement at both of them. She cries out, "Oh my goodness, there're for me?" "Yes, of course they're for you! Don't you like them?" Tess questions her daughter. Jumping up and down Elena shouts, "Yes, yes, I love them!" She reaches over to her mother hugs and kisses her. She rushes over to her father and embraces him.

After she expresses her immense appreciation, Elena begins to take off her tired looking slippers and carefully puts the jeweled velvet ones on - they fit perfectly. She admiringly stares at them. Slowly her velvet slipper-clad feet, like magic, moves rhythmically. Mike runs to the record player and puts on one of Elena's new record albums. To her parents' delight, Elena twirls and dances all over the living room around the Christmas tree. She resembles the beautiful Snow Princess in the Tchaikovsky's infamous ballet *Swan Lake*. The song ends, Elena looks sad and questions her mother, "Where will I wear them? They are so special!" Tess quickly reminds her daughter, "Aren't you invited to a New Year's Eve party to celebrate Ginny's brother Angelo's 17th birthday?" "Yes, but I didn't think I would go." Immediately she blurts out, "With these beautiful ballet slippers, now I must go!" Under her breath she whispers, "My own magical shoes." It truly was a Merry Christmas morning for Elena and her parents; especially for Tess who has been concerned about her daughter.

Tess and Mike also loved their gifts from their daughter. Black woolen gloves for Mike and a beautiful white and pink floral scarf for Tess. Aunt Mary Grace helped Elena pick them out from a Macy's catalogue the day of Thanksgiving. She ordered them for her niece and had them mailed downstairs to Ettie's house. After Tess, Mike, and Elena open their Christmas presents, consume their traditional hot chocolate, and the nut and dried fruit filled German Christmas Stollen, Elena announces she is going downstairs to wish Aunt Ettie a "Merry Christmas." First she carefully places her special gift in the box and puts the velvet slippers safely in her bedroom closet.

Coming out of her bedroom Elena immediately attempts to head downstairs to visit her Aunt. "Wait a minute!" Tess calls out while removing a large beautifully wrapped Christmas present from under the Christmas tree. She motions for Elena to come and get it. Tess instructs Elena to bring it downstairs and give it to Aunt Ettie. Her mother cautions Elena not to be a nuisance and return soon so they could get ready to go to Aunt Mary Grace and Uncle Geoff's house for Christmas dinner. With great excitement Elena heads downstairs to bring the beautifully wrapped gift tied up with a huge red bow to her Aunt Ettie's.

"What did you buy for my sister?" Mike interrogates Tess. "I got her a lovely robe and nightgown." Noticing Mike is not pleased, Tess reassures him, "She'll like it! Don't worry Mike I did well!" Sarcastically she comments, "It's probably the only decent present she'll get." Convinced, Mike held up his present. He tells Tess how thrilled he is with his new Remington electric shaver. "I always wanted one of these; no more stubble to scratch your baby-soft face," he teases. Tess is content with her Lanvin Arpege Perfume. Dabbing some behind her ears, she says, "Mike, this is too extravagant. You should have bought cologne. Perfume is too costly." Feeling proud, he assures her, "Nothing but the best for my gorgeous wife."

The good spirit dissipates quickly when Mike stands up, places his gift under the tree, pecks Tess's forehead announcing he is going out for a while. Placing a dab of perfume behind her ear hearing this, in anger, Tess screws the top of the bottle of perfume. She gives her husband a look to kill. Disappointed, she pleads, "It's Christmas, where are you going?" He hollers, "Out! I'll only be gone for a while." Hurt, Tess shouts, "Go ahead! Who cares?" With fury in his eyes Mike glares at her complaining, "There you go again Tess ruining a perfectly good morning and Christmas at that." He continues, "You're not happy unless you start trouble."

Mike reminds Tess, "Did you see how Elena was thrilled with her gifts; especially the record albums of all the latest Broadway Show tunes, the artist easel, and those shoes." He emphasizes his daughter's pleasure, "She was even dancing around in those fancy slippers." Betrayed that Tess picked them out without him, and Tess receiving all the credit, he walks over to Elena's new easel. Mike picks up a paint brush and swishes it around bragging, "Elena can't wait to paint on her new easel that I picked out!" Tess interjects, "Sure, she was putting on a good front." "Front my eye! Why are you are always looking to find something wrong with me and our daughter!" Tess defends herself, "You can think all you want, but I'm the one who hears her crying at night, tossing and turning and unable to sleep." "Bullshit," Mike stammers. Ignoring Mike, Tess resumes, "I see the blank stare in her eyes which comes and goes in a flash and you ignore it." Mike retaliates, "I didn't see any blank stare in her eyes this morning. They were sparkling. She was happy!" "That's for our sake," Tess shoots back.

Enraged, Mike closes his eyes, raises his hand to his ears not to look at his wife or listen to her any longer. Infuriated, Tess runs up to Mike pulls his hands from his ears, shouting, "Mike, you're going to listen to me! You turn a blind eye and a deaf ear to everything. You're a coward, you run away when things get tough!" Mike opens his eyes and darts a glaring intent look back at his irritated wife. He throws his hands up in the air shouting, "I give up!" He storms out of the room; grabs his coat. Heading down the stairs he yells out, "You don't know what tough means. I'm out of here!" Filled with pent up anger Tess throws the perfume bottle at him. It didn't hit him or break, but, when it landed on the hardwood floor, it made a loud bang - but not as loud as the bang from the front door, as Mike slams it shut. Storming out of the house he calls out, "And all that so called 'gaudy tinsel' looks great!"

All excited, Elena tells Aunt Ettie all about the first midnight mass she attended last night with her parents. Her aunt is pleased. Aunt Ettie tells Elena she is sad she missed it. "Uncle Carlo was not feeling well," she mentions. Handing her Aunt the present, Ettie seems shy about taking it. Opening it, a broad, happy smile beams across Ettie's face. "This is so beautiful. I always wanted a long blue robe and what a pretty nightgown. These blue and yellow flowers on the nightgown are beautiful," she exhorts. As the young niece and Aunt are fussing over the gift, they hear a loud noise from upstairs. Aunt Ettie questions, "What's that racket?" Rising to go upstairs, Elena's caring Aunt, sensing trouble, convinces her niece to stay, "Sweetie stay, something must have dropped by accident." Ettie tempts Elena to stay by offering her the sumptuous homemade Italian cookies she made. Aunt Ettie reaches for a plate filled with sugary delights. "Here, take one; I was going to send them upstairs later but since you are my dearest brother Mike's daughter, you can have the first one. Besides, it's Christmas."

Aunt Ettie adores her younger brother Mike. After their parents died, the older sister and younger brother bonded like cement. Ettie was a surrogate mother to Mike when their mother died. Their intense closeness always disturbed Tess. It was not unfounded, Mike ran to his older sister whenever he needed to get away from a situation that should have been handled between a husband and wife. Meaning well, Ettie made excuses for her brother all the time. She never deliberately did it. Unfortunately, it alienated herself from Tess.

Tess wanted to move into another place years ago but Mike never wanted to leave his sister or his family home. He felt obligated to Ettie since she raised him after his parents died. Ettie loves her husband Carlo and her two adult children but Mike was clearly her joy. Mike felt responsible to stay and maintain the house their parents bought years ago from their *blood sweat and tears.* As Italian immigrants, his humble parents slaved relentlessly to earn enough money to buy their own home in a clean, safe, up-scale neighborhood. *The American dream!* Mike selflessly took on the cloak of protector of the family and the house but *at whose expense?*

Elena nervously gobbles down one of her aunt's homemade cookies. Recalling her mother's warnings not to stay too long, and upset by the noise upstairs, she kisses and hugs Aunt Ettie. She thanks her for the treats and promises that she will come back down later when Aunt Ettie's adult children come to have dinner with their mom and dad. Actually, Elena liked being alone with her Aunt. She could never warm up to her Uncle Carlo. Ettie's adult children Blaise and Rosaria are considerably older than Elena for her to have much in common with them.

Ettie's husband Carlo is out visiting his old cronies, even on Christmas morning. He is very old fashion, frugal, and doesn't believe in frivolous gift giving. Ettie never receives a Christmas present from him; if she did, it was always practical. Something for the kitchen. Fortunately, Tess, Mike, and Elena always give her something special, as do Ettie's children. Ettie is content just to be with her family; gifts do not matter to her. Family is the most important thing in her cloistered life along with maintaining a harmonious, intact family. Loyalty and family are paramount in Ettie's simple life. These are the only gifts she desires. Ettie does everything in her limited power to achieve and fiercely maintain it.

 *

Racing upstairs, Elena flings open the door. Seeing her mother sitting on the floor next to the Christmas tree cradling her bottle of perfume in her shaking hands upsets Elena. Tess's head is hung low on her chest.

When her daughter comes in, Tess immediately pretends to be happy. Wiping the tears from her eyes, Tess calls out to Elena, "How did Aunt Ettie like her presents?" Elena goes into her bedroom and bangs her door shut. She refuses to deal with this drama anymore. Elena's record player is in a corner of her bedroom. She takes one of her records out of its album cover; places it on her record player; puts the needle on it; and plays her favorite Christmas album by Bing Crosby: *I'm Dreaming of a White Christmas.* This beautiful Christmas song fills Elena's bedroom with pleasant comforting harmony. Through music Elena attempts to find joy on this special supposedly joyful holiday.

Unfortunately, it dissipates quickly when she hears her father climbing up the steps and her mother's bedroom door slams shut. As if nothing happened, Mike asks, "When do we leave for your sister Mary Grace's house?" No answer. He screams, "Tess, I said, when the hell *do we* go to Westfield to have dinner with your so-called precious sister and her loony family?" From inside their bedroom Tess hollers, "Elena and I are leaving here by noon and I'm taking the car!"

Tess defends her family and defiles Mike's, "You call my family loony, what about your brother-in-law Carlo? He rode that broken-down motorcycle till he crashed and totaled it." Laughing, she mockingly adds, "Then he goes out and buys an old wreck of a car, a real hunk-of-a-junk." Mike defends the situation, "It gets him to and from work." "Really?" Tess sarcastically calls back, "He's so brilliant he took out the entire front windshield deliberately." Mike once again defends Carlo's actions, "He had to break the windshield; it had a crack in it and it wouldn't have passed inspection." Annoyed, Mike defiantly explains to Tess, "Carlo was smart enough to know that no windshield was better than a cracked windshield." "Brilliant," Tess hollers back. He yells out, "He passed inspection!" Scornfully Tess questions, "What does he do in the snow, rain and cold?" Mike calls out, "Very funny; he puts a blanket over himself." "Real clever!" she shouts. Sardonically laughing, Tess stresses, "I rest my case; your sister's husband is beyond odd. You, Mike a narcist and your sister's false idol." She pauses a minute. Tess then adds, "Oh, excuse me, I meant to say, idiot!" Fuming mad, Tess continues her rampage, "Also, I hate this city. Who ever heard of a place that doesn't allow its children to go

Trick-or-Treating? Instead, they let them go "Begging-for-Thanksgiving." She screams out, "It's un-American!"

Mike ignores Tess's insulting comments. He returns to the issue at hand, "What in hells name do you mean you and Elena are leaving at noon? What about me?" Angry Mike asks. No answer from Tess. "You don't take Elena or the car without me," he warns his wife. "It's mine. I paid for it!" Mike shouts out. Tess answers back, "Yes, you paid for it but I helped too."

Hearing her parents heated argument, sitting with a huge book on her lap, Elena calls from behind her bedroom door, "I'm not going! I'll stay here with Aunt Ettie." Mike taunts his wife, "Good idea. Elena will stay home with me. Besides my sister Ettie cooks a hell of a lot better than your sister Mary Grace." He continues to provoke, "Speaking of "odd" that nephew of yours, Tim, is a weirdo and I think he gets it from his perverted father." Tess does not respond. Mike emphasizes, "I don't want my daughter near wacky Tim or his racy father." This sends Tess over the brink, "You try to stop me from going." Tess calls out to her daughter, "Elena, you're coming with me!" "No!" chimes Elena. Fearing her mother will come in the room, Elena takes the two large books one about the Civil War and another an old family photo album she got from Sister Margaret Mary and quickly hides them back under her bed.

Tess accuses, "Mike, see what you've started - you and your sister." Mike impulsively hollers back, "My sister?" He retaliates, "What about that bleached blond, over-made-up, dizzy-in-the-head sister, Mary Grace." Calling out, "She's nothing but a wanna-a-be Marilyn Monroe." Mike stops to catch his breath then adds, "Even though she thinks she is Shirley Temple, the only sane one in that family is Regina." Tess retorts back, "Leave my sister Mary Grace and her family out of this." Recognizing that it is getting way-out-of-hand Tess pleads, "Please Mike, let us go in peace." Mike threatens, "Over my dead body!" Tess's fiery temper returns. She blurts out, "Get out of here. Go to that drunken lonely hearts club Walsh's Tavern where you can cavort with those female floozies with their numbers racketeer pimps." Stamping his feet Mike responds, "I get more respect there than I do here!"

No longer able to tolerate her parent's fighting and accusations, Elena goes into an out-of-body mode. The crooning sound of Bing Crosby singing, *I'm Dreaming of a White Christmas. Just like the ones I use to know,* raises Elena mentally up and away. The disharmony and friction between her father and mother, along with her repressed fears, make this innocent young girl once again escape to another time and place to a disguised unreality where fact and fiction merge.

CHAPTER TWELVE

"Away in a Manger"
Christmas Morning
Walpole, New Hampshire
1866

ON THIS SERENE Post Civil War Christmas morning, the snow is falling like fluffy cotton from the winter skies. The New Hampshire landscape is blanketed with virgin pure white snow. The skeleton trees' swaying movement in the wind makes them look like a ballet troupe from *Swan Lake*. Anna Lee, Austin, and Theresa Edith are sitting near the twinkling candle-lit, mammoth blue spruce Christmas tree sharing and viewing their presents. Theresa Edith is ecstatic over her new porcelain Victorian doll and handmade wooden rocking horse. Austin loves the navy blue and gold scarf his wife knitted. Anna Lee adores the hand-carved wooden cradle her husband, with the help of Zeke, made for their future second child who is due early spring.

Feeling chilled, Anna Lee requests that her husband put more logs on the fire. As he slowly and painfully moves to the huge stone fireplace, Anna Lee notices that his limp is more pronounced. She is now grateful that she engaged Zeke to make a beautiful walking stick for her husband with an elaborate brass horses head on the top for her to give to him for Christmas. Austin is thrilled with it but his pride takes hold. He announces, "I really don't need this walking stick right now; maybe when I am twenty years older." Observing the disappointed look on his wife's face and the smirk on Zeke, he retracts his previous statement stating, "It is so handsome. I'll use it for show." He holds it up proudly and labors with it over to the fireplace.

During the Civil War, Austin Nicholas Stevens was a Lieutenant in the 5th New Hampshire Regiment. In 1863, during a fierce battle against the Confederates, he was shot in the leg. His leg was so badly shattered that they thought they would have to amputate it. Amputations were frequently done during this deplorable war between the states. Austin was one of the lucky ones from his regiment. About fifty-seven men were killed from the 5th New Hampshire regiment during the war between the states. Austin's older cousin, Col. Edward Everett O'Brien Cross, was mortally wounded at the young age of thirty-one during this tragic war. These horrific memories of not so long ago, not only permanently wounded his leg, but his soul. Austin feels guilty that he came home alive and in one piece while so many, including his heroic cousin Col. Cross, did not. This is a permanent wound that will not heal. Seeing his budding pregnant wife and beautiful, health-young daughter, Austin O'Brien-Stevens feels blessed and courageously accepts his fate.

The American Civil War was a conflict between the Northern states of the USA, the Union, who fought to maintain the United States as one nation and the Southern states, the Confederacy. The South seceded from the union. The war lasted four, long hard years from 1861-1865. It cost more than 750,000 lives young and old. Brothers against brothers; fathers against sons; friends against friends; and neighbors against neighbors; fought one another from maiming to death.

The long standing, brutal disagreement over slavery was one of the predominate conflicts between the North and the South. The economy of the eleven Southern states including Virginia depended on slavery. In 1864, bloody campaigns in Virginia, Georgia, and the Carolinas depleted the South's human and material resources. It created great devastation and famine in the region.

On April 9, 1865, the South surrendered. Confederate General Robert E. Lee surrendered to the Union Army General Ulysses S. Grant. Sadly, Civil War President Abraham Lincoln, who fought fiercely to preserve the Union, was assassinated five days later. His legacy lives on as the President who preserved the United States as one nation and assisted in freeing the slaves. This dreadful "War Between the States" pitted brothers, fathers, and sons against one another; lovers and neighbors. Anna Lee from the

South and Austin from the North were divided geographically but joined together by a greater force. Love!

In 1861, Anna Lee and Austin were married only a short time when Austin officially became a soldier in the Union Army. He left immediately thereafter to fight with the Union Army. While Austin was away fighting, he felt confident that his young, newly pregnant bride was in good hands. He trusted and felt confident that Zeke his new farm hand would watch over her. Anna Lee's Virginia family were unable to help her since she now lived in enemy's territory New Hampshire.

Rumors have it that Zeke found his way to New Hampshire as a traveling farm hand or, as some around these parts assumed, an indentured servant or wounded soldier. Just before Anna Lee and Austin got married, with no questions asked, Austin hired him. Austin liked him because he was a hard worker. He admired that he quietly and faithfully did his chores and took first-rate care of the animals. More importantly, he took excellent care of Austin's favorite horse, Buck. Buck responded well to Zeke which was unusual for this finicky gelding.

Anna Lee was a little leery of Zeke. She felt uncomfortable being alone in that big house while an odd, mute man was living in the quarters next to the barn not far from the main house where she resided. Zeke rarely uttered a word he just murmured odd guttural sounds. Anna Lee found him strange but she trusted and went along with her husband's decision.

Anna Lee misses her family from Richmond, Virginia. Like so many other families, the War separated her from her biological family. Her father, Sherman Campbell, a wealthy tobacco farmer, was a Confederate loyalist. He was against abolishing slavery since he needed numerous slaves to keep his tobacco plantation financially viable. Her brothers, Tyler and Hamish, fought for the Confederate Army. Due to the war, with her husband fighting for the Union Army, Anna Lee was painfully separated from her Virginian family both physically and emotionally.

Anna Lee misses her mother Sarah Hall Campbell and her younger sister Beatrice terribly. This young woman was deeply worried for her husband and her brothers' safety. Anna Lee feels powerless, therefore she channels all her energy into her future baby and making her new home welcoming for her husband's safe return. This gentle young wife and daughter prays that when the war is over her entire family from either North or South will be together again amicably and peacefully.

It took awhile for Anna Lee to get used to New England and the remote people who live there. Anna Lee met Austin before the war at a cotillion while he attended a military school in Virginia. It was love at first sight. This handsome young man asked Anna Lee's father for her hand shortly after they met. Her father hesitated knowing that war was pending and he would have to relinquish his daughter to a future Union Army man. Love won out. Immediately after the wedding in Richmond, Virginia, Anna Lee moved to New Hampshire to the estate Austin inherited from his grandfather after he died. He was an only child. He lost both his parents as a young boy. He was raised by his paternal grandfather Austin Thomas Stevens the First. Being an only child with no parents Austin's ambition was to fill his grandfather's home with his future wife and numerous children. He believed he and Anna Lee would make it happen.

Anna Lee was a young, naïve, love-struck eighteen- year old Virginian Southern bride when she came to Walpole, New Hampshire. In the beginning she was extremely lonely and terribly homesick. This young well-bred southern girl, pious Christian felt misplaced as a new southern bride living in patriotic New England. At first, her New Hampshire neighbors were distant from her since they knew her brothers fought for the Confederacy and her southern ancestors and father were slave owners. At times, this young woman feared for her safety in this unwelcoming environment. Her deep love for Austin was so intense that she put aside her parents' and her concern. Anna Lee made it a priority to diligently strive to make her new husband and home happy and serene.

The warm springs, hot summers, cool autumns, and endless freezing New Hampshire winters passed uneventfully for Anna Lee while Austin was away fighting in the War. The newly pregnant Anna Lee managed alone with Zeke but she was always longing and praying ceaselessly for her husband's safe return. Anna Lee and Zeke are not fast friends but accept one another. A few days before Christmas while her husband it still at war, Anna Lee goes into premature labor. It is Zeke who rides Buck in the middle of the night during a fierce snowstorm to get the midwife, a local farmer's wife Emma Johnson to assist in the forthcoming birth.

Emma and her husband Joshua own and run the dairy farm up the road. It is Emma and Zeke who first lay eyes on the beautiful newborn. Anna Lee had a difficult delivery and fell into a deep sleep soon after the baby was born. When she finally wakes up she notices Zeke sitting on the wooden rocking chair he made. As if it were a new-born calf, he is holding securely onto the infant. Anna Lee is disturbed when she sees her infant in Zeke's arms. She immediately reaches out for her child and asks, "Please hand me my baby." Zeke hesitates. The young mother pleads for Zeke to give her the baby. "I asked you to give me my child," she repeats. After her persistence, he reluctantly hands the infant to her. Anna Lee is relieved and happy to have her child in her arms. She ignores Zeke's unfriendly look.

Cuddling her precious first-born daughter, and filled with immense love for this miracle, she looks around for Emma, the neighbor midwife. Realizing who Anna Lee is looking for, Zeke motions that she left. Concerned, Anna inquires as to who will help her with the baby. With his large index finger, Zeke boldly points to himself. Anna Lee is not pleased with this unexpected arrangement. She does not want him to care for her or the baby. Being a well-bred, southern woman, she politely and diplomatically thanks Zeke and reassures him that she and the baby will be fine by themselves. The farm-hand Zeke is upset. He defiantly stands there without moving. Observing his standoff, Anna Lee firmly requests again that he leave, "I do not wish to repeat myself but I must. Please leave!" She reminds him that in the absence of her husband, "I am the lady and head of the estate while my husband is gone. Your responsibilities are only to take care of the barn, the animals, and the property." He boldly stands there. Anna Lee equally as bold and defiant adds, "My husband made it clear to you Zeke that you are required to supply wood for the fireplace and provisions for me and the baby and nothing else unless I request it."

Zeke ignores her and with intimidation lingers. Anna Lee's eyes harden as she insists and orders, "Zeke, go back and resume your duties around the farm immediately!" She again reassures him, "I am fine and perfectly able and willing to take care of my child!" To soften the situation, she reassures him, "I will call you if and when I need you." Shamefaced but grudgingly, Zeke storms out.

Anna Lee hears the front door shut, holding tightly onto little Theresa Edith. Theresa was Austin's deceased mother's name and Edith was his grandmother's name. Anna Lee slowly rises from the rocking chair and walks over to the partially opened shuttered window. Intentionally hiding herself from view, she peers outside. The young mistress of the estate and new mother wants to make sure that Zeke goes back to his quarters behind the barn. Shielding her eyes from the blinding white snow pounding on the window, Anna Lee observes him as he slowly trudges through the snow which covers the entire property toward the barn. Chills shiver up her spine when she sees him turn and look up at the window where Anna Lee is shielding herself and her infant. She quickly closes the shutter tightly trying to shut out her fears as she cradles her new baby daughter tighter. Lovingly gazing down at this precious baby, Anna Lee believes that this special child will be her saving grace.

Anna Lee wishes Austin could be here with her to share in the abundant joy she feels for this new child and for him to reassure her that all will be fine. She patiently waits for his letters comforting her that he is safe and out of danger. Anna Lee writes to her husband daily yet she is never sure if he receives any of her letters. She gives them to Zeke praying he mails them and they reach her husband. A week later, Emma the midwife returns to inform Anna Lee that she can only stay a few days longer–she informs Anna Lee that unfortunately she is needed elsewhere. Before Emma leaves, and when the opportunity arises, Anna Lee asks Emma if she knows anything about Zeke.

Emma responds to Anna Lee's query, "Very little. I only know that he showed up one hot summer day during the early days of the war needing a good meal, medical attention, clothing, shoes and a job." "He was a

Helena C. Farrell

mystery!" she reiterates. Emma shares that she heard he lost his speech in a fiery battle. In a hush tone she adds, "Mrs. Stevens no one knows which side he fought on. For all anyone could surmise, he could have been a Confederate or a Union soldier or even a despised deserter." Emma continues, "Some thought Zeke never even participated in the war. They called him 'a chicken liver wimp.'" Whispering she says, "The word spy was also mentioned regarding Zeke."

New Englanders commonly mistrusted strangers. Emma Buffton Johnson, whose husband was a third generation Johnson from New England, seeing how upset Anna Lee is, tries to reassure her by saying, "If Austin hired him, then Zeke must be okay." She reinforces this by reminding Anna Lee, "Austin is a pure-blooded, native New Englander and a person to be trusted." Emma's remarks did not console or make Anna Lee feel any safer. She senses that Emma mutually feels the same mistrust about Zeke. Emma is good at keeping a façade when needed. As a proud New Englander and a long-time neighbor of Austin, Emma will do or say anything to make Anna Lee feel content and safe in Walpole. Therefore, she will not reveal *her* true feelings about Zeke.

After Emma leaves to help her husband with their dairy farm duties, it is just Anna Lee, baby Theresa Edith, and Zeke alone on the isolated farm. Zeke makes every excuse to come in the house just to stare at the baby; in fact, one time, while Theresa Edith was sleeping in the cradle in the nursery, Anna Lee heard a strange noise upstairs. She rushes up, and similar to a huge dark imposing shadow she observes Zeke lurking over her baby. Startling him, Anna Lee cries out, "What are you doing in here?" Shuddering, she runs over to the cradle, grabs the baby, shelters the infant in her arms, and points to the door. Zeke never utters a word; he just slithers his way out of the room with a sinister sulking look on his stoic face.

The next couple of years, while Austin was fighting with his regiment, Anna Lee experiences other strange encounters with Zeke, but they never amounted to anything serious. In the numerous letters Anna Lee writes to Austin she never mentions her concerns; she does not want to give her husband undue worry. She knows he would defend Zeke and claim that she was imagining things.

CHAPTER THIRTEEN

Brotherly /Sister Devotion
Christmas Day
Jersey City/Westfield, NJ
1955

MIKE JUMPS UP as Tess slams the front door, dragging a very angry Elena by the arm. A furious Mike screams through the door, "Get out of here; I'll have a better time without you!" Trembling and trying to appease her father, as she is leaving Elena calls out, "I'll be home early Daddy and we can celebrate later. I love you!"

Despondent, Mike goes to the refrigerator, grabs a beer and takes a long swig. Hearing music in Elena's bedroom, Bing Crosby's *White Christmas* is still playing, Mike goes in to shut it off. He accidentally scratches the record as he pulls the needle off. "Damn it!" he shouts. Christmases are not like they use to be. Peace and joy and all that crap is nothing but *Hum Bug*, a lot of bullshit." Trying to appease himself, Mike remarks, "Tess needs help, not my Elena." He consoles himself saying, "Tess is an out-of-control fighting tiger. I was warned not to marry a woman with red hair. I should have listened!" He gulps down the rest of the beer, crushes the can in his hand like a basketball tosses it in Elena's waste basket.

Mike goes to the side door, opens it and bangs it shut as he heads downstairs to his sister Ettie's where he knows he will get respect, comfort food, and unconditional love. When he opens the door and Ettie sees him, she is thrilled. She rushes over to him and leads him to the table. "Come Mike I made all your favorite Christmas food. She grabs a plate, starts to fill it to the brim. Her husband Carlo pours his brother-in-law a glass of homemade red wine. Clicking glasses Mike shouts out, "Salute! Buona Natale." Ettie and Carlo respond in kind. Ettie looks at her brother in awe.

It's as if the baby Jesus was born, not in a manger in Bethlehem, but right there in her humble dining room.

Filling his mouth with his sister's mouth-watering food, Mike stops, wipes his mouth with a large napkin and inquires, "I thought your kids were going to be here. Aren't they coming?" Ettie answers, "Sure. Rosaria doesn't get off duty from the hospital until later and Blaise's train arrives in about an hour." She immediately adds more food onto Mike's empty plate mentioning, "Rosaria and Blaise insist we start eating without them." Taking more bread, Mike recalls, "I haven't seen Blaise and Rosaria in a while." He pulls apart a piece of the hard crusted Italian bread and swirls it around his plate filled with rich red tomato sauce and comments, "You should be proud of Blaise, a US Marine." Slams his fist and shouts, "Now that's a man!"

Mike drinks another glass of wine. He asks, "How is gorgeous Rosaria? She's a RN now, right?" Ettie proudly remarks, "Yes Mike, my Rosaria has been working at the Margaret Hague Maternity Hospital a few months now!" Mike comments, "That's nice." He brags, "As usual, my call to the head of the hospital about giving her a job worked." "That's right!" Embarrassed Ettie asks, "Mike, didn't Rosaria call to thank you?" He responds, "No worries. I've got jobs for plenty of others. Why not for my own flesh and blood."

With his fork in hand, Mike reaches over for another pillow soft, ricotta cheese-filled ravioli. He places it in his mouth and swallows it down whole. Carlo gives his brother-in-law an ugly smirk. Mike resumes his talk about his niece, "Rosaria is real pretty. Isn't she close to thirty?" Ettie shakes her head up and down. He inquires, "Why doesn't she have a boyfriend or husband yet?" Noticing that Ettie and Carlo are avoiding answering, Mike suggests, "There must be plenty of eligible men in the hospital; a doctor would be nice." Ettie remains silent as she moves the meatballs and sausages closer to her brother. Mike, recognizing that he hit a sensitive nerve, tries to comfort his sister by remarking, "She's better off single." He reaches for another meatball.

Irritated, Carlo questions his brother-in-law, "Where's your wife and Elena?" Mike does not answer. Ettie quickly pours her husband another glass of wine to keep him quiet while adjusting the large white napkin around his stout neck. Ettie insists that her husband not dirty his Sunday white shirt she meticulously washed, starched, and ironed for him to wear on Christmas. She lectures, "Carlo, don't spoil your nice clean white dress shirt." Proudly she adds, "I want Rosaria and Blaise to see you all spruced up." Carlo pushes her hand away and pontificates, "Who cares about a clean white shirt!" He shouts, "My kids have seen me in soiled work clothes my entire life from hard, honest work. I'm not ashamed of any dirty shirt." Mike is ready to defend his sister. Ettie gives her brother the high sign not to comment.

After eating as much as he could to please his sister, Mike pushes himself from the table and rises. Stretching himself and loosening his belt, he thanks his sister, "That meal was fabulous. I must have put on five pounds." He announces, "I must go!" Ettie is disappointed. She begs him to wait for her son Blaise and daughter Rosaria. Mike hugs Ettie and promises her, "Of course I'll be back! I don't want to miss your delicious home-made Italian cookies like Mom used to make." He adds, "And your delicious ink black espresso." Carlo smirks saying, "You'll need that espresso if you continue to drink like you do." Seeing his sister upset by Carlo's comment and her disappointed face, Mike winks at her and reassures, "You know I'll be back Sis." Ettie smiles as she removes the food from the table. Frustrated with brother and sister's bantering Carlo quickly downs another glass of wine to repress his coughing fit.

Looking at his sister closely Mike painfully notices her aging before her time. Ettie's premature graying hair in a tight low bun, her shrinking stature, and wearing her usual red and white checkered apron, she reminds him of their late, sweet mother, Antonella. Mike stops, turns, smiles at his sister and insists, "Tell my niece and nephew to wait for their favorite uncle and make sure they save me some of those Italian pastries." Now really irritated Carlo pours himself more wine. In a harsh voice he orders his wife, "Let him go Ettie. He's a big boy now!"

Mike frowns back at his brother-in-law and heads toward the front door. Ettie runs after him and whispers in his ear, "Mike, I went to the cemetery yesterday and put flowers on our sister Rose's grave. Mike's large round, coal black eyes instantly get misty. He questions, "I hope they were red roses?" She reassures him. He bends over and gently kisses the top of his sister's head and goes out the door. Ettie stands there a moment wiping the tears rolling slowly down her puffy, aged cheeks with the bottom of her well-worn apron. Carlo calls out to her, "Ettie, where are you? Get me my cigarettes." Ettie is a selfless caregiver and dutiful wife. She shoves her pain deep inside. Not to aggravate Carlo further Ettie rushes back to her demanding but hardworking loyal husband.

CHAPTER FOURTEEN

"Sisters, Sisters, There Were Never Such Devoted Sisters"
Christmas Afternoon
Westfield, NJ
1955

AFTER AN HOUR of driving and dealing with heavy holiday traffic in icy sleet, Tess Adeline and the pouting Elena arrive late but thankfully safe at her sister Mary Grace's home. It is a typical 50s split-level, white house in suburbia Westfield, New Jersey. Looking out the front window seeing the red auto pull up in front of her house with her favorite cousin Elena and Aunt Tess, Regina runs to the front door and flings it open. With no coat on she shuffles outside through the snow and rushes over to the ice covered four-door red and white Chevy. Regina has her Christmas present in her hand; a new Brownie camera. She immediately begins to take pictures of Elena as she laboriously crawls out the car. Tired and freezing cold Tess quickly hands packages for both girls to help carry inside.

Similar to the Three Wise Men bearing gifts, in the wet snow they trudge toward the glitzy, multi-colored lighted Christmas decorated house. They enter through the wide opened front door, pull off their snow-covered boots, and leave them in the foyer to dry. Mary Grace hears them coming into the house and calls from the kitchen, "Merry Christmas. You're late!" Tess responds, "Late? Thank god we made it here safely. It is treacherous out there." Taking off her Camel Hair beige coat with fox trimmed collar, Tess further explains, "It's a miracle we got here in one piece." Not paying attention, Mary Grace orders, "Take your coats and boots off, and get ready to have your frigid bones warmed." In unison Elena and Regina holler back, "Done." Running over to the Christmas tree. Mary Grace calls out, "Tess, I have eggnog waiting for you and it is laced with plenty of dark Cuban rum." Tess shouts back, "Just what I need!"

Nephew Tim saunters up to his Aunt Tess and reluctantly kisses her cheek. Looking around, he tauntingly questions, "Where's Uncle Mike? Playing Uncle Scrooge again?" Tess has all she can do to ignore his sarcastic remarks. Getting off the couch, Geoff goes over to Tess and hugs his sister-in-law. He turns and tells Tim, "Go check on Uncle Danny." Danny is Geoff's bachelor brother, who fought at the battle of Pork Chop Hill in Korea. He is quietly sitting on the couch stone-faced unaware as to what is going on around him. He does not acknowledge Tess and Elena.

Regina and Elena are in the living room where a white artificial Christmas tree is gaudily lit. Elena spreads their wrapped gifts around the already cluttered tree which is filled with opened presents. In the foyer with Tess, Geoff looking around and similar to a machine gun shoots questions at Tess, "Is Mike parking the car?" Before she can respond he says, "He can park in our driveway. I just shoveled it. My new 1956 black Buick is safely in our garage." Tess is ready to explain when he moves and says, "I'll go tell him." "Stop! No," Tess yells, "He didn't come." Sensing a sensitive subject, Geoff stops on the spot and recommends that Tess head into the kitchen. "Oh, in that case Mary wants you in the kitchen she has a mean eggnog for you."

Geoff quickly leaves Tess and heads into the living room. He plops himself back on the couch, looks over at his expressionless brother Danny, and finishes off his well-spiked eggnog. He proceeds to light a Camel cigarette for himself. He inhales deeply, shakes his head back and forth as he glances over at his somber brother staring into space. Geoff lets out a sigh and remarks, "This is going to be a tricky Christmas dinner. I can feel it in my bones."

In the kitchen Mary Grace calls out and threatens, "Hey Sis, hurry and get some of this eggnog before I drink it all." Instead of going directly into the kitchen, Tess heads to the pink and black tile elaborate powder room. Tess quickly freshens up by combing her hair in the fancy pink- marble guest bathroom. Feeling more relaxed she heads toward the kitchen while taking note of the elaborate decorated candle lit dining table. "Wow, you would think your guests were royalty," she hollers out to her sister.

In the kitchen Tess kisses Mary Grace, takes the eggnog from her sister's bright red nail polished hands and drinks it quickly. Mary Grace quietly remarks, "I heard you tell Geoff that Mike didn't come." Upset for her sister and niece Mary Grace attempts to lighten things up. She teases, "Don't worry we'll have a great Christmas like the old days when it was only you, me, Mom and Dad in little old Keyport, NJ."

Swinging her hips back and forth Mary Grace sings out, "We Rapp sisters don't need anybody to make us have 'A Holly, Jolly Christmas.'" Tess grabs her sister by the waist and warns Mary Grace, "Settle down, little Sister! No more spiked eggnog for you." Mary Grace calms down and hands her sister Tess a hefty platter of ham and pushes her toward the dining room telling her, "I made this ham the way Mom always made it. Remember? With pineapple and cherries on top and basted with brown sugar and honey?" "Sure do," Tess chimes. Moving her sister out of the kitchen Mary Grace calls out, "Let's eat! Everyone is starving!" Tess carefully carries the huge plate of baked Virginia Ham into her sister's ultra-modern Danish dining room table.

The dining room table is beautifully set with festive red, green and gold Christmas Holly- covered place mats. No old-fashioned lace-heirloom tablecloth in this up-scale 50s contemporary house. "I'll manage the turkey and the other food," Mary Grace assures Tess. Mary Grace shouts to the others, "Last call. Come and get it!" With sarcasm, Tim yells back, "It's about time. If we waited any longer, it'll be 1956!" Geoff places his hand over his son's mouth and reprimands him, "Keep that mouth shut." Loudly he tells Tim, "Show a little respect for your mother and our guests." Tim pulls his father's hand away, rushes to the table and places his long lanky body down onto a dining room chair. With a sarcastic tone Geoff says to his son, "Just because you're pretty little girlfriend Nancy can't be here for Christmas, don't take it out on all of us." Similar to a petrified mummy, Danny, follows his brother Geoff into the dining room. He quietly sits down next to Tim and begins to absentmindedly fiddle with the silverware. Oblivious of what is going on around him or where he is, Danny looks long and hard at a sharp knife he is holding in his hand.

Holding onto the hot plate Tess places the luscious ham on the table. Hearing Geoff's remark to Tim and attempting to make her nephew feel better she counsels him, "Tim, most girls spend Christmas with their parents. I'm sure you'll see Nancy later." "No, he won't," comments the dramatic Regina. "Pretty little Nancy went to New Hampshire to visit her family for the holidays." She looks over at Elena and mocks, "Unlike Elena's imaginary grandmother, Nancy's uncle really lives in New Hampshire." Defiantly Tim points to his sister and says, "You're dead meat." He begins to fill his plate with Virginia ham. Tess does not hear Regina's snide remark. She takes the platter away from Tim and reminds her nephew, "Wait until everyone is seated."

Geoff, not wanting any more trouble, calls for Mary Grace to, "Come in, Pronto!" The outburst startles Danny. He jumps up and drops a knife on the floor. Geoff gently pushes Danny back into the chair, picks up the knife from the floor, puts it safely away on the serving table. He places his arm on his brother's shoulder, whispers in his ear to calm him down. When everyone is seated and settled in, the Glakowski family is prepared to enjoy a hearty, happy Christmas meal.

After Geoff's short toast, this distinctive group partakes in a typical American Christmas dinner. No ravioli and meatballs at this table. The conversation is tensely guarded. No one dares to mentions the missing Mike or absent Nancy nor do they entertain the illusive Uncle Danny. Once the meal is consumed and praises about the meal are offered, small talk emerges. Mary Grace inquires if Tess saw their favorite holiday movie on TV last night, *It's A Wonderful Life.* Tess quietly responds, "Not this year." Geoff mentions, "That film is dated." He asks, "Did any of you see that new movie, *Rebel Without a Cause,* I hear it's pretty cool." Tim smirks at his father and questions, "Why, did you see it Mr. Wanna Be Cool Cat?"

Since no one else at the table dares to comment, Geoff gets up and says, "Since I'm not getting any attention in this group I'll go get a smoke." Tess responds, "That movie is controversial, Geoff." Mary Grace mentions, "I think Mom worked on the wardrobe for that movie, Tess." "Yes," Tess answers. "She dressed that young starlet Nathalie Wood." Regina is thrilled to hear about her grandmother working on the film but Elena and Tim let it pass unfazed.

While the two sisters are taking the dishes off the table Mary Grace asks Tess, "Do you have any plans for New Year's Eve?" No response from Tess. "If not," she suggests, "Join Geoff, Regina and me at our favorite local Chinese restaurant, The China Garden." Tess is silent. To entice her

Mary Grace adds, "They make great frozen drinks with fancy little colorful paper umbrellas on them." Mary Grace uses her sister's indulgent palette by adding, "Their egg rolls, spareribs, and shrimp fried rice are the best!" Mary Grace continues, "You can stay here overnight after we have our Chinese dinner; it will be fun." Looking at her sister's somber face Mary Grace adds, "Tess, we can bring in the New Year together watching Guy Lombardo on the television and toast in the New Year with an ice cold bottle of Moet Champagne like Mom and Dad did every New Year's Eve."

Elena looks at her mother and whispers, "What about my New Year's Eve party and the velvet slippers?" Overhearing Elena, Regina, with an envious look on her face, questions, "Slippers? New Year Eve Party?" She laughs and taunts Elena, "What, glass slippers? Who are you Cinderella?" Tim shouts out, "You two are more like the freaking, ugly stepsisters." To defuse the situation Tess, responds, "Let's get Christmas over with first before we talk about New Year's." Geoff comes back with his pack of cigarettes and inquires, "What's this about New Years? I'm not sure if I will be here." Mary Grace gives her husband a questionable look. No one responds, as tension builds.

Tess insists they clean up so they can open their Christmas presents. The women return to the kitchen and the men return to the living room. Geoff leads his brother Danny to the couch and they both sit down. Tim plops down on the Oxblood colored Lazy Boy recliner. In the kitchen, the sisters shoo Elena and Regina out so they can be alone and talk. Since the snow and sleet have subsided, they advise the girls to go outdoors while it is still light. They assure the girls that they will call them in as soon as the kitchen is clean and promised they can open their gifts soon after. As Elena and Regina prepare to go out, Mary Grace warns, "Dress warm." Tess hollers back, "That's right! We don't need anyone to get sick."

The two cousins run out the house with their winter coats, wool hats and mittens on while pulling on their snow boots. Since the winter days are short there is little time left of daylight. Regina brings her new Kodak Brownie camera out so she can take pictures before it gets too dark. She proudly announces, "Someday I'll be in front of the camera." Elena enthusiastically agrees, "I bet you will! Not only will grandma be in Hollywood but so will you, as a famous star." She grabs the camera from Regina and orders, "You pose and I'll take your picture." Regina exaggerates a dramatic pose and shouts," "Shoot." Elena snaps it and comments, "You look like Judy Garland's Dorothy in *The Wizard of Oz.*" Regina retrieves the camera from Elena and says, "She was a little hick girl. I'm going to be glamorous like Bette Davis!" She insists, "Elena let me take a picture of you now." Regina orders, "You've been so glum lately give me a huge smile. Show me your pearly whites!" Elena, to appease her cousin, exaggerates a fake smile. After the photo is taken, she sticks her tongue out at Regina.

Inside the warm and well-lit house, Geoff opens the drawer of a glass and chrome side table and pulls out a deck of playing cards. He convinces his son Tim to play with him since Mike isn't around and his brother Danny lacks interest. Tim wants nothing to do with it but knowing that his father expects him to stay home for the holiday and amuse him, he complies. While playing cards, Tim desperately wants to go out and wring his sister's neck for mentioning the absence of Nancy. After a few hands, he tells his father that he is going to take out the garbage, knowing that Elena and Regina are out back. His father looks at him quizzically. Tim slyly remarks, "Well someone has to do it since the real garbage man didn't show up." Geoff is ready to jump all over his son. Tim quickly heads toward the kitchen calling out, "Hey Mom I'll throw the garbage out." Before he leaves the room, Tim sneaks a cigarette from the pack his father left on the side table next to the couch.

"Wow, I'm shocked," exclaims Mary Grace from the kitchen. Tim enters the kitchen. She teases, "Tim is this another Christmas present for me?" He smiles at his mother and slings the garbage bag on his strong youthful back and hurries outside. Tess comments, "Isn't he in rare form and you're always complaining about him Mary Grace." Chuckling, Mary Grace says, "This is a better gift than the cashmere purple sweater set Geoff bought me for Christmas along with a beautiful pearl necklace." Bragging she adds, "He purchased them at Saks Fifth Avenue." "Wow, I'm impressed. Saks, cashmere, pearls, and a spanking new Buick," Tess mocks. Noting sarcasm in her sister's voice, Mary Grace does not respond. Tess continues to annoy Mary Grace and says, "Looks like the insurance business is good these days for Geoff." She continues, "You bought new furniture too. It looks very expensive." Mary Grace retaliates back, "Well, well, well, the green eye monster has awoken. Don't you remember what happened in *Othello*." Tess responds back, "Desdemona was innocent and naïve. I'm smart."

Pointing at the artificial Christmas tree in the living room, Elena continues to taunt, "What's with that ugly looking fake white Christmas atrocity?" Mary Grace defends the tree, "That's the newest trend. No needles falling all over the rug or watering like you have to with dried up natural trees." Tess shoots back, "Looks like something our Hollywood Mother would have in her so called glamorous gaudy abode." She continues to taunt Mary Grace, "Not my taste, but you always were more like mother than I was." The sisters recognize this is a hot family topic; therefore, they stop tormenting one another and resume washing the dishes. Both mention that they called their mother in California on Christmas Eve to wish her a "Merry Christmas." "Happy to hear she is spending it with Uncle Albert again this year," Mary Grace comments. Tess quickly responds, "Wouldn't it be nice if she came here one year and spent the holidays with her daughters, their husbands, and her only grandchildren." Mary Grace defends her mother, "That's a long trip for a woman of her age to take."

Out of the blue Mary Grace suggests, "Why don't you go out to California and visit Mom, Tess? It might do you some good to get away and take Elena with you." Tess does not respond and offers, "I'll take the dessert plates in the dining room." Under her breath she comments, "And you, Sister keep your opinions to yourself." Infuriated by her Sister, Mary Grace slams down a pot she has in her hands. Hearing the loud crash in the kitchen Danny bolts up out of his chair. Geoff protectively guides his frenzied brother back down.

In retaliation, and finally getting her nerve, Mary Grace follows Tess into the dining room carrying the coffee cups and with sarcasm questions, "Why didn't Mike come Tessie?" Tess turns with raw emotional and shouts, "Because I asked him not to come! Simple as that!" Mary Grace blurts out, "What?" Tess shoots back in defense, "I desperately needed to be away from him." Shocked, Mary Grace shouts, "On Christmas!?" Mary Grace stares at her sister and further questions, "What about Elena?" Chastising her sister, she lectures, "You should be thinking of her. Especially after what you told me on Thanksgiving what she's been going through lately." Knowing that she would receive a harsh rebuttal, Mary Grace whispers to herself, "You always did think of yourself first, Tessie."

Disgusted, Mary Grace leaves her sister and returns to the kitchen to prepare special French press coffee. Tess follows her Sister into the kitchen and scoops out the last of the eggnog on the bottom of the silver punch bowl and gulps it down. She gives her Sister the cold shoulder. Not one to back down, Mary Grace continues, "I hate to get involved, but I think you are making a huge mistake." "Then don't get involved," Tess strikes back. Grabbing the sugar and creamer Tess explains, "You can think what you want. But Mary Grace, you don't live in my house." Getting choked up Tess cries out, "You have no idea what's going on."

The tension is temporarily broken when Geoff calls from the living room, "Did Tim come back in yet?" He takes his pack of cigarettes off the side table; looks inside; stomps his foot down hard; and screams out, "I'm going to strangle that kid! He stole one of my Camels." Geoff's booming voice startles his brother Danny so that he again leaps out of his seat. Instinctively Geoff pushes him back down. "Stay!" he shouts at his perplexed brother. Mary Grace hears Geoff but ignores him—she is engrossed with Tess. The sisters are clearly not in agreement; therefore, they end their edgy verbal exchange.

Tess looks out the window and notices Tim taunting Elena by holding something in his hand and flagging it in her face. Regina is trying to pull her brother away from her infuriated cousin. Elena is desperately trying to grab the item in Tim's hand. (*It is Elena's polka dot underpants which he pilfered from her bedroom on Thanksgiving.*) Tess can't make out what it is. Elena eventually pulls it from Tim's hand and runs with it to the front of the house.

Rushing out the back door, Tess screams at her nephew, "Leave her alone; you bully!" Turning quickly, Tim defends himself, "What's wrong Tessie? She's a big girl now. Elena can defend herself." He kicks at the snow and shouts, "She doesn't need her Mommy coming to her aid." Hearing his haughty remarks provokes Tess further. She runs up to him. The outraged

Tess grabs Tim by his sleeve and yells, "Aunt Tess to you; you arrogant brat." Holding him tightly so he can't get away she infers, "You're worse than those teenage hoodlums in the movie, *Rebel Without a Cause*." Tim tries to pull away from his Aunt but she has a tight hold. He screams in her ear, "You mean that sexy heartthrob James Dean? Thanks! I'm flattered. Why Tessie, does he turn you on?" She releases him but he stands there looking directly into her contorted face and continues to goad his enraged Aunt Tess, "You're like that horrible mother in the movie who makes Sal Mineo's character commit suicide." His insult infuriates her.

Tess is all pent up from what has been going on this year. She takes hold of her nephew's ear and pulls it taunt. Tim screams for her to let go. "Stop, you crazy, deranged witch." The enraged Tess shouts in his ear which is turning blue, "I'll pull your ear off and you'll be like Van Gogh, you bigheaded creep!" Tim calls out, "As my Uncle Mike calls you, you are a crazy raving red headed loony bin. No wonder your husband didn't come today." "You leave my husband out of this. And to think I defended you when Regina teased you about Nancy. She is a smart girl not to come today!"

Regina is taking photos of the entire encounter. In defense of her brother she shouts, "Leave him alone Aunt Tess, he's upset! Nancy broke up with him yesterday." Standing by the back-door Geoff hollers out to his son, "Get the hell inside Tim and I'll break your neck if you ever take a cigarette from me again." Tess interjects, "Forget the cigarettes tell him to leave my daughter alone!" Geoff responds, "Tim, how many times have I told you to leave those girls alone?" Adding insult to injury, he mockingly says to his son, "Maybe pretty little Nancy did the right thing." Tess shouts back to Geoff, "Evidently you didn't tell him enough to leave girls alone. Perhaps he has the wrong male role model."

Geoff rushes out the door and heads over to Tess and Tim. Tess lets go of Tim's now purple bruised ear. Embarrassed and irate, Tim spits on the white snow leaving a brown tobacco stain. While hustling back to the house and rubbing his bruised ear and manhood, he shouts out to his father, "You should practice what you preach, old man." Geoff does not hear his son's sly remark he is trying to calm Tess down. He takes hold of his sister-in-law and squeezes her tightly. Tess can hardly breathe. When she feels his hands moving inappropriately around her, in disgust, she pushes him away while shouting, "Get your filthy hands off of me." He releases her. Ready to cry, Tess moans, "I should never have come here! You're both disgusting deviants." Geoff reaches for her again. Tess slaps him hard across his face and calls him despicable as he falls to his knees into the cold wet mushy snow which is now streaked red from Geoff's bleeding mouth.

Covering his bloody lip, humiliated and insulted, Geoff blurts out, "No wonder Mike stays far away from you; you are one cold, hard bitch." Next thing you know, Geoff is flat on his back with blood spurting out of his mouth from Tess's second hard slap across his face. Ironically, it was her sharp wedding and engagement ring that cut his mouth. Tim is lurking behind the backdoor with a huge look of satisfaction on his face. He shouts out to anyone who will listen, "As soon as I turn eighteen, I'm going to join the Army like Uncle Danny and get far away from this house of horrors."

Shook up, Regina runs to the front of the house to check on Elena who is looking around the house at this shocking family scene. It is tortuous for her. "When will I ever find peace?" she whispers to herself. Greatly confused, Uncle Danny goes to the door and stands behind Tim. This former US Army sergeant is brandishing a knife. When he heard his nephew say he was going to join the Army, he shouts out a horrible blood-curdling groan and throws the knife over Tim's shoulder. It lands in the snow not far from the injured Geoff. Tim compassionately grabs his Uncle Danny and tries to calm him. Mistakenly thinking Tim threw the knife, Tess calls out to her nephew, "Join the Army? You'll be AWOL or dishonorably discharged soon after you arrive."

Hearing and seeing most of this calamity, howling, Mary Grace runs to the back door. She shoves Tim and Danny aside and goes directly to her injured husband. Geoff is lying motionless and bleeding in the cold, blood-soaked snow. When she reaches him, she kneels and takes his head into her shaking hands. Holding her husband's head, Mary Grace wipes the blood from his cut mouth with a dish towel. Standing nearby, Tess apologizes to her sister and says she is going to leave. Not looking up at her Sister, the angry Mary Grace strongly agrees, "Yes, you've done enough damage around here; you better leave now!"

Tess goes into the house and calls for Elena to come. Confused and upset Regina and Elena follow Tess in. The shaken and wounded Geoff attempts to get up. His angry wife Mary Grace attempts to help him. He pushes her away. Not only does his face hurt but his male ego is shot down with each of Tess's slaps. Distressed Mary Grace heads back in the house followed by the staggering Geoff. He immediately heads into the bathroom and bangs the door shut. The others can clearly hear him holler, "That son-of-a-bitch!"

Mary Grace runs into the living room to pack up the Christmas presents she has for Tess, Mike, and Elena. To diffuse the situation, this unhappy woman is anxious for her sister and innocent niece to leave as soon as possible. Mary Grace fears Geoff's retaliation. She is also fuming mad that Tess upset this seething man she calls her husband. Geoff is like Mt. Vesuvius who looks majestic and peaceful but underneath is a boiling volcano ready to erupt. From past experience, Mary Grace learned how to maneuver around him. *At whose expense?*

Before any more eruptions can occur, Tim rushes to get Tess and Elena's coats. He wants his Aunt out of his life as soon as possible, along with his immediate family. Mary Grace hands her fuming sister the huge shopping bag filled with beautifully wrapped gifts. Elena and Tess prepare to leave. Regina is disappointed but smart enough to recognize its better they separate for now. "See you on New Year's, Elena," Regina calls out. Tess comments, "Surely that will not happen!" Under her breath Elena says, "I hope I have other plans."

The phone is ringing in the house while everyone is hustling about to get Tess and Elena ready to leave. Regina picks up the phone, "Hello?" The caller hesitates. Regina asks, "Who is this?" No response. She asks the person on the other line, "Who do you want to talk with?" Mary Grace shouts, "Who is that?" The person on the other line asks Regina, "Is he there?" "Who?" questions Regina. The person on the other line hangs up abruptly. With a puzzled look on her face, Regina stares at the deadline and gently puts it back on the receiver. She answers her mother, "Some woman." Her mother questions, "What did she want?" Regina explains, "Mom, when she heard you ask, 'Who is it? She hung up!" She neglects to tell her mother that the strange woman asked, "Is he there?" Mary Grace comments, "Probably a wrong number?" Holding an ice pack on his face, Geoff peeks into the living room and stares at the phone. Tim contemptuously shouts out, "Another one of those hang ups - from a woman? It happens all the time!" He turns and shoots a look-to-kill at his father.

Tess, grabbing Elena shouts out, "Come on Elena, we are out of here." She turns and glares at the family staring at her and says, "Goodbye!" Tim yells back, "Good riddance!" Geoff adds, "You can say that again!" He screams, "Don't let the door hit you on your ass as you leave, bitch." Mary Grace runs out of the room with misty eyes. Regina heads to the living room, peeks out the window to watch her Aunt and cousin prepare to leave. Uncle Danny, now calm, is in the living room watching the movie, *It's a Wonderful Life*. Smirking and looking around at the others, he whispers, "Peace on Earth Good Will to Men."

When Tess clears the snow off the red Chevy she drives off with Elena in the back sniffling. This despondent woman is fuming mad, deeply hurt, and disillusioned with the way this Christmas is ending up. Even though she is mad at Mary Grace, Geoff, Tim and Mike, she is mainly disheartened by the way life has been going lately. She had hoped that Christmas would bring peace and resolution - especially for Elena. Huddled in the back holding tightly onto her polka dot panties, Elena feels both violated by her cousin Tim and guilty. She believes that she is the one who caused the commotion both here and earlier at home. As hoped, Tess and Elena did not have "A Holly Jolly Christmas!" Unlike the ending in the film, *It's a Wonderful Life*, the Policano family is not experiencing a Merry Christmas.

CHAPTER FIFTEEN

Brother's Keeper
Christmas Evening
Jersey City, NJ
1955

ETTIE IS COAXING her beloved brother *Mickey* to come back into the house and eat more, "Why you only had one helping of ravioli and a little turkey; you hardly had any dessert, what's wrong, is it my cooking?" Mike consoles his sister, "Hey, this was the best meal I've had in a long time. You're still the best cook ever Sis!" To reassure her, he kisses Ettie on her flushed cheek from being by a hot stove all day; actually every day. She brushes away her brother's hand in embarrassment. This shy unassuming woman is not used to compliments or affection. Carlo is calling out to his wife to bring him his cigarettes, "Hey cut that soupy talk out and get me my Camels!" He is unaware of his wife's need for compliments and attention. Mike thanks his sister and tells her he is leaving. Ettie is disappointed; although, she never questions her brother or any man for that matter. Her husband, who is envious of his wife's persistent attention to her younger brother, hollers from the dining room to his brother-in-law, "Guess you have to go and look for your lost wife and child?" To add fuel to the fire, he sarcastically jokes, "Maybe the Three Wise Men will locate them." To make matters worse, Carlo laughs at his own levity. Ettie never reprimands her husband. She ignores his cryptic remarks. Mike responds by shouting back, "Very funny; you think you're Groucho Marx?" He notices Ettie is upset. He consoles her, "He's just jealous." Then he shouts out, "Hey, old man, some things are better left unsaid." Mike praises his sister again and flatters her, "You're the best cook and sister in the entire world."

Buttoning up his pea coat he tells Ettie, "I'm heading out to check on a few things." She pleads with him. "But you'll miss Blaise and Rosaria." "I'll see my niece and nephew when I get back," Mike reassures Ettie. "Good, good, good." She replies, "I don't know why they are so late. But I'll ask Blaise and Rosaria to wait for you." Mike says, "You do that!" Ettie seems satisfied. She tells her indulged brother, "I already set aside pastries for you." While leaving, Mike smiles and hollers out, "You're the greatest!" Ettie does not need praise; she is defined by her cooking. The complements from her brother are better than any thank you. She rushes back into the house to attend to her needy and demanding husband. *Ettie pleases everyone but herself.*

After Mike leaves, Ettie hurries back to the living room to bring her husband his cigarettes. She pleads with him, "Carlo you should stop smoking; your cough is not getting any better. Dr. Sacks told me they're not helping your condition." It falls on deaf ears. He ignores his concerned wife. Carlo takes the cigarettes and tells his wife, "I'm going outside. I need to stretch my legs and have a smoke." He hollers back at Ettie, "Dr. Sacks doesn't know everything." The compliant wife runs to get his coat and while helping him on with his coat insists, "Now button it up; your cough will get worse if you catch a chill." He grudgingly grabs it from her and heads out.

Mike, with his coat collar turned up to keep his ears warm, is on the front stoop lower step scoping out the neighborhood. On the top step of the red brick porch, Carlo immediately lights up a Camel. Mike smells the smoke, turns, looks up and seeing Carlo questions him, "You smoke at least a pack or more a day, don't you?" Carlo ignores Mike and takes a deep drag on his cigarette and blows it out toward Mike. This annoys Mike but his love for Ettie is too great to agitate her defiant husband. He warns his brother-in-law, "Hey Carlo, I can hear you coughing at night from upstairs. You better kick that dirty habit." Aggravated, Carlo retorts back, "Me? What about your uppity wife? She smokes those Chesterfields like a stinking smoke stack." He continues to taunt Mike, "Why, I've even seen her light up a butt from an overflowing, disgustingly dirty ashtray." In anger Mike kicks away the snow from the step with his heavy shoe.

Frantically Mike tries to keep his cool until Carlo unravels Mike when he resumes his verbal accusations, "Did you know Mr. Know-It-All, that during a heavy electrical rainstorm, your prissy wife sent that innocent little Elena out to buy her a pack of cigarettes?" Mike stares at him as Carlo adds, "That poor kid could of got killed out there." Troubled to hear this, Mike tries desperately to pay no heed to his brother-in-law who is always trying to upset him. But it doesn't last a second. Carlo intentionally says something that turns Mike's insides out, "You know, Mikey, maybe that's why Tess lost the baby a few years ago. I hear smoking is not good for pregnant women." Continuing his assault, Carlo, as he blows out circles with his cigarette, hits below the belt with this cutting remark, "Hey, maybe it would have been a boy; a son to take over the infamous garbage business." Outraged and ready to punch his brother-in-law smack in the face, Mike leaves the porch. He tries to get away from Carlo's arrogant talk before he ruins Christmas for his sister and his niece and nephew.

Filled with pent up rage; heading down the snow blanketed street toward Walsh's Tavern, Mike shouts out to Carlo, "Go to hell you pompous, want-to-be scholar. You think because you read those Encyclopedias you know it all." Mike raises his fist and calls out, "You're nothing but an empty- headed, heartless loser." Carlo laughs and begins to cough profusely then spits out blood on the white snow which covers the porch stoop. Mike shouts back, "My sister and those two kids are too good for you. You're nothing but a stinking smokestack." Carlo laughs while Mike retaliates, "Your lungs must be as black as the devil's." Trying to act unfazed, Carlo takes a long drag on his cigarette, inhales deeply, blows out the smoke in circles and flippantly flicks the butt of his cigarette into the encrusted snow. Mike screams out, "My angelic sister should have never married you!" This last remark from Mike makes Carlo fuming mad. He goes back in the house and hollers out to his wife who is in the kitchen, "Hey woman, make me a cup of coffee and make sure it's strong and steaming hot." He pauses and shouts, "Put lots of Anisette in it!" Ettie hears him but remains motionless.

Infuriated, Mike shuffles down the snow-covered street while looking around to see if the red and white Chevy is parked nearby. Not seeing it, he fears that Tess and Elena might not come home. For spite, he goes into Walsh's Tavern, which never closes, not even on holidays. It is the only place where lonely people can go and feel welcomed and comfortable 365 days a year. Some neighbors coined it the 'Lonely Heart Club' joint. Mike enters and sees his old buddy Ray Sinnotti, the local, popular pharmacist, and Brendan O'Connor, a former Philosophy/Literature Fordham University professor, sitting alone at the bar. A few homeless stragglers are hanging around or sleeping on the side tables behind them. As usual, Brendan O'Connor is at the end of the bar unaccompanied and feeling no pain. Ray is sitting at the other end dressed in his holiday finery carefully winding a wrist watch. Avoiding Brendan, who is a goner, Mike sits down on a bar stool next to Ray. He wishes his friend, "Merry Christmas, Ray." Looking perplexed, he asks, "Why aren't you at home with your family?" At first Ray ignores the question then putting the watch back on his wrist he responds, "Just taking a break; too many people at the house. They don't even know I left. What about you?" Mike acts as if he didn't hear him. Ray remarks, "The holidays bring out the best and worst in people. It was best for me to get away for a short time."

Mike slaps his former prep school buddy on his back and calls out to the bar owner, "Hey Walsh, my man, pour a Christmas drink for me and my bro Ray and one for you." Taking off his pea coat he shouts out, "Make it the good whiskey and don't be skimpy." The ruddy-faced, pleasant older tavern owner sets them up. The three men clang their glasses and make toasts. Mike says to Ray, "Salute, Pisano," "Slainte," the Irish pub owner calls out to the entire saloon waking Brendan at the end of the bar. They down their whiskey in a flash. The tavern owner slams down his shot glass, wipes his mouth with his sleeve and proceeds to clean up while humming an old Irish ditty.

As usual, Mike and Ray decide to arm wrestle. While arm wrestling, the former high school buddies brag about their glory football days at St. Peter's Prep. They proudly reminisce how they were football State Champions and undefeated during their four years at the Jersey City Jesuit Preparatory High School. Like always, Mike smashes Ray's arm onto the bar. Embarrassed, Ray cries out, "Hey, look out, you'll break my new watch." Checking his watch and rubbing his sore arm, he sighs, "It's a Christmas present from my wife Maize. She'll be fuming mad if it breaks!" Brendan hears the noise, lifts his head off the bar and yells out, "Stop your belly aching, Ramondo!" He hollers at both of them, "I'm sick and tired of hearing you two blokes always bragging about those 'good old Prep days.'" He stresses his annoyance, "Why can't you get it through your bloated heads that those days are over. Gone with the wind!" Disgusted, Brendan finishes the last of his Irish whiskey. Slurring his words, he pontificates, "You guys are living in the past and that's futile." He shakes the empty glasses on the bar when Brendan slams his bony fist down hard. Ray and Mike humor him. In unison they call out, "We hear you Socrates." Ray humorously remarks, "Now he's not only a philosopher but a poet, a Dante Alighieri." Walsh adds, "No he thinks he is the Irish writer Flann O'Brien." Hearing this, Brendan quotes O'Brien, "*When money's tight and is hard to get and your horse has also ran, When all you have is a heap of debt A PINT OF PLAIN IS YOUR ONLY MAN.*" Mike and Ray are ready to further tease him. The tavern owner goes to his fellow Irishman's aid.

Tom Walsh, the long-time pub owner, takes the empty glass from Brendan and orders the three antagonists, "Stop all the shenanigans; you three are acting like a bunch of hooligans." Walsh turns to Brendan and tells him, "Faith and be Golly better get home Professor. Your dear old mother will be worried about her 'wee little one.'" Walsh walks around the bar, grabs Brendan's jacket, attempts to put it on him, and warns him to be careful going home. Brendan pushes Walsh away. The inebriated Professor refuses to leave. Walsh hovers over him. But recognizing that it is futile to get him to leave; he goes back behind the bar leaving the Professor to sit alone on an old barstool with his thinning ginger-red haired head resting on the bar. Mike tells the tavern owner, "He's hopeless. Let the poet sleep it off."

To remove the attention from "Socrates" Mike asks Walsh, "Why do you keep this place open 7 days a week, 12 months a year; even on Christmas? Don't you have a wife and family?" Walsh remains mute. "If you do, you never talk about them," Mike comments. Ray punches Mike's arm and reprimands him, "Why the hell are you asking him that after all these years?" Flustered, Walsh answers, "Sure I have a family; they live in Ireland - County Longford." Mike and Ray look at one another shocked. Brendan raises his head and exclaims, "What's this, Confessions of St. Augustine's!" Ray shouts back to Brendan, "Are you the Pope now?"

The Leprechaun-looking tavern owner takes out a bottle of good Irish whiskey and pours himself a double and two more for his bar companions, excluding the highly inebriated Brendan. He calls out his Irish toast, "Slainte" and pours himself another double. With a loose libido and tongue the old Irish tavern owner tells his long tale, "I was married at a young age to the girl of my dreams." With a huge, rare smile on his craggy face he adds, "The beautiful Maura Sharkey. A wee Colleen; a local gal, with the bluest eyes you'd ever seen with long, silky, black velvety hair down to her wee little waist." Mike, Ray, and even Brendan are mesmerized with Walsh's shocking revelation. He sighs and with his heavy Irish Brogue he calls out, "God Bless her! My beautiful Maura was full breasted and more than able to nurse many future babies." With a sullen look, Tom Walsh resumes his tale, "We had four healthy kids and a little cottage near the village where we both grew up."

Reflectively, the tavern owner proceeds to expose the long account of his past life, "I was a steam-pipe fitter in Ireland. There was a union strike and I got heatedly involved in it. During the strike we formed a march in protest against the rotten to the core greedy establishment. The march was heavily guarded by local police and filled with planted rebel rousers." Brendan speaks, "What else is new Macbeth." Ray shouts, "Quiet Shakespeare let him finish." Walsh continues, "A vicious fight broke out; there were sharp broken bottles, metal pipes, and even loaded guns." Mike and Ray listen attentively as Walsh continues, "In all the commotion, I accidently hit a man in defense with my solid hard fists. Sadly, the man hit his head on the cement pavement and died instantly." The men listening are speechless even Brendan. Walsh reflects, "Thank the Lord; the poor soul didn't know what happened to him nor felt any pain."

While the stunned mesmerized men listen quietly, Walsh resumes his tragic tale to his captive audience, "There were witnesses." Brendan shouts out, "Stool pigeons, squealers." Walsh looks at him and nods and adds, "The police soon came looking for me." Taking another shot of whiskey, Walsh resumes, "My wife feared for my life since I was always a hot head and loved a good fight." He bragged, "In the old country they said, I 'could lick any man before me.' My concerned, fearful wife had family in America and begged me to leave Ireland immediately undercover." Walsh takes another swig of his whiskey and continues, "She felt, and I also knew, I would never get a fair trial there. I was a dead man!"

Ray whispers to Mike, "Sounds like he lived like Marlon Brando in the movie, *On the Waterfront*. Did you know that before he bought this place, he was a dockworker in Hoboken?" Mike asks, "Walsh, I didn't know you were a dockworker in Hoboken." Brendan corrects Mike, "You mean a longshoreman." Ray shouts for Brendan to be quiet. Brendan is not deterred he continues, "Hey, old-man Walsh, I guess you were a boxer too?" "I did my far share in the ring," Walsh answers. "You need to be to work on the docks," Walsh responds. He surprises his captive audience by defending himself and revealing, "But I was no punk; but I had to deal with a lot of them savory mob bosses." He proudly comments, "But, I was respected by the workers." Mike, Ray, and Brendan look at the bar keeper with new respect and awe. Mike tries to absorb all of this and coaxes Walsh, "Go on, continue with your original story." The bar owner asks, "Refresh my memory." Ray reminds him, "We left off with you in trouble in Ireland."

Walsh continues, "Secretly I left Ireland My Mother Country one night and sailed as a stow-a-way on a cargo ship heading for America. It landed in Hoboken, NJ." He stops to pour himself another whiskey. In unison the anxious men call out, "Go on!" Walsh doesn't need to be encouraged; he is on a drunken catharsis roll, "Through Maura's family in the United States and their connections, as I told you, I got a job as a longshoreman on the docks in Hoboken." Brendan, listening attentively teases, "Walsh did you meet Marlon Brando?" The frustrated tavern owner slams his fist on the bar and hollers out, "This is no joke, Professor, it was back breaking work. I took a lot of sh-t; but, hell, I made good money." Brendan holds up his empty glass and requests, "My good man Brando, pour me another." He then mockingly recites, "'I coulda had class. I coulda been a contender. I coulda been somebody,'" mimicking Brando's iconic line in the movie *On the Waterfront*. Mike hollers out to Brendan, "Shut the hell up; go back to Fordham." "Or your saintly Mother," Walsh adds. "Go on!" yells, Mike and Ray.

While placing the dirty glasses in the sink Walsh further explains, "I sent money home faithfully to the old country and my dear blessed family." He stops and wipes his misty eyes and adds, "When I found out I could never go back to Ireland, I saved enough to buy this little bar." He again pounds his tight fist on the bar and shouts, "Faith and Be Golly. Here I am." The shaken Walsh with blood shot eyes turns his back from the captivated men and exclaims, "End of story!"

Stunned and moved by Walsh's story, Mike slugged down his second double whiskey and inquires, "Walsh, what happened to your wife and kids?" The tavern owner grabbed a towel and wipes the bar vigorously making the blue veins in his arms pop out. After a few minutes he slowly and reflectively responds to Mike's query, "I never saw or heard from them again even after I sent my wife enough money so she and the kids could come here and live with me. I wanted my family back!" His eyes well up with tears as he groans, "She never showed up." Mike feels Walsh's pain. Walsh takes ice out of the freezer and puts it in a large cast-iron bucket and timidly says, "Guess she found another man in Ireland." Brendan pontificates, "Time moves on and life changes for all." Upset hearing this Mike says to Brendan, "Shut that fancy mouth of yours."

The tavern owner looks at the perplexed Mike and comments, "The Professor is right; that was so many years ago." "Didn't you check with her family here in America?" Mike questions Walsh. Sardonically, the Irishman responds, "Her family here in America acted dumb when I questioned and begged them to let me know what was going on." He makes the Sign of the Cross and with reverence says, "Faith and Be Golly I pray every day that they are well." He puts away the whiskey bottle and nonchalantly professes, "Now the people who come into this bar are my family." Ray and Mike look at him and recognize that he truly wants to end the conversation right then and there. They cease asking any more questions. Brendan once again lifts his head and repeats, "It is futile to talk about the past." After his bold statement, his head plops down again on the wet-oak bar.

Walsh's revelation disturbed Mike terribly. In fact, Ray was so troubled that he gets up from the bar, thanks Mike for the drinks and commences to leave Walsh's establishment. As he prepares to leave Ray announces, "I better get back to my dear wife and sweet kids." Waving his hand, he shouts out, "Merry Christmas to all and to all a good night." Brendan whispers, "Good Night, Good Night, Parting is Such Sweet Sorrow." The poet/theologian slowly raises his head once more and dramatically recites, "Merry Christmas to all and to all a good night." Feeling melancholy, with a ruddy face from years of drinking, Walsh shouts out to Brendan as his head hits the bar again, "Sweet dreams, Tiny Tim." Brendan calls out, "Thanks Scrooge!" To lighten the dark mood, the men all laugh in merry humor.

As Ray walks out the door, 6'2" Tony, Mike's long-time employee covered with soiled work clothes barrels in. He is freezing cold. This Goliath figure removes his gloves and like a fiery dragon blows on to his rough hands to warm them. Happy to see Mike there, Tony goes over to his employer and with his powerful pumped-up-muscled arms slaps him on his back. He vigorously shakes his employer's hands and offers a holiday greeting, "Merry Christmas boss." With a booming voice Tony shouts out for Walsh, "Pour me a stiff one, you jolly old Irishman." Walsh shouts back, "The usual Big Guy?" Looking his employee up and down Mike inquires, "Tony, you look like you just got back from work." "Yes!" He reminds his boss, "You forgot I had to go over to the church and pick up all the accumulated garbage. There was an overloaded from all the holiday services and the Christmas parties they had this week." Confused Mike confesses, "Forgot all about that." Tony looks at the morbid Mike and inquires, "You forgot boss?" He calls out, "There was tons of garbage and lots of shit spread all over there." Mike apologies, "Sorry I made you work on Christmas."

Walsh slams the drink in front of Tony. "Triple time on holidays; right Mr. Mike?" the bar owner teases. Tony grins at Walsh, "No union wages; the boss runs a private organization, right boss?" Slapping him on his back even harder this time. "Besides, the Big Guy brags, "He takes good care of me!" Mike reassures his favorite long-time employee. "The drinks are on me Big Guy; so splurge," Mike says.

This colossal man laughs out loud and speedily drinks down his "stiff one" followed by a pint of beer. Tony immediately motions for another and orders, "And keep those Boiler Makers coming, Irishman." Wiping the foam from his mouth with his torn sleeve, Tony turns and looks straight at Mike and says, "I hate to trouble you boss but that new young janitor at St. Victor's is still giving me a hard time and that new younger priest is a wierdo." Angry, Mike quickly responds, "What the hell!" Tony quickly explains, "When I went and told that new young priest, Father Schultz, he defends him and told me not to mention it to Monsignor Kelly or you for that matter." Tony quietly comments, "I even saw that sweet old nun Margaret Mary hidden in the background and I think she looked upset too." Mike is beyond frustrated. Annoyed, he reassures Tony, "No worries, Big Guy, I'll take care of it after the holidays." Touching Tony on his muscular back, Mike tells him, "Relax and enjoy the rest of your Christmas. Did you eat?" "Naw," groans Tony. Mike quickly responds, "If I knew you were going to be alone, I would have invited you to my sister's house for dinner." He stands up and orders, "Come with me now!" Tony reassures his boss, "No, I'm fine; I'll eat when I get home. I have a frozen TV dinner in the freezer to make." Mike makes a face and comments, "What, like a skimpy Swanson pot pie? That crap won't fill your molar." Hearing Walsh, he offers the Big Guy a Spam sandwich. Tony shakes his head *no*. Brendan adds his two cents and hollers over to Walsh, "Why not offer him a fine fat goose with sweet plum pudding, eh Scrooge." "Put a sock in it Professor," Mike hollers back.

Tom Walsh bangs Tony's third set of drinks in front of him and inquires, "Hey Big Guy, since we've all been going to confession here, don't you have any family?" Tony wipes his mouth with the back of his huge olive-skinned hand and brags, "Sure do! I have a four-year-old daughter, Angela Maria." Mike looks perplexed and shouts out, "What? When did you get married and have a baby?" Tony comments, "I didn't say I had a wife, I said I have a daughter and like her name she's my precious angel." He quietly adds, "Maria Angela's my everything; the sunshine of my life." Again, the men look at Tony puzzled. He resumes, "I support her and will forever in any way I can." Walsh quickly pours him another bourbon followed by a tall cold beer. Tony drinks his third "stiff one," and mumbles; "She lives in Columbia, South America with her Madre." Tony takes out his stuffed wallet and pulls out a photo of a little girl dressed in a rainbow-printed flowing dress with a huge red bow on her pretty little head. The Big Guy proudly shows it to Mike and Walsh.

Questioning Tony, Mike asks, "Is the tattoo heart on your arm for her?" Tony sneaks a smile saying, "Man, that's for me to know and for you not to ask." Brendan mockingly comments, "A love child. the Immaculate Conception." Tony gulps down his bourbon followed by his tall cold brew. A Boiler Maker, his favorite drink. "It puts hair on your chest," he jokes. Warningly Tony shouts out to the professor, "Don't ever make a joke about my daughter. Let's leave it at that Mr. Wise guy and I don't mean wise like a smart owl!" Clearly the Big Guy wants to end the conversation. Walsh brings over a ham and cheese sandwich which he had in the back for a snack, and hands it to Tony. The Big Guy thanks Walsh saying, "Keep pouring. I don't need food." Brendan lifts his head singing out, "Amen! Man does not live by bread alone."

True confessions and stories of ghosts-of-the-past have ended, at least for now. The rag-tag bunch finally settle down. Tony and Walsh begin to discuss sports and who won "the numbers" recently. Mike doesn't join in; he is truly upset and angry about what happened earlier in the day with his wife Tess and his daughter spending Christmas without him. What Tony told him about the church janitor and the new priest and his surprise revelation about his ten-year old secret love child added fuel to his discontent. The upheaval of the entire day has taken its toll on Mike. Tess and Elena leaving him alone on Christmas; Carlo's ugly remarks; Walsh and Tony's surprising and shocking revelations, and drinking entirely too much, all contribute to his inability to make rational decisions. There is also something which is disturbing him greatly; something he is unable to share with his wife or anyone for that matter; at least for now. Life for this bewildered husband, father, brother, friend, employer, and man is dangerously overwhelming and distorted on this holy night.

Women were not allowed in taverns or bars in the 50s but daring and questionable women would sneak in the back of Walsh's Tavern and make their presence known. Mike was a favorite of the few women who frequented the bar. Some of these colorful women were "skillful numbers-runners." It was common knowledge that in Hudson County the illegal numbers, gambling racket was going on daily; giving much needed but illegal money to the local unemployed making the racketeers rich. Even housewives and church-going people were involved in the "numbers racket" which kept the mob's palms heavily greased and gave the lower working class families extra pocket money. The local police, politicians, and even the clergy turned a blind eye on the illegal numbers racket and their local runners. Eileen Moriarity was one of them. Rumor had it that her notorious ex-husband, Marty Goldstein, was one of the big guys and number one organizer in the illegal numbers racket in Hudson County and that he was backed by the Italian Mafia since his mother was born in Sicily. Marty, the kingpin, prided himself and greatly profited by having the largest numbers' clientele in all of Hudson County.

Eileen, his estranged wife, was used and abused by him. Yet, she had the womanly knack and knowhow to satisfy a man's weak ego when necessary to save herself from his unorthodox method of keeping her in line. Underneath that brash façade she was a pathetic and needy woman. Sadly, she was alienated by others and her dangerous racketeer husband abused her most of her married life. Her parents, who were from Ireland, died and her older brother Sean was plagued by the Irish curse, alcoholism. She desperately tried to get her brother cured. She cared for him when he was at his lowest point. Having no family support and desperate Eileen was willing to please a man at any cost. *She had no other choice!*

Eileen's willingness was easy bait for the vulnerable-insecure male. She had an obsessive crush on Mike for years. It began the day he came into the dinner on Five Corners where she was a young, innocent waitress years before she met her unsavory mobster husband. Mike was charming and handsome. He was active in the political scene and well respected in the Jersey City community. The moment this Valentino-type man, with his main employee Tony, walked into the diner he immediately caught Eileen's wandering lustful eye. Mike always ignored her but Tony tried in vain to capture her attention to no avail.

When Eileen came into the bar this Christmas night in 1955, Mike was highly inebriated, susceptible, and feeling rejected. Eileen saw he was sullen and alone on Christmas and took advantage of his vulnerability. She coyly invited him back to her place, a few short blocks away. This black haired, blue eyed, disadvantaged but shrewd woman told him she could use a strong man to fix her burnt out light bulb on her "too hard to reach ceiling." For payment she promised to give him a strong holiday drink and insinuated "more," if need be. Observing the web this spider woman is weaving around his boss, the envious Tony goes up to Eileen and whispers in her ear. She pushes him away and says, "That big lug of mine the cad is in deep-shit trouble; I hope I never see him again." Tony, angry and feeling rejected by her tells her, "He better magically appear; he owes me plenty of money."

Holding tightly onto her coat Eileen walks away from Tony and begs Walsh for a drink. Walsh tells her, "You know women aren't served at the bar." Eileen laughs and proudly sings out, "Perhaps not a woman but I'm a lady!" "Okay, My Fair Lady, since it's Christmas I'll pour you a short one." The Irishman places it in front of her and instructs, "Drink it fast and go home. When you get there take care of that squawking parrot of yours." He stops a minute and being a compassionate soul, he asks, "How's your brother Sean doing these days; thankfully he hasn't been in here lately." Eileen sits at one of the side tables, ignores his query about her brother and throws the bar owner a kiss. With hungry eyes, Tony looks seductively over at Eileen. She is unaware but the tavern owner doesn't miss a thing in his bar. Walsh shouts over to Tony, "Hey Big Guy I've got the perfect song for you." He sings, "I've only got eyes for you . . ." Tony throws Walsh a look that could kill. Eileen is oblivious to the antics going on; she is thinking about her brother Sean.

"It Came Upon a Midnight Clear." Mike is outside the bar looking up at the brilliant stars. When he hears a car, he looks down the street. Hoping it is Tess and Elena. *It is not Tess's car.* This further enrages him. Full of resentment he goes back into the bar. Eileen runs up to him and pleads with him to go and help her at her apartment. Irritated that Tess and Elena are not back and inebriated, he foolishly agrees to go with Eileen. He was drunk, fuming, and since his younger sister Rose died suddenly on Christmas day he was feeling extremely melancholy. It didn't help that he erroneously felt misunderstood by his wife. Along with not being with his daughter on Christmas, Mike felt he would make a standby going with Eileen.

Mike imagined that Eileen looked somewhat like his sister Rose. Along with erroneously convincing himself that she was a lady in distress, he defiantly leaves with her. Thrilled, Eileen holds on tightly to Mike's arm. She shrewdly tells him how strong and manly he is. As they are walking out, Mike wobbling, Tony and Walsh look at one another fearing Mike was making the wrong decision. Walsh says, "What's with Mike tonight; he's not himself." Under his breath, frustrated Tony remarks, "Women are not his only problem."

Brendan murmurs, "Jezebel has risen." He slowly lifts his head again, looks over at Mike and Eileen leaving together and shouts, "Adam bites the Forbidden Fruit!" Laughing he says, "The Fall of Man." Disappointed that Eileen is leaving with Mike, Tony slugs down the rest of his Boiler Maker. With desire and envy in his eyes he lashes out, "You can say that again, Professor Big Mouth!" This adds fuel to Brendan's ranting. With his literary prowess Brendan bellows, "Watch out for Flaubert's parrot, Mike." As she is walking out the door with Mike, Eileen hears his cutting remark. She stops dead by the opened door, turns to face the inside of the bar, and gives Shakespeare the finger. Tony laughs and shouts out, "She my kind of woman; sassy and sexy."

Eileen and Mike are finally leaving. They bump into Father Arthur Shultz and Juan who are going inside the bar. The four awkwardly greet one another. Father Schultz guilty attempts to explain to Mike, "It was a long day of services, numerous house visits; and Juan has been shoveling snow all day. I wanted to give him something substantial to drink to warm him up." Mike, not in great shape, looks at the priest with repulsion. Not uttering a word Mike walks away. My Fair Lady, Eileen sprints right after him.

Inside the bar, Brendan, who observed the entire encounter, smirks and shouts out, "Saint and Sinners meet." Laughing grotesquely, he begins to sing, "God Rest Ye Merry Gentlemen." Still fuming over Eileen going with Mike, Big Tony moves down the other end of the bar to avoid the priest and the mute Juan whom he also is frustrated with. His resentful envious sentiments are palpable. Brendan doesn't miss a thing and calls out, "Hey Big Guy watch out before you become the green-eye monster Othello. Desdemona is off with . . ." "Shut your mouth before I shut it for you permanently," the aggravated Big Guy threatens the taunting Professor.

Outside on this peaceful Holy Night Eileen, covered in a warm emerald green coat, matching gloves, and a woolen hat, cuddles next to Mike who has his black Pea Coat collar up to hide his face; hoping to be incognito. He is wearing the new black woolen gloves his daughter Elena gave him for Christmas. This pathetically lonely woman seductively leads the secret love-of-her-life fantasy to her sparse, rented attic apartment. It is a few short blocks away from Walsh's Tavern in this working-class urban city. When they arrive at this pre-World War II brick, dilapidated apartment building, they enter the putrid smelling dark hallway and walk up the creaking stair to Eileen's small attic apartment.

A tacky plastic Christmas wreath is hung loosely on the entrance door. It has a tired, warn-out red bow on it. The sound of a parrot is heard squawking: "Merry Christmas, you fools." Mike backs up in surprise. Eileen giggles and reassures Mike that her parrot is in a cage and harmless. She calls out, "Flaubert, Mommy's home. She has a guest." He squawks loudly, "Cutie, another looser?" Eileen and Mike enter the tiny sitting area. Eileen tells Flaubert her parrot to be quiet. He is still squawking so she runs over and covers the cage with a white sheet and whispers, "Please be quiet baby! If you're good, Mommy will give you a treat later." Flaubert squaws back, "After you get your treat Cutie?" Eileen hits the top of the cage. "Quiet, Pecker head!" Eileen runs into her makeshift bedroom, removes her clothes, and puts on a flashy short red Chinese Kimono. She slinks back into the dark living room. Mike has his back to her. She rushes to get two glasses and a bottle of cheap wine from the small bridge table in the corner of the sitting room.

Looking around the tiny dim-lit room, Mike observes that no light bulb needs to be replaced. He becomes upset. "It looks like all the lights are working fine in here." Eileen tries to convince him that her landlord must have fixed the light after she left. She coaxes Mike to stay by offering him some cheap holiday cheer and womanly comfort. "Take it you fool," Flaubert screeches from behind the covered cage. The faithful parrot warns, "Hey Cutie; be careful; the goon is coming!" Flaubert keeps chanting this. Eileen hollers, "Be quiet!" She lifts the sheet from the cage and bribes the parrot with a carrot and croons, "Be good and there will be more later." He pecks at the food and begins to frantically tug at his red, yellow and green colorful feathers. *This astute feathered friend can hear and sense trouble.*

Mike was ripe and this lonely woman was longing for some long-awaited loving. Unbeknownst to the both of them, something was outside the door while Eileen was plotting to indulge her loneliness with unbridled passion. Without warning the door bursts open causing Eileen to scream along with the loud sounds of a parrot screeching, "Cutie, run for cover, run!" Mike yells at Eileen, "Hey is this some kind of freaky trick?" She yells to her pet parrot, "Quiet!" Mike blurts out, "What the Hell is going on around this place? It's like a zoo." Racing out the door, Mike plows into this unknown intruder, who is masked and brandishing a huge silvery-bladed knife. Mike crashes into the masked "thing" and knocks it down. Screaming like a banshee, the frantic Eileen leaps over the person lying on the floor and runs after the mystified Mike.

"Silent Night, Holy Night" is filled with shattering, ear-piercing monstrous sounds of a frightened out-of-his-mind Mike and the ferocious unknown creature. In the background you can hear Flaubert screeching, "The Goon, the Goon, the Goon."

Along with the horrendous screams and squawking coming from Eileen and Flaubert, the screeching of tires on an icy city road is heard simultaneously. It is the sound of Tess's car turning the corner near Walsh's Tavern. She desperately drives around trying to find an available parking space. Tess was losing her patience; she had to go a few blocks away to find an available space near her house. It was a long treacherous drive home from her sister's, she had too much spiked eggnog, was angry, tired, and frustrated. Elena did not talk to her mother the entire way home. She hovered in the corner in the back seat pretending to be asleep. This upset teenager did not want to discuss what happened between her and her cousin Timothy. More so, Elena was upset that she did not spend Christmas with her father.

As Tess turns the corner, she hears loud screams coming from a nearby old multiple dwelling. It was so loud that even Elena sits up and asks, "Where is all the noise coming from?" Suddenly, they see a man running frantically down the middle of the icy street. He is being chased by another who was brandishing a huge shinny-blinding knife as it reflects off the snow. At first they appeared as two dark shadows against the white snow but, as they came near the lighted lamp post, one of the figures became scandalously familiar. Tess was shocked to see it was her husband Mike. Elena was amused that it was her father until she saw a woman in a red flowing open rob screaming running after the two figures. Deeply distressed, Tess revs up her engine and drives head on toward the figures. She beams her head lights brightly over Mike. Who, like a stunned deer, is frantically looking at the car's blinding, beaming headlights in disbelief. Like a frozen ice statue, Mike stops cold in his tracks. Desperate and mortified, he calls out, "Tess, it's not what you think."

The masked man mysteriously disappears. The shaken other woman/ Cutie, Eileen, runs toward Mike to help him. He put up his hand vigorously waving her to go away. Seeing this half clad woman running toward her husband infuriates Tess. She recklessly backs the car away from Mike and that Jezebel woman and speedily drives away. Tess finally locates a spot near her house to park the car. Confused, Elena is not sure what happened or what she saw, but she knew it was not good. Tess knows exactly what happened with that Jezebel and knows exactly what she will do.

Mike, drunk and dazed, desperately gropes trying to get up but to no avail. He keeps falling down in the wet, slushy snow. Out of sight, the mysterious man holding onto the knife hovers. Seeing the masked man vanish around the corner and Tess's car speed off, Eileen rushes back over to help Mike. She attempts to comfort him. He pushes her away. Shunned and nervous Eileen moves away. Getting his bearings, Mike laboriously gets up from the street and attempts to stagger home. He is brutally aware that he is in serious trouble, not only with his wife, but in every aspect of his disintegrating, unraveling current life.

The disappointed and equally inebriated Eileen watches as "the man of her dreams" pathetically mopes away. Eileen boldly calls out to him, "Hey handsome, if you ever need me, you know where to find me." As the disappointed and perplexed Eileen trudges through the snow back to her lonely attic, she sarcastically sings, "I'm dreaming of a White *bitchy-witchy* Christmas…" The once buoyant mood is now dismal and sinister. Coming to her senses, suddenly Eileen stops singing. A creepy feeling of dread consumes her. Lights from the surrounding, festively decorated houses glisten brightly in the snow but a dark morbid shadow is lurking casting a ghostly image. *It Came Upon a Midnight . . . fear!*

Out of the shadows a huge man runs toward Eileen as she is despondently walking away. It is Eileen's estranged, sick monster of a husband. He is hiding waiting for Mike to leave. When he is sure Mike is out of sight, he takes out the knife and sneaks up behind his prey. Tony,

Mike's loyal employee, shouts for Eileen to get down and immediately lunges toward Eileen's ex as Marty attempts to stab his wife. Tony grabs the knife from him and the two men roll around in the snow. The huge knife is still in the estranged brutal husband's gloved hand. Eileen's ex Marty is screaming at Tony, "You'll pay for this you stinking piece of garbage." Tony, with his huge muscles and herculean power, overtakes Marty and shouts, "Don't threaten me you poor excuse of a gangster; you own me plenty of money and I intend to get it!" The struggle resumes until there is a loud blood curdling gasp. Eileen's brutal, enraged ex-husband lies still on the wet snow which is now soaked with oozing, fresh-red blood.

Big Tony jumps up, moves away from the bleeding Marty, runs over to Eileen, pulls her up and orders, "Get the hell out of here! Run home, lock your door and don't answer to anyone. I'll check on you later." Shocked, Eileen turns and sees her ex lying in the snow surrounded by a pool of blood. She screams, "Oh, god, no; what happened?" Tony shouts, "Nothing, just get the hell out of here, now!"

Seeing the dazed and frightened Eileen finally heading toward her apartment, Tony pulls the bloody knife stuck in Marty's chest, wipes it clean and checks to see if he has a pulse. He looks to see if anyone is around, seeing no one, he runs through the dark night leaving the good for nothing, bastard, cheating, wife-beating, gangster/husband drowning in a pool of blood. Tony gets rid of the deadly weapon where it will never be found. *The Ghost of Death is lurking and hovering over this holy peaceful night. Echoes of Brendan crying out, "Et Tu Brutus."*

Around the corner in the gloomy night, the Irish tavern owner, Tom Walsh, secretly observed the entire monstrous events that just occurred. When the coast is clear, Walsh runs over to the bleeding man. Walsh recognizes him immediately. He takes off his coat and covers him. Brendan secretly follows Walsh and when he sees the body he shouts, "Ah Tu Brutus." Sirens are now sounding. Two police cars race around the corner, stop abruptly where Walsh and the body are. They jump out of the patrol cars and rush over to Walsh and quickly exam the body on the ground. He is pronounced "dead on arrival (DOA)!" Walsh, knowing almost all of the police in the Jersey City Police Department and well respected by them, tells them he saw the whole thing. Walsh convinces and swears to the police that it was a mob hit. When Marty Goldstein is identified, the police write the death off as another unsolved brutal mob murder. *Thanks to Walsh and also to Brendan, who for once keeps his mouth shut, Big Tony walks away as a free man and Eileen can hopefully safely rest in peace.*

CHAPTER SIXTEEN

Strangers in the Night
Christmas Night
Walpole, New Hampshire
1867

AUSTIN RUNS TO the front door where the eerie banging sound is coming from. The front door is wide open from the harsh winter winds which are slamming this portal against the house. Cautiously standing by the opened door, Austin looks out at the pitch black night and sees nothing. He grabs the handle of this solid door and tries to close it but he is unable to do so. The powerful gale is no match even for this man. Out of the dark night a large gloved hand grabs Austin's arm. Alarmed, Austin tries to release himself. He hears a groan he recognizes. It is Zeke's sound. Austin allows Zeke to help him hold the door. Before they close the door, Zeke turns and motions to a shadowy figure hiding behind a mammoth Maple tree. Seeing Zeke waving, the lone figure gradually comes out from behind the monster-sized tree. The brilliant moon sheds its bright light on this lovely looking young girl who is wrapped in a magenta shawl and matching wool hat. She hesitantly moves forward after Zeke vigorously motions her to come to him. Stunned, Austin immediately asks his farmhand, "Who is that?" The young girl with long blond hair moves closer toward Zeke. Staring at this unfamiliar girl, Austin questions her, "Who are you?" Noticing that Zeke nods affirmatively to her, the shy girl of about sixteen, barely audible whispers, "I'm Nannette." Confused, Austin continues to question her, "How do you know Zeke?" Frightened she whispers, "I'm Zeke's ward." Austin looks at Zeke. Zeke nods yes. Hearing an unfamiliar voice and strange sounds, Anna Lee calls out to her husband, "Austin, what's wrong; are you alright?" He does not respond immediately so she calls out louder, "Please answer me! I'm concerned." Austin reassures his wife, "I'll be right there Anna Lee. Everything is fine."

Austin turns back to Zeke and interrogates him, "What are you two doing out on a night like this? You'll freeze to death." Since Zeke does not verbally communicate, the strange young girl Nannette explains, "We came to tell you about Buck." Alarmed, Austin shouts frantically staring at Zeke, "Buck! What's wrong?" Nannette spontaneously responds for the voiceless Zeke, "He received a deep cut on his front leg and was bleeding." The terrified girl hands Austin a paper. "This will explain everything." She further informs, "We were bringing this over to you when your door suddenly flew open." Austin takes it and looks at Nannette with a questionable eye. "Read it and you'll be relieved to know that the horse will be fine," Nannette sheepishly tells him. While Austin is reading it, she continues, "Zeke will go tomorrow to get the veterinarian." Austin looks over at the stoic Zeke for confirmation. Zeke nods yes. Austin blurts out, "I must go and check on Buck immediately!" Nannette quickly puts her hand up to stop him and reassures him, "No, it is not necessary. Zeke cleaned the wound." Zeke shakes his head in agreement.

"Buck was resting peacefully when we left the barn to come here," the young girl reassures Austin. Austin staring at Zeke, questions, "Is that true?" Zeke vigorously shakes his head affirmatively. Austin feels satisfied. He believes and trusts his dutiful and competent worker. Besides, he knows how much Zeke cares for Buck and would never let anything happen to him. "Thank you Zeke, for taking good care of Buck," he tells Zeke as he reassuringly pats him on the back.

Feeling relieved about Buck, Austin motions for Zeke and the girl to follow him into the house. "Please come in; you'll both get frost bite. You will get warmed by the hearth; the fire is blazing and we have plenty of hot apple cider too." He adds, "Besides I want to know in detail how Buck got wounded." The freezing and uncertain Nannette does not move; she turns to Zeke for reassurance. His reassuring look makes this shy young girl feel comfortable. Following Austin, they enter the warm festive house.

Anna Lee is greatly relieved when she sees her husband, as he limps slowly into the parlor. His concerned wife and darling little daughter are standing by the fire not far from the magnificent candle lit Christmas tree. Anna Lee sees her husband enter first and inquires, "Austin, what is going on?" Before he can answer, Anna Lee is shocked to see Zeke holding the arm of a young girl, as they follow her husband into the parlor. She warily eyes this strange young girl.

Austin goes up to the hearth where Anna Lee and Theresa Edith are waiting. He tries to reassure his shaken wife. Giving her a peck on her cheek he says, "All is fine dear." He hugs his little daughter Theresa Edith. Noticing that Anna Lee is staring at the unexpected stranger, Austin immediately introduces Nanette as Zeke's visitor. Anna Lee's husband deliberately does not mention the situation with Buck. He politely asks his wife to fetch warm apple cider for the shivering young girl. Anna Lee halfhearted goes. Her good manners and Southern etiquette make her heed her husband. As a good host, she must dutifully obey her husband and make her guests feel welcomed. Like a mummy, Zeke stands there with the uncertain Nannette close by. "Sit down by the fire," Austin insists. The two glacially cold guests timidly comply. Zeke and Nannette sit side-by-side on a crimson soft velvet loveseat.

Austin moves to a mahogany buffet server which holds a large, oval shaped Paul Revere Silver Tray which has beautiful family heirloom cut crystal stemware with elegant carafes filled with fine, rare liquors next to them. He delicately pours two glasses of brandy into two fine crystal cut brandy sniffers. One for Zeke and the other for himself. Austin walks over to Zeke and hands it to him. He stands tall and lifting his sniffer, he makes a toast, "A warm welcome to Nannette and thank you Zeke for always taking excellent care of Buck." Austin savors his fine aged amber colored brandy. Zeke stares at the fine cut-crystal brandy glass with its rich amber colored liquid swirling inside it.

Nannette apprehensively sits quietly observing the beautiful home. She smiles at the little girl quietly standing by the magnificent Christmas tree. Austin announces, "I will feel better when the new veterinarian Dr. Jeremiah Holden comes and examines Buck tomorrow." Looking at the dismayed Zeke, Austin firmly comments, "I am sure you did a fine job cleaning and dressing the wound Zeke." Looking serious and concerned Austin inquires, "How did he get cut?" Nannette interjects, "Zeke was sharpening his whittling knife in the barn when Buck sneaked up behind him. Unaware, Zeke turned quickly and accidently cut Buck's upper front leg."

Austin does not respond. He finishes his aged brandy, goes to a side table and takes out two cigars from an elegantly carved wooden humidor. He meticulously rolls one of the cigars between his long fingers, cuts off the end, lights it and hands it to Zeke. Austin repeats it for himself. Standing tall and stately he puffs on his cigar. Austin inhales deeply and blows the white cigar smoke out slowly. It circles like a fleeting cloud. He sighs, "Wonderful!" Noticing that Zeke has not touched his brandy or puffed on his cigar, he reassures his trusted worker, "Go ahead Zeke. It is Christmas; indulge!" Mesmerized, Zeke stares at the red flame of the cigar and stamps it inside his rough hand and puts it aside next to his untouched brandy.

Anna Lee enters with a steaming mug of hot brewed apple cider and hands it to Nannette along with a fine embroidered linen napkin. Quietly Nannette takes it and whispers, *"Merci."* This beautifully dressed and lovely lady of the house inquires, "You speak French and English?" Nannette shakes her head affirmatively and whispers. *"Oui."* She glances over at Zeke whose eyes open wide when Anna Lee inquires. Austin's perplexed young wife is feeling extremely chilled. She meekly asks her husband to add more logs to the fire. "Darling, please add more logs to the fire; I'm feeling chilled, as I am sure Zeke and his guest must."

Placing his cigar down in a porcelain ashtray, Austin gets up and walks to the fire and adds more logs. The flame rises quickly and violently Austin steps back. Zeke, seeing the out-of-control flames, cringes and lets out an ungodly groan. "OHHHH!" He stops when he notices the others looking at him. "Zeke, I have it under control," Austin assures him as he pokes the fire. Once the flames are tamed and the guests are warmed, Austin questions Zeke further, "Now Zeke, I know it is difficult for you to communicate but perhaps Nannette can shed some light as to how and when this beautiful young lady came here and, why was I not told about this charming woman- child previously?" Zeke glances at Nannette, gives her a nod, which infers she may answer.

Before Nannette can respond, little Theresa Edith jumps up from her child-sized wooden rocker and heads toward Nannette. She surprises everyone as she goes up to this new, unfamiliar young woman. Austin and Anna Lee are astonished to see their daughter go so readily to this stranger. Nannette puts down her hot cider, smiles at little Theresa Edith, lifts her onto her lap, and holds on to her tightly.

Feeling more at ease, Nannette answers Austin's questions. Nannette explains that she just arrived a day or so ago. Prior, she explains that she was an orphan in a small town in West Virginia. She further informs that the rules at St. Francis Orphanage are when a ward turns sixteen they are no longer permitted to stay. Nannette emphasizes that they must go out on their own and make a life for themselves. She hesitates to further her story when Austin pressures her, "Please clarify, I am still not sure how you got here and found Zeke." Nannette is reluctant to continue until Zeke gives her a nod of approval, "I turned sixteen a few months ago." "Go on," Austin prompts her. "Before I left, a kind woman who works at the orphanage did some research and found out that my father was killed in the Civil War in 1864, in the terrible Battle of the Wilderness." This statement deeply upsets Austin and he shouts out, "My god child, how dreadful!" Anna Lee asks, "What about your mother?" "Long before my father died, my mother passed away from Tuberculosis in New Orleans, Louisiana; I was told." Anna Lee further inquiries, "Do you have any siblings or other relatives?" "Unfortunately," Nannette reveals, "I was an only child and have no other known relatives." She pauses. "Go on," Austin requests. "I was told that my parents came from France and settled in New Orleans around 1845," she offers and pauses. "Continue!" Austin calls out. Nannette explains, "Checking the records further, the woman at the orphanage, Miss Elizabeth, heard that a person contacted the orphanage about me. It was Zeke." Miss Elizabeth claims that, "He was sending money to the orphanage for my expenses since 1862."

Meekly Nannette continues, "Miss Elizabeth at the orphanage found an old envelope with a Walpole, NH postmark on it in my file and, before I had to leave, she gave it to me and encouraged me to follow up knowing I had no other options." Impressed and amazed, Austin praises her bravery, "With only this information and no other family or friends, Nannette, you bravely traveled to Walpole New Hampshire in search of Zeke?" "Yes," Nannette responds, "The kind woman at the orphanage gave me money, food, a ticket for a train, and vital information about traveling to New Hampshire." she informs. Austin and Anna Lee are beyond shocked. Austin blurts out, "This is unbelievable for a young woman to be able to find us and to heroically travel alone not knowing if you would ever find Zeke."

Nannette boldly reveals, "I had no other options but to find Zeke. After a long and frightening journey, I praise God I finally arrived in Walpole." Anna Lee chimes in, "How did you know he was at our farm?" Nannette immediate explains, "I met Emma Johnson in town who directed me to the place where she said Zeke would be and here I am." She puts her head down and whispers, "I thank God he is a good man and accepts me."

Austin and Anna Lee sit quietly listening attentively while this extraordinary young girl shares her ill-fated tale with a hopefully happy ending. Austin looks over at Zeke and inquires if this is true. Zeke awkwardly nods yes. Austin questions Zeke further, "How do you know her?" Nannette blurts out, "My dad and Zeke met during the war." She gently hugs Theresa Edith for comfort who is still sitting on her lap playing with Nannette's shawl. Theresa Edith looks up and smiles at her new friend.

Austin, noticing how Theresa Edith is warming up to Nannette, fearlessly suggests that she move into the main house. "You cannot live in the same quarters as Zeke and the barn is unfit for a young girl." Austin continues, "You can assist Anna Lee with the chores and be a companion to our dear Theresa Edith. It is evident that she has taken a real shine to you." Noticing that Zeke is looking at Austin, he adds, "Of course, we will provide new clothes, food, board, and an appropriate stipend." Anna Lee is leery of her husband's daring invitation. "Besides," he informs, "Shortly I must leave for Australia for a few months to check on my sheep farm and property along with other pressing business matters." He looks over at his perplexed wife and reassures all, "I will feel much better knowing that Anna Lee has extra help and my precious Theresa Edith has a female companion."

Anna Lee passively sits quietly and reluctantly accepts her husband's decision. Looking over at Nannette who seems pleased, Zeke nods affirmatively. Nannette kisses little Theresa Edith on her cheek. Seeing that all are in agreement, Austin stands tall and gallantly commands, "It is settled!" Anna Lee, the dutiful wife, charitable Methodist, and caring woman, smiles and walks over to Nannette. She removes her daughter from the young woman's lap and comments, "It will be a delight and a privilege to have you Nannette." Walking away, a look of sadness clouds Anna Lee's striking vivid violet eyes.

Noticing his wife getting melancholy he requests, "My dearest, why don't you play something on the harpsichord for us. I am sure your parents would be pleased to know that the Christmas present they so generously sent you is being put to good use and making you and their granddaughter happy." Anna Lee looks at Austin and quietly answers, "I would love to accommodate you dear and our guests, but I fear I am too tired." She austerely looks over at her disappointed husband, daughter and Nanette and with confidence adds, "I am sure my generous and caring parents would understand therefore I pray you will also my dearest husband." Disappointed Austin nods his head in agreement to appease his wife.

Nannette chimes in, "I learned to play the harpsichord at the orphanage perhaps I can play something." Looking over at the dismayed Anna Lee, Nannette cleverly remarks, "Although I am sure I do not play as well as you." Austin seeing his wife becoming extremely put out says kindly to Nannette, "Perhaps another time." Things calm down and Anna Lee recognizes that her husband is not pleased with her cryptic behavior. Wanting to redeem herself, she resumes being a polite host. She calls out, "Now let us all relax and enjoy the rest of our precious time together."

Hearing Austin say that he is leaving for Australia for a few months to check on his sheep farm, which he also inherited from his grandfather, Anna Lee had no other options but to accept her husband's decision to welcome Nannette into her home; especially since she dreads being alone with Zeke. Besides, Anna Lee's parents are older and not well enough to travel from Virginia to spend time with her and their first grandchild. Sadly, Anna Lee lost her favorite brother Hamish in the Civil War. Her sister Beatrice is currently pregnant with her first child. After Anna Lee's older brother Tyler returned from the Civil War, he dutifully remained in Virginia to care for their aging parents. Also, he stayed to be near his sister Beatrice whose husband James Ferris is missing in action. Tyler was badly burned in the Civil War and is also healing his wounds both externally and internally. He is now the head of this Virginia family plantation since their father is melancholy over the loss of his son and missing son-in-law and is almost nonfunctioning. This horrible war has taken a devastating toll on so many families both North and South.

Anna Lee is unsure of and not impressed with Nannette. She finds her story unreal and bizarre that she just drops into Walpole and miraculously finds Zeke out of nowhere. Anna Lee mutters, "Isn't it ironic, this strange young woman comes at the right time to solve the dilemma of Austin leaving and abandoning me while I am pregnant. Not to mention that Theresa Edith will miss her father terribly." The once peaceful and pleasant Christmas night becomes an evening of unexpected surprises and unresolved questionable revelations.

In a short time, the parlor and the people inhabiting it become jarringly silent. Noticing the tension, Austin breaks the creepy mood. He rises, faces the others in the room, and with a strong solid voice, pronounces, "Merry Christmas to all" and looking directly at Nannette chants, "And a very hearty and cordial welcome to our new family member." Nannette shyly flutters her big blue saucer -shaped eyes and demurely lowers her head when she notices Anna Lee gazing oddly at her. "Merry Christmas to all" shouts little Theresa Edith. Anna Lee and Austin's precious little angel begins to clap her tiny hands while jumping up and down enthusiastically. Clearly, Theresa Edith is overjoyed with her new friend. Grudgingly Anna Lee sits silently and sips her cooled apple cider. Suddenly it tastes bitter to her and the warm room becomes eerily frigid. Zeke is immobilized as he glaringly stares at the *threatening* fire and is vividly aware that Anna Lee's tranquil facade is fuming and raging inside her.

Everyone is startled when Austin shouts, "One more thing, how did that front door blow open?" Anna Lee repeats, "Yes, how did it open?" Nannette gives Zeke a shy look. Seeing her look; he nods to her affirmatively. Nannette stands up and attempts to explains, "I think I know what happened." Austin prods, "Go on!" Hesitating, she resumes, "While you were all at church today, Zeke and I came into the house from the backdoor." "What?" Anna Lee blurts out. "Be silent; let her finish," Austin quiets his shocked wife. Zeke nods to Nannette to go on, "Zeke wanted to leave something under the Christmas tree for your daughter." She points behind the tree. Austin insists she go and locate it. Nannette goes over to the Christmas tree. Hidden way behind in the back she retrieves a large wrapped package. Carrying it, she walks over to Theresa Edith. With a huge smile on her face,

Nannette hands it to the excited little girl. Theresa Edith smiles, looks at her father who gives her permission to open it. She excitedly unwraps the package and looks inside. While holding tightly on to the item, Theresa Edith squeals in delight. It is a beautifully handcarved, brightly painted wooden Nutcracker. Therese Edith runs over to her mother to show it to her.

Nannette proudly calls out, "Zeke made it!" Anna Lee is happy for her daughter, "Very nice." She turns and looks over at Zeke and questions him, "Again, may I ask how did the front door fly open?" Zeke motions for Nannette; she further explains, "After we placed it behind the tree, we were ready to leave by the back door but we heard you coming in that way therefore, we rushed out the front door." Guiltily, she confesses, "In our haste, we must have left the front door slightly ajar. I'm so sorry." Zeke nods in agreement. Anna Lee, while pleased for her elated daughter, is upset to think that Zeke feels free enough to come into her house without permission. Anna Lee knows that if she addresses this with her husband, he would defend Zeke. He would also remind her that Zeke is part of the family; as she resentfully assumes Nannette eventually will be. Zeke stands silently as stoic as the Nutcracker he created while Nannette was explaining the situation to the others.

Anna Lee remains silent. A lady of this time period must always acquiesce to her father, husband, and brothers. While everyone remains quiet, Austin goes over to his daughter and examines the Nutcracker. Holding it in his hand, he raises it up and glares over at Zeke and comments, "Your whittling knife must be dangerously sharp to carve this intricate item." Looking directly at Zeke he questions, "Am I right, Zeke?" Zeke shakes his head affirmatively. Austin hands it back to his overjoyed daughter. While walking away to stoke the withering fire, under his breath, Austin remarks, "I'm anxious to hear what the veterinarian has to say tomorrow." Trying to restore the earlier holiday spirit, Austin turns to his wife, daughter, and guests and request they sing along with him. In a booming voice the head of the house begins to sing out, "O Come All Ye Faithful…" Zeke taps his foot in tune while the others sing out joyfully. Anna Lee pleases her husband by singing loudly.

CHAPTER SEVENTEEN

Silent Night, Holy Night
Late Christmas Night
Jersey City, NJ
1955

AFTER EXPERIENCING A miserable Christmas at Mary Grace and Geoff's house and seeing her husband Mike lying in the cold wet snow with a strange woman hovering over him, Tess enters their darkened house deeply and hotly disturbed. Equally distraught Elena follows her mother carrying the gifts Aunt Mary Grace gave them to take home. Tess Adeline puts the lights on in the darkened house, takes off her heavy winter coat, and asks Elena to put the gifts from Aunt Mary Grace under the Christmas tree. Defiantly Elena throws them down in the hall right where she is standing, runs to her bedroom, and slams the door shut. Shortly after, music is heard coming from her room. This deeply wounded teenager wants to blur out what occurred today. *Music always distracts and comforts her.*

Tess heads to the kitchen and puts on the tea kettle. When she was a young girl and upset, her mother always made her a cup of hot tea with honey and lots of fresh-squeezed lemon. *Even the soothing tea will not comfort this troubled woman tonight.* Waiting for the tea kettle to boil Tess goes to Elena's bedroom door and inquires, "Are you all right? Can we talk?" No response from her daughter only the sound of music playing; it is from Elena's new Broadway Show album, *Oklahoma*. Ironically, the song playing was "Lonely Room." Tess hearing the lyrics: "By myself in a lonely room," filtering through Elena's closed bedroom door makes her feel even more despondent.

The tea kettle is whistling loudly. Tess runs to shut it off. The front door opens; it is Mike, staggering in. Tess rushes to get her tea, goes directly to her bedroom and locks the door. She wants nothing to do with her husband tonight or ever, for that matter. Tess does not want to upset her daughter any more this evening therefore she sequesters herself in the bedroom. Mike knows that he is in deep trouble, so he quietly goes into the guest bedroom in the front of the house. He takes off his wet jacket and prepares to undress when he remembers he promised his sister Ettie that he would go down and visit with his niece and nephew.

Not to disappoint his sister Mike quickly cleans himself a bit and quietly heads downstairs. As he enters Ettie and Carlo's place, Rosaria and Blaise are preparing to leave. They are thrilled to see their Uncle. Blaise immediately goes and bear hugs him. Mike comments on how great his Marine nephew looks in his uniform. Rosaria is a little caution and just smiles at Mike and inquires, "Hope you, Aunt Tess and Elena had a nice Christmas." Mike, to save face, responds, "We did." Rosaria wants to leave to avoid further talk with her Uncle. She explains, "I must leave. I have to be at the hospital first thing tomorrow. I have the early morning shift." She runs out. Blaise, shocked by his sister leaving so suddenly says, "Hey Uncle Mike, I'll stay and have a drink with you; we have a lot to catch up on."

Aware that her brother Mike is inebriated and looks disheveled, Ettie suggests, "Let's wait till the next time Blaise." Blaise responds, "Okay, besides I want to visit Robbie Savini tonight. I must catch a train back to my post first thing in morning." He kisses his mother and adds, "Don't expect me back Mom." Carlo interjects, "Yes, you better get going. Scrutinizing Mike closely he sarcastically remarks, "Your Uncle looks like he's had too much already and then some." Mike is too sick to argue with Carlo therefore, he wishes his nephew well. They make plans to get together next time Blaise has leave from Parris Island, SC. Rosaria has already left. Mike, also anxious to leave, says his goodbyes and sneaks back up the stairs to his place. He knows well enough after tonight fiasco to go directly to the guest room. Tess hears him but is too upset to confront him. "All's Quiet on the Western Front," for now, Mike erroneous thinks.

In the front guest bedroom Mike is sleeping off his hangover. In their bedroom, Tess is unable to sleep. She is unnerved, experiencing extreme anxiety, and feels as if she is losing her mind. As a concerned mother, Tess knows she must go and check on her daughter. She quietly gets up and enters Elena's bedroom. She is shocked to see Elena shivering in her bed, even though she is covered with multiple heavy blankets. Tess immediately feels Elena's forehead. It is burning hot. Elena is running an extremely high temperature. Tess tries to talk with her but Elena is incoherent. Petrified, Tess goes to the bathroom and retrieves a thermometer. In the bedroom she takes Elena's temperature. It is almost 104. Tess instantly calls their family doctor Dr. Saul Sacks (in the 50s doctors made house calls). Hearing the dangerously high fever the concerned physician instructs Tess what to do until he gets there. Dr. Sacks reassures her that he will leave immediately. He is only a few blocks away.

Suffering from a horrible headache and hangover, Mike overhears his wife's urgent call to Dr. Sacks about Elena. He runs in to see what's happening. "What's wrong with Elena?" he shouts. Tess is busy preparing an ice pack to put on Elena's head; she deliberately ignores her husband's query. This infuriates Mike. He rushes into his daughter's bedroom and is greatly alarmed to see the terrible condition Elena is in. Not sure what to do; he holds her in his arms and strokes her head. He hollers out to his wife, "We should take her to the hospital; it may take Dr. Sacks a while to get here." "No!" screams Tess. She warns and accuses him, "Stay out of this; you caused enough trouble this Christmas."

Tess hurries in with an ice bag. She pushes Mike aside. He slides down on the floor. She places the ice bag on her daughter's burning head and puts ice cubes near Elena's parched lips. Tess insists her daughter suck on them before she becomes too dehydrated. Mike is greatly alarmed. He struggles to get up and repeats, "She should be in a hospital!" Tess is ready to demand he leave when she observes Elena's eyes rolling back into her head. Tess panics, she fears that Elena is having a convulsion. Immediately she pulls her daughter's tongue out of her mouth. Pushing Tess aside, Mike grabs his daughter in his trembling arms and shouts, "We're going to the hospital." Hearing her parents fighting, this very ill young girl forces herself into an out-of-body situation. The doorbell is ringing while the familiar comforting voice of Dr. Saul Sacks is heard.

CHAPTER EIGHTEEN

Dr. Frankenstein Revisited
Day after Christmas
Walpole, New Hampshire
1867

IT IS THE day after Christmas. The Stevens family had an interesting Christmas. A door suddenly flung open; Buck is injured; an unexpected stranger enters their lives; and Austin announced he is going to Australia after the New Year. He also boldly invites the new girl Nannette, Zeke's ward, to live with Anna Lee and Theresa Edith without consulting his wife first. Tension is palatable in this once serene and orderly home.

It is December 26, 1867, early morning before the sun has risen. Austin enters the cold kitchen to start a fire. He is surprised to see Anna Lee already there. She started the fire, made coffee and is preparing breakfast. This dutiful wife is cooking her husband's favorite bacon and biscuits. Austin praises her for being such a great cook yet comments, "No breakfast for me; I'm going immediately to the barn." Noticing his wife's disappointed expression, he explains, "Dr. Holden will be here shortly to check on Buck."

Looking at her husband Anna Lee halfheartedly inquires, "Is Buck going to be all right?" She really wants to ask him what possessed him to invite that strange young girl to come and live with her especially now that he is going away. Anna Lee is afraid to speak her mind. It is not proper for a wife to question her husband. Austin notices that Anna Lee is exceptionally quiet this morning, therefore he offers, "When I come back from the barn, we will discuss my trip to Australia and the arrangements for Nannette." He grabs his coat hanging on the hook on the kitchen door. Before he leaves he reassures his wife, "Anna Lee, please know that I will be back before our baby is born." She nods. Austin leaves by the back kitchen door.

Walking over to the door to lock it Anna Lee peeps through the misty glass windowpane. She watches her husband struggle through the snow to the barn; she notices his limp is getting worse. Anna Lee turns suddenly when she hears Theresa Edith coming down the stairs adoringly carrying her Christmas gift from Zeke, the Nutcracker. She runs over to her mother and hands her the Nutcracker and announces, "Mama, he's hungry." Anna Lee hugs her daughter tightly.

Dr. Jeremiah Holden, the new veterinarian, is in the barn with Zeke. He is a tall, thin, bespectacled man in his late thirties with dark cynical looking large eyes and a beard growing on his sharp pointed chin. He has a pipe tightly gripped in his teeth. He is married to a zealot-religious woman, Rebecca Watkins Holden, who has been bedridden most of their childless married life. People in Walpole knew little about him; those who heard rumors regarding this stranger greatly question the reason he married this sickly, frail young woman.

Dr. Holden came to Walpole shortly after the Civil War was over and married Rebecca Watkins soon after. He replaced the elderly, local, highly respected veterinarian, Dr. Abraham Goldsmith, who died in his late eighties prior to Rebecca and Jeremiah's wedding. Dr. Goldsmith was a close long-time friend to Rebecca's well-to-do New England family, who settled in Walpole over a 100 hundred years ago and has resided there ever since. The well-respected Dr. Goldsmith was also close friends with Austin's grandfather and was the Stevens family's highly respected and long-associated veterinarian. *Dr. Jeremiah Holden had large shoes to fill.*

As Austin entered the barn, he was surprised to see Dr. Holden had already arrived. He comments, "Sorry, I didn't know you were here." He extends his hand to the new veterinarian. "Thanks for coming Dr. Holden." Wearing thick eyeglasses, he looks at Austin, shakes his hand vigorously and requests, "Please call me Jeremiah." Austin does not reply. Dr. Holden informs Austin that he finished examining and administering to Buck and reassures him, "Buck will heal nicely and be as good as new in a short time."

Austin is pleased to hear this but further inquires as to the nature of the wound. He questions as to how long it will take to completely heal. He asks, "Will there be any future ramifications from the wound?" Dr. Holden informs, "No Buck will be fine. As to how the stab wound occurred, you'll need to have Zeke explain it to you." He stops and adds, "Clearly he was stabbed with a sharp instrument. It deeply punctured his front upper leg causing heavy bleeding." The veterinarian continues, "Zeke had the good sense to put pressure on the wound, clean it with water and alcohol, and tape it tightly."

Austin is looking perplexed, he turns and stares at Zeke. Dr. Holden looks over at the sheepish Zeke and comments, "Although, I did have to give him a few stitches." Dr. Holden goes over to Zeke and hands him a bottle and instructs him, "Keep the wound sterile and put this ointment on it daily." The vet also reminds him to keep Buck quiet until it heals and instructs Zeke, "Come and get me if it becomes infected."

Dr. Holden turns to Austin and informs him, "I'll be back in a week to check up on Buck and remove the stitches." He also reminds Zeke to keep the other animals away from Buck, "Even the black and white barn cat Edgar Allan whom Buck adores?" Austin asks. He further inquires, "Did Zeke show you the tool that punctured Buck?" Dr. Holden quickly responds "No! No need to see it." "Well," Austin murmurs, looking directly at the stunned Zeke, "I would like to see it."

Before the conversation continues, Nannette enters the barn holding a large pale of swishing water. With the door slightly ajar, the rising sun makes her long golden hair glow. It is as if a hallo is surrounding her. Nannette is a vision of rare beauty like the Italian artist Botticelli's magnificent painting, *The Birth of Venus*. She looks even more radiant and beautiful than the night before when Austin saw her hiding behind the tree. Dr. Holden is taken back by this magnificent young girl standing motionless by the slightly ajar barn door. His eyes widen as he stares at her in a peculiar manner - clearly he is mesmerized by her striking beauty and youth. Austin is uncomfortable with the way the doctor is looking at Nannette, as is Zeke.

Austin distracts the vet by taking him over to the other end of the barn where the tools are stored. He points to the paraphernalia and inquires, "Do you think any of these could have punctured Buck so deeply?" Still preoccupied with the gorgeous young girl standing next to Zeke, Dr. Holden barely looks at the tools. He turns his head and continues to stare at this breathtaking beauty. Austin coughs loudly startling the vet and reminds him, "The tools?" Dr. Holden hastily comments, "That's difficult to decipher," while continuing to stare at Nannette who is now nervously standing close to Zeke.

Austin calls over to Zeke and Nannette, "Both of you, please come here. Show me the tool that harmed Buck." They both walk to the tool shed. Nannette stays as far away from the veterinarian as she can. Zeke rummages through the tools he pulls out a pointed sharp carving instrument. Austin takes it from Zeke, looks at it closely, and inquires, "Dr. Holden can this be the culprit?" Annoyed, he once again claims, "As I said, it is difficult for me to know; I am a doctor that heals not harms." He then turns and continues to stare at Nannette. Zeke gives the doctor a menacing look. Nannette sheepishly backs away and places her shawl over her head almost covering her face.

Dr. Holden hesitantly leaves the barn with Austin's encouragement. He reluctantly follows Austin out. Outside Austin shakes Dr. Holden's hand and places money in his broad gloved hand. The veterinarian puts it in his coat pocket and with great interest, he inquires, "Who is that striking young girl with Zeke? I've never seen her around here before?" Austin responds, "She's a friend of Zeke's and will be helping my wife Anna Lee while I'm away in Australia." "Interesting," Dr. Holden reassures Austin, "While you're away, I can check on your animals and your family for you."

Skeptical of his last remark, Austin sarcastically responds, "If Zeke needs you to take care of the animals, he will contact you. As far as my family is concerned, absolutely no need!" Dr. Holden tries to interject but Austin comments, "Besides, I'm sure you have enough to do with your poor wife Rebecca being bedridden and also with your active practice." Dr. Holden stands there in the deep snow stunned with a strange look on his stricken face. Limping, Austin walks away from him and shouts out, "Goodbye, Jeremiah!" The veterinarian eyes harden as he grudgingly hollers back, "Call me Dr. Holden!" Austin brusquely continues to limp toward the house and again emphatically hollers, "I said, goodbye, Jeremiah Holden!" Annoyed, boldly he calls out, "Wish your family a Merry Christmas for us. Especially your sweet wife Rebecca. Jeremiah!"

On this unsettling day after Christmas, Zeke and Nannette, hearing the two men talking, go over to the slightly ajar barn door and peer out. The veterinarian reminds Nannette of the main character in the book, *Frankenstein,* by Mary Shelley. Nannette quietly saunters over to Zeke and meekly asks, "Do you like that man?" Zeke looks at her gloomily and lets out an odd *groan.* The confused girl quickly slams the barn door shut. Fearing he upset the girl, Zeke gently pats the top of her head to assure her all is okay.

Zeke heads over to check on Buck. The black and white barn cat, Edgar Allan, lazily sleeps next to the wounded horse resting on soft hay. It's as if the feline knows his buddy is ill and wants to comfort him. Zeke bends down next to Buck and gently rubs the ailing horse's sore leg and checks to make sure it is not oozing, red, and swollen. He looks at Edgar Allan and pats him too making it clear that he will not separate the two buddies even if that weird vet said so. Feeling confident that all is currently alright, Zeke motions for Nannette to bring the pail of water she has been patiently holding. She dutifully carries the full pail of sloshing water over to Buck. Smiling Zeke whispers "Thank you." Hearing Zeke speak for the first time shocks Nannette and makes her very happy.

Zeke knows enough about horses that Buck is terribly weak but also that it is not good for a horse to lay down for long periods of time. The wise caretaker makes a makeshift harness to wrap around the body of the horse. He uses strong, heavy-duty rope to go around a weighty wool blanket which will be placed under Buck. The ropes will be thrown over the strong barn wooden beams. After Zeke tests it for its safety and ability to hold up Buck, he places it under Buck and hoist him up thereby allowing the weak horse to comfortably stand up on all fours with little or no weight on his wounded leg. Nannette gives Buck the water and pats his wet noise. She watches him greedily lap it up. Even though she realizes it was necessary in the healing process of Buck, Nannette becomes anxious when she observes

Zeke adjusting the mechanism to keep Buck upright. On her journey to New Hampshire, it brought back the horrors that continue to haunt her of seeing black runaway slaves being hung with nooses.

Dr. Holden is not willing to leave at the demand of Austin. He defiantly stands knee deep in foot high snow near the front of the main house watching Austin struggling back toward the outside kitchen door. Ignoring the veterinarian, Austin looks up at the rising sun. White smoke lazily is curling out from the kitchen chimney where Anna Lee is preparing a hearty breakfast for him and his daughter.

The veterinarian throws his medical bag into the front of his sleigh, jumps in, hastily grabs the snake-like long leather whip and with great force cracks it violently on his horse's broad back making it leap forward. The cracking sound on the solid snow from the horse's hoofs is deafening. Dr. Jeremiah Holden's black-raven horse Diablo is working hard as the sleigh moves down the polar white Watkins Hill Road.

In the background the low whining of the ailing Buck and the heartache moaning of Zeke in the barn comingles with the sound from Dr. Holden's sleigh. Inside the barn, the rapid lapping of water is heard while Buck continues to greedily devour the water. Getting Buck back to his former good health is priority for Zeke and also for Nannette who has grown fond of the gelding. Zeke feels guilty for harming Buck while Nannette is sad it happened soon after she arrived. A cloud of darkness circumvents the age-old historical barn and these two mysterious residents.

Realizing she is moving into the main house this morning, Nannette nervously asks Zeke if he needs her any further. He shakes his head negatively and motions with his hand for her to get going. This nervous young lady returns to Zeke's small living quarters behind the barn and hurriedly packs her few meager items of clothing: her only pair of boots and her deceased mother's bible. She takes them to the main house where her duties as companion to little Theresa Edith will commence today.

Nannette puts on her special hand knitted magenta hat and shawl. Mrs. Elizabeth, the kind woman at the orphanage, gave the hat and shawl to her the day she left the orphanage. Miss Elizabeth explained to Nannette that the day she arrived at the orphanage the magenta hat and shawl were in a sealed package with her name written on it. Nannette was not aware of it at the time.

Miss Elizabeth was required to open and inspect all packages that came with the orphanage's wards. After seeing how beautiful these hand-knitted items were, this insightful woman decided to give them to Nannette at the official time of her departure. She feared others at the orphanage, jealous of this stunning, sensitive girl, might be tempted to steal them from her. Miss Elizabeth felt a special kinship to this lonely but beautiful, golden-haired beauty with delicate porcelain skin and greenish-blue piercing eyes.

Dressed in her *special* magenta shawl and hat, Nannette leaves Zeke's room and drudges through the weighty snow toward the main house looking similar to the fairy tale character, "Little Red Riding Hood." Similar to the young *Jane Eyre*, Charlotte Bronte's famous character and Nannette's favorite book, she carries her meager personal items to the main house ready to be a nanny for this family. Against the luminous white snow, this fragile young lady mimics a brilliant red cardinal as she heads toward her new home. Nannette holds on tightly to the few private items she owns. While outside Nannette becomes anxious when she hears the fading sound of sleigh bells coming from Dr. Holden's horse-drawn sleigh as he rushes down Watkins Hill Road. "Dashing Through the Snow in a One-Horse Open Sleigh…"

This shy young woman experiences a creeping feeling as she recalls Dr. Holden's dark, remote eyes gazing at her strangely. His deep-set obtrusive eyes seem demonic to her. She felt them piercing deeply into her being–like a sharp knife piercing her tender heart. She hopes he doesn't come back. If he must, Nannette wishes she will not encounter this "Dr. Frankenstein-like" creature again.

CHAPTER NINETEEN

Strangers in the Night
Late Christmas Night
Jersey City, NJ
1955

THE ELDERLY, KIND, and competent Dr. Saul Sacks, in his usual black-worn suit and twisted blue-black and white striped tie, attempts to comfort Tess and Mike by reminding them, "Elena is a strong girl. If her fever breaks tonight, she'll get through the crisis and be well soon." Mike respects Dr. Sacks but tonight he is not convinced that Elena will get through this. He challenges Dr. Sacks and confronts him, "What makes you think that the medicine you gave her will work?" Before the good doctor can respond, Mike insists, "We should bring her to the hospital! I have a lot of connections there and I can get her a bed and the best care immediately." Tess immediately interjects, "Mike, Dr. Sacks knows Elena since the day she was born. He just gave her a penicillin shot." Frustrated Tess tries to convince her highly disturbed husband, "Mike, give it a chance to work." Tess goes to her daughter and kisses her forehead. She turns to Mike and attempts to reassure him, "See, she's sleeping peacefully now."

Before anyone has the opportunity to say another word, there is a knock on the back-hall door. The door is always unlocked therefore Ettie lets herself in. She is carrying a coffee pot and a plate of her homemade Christmas cookies. Mike, looking overwhelmed, rushes over to his sister and grabs the items from her. Ettie pats her brother gently on his slumped shoulders. Tess gazes over at the two of them. Ettie immediately runs to Tess and puts her arms around her while tears are slowly rolling down Ettie's worried, doughboy-sullen face. Tess stares at her quizzically, "How did you know?." Ettie explains, "I couldn't sleep since Carlo was coughing so much and many other things. I went to the living room and was looking out my front window." She puts her hand over her heart and cries out, "Oh, my god, when I saw Dr. Sacks' car and saw him rushing over to our house, I ran over to open the front door to the entrance way." She explains that the doctor told her why he came, "When he told me my sweet Elena was sick, I had to come up." Tess tells Ettie about Elena's high fever, her hallucinating, and told her Dr. Sacks just gave her niece a penicillin shot.

Worried Ettie immediately goes over to the bed where her beloved niece is sleeping. She kisses her on the forehead. The concerned Aunt feels her niece is burning up. She piously makes the Sign of the Cross on Elena and quietly prayers over her. Ettie, deeply distressed, stands up and returns to her distraught sister-in-law, "Tess, I can't image how hard this must be for you. Please forgive me for intruding but I wanted you to know that I am here for you." Ettie reassures her sister-in-law, "I prayed a rosary soon after I spoke to Dr. Sacks and heard Elena was sick." Ettie is deeply religious and only knows how to comfort people through offering her prayers and food. Tess thanks her and returns to her daughter Elena.

Mike is in the kitchen drinking the coffee which he desperately needs. The elderly physician comes into the kitchen to wash his hands. Mike offers him a cup of coffee. The doctor politely declines. Dr. Sacks explains to Mike that he has to leave and asks Mike to contact him as soon as Elena's fever breaks. He reassures Mike that Elena will come out of it in a few hours. Mike is still hesitant but knows that after what occurred earlier tonight Tess would never agree to anything he suggests. Dr. Sacks is the only one she will listen to at this point. Stooped over and slow moving the long-time family physician goes back into Elena's bedroom and insists that Tess call him if the fever does not break by morning. He again checks on Elena; takes her temperature and pulse one more time. Looking relieved, he announces, "The fever has definitely gone down and her pulse is returning to normal." Satisfied he comments, "This was the positive sign I was looking for."

Still fearful, Tess asks if he will come back the next day even if Elena's fever breaks. Dr. Sacks nods his head and reassures her, "I'll stop by first thing in the morning; but please don't hesitate to call my emergency service if need be." Gently stroking Tess's back he reminds her, "I'm only a few short blocks away and I will get here immediately." Seeing how stressed out Tess is and Mike still insisting taking his daughter to the hospital, the good doctor cautioned Tess to call an ambulance if the high fever returns and if Elena begins to hallucinate again. He smiles and remarks, "I highly doubted it will be necessary but always wise to be safe. Besides Mike with his political connections at the hospital, and my son David being a resident there, we'll have no problem healing Elena."

Slightly relieved, Tess thanks Dr. Sacks profusely and calls for Mike to walk the doctor out. Similar to a life-saving Saint Bernard or the Three Wise Man at Jesus manger, Ettie stands by Tess and Elena. The caring aunt pulls a clean cotton hanky from her bathrobe pocket and gently wipes Elena's brow while whispering a prayer to St. Jude the Patron Saint of hopeless cases. She asks Tess if Dr. Sacks left. Tess tells Ettie that he did. Her sister-in-law is disappointed. She was hoping he could check on her husband Carlo.

While escorting their devoted family physician out, unsteady on his feet, and with a major headache, Mike apologizes for his earlier behavior to the good doctor. Dr. Sacks looks at Mike and seeing the terrible condition he is in, he recommends that Mike take better care of himself and to also watch Tess. "I think both of you need to calm down and keep Elena foremost in your minds," he advises. He shakes Mike's hand and calls out, "See you first thing in the morning; hopefully not before." Mike, standing on the front porch, watches Dr. Sacks get into his old black Oldsmobile and cautiously heads down snowy, sleepy Armstrong Avenue.

To clear his head, Mike breathes in some much needed cold fresh air. He reflects on the horrors of this supposedly Holy Night. He looks up at the night sky and speaks to his deceased sister, "Rose, I beg you, please watch over and protect my daughter." He continues to plead, "I know I've been a looser lately but my innocent, sweet daughter is a good girl." He gazes up at the bright night sky and studies the heavenly stars. One is brighter than all the others. Mike smiles, he is confident his sister Rose hears him and Elena Rose's fever will be gone by morning. Mike turns to go back in, he stops, looks up again at the heavens and calls out, "Say Merry Christmas to Ma and Pa for me Rose."

In Elena's bedroom, Ettie brings Tess a cup of hot coffee and a few Christmas cookies. Tess sips the coffee but refuses the cookies. "I can't eat a thing!" Looking appreciatively at her sister-in-law, with a hush voice she says, "Thank you, Ettie." To distract Tess from thinking about her daughter's condition, Ettie timidly shows her appreciation, "Tess, I love the blue flowered nightgown and robe you gave me for Christmas. I know you picked it out and it was you who thought of me. Thank you so much!" Surprised by her sister-in-laws talkativeness and thanking her and not Mike, Tess gives her a gentle hug. Not used to open affection, Ettie shyly excuses herself, "I better clean the coffee cups. You stay with Elena Rose."

Feeling a little better from the night air and seeing the special star, Mike goes back into the house and goes directly to Elena's bedroom. Tess is kneeling by Elena who is still sleeping but her breathing is labored. Not wanting to disturb mother and daughter, Mike quietly returns to the kitchen. As he enters, Ettie automatically pours her brother another cup of dark-black coffee. "Here drink this; looks like you need it!" She plops it in front of him then reassures her brother, "Mike, Elena will be fine. The Blessed Mother will take care of her." He sheepishly drinks the bitter, hot coffee.

Mike looks at his aging sister and tries to explain himself, "Ettie, this was a horrible night. I did something awful." Ettie whispers, "You are so right." He slams his fist on the table spilling the hot coffee on his already soiled shirt. Ettie rushes to wipe it off him. He pushes her hand away and blurts out, "I know Tess will never forgive me and I think God is punishing me through Elena for what I did." Ettie moves back from her brother and to distract herself she rinses the coffee cups and remarks, "That's between you and your wife."

Ettie stares directly at Mike and in a stern and lecturing tone retorts back, "From now on little brother you better grow up and take care of your own problems." Mike was taken aback. "Hey, I thought you would be on my side?" Ettie takes the dish towel and comes toward her brother. Annoyed she reprimands him, "You are a grown man Mike; you wipe up your own messes and accept responsibility for them!" Mike retorts back, "Hey, you don't even know what happened!" The usually placid Ettie raises her heavily veined work hand and slaps her precious brother Mike hard across the top of his head and warns him, "Trust me little brother, I have eyes behind my head!" This usually passive woman is full of rage. Ettie grabs Mike's arm and shouts, "Make it right!" Mike shrivels down into the kitchen chair. Ettie stands over her cowling brother, moves away and demands, "Now I'm going to take care of Tess and Elena which is really your job Mike." Angry, Ettie heads toward Elena's bedroom.

Tess is standing by the opened bedroom door looking at Ettie in astonishment. She compassionately touches Ettie's arm and whispers, "Thank you Ettie." Acting naïve, Tess's sister-in-law questions, "For what?" Tess explains, "I heard what you said to Mike." Ettie ignores her sister-in-law. Tess, realizing Ettie doesn't want to acknowledge it, with much relief says, "Elena's fever just broke. She is sweating profusely just like Dr. Sacks said she would when she comes out of the crisis." Ettie breaks down and cries into her mangled hanky which she pulls from her old plaid cotton robe. Tess hugs her sister-in-law and tells her, "I was coming into the kitchen to get a clean washcloth to wash Elena up when I overheard you talking to Mike. I want to thank you over and over again." Not one to show her emotions, Ettie blushes, "No need to thank me Tess. I'm a woman too; an old one but I am aware of men's faults, even my brother's; this was long overdue!"

This woman, who speaks little, continues, "I was taught it was not my place to speak up; especially to men." She explains further, "Seeing innocent Elena suffer so, I thought of my sister Rose and realized I have to speak up once and for all." Tess stands there in shock. Ettie, not used to revealing herself, quickly changes the subject and gently guides Tess, "Enough, let's get my sweet niece Elena Rose all cleaned up." Gaining control of her emotions she boldly announces, "This has been one strange Christmas." Ettie looks distraught and under her breath moans, "I pray we can all get through this year."

Carlo is calling from downstairs, "Ettie, where the hell are you? I want you down here now!" Ettie goes to the door and boldly calls down to her husband, "You wait till I'm good and ready!" Carlo is fuming mad, "What did you say?" "You heard me," Ettie responds. Shocked by his wife's sudden change, Carlo slams the door making a fearful noise. Tess gives Ettie a concerned look. "Is he alright?" Ettie reassures her sister-in-law, "My Carlo can't fall asleep without me next to him." She takes hold of Tess's arm as they go back into the bedroom where Elena is gradually coming to. Elena's eyes are slowly opening. She sees her Mother and her Aunt Ettie smiling and holding onto one another. Elena's mouth opens slightly as she tries to talk. It makes Elena extremely happy watching her mother and Aunt Ettie, once two *strangers in the night,* embracing. Elena whispers under her weak breath, "What a treat it would be if mother and father would do this!" *The trick is, how to make it happen.*

Mike overhears Tess and his sister Ettie talking. Thinking they are arguing, he jumps up out of the kitchen chair and rushes toward his daughter's bedroom. Mike heads to the Elena's bedroom door and peeks in. He is amazed to see the three most important women in his life bonding - he feels pleased but oddly, left out. Standing by the door and attempting to assert himself, he questions, "Did I hear Elena's fever broke? She's going to be okay?" "Yes!" Tess exclaims. Relieved, Mike moves toward his daughter who is being comforted by her Aunt Ettie. Tess rushes to him and takes hold of his arm. "No, Ettie is fine with her." Mike insists, "But I want to see my daughter." Tess keeps him at bay, "Elena is still half asleep; I don't want you disturbing her peace."

"Come with me Mike," Tess employs. "I need to get a washcloth to sponge Elena down with alcohol." Feeling alienated, Mike confronts his wife, "I have a right to go in there; she's my daughter too." Tess, calmly, yet with conviction, pulls him into the kitchen and exclaims, "You forfeited that right! Elena was in the car tonight and saw you on the snow and that tramp hovering over you." Mike becomes defensive, "What? Are you blaming me for Elena getting sick?" He pulls his arm away from her and shouts, "You never gave me a chance to explain what happened tonight." Tess quietly employs, "Hush, you don't want Elena to hear us fighting."

Mike recalls what Dr. Sacks said and what his sister just said. "Okay!" Mike accepts, "But, when Elena is fine and we are all settled down, we must discuss this with an open mind." Tess moves away and gets a clean washcloth and puts it under the water spout in the kitchen sink. She turns to her husband and declares, "Mike, I've already decided what I am going to do." Mike looks at her confused and quickly defends himself. He attempts to place some of the blame on Tess. "It was you who ran off on Christmas Day to your sister's house with Elena and left me alone." He stamps his foot and accuses, "You took Elena out in this miserable weather." "Enough!" Tess demands. "I have to call Dr. Sacks to let him know about Elena."

Tess tries to calm Mike down by suggesting, "Your daughter still needs lots of undivided attention, rest, peace, and lots of love." Tess gives her troubled husband some reassurance, "Yes, you are her father and we should have spent Christmas together but you went beyond what a marriage represents tonight." She pushes him toward Elena's bedroom, "Go and kiss your daughter. I know she is waiting for you." Tess is exhausted, wrought, and bewildered. She wants to be strong for her daughter but she knows she has many decisions to make on her own. For the first time in a long while Tess has a definitive plan that does not include Mike.

Collectively the Christmas of 1955, for Elena, Tess, Mike, and Ettie was filled with unbelievable offensive and rare awakenings. For Tess the confrontation with Mike this morning; followed by Christmas dinner at her sister Mary Grace's house with Tim and Geoff unmoored her. Arriving home and seeing Mike lying down in the snow earlier tonight with that intolerable woman and worst of all, Elena, her fragile precious daughter, becoming dangerously ill, this was enough to make any woman fall apart.

For Mike, he was devastated that Tess and Elena left him on Christmas; his brother-in-law Carlo making accusations about the miscarriage; the revelations at Walsh's Tavern from his friends; the disastrous decision he made going with Eileen to her apartment and the masked stranger breaking in. The final and most horrific of all was Tess and Elena seeing him like a broken, drunken man lying in the snow with a strange woman hovering over him. The most devastating was Elena's sudden and perilous illness.

The one bright spot of this unforgettable horrible Christmas, the Shining Star of Bethlehem, which brings peace and love, for Tess and Ettie was their coming to terms with their fragile, confrontational relationship. After so many years of alienation, mistrust, and fighting for Mike's attention, Tess and Ettie finally are true sister-friends. *Women empowering women*!

This night's revelations made Mike aware that he must tell Tess the truth, not only about tonight's encounter with Eileen. More importantly he must share what is going on in his fractured life right now. His sister Ettie finally telling him to grow up; seeing that brilliant huge star in the heavens tonight, which he believes was his sister Rose; gives him the courage to sit down with Tess and finally reveal all. Mike hopes that Tess will give him the opportunity. He recognizes he must make it his priority to strive for his wife's understanding and hopefully, eventually her forgiveness. As the New Year, is approaching, Mike's resolution is that they become a happy, healthy bonded family again. He is willing to work endlessly toward this goal especially for his precious daughter Elena Rose.

"What Child is This, Who Lays to Rest..." On this transformative Christmas night, surrounded by her cherished mother, concerned father, and her devoted Aunt Ettie, Elena is finally resting peacefully.

CHAPTER TWENTY

Breaking Bread, Breaking Bad
Walpole, New Hampshire
1856

AUSTIN, ANNA LEE, and little Theresa Edith are sitting at a long, sturdy oak table eating a hearty breakfast of homemade biscuits with sweet maple syrup from the rich sap from the maple trees on their property. Along with fresh eggs from their neighbor's hens, and cured bacon from their hearty pigs. While pouring more steaming coffee for her husband Anna Lee comments, "Austin, I am so pleased that Buck is going to be fine." She shyly inquires, "Do you like Dr. Holden the new veterinarian?" Austin savors his biscuit smothered with rich golden-brown maple syrup and savory cured bacon. He responds, "He seems to know what he is doing but he is not like old Dr. Goldsmith." Anna Lee sits down and suggests, "Give him time dear; he is new around here." With a hushed voice she murmurs, "I know how that feels." Austin shrugs his shoulders hesitantly and offers, "It will be difficult, but I'll try."

Anna Lee, while coaxing her daughter to eat, says to her husband, "It must be terribly hard for him. You know his wife Rebecca, the poor thing, is terribly ill and unable to be with child. I'm sure all of this must be a huge burden on him." Austin responds quickly, "He knew when he married her that she was ill and that she can never have children." Pouring her husband more coffee, Anna Lee questions, "Why then did they marry?" Austin inaudibly comments, "Money." Gently touching her husband's shoulder she questions, "What do you mean dear?"

Austin explains, "When Rebecca's father, Sebastian Watkins and her Uncle Bartholomew Watkins died, Rebecca inherited a monetary fortune from them along with the entire Watkins Hill area." Tess defensively comments, "Austin, I am sure he loves her dearly." Austin smirks and takes another sip of his coffee. He slams the cup down on the table and laughs, "She is a woman of immeasurable means; it makes perfect sense to me why he married her and I doubt love had anything to do with it." Anna Lee pats her husband's arm and reprimands him, "Why Austin you shouldn't say such things." Austin further explains, "Dr. Goldsmith, the old veterinarian, was very close to the Watkins family. Isn't it convenient that when he died, Jeremiah, the conniving sneak, took over Rebecca's father's best friend's lucrative practice." Smirking he further infers, "To make matters worse this joker..." Laughing loudly, Austin adds, "He even dresses like a wealthy aristocrat from European Royalty?" Anna Lee is shocked by these disturbing revelations. She looks at her husband and notices how upset he is. Distraught and feeling weak Anna Lee sits down. She tries to eat something but she is not able to keep food down these last few months.

The dim mood is broken when little Theresa Edith quietly requests, "Mamma, can we have more milk, please?" Looking around Austin questions, "We?" Entering her seventh month of pregnancy, Anna Lee rises slowly from her chair to obtain the milk while humorously explaining to her husband, "Austin, don't you know that Theresa Edith wants to make sure her Nutcracker grows up big and strong too." Austin notices that his daughter has the Nutcracker sitting on a chair next to her placed on her large *Mother Goose Fairytale* book. Winking at his wife he praises his daughter, "Good girl, Theresa Edith."

With a frown on his face and pointing to the Nutcracker sitting majestically on the chair next to Theresa Edith, Austin whispers to his wife, "That's the culprit that caused Buck's almost fatal injury." Pouring milk from a large ceramic pitcher into Theresa Edith's cup and a small amount into a tiny cup sitting in front of the Nutcracker, confused, Anna Lee blurts out, "How's that?" While vigorously smothering another biscuit with sticky, gooey syrup, Austin whispers to his wife while his daughter is putting the little cup of milk into the Nutcracker's wooden mouth, "Zeke revealed to Dr. Holden and me that the pointed whittling instrument Zeke used to carve the infamous Nutcracker was what accidently pierced Buck's leg."

Austin further explains to his baffled wife, "After Dr. Holden and I viewed it, Nannette, who was also in the barn at the time of the accident, further verified that Buck walked into Zeke while he was holding onto the sharp instrument while carving the Nutcracker." Anna Lee is still not sure exactly what happened, "I can't exactly understand the nature of the accident." Austin tries to explain once more by emphasizing what Nannette claims she saw, "Nannette said that Zeke hearing a loud noise like a gunshot startled him. He suddenly turned around while still holding the sharp instrument and it accidently pierced Buck." Anna Lee perplexed listens cautiously. Austin further states, "Guiltily, Zeke nodded affirmatively to verify Nannette's explanation; now let's leave it at that!"

Anna Lee is ready to reply when a single knock on the kitchen door disrupts their attention-grabbing conversation. Anna Lee rises from her chair and heads to the kitchen door. She peeks through the glass pane and sees Nannette standing outside the door holding onto her few personal items. Theresa Edith seeing it is her new best friend, jumps up, almost spilling her milk. She excitedly runs over to the door, pushing her mother aside. Theresa Edith pulls open the door. Elated she greets Nannette. Sensing she has disrupted their breakfast, Nannette shyly pats Theresa Edith on the top of her head. The little girl is hugging and squeezing Nannette so tightly that she can hardly breathe and is unable to apologize. Theresa Edith's head is firmly planted into Nannette's budding bosom while holding tightly around Nannette's slim waist. Theresa Edith looks up lovingly at Nannette and pleads, "Please, please stay and play with me!"

Appalled and envious of her daughter's behavior toward Nannette, Anna Lee pulls her daughter's arms from Nannette's waist and emphatically instructs her daughter to go back to her seat at the table. In an unusually forceful voice and pointing her shaking finger, Anna Lee orders her daughter, "Go sit and finish your milk!" The determined little girl ignores her mother and defiantly cries out to Nannette, "Please, please stay!" Austin, this stately military man, sensing tension building, attempts to alleviate the strain surrounding the once peaceful kitchen. He goes over to his distraught wife, pecks her flushed cheek, turns to his frustrated daughter and gently kisses her little soft cheek and tries to convince her, "Sweetheart, listen to your mother. Go back to your seat at the table and finish your milk." Looking into his daughter's determined eyes, he teases and seduces her, "Your friend the Nutcracker needs to finish his milk; he looks very thirsty and lonely."

Anna Lee, defused by her husband's intervention, and knowing that a southern lady is always polite, invites Nannette to sit down and have some tea and biscuits with the family. As she goes to the stove to get the tea and warm more biscuits, Anna Lee turns slightly and glares over at Nannette. Clearly she is not happy about having this young, flowering beauty in her home. Nannette is a competitor for her daughter's love and fears her charm will also attract her handsome-vulnerable husband.

Austin takes Nannette's items and suggests she go sit at the table. "Give me your belongings Nannette." Motioning to the kitchen table he suggests, "Please take a place at the table; the biscuits are delicious." She looks over at the mistress of the house and notices the haunting look on Anna Lee's face. Theresa Edith gleefully invites Nannette to sit next to her and her beloved Nutcracker.

Having been an orphan for so many years, Nannette knows loneliness and being unwanted; therefore, Nanette is overjoyed with Theresa Edith's warm and inviting acceptance of her. For years she longed for a stable family life and unconditional love. Anna Lee is standing next to the warm stove. Her violet-blue, striking eyes pierces a cold icy stare at Nannette. The extremely astute young woman is aware of Anna Lee's frigid demeanor and of the mistress of the house's intense distrust of her. *Nannette fears rejection.*

As a male, Austin has no patience for women's jealousies and insecurities. He finishes his coffee, slams it on the table and boldly announces he wants everyone to sit down and finish breakfast. A chill surround this once warm kitchen between these two needy yet competitive young women. Austin, this stern military head of the household, has seen enough fighting on the battle fields and wants none of it on his home turf. Only the innocent Therese Edith is unaware of the competitive vibe in this respectable family and stately farmhouse.

CHAPTER TWENTY-ONE

Auld Lang Syne
New Year Resolutions
1956

DOCTOR KNOWS BEST. As Dr. Saul Sacks predicted, and much to Tess, Mike, and Ettie's relief, Elena is much better the day after her Christmas night unexplained illness. This once extremely ill young girl is up and about painting, listening to her record albums, and eating lots of cookies her Aunt Ettie made especially for her. Adding to her high spirits, Elena's Aunt Mary Grace and cousin Regina visits the day after Christmas to cheer her up. The two sisters put aside their anger and reconciled on the phone the night Elena was ill. After Mary Grace heard how dangerously ill Elena was, she insisted on coming the next day to give support to her distraught sister and to assist in the care of her recuperating niece Elena. Mary Grace also hopes that Regina would brighten up her cousin Elena. Tess whole-heartedly agrees. Actually, Tess desperately wants to discuss with her sister what occurred with Mike after she left Mary Grace's on Christmas night prior to Elena's unsuspected illness.

Elena, still deeply disturbed about what happened on Christmas night before she became sick, is pleased to hear her cousin Regina and Aunt Mary are coming over. She very much needs a distraction from what occurred on Christmas night and she must keep an eye on her battling parents. What happened in the street Christmas night with her father and those strange people overshadowed what occurred at her Aunt Mary Grace's house with her erratic cousin Tim and Uncle Geoff. Elena temporarily stores that mysterious street scene in the deep recesses of her mind.

Mary Grace and Regina arrived around 11 a.m. bringing leftover food from Christmas and their earnest desire to make things right between the four of them. The two sisters warmly embrace and put aside what occurred on Christmas Day at Mary Grace's house with Tim and Geoff. As soon as they arrive, Aunt Mary Grace goes to the bedroom where her niece Elena is resting and indulgently fusses over her. She gives her a huge hug, smothers her with wet kisses, and insists that she take care of herself.

Fuming mad, Regina hotly watches as her mother showers her cousin with love. Regina boldly goes up to her mother and pushes her away from Elena and orders her to stop babying her cousin. She cries out, "You never did that for me when I was sick." Tess goes over to Regina and gives her upset niece a much needed hug. Mary Grace reassures her daughter, "Why, baby you know I love you." Regina retorts back, "Not as much as you love Tim." To ward off more conflict, Elena asks her Aunt and Mother to leave the bedroom. She tells Regina to stay and says, "I want to show you something very special." Regina is suddenly intrigued. When the sisters remove themselves, Elena takes out the box with her magical velvet slippers. With much enthusiasm, she shows them to her cousin expecting her to be as excited and happy for her as she is.

Pleased to see the two cousins happy to be together, the Rapp sisters head to the kitchen. Tess makes a fresh pot of coffee and prepares to explain to her sister all that happened last night with Mike and what she plans on doing. Relieved that her daughter is on the mend, Tess shares with her sister that she is determined to implement radical decisions about her marriage for her daughter's wellbeing.

Well aware that he is not out of the woods, Mike leaves the house early to check on his employees. Knowing that Tess and Elena would be occupied with Mary Grace and Regina's visit, he feels confident to leave since his sister Ettie is downstairs in case of an emergency. Mike knows it is prudent for him to leave. Also, he does not want to face Mary Grace knowing full well that Tess will fill her sister in on what happened the night before. With Mike now gone and Elena resting in her bedroom with her cousin, Tess feels secure to converse with her sister. After listening to Tess explain her future plans, Mary Grace is in shock and fuming mad.

While the sisters are in the kitchen, they are relieved to hear their girls busy in the bedroom, so their talk intensifies. Tess shares with her sister about finding Mike in the pitch dark lying in the snow covered street with a strange figure of a man and a hysterical woman in pursuit of him. Tess assures her shocked sister that as a concerned mother her priority is to make sure her daughter is physically and mentally well therefore she has made some poignant decisions. She explains that although she and Mike did not settle their differences, they have decided to be civil with one another for the sake of Elena. Tess and Mike mutually agree to a truce until after the holidays. Tess's mind is made up about what she must do. She is well aware that her plans will not sit well with Mike, Elena, or with Mary Grace.

Back in Elena's bedroom, Elena is in good spirits. She shares with her cousin that she is anxious to attend the New Year's Eve Birthday party at Ginny's house for her brother Angelo's 17th Birthday. She is excited to go because she wants to wear her beautiful black-velvet, multicolored stones shoes she received for Christmas from her parents. Even though Elena is shy and this is her first girl/boy party, she explains to Regina that she is anxious to go to Ginny's brother birthday just to show off her new velvet shoes. Acting disinterested, Regina desperately tries to look unimpressed. Elena unaware of her cousin's blatant envy, says, "With my new shoes as my support I am thrilled to go!" *In her heart of hearts this fragile young girl believes that the Christmas shoes would be a source of strength for her. This impressionable, insecure young girl feels they have magical powers.*

Elena gently lifts the *magical* shoes out of the box, as if they are the Holy Grail, to show Regina. Holding them temporarily dissipates her previous fears about what occurred on Christmas Day with Tim and on Christmas night on the dark icy street with her dad. Her bewildering illness is also blurred from her conscious mind for now. As Regina looks at the shoes, her eyes grow wider and she looks like the green-eyed monster. Regina aggressively grabs them from her unsuspecting cousin and boldly puts them on her petite feet. They are too big! Regina begins to dance with them on all over Elena's bedroom. At first Elena is happy but she is concerned when Regina defiantly runs off into the kitchen. Elena calls, "Regina, come back in here; I don't want you to get them dirty." Regina ignores her cousin's plea. Elena starts to go into the kitchen to retrieve her precious shoes. Suddenly she begins to sweat profusely. She is extremely dizzy so she throws herself on the bed. The room is spinning all around. Elena goes into a state of frenzy. The sound of her cousin Regina's feet tap dancing on the kitchen floor with her precious velvet slippers on is the last thing she hears before she blacks out.

In the kitchen Tess and Mary Grace are in a heated discussion as Regina barges in tap dancing. She falls down from the too- big shoes. Tess asks Regina, "What are you doing with Elena's new shoes?" Regina tells her that Elena asked her to wear them to break them in while she takes a nap. Tess is pleased that Elena is resting and politely requests Regina to put the slippers back in the box. "They are too big for you." Regina acts as if she does not hear her Aunt. "Those shoes mean everything to Elena. Please return them and do so quietly. I don't want you to wake Elena up!" Tess orders Regina. Seeing how upset her sister is getting, Mary Grace warns her daughter, "Do not disturb Elena while she rests and do what your Aunt asked you to do." Ignoring her mother also, Tess yells, "Put those shoes back immediately." Regina is bothered, to defuse the matter Mary Grace kisses her seething daughter and pleasantly asks her to leave the kitchen and return the shoes. Regina pushes her mother away.

Tess desperately needs her privacy and wants Regina out of the kitchen pronto. "Do what your mother tells you. Leave the kitchen and quietly return the shoes." Regina storms out of the kitchen. Tess calls after her and asks her to come and get her if Elena needs anything when she wakes up. In anger Regina pulls off the slippers. Unbeknownst to her mother and aunt, Regina sneaks into the bathroom and quietly locks the door.

Mary Grace apologizes for daughter's behavior and reassures her sister that her daughter will put the shoes safely away and that Regina will check on her cousin Elena. Seeing that Tess is comfortable again and anxious to learn more, Mary Grace encourages her sister to resume her unimaginable revelations. Tess and Mary Grace resume their unsettling conversation about what occurred with Mike on Christmas night along with the unfathomable course Tess decides to take soon after the holidays.

Mary Grace goes over to the stove, takes the coffee pot, brings it over to the kitchen table and pours another cup of coffee for both of them. Tess is cautiously trying to tell Mary Grace about Christmas night while she was searching for an available parking space near her house. Mary Grace places the coffee pot back on the burner and inquires, "What exactly did you see?" Looking around to make sure Regina is not near and that Elena is sleeping, she hesitates to share with Mary Grace. When Mary Grace attempts to apologize for what happened at her house on Christmas, Tess puts up her hand to stop her and says, "We'll save that for another time."

Mary Grace is relieved and requests, "Go on, finish your story about after you left my house. Tess elucidate how while searching for a parking spot she had to abruptly stop the car when she sees this dark, imposing figure running toward the car. Fearing she might hit him, Tess, with a quivering voice, explains how she slammed on the brakes and skidded on the icy road. With anger now rising in her voice she shouts out, "The head lights of the car illuminated a terrified man falling on the icy ground while two figures were fiercely pursuing him." Getting close to Mary Grace's shocked face she screams in her sister's ear, "It was Mike, my husband." Elena's adored father looking at me followed by a strange man who looked like a petrified deer staring at my headlights in the night!" Mary Grace grabs her sister's anguished face with her manicured hands and peers in her sister's teary eyes and cries out, "That's horrible!"

Tess pulls away and continues, "Not as horrible as when the pursuing ghostly man with a weapon disappears into the shadowy night and a hussy of a woman rushes toward Mike and bends over to help him up." Mary Grace lets out a gasp, "Oh my god, who is she?" The sisters hear the bathroom door open and close. Tess motions for her to lower her voice. "Her name is Eileen Moriarity." "Who?" Perplexed Mary Grace questions. Tess gets up and listens to hear whether Elena and Regina are in the proximity. She mockingly answers, "She is the out-of-work waitress, illegal numbers runner, who hangs around Walsh's Tavern hustling men." With sarcasm she mentions, "As Mom would say 'a real tramp!'" Tess continues her verbal rampage about Eileen, "Her notorious gangster ex-husband Marty Goldstein or one of his brainless, tough goons, will kill Mike and that hussy if they found them," Tess exclaims to her shocked sister.

For once, the talkative Mary Grace is speechless. When she gets her senses back, Mary Grace tries to make light of it by suggesting, "Maybe Mike was just a casual bystander who got caught up in a fight between a husband and wife." "Mary Grace!" Tess defends, "I'm no fool, Mike and I have been fighting for over a year now. He has been acting strange as I told you on Thanksgiving." She slams her hand on the table making the coffee cups rattle and adds, "This lady of the night has had an obsessive crush on Mike for years." "Well," Mary Grace suggests, trying to lighten things up, "Mike has better taste then a woman like that. He's most likely going through his middle-age crisis like most men his age. Didn't you see the new Marilyn Monroe movie, "The Seven Year Itch?" "Are you crazy Mary Grace talking about a movie when my marriage is in crisis," Tess admonishes her sister.

With a pained look Tess explains further, "Open your ears. Didn't you hear me? This woman was married to a hoodlum, a mobster. A head of the numbers racket in Hudson County and before her divorce from him she pursued Mike." Mary Grace continues to defend her brother-in-law, "But Mike can't help it; he's flattered!" She adds, "You two aren't getting along!" She stands over her sister Tess and suggests, "That makes it easier for that tramp to take advantage of a vulnerable confused man." "Vulnerable my eye!" Tess blurts out. Forlorn, Mary Grace lowers her voice and confesses, "Even my husband Geoff has a wandering eye these days." "What? What are you saying Mary Grace?" Mary Grace shares, "Someone keeps calling our house and hangs up if I or the kids answer." Not totally surprised Tess questions her sister, "How long has this been going on?" Mary Grace whispers, "A long time. I also hear my husband late at night downstairs on the phone, secretly talking to someone."

Extremely upset, Tess jumps up from the table, grabs the coffee cups and crashes them in the sink. The noise startles the girls. Tess goes to a cabinet; removes a hidden cigarette out of an old cracked sugar bowl; grabs matches from a kitchen junk drawer and defiantly strikes the match and lights the cigarette. Like the 40s movie star Lauren Bacall she takes a long deep drag and blows it out slowly and methodically. Mary Grace jumps up and opens the kitchen window so the smoke does not fill up the kitchen. She fears the girls will smell it and squeal on Tess. Mary Grace moves from the opened window and walks over to her sister and takes the cigarette from her and inhales a long deep drag on it and shouts out, "Wow, this tastes good."

Elena's voice is heard calling out to her mother. "Mom is everything all right? I smell smoke." Regina laughs out loud and comments, "You got to be kidding me Elena, that's a ciggie you smell." Tess takes the cigarette from Mary Grace and immediately puts it out in the sink, runs water over it and takes a mint out of her apron pocket to camouflage her tobacco breath and calls out, "Elena everything's all right sweetie." Tess rushes to her daughter's room.

Tess enters her daughter's bedroom. Elena is sitting up in a daze. She tells her mother that she got dizzy and must have blacked out. Tess immediately takes her temperature. Relieved, thankfully it is normal. Mary Grace overhears and suggests that perhaps Elena needs nourishment. "I'll go and make her tea and toast. She grabs Regina and orders, "Come with me." Tess sits next to her daughter, strokes Elena hands gently and asks her if she is feeling better. Elena reassures her worried mother that she is. Shortly after, Regina and Mary Grace come in with hot tea with honey and lemon and two pieces of thickly buttered cinnamon toast. Elena finishes it all and confesses that she needed food.

Noticing that her cousin is feeling better, Regina suggests that she and Elena listen to music and insists that the mothers go back into the kitchen and relax. Tess is hesitant but Elena assures her mother that she is feeling much better. Regina adamantly insists that the mothers leave. She opens the door wide and with flare and pomp and circumstance the dramatic Regina bows and stretches her arm out the door and pronounces, "Madams your High Tea is waiting for you in the sitting room." Laughing, Mary Grace and Tess leave feeling reassured. With the coast clear, the two cousins look through the numerous record albums trying to decide which one to play. *Clearly, Elena has forgotten all about her magical velvet slippers but not Regina.*

Back in the kitchen, Tess immediately reveals to her sister that as soon as the New Year arrives she is planning on arranging an indefinite leave of absence from work. She further informs that she and Elena will leave for California to visit with their mother in Hollywood, California for an undecided period of time. Before Mary Grace can respond, Tess obstinately reminds her sister that this is her life and no one is going to tell her what to do. Tess, anticipating her sister's numerous questions and disapproval, she explains, "I will tell Mike and Elena that mother is ill and needs me there to assist her while she is convalescing." Mary Grace immediately interrupts, "What about Elena's school?" "She will go to school there," explains Tess. Rationalizing, Tess explains, "I truly believe that being with her loving grandmother, in a warm climate, and a change of scenery will benefit Elena greatly." Mary Grace vehemently interjects, "What about Mike?"

"We need space from one another! Didn't you hear one word I said about Christmas night?" Tess shouts. Again, Mary Grace is speechless. Quickly, Tess assures her sister, "Mike has the house, his time-consuming business to deal with, and foremost his over indulgent sister Ettie to take care of him." She pauses and adds, "Also, his Walsh's Tavern cronies to keep him occupied." Tess is convinced that since she and Ettie have made peace and that her sister-in-law understands the situation between Tess and her brother Mike, that she will be supportive of her decision.

Infuriated, Mary Grace blurts out, "What about this so-called hussy and Mike's so-called wandering eye?" Tess smirks and repeats. "Space, we need space." This annoys Mary Grace further, "Are you out of your mind Tess?" Mary Grace stands up and hovers over her sister, "This is insane; what does Mom think?" Guiltily, Tess confesses, "I haven't told her yet; but I plan on calling her on New Year's to tell her." "What?" shouts out Mary Grace. "Calm down Mary Grace," she orders her bedazzled sister. "As soon as I get Mom's approval, which I'm sure I will, without delay I'll make train reservations for the middle of January for Elena and myself." Tess's flustered sister further questions, "What about Mike?" When Tess does not respond, Mary Grace pounds on the table and hollers, "If you don't give a damn about Mike what about your daughter? How do you think Elena will take this?"

With trepidation Tess whispers, "I will not tell Mike or Elena until all the plans are finalized and confirmed." Tess further explains, "I am planning on having Mom call Elena and invite her to come and visit while she is recuperating." Before Mary Grace can interject, Tess continues, "While there, I will have Mom convince Elena that staying in California for a long period of time is best for her."

Mary Grace is beyond shocked. For once this chatter box is speechless! Tess puts her arms around her sister trying to comfort her. She promises, "Don't worry little Sis, I know exactly what I am doing!" Advising Mary Grace Tess adds, "I think you should take care of your own problems at home with Tim, Regina and Seven Year Itch, Geoff!" She takes Mary Grace's hand and with an edge of sarcasm recommends, "I strongly suggest you figure out what your shifty husband is up to without delay."

Their disquieting conversation is interrupted by Elena shouting, "Regina, where did you put my velvet shoes?" In the bedroom, Regina blankly stares at her infuriated cousin. She coyly shrugs her shoulders as if she has no idea what her *flakey* cousin Elena is talking about. Hearing the commotion, the alarmed sisters rush to the bedroom while an incensed Elena is pointing at Regina with a trembling hand shouting, "You diabolical, pathetic liar!" Regina nonchalantly saunters out of the room. She abruptly stops by the bedroom door and with a comical sneer on her face remarks to her Aunt, "Maybe you can calm down your neurotic daughter." Ignoring her niece Tess goes to her daughter and puts her arm around her. "What's the matter sweetheart?" pleads Tess. Acting as if nothing is wrong, Regina points at her cousin saying, "She isn't sick, she's a crazy lunatic!" Elena shouts, "Regina was wearing my new velvet shoes just before I got dizzy and fell asleep and now she says she has no idea where they are?"

Trying to be as calm as possible, Mary Grace turns to her daughter and asks, "Regina what did you do with your cousin's shoes?" Regina acts innocent and claims, "As you instructed me, after I left the kitchen, I went to her bedroom and gave them back to her." Tess gives her niece a puzzled look. Seeing this Regina coyly comments, "Ask her," sneering at Elena. She points at Elena and says, "Since she has been acting like a loony lately, perhaps Elena can't remember or maybe she threw them out the window." Tess is fuming. She loses her cool and runs over to Regina and begins to shake her. "I saw you wearing them and you told me Elena was sleeping." Mary Grace jumps up and pulls her sister away from her daughter. Trying to settle things down she pleads, "Now let's all calm down!" She states, "These shoes couldn't mysteriously disappear. Let's look around!" With a huge smirk on her face Regina sings out, "Maybe they flew away on a magic carpet." Looking at her cousin, Regina resumes her taunting, "Didn't you say Elena that they were magical." Sitting on the edge of her bed Elena weeps, throws her trembling body across the bed, and pulls the blanket over her head.

The situation is extremely tense. Mary Grace takes Regina into the kitchen to have a private talk with her daughter. Tess goes over to comfort her distraught daughter. When things settle down a bit, they look all over for the shoes to no avail. Regina does not help. She quietly hums tauntingly under her breath, "The magical shoes magically disappeared." Mary Grace assures Elena that if they don't turn up she will buy new shoes for Elena. Hearing this, in a jealous rage, Regina shouts out, "No!!"

Fed up with the whole situation and seeing how disturbed Elena is becoming, Tess asks her sister and niece to leave, "I have had enough with Regina's theatrical antics and temper. You better leave now." Mary Grace is terribly upset; she thought today would make up for the appalling events that happened at her house on Christmas Day, "Tess, I am so sorry. I thought today would be a way to resolve all that happened yesterday." She gives her sister Tess a hug. Tess feels bad too. To placate her sister, Tess assures Mary Grace that there are no hard feelings even though she would love to teach her niece a good lesson in manners. Under her breath Tess comments, "I can see the devil in her; it must run in that family!" Mary Grace and Regina leave.

Tess goes over to Elena, pulls the blanket from over her moist, distressed face, and reassures her hysterical daughter, "No worries dear we will find your precious shoes." Elena ignores her mother and continues weeping. "All will be well Sweetheart," she whispers in her daughter 's ear. Elena sulks and cries out, "I am not going to Angelo's New Year's Eve Birthday party!" Her mother tries to console her, "All will be fine. We'll find the shoes and you'll have wonderful time at the party." Elena emphatically insists and shouts, "Evil Regina stole them!" *Elena needs the magical shoes as her support.*

This is the last straw for Tess. She is overwhelmed by all that has occurred this Christmas. This distraught mother and wife is now convinced more than ever that she must get out of New Jersey as soon as possible and as far away as possible. California is her destination! *She must make it happen soon.* Elena settles down; she pulls a book from under the bed and quietly reads. Flustered but convinced she must do something immediately, Tess goes to the kitchen, picks up the receiver of the kitchen phone and asks the telephone operator, "Long distance please and hurry."

CHAPTER TWENTY-TWO

By the Light of the Silvery Moon
Winter, Walpole, New Hampshire
1868

AUSTIN SLOWLY RISES UP from the kitchen table after a very tense breakfast with Anna Lee, Theresa Edith, Nannette, and the infamous *Nutcracker*. Extremely confounded, Anna Lee laboriously slowly rises from her chair and starts to remove the dishes off the kitchen table. The petite woman has put on a lot of weight with her second pregnancy. Seeing Anna Lee moving with great effort, Nannette jumps up to assist her. Anna Lee raises her hand up and insists, "No need; I am totally capable of taking care of my kitchen and my house for that matter."

Austin goes over to his wife places his long, strong arms around her fragile shoulder and attempts to defuse the edgy situation, "As always, my dear wife, what a fine breakfast." Anna Lee bows her head slightly, out of respect turns but glares at Nannette. Sharp as a tack, Austin suggests, "Theresa Edith why don't you show Nannette her room next to yours and bring your Nutcracker with you." Theresa Edith takes hold of Nannette's slender and graceful hand. This innocent child, holding on tightly to her beloved Nutcracker, gleefully pulls her new friend upstairs. You can hear the excitement in Theresa Edith's voice as she tells Nannette all about her pretty room.

Austin convinces his wife to leave the dishes for Nannette to do later. Dutifully, but hesitantly, Anna Lee heads toward the parlor with her knitting. Her husband goes up behind her, puts his arms around her expanded belly and kisses her milk-white neck affectionately. Anna Lee resentfully pulls away. Austin grabs her arm and begins to lecture, "You have to get used to having Nannette in the house; clearly you need the help especially when the baby comes while I am away." Anna Lee turns from him and without a word whispers to herself as Austin heads out the back door, "Zeke and now Nannette." Anna Lee grudgingly hears Theresa Edith and Nannette giggling and enjoying themselves upstairs. She sits down on the rocking chair in the parlor, grabs hold of her knitting, places her hands in her face covering it. The baby booties she is knitting fall to the floor. Anna Lee begins to silently weep and comments, "I miss my old home in Richmond and my Virginian family."

Not interested in dealing with *petty* women issues, Austin leaves the house. He decides to remove himself from the women folks and heads to the barn to check on Buck and have a heart-to-heart talk with Zeke. He needs answers about the accident with Buck, Nannette's mysterious arrival, and Zeke miraculously finding his once muted voice which seems to coincide with the coming of Nannette.

Zeke is cleaning out Buck's stall when Austin enters the barn. Seeing his boss, he immediately heads over to Austin and says, "I want to thank you for giving Nannette a job in your fine house. She won't disappoint you." Austin just shakes his head and comments, "I will never understand women!" Zeke remarks, "And you never will!" Concerned, Zeke asks, "Is there a problem?" "No, not as long as I am head of this house!" He slaps Zeke on the back and boldly orders, "When I am not here Zeke, you better check on the women of the house. Keep peace if you can or at least keep them apart." "You sure enough know I will, Sir!" Zeke reassures his worried boss.

Austin looking at his barn hand quizzically comments, "Zeke that young woman has done wonders for you; you never spoke a word before she came and now you speak freely and frequently." He looks at Zeke and boldly requests, "Can you explain that to me?" Before Zeke can answer, Austin adds, "And how do you know this charming young woman?" Zeke shakes his head and calmly explains, "I had no reason to speak before she came." Austin, scanning Zeke from head to toe replies, "Well I never thought I'd see the day but you are a new man now; you even shave and dress better." With a contented look on his face, the loyal barn hand slyly smiles at his boss and proceeds to head over to Buck. *Once again he is at a loss for words.* Not fully convinced as to what Zeke told him, Austin decides to leave it for now. He has more than enough to do before he departs for Australia.

To keep his fluttering mind busy, Austin grabs a bucket of feed and heads over to his prized Buck. Zeke is cleaning the area where Buck is. Austin asks him if the new veterinarian Dr. Holden is coming by to check on the horse today. Zeke, looking aggravated, answers, "Not sure, but if I know that phony, he'll be coming by but not to check on Buck." "What?" stunned, Austin questions. Zeke explains, "I swear that so called dandy, slithering snake has his evil eyes on my sweet innocent Nannette." Austin drops the bucket he was using to feed Buck and comes face to face with Zeke and demands, "You want to explain that to me!"

Zeke kicks his foot and moves the hay around and spitting in the ground says, "Just have a hunch!" He continues to explain, "Nannette mentioned that while she was in town looking for me, and before she located me, she ran into him!" Anxious to learn more Austin questions, "What happened?" "She said he gave her the creeps and that he looked like a corpse until Sue Buffton came over and saved her from his menacing antics." Austin insists, "He's a professional married man with a sick wife." He laughs and jokingly adds, "Why Nannette could be his daughter!" The barn hand slaps his hip and shouts, "I know that, but I still feel it in my bones and I am going to keep a sharp eye on that one!" Zeke spits out another brown tobacco stain, grabs a shovel and begins feverously picking up manure. Out of nowhere Zeke calls out, "He is full of manure with his sweet talking, eye lurking and drooling mouth." He slams the shovel down and yells out, "I'll give a piece of my fist, kick his fat smartass and then some if he even dares to go near any of the fine ladies in this swell place."

Austin is beyond upset. He looks Zeke straight in his angry face and orders him, "If your so called instincts are correct, you have my full permission to do whatever it takes to put that questionable scoundrel in his place." Calming himself down Austin ponders, "If he wasn't the only vet in this area, I'd get rid of him this day but unfortunately we need his services while I'm away to take care of the animals." Austin pounds his good leg hard on the ground and demands, "And I mean the animals only!" He stares Zeke in the eye and firmly repeats, "Hear me, the animals only!" Austin once more orders Zeke, "Keep a sharp eye on him and never leave sight of him while he is on my property." Standing erect and stately like a true military man, Austin emphatically commands, "If he dares to go over to the main house, or tries to get near the women, you know what to do; got me Zeke!" Zeke spits, kicks the hay and shouts, "Sure do Mista Austin and I won't hesitate to do it either!" They shake hands and seal the deal, man to man.

That matter settled, Austin reminds Zeke, "I'll be leaving soon for Australia and we must go over what needs to be done with the animals, the property, and most of all taking care of the women and my future baby before I depart." Calming down, Zeke suggests, "Maybe you'll have a strong baby boy who will grow up like you." Austin smiles and states clearly, "As long as it is healthy it doesn't matter whether it is a boy or a girl, but it would be nice to have a son." Zeke nods in agreement.

Austin reiterates, "Remember Zeke, until I return from Australia, you are in charge of the barn and the safety of my dear wife, my precious daughter Theresa Edith, and Nannette." With a broad smile on his handsome face Austin adds, "Perhaps, even my future son and heir." Feeling proud, Zeke stands tall, looks Austin squarely in the eye and boldly reassures his boss, "You sure enough can trust me, Mista Austin." Under his breath, Zeke ponders, "Hope Mistress Anna Lee understands." Austin does not hear this; to him Zeke is his right arm and trusted barn hand. *Even though the two men come from different worlds and their lives are totally dissimilar they have an unspoken bond and mutual respect for one another.*

CHAPTER TWENTY-THREE

Those Wedding Bells are Breaking Up That Old Gang of Mine
New Year's Eve
New Jersey
1956

THE OLD GANG is at Walsh's Tavern talking and gossiping about what happened over Christmas and the week leading to the New Year. Walsh, the surly tavern owner, is washing glasses but listening intently to Tony, the Big Guy, Mike's top employee. Tony bangs on the bar, shaking the glasses that Walsh just cleaned and lined up in military fashion on the bar top. He screams out, "That scum bag, bum, bastard, is six feet under." Brendan, sitting at his usual spot at the end of the bar, lifts his head and turns to look at Tony. "You mean your new girlfriend's racketeer ex-husband, the one who almost killed your boss Mike on Christmas Eve?" Looking over at Brendan, the Professor, Walsh chimes in, "You know very well he's the guy but you better keep your smartass mouth shut or you'll be underground in the dirt." Walsh fills a shot of Irish whiskey in a tall glass and gives it to Brendan and then gives a double bourbon to Tony. He warns them, "Now Big Guy and Professor Smartass, hope this keeps your traps shut before my place gets blown up."

Walsh turns to Tony and coyly questions, "Is it true you saved your boss's life Christmas night and Eileen's too?" Tony ignores Walsh. The gossipy Irishman doesn't give up, he continues to interrogate, "I heard the police got involved but I'm sure they got paid off quickly." Tony slugs down his double bourbon and ignores Walsh's intrusive remarks. Brendan holds his drink up and makes a toast, "Cheers to the corrupt Hudson County police, politicians, and their crooked cronies in this fair city of promiscuity and sin!" The Professor finishes pontificating, drinks his Irish whiskey in one long gulp; slams his glass down hard; and shouts out, "May that crooked criminal rot in jail or wherever he is hiding." He plops his head back on the bar and whispers, "Me thinks he is six feet under or swimming with the sharks." Walsh responds, "There ain't no sharks in the Hudson River but plenty walking the streets around here."

Walsh turns to Tony and inquires, "Do you know where Eileen's ex-husband is? I hear rumors that he is a goner." Again, Tony ignores him. Brendan shouts out, "If he isn't with the sharks, he's in Dante's Inferno with the other goons." He grins and shouts out, "His ex-wife better say a novena for his soul." Walsh, seeing Tony getting pissed off by Brendan suggests, "Hey Big Guy ignore that wind bag." Yet, to satisfy his own inquisitive nature, he asks Tony, "Is it true; you are seeing that two-timing Eileen?" Enraged at that remark, Tony shouts, "What's it to you; besides she's a woman who can stand on her own two feet and I like that in a gal." "But," interjects Walsh, "I thought she only had eyes for Mike, your boss, and if her husband Marty comes back from wherever he is he'll make sure you're five feet under." Brendan shouts out, "With cement shoes in the polluted Hudson River." Tony looks at them with a strange grin and says, "Do I look like I am shaking in my boots?" Still wearing his gloves with shaking hands he then slugs down his drink.

Brendan antagonizes Big Tony further, "What you got hidden in those black gloves of yours or are your hands cold from fear?" Big Tony responds, "I'll wear what I want when I want." He looks over at Brendan and threatens, "I gotta keep my hands in good shape for when I smash your wise-guy-face in if you don't clamp it up now!" Walsh shouts out, "Nobody likes a stool pigeon especially those hoodlums! So why don't you all keep quiet." He laughs and adds, "As my uncle from the old country always said, 'If you keep your mouth shut, you'll catch no flies.'"

The sloshed Professor plops his head on the bar. Seeing he will not get any more mouth from him, Tony stands up and puts his angry face right into Walsh's craggy face and gruffly warns, "And for you, Mike is married and besides, he has enough problems right now and I don't mean just with his wife." "Yeah," says Walsh, "Words got around that the county took away the contract for his garbage company to pick up any and all of the refuse in this fair city and Hudson county permanently." Walsh, like a good Irishman who never backs down from a good fight, continues, "If

I were Mike I would stay low. Words out that the higher ups in the Mafia are on his tail too."

Recognizing that he said too much, Big Tony sits down and gestures to Walsh to fill his glass again. The curious bar owner, complies and edges him on, "Is this true?" Tony slugs down his bourbon and beer, a Boiler Maker, his favorite drink. He stands and grabs Walsh by his white, starched shirt and responds, "That's not for publication but since you like Mike, I'll tell you the rumor is no longer a rumor." "Wow," says Walsh, "What's going to happen to Mike and you?" Brendan lifts his head up off the bar and adds fuel to this heated conversation, "Why, my man, Big Tony, I'm sure Eileen's shady husband Marty would love to set you up as his muscle man in his racketeer organization that's if he is still walking this earth."

Tony shoots Brendan a look to kill. To calm him down Walsh changes the subject, "What are you up to, Big Guy." The Big Guy proudly tells Walsh, "I'm going to take a long vacation and visit my daughter Angela Maria." Walsh comments, "You don't say." Tony takes a slug of his drink and continues, "I'm going to convince her mother to let me take Angela Maria here to America to permanently live with me." Brendan overhears, laughs and taunts, "You think her Madre will let her come here with you?" Tony shouts back, "Listen Professor Know-it-All, her Madre is married and has two more kids and her poor husband can't afford to feed them all." To defuse the tension, Walsh tells Brendan, "Keep the Malarkey to yourself! Now go home to your sweet, aged mother." He turns away from Brendan, pours Big Tony another drink, and offers his unsolicited opinion, "I sure hope you can bring your little angel here." With sincere advice, Walsh resumes, "You know Big Guy, if you are serious about Eileen, I think what she needs is a good man like yourself and a sweet little girl like your Angela Maria to change her life around."

Tony perks up and says, "Hey, Walsh you are one smart man! I'll get on it right away." Walsh reflectively says, "I wish I had tried harder to bring my wife and kids here. So Big Guy don't delay." Brendan yells, "How the hell do you think you are going to get her into this country legally?" Livid and without thinking, Tony shouts back at the Professor, "Mike has connections in South America. His grandfather lived there after he snuck out of Italy before he came to America."

Walsh comments, "Yeah, that's right. There was talk floating around that Mike's father killed a man high up in the Mafia in Salerno, Italy to protect his family." All in the bar keep quiet and listen intently to the barkeeper as he explains further, "They claim they had to slip him out of Italy before the opposing gang killed him and his entire Italian family." Brendan shouts out, "Whose they?" Tony hollers back at him, "Shut up smart mouth, before you're swimming in the Hudson River with your own cement shoes." Tony adds to the 'talk', "You know I always thought Mike was secretive about his father." He pauses commenting, "Come to think of it, he never answered me after I questioned him how is grandfather came to America." Walsh adds, "I heard they even had to change his last name."

Listening intently, Brendan chimes in again, "Everybody has a hidden secret but sooner or later it comes out to haunt you!" Tony is speechless. He tells Walsh, "I'm not worried, my boss Mike knows all the right people." He wipes his sweaty brow and shouts out, "I'll get my precious daughter here and we'll be one big happy family!" To lighten things up, Walsh comments, "Faith and be Golly I can just picture you three and that squawking parrot of Eileen's." He continues, "Big Guy, you'll be the perfect American family, apple pie and all." "Amen! Like the Holy Family in Bethlehem. Mike, Walsh, and Yours Truly will be the Three Wise Men," the Professor mocks. *God Rest Ye Merry Gentleman.*

After all of these scandalous revelations sprinkled with sound advice, the tavern door opens and in walks the unsuspecting Eileen carrying a large round plate covered over with a Christmas dish towel. "I brought you guys something to eat," she proudly announces. Brendan shouts out, "Here comes Jezebel." Eileen gives Brendan the finger and confidently struts over to the table where her new love Tony is sitting. With flair she uncovers it. It is a home baked Irish Soda Bread. Always having to say something, Brendan looks at the bread and calls out, "Man does not live by bread alone." Walsh looks over at him and shouts, "Enough!" The tavern owner walks around the bar and hands Eileen a sharp knife. She immediately proceeds to slice them a piece. Taking a big slice and smiling Walsh whispers to Tony, "You got a good one there." Professor adds, "A reformed one but I agree a good one. You have my permission Tony!"

Eileen looks quizzically at them and questions, "What are you guys squawking about?" Tony places his muscular arms around her tiny waist and gives her a big smooch on her Wild Irish rosy cheek. Unusual for this 'been-around-the-block' woman, Eileen turns beet red. After eating a piece of the warm Irish Soda bread, Walsh pats Tony on his strong shoulder, winks, looks at Eileen and comments, "Hey Big Guy, sexy and a great baker too!" Slouching at the end of the bar on his permanent stool, the Professor extols, "The blushing bride and her love sick Godzilla!" Brendan stands up and sings, *Those wedding bells are breaking up that old gang of mine!*

Eileen turns to Tony and questions, "What's got into these guys lately?" Grabbing Eileen he whispers in her ear, "We have no time to waste Babe, I'm planning a trip and we're going to bring my little daughter here and be a family." Eileen reaches up and kisses Tony on his full desirous lips and screeches, "I'm ready Big Boy!" He hugs her tightly and shouts out, "Me too Babe!"

Not one to miss a thing, Brendan shouts, "How in heaven's name did you two love birds pull this off with Marty the Killer around?" With a smirk on his rough broad face Tony responds, "No worries, I've had my eyes on Eileen, this sexy siren, for a long time." Kissing Eileen again, Tony ironically states, "In fact, her so called loser hubby owes me plenty of money but he can forget it! I got the real prize now." He smiles broadly at Eileen. To deflect any knowledge of Marty's death, Walsh comments, "No worries about that phony con man, he owes a lot of people money in this town." The tough as nails Irishman pours himself a stiff one and murmurs, "He's is a walking dead man now." Eileen does not hear a word. Feeling the whiskey throughout his body Walsh fearlessly adds, "It's a smart thing he disappeared after that Christmas Eve fiasco." "Perhaps he is in Cuba with that crazed dictator Batista," shouts Professor 'Smart Mouth.'

With a strange look on his face, Tony bangs on the table with his gargantuan hand and shouts, "Enough about that son of a bitch beast!" The others at the bar become quiet and motionless as Big Tony gets up and walks over to the bar and reaches over to get a bottle of bourbon. Tony comments under his breath, "Hell is where he belongs." Taking a huge slug right out of the bottle of bourbon, and wiping his mouth with the sleeve of his woolen work shirt, he shouts, "The devil and demons will deal with him now!" Frustrated he again bangs his enormous muscular fist on the bar once more shaking all the glasses. Brendan begins to say something but Tony screams, "I never want to hear that scum bag, bastard bum, cheater, wife-beater's name again!" Everyone at the bar looks at him and recognizes that the name Marty will never be mentioned again in front of the Big Guy ever again. "Dead as a Door Nail," Brendan stands tall. He acts out he is being stabbed and shouts out, "Ah Tu Brutus!"

Changing the subject immediately, Walsh teasingly questions the blushing, future bride who is trying to soothe Tony by hugging and kissing him. "Hey little Colleen, Tony and you make a great couple," Walsh compliments. Eileen immediately interjects, "I always had my good eye on Tony but I thought he never noticed me. I only flirted with Mike because I felt sorry for him. He thought I reminded him of his deceased sister Rose." As the Professor said earlier: "New beginnings. I wish you two all the best," Walsh says. "Me too," chimes in Brendan. Walsh pours more drinks for everyone. Holding up his glass Walsh makes a toast, "Happy New Year and all the best to the love birds." Eileen hugs Tony. He kisses her and warmly says, "You are my Christmas Present Babe all wrapped up in lots of loving." The Professor sings out, *Love and Marriage go together like…* Walsh overrides Brendan's words and shouts loudly, "We'll drink to that!"

The door to Walsh's tavern swings open letting cold wind blow in like a warning of impending doom. The new younger priest Father Arthur Schultz and Juan Flores the church's new maintenance guy comes traipsing in. Seeing them, Brendan, pointing to Tony and Eileen, announces, "Just in time to marry these two, Padre!" He turns to Juan and sings out, "Feliz Navidad." Tony ignores Brendan but gives the priest an ornery stare. Under his breath swears, "Over my dead body will that so-called holy man marry me or get near Eileen, or my precious Angela Maria when she comes here." Brendan shouts out, "New Year, new beginnings."

Taking off their winter coats, the priest's long, black cashmere and Juan's flimsy, hand-me-down snow jacket from a kind parishioner, they sit down at a quiet table in the corner. The priest motions over to the bar owner and requests Walsh to bring them two fine brandies. Surprisingly, Juan boldly says, "I'd prefer a tequila." Walsh comments, "Juan how's our

New Jersey winters treating a Mexican from El Paso, Texas's hot desert climate?" Father Schultz defensively immediately responds, "Juan is taken excellent care of here." He pats Juan on the shoulder and brags, "We at St. Victor's make sure he has plenty of heat and all the spicy food he wants." Tony shouts out, "Too hot for my liking." Professor Brendan, comments, "Me thinks." He then continues to address Juan, "Did you have your hot tamales today, Amigo?" Juan ignores the Professor. Father Schultz comments back, "You need to watch your tongue my good man."

Tony, ignoring Brendan, defiantly walks over to the priest's table and tells Juan, "Juan, remember you can always come to me if you need anything." He stares down Father Schultz and continues, "I know Amigo we got off on the wrong foot when you first came here but I finally figured out why." Glaring demonically at Father Schultz, he reassures Juan, "You can depend on me, hear me?!" Tony gives him a friendly pat on his back. Juan nods his head passively at Tony. Looking over the brandy sniffer Father Schultz keeps a sharp eye and ear on Juan and Tony. The priest requests another brandy even though he has not finished the one he has.

Calculatingly, Father Schultz acts as if he doesn't take notice of Tony's comments to Juan. Defiantly, with a smirk, the annoyed priest turns to Tony and sarcastically questions, "Where is your boss, Mike? Last time I saw him, his red-headed wife and their sweet little daughter were at Christmas Eve mass." Nervously, Juan slugs down his tequila and motions Walsh for another. Tony stares at the clergy and warns him, "None of your GD business preacher man!" Father Schultz calmly and very much in control comments, "If and when you see Mike, my dear man, please tell him I am here for him if he needs repentance." He continues, "Monsignor Kelly informed me that his wife Tess is contemplating on leaving our fair city without Mike and taking his precious daughter Elena too." Schultz sips his brandy and adds, "I believe it was predicated by Christmas night's horrific fiasco in the streets." Walsh, Tony, Eileen, and Brendan stare back at him. Incensed, Tony stands up. Eileen reaches over to Tony to stop him. She is desperately trying to keep the priest and her new love from a disastrous altercation.

The pompous Father Schultz continues to taunt Tony, "Good man, I believe Eileen was present at that unsavory occurrence and me thinks you came to her and Mike's rescue." Not afraid of anyone, Father Schultz stands up and faces Tony square in the face and defiantly asks, "Whatever happened to Eileen's infamous husband? Perhaps you can tell us Big Guy?" Tony is ready to pounce on him when Walsh rushes over and holds him back. The priest has no fear and continues, "God only knows; right Tony?" He adds more fuel to the fire, "My good man you are close to Mike's family. Tell his sweet innocent daughter Elena that like a lost sheep, if she needs comfort, she can always come to her fold where her church's pious Shepherd's will guide her." The enraged Tony defiantly shouts smack in that antagonizing priest's stone-cold face, "What? You'd shepherd them!" "Where? To the slaughterhouse?" The priest smiles back and calmly accuses, "As you should know my good man!"

Fearful of this getting out of hand, Juan stands up and takes the furious Tony by the arm and begs him to go back to the bar and away from them. Juan has no control over his superior Father Schultz but he feels a kinship with Tony. The aggressive priest pompously finishes his smooth brandy and resumes to antagonize, "Come to think of it, I haven't seen Elena in a while; she used to take piano lessons from Sister Margaret Mary at our fine parish, St. Victor's." With a demonic smile he adds, "I loved hearing her play and watch her dainty fingers go delicately across the ivory white and black keys."

Juan gets fearfully alarmed when he sees Tony raise his powerful arms again as if ready to box the priest. "You'll not go anywhere near that girl!" Tony heatedly warns the arrogant priest. Juan jumps up and stands between the priest and Tony. He desperately tries to calm them to no avail. Eileen, fearing another night like Christmas night, pleads with Tony, "Please Tony don't let that so-called religious gossiper upset you." "Elmer Gantry is in our mists," chimes in Brendan. Tony is beyond furious but listening to Eileen and fearing another Christmas night fiasco, he reluctantly storms away. With her heart palpitating fiercely, Eileen takes hold of Tony's mammoth-gloved hand and pulls him away. Holding tightly onto her new man's huge fighting hand, Eileen is desperately hoping to defuse the situation. She whispers, "Tony, please calm down! He's not worth it!" She kisses him and pleads, "Don't ruin our happy future."

Smirking, Father Schultz puts on his long black draconian like coat and orders Juan to get ready to leave. This so-called holy man senses a dark violence overcoming him. He scoffs at the others and commands,

"Let's leave this den of iniquity Juan before we are tainted." Nervously, Juan grabs his shabby coat and obediently follows the priest out the door. Before he exists, he turns quickly and gives Tony a look of appeal. Tony is overwhelmed with anger and rage. To distract Tony from chasing after them, Eileen gives him a sexy kiss on his trembling lips and rubs her tempting body close to his quivering one. Like the lost sheep following the shepherds on that Holy night in Bethlehem, Juan dutifully follows the priest out the tavern door.

Relieved to see them leave, Walsh and Brendan go back to their mundane typical routine at Walsh's tavern. Walsh scrubs the soiled glasses with scalding, sudsy water symbolically trying to wash away the emotional soil that just occurred in his pristine bar. The inebriated Professor swallows his shot to the very last drop and pounds the empty glass on the bar motioning Walsh for another while shouting out, *"A New Year! New Beginnings!"* Like long-lost lovers who have finally found one another, the smitten love birds, Eileen and Tony, cling tightly to each other for dear life. Peace has finally come to Walsh's Tavern at least for now. In the background you can hear the Professor with his fine Irish tenor voice singing, "God Rest Ye Merry Gentleman. . ." After Brendan finishes his Christmas carol, a remorseful Walsh, seeing Eileen and Tony kissing, quietly sings, *Those Wedding Bells are Breaking up that Old Gang of Mine.*

 *

That same night back at 391 Armstrong Avenue on New Year's Eve, Tess places the receiver on the phone after she finishes talking with her mother. Tess finally convinced her mother to let she and Elena come to California to stay indefinitely. She explained that Elena has been ill and needs to recuperate in a warm climate. To her confused mother Tess emphasizes her desperate need to get away from recent upsetting distractions at home. While Tess is on the phone with her mother, Elena overhears. She runs to her mother as soon as she ends the phone conversation. Immediately Elena questions, "Where are we going?" Trying to settle Elena down, Tess assures her daughter that all will be fine. Stating that her grandmother in

Hollywood is ill and they need to go to California and care for her until she is completely well. Elena demands to know why she has to go. "Why do I have to go? You go!" She tells her mother, "I'll stay here with Dad and Aunt Ettie." Tess loses her patience and shouts, "You will do as I say!" Elena screams back, "I'll do whatever Dad says!" She rushes to her bedroom and slams the door. Tess, trying to calm things down, calls out to her daughter, "We'll discuss this further; now get ready to go to Ginny's brother's New Year's Birthday Party." Tess, to appease her daughter reminds her, "We found your special slippers so no excuse." Elena sarcastically calls back, "You mean the ones that sneaky Regina hid in the bottom of the laundry basket and no one believed me when I said she did it?" "Now, now, Elena, we are not sure how they got there. The important thing is that we found them and they are as good as new." Feeling anxious Tess runs to the kitchen to make tea and to check out dates to leave for California.

A little while later, Elena reluctantly comes out of the room dressed in a lovely green velvet dress and wearing her "magical shoes." Tess runs over to her and compliments how wonderful she looks. "My dear, sweet daughter, you look so grown up and so beautiful." She remembers something, rushes over to the Christmas tree and retrieves a huge box covered with some festive Christmas wrap and carries it over to Elena. Tess tells her daughter, "I forgot to tell you, your Aunt Ettie came up here earlier today and asked me to give this to you." Elena is confused. Tess explains, "She said she is sorry it is so late but she had to finish it." Elena immediately takes it from her mother. She quickly tears off the wrapping, opens the box, removes the tissue paper and finds a lovely hand-made, red knitted wool shawl. Elena is speechless. Tess encourages her daughter, "Elena, put it over your shoulders." Tess gently places it on Elena. She is thrilled and begins to twirl around. Tess, cautions her daughter, "You better get going; you can thank Aunt Ettie tomorrow." The proud mother lovingly looks at Elena and comments, "You look fantastic! Now let's get a move on!" Between her Aunt Ettie's comforting, striking red shawl and her magical black gem-studded velvet shoes, Elena is more than ready to bring in the New Year celebrating Ginny her best friend's brother Angelo's 17th birthday.

Mike calls out, "I'm home; is Elena ready to go to Ginny's house?" He looks over at Elena all dressed up and becomes teary eyed. Seeing his daughter looking so mature and gorgeous he is overwhelmed. Mike saunters over to Elena, gently touches her cheek and says, "Ready to go my precious angel?" Giving her a peck on her cheek he teasingly remarks, "Remember, you are daddy's little girl no matter what other men come into your life." Giving him an annoying look, she pleads, "We better hurry Dad, it's a surprise party and I don't want to spoil it by being late." Mike turns and gives Tess a look of remorse as he reassures Elena, "Off we go my princess, your chariot is waiting." As they are leaving, Tess hollers out, "Have a great time." She reminds Elena, also hoping Mike hears, "Dad will pick you up at 1 a.m. after the New Year."

As father and daughter are heading out the front door, Aunt Ettie comes out her door, sees her niece looking so mature and beautiful, hugs her and comments, "My you look like an angel, a very special angel." Elena hugs the red shawl, smiles and whispers, "Thank you, thank you!" Mike pleads, "Okay, no more emotional outbreaks. We've got to go!" "When you come back Mike," Ettie requests, "Please stop in to see me I have something very important to tell you." Mike reassures his sister he will. He tightly holds onto his daughter's hand. *Off they go! Not in a sleigh across a snow-covered farmland but in the little red Chevy heading up Armstrong Avenue in Jersey City.*

CHAPTER TWENTY-FOUR

Haunted by the Ghosts of the Past
New Year's Eve
Walpole, New Hampshire
1866

THE MAIN HOUSE on this bucolic New England gentleman farm is all aglow with lightened candles to welcome in the New Year of 1867. The large stone fireplace in the beautifully decorated parlor is ablaze with a roaring fire to keep at bay the extreme fridge night on this wintery evening. Outside the snow is falling furiously adding layers upon layers of snow to the already mounds of snow accumulated since late fall.

The young woman of the house Anna Lee is in the kitchen with her young daughter Theresa Edith and Nannette, Zeke's ward and the Stevens' new family helper. The women are preparing special food and potent drinks to celebrate the ending of an interesting year. The Stevens family and their small extended help are anxious to welcome in a New Year. Especially Anna Lee, Austin, and Theresa Edith as they patiently wait for the birth of a new child to add fresh life and happiness to their blissful family. Anna Lee is blooming in pregnancy. Theresa Edith is overly excited to welcome a new brother or sister. Nannette is anxious and thrilled to be a nanny for the future baby. Zeke is hoping it is a boy so Austin will have a namesake to add to the family lineage and he can teach him to care for the animals and to make fine wooden crafts.

While the women are busy in the kitchen, Austin and Zeke are out in the barn checking on the animals, food supplies, firewood, and making sure the barn is secure with all the heavy snow that is accumulating on the old barn's wooden roof. On this last night of the year, the temperature dropped 10 below zero. The men are making sure all is safe and sound.

Once the animals are warm, sheltered and fed Austin and Zeke very much look forward to going back to the warm house to bring in a New Year. Seeing everything is fine with Buck and the other animals, and all is safe and secure, Austin goes to the far end of the barn and retrieves his favorite rifle the infamous Henry Rifle which his grandfather gave him when he was just a boy. Taking a key out of his jacket, Austin unlocks the cabinet where he safely keeps his special rifle. It is a Stevens family tradition for the man of the house to shoot the Henry Rifle a dozen times at the stroke of midnight on New Year's Eve into the starry-dark night.

Austin fondly recalls years past as a youngster when his grandfather and their neighbors always performed this festive ritual. On the other hand, Zeke finds this tradition appalling. He does not join his boss outside at midnight for this local occurrence. He stays indoors with the women folk or in the barn calming the frightened animals from the blasting shots being fired. Zeke's New Year's Eve custom is to have plenty of moonshine and traditional black-eyed peas like he did when he lived in Louisiana.

Carrying his special Henry Rifle with great care, Austin enters the main house and heads into the parlor with Zeke following far behind. The women are still in the kitchen. First placing the antique rifle safely high up on the mantle, Austin walks right up to the blazing fire to warm his frigid hands. While his boss is rigorously rubbing his hands, Zeke stays away from the fire and stands stoically near the door. "Come up and warm your hands Zeke," Austin shouts out. Zeke ignores him. "Your hands must be frozen," Austin suggests. "I'm okay," Zeke assures his boss. Seeing Zeke being firm in his choice, Austin accepts his decision, "Whatever you say, my good man. You are a sturdy and solid specimen."

Although Austin proudly praises Zeke, there are some things about his loyal farmhand that perplexes him. Noticing that Zeke always avoids being near fire, Austin questions him, "I've noticed you become very squeamish near fire. Why is that?" Zeke, shuffles his feet while vigorously rubbing his frigid hands together barely audible hesitantly responds, "No disrespect Mista Stevens but that's a story for another time and place." Respecting his wishes, Austin ceases further questions. Reflecting back, Austin recalls a deadly fire that permanently altered his young life forever.

The conversation between Austin and Zeke abruptly ends when Anna Lee walks in carrying mugs of hot cider, followed by Theresa Edith who is carrying a tray of warm, homemade biscuits, followed by Nannette holding a huge pot of slow-cooked New England baked beans laden with thick chunks of savory bacon. The smell is tantalizing and everyone prepares to eat, drink, and welcome in the New Year. "The food is ready," Anna Lee proudly announces.

Placing the homemade food and drink on the long table near the candle lit window, the busy women cheerfully prepare to serve the hungry men. Pleased, Austin holds up his hand and politely asks the women to wait, "Please, first let me get a special bottle of brandy from the cellar." He heads to the kitchen as the others hear his heavy feet plopping down the rickety cellar stairs. Anna Lee, the lady of the house, suggests that everyone sit down and wait for her husband Austin. Theresa Edith begs Nannette to sit next to her on the Victorian sofa. Anna Lee walks slowly to her rocking chair and patiently waits. Zeke remains standing by the door.

It is almost nine o'clock in the evening and Theresa Edith is looking sleepy. "Theresa Edith," Anna Lee calls over to her tired-looking daughter, "I wish you would have taken a nap this afternoon. I doubt if you will be able to stay awake until midnight." Nannette defensively chimes in, "She will be fine." "I will Mama," Theresa Edith pleads. Nannette continues to defend Theresa Edith, "She didn't want to take a nap because she was excited about helping me prepare and cook the beans and biscuits. We also had fun cutting up colored paper to throw into the air at midnight." Anna Lee, too tired herself to argue, acquiesces. "Well my dear, I hope you are able to stay up till midnight." Zeke knew enough about women not to comment. He hopes Nannette doesn't push the matter too much further and aggravate Anna Lee.

Shortly after Austin leaves to retrieve the brandy, a loud boom and crash is heard coming from the cellar. Theresa Edith cries out, "What is that?" Anna Lee jumps up from her rocker. Nannette grabs hold of Theresa Edith. Zeke, running to see what happened, reassures the frightened women and child to stay put. "I'll take care of this." He notices the concerned look on their faces. "I'm sure all is fine," Zeke tries to ease the anxious ladies. Zeke runs to the cellar door and hollers down, "Everything alright Mista Stevens?" Austin shouts back up, "Get down here right away!" In a flash, Zeke flies down the steps and is shocked to see Austin lying flat on his back with a broken bottle of fine brandy spilled all around him.

Helping Austin, Zeke inquires, "Are you okay? What happened?" "I don't know. I was carrying the bottles up when Hocus Pocus I felt something or someone push me down," Austin whispers to his handyman. Zeke stops and gives his boss a questionable look. He asks, "Are you sure you're alright? Does anything hurt you?" "Get me up and grab the other bottle that did not break," Austin insists. Zeke helps his boss up. Austin tries to make light of it and jokingly comments, "My war-wounded leg likes to let me know now and then that it is my Achilles Heel." Getting him up on his feet, Zeke offers, "I'll take the bottle. Hold onto me while I get you upstairs and let the women folk know you are okay." Embarrassed and confused Austin agrees. "Please assure my wife and daughter that I am fine."

Anna Lee, Theresa Edith and Nannette are standing like stone statues waiting anxiously to hear what happened. Anna Lee seeing her husband holding onto Zeke barely walking frantically rushes over to him and cries out, "What happened to you darling? Are you alright?!" Making light of it, Austin assures his wife, "I am perfectly fine." He hugs her and further explains, "I stumbled on something in the cellar. I am fine other than angry. I broke a fine bottle of rare brandy which came all the way from England made by the Benedictine Monks." Anna Lee kisses her husband and says, "Who cares about the brandy as long as you are well my dear."

Zeke trying to make light of it chimes in, "You can't keep a good military man down. Mista Austin can take a licken better than any man. Not even a bottle of fancy brandy can harm this brave soldier." Zeke carefully brings Austin over to his fireside chair and sits him down. Seeing that Austin is fine, he quickly moves away from the fire. Zeke walks over to the table and puts the good bottle of brandy next to the crystal sniffers and heads back to the door. He stands there quietly like a regimented soldier. *He is in deep thought.*

Safe and securely seated, Austin lightheartedly questions, "Now where is that delicious food you have been preparing all day?" Anna Lee motions to Nannette to assist her. The young lady obediently helps Anna Lee serve the much awaited and desired food with Theresa Edith not far behind. As the women are busy preparing to serve the food, Austin motions for Zeke to come over to him. Austin whispers to Zeke, "Tomorrow, clean the mess up in the cellar." Making sure his wife cannot hear, he insists, "When you do, look around to see if anything unusual is down there and give me a report if there is." Austin looks Zeke squarely in the eye and comments, "I swear I saw a strange shadow and felt something shove me." He groans and adds, "Next thing I know, I am flat on my back on the cold ground. "Yet," he continues, "I saw no one." Zeke looks at Austin, confused. Austin, shaking his head back and forth and with a puzzled tone adds, "I can't make heads or tails out of it." Zeke nods affirmatively with a strange look on his face. The women insist Zeke come to the table to get a plate of food.

Austin, noticing the women are able to hear now, changes the subject. He teasingly suggests to Zeke, "You better hurry before they eat all the food." Austin tells Zeke, "Make sure the women bring me a plate full too." Anna Lee is happy to see her husband acting like himself. Nannette is filling Zeke's plate to the brim. Sweet Theresa Edith is carefully carrying a plate over to her father with her mother following right behind. Anna Lee is carefully carrying a beautiful cut crystal brandy sniffer filled with the amber-colored, well-aged fine Benedictine brandy to bring to her husband.

After the family finish eating, the men indulge in the brandy and the women savor warm, spicy cider and while Theresa Edith enjoys rich hot chocolate. Austin reminds them to prepare to count down to twelve midnight. First he requests that they all share the best that has happened to them in the year soon to pass and the worst so it will pass on permanently. Standing up steady on his feet now, Austin orders, "The youngest goes first. My precious Theresa Edith, what made you the happiest this year and what not so happy?" His sweet daughter jumps up, looks over at Nannette points at her and says, "Nannette and my Nutcracker are the happiest." She pauses to think and adds, "Not happy because I have not seen my Princess Angel in a while." Nannette smiles and throws her a kiss. Anna Lee reassures her daughter, "Don't worry Sweetheart, you are our princess and will be forever." Theresa Edith looks at her mother curiously, runs to the window and looks out and begins to jump up and down in delight pointing to the stars high in the sky.

CHAPTER TWENTY-FIVE

Love is Stronger Than Death
New Year's Eve
Jersey City, NJ
1956

MIKE DRIVES ELENA to the New Year's Eve Birthday Party for Angelo. Feeling confident his daughter is safely in Ginny's house, he immediately drives back home. Mike parks the car and starts to walk over to Walsh's Tavern. He is startled hearing his sister Ettie yelling out to him from the stoop in front of the house. "Mike, please come over here!" Mike immediately turns and heads over to his sister who is looking forlorn and extremely upset. "What's wrong Ettie, you look like you've seen a ghost?" She pulls him closer to her and mumbles, "Everything in my life is going wrong. I pray to the Blessed Mother, St. Therese and St. Jude but still I have problems." Concerned, Mike shouts out, "What the heck are you talking about? Tell me!"

Ettie explains what has occurred these last few months. Crying and shaking she reveals, "My Carlo was recently diagnosed with lung cancer. He's been spitting up blood and coughing for a year now." Shaking his head back and forth, Mike cries out, "Holy heck and you never did anything about it?" In defense, Ettie says, "He is so pig headed; he refused to go and see a doctor. A month ago, my Rosaria finally convinced her father." She pauses to wipe her teary eyes and catch her breath. Mike is trying to absorb all this information. Although, hearing his brother-in-law's persistent cough many nights, and aware of Carlo's long-time chain-smoking, Mike wasn't totally surprised but saddened. He patiently further probs Ettie, "When did he go to the doctor and who did he see?" Ettie informs, "Dr. Sacks' son David. He is a cancer specialist at Jersey City Medical Center."

Not wanting to believe this, Mike questions, "What makes them think it's cancer?" Ettie clarifies, "Dr. David Sacks took numerous tests and just before Thanksgiving he gave Rosaria the fatal report." "Oh my god Ettie why didn't you share this with me sooner!" Mike cries out. He further questions, "Does Carlo know?" Ettie begins to whimper mumbling, "No he doesn't. I haven't told anyone only Rosaria and the doctor know. Now you." "Why not?" he pleads. "I didn't want to upset anyone for the holidays and my poor Carlo can't handle it."

Ettie is trembling. Barely audible she says, "Dr. David Sacks says he only has a few months." Crying she shouts, "I don't want him to deal with this." Mike grabs his sister and holds onto her tightly. She whispers in his ear, "Mike, sometimes I think there is a curse on our family." Annoyed Mike shouts, "What the hell are you talking about." She adds, "I think we are paying for the sins of our ancestors in Italy." Mike cautions her not to think like that and reminds her, "We'll get through this together like we've done in the past." Wiping her teary eyes he suggests, "First we have to tell your son Blaise. I will talk with Rosaria and we'll get in touch with the doctor and get all the facts."

Startled by his suggestion, Ettie pushes her brother away and adamantly demands, "NO! I want to handle this myself and I don't want my son to worry he has enough going on, as you do." Mike tries to convince his sister, "But you can't handle this alone." Ettie is heartbroken yet her inner strength is strong from many years of dealing with hardships. She has endured so much in her life she has become immune to pain. *Ettie will bravely endure whatever is ahead.*

Still trying to absorb all of this, Mike stands back, looks at his defiant sister, rubs his face, kicks the ground and screams out, "This is bull shit; what more can this family take?" Ettie takes her brother's troubled face in her trembling hands. She reminisces, "We lost Mom, our dear sister Rose, and Dad. We will handle this too." Mike realizing he cannot convince his sister to tell her husband or son, kisses her tenderly on her shaking cold hands and insists that she go back inside and get warm. He comforts her by reassuring her that they will talk first thing in the morning and get a viable plan. Ettie wipes her face, turns and says to Mike, "I know you have lots of your own problems right now so I don't want you to worry about me. I am stronger than you think." Now more than ever, Mike needs a drink and comfort. Seeing his sister opening the front door to the house, he walks toward Walsh's where he is sure he will find both drink and comfort.

Ettie does not go in; she turns and calls out, "Mike, wait," Ettie stops him in his tracks, "There is something else I have to get off my chest." Ettie's totally flustered brother, stops short, turns, looks at his sister and groans, "What the hell! What more can you tell me?" This agonized woman looks around to make sure no one is near. When Mike gets close to her she blurts out, "Rosaria is pregnant!" Mike screams out, "What in god's name are you talking about?" Confused he reminds Ettie, "You said yourself that she doesn't have a boyfriend!" He stamps his feet and calls out, "What next the Immaculate Conception?" Ettie is shuddering and sobbing. He stares at his hysterical sister and demands to know, "Who's the father? This worthless maggot? I'll have him torn to pieces and thrown to the sharks." Crying Ettie pleads, "Please, no Mike, let me explain." Mike looks at her with compassion now and listens as she explains. "He is a nice guy but married." "Nice guy? Married!" Mike screams. "Are you crazy?" infuriated, Mike walks away in a rage ramblingly. Ettie calls after him, "Mike, please let me finish." He turns, seeing his sister about to collapse, he runs over to her. She puts her head into his shoulder and moans in his ear, "He is our Dr. Sacks' son David, Carlo's doctor." Mike is shocked and enraged. Ettie continues before her brother can say another word. "Rosaria met him at the Jersey City Medical Center. She was frequently assigned to his cases before she went to the Margaret Hague Maternity Hospital. Sadly, his wife is ill and one thing led to another." Mike is too stunned to reply. He wipes Ettie's tears with his coat sleeve.

Trying to convince Mike and herself Ettie adds, "My Rosaria says he is a good guy. Mike, she loves him but they were caught in a bad situation." Mike is overwhelmed and can't believe his Holier-than-Thou Saint-like sister is making excuses for his niece and that two-timing, cheating physician. He questions her, "What is Rosaria planning on doing to make this right?" He stops and shouts out. "I hope you didn't tell Carlo!" Ettie explains, "No, Carlo can never know." Wiping her tears she cries out, "He would never forgive his daughter and most likely will die hating her." "It will probably kill him before the cancer does," Mike blurts out.

He adds, "Blaise will have his penis cut off." Ettie screams out, "Please don't say that!"

Mike calms down and inquires. "What in god's name is Rosaria planning on doing? Is she going to keep the baby?" Fuming mad, Ettie pushes her brother away, "She will keep the baby! What are you implying if it is what I think it is that would be a mortal sin and I wouldn't allow her to do away with it." "Well speaking of a mortal sin," Mike quickly responds, "Having a baby out of wed lock is considered a sin if I remember my Catholic teachings correctly."

Ettie ignores Mike's last vile comment. She resumes to pontificate, "How can you even ask or suggest such a thing, Mike?" Ettie scolds her perplexed brother. Mike shouts out, "God damn it Saint Ettie, say it abortion! How is she going to have a baby without a husband and Carlo and Blaise not finding out and the gossipy neighbors?" Ettie barely audible informs her brother, "Rosaria is definitely going to have the baby. David promises he will support the child and eventually marry her when he can." "Big deal," Mike chimes in. He mumbles, "He better!" Ettie, knowing her son Blaise would be beyond enraged and fears what he might do, insists, "Blaise is not to be told a thing about her pregnancy." Getting her strength back Ettie, staring at her brother with warning eyes, she threatens, "You hear me little brother!"

Mike catches his breath. He stares back at Ettie. "What in god's name is your brainless daughter planning to do, big Sister?" he angrily taunts her. Ettie takes a deep breath and calmly explains, "Rosaria is going to move to New Hampshire where her close nurse friend lives. She'll have the baby there." "Then what?" Mike shouts out. "What does our infamous, favorite family doctor Dr. Saul Sacks think about his pathetic son?" She threatens her brother, "He knows nothing about it and will not be told and you will not tell a soul, not even Tess."

Mike is fed up. He asks his sister, "After Rosaria has the baby then what?" Ettie continues to reveal her daughter's plan, "Like I said, Rosaria is going to New England next month. She will tell people she got married to a man in New Hampshire. After a time she will say her husband and she had a baby but soon after the marriage failed." Mike, shaking his head in disbelief, sarcastically asks, "Then what!" "She will come home. I will take care of the baby and Rosaria can go back to nursing." Under her breath she murmurs, "I pray to God by then David will be free to marry my Rosaria." Mike is in disbelief but feeling pain for his sister, insists his freezing-cold distressed sister go back in the house. He is unable to listen to any of this any longer.

Mike feels terrible for his sister. Her entire life she broke her back for others never thinking of herself and now she has to endure these unbearable, heartbreaking hardships. Mike needs time to think about these mind-boggling secrets and his own troubling personal and business issues. Before going inside, Ettie again vehemently pleads with Mike not to tell anyone and begs him to try to understand and forgive his niece and pray for her Carlo. Not ready to accept this but loving his sister dearly he reassures her. Mike has great concern and compassion for his selfless older sister.

Mike promises Ettie. Once again he vehemently insists she go back in the house. Grief-stricken Ettie heads back in with her eyes watering as she prepares to put on a happy facade for her dying, unsuspecting husband and to pray for her daughter's soul and her future grandchild. More than ever, Mike needs that drink before going to pick up his daughter Elena from the party. Seeing Ettie finally entering the house, Mike, still in disbelief, heads toward Walsh's Tavern.

As Mike is lethargically approaching Walsh's Tavern, he sees his friend Ray Sinnotti standing by the tavern's door. Surprised to see Mike, Ray holds the tavern door open for his buddy. As he gets closer, he notices Mike is in a foul mood, he calls out, "Hey Mike why you look so gloomy? It's New Year's Eve; come on in, let me buy you a stiff one." Ray puts his arm around Mike and the two high school buddies enter Walsh's Tavern.

Walsh is pleased to see the two of them and hollers, "Well look who the cats dragged in." Waving a wet towel he says, "Come on in; drinks are on the house." Ray and Mike go over to the bar. They sit down at their usual spot. Walsh pours them each a double of fine whiskey. "Salute," Ray shouts out as he taps his prep school buddy's glass and Slainte to you Walsh. Brendan is at the end of the bar absolutely wasted. Quiet as a church mouse, Walsh recognizing that the guys want their privacy, goes over to Brendan and tries to wake him so he can head home to his widowed-elderly mother.

Ray, keenly aware that Mike is not himself and having heard the rumor about Mike losing the City Refuse Contract, gently eases his friend into conversation, "Mike what are doing here on New Year's Eve? I thought you and Tess would be at her sister's or having Chinese Food at Canton Tea Garden where you usually go every year." Mike, gulps down his drink and comments, "Tess and I decided to stay home since Elena is at a New Year's Eve party. I have to pick her up soon after midnight." Annoyed being questioned, Mike looks Ray up and down and comments, "What the hell are you doing here, Mr. Question and Answer guy." Ray blurts out, "My wife is with her sick parents and the kids are with the neighbors. Their children are close friends with mine."

Sensing his friend's continuous testiness, Ray changes to a lighter topic, "Wow, Elena's at a New Year's Eve party? You better keep a close eye on her! She's turned into a real beauty like her mother." Mike sarcastically comments, 'Her mother is more like the Wicked Witch of the West these days." Mike orders Walsh to give a round to everyone at the tavern. Ray cautions his buddy, "Take it easy Mike you have to pick up your daughter. I doubt Tess would like to see you drunk when you get home." Brendan overhears the two friends' conversation and adds his two cents, "You mean he will be Two Sheets to the Wind as you low life's call it."

Walsh shouts over to the Professor, "Mind your own business and get home to your poor widowed mother." Brendan again hears his mother being mentioned. He becomes extremely agitated. He hollers out loud, "Leave my blessed Mother out of this!" The Professor calms down and with a choking, barely audible voice says, "She is no longer with us." Walsh is taken back by this comment, "What do you mean by that Professor?" Mike and Ray stop and stare at Brendan who for the first time is at a loss for words. The Professor makes the Sign of the Cross and in a prayerful tone says, "The Good Lord took her in her sleep last night." You can hear sighs from those listening.

Walsh is saddened. He proclaims, "Faith and Be Golly this saintly woman is in Heaven now." Mike says, "Truly sorry." Brendan nods in appreciation and adds, "My sweet pious mother was holding tightly onto her favorite crystal rosary beads blessed by the Pope while Father Kelly gave my blessed Mother the Holy Sacrament of the Last Rites." Brendan wipes his watery bloodshot eyes and adds, "She smiled at me, held my hand, and fell asleep forever."

Walsh is devastated. He whispers, "It happened today?" Brendan nods affirmatively. "Where is she now my good man?" Walsh asks. Brendan responds, "Her blessed remains are at Healy's Funeral Parlor until I can make the proper arrangements for her funeral, mass and burial." Mike and Ray are speechless. Saddened, Walsh walks over to Brendan, puts his arms around him and compassionately offers his condolences, "Sorry to hear this; she led a good life and I know the Lord and his heavenly angels are taking excellent care of her like you did." The tavern keeper turns to the others and announces, "The next round of drinks are on the house in honor Peggy O'Brien a grand old lady of a devoted son, Brendan Aloysius." He raises a glass and offers a toast, "Slainte!" Brendan solemnly adds, "The Lord Giveth and the Lord Taketh." In unison they all say, "Amen!" and finish their drinks in honor of Peggy O'Brien.

Seeing Brendan solemn, to lighten things up and change the subject, Walsh goes up to Mike and Ray and says, "You guys missed all the fun earlier this evening." Mike looks at Walsh and stammers, "I got my own problems!" Disappointed Walsh walks away and remarks, "I'll tell you when you're in a better mood. I'm sure you'll want to know all about it." Mike nods his head, looks over at Brendan and with respect comments, "Later. We've had enough sad news tonight."

Ray glances at Mike's sullen face. Making sure no one can hear, he questions, "Listen Mike, I've been hearing rumors about your company losing the city contract." Mike ignores his friend but Ray persists, "I hear the big boys are after you too; what is this all about?" Turning to make sure no one else can hear he offers, "You know you can trust me." Slamming his fist on the bar, Mike turns and cries out, "None of your GD business; do I question your pharmacy activities?" Out of the blue Mike begins to shake and starts to verbally vomit all that has been happening in his life with his business, wife, and daughter to his intimate and long-time best buddy Ray, (leaving out his sister Ettie's recent revelations.)

Ray is deeply saddened and disturbed to hear all the recent harrowing things his best buddy is enduring of late and more importantly fearful for his life. Ray cautions Mike to be careful with *those guys* and to forgot about the garbage company. He tries to comfort him by reassuring his best buddy, "Mike, you'll have no problem starting a new career even at your age. With your political pull in this county, your family name in this city and the church behind you, Bro, you can do whatever you want." Mike ignores his best friend. But Ray will not give up, "Why the police, fireman, and every business in this town respects you. You've done a lot for almost everyone in this city and they will all back you and defend you."

Mike shakes his head and says, "I know Ray, but there is more going on in my life than the business and those racketeer goons. I can handle them and I will!" Ray, concerned, questions his bro, "Are you sure? They are deadly and ruthless if crossed," Ray warns Mike. He adds, "I'm glad you are getting out of that business, you never wanted it." "I had no choice Ray, you know that I was the only living male in the family and I had to take it over. You should know, you're Italian," Mike reminds him.

Standing up and taking off his tie, Ray again whispers, "But what about the opposing family Mike. The Sicilian bosses. Naples is enemy to them." Mike grabs Ray's tie and puts it around Ray's neck and says, "I can take care of myself; no noose around me buddy!" Ray pulls it off and shouts, "That's your problem Mike, you think you can solve everything." Mike grabs Ray and reveals, "No worries, I have more on them and they know it. My name and family ties will protect me." He orders another drink and adds, "Let's end this conversation once and for all. I have other problems to deal with." "What?" Ray shouts out making the others in the tavern look up.

Whispering to Ray Mike explains, "My daughter, that's my real concern." Ray is shocked, "What? That sweet, innocent girl of yours in trouble! What in hells name is going on?" Mike attempts to explain, "This is not for publication Ray but as Tess has been telling me, but I have turned a deaf ear to her, there has been something not right with Elena for a while now." Wiping his sweating brow, Mike continues, "I intend to get to the bottom of it soon." Ray is in disbelief, he shakes his head, pounds his fist on the bar and shows his loyalty by announcing, "I am here for you Bro and I'll use everything in my power to help you and that sweet little girl of yours."

Ray stands tall and proclaims, "Why Elena is like my own daughter!" He slaps Mike on the back and exclaims, "We might not be blood brothers, but I'll put my life on the line for you and yours and I know you would do the same for me." Mike and Ray put their arms around one another while Walsh and Brendan look on amazed. The two elderly Irishmen turn their heads away from the two Italian Pisano's to allow the two bosom buddies privacy as they show their loyalty and love in an intimate but manly manner which is a tight bear hug and kisses on both cheeks. *A seal of fidelity and respect to the end.*

Not one to show affection in public, Mike immediately separates from Ray. He glares at Walsh and Brendan and hollers, "What, you never see two bros show affection." To change the subject, Mike calls Walsh over to him. "Okay, Walsh, you've been dying to gossip about what happened earlier today. Spill the beans quickly I have to leave here before midnight. Open that big Irish trap now and share that Irish malarkey now!" Before Walsh can say a word Ray interjects, "Mike, you're going to get Elena before midnight? What fun is that for a young girl? Midnight is just when the party gets started." "No," Mike calls out, "I have to shoot my father's special gun outside at midnight. It's our family tradition to shoot twelve shots into the air announcing a New Year." "That's right!" Walsh comments, "Ryerson Steel let's their huge whistle blasts twelve times at the stroke of midnight every New Year's Eve since their opening in the 20s." Mike adds levity and says, "My father's faithful gun is louder than that old Ryerson Steel whistle."

Ray announces he better get going. As he is preparing to leave, he tells Mike to get in touch with him soon. A little embarrassed by their prior intimate hug the two prep school football players bang each other on the back and call out in unison, "Happy New Year, Bro!" Ray winks at Mike and says, "Give my beauty Elena a hug and kiss from her Uncle Ray." He stops and stares at his buddy and with sincerity assures Mike, "Remember I am here for you Bro." Mike gives Ray a thumbs up.

Mike and Ray both look at the pathetic Professor Brendan and add, "We'll keep your dear mother in our prayers, good man!" Brendan turns and gives them a sly grin; a half of a smile. Something no one has ever witnessed him do in all the years they have seen him at the bar. Walsh adds, "As soon as you know your sweet Mom's funeral arrangements Brendan, let us know. We'll be there for you."

The gruff but compassionate bar owner, in a low tone says to Mike and Ray, "The poor old geezer was his dear Mom's only child. She's been a widow since Brendan was a young toddler. She adored him and did everything for him." Mike and Ray, look at Brendan with empathy. Walsh continues, "His sweet old mother lived a long, holy life; the church and her son were everything to her." He whispers to Mike and Ray, "I think the Professor never married because he felt obligated to his dear widowed mother. She was always his top priority!" The pensive bar keeper takes a glass and begins to wipe it vigorously and adds, "She lived to be ninety-six. I know it's because of her faith in the Good Lord, her church, and her devoted son."

Astonished, Mike and Ray look over at Brendan with new respect and admiration. Mike insists, "Let us know when the services are Walsh. We'll make sure we attend. We will send flowers and make a considerable donation." Ray nods emphatically in agreement. The two pensive men leave the tavern. Walsh and Brendan remain in deep thought. While Mike is walking home, he is thinking about Brendan's sweet mother. It brought back fond memories of Mike's deceased mother Antonella and his sister Ettie who also devoted their lives to their family at their personal expense.

CHAPTER TWENTY-SIX

Baa, Baa, Black Sheep
New Year's Day
Walpole, New Hampshire
1867

IT IS A bright, blistery New Year's Day in Walpole, New Hampshire. Austin O'Brien-Stevens pregnant wife Anna Lee, their young daughter Theresa Edith, and recent home helper Nannette are in the kitchen cleaning up after last night's festivities welcoming in a New Year. Austin and farmhand Zeke are in the barn discussing Austin's up and coming business trip to Australian. Austin reminds Zeke that while he is away he is to take care of the barn, the animals, property and especially keep a close eye on his wife, daughter, and address their needs as requested by his wife Anna Lee.

Zeke found his mute voice after Nannette arrived. He is now more vocal and has been questioning his boss Austin liberally. While brushing Buck, he asks his boss, "How is it that you have property and business in that faraway place Australia, Mista Austin?" Zeke boldly questions. Austin has great respect for Zeke therefore he shares this information. "My family has its roots in Australia as far back as in the 1700s."

Interested, Zeke inquires further, "How did you get involved with the sheep business?" Austin proudly explains, "Captain John Macarthur, a distant relative of my family, is regarded as the father of the Australian sheep industry." He boasts, "MacArthur first developed a flock based on British rams and Indian ewes shipped from South Africa to Camden near Sydney in 1797." Zeke lets out a holler "Wow, and this Macarthur sheep man is how you all got started there?" he questions. Austin smiles and continues, "My paternal grandfather and Macarthur got into the lucrative

Merino wool industry and did extremely well." "And now it is yours, Mista Austin?" Zeke asks. "After my grandfather died, I inherited the land, the business and all the herds of sheep." Austin explains. Zeke is impressed yet feels his loyalty is to the animals at the Walpole farm. "Mista Austin, what about you raising sheep here? I can help and that way you can always stay home and be with your growing family." Austin ponders and says, "I hate leaving my family especially now with my future second child on the way." He looks despondent and with a hushed voice says, "Zeke, my good man, it is not as simple as it seems."

Leaving the barn Austin turns, pats Zeke on his back offering, "Zeke, as you know, I am anxious to get ready to leave for Australia shortly, therefore, we will have to leave this discussion until I return from the Land of Down Under." "One more thing, I can't stress it enough, keep a sharp eye on Dr. Jeremiah Holden." Zeke nods affirmatively. "Be vigilant when he is around," Austin cautions. He pounds the barn door with his fist and states, "I don't want him to come here unless you request it." "Sure enough, Mista Austin!" Zeke promises.

Seeing his boss angry Zeke apologizes, "Sorry if I asked too many questions before." Austin does not reply, he has other important things to think about. Austin heads back into the house to pack. Zeke has his chores to finish. He shakes his perplexed head and goes about cleaning the barn stalls and taking care of the beloved animals, especially Buck. *The thought of the new veterinarian disturbs both of these men.*

Austin enters the side door into the kitchen. His pregnant wife Anna Lee is sitting at the table finishing another cup of sweet tea to sooth away her nausea. Theresa Edith is helping Nannette clean up the kitchen. As soon as she sees her husband, Anna Lee stands up and walks over to him. They embrace. Theresa Edith runs over to her parents and holds on tightly to both. The three stand there tightly hugging like a perfect triangle of love.

Embarrassed seeing their intimate embrace, Nannette goes over to remove Anna Lee's empty cup of tea from the table. Suddenly it drops on the ground and shatters all over the floor startling the perfect family embrace. Nannette shouts out, "I am so sorry! I don't know what happened?" She rushes to pick up the broken pieces and cries out, "I will clean it up immediately." Austin comforts her, "Fear not, as long as you didn't cut yourself." Anna Lee looks frazzled. She groans, "That cup and saucer was part of my mother's favorite China tea set." Tears begin to roll down her check. Austin tries to calm his wife. Nannette and Theresa Edith look at Anna Lee perplexed. Anna Lee cries out staring at Nannette, "It was my maternal grandmother's!" She reminds her husband, "My mother gave it to me when we got married, Austin." Like a lost sheep, petrified Nannette looks down at the shattered china cup pieces. Seeing her standing there like a statue, Austin asks her politely, "Nannette please clean it up now and be careful we don't want you to hurt yourself." Hearing this Anna Lee begins to whimper and holds on tighter to her daughter who runs over to her mother to comfort her.

Austin, trying to defuse another misunderstanding between competing women, again asks Nannette to immediately clean up the shattered tea cup and saucer. He turns to his wife and reassures her that all will be fine. The father, who feels it is his duty to make things right, smiles at his daughter Theresa Edith, who is hugging her flustered mother tightly. "Please Anna Lee, it is not worth your getting upset," he lectures his wife. He tries to appease her, "We will try to replace it or I will purchase you your own fine china tea set which you can hand down to our daughter." Theresa Edith looks up at her mother and offers, "Don't cry Mama I'll give you my doll's tea set." Her sweet daughter's generous offering spreads a huge smile on Anna Lee's distressed face making Austin very happy. They once again embrace in that beautiful triangle of love.

Standing over the ceramic kitchen sink, Nannette is washing her hands which is covered with blood from a sharp broken piece from the china cup which pierced her thumb. Suddenly there is a loud knock on the kitchen door. All stop what they are doing and look over at the door. From the misty glass kitchen door a huge silhouette figure is omnipresent. The women stare frozen in time. Austin walks over to the door, peers out to get a better look and then opens the door vigorously. "What do you want!?" he shouts out to the man standing there. It is the veterinarian. Shaking from the cold the veterinarian retorts, "Why my good man is that the way to greet a neighbor and friend?" Austin remains silent. Frustrated Dr. Holden remarks bitterly, "What kind of a man are you to leave a friend out in this frigid weather?" Austin comments, "I'll give your comment 'the good man' credence but 'friend?'"

Austin is stubbornly posed by the door and obstinately does not invite him in. "What are you doing here?" he asks. "I don't recall Zeke informing me that you were expected; is there a problem with the animals?" The veterinarian pleads, "Let me in and I will explain." Waiting for Austin to comply which he does not, Dr. Holden adds, "It has nothing to do with the animals, Zeke, or my professional services." Anna Lee chimes in, "Austin, where are your manners? Our neighbor is freezing, let him in." Austin, observing his wife, daughter, and Nannette anxious, he reluctantly invites him in, "Come in and it better be for a good reason."

Anna Lee runs over and insists, "Come near the fire and warm up right now." She takes his coat and hands it to Nannette and asks him, "How is your dear wife?" He immediately explains, "My poor, dear sick wife is exactly why I have come. Bless her innocent soul, she is not well at all; in fact, I fear her days are numbered." "Oh dear, how truly sorry to hear this," Anna Lee says in a low pious tone. "Is there anything we can do?" she compassionately asks. The frustrated veterinarian immediately offers, "Yes there is and this is why I have come to your fine home." Anna Lee inquires, "Please tell us so we can accommodate you." Sheepishly he pleads, "I have no one to help me care for her to make her last days left here on earth comfortable." Wiping his eyes, he requests, "It would be extremely kind, altruistic and compassionate if you would allow your new boarder Nannette to come and assist me with her care during my beloved wife's final days." Dr. Holden lowers his head and wipes tears from his bulging eyes. Before the shocked Anna Lee or Austin can answer, Theresa Edith shouts out, "No, Nannette is mine; I will not share her with anyone!" *Nannette is petrified.*

Astute Austin suspecting and believing the veterinarian has a sinister reason for wanting Nannette is absolutely enraged that this person has the audacity to even suggest such a thing. He suggests sarcastically, "I believe it would be prudent and wise for you to speak to your clergy, my good man." The infuriated and disappointed veterinarian stares at him. Austin adds, "I am sure there are many fine churchwomen or young girls that would be willing to help you with the care of your sweet, pious wife."

Before Dr. Holden can respond, Austin informs him, "My wife and I have no authority to make this decision, nor does Nannette." He further explains, "Zeke is her sole guardian. He alone has the final say and I know what his answer will be." Austin takes the coat which Nannette is still holding; shoves it back to the disappointed vet; opens the door; boldly and loudly tells the stunned vet, "Be careful going home, my good man" Anna Lee calls out, "Please give your angel of a wife our love and prayers." Austin pushes him out the door. He slams the door so hard it knocks the vet down.

Zeke hears the loud slamming of the door; peeks out from the barn where he is cleaning out the stalls; sees the vet spread out on the ground with his face in the cold wet snow; and immediately runs over to him and angrily hollers out, "What are you doing on the ground; too much moonshine? Or should I ask what you are doing here by Mista Austin's house?" Annoyed he helps the stunned vet up and informs him, "Your duty is with the animals only, not the fine folks who live in this respectable establishment." Dr. Holden, trying to stand up, grabs onto Zeke. Once free to stand independently, he gives Zeke a look that could kill and stomps off to his sleigh. He hops on and cracks the whip so hard that his stunned horse rears up almost throwing the frustrated vet out of the sleigh. Extremely perturbed he turns and gives Zeke a leering look and threatens him, "You are nothing but a lowly servant to your Mista Stevens and that young lassie of yours is not your legal ward."

Zeke spits into the snow and raises his arm and makes a fist. The vet hollers as he rides off, "You are a scoundrel and a misfit and I have my reasons to believe a Confederate deserter!" Enraged Zeke hollers back, "You're a sick pervert and wife abuser!" Incensed he shouts back at Zeke, "Why you no good bastard, I am unquestionably going to find out the truth about that girl you call your legal ward." Zeke picks up a heaping handful of hard snow; hastily makes a hard snowball; throws it at the horse's back hind leg; making it rear up. It immediately aimlessly gallops down the icy road with the hopping mad vet holding on for dear life. Zeke, one who never laughs, begins to shake vigorously laughing uncontrollably. He stops abruptly when he hears a crash and blood curdling scream from down the road.

CHAPTER TWENTY-SEVEN

Sentimental Journey
Jersey City, NJ
January1956

TESS IS PULLING a large suitcase out of the bedroom. She calls out to her daughter, "Elena are you finished packing? Hurry and bring your suitcase out of the room so I can have the taxi driver bring our luggage downstairs." Tess hears a lot of banging in the room and hollers out again, "Elena did you hear me?" The door opens Elena is dragging an old suitcase out of her bedroom door. "Mom stop bugging me; we have plenty of time," she says further annoying her frustrated mother. "The train leaves at two this afternoon and I have to check our luggage and make sure the tickets and transfer tickets to Los Angeles are okay," Tess desperately explains to her defiant daughter. "Why isn't Dad taking us to the train station?" Elena asks. "As you heard last night at our farewell dinner at Aunt Ettie's, he has an important business meeting downtown today. Besides, I don't want another intolerable goodbye." Tess further emphasizes, "We said our goodbyes last night to everyone."

Noticing her daughter getting melancholy she reassures Elena, "We'll call your Dad when we arrive in Chicago before we transfer trains to Los Angeles." Elena stops dead and cries out, "I want to call Ginny right now! I have something important to tell her." "No, you saw her last night at Aunt Ettie's farewell dinner. You can write Ginny a post card when we get to Chicago." Elena stamps her feet. Tess goes right up to her, hugs her and reassures her daughter, "You're just nervous and want to avoid leaving." She kisses her insecure daughter and remarks, "I promise you all will be fine and someday you'll thank me." Elena begins to cry. Her mother wipes the tears encouraging her, "Now Elena, let's get this party started!" She heads over to the door calling out, "I'll let the taxi driver in." She sees her daughter standing stoically. She pleads, "Now go wash your pretty face." When Tess is downstairs ready to ask the driver to retrieve the suitcases, she is shocked to see her sister Mary Grace and Regina standing by the front door.

"What are you doing here? We spoke last night; enough goodbyes!" Annoyed Tess lectures, "It's making Elena nervous, all these farewells." "Tell her Mom!" Regina immediately chimes in. "Tell me what?" confused, Tess asks. "We want to go with you!" Mary Grace blurts out. "Go with me!? Are you crazy Mary Grace?" Frustrated, Tess calls the taxi driver to come and get the luggage. Annoyed with her sister she shouts out, "I have no time to play your games, Mary Grace. Now go home!" "I am not playing games; we are going to California too. I already spoke with Mom and she agrees," Mary Grace quickly informs her sister. Elena comes down the stairs and is surprised to see her aunt and cousin standing outside next to her mother. She wonders what is going on. "What is this? Another farewell party?" she sarcastically hollers.

Noticing Tess motioning him, the irritated taxi man quickly grabs the two huge pieces of luggage and begins to place them in the trunk of his taxi. He calls out, "Ladies we better get going. I don't want to hit traffic." Regina further explains, "I was offered to take an audition for a part in a movie in Hollywood." Looking around, she murmurs, "I think my Mom and Dad are breaking up."

Tess and Elena stand there shocked at Regina's last comment. Mary Grace immediately admonishes her daughter, "Regina, we are not breaking up; we are taking a break from one another!" Laughing sardonically, Regina yells, "Yeah, a break so he can have more time with. . ." Before Regina can finish, Mary Grace slaps her daughter hard across her giggling face. Tess runs over to control her sister. Elena walks over to Regina and pulls her aside. Ambiguous about her feelings, Tess has no time to comfort her sister. They have to leave immediately.

The anxious taxi driver is waiting to take them to the train which will take them to Chicago. From Chicago, Tess and Elena will catch a connecting train to Los Angeles. Tess informs her sister, "This is all so sudden and shocking, but I must leave now. When I get to Chicago I will call you." Mary Grace kisses her sister Tess and says, "I am fine! Regina has a chance of a lifetime if she gets this part. Now is the time to take advantage." She wipes a tear from her eye and adds, "Geoff and Tim will have to take care of themselves. I've done it long enough as you so well know Tess." The taxi driver, sitting in the driver seat, blows the horn motioning to Tess and Elena to get in the car. The sisters and cousins, hug and kiss and say their goodbyes. As the taxi speeds down the street, Tess and Elena wave back at Mary Grace and Regina.

While the taxicab is turning the corner onto Westside Ave, the front door at 391 Armstrong Avenue opens. Ettie is standing there like a lone, sad soul. Seeing Tess's sister Mary Grace and niece Regina, she calls to them and graciously invites them in, "Please come in, you'll get a cold. I have a nice pot of fresh hot coffee brewing." Mary Grace hesitates, but Regina chimes in, "Do you have any of your homemade cookies?" Ettie smiles proudly and shouts back, "Of course I do! Now come on in." Mary Grace is hesitant but Regina runs up the stoop and heads inside Ettie and Carlo's place. Ettie stops Mary Grace and mentions, "I know you will miss your sister and Elena, as I already do, but I think Tess knows what she is doing?" Ettie whispers, "It will be good for Elena too; she has been going through a lot lately."

Mary Grace nods in agreement. She forgoes telling Ettie that she is planning on going to California also. A black Oldsmobile car pulls up. Ettie sees it and explains to Mary Grace, "Please go into my house." Seeing Mary Grace looking at the man in the Oldsmobile, Ettie explains, "That's Dr. Sacks. I called him to check up on Carlo. My husband is not feeling well." Mary Grace stands there staring at the Oldsmobile. Ettie coaxes her, "Go straight into the kitchen and pour yourself coffee. Milk is in the refrigerator and sugar is on the counter. Plenty of cookies are on the table." Mary Grace asks about disturbing Carlo, Ettie reassures her, "No you won't. Carlo is sleeping in the bedroom with the door shut." Convinced, Mary Grace heads inside, turns and asks, "Is Mike around?" Ettie ignores her question and calls out to Dr. Sacks, "Thank you so much for coming Dr. Sacks. Carlo is sleeping; can we talk before you go in and check on him?" Dr. Sacks is standing next to Ettie; he puts his arm gently around her and answers, "Why of course." "Come into the living room my brother's sister-in-law and niece are in the kitchen; we will have privacy there," Ettie tells him.

The family doctor follows Ettie into the living room. She politely asks him to sit in the huge chair that Carlo usually reclines in. When he is seated, Ettie plops down on the well-worn, brown sofa. She calls into the kitchen for Mary Grace and Regina to make themselves comfortable. "We are fine Ettie," Mary Grace calls back. Mary Grace noticed Dr. Sacks' car as she was entering the house and also heard from her sister recently that Carlo was not well. Before the doctor can say a word, Ettie blurts out, "Carlo is still coughing up blood. He is in a lot of pain and sleeps only when I give him the medication you gave me to give to him." The doctor is temporarily at a loss for words. "What did the new tests show?" Ettie inquires. Dr. Sacks gets up, takes Ettie's shaking hands and whispers to her, "The tests did not come back good. There is nothing more we can do for him." Ettie questions, "What does that mean? What about this radiation you mentioned?" With stoic composure but looking forlorn, Dr. Sacks answers the confused wife, "Terribly sorry to tell you that your husband has advanced lung cancer. It is inoperable and radiation will not help." Ettie is shocked but shows no immediate emotions. She has endured so much pain and sorrow in her life that she is immune to tragedy.

The sympathetic and concerned doctor puts his comforting arm around Ettie. He attempts to console her with his personal and professional advice, "Ettie, just make him comfortable." With great compassion he reluctantly gives her more dreadful news, "It breaks my heart to say, Carlo does not have long. It would be a blessing if he goes quickly and as peacefully as possible." Hearing these fatal words, this typically solid-as- a-rock woman makes the Sign of the Cross and whispers a short prayer after, she quietly weeps. The good doctor, at a loss for comforting words, takes on the cloak of a professional. Heading towards Carlo and Ettie's bedroom he tells her, "I'll go and check on Carlo now and administer another shot to relieve his pain." He motions for her to go inside, "Go and have coffee with your guests in the kitchen. I will call you if I need you."

Quiet as mice, Mary Grace and Regina are sitting in the spic-and-span kitchen. Mary Grace notices the doctor going into Carlo's room looking extremely fraught. Ettie moves slowly into the kitchen. Mary Grace goes up to her and instinctively hugs her. Regina sits there not sure what is going on. Ettie moves away from Mary Grace and sits on the kitchen chair. Mary Grace rushes over to get her coffee. Regina automatically retrieves a clean glass on the counter and fills it with water from the faucet. Neither mother or daughter heard what the doctor said. They erroneously assumed Ettie's morbid look was about Tess and her dear niece Elena leaving. Observing the doctor's solemn face and Ettie's tearful eyes after conversing with him Mary Grace figures something bad is going on.

Regina brings Ettie the water. Ettie drinks the water ignoring the coffee. She thanks them and explains that Carlo hasn't been well and the doctor is going to check on him. Half truths are told. Ettie, like Mike, was raised not to tell anyone personal information. Only immediate blood. Mary Grace, knowing enough to leave, stands up and asks if there is anything she can do, "If not Ettie, Regina and I will leave." She thanks Ettie and tells Regina to put the coffee cups in the sink and get ready to go. Regina, not fully aware of the severity of Carlo's illness, asks, "Why aren't you telling Aunt Ettie that we are going to California too?" Ettie looks up at them puzzled but does not ask questions. Regina is flustered that no one is paying attention to her, she blurts out, "I'm going to be in the movies and my Mom and Dad are separating." Ettie is shocked. Mary Grace grabs her daughter ordering, "Keep quiet Regina! Aunt Ettie has enough to deal with." Mary Grace pushes her daughter toward the door, gently places a kiss on Ettie's sweating forehead. She encourages Ettie go check on her husband and Dr. Sacks.

"We hope all turns out well for Carlo," she comments as she is leaving. Mary Grace thanks Ettie for her kind hospitality. "The coffee was wonderful and we are warm now." She looks over at Regina who is looking perplexed and adds, "Ettie we are leaving unless you can think of anything we can do." Ettie nods negatively. Regina says, "Delicious cookies! Goodbye. We are out of here!"

When Ettie is certain Mary Grace and Regina are out of the house, she goes into the bedroom where Dr. Sacks is tending her sick husband. Dr. Sacks is standing over Carlo who is in a daze. The fatally ill man glances up at his wife for a quick second and weakly grins. Ettie bravely smiles at him. Feeling she must do something, she pulls the warm blanket over her husband to comfort him. Dr. Sacks motions for her to leave the room. "He will sleep comfortably for a while now. Let him be," he suggests. They both leave the room. Ettie shuts the door.

Dr. Sacks hands her a prescription for a pain killer. He instructs Ettie to give it to Carlo every four hours as needed. "Lung cancer?" she whispers. "How did he get it?" Ettie questions the doctor. "We have no idea but some researchers now believe cigarettes are a factor. Carlo works at Ryerson Steel factory with questionable chemicals and has smoked heavily for many years. These could have been the source, but we aren't sure yet," the doctor answers. Feeling overwhelmed Dr. Sacks wipes his sweaty brow with his sleeve from his typical crisp white shirt.

Dr. Saul Sacks face is sullen and sad. "You will need round the clock help caring for him Ettie. What about your daughter Rosaria the nurse? I am sure she would be willing to move in with you temporarily?" he recommends. Ettie gives him a strange look. "Rosaria has more important things to attend to." She looks him dead in the eye and asks, "Perhaps you are aware?" she sarcastically responds expecting a response. The good doctor is at a loss for words. He coyly changes the subject and again mentions she needs help.

Dr. Sacks suggests to Ettie, "I hope Tess and Mike will be able to assist you or your church lady friends." Ettie blurts out, "I'll take care of my own husband! I did it for my mother, father, and sister." She continues, "Any way, Tess and Elena are on their way to California to care for Tess's ill mother." Dr. Sacks is taken aback, "Interesting. Perhaps it is good medicine for Elena." He stops, ponders and cautiously inquires, "How is Mike handling them leaving?" "Mike is fine with it and will be fine," Ettie shoots back defending her brother. Sensing tension, the family physician prepares to leave. He ardently asks Ettie to call anytime if need be. He looks at this distraught woman and reminds her, "You must take care of yourself too. You are older now and you have to watch your blood pressure and diabetes." He pats her gently on her head and warns, "Now don't be a martyr." Seeing Ettie's ambiguous look on her waned, pale face, and recognizing there is little else he can do, the doctor leaves.

Ettie is relieved the doctor left. She is anxious to go and check on Carlo. Before she enters the morose bedroom where her very sick husband is sleeping, she recalls all the good times she had with Carlo when they first met as carefree teenagers. She recalls back to when he rode past her house riding his motorcycle daily trying to get her attention. After months of trying to get her interest, Carlo finally wooed her. She smiles as she reflects on how he always made her laugh with his strange humor and silly, quirky antics. Only she understood this complex man. This woman, who has been through so much in her life, even after hearing this dreadful news, puts a false smile on her face as she enters Carlo's room.

Calling to mind the mantra her cheerful, late sister Rose frequently preached, *Laughter is Good Medicine.* She puts her stooped shoulders back, puts a pleasant smile on her aged face and boldly marches into the room calling out, "Want to hear a good joke, Carlo?" He longingly looks up and weakly smiles at his devoted-loving wife as she does the performance of her life; making her sick stoic husband smile. *Laughter is Good Medicine!* Carlo falls asleep with a huge peaceful smile on his shallow-emaciated face.

Ettie's back door opens. She hears her brother Mike call out to her, "Sis, where are you?" Fearing he will wake her husband, Ettie makes sure Carlo is sound asleep. Lovingly brings the blanket up further to cover his shrinking body. Seeing he is comfortable for now, she heads into the kitchen where her brother is standing there motionless. Mike looks perplexed and gloomy. Not one to show much affection, he immediately takes hold of his sister when she runs over to Mike. Without thought Ettie throws herself into her brother's protective arms. He holds her trembling body tightly.

In her brother's protective arms Ettie begins to sob. Suddenly she feels ashamed. Ettie pulls away. With his caring hands, Mike gently wipes away the pool of sorrowful tears cascading down Ettie's swollen cheeks. Ettie looks at her brother ready to speak. "Don't say a word Ettie," Mike compassionately suggests. Mike puts his hand gently near his sister mouth and explains, "I met Dr. Sacks outside as he was leaving. He told me everything." Ettie looks deep into her brother's velvety black eyes that are now also rimmed red and misty.

Before Mike can say another word, randomly Ettie cries out, "I told him to stop smoking! I told him to retire early and that his job was killing him, but he wouldn't listen." Wiping the tears from her face with her trembling hand she moans, "He was always so stubborn! Pig headed as Blaise calls him!" Mike patiently listens to his hysterical sister purge herself of years of suppressed anger and hurt. Like himself and their late parents, he always felt she held things in too much. Only their younger sister Rose expressed her feelings openly. "Rosaria is like her too," Mike muttered to himself.

Holding her tightly Mike leads Ettie to a kitchen chair and insists, "Let's sit down and discuss what we have to do next." Like an android she sits and continues to weep. "I don't know what to do! Dr. Sacks says I need help but Rosaria is unable and Blaise is in the Marines. He can't take time off." Sitting next to her and holding onto her hands tightly Mike reassures his sister that he will find someone, "I'll call Father Kelly later. There must be some capable lady at the church who can help or perhaps Rosaria has a nurse friend who needs work."

In a daze Ettie hardly hears what her brother is suggesting. Talking to herself she whispers, "Everyone said that Carlo was not good for me but he was always faithful and a good earner." Mike tries to console his sister, but she is on a roll. "We always had plenty of food on the table; our bills were paid on time; and my Carlo never missed a day of work," she defends her husband. "Yeah, yeah, I know Sis, but now we have to think of you," Mike insists. Ettie cries again, this time with such agonizing emotion. Mike's heart is breaking for her but he is at a loss as how to comfort her or how to make things right. Mike realizes that only a woman can express emotions openly.

Feeling out of control, Mike is extremely angry! He stands up. Pacing the floor he shouts, "I can't believe Tess and Elena left. Especially now when you need them!" Ettie tugs at his arm and makes him sit back down. She asks her brother to be quiet and informs him, "Your wife didn't know about Carlo and I'm glad they left when they did!" She looks straight at her brother and wisely states, "Elena is just starting to be her old happy self again. Telling her about Carlo would make her very sad and will most likely bring back her depression." Mike shakes his head back and forth and keeps quiet.

Changing the subject, Ettie informs, "You know that Mary Grace and Regina were here. In fact, they left just before you came." "What?" asks Mike. "Did you tell them about Carlo?" Ettie replies, "No, only that he is not feeling well." She adds, "I was surprised to hear they are going to California too." In a hushed voice she reveals, "Regina said her parents are separating." Mike is shocked by his sister's revelation about Mary Grace and Regina going to California and especially about Mary Grace and Geoff separating. Frustrated he shouts out, "What the hell is going on with those two crazy Rapp sisters? Dragging those two innocent girls into their little secrets and plots." He continues his dissatisfaction, "Tess leaving and now Mary Grace following suite!" From the bedroom Carlo is moaning loudly. Immediately Ettie jumps up and rushes to her terminally ill husband. Mike is touched with immense emotion and admiration hearing Ettie soothing her moaning husband while praying over him. Carlo quiets down and a semblance of peace embraces the house until the phone rings starling Mike temporarily out of his fog and dark mood.

Mike answers the phone. He is relieved to hear it is Rosaria. Before she can even speak, he tells his niece about the father's prognosis which she assures him she unfortunately is well aware. Choking on her words she tells her uncle, "I just spoke with Dr. Sacks and he told me the fatal diagnosis." Rosaria asks for her mother. Mike explains that her mother cannot come to the phone because she is with her father Carlo. She instructs her uncle to let her mother know that she will be over in a few hours as soon as her nursing shift at the hospital ends. Rosaria also asks her Uncle Mike, "Please tell my mother I will get in touch with my brother Blaise and let him know about our Dad." The doorbell rings just as Mike is hanging up the phone from his worried but in control niece. He labors over to the door to see who it is.

Mike is surprised to see his top man Tony standing there with his huge hands shoved deep into his heavy work coat. Seeing Mike looking disturbed, Tony explains, "Sorry to disturb you boss but I was passing the house earlier and saw people outside, a taxicab, and Dr. Sacks' car and I got real concerned." Mike motions for him to come in. Tony continues to talk, "Later I saw you going in the house too and I needed to talk with you so I took the liberty of ringing the bell." Noticing how somber it is in the house Tony becomes silent. The two men head into the kitchen. Mike fills Tony in about Carlo. Tony feels terrible. Mike mentions how concerned he is for his poor sister Ettie. "It's too much for her to take care of him alone. She needs help and I know she will never ask for it or put him in a hospital."

Tony slaps his thigh and shouts out, "No worries Boss, I have the solution." Mike gives him a questionable look. Tony says, "My Eileen is looking for work; she took care of her elderly sick aunt for a few years. She will be perfect. I will tell her today. Trust me Boss I vouch for her and promise you she'll be a godsent." Mike does not answer but asks, "Tony what was it you really wanted to talk to me about?" Tony laughs, "You won't believe this I wanted to ask you, with all your connections, if you can find a job for my Eileen." Mike smiles calling out, "Problem solved! Ettie will not dare refuse me when I tell her I got her help." Both relieved they automatically embrace.

Tony releases himself from their grip and somberly looks at Mike. "Boss, I have to leave for South America ASAP." Mike looks at him and questions, "What, to bring your daughter back here?" Tony hesitates a moment and continues, "Well that is one reason, but as you know I must get out of here pronto; the heat is on." Mike looks at Tony's raw, red hands which have deep lacerations all over them. He looks up and sees a huge slash across Tony's left eye. Tony, noticing his boss looking at his multiple slashes, shares his fears, "People surmise they know what happened to Eileen's scum bag husband," pointing to himself with his mangled hand. He announces, "The finger is pointed at me." Puzzled, Mike stares at Tony.

Looking again at Tony's slashed hands and swollen eyelid, a bolt of lightning suddenly strikes Mike. He blurts out, "Oh my god Tony, it was you who saved my life Christmas night." Mike wipes the perspiration dripping from his bulged veined forehead and says, "I was totally out of it; now I recall a huge figure hovering over me and Eileen. I remember now seeing a struggle between the freak who was trying to attack me and a towering figure fighting to get hold of the deadly blade and two figures pounding one another."

Tony is silent, recognizing the less said or admitting anything is better for all. Mike is dumfounded. Tony warns his boss, "Mike, things are going to get real bad around here and I fear for you too. The mob is out for blood and I know they want you out of the picture too." Hiding his real concern, Mike reassures Tony, "Don't worry about me! Get out of here as soon as you can." He displays his loyalty, "Lay low Big Guy until I let you know how thing are." Mike mumbles, "We'll find a way to keep in touch." He warns Tony, "Stay incognito." Tony is mainly concerned about Mike and his precious Eileen, "You take care too Boss and please keep an eye on Eileen." Mike reassures Tony, "Don't worry about me!" He promises, "You can be sure I'll watch out for Eileen." Angry, Tony shouts, "It isn't only Eileen I am worried about, it's you too Boss!" Mike pounds Tony on his chest saying, "Leave all to me; now get the hell out of here pronto!"

Hearing raised voices, Ettie opens the bedroom door and calls out, "Mike is everything alright?" "Yeah," Mike responds. He opens the door for Tony and pushes him reminding him, "Take care of yourself Big Guy. You saved my life. I owe you one!" With a huge smile on his broad, black-bearded face Tony hollers out, "There is one more thing I have to do before I leave." He proudly announces, "Make my new lady an honest woman. I want you Boss to be my best man." Mike shoves Tony out the door. With a questionable grin on his face, Mike warns, "I hope you know what you are doing, Big Guy!" He shuts the door before Tony can respond. *Love and Marriage temporarily overshadows Death and Dying.*

Exhausted, Mike leans against the door. Like a rushing waterfall, perspiration is pouring down his fatigued face. Mike is desperately trying to figure everything out. Even though he hates to admit it, Mike is relieved Tess and Elena are on a train heading to the west coast. Mike fears the ones he loves are hovering and flirting between life and death and he is to blame. This confused man never shows his emotions. He is not one to back down or hide from danger. Mike convinces himself that he will finally confront his enemies.

Mike's family background with its strong Italian bloodline runs through him deeply. When the right time comes, he is confident he will face his pressing and perilous issues head on. Mike is keenly aware that he has to take care of things in this house first. With Carlo's death imminent, and his sister Ettie soon to be a widow, Mike recognizes he has a responsibility to her and her children. *Family is priority!*

Alone in Ettie's kitchen, Mike looks around and focuses his eyes on all the holy pictures of saints his pious sister has. He softly prays, "St. Joseph, St. Anthony, Blessed Mother and God please take care of my family." He walks toward Ettie and Carlo's bedroom and peeks in. Ettie is praying the rosary over Carlo. Quietly Mike offers Ettie a comforting smile. Seeing her brother makes her happy; she returns his smile. Aware that Ettie and Carlo need their private time during this sacred moment, Mike respectfully closes the door. Ettie's prayerful voice is heard through the closed door.

The sound of a distant train is heard as Mike goes upstairs to his empty house to attempt to address the serious, pressing issues confronting him. His blood is fiery as he begins to strategize. Intensely, Mike craftily plots his next step. Knowing that his Tess and adored Elena are heading to California and hopefully, "Out of Harm's Way."

CHAPTER TWENTY-EIGHT

Triangle of Love
Walpole, New Hampshire
January 1868

AUSTIN IS DRAGGING his huge steam trunk down the stairs followed by his very pregnant wife Anna Lee who is carrying a valise. Turning and seeing his wife struggling with the bag Austin calls out, "Nannette please come here and help my wife, she is struggling with my heavy valise." Nannette is in the kitchen playing with Theresa. Hearing Austin's command, she instantly jumps up. Anna Lee is annoyed, "Please Austin do not call her. I am more than capable of handling this little valise." Austin stops and kindly remarks, "Anna Lee I am only thinking of you and the baby." He smiles at her warmly and adds, "While I am away I insist you make sure you take all precautions to take care of yourself and our future son." "Son?" cries out Anna Lee. "Why do you assume it will be a boy?" "Well," he turns and responds, "If you want to know, Zeke feels it is going to be a boy." Annoyed, Anna Lee responds, "Zeke thinks it is going to be a boy? How interesting!" Austin defends his suggestion, "I believe he has some unique abilities of predicting the future. Zeke lived in New Orleans at one time and I've heard it said that people from there have the gift of making solid predictions." Mockingly, Anna Lee burst out laughing commenting, "Like Voodoo?"

Before the conversation continues further, Nannette rushes over. In good nature she attempts to take the valise from Anna Lee. Resisting Nannette, Anna Lee holds tightly onto the bag. Powerless, Nannette stands back and waits for Austin to solve the testy situation. Austin kindly takes the valise from his wife and manages it along with the trunk. He brings the two to the bottom on the stairs. Motionless, Nannette stands there.

Austin tries to soothe things over, "It is okay Nannette, I should not have disturbed you." He kindly guides her toward the kitchen and instructs her, "Go and continue playing with Theresa Edith!" He stops a second and further requests, "First, please let Zeke know my bags are ready to be put in the sleigh." Nannette nods affirmative. Theresa Edith is in the kitchen waiting patiently for Nannette to come back and play with her. Nannette assures the impatient little girl that she will be right back. Austin turns toward his moody wife noticing she is standing there defiantly. He gently takes his wife's petite hands and leads her into the parlor.

In the stately Victorian formal parlor, Austin pecks his stoic wife on her flushed cheek. In a comforting and reassuring manner, he attempts to comfort her, "Please darling all will be fine while I am away." Stubbornly she does not respond. He sternly instructs her, "You must, and I insist, let Nannette help you! That is why I engaged her." He states firmly, "While I am gone you and Theresa Edith's well-being are priority. Also, the safe birth and health of our future child."

Standing tall and firm, Anna Lee glares into her husband's stern eyes and rebelliously reminds him, "I lived here alone with Theresa Edith as an infant while you were fighting in that ghastly war." "Yes, I know that only too well dear," Austin retaliates. She continues, "Even though Zeke was around, I did perfectly well without a female helper..." "May I remind you," Austin overrides her final words, "You will have two young children to care for, one an infant and I will be much farther away in Australia."

Not convinced, Anna Lee cries out, "You should have let Nannette go and live with Dr. Holden and care for his sick wife!" "Now, now, Anna Lee!" Austin pleads. "You are getting hysterical. I would never allow that innocent young girl live with that questionable man!" He takes his wife in his arms and begs her, "Now dear, please, for my sake, let's end this foolish conversation!" Not wanting to upset her husband further before he leaves Anna Lee listens as he pleads, "Please darling try to get along with Nannette so I can take care of my business in Australia with no concerns about you and my dear family back home." He reaches over to give her a reassuring embrace. She accepts it willingly falling into his arms with her head firmly planted on his safe, strong pulsating chest trying desperately not to cry.

As they are in a warm embrace, banging is heard coming from the backdoor startling Anna Lee and Austin. It is Zeke. Nannette lets him in. Austin runs into the kitchen and before he can say a word Zeke shouts out, "There has been a serious accident down the road." "What, who, when?" Austin questions. With sarcasm Zeke explains, "Dr. Jeremiah Holden's magnificent black horse Diablo skidded on the ice and broke his leg. Sadly, he had to be taken out of his misery." With immense sorrow Zeke adds, "He was shot."

Hearing this, with concern, Anna Lee kindheartedly inquires, "What about Dr. Holden? Is he all right?" Zeke looks at Anna Lee strangely and responds, "He might have a broken a leg." He coldly remarks, "It would have been better if he broke his neck and had to be shot rather than that fine specimen of an animal." Zeke is on a verbal rampage, "That bastard pushed that fine strong animal too far; right to his untimely senseless inhumane death." Almost in tears Zeke cries out, "I know he caused the accident; he murdered that helpless animal." "My god Zeke, how insensitive and unkind of you to say such a horrible thing!" Anna Lee immediately lectures. Austin again has to make peace. "Sorry to hear about the horse and the accident. How is Dr. Holden? Is he in good hands now?" "I am afraid so," Zeke answers after giving a sly look at Anna Lee. "Well I am sure things will work out," Austin remarks trying to soothe matters over so he can leave confident that his family and his home is at peace.

Anxious to be on time, Austin instructs Zeke, "I'm sure matters will resolve themselves with Dr Holden." He turns and requests, "Zeke, place my trunk and valise in the sleigh immediately. I must leave shortly or I fear I will miss my connections." He turns to Anna Lee, holds onto her and calls to Theresa Edith to come. Once again the three become a perfect *triangle of love.* Nannette looks on longingly. If only she could experience such family devotion. Zeke notices Nannette is upset. To distract her he asks her to help him. Unassumingly Zeke gives Nannette a slight hug and peck on her flushed cheek. Not one to expose his soft side, Zeke orders, "Nannette hurry!" He reminds her, "Mista Austin is ready to depart and I don't want it to be my fault for his missing his travel connections."

Austin O'Brien-Stevens, Anna Lee, and Theresa Edith reluctantly release themselves from their impenetrable strong bond. Zeke slides over to Austin and whispers in his boss's ear, "I did what you asked me. I found the perfect watch dog for your family and it will be great pal for Buck." Austin breaks away from his wife and daughter and calls out, "Well done my man!" Austin grins happily ear to ear. Zeke proudly tells him, "He is a Terrier Bull dog and was once a beloved mascot in the Civil War." Excited, Zeke asks, " If you don't mind Mista Stevens can I call him Brutus? That's the name the soldiers in the old regiment called him." Waiting for Austin's approval, he adds, "The soldiers named him Brutus. He'll be here in a few days." Austin shouts out to Zeke with much zeal, "Brutus it is! Now I must leave!"

Similar to a brave soldier facing what is ahead, Austin leaves the house finally confident all is in order. He swivels around and gives his wife and daughter another warm embrace and covers their sweet faces with gentle kisses. Pulling away from them, Austin calls out, "Be good everyone and take care. God be with you." He winks at Zeke proudly announcing, "When spring comes I will be home to welcome my new son!" He slyly smiles at his wife as she tweaks one back. Theresa Edith calls out, "I want a baby sister." Austin attempts to leave on a pleasant note whereas Anna Lee's heart is very heavy. Seeing her father leaving, Theresa Edith whimpers. Her comforting mother takes hold of her tightly. Anna Lee kisses her young daughter's sweet face. Not being an intricate part of the inner circle of this tight family, Zeke and Nannette look at one another somberly. Although they appreciate being a small part of the Austin O'Brien-Stevens tightly knit clan.

Down the foot of Watkins Hill Road is Dr. Jeremiah Holden in his wife Rebecca's ancestral home. He is mopping around in their grey-stone, dark house which his sickly wife inherited. Dr. Holden is glancing out the front bedroom window which he shares with his young-fragile wife. Sadly, Rebecca is now laying semi unconscious in their once conjugal bed slowly dying. Seeing Austin's heavily laden sleigh with trunks and travel gear heading past his property gives Jeremiah an idea.

As Austin's sleigh passes Holden's wife's family home, the Watkin's Estate, he is unsettled leaving his family. Although, Austin is confident that Zeke, Nannette, and the new watch dog Brutus will be his loyal support system protecting his beloved family while he is away on extremely important, private business. The sturdy O'Brien-Stevens' sleigh overburdened with a heavy trunk, driven capably by Zeke with Austin as sole passenger, smoothly glides swiftly down the long winding Watkins Hill Road. As they travel down the meandering road, Austin notices where Dr. Holden's recent accident occurred. He feels terrible about the horse. Pondering how mortified he would be if it was his loyal horse Buck. Continuing down the road Austin's sleigh also passes the house where Dr. Holden's ill wife is laboring on her deathbed. Austin happens to peer into an uncovered window and notices the veterinarian administering something to a ghost-like figure, Dr. Holden's young-innocent wife. This immediately startles Austin. He makes a mental note that when he gets out of his sleigh he will caution Zeke to be extremely alert if Dr. Holden should come to his house unsolicited.

Uneasy about Dr. Jeremiah Holden, Austin will emphasize to Zeke that Dr. Holden should only be on the Stevens premises to care for the animals; called to do so only by Zeke or Anna Lee. Zeke prides himself on having remarkable intuition therefore he is intuitively well aware of this. For now, Austin must forgo obsessing about this any further. He must concentrate solely on his urgent dealings in Australia and trust Zeke's special instincts to act accordingly. Austin's immediate concern is for his wife to have a safe birth and that their future child is born healthy. Also, secretly wishing the infant will be a male heir to eventually inherit the O'Brien-Stevens estate and to maintain the legacy.

CHAPTER TWENTY-NINE

CHICAGO, CHICAGO THAT HUSTLING TOWN
Chicago
January 1956

ON THE JOURNEY to Chicago, besides spending time with her new friend Rodney, Elena is deeply engaged in reading a book. The book is old and tattered; therefore, Tess inquires as to what her daughter is reading. At first Elena is very evasive. Noticing her mother is ready to further question her, she blurts out, "Sister Margaret Mary lent it to me." Tess is interested and further inquires, "Is it a history book?" "Yes, but not exactly," is her daughter's immediate response. Tess is confused and curious. "What is that supposed to mean?" annoyed she asks. Elena shuts the book and places it under the seat. Frustrated she answers, "Well, if you really have to know, it's about the Civil War." Looking straight at her mother Elena says, "It's a diary written by Sister Margaret Mary's great aunt who lived in the 1800s in New England."

Tess is surprised. She spontaneously questions, "Really?" Noticing her mother is confused and will require a better explanation, Elena further offers, "Sister Margaret Mary's aunt's husband fought in the Civil War." Tess exclaims, "Interesting!" She adds, "May I read it?" "No!" Elena spontaneously responds. Baffled, Tess further inquires, "But why would she give you such a personal family heirloom?" Elena calls out, "You may NOT read it. Besides, it is none of your business why she gave it to me." Tess is shocked by her daughter's haughty and mystifying response. At a stalemate, Tess leaves it at that; at least for now.

Walking through the quaking train cars, the stately, elderly black Pullman train porter, elegantly dressed in a formal black and white uniform with a black cap perched on his firm head, rings the chimes while calling out, "First call for dinner! Served in the dining car." Elena bolts up and heads to the dining car. The gentlemanly porter smiles at the frustrated Tess who is standing there confounded. With a warm but professional manner he reminds Tess dinner is being served. Elena is standing outside the dining car. She is peering at the window as the train speeds by making everything outside move in a flash similar to a speeding bullet. Tess finally catches up with Elena. Trying to smooth matters over with Elena, Tess suggests, "What we need is a nice meal. Let's get seated before too many people arrive." Not sure whether to seat themselves or be escorted to a table, they remain there stupefied.

Observing mother and daughter standing there, the dining room host comes up to them and offers to show them to a table. In a sour mood Tess and Elena sit down at a formal table set gracefully with fine linens, beautiful china and shiny, highly polished silverware. The waiter sensing tension between the woman and young girl immediately presents them with a menu. He announces he will be back shortly to take their order. Silence is deafening as mother and daughter just look at the menu not engaging one another.

Other passengers are now entering the dining car and escorted to a table. One young fellow, a little older than Elena, sits alone at a table across the aisle from mother and daughter. At his youthful age, he presents himself as confident and sure of himself. Elena shyly glances over at him as he smiles at her. Tess notices this and teases Elena, "Didn't I say you were going to have a very interesting trip." Blushing and to distract her mother, she motions for the waiter to take their order. Tess sneaks a smile over at the young man. He returns it in kind.

The distinguished and superbly uniformed waiter walks over to the table and introduces himself, "I am Simon. I will be your waiter for the duration of your trip." He takes the fine linen napkin from Tess's table setting and with flair unravels it and places it on her lap. He does the same for Elena. While expertly performing this he announces, "It is my honor to make this trip as pleasant as possible for you in this fine dining car until you reach your final destination." He adds, "Chicago being your final destination?" Tess answers, "Yes and no. We are transferring trains in Chicago and heading to Los Angeles." "My grandmother lives there," Elena chimes in. Impressed and feeling the tension release between them, Tess and Elena eagerly give Simon their meal order.

When the waiter leaves, the young man seated across from them is keenly observing Tess and Elena. Rising he walks over to the table where they are sitting. He puts his long, slim arm out which is encased in a beautiful starched-white dress shirt and proceeds to individually shake their hands. Politely he introduces himself, "Good evening, my name is Rodney Sheridan. I thought perhaps if you don't mind, I might join you for dinner." The self-assured young man is particularly tall and lanky but sturdy. He has long shaggy, white-blond hair which almost covers his perky-pointed ears. Elena, startled by this bold request from a total stranger, peers at her mother in disbelief. Tess, also surprised but not wanting to act unfriendly, responds, "Why of course; aren't you waiting for your parents?" Rodney laughs out loud and answers, "Why no. I always travel alone." "Sorry," embarrassed Tess says. Rodney explains, "I am going back home to California after visiting colleges in New York." Startled by his boldness, Elena tries to ignore this daring interloper. Whereas Tess is instantly fascinated with the young man who is gazing at Elena with his azure-blue, mesmerizing eyes.

Turning, Rodney calls over to the waiter, "Simon, please set a place for me here. I will be joining these lovely ladies for dinner tonight." Simon rushes over and immediately sets a place and inquires, "Sir, will you be having your usual?" While placing the large white linen napkin on the young man's lap Simon continues, "Sliced steak, medium rare, French fries, and string beans almandine?" "Yes, thank you Simon and please bring us bottled water also," Rodney responds to the waiter. It is apparent they know one another. Simon rushes off. Tess is amazed. She continues to question this mature-acting young man, "Seems as if you have been on this train frequently." "Why, yes, I have!" he proudly interjects. He turns and gives a broad, warm smile to Elena who is trying to act nonchalant. Feeling uncomfortable and shy Elena nods politely. She knows enough not to be rude.

The seasoned waiter Simon takes excellent care of the two women and Rodney. These three complete strangers have now become acquainted and cordial. After dinner, Rodney suggests they go to the top of the observation deck for a better view of the magnificent vista outside. He is enthralled to show them, "something spectacular." Poetically Rodney announces, "When the sun falls asleep there are a thousand brilliant stars out there in the dramatic celestial night sky." Tess is excited but Elena does not respond. "I would love for you to see it and experience its breathtaking beauty," he eagerly probes his new acquaintances. Rodney especially is eager to convince Elena. Cleverly, Tess does not accept, "Thank you but I have a few things to take care of." She turns to her daughter encouraging her, "Elena you go. I know you will enjoy what Rodney is so kindly offering." Elena gives her mother a look to kill, "No, Mom, I told you I have to write a letter to Ginny." With a gloomy face she tells her mother, "Since I was unable to call her before we got on the train." Disappointed yet Rodney takes no insult, "No problem." Further suggesting, "Perhaps we can have breakfast together tomorrow." "Yes, that would be lovely," Tess chimes in.

Rodney leaves immediately without signing the dinner check. Elena tells her mother she is going to their car to write her letter. Simon, their competent waiter arrives and hands Tess the tab to sign. Tess offers to pay for the young man. Simon, who is usually extremely professional, lets out a chuckle, "No, not necessary! You see," he whispers, "Rodney Sheridan's grandfather is one of the owners of this fine train line owned by Atchison, Topeka, along with the Santa Fe line which also owns the El Capitan." Tess squeals, "The El Capitan too?" "Yes," responds Simon and adds, "I believe Madam you will be transferring onto to it to take you to your final destination Los Angeles as will Mr. Rodney." Hearing this, Tess is stunned yet impressed by this good fortune. Her intention for this adventure is that Elena would meet new, exciting and interesting people on this *healing* journey. *Could Rodney be the first in this transformative experience?*

Back in their train car Elena is fervently writing. Tess sits down next to her daughter and comments, "Wasn't that nice to meet someone from Los Angeles? Did you know that he is the grandson of one of the owners of this renowned train company and also the next train we take?" Elena deliberately pays no heed to her mother. Annoyed, Tess heatedly remarks,

"Elena, you must learn to let down your defenses. Please try to make the best of this trip."

Elena frets, "Mom, you know how difficult this is for me leaving Dad, Aunt Ettie, and my friend Ginny." Elena hesitates a moment then reveals to her mother, "At night from upstairs in my bedroom I hear Uncle Carlo coughing and crying out." She looks at her mother questioningly and asks, "Is he alright?" Tess grasps her daughter's trembling hands and holds them tightly. "Elena you must not concern yourself with the family back home. You are too young to be worrying about everyone." She attempts to comfort her concerned daughter, "No worries! Dad and Aunt Ettie will take good care of Uncle Carlo. They are well aware of his hacking cough." Noticing that Elena is still gloomy Tess adds, "I am sure Dr. Sacks will give Uncle Carlo medicine and that will be that." She squeezes Elena again cautioning, "You are too young to be worrying about everyone."

Tess holds onto her daughter's tender hands and pontificates, "Believe me Elena, I know this trip is going to make you forget whatever is going on back home." Under her breath she murmurs, "Or whatever unpleasant situation that has made you upset and not yourself lately." This caring mother lovingly pecks her daughter's soft moist cheek and pleads, "I only want the best for you, sweetheart." Elena leaps up. With her voice filled with suspicion, she mutters, "I don't know who to trust anymore!" Tess quickly responds, "Then trust me!"

Discouraged and mystified Tess mentions, "Perhaps it's good that Aunt Mary Grace and your cousin Regina will be joining us." She puts her arms around her daughter and offers, "It might be nice to be around my family for a change." Exasperated, Elena bolts up, leaves their train car, and heads to the club car. Tess stands there bewildered. Incensed, under her breath, walking away Elena grumbles, "What good will Aunt Mary Grace and Regina be?" Rushing to get away from her mother she chatters, "They need help themselves!"

Walking through the speeding train cars, Elena places her hands on the walls to steady herself. Crossing through the narrow, swaying platform into the next car is a physical challenge. Suddenly a man of the cloth, a minister or priest in a black suit, enters the train car she is in. He stops, reaches over and holds the heavy door open for Elena. As they both enter the next car, he attempts to introduces himself. Elena, seeing his black suit and noose-like collar shudders. She races ahead completely ignoring him.

The distinguished man in black is not offended. From years of experience he well understands the youth of today. This wise, elderly man of the cloth works daily with many young people; therefore, he is well aware most are totally into themselves. With a relaxed look on his face, he stands tall and walks ahead with no concern whatsoever. He comments to himself, "What a smart young girl. I admire her for not talking to strangers." He makes the Sign of the Cross and comments, "God Protect the Innocent." *This is his adored prayerful mantra.*

Safely away from this strange man in black, Elena anxiously asks one of the porters to direct her to the observation deck. He professionally and politely escorts Elena to the stairway leading up to the observation deck. She thanks the porter and carefully climbs up the winding stairs holding on tightly to the railing as the train is rocking to and fro. Once safely on top, she is captivated by the multitude of stars beaming brightly from the bubbled shaped glass ceiling. The train suddenly jerks. Elena is about to lose her balance. She begins to fall. An arm reaches over to grab her.

It is Rodney. Seeing Elena flustered, he asks, "Are you alright?" "Yes," blushing she replies. He is smiling ear to ear. "I am so happy you are here." Elena relaxes a bit. Rodney poetically sighs, "Ah, tonight the stars are beyond spectacular and the moon is in all its glory." Beaming, Rodney reveals, "It reminds me of "Starlight Night" by the English poet and Jesuit priest Gerard Manley Hopkins." Elena is mute. "This poem captures tonight's sky perfectly," Rodney adds. This young romantic, anxiously guides Elena to a seat, "Follow me, I'll show you where to sit to get the best view." Pointing at the stars Rodney quote's Hopkins' poem, *"Look at the stars! Look up at the skies! O look at all the fire-folk sitting in the air!"* Elena is both in awe and startled by this young man's range of interests.

To add to the spellbinding mood, Elena modestly expresses her limited knowledge, "I only know about stars from a rhyme my mother used to sing to me before I went to sleep." She pounders a second. Blithely Elena mentions, "That was a long time ago." Shyly she poetically quotes, *"Star Light, Star Bright, the first Star I see Tonight."* No one speaks for a while. Elena and Rodney sit at a safe distance from one another. Both are mesmerized by the celestial showcase up high outside as the train is racing along. The full magnificent moon beams as it is surrounded by a burst of millions of brilliant stars. This burst of beauty shines on these two impressionable young people. *"When you Wish Upon a Star."*

Gazing up at the sky, Rodney slyly moves closer to Elena. She is suddenly uncomfortable. This young girl does not know how to act around a strange boy especially in an unfamiliar environment. Elena's fears take the best of her but are soon abated since Rodney is very kind. Surprisingly he makes her feel at ease. No real words are spoken between them. Words are not necessary as they silently peer at the heaven's brilliant dazzling showcase. After a while, Elena decides it is time to leave. Before she leaves, getting her nerve up, she inquires, "Rodney, is it true your grandfather is one of the owners of this train line?" Rodney hesitates at first and then explains, "Yes, that is true. Although, I am one of many grandchildren." Elena's curiosity is active, "Do you have brothers and sisters?" Rodney further informs, "I am an only child." He pauses and solemnly says, "My parents are divorced." His face is gloomy. Elena picks up on this and comments, "I didn't mean to make you upset." "No, no, please," he blurts out. "I am fine; it is just that my family is not close. I find meeting new people fills my loneliness." He notices Elena's quizzical look. In defense Rodney questions, "I hope you don't find me pushy, a pompous snob, or an intrusive person." Feeling terrible, Elena reassures, "Why not at all; it is just that I am also an only child." She reveals, "Ironically, I am concerned that my parents are having a difficult time."

Putting aside her own fears, in a mature way, Elena tries to console Rodney, "I hope I don't come across as if I don't like you? You are very nice." Relieved, Rodney beams at Elena as they leave. "See you for breakfast, I hope?" Rodney coyly asks. Elena, wanting to sound nonchalant, flippantly responds, "Sure, why not." Rodney halts, looks up at the moon. With a huge happy smile and like a wolf in the night, he howls, "Bella Luna!" Embarrassed Elena moves on quickly. He chases after Elena.

The enormous silvery gossamer moon is brightly illuminating the landscape as the train speeds along determinately to reach its destination. When Rodney catching up to Elena, from a window in one of the trains connecting car platform where they stand, he once more points at the brilliance of the moon outside. Poetically, Rodney quotes to his new friend Elena, *The only light we have in all this darkness*. He gazes at her pontificating, *Is out there and in our hearts*.

Moonlight Sonata is playing in the background as these two young moon/star struck travelers are alone. Elena stops, looks up once more at the starry moon lit night, softly she asks Rodney, "When you look up at the stars and moon do you ever see anything special?" He ponders over this a moment and quizzically responds, "Well, let me think. I recall the poem you mentioned earlier, 'Star Light Star Bright.' I always make a wish but so far it hasn't been granted."

Looking over at Elena, Rodney inquires, "What do you do or see?" Surprisingly Elena lets down her guard and immediately responds, "Sometimes I see a special Angel and I feel like flying away with her." She hesitates and murmurs, "At times I do fly away into another realm." Rodney does not disallow her remarks. He politely looks at her in wonder. In a melancholy tone he offers, "I once heard someone say that when you save someone from death they become your angels." Elena looks at him murmurs, "I believe I understand what that means." She does not wait for him to respond further. In a state of euphoria Elena runs ahead leaving Rodney standing there bewildered and awestruck or *moonstruck*.

Feeling light and happy Elena is swaying while holding on as she carefully walks through the many wobbling train cars trying to reach where her mother and she have their seats. This young lady finally seems to be finding her soul's balance. As she struggles to open the heavy doors in between the swaying platforms, she enters another car. Elena again runs into the man in his stark black suit. He smiles at her but Elena once more ignores him and rushes by. Rodney is standing in the car the priest is entering. He immediately stops the priest. The two begin a lively and very friendly conversation. Elena turns, she notices them pleasantly conversing. She continues to walk ahead to reach the car where her mother is waiting patiently for her.

"Elena," cries Tess when she sees her daughter, "I was beside myself looking for you until Simon the nice waiter informed me that he saw you go to the observation deck." Elena stands there silently. Tess continues,

"He was kind enough to reassure me that you were fine; he mentioned you were with Rodney Sheridan." "Mom, why do you worry so much? I am older now and can take care of myself," Elena answers cryptically. Tess decides not to go any further. "Well, let's get a good night sleep. We have a busy day tomorrow." She motions for Elena to sit, "We arrive in Chicago early afternoon and I have wonderful plans for us while on layover there."

Half listening to her mother, Elena sits down, takes out her pen and begins to write in her pad. Inquisitive Tess probes her daughter with a litany of questions, "So how was the observation deck? How did you and Rodney get along?" "Mom, please, no questions!" Elena shouts back at her mother. "Well, I am only inquiring. He seems like such a nice young man." Tess pauses waiting for Elena to respond. Since her daughter does not, she adds, "You know he will be in California too. Perhaps you can keep in touch and get to see one another there."

To distract her mother from the Rodney track, Elena insists, "He isn't interested in me Mom. I am not his type." She smirks and adds, "More importantly, Mom, I am not interested!" Her comment disappoints her mother. Tess is ready to respond when Elena blurts out, "He has big ears that stick out." "Elena," shouts Tess, "How cruel of you." Tess adds, "I didn't think you were like that." She stops and stroke's Elena's hair and whispers in her daughter's ear, "He has other great assets." "What Mom? Money and because he has a famous, rich grandfather?" Elena sarcastically responds. "No!" Tess interjects vehemently. Elena gives her mother a pleading look. She begs, "Please Mom, leave it alone." Seeing her mother upset she shares, "You will be happy to know that he wants to have breakfast with us tomorrow." Tess smiles. Elena closes her notebook, puts her pen down and quietly says, "Goodnight, Mom." Tess kisses her daughter and remarks, "Sweet dreams sweetheart." Elena looks up at her mother. Feeling sad she was mean to her mother she asks, "Did you see the stars and bright moon tonight, Mom?" Tess nods affirmative. She is pleased when Elena shares, "I made a wish."

In a private luxurious suite in the frontage of the train Rodney is alone trying desperately to fall asleep. In the back of the train in coach, Tess and Elena's disturbing sleep patterns are due to their haunting past and fear of the unknown future. In another section of the train Rodney is pondering over his lonesome life. Sadly no one is wishing him "sweet dreams." The massive, faster than a speeding bullet-like train is racing along in the dead of night. Fortunately for some of the various and ample passengers they are lulled to sleep by the cradle- like rocking movement of the powerful iron horse. In another section of the train, away from the paying passengers, the hardworking personnel, Simon for example, are readying themselves to assist their passengers for their auspicious arrival in Chicago's infamous Windy City.

In the break of dawn, the gracious porter walks through the train cars announcing, "First Call for Breakfast." Since they had a restless night, Tess and Elena are up early and dressed. "Mom, I'll meet you in the dining car. I'm very hungry," Elena informs her mother. "Wait for me, Elena." Tess pleads. "I'll be ready in a jiffy." Hesitantly Elena decides to wait. Tess closes her overnight bag, locks it, and grasps Elena's hand. Mother and daughter walk one behind the other in tandem with Elena leading through the narrow swaying train to the dining car. Simon is waiting for them. He immediately escorts Tess and Elena to the table where Rodney is patiently sitting anxiously waiting their arrival. As Elena and Tess enter and come to the table, he immediately leaps up, pulls the chair out for Elena. Simon does so for Tess. Tess is elated that Rodney is joining them for breakfast.

As Tess, Elena, and Rodney are scanning the menu, the man-of-the-cloth walks in alone. Rodney sees him and calls out to him, "Monsignor Cooney, would you like to join us?" He immediately notices Tess's surprise look. Rodney apologies, "Sorry I was so presumptuous. Do you mind if he joins us?" In a lower voice he suggests, "If you do, I will join him for breakfast. I hate to see anyone eat alone." Elena gives Rodney an annoying stare. Tess is at a loss for words but then responds, "Of course he can join us for breakfast." She smiles over at the clergyman who is smiling back. Tess questions, "You know him?" Rodney nods affirmatively.

Clearly, Rodney knows the priest. Having the priest join them for breakfast does not bode well with Elena. Tess comments, "It is always nice to meet new people." The astute waiter Simon brings the man in black over to the table and immediately adds another place setting. He hands the priest a menu. He informs them, "I will be back shortly to take your order. May I remind you we arrive in Chicago early afternoon."

Rodney takes the waiter's cue that time is of the essence therefore he quickly introduces Tess and Elena, "I want you to meet a good friend of mine and my family's, Monsignor James Cooney. He is from Notre Dame University in South Bend, Indiana. "The Fighting Irish," the priest proudly adds. Rodney smiles at the monsignor and reveals, "We were able to spend some time in New York together at Fordham University. Another school I am interested in attending." Elena whispers to her mother, "Isn't that where cousin Blaise's friend Robbie graduated from?" Tess does not respond. Monsignor stands up, reaches over, extends his long-crooked fingered yet smooth cool hand and shakes Tess's warm hand. Reaching over he then offers his hand to Elena's vacillating hand. With head bowed Monsignor gracefully addresses them, "It is a great pleasure meeting you. If you are one of Rodney's friends, then you will be my friend also." Simon comes over to the table and takes their orders.

Monsignor Cooney questions Tess and Elena. He asks where they are from and where they are going. He is very excited to learn that they are from Jersey City. Monsignor Cooney mentions that he knows a Monsignor Jack Kelly from St. Victor's Church and the fine Sister Margaret Mary also from the Jersey City parish. Tess and Elena are surprised. Tess instantly tell him that they attend that parish and know Father Kelly and Sister Margaret Mary very well. Rodney is amazed, "This is such a rare coincidence but then again Monsignor Cooney was born and raised in New York." Tess further adds, "My husband and his family have been long-time parishioners of St. Victor's parish and close friends of Monsignor Kelly." Looking over at her daughter she adds, "Elena has Sister Margaret Mary for history. Elena also has been taking piano lessons from her since second grade."

With a sulking look on her face, Elena makes a grunting sound. Rodney looks at her and whispers, "You seem upset; is there a problem?" Elena blurts out to Monsignor Cooney, "Do you know Father Arthur Schultz too?" Hearing this, Monsignor Cooney is stunned and at a loss for words. He looks extremely mystified and questions, "Why do you ask young lady?" Elena looks at her mother's stern stare. She ignores it and calls out, "I think he's a creep!" Tess immediately lectures Elena, "Why Elena what an unkind thing to say. Apologize immediately to Monsignor Cooney." The Monsignor pauses and ponders before he speaks.

He vehemently responds, "This is impossible! The Father Arthur Schultz that I know is based in El Paso, Texas. He works with the poor Mexicans in Juarez, Mexico, a frighteningly violent and dangerous city." Under his breath Monsignor Cooney utters. "He is missing."

Responding immediately, Tess calls out, "This cannot be!" Monsignor James Cooney informs, "It has been months since we last heard from Father Schultz." Tess questions, "El Paso, Texas borders Juarez, right?" "Yes," the priest quickly responds. Tess mentions, "The Father Schultz we are referring to brought a young Mexican with him named Juan. I think Sister Margaret Mary mentioned he was from Juarez originally." Tess continues, "We saw both of them at Midnight Mass this past Christmas Eve." Rubbing his hands together Rodney, in exhilaration, chimes in, "Why this is absolutely intriguing."

Before the perplexing conversation resumes the waiter Simon brings the food. He carefully distributes it to the guests. When everyone is served, Monsignor Cooney makes a pithy blessing over the food. At this point, no one other than Rodney seems hungry. "What does your so-called Father Schultz look like?" the confounded priest inquires. "Why, I hardly see him, but I think he is in his late thirties; very tall; lean, with dark hair cut short; with I believe gray eyes." "That is strange!" shouts out Monsignor Cooney. "That does not fit his description." He ponders, "This cannot be the same person!" Hearing this, Elena loses her appetite. She asks if she can be excused. Tess takes a sip of her coffee. Looking over at Elena, who is extremely upset she begs her daughter, "Please eat at least a small piece of toast." Rodney eats ravishingly.

Monsignor Cooney also sips his heavily creamed and sugared coffee. He reassures Tess that he will look into the strange matter about this Father Arthur Schultz from St. Victor's parish as soon as he arrives at Notre Dame. "It would be wonderful if the Father Schultz you know is the one that is missing." He continues to add, "There must be an explanation as to why we have not been informed." Bewildered the Monsignor exclaims, "This is very strange indeed!" He takes the large white linen napkin which is on his lap, unravels it, and gently wipes his moist brow. Sweat is dripping down this holy man's contorted face which only a short while ago was serene. "This mystery is extraordinary in the ordinary," Cooney pontificates.

Since Elena has left, confused, Tess rises up. She requests Monsignor to give his contact information to Rodney whom hopefully she will see in Los Angeles, California. She is determined to keep abreast of this complex situation. With a troubled look on his face, Monsignor Cooney pleads with Tess, "Please, I beg of you do not discuss this with anyone. Inform Elena not to mention it either. This is sacred." Looking around he groans, "This has all the elements of something sinister and perhaps dangerous." Profusely in agreement, Tess nods. Monsignor Cooney stares sternly at Rodney. He insists that he keep this information to himself. "Young man, it is imperative that you speak not a word or reveal any of this conversation to anyone." The Monsignor continues to stare at Rodney adding, "Like confession, myself and only Our Holy Father in Heaven should know this." "Don't fret Monsignor Cooney," Rodney promises. To add to the drama, Rodney puts his hand up and pronounces, "Mum's the word. So help me God."

The priest is extremely disturbed. He blames himself. Looking directly at Tess and Rodney, he remarks, "My biggest mistake I fear was sharing this private-church information with you lay people." He again rubs his distraught face with the napkin in his pure white soft shaking hands. Under his labored breath Monsignor Cooney pleads, "God forgive me. I don't know what I was thinking." He makes the Sign of the Cross. Repeating, "This should never had been spoken of and I am appalled with myself." He gazes over at Tess and Rodney. He sadly infers, "I might have placed your lives in peril."

The flustered Monsignor glances again at Tess and is deeply saddened to see how upset she is. He attempts to soften his fears saying, "My dear young lady, I believe you and your sweet daughter are honest decent people. I feel deep down inside my soul I can trust you to keep this between us." Again, Tess reassures him and gently places her hand in his. For once Rodney is at a loss for words but has a queer, sneaky smirk on his young smooth face. Monsignor Cooney is overwhelmed as he speaks these profound words, "The wounded world is full of wounded people; we must pray for those lost souls." He looks up calling out, "God Protect the Innocent."

The Monsignor looks back at Tess and with solemnity pronounces, "Bless you Woman." He adds, "I believe the Divine Father made us meet like this so that the ghastly unknown about our dear Father Arthur Schultz's mysterious disappearance is to be resolved soon." He makes the Sign of the Cross once more and remarks, "Our prayers will be answered through Jesus Christ our Savoir." He wipes the perspiration from his somber face and with a quivering voice reveals, "We greatly feared he was killed by the Mexican drug cartel." Tess stands there in trepidation and fear but refuses to let this ruin her plans for her and Elena's time in Chicago. The priest leaves and heads to his coach car to prepare to disembark shortly from the train. Anxious to remove herself from this tense environment, Tess excuses herself politely and heads toward her train car.

Rodney is excited. He murmurs to himself, "This will be a great movie! I want to write, produce, and direct movies in Hollywood." He is in a state of euphoria and continues to brag, "Like Alfred Hitchcock I will shock the movie industry!" Rubbing his hands together, he brags, "This will be my first big hit. A true blockbuster!" Thankfully no one hears Rodney's chatter about his future in the movie industry and what provoked it.

Tess is anxious to fill her daughter in on the part of the conversation that it is absolutely imperative that Elena not discuss the mystery surrounding Father Arthur Schultz and Juan with anyone. This concerned mother does not want to upset her sensitive daughter just when Elena seems to be upbeat. Tess is careful how she presents it to her daughter. Tess recognizes she must insist that this be kept an absolute secret. Tess questions whether her decision to leave her husband and Jersey City and head to Los Angles was right. She ponders over this and comes to the conclusion that this is not the right time to question it. Hence, she convinces herself it is for the best. Tess decides she will deal with what comes out of this absurd mystery when the time is right.

Leaving the car, Rodney is all excited about this baffling but fascinating situation. Monsignor Cooney ignores Rodney's quirky reaction. Monsignor Cooney silently continues to interrogate, "Why would Father Schultz go to another parish without anyone knowing?" He wipes the sweat from his reddening face and gasps, "I fear the worst!" Monsignor is determined to once again caution Tess the importance of her not revealing this to anyone including Elena. He is especially anxious to make sure Rodney understands the urgency in keeping this an absolute secret.

Monsignor Cooney will assure Tess that he will contact the proper church authorities to confirm the true nature of this strange Father Schultz at St. Victor's as soon as he gets to Notre Dame University. The perplexed Monsignor questions, "It is strange as to why Monsignor Kelly the pastor did not notify the church's higher ups?" He further ponders, "Every parish church and seminary in the country and I believe the Vatican was notified of Father Schultz's mysteriously missing without a word or clue." He convinces himself that the church higher ups have diligently kept it quiet from the unsuspecting lay people because of the obnoxious press which distorts everything and is not loyal and at times unfaithful to the Roman Catholic church.

Since this unsolved secrecy is an internal church affair, this loyal and pious clergy is appalled with himself that he dared to share and reveal this with complete strangers. Rodney is the exception but Monsignor Cooney is concerned he is young and frivolous and unable to keep this to himself. He wishes he had adhered to the old profound statement: "Hear No Evil, Speak No Evil, See No Evil." He cries out to himself, "What is done is done! What is said is said!" Monsignor comforts himself by professing, "I must place it all in God's hands and ask for his guidance."

Elena is not in a good frame of mind as is Tess after hearing these shocking revelations about the questionable Father Arthur Schultz from Monsignor James Cooney. When not spending time with Rodney, Elena keeps to herself on the train and does not further frustrate her mother about leaving Jersey City. Tess, seeing that her daughter is deeply upset upon hearing the news about the strange situation with Father Arthur Schultz, she promises herself that as soon as they arrive in California she will make it her top priority to explore Monsignor Cooney's disturbing conjecture about the mysterious double Father Schultz. Tess keenly recognizes that it is imperative she keep this clandestine revelation a top secret. *Mums the word!*

Tess Adeline and Elena Rose prepare to disembark from the train. In Chicago Tess checks on their transfer tickets to Los Angeles. The new El Capitan Super liner will take them to their final destination, Los Angeles, California *The City of Angels*. There is a six-hour layover until they board the El Capitan. Tess is anxious to take Elena to the famous Marshall Fields and Company Department store in downtown Chicago for lunch at their famous tearoom on the fourth floor. After lunch she is excited to bring Elena to the renowned Art Institute of Chicago to further enhance Elena culturally.

Tess eagerly tells Elena, "At the famous tearoom at the renowned Marshal Fields Department Store, they use the finest linens, elegant bone china, and every woman gets a long-stemmed gifted rose." Elena listens but she is in another realm. With extreme enthusiasm Tess adds, "After lunch we will go to the Art Institute of Chicago." She informs, "The rare and famous works are exceptional! I know Elena you will love seeing them up close." Tess Adeline's intention is to make this trip as stimulating and educational for her daughter as possible. Elena recognizes and appreciates what her mother is doing for her but she misses her father and is deeply disturbed by what she heard from Monsignor James Cooney about Father Arthur Schultz.

Preparing for the next phase of their journey to Los Angeles, it is comforting for Tess knowing that Rodney, young as he is, but a seasoned traveler, will also be accompanying them on the El Capitan to Los Angeles. Monsignor James Cooney of the Order of the Holy Cross's final destination is Chicago, Illinois. From there, as he informs them, he will be going straight to Notre Dame University in South Bend, Indiana where the Fighting Irish's illustrious football team call's home. The clergyman alludes confidently that he will solve the strange unknown about the identity of the questionable, perhaps impostor, Father Arthur Schultz who is currently at St. Victor's parish in Jersey City. Tess has no doubt that Monsignor James Cooney, with whom she recently became acquainted, will go to any and all ends to solve the mystery surrounding the dubious Father Arthur Schultz. Who ironically is the newest priest at St. Victor's Roman Catholic Church in Jersey City.

Sensing there might be real danger, and respecting Monsignor James Cooney's plead to keep it a secret, Tess is determined to lock it up in her mind and heart for as long as necessary provided it doesn't endanger her immediate family. As a cautious mother, she insists Elena pledge and swear to do the same. Elena guardedly agrees. *This perceptive young girl fears she already knows the answer.*

Having a dramatic and cynical curiosity and a relentless determination, Tess is evolving into a novice sleuth. She is restless and eager to find out whether the bizarre Father Schultz is a charlatan or, perhaps even worse, a murderer or, an innocent, falsely accused man. *Echoes of Agatha Christie's "Murder on the Orient Express" surrounds Tess.* Alone in the train car preparing to disembark, Elena Rose is deeply disturbed. She shudders, "Trouble seems to follow me wherever I am."

The powerful iron horse which originally embarked at Pennsylvania Station in New York City for Chicago, Illinois, arrives on time at Union Station in the Windy City Chicago or some call it *Sin City*. Tess is relieved since she needs time on the lay over to give Elena a chance to call her father. More importantly, Tess has to check on her transfer tickets for the Santa Fe Line's newest super train, The El Capitan which will be taking them to their final destination Los Angles, California in a few days. The trip from New York to Chicago was interesting, exhausting, and shockingly surprising. Tess hopes the second leg of this journey is successful and transforming. Tess Adeline is determined to put aside her fears for now. She is anxious to be in Chicago, visit the places she wants Elena to see; contact home; get settled on the El Capitan; and prepare to see her mother in Hollywood, California. *Hooray for Hollywood!*

CHAPTER THIRTY

Life and Death
Jersey City, New Jersey
January 1956

MIKE IS ALONE upstairs in his home getting ready to go to work. He misses Tess and Elena but having a lot of pressing and disturbing issues to deal with he keeps his frazzled mind temporarily off their absence. It snowed during the night therefore, before he leaves for work, Mike plans on shoveling the snow off the front stoop and walkway so his sister Ettie will not go and do it. During the entire unsettling night, Mike heard Carlo's endless hacking cough and the rustling sounds of his sister Ettie up most of the night. Thankfully Ettie finally agrees to get help. Eileen Moriarity is more than willing and able. Tony told Mike that she took care of her ailing aged, sweet Aunt Emma for a while before she passed away. Mike is pleased Eileen will start this morning at nine. He recognizes his exhausted sister is worn out and desperately needs full-time help. He hopes Eileen will stay the night. Mike will suggest it to Eileen this morning.

With his heavy, navy-blue pea coat buttoned to the top of his neck, black gloves on his strong hands, knit hat pulled down over his ears; and black sturdy boots securely on his feet, Mike heads down to the basement to get a snow shovel. As he passes Ettie's sidehall door, it flings open. His anguish looking sister stands there holding a cup of hot coffee for her brother. She hands it to him. Ettie doesn't speak a word. Mike annoyed shouts, "What's wrong with you Ettie? Take care of yourself. I will get coffee at the diner." Ettie insists. To please her, Mike takes it and gulps it down immediately. He hands the empty cup to his sister and inquires, "How's Carlo this morning?" With agony in her voice she mutters, "He had a rough night; even the pain killers aren't working."

Mike looks at his exhausted sister and comments, "I'm glad Eileen starts working for you today." Ettie responds, "I wish I never agreed!" Mike responds, "What are you talking about. You need help!" Sneering Ettie blurts out, "What would Tess think if she knew Eileen is staying here with you upstairs?" Upset she says, "What kind of a sister-in-law would I be?" Mike responds, "It doesn't concern her." To appease his sister's apprehension he reveals, "For your information Eileen is now married to Tony Rivera." Ettie is stunned. She cries out, "What? How in heavens name did that happen?" Ettie's brother smirks and says, "You live in the kitchen too much Sis; people have lives outside 391 Armstrong Ave."

Mike pecks his sister on her flushed cheek and insists, "Now listen, when Eileen comes, make sure you rest and let her take care of Carlo." Ettie, who has had to be frugal her entire life, is guilty and feels unworthy that Mike is paying for Eileen's services to nurse Carlo. "If Carlo knew I was taking money from you, he would divorce me!" She sighs, "He would never want anyone else taking care of him but me." "No worries Ettie you have done more for me than I can every pay you back for." He adds, "In the state Carlo is in he has no say." Mike orders, "Now get inside!"

Mike suddenly stops in his tracks, before he heads down to the basement to retrieve a shovel, he swerves and asks Ettie, "Wait, how is Rosaria doing?" Ettie ignores him. He questions further, "What decision did she make about you know what?" His sister stares at her brother gravely. He whispers, "The baby?" Ettie quietly says, "Like I told you, as soon as she starts to show, she is going to her friend's house in New England to have it." Mike is mute. Ettie pathetically reveals, "She fears she will not be here to help me with Carlo." Annoyed Mike says, "That's nonsense! Tell her to go when she has to."

Having immense love for his selfless sister, Mike places his strong arms around her. Ettie's eyes are now welled up with tears. He compassionately reminds her, "Let's be truthful with one another Sis, Carlo has only a short time." He wipes Ettie's eyes gently with his gloved hand and consoles her, "Carlo is ready to go. Even Dr. Sacks said so." She puts her head into Mike's chest and weeps. Tenderly Mike adds, "You're a religious woman Ettie. It's time for you to accept it and put it in God's hands." Slurring her words, this devoted wife soberly responds, "I hate to see my Carlo suffer so. I hope God does take him soon but I feel guilty thinking like this." "Hell with guilt! You've been a fantastic wife and mother! Stop being a martyr!" Mike continues, "Carlo, Rosaria and Blaise were blessed to have you; as I am." Ettie cries out, "What am I going to do now? No husband or children to care for; they've been my whole life." Startled by Ettie's doorbell ringing, Mike kisses his sister. Wiping her eyes on her apron Ettie rushes to answer her front door. Saddened for his sister to distract himself, Mike heads down to get the shovel. He needs to get outdoors to clear his head.

Bundled up in full winter gear, standing at the front door is Dr. Saul Sacks. Alongside of the good doctor is Eileen. Ettie opens the door and warmly welcomes Dr. Sacks but barely acknowledges Eileen. Dr. Sacks inquires, "How is Carlo this morning?" Before Ettie can respond, Eileen introduces herself. "Dr. Sacks, I'm Eileen Rivera." She puts out her petite gloved hand for him to shake and politely says, "Pleasure to meet you. I will be helping to care for Carlo." Dr. Sacks is pleased. Looking at fatigued Ettie, the doctor comments, "Happy to hear that you have finally agreed to engage help."

Ettie is annoyed with Eileen's intrusive behavior. Having to admit she needs help disturbs her. Ettie ignores Eileen. The brokenhearted wife takes hold of Dr. Sacks free hand; in the other he is holding onto his black, well-worn leather medical bag. Ettie insists, "Come in now doctor." She gives Eileen a distained smirk. The two head inside with the door ajar leaving Eileen standing there left out. Ettie leads Dr. Sacks directly into the bedroom where Carlo is semi-conscious.

Eileen musters up confidence and prepares to enter Ettie and Carlo's house. As she is entering, she notices Mike coming around from the alley carrying a shovel. Eileen stops and hollers, "Mike, I need to talk with you for a minute?" He stands frozen and hesitantly shakes his head affirmatively. Eileen carefully walks back down the snow-covered steps and asks, "What are you planning to do with that shovel?" "Shovel the snow! Why?" he inquires. "Oh," scanning up and down the street, "I thought you were going to defend yourself with it." "Why would I do that?" annoyed he asks. "Rumor has it that the head man's goons are looking for you." Mike smirks and starts to shovel the snow. "Before Tony left he insisted I warn you!" anxiously Eileen informs Mike.

This does not bode well with Mike. Angrily he throws the shovel down and grabs Eileen's long wool scarf which is around her neck. "Listen Mrs. Rivera, you are to stay out of my life and my business." Eileen pulls away. He curtly reminds her, "You are here only to take care of my sister and her husband." This feisty Irish lass stands her ground, "You must listen! I know what these mobsters are capable of doing. I was married to one." Mike settles down, picks up the shovel and remarks, "Okay, you told me what Tony asked you to do now go inside and do your job." Ettie comes to the door and calls out, "Eileen, the doctor wants to talk with you." Mike roughly snaps at his sister, "She's coming now!" Eileen trudges up the snow-covered porch steps. She follows Ettie into the house but turns to see if Mike is okay.

Now riled up, Mike glances up and down the street. He quickly shovels the snow from the stoop; the walkway; and cleans the blanket of snow off his Chevy which is parked in front of the house. After cleaning the snow from around the house and removing the snow off his car, Mike enters the red and white Chevy Bel Air. In the driver's seat he puts the key in the ignition, switches it on making the motor turn over. While the motor is purring, spooked by Eileen's warning from Tony, Mike uneasily sits in the car waiting for it to heat up. Out the rear view mirror he spots an unfamiliar black sedan creeping slowly down Armstrong Avenue. It slows down as it approaches the red Chevy where Mike is sitting. Suddenly, the door to Armstrong Avenue swings open and Dr. Sacks shouts out, "Mike, get in here immediately!" The unfamiliar man behind the wheel of the strange black sedan observes the elderly man at the front door calling Mike. The unknown driver accelerates immediately and speeds down Armstrong Avenue passing Mike in the car. Mysteriously, it turns onto Westside Avenue and disappears. Observing the strange car turning the corner vanishing, Mike jumps out of the Chevy, races up the porch steps, and follows the panicked doctor into Ettie's place.

Dr. Sacks and Mike go directly into Carlo's bedroom where anguished Ettie is holding onto Carlo's cold hands sobbing. Alone in the kitchen Eileen is trembling. "What's going on?" Confused, Mike blurts. Ettie cries out, "He's gone. My Carlo is dead!" Mike reaches for his sister but she pushes him away. Weeping she pleads, "Please, leave me be. Leave me alone with my husband." In a state of shock Mike steps away. Ettie bemoans, "I never had a proper chance to say goodbye or tell him how much I loved him." Dr. Sacks motions for Mike to leave her be. After hearing Ettie's painful comments, in a hush tone the wise doctor comments, "Mike, one thing I learned after years of practice and seeing people die, if you love somebody, tell them when they are alive, well and, able to feel it." Mike stops and ponders over this for a moment. The good doctor motions for Mike to leave the room. The two head into the kitchen where Eileen is helplessly standing by bewildered.

Ettie's perplexed brother Mike looks over at the doctor and questions, "What happened? So fast! I thought he had a month or so." Confounded, Mike continues to interrogate Dr. Sacks. With compassion and professionalism Dr. Sacks responds, "I knew it would be days but I wanted to give Ettie time to process it." The devoted family physician wipes his brow which is moist with sweat. He kindly comments, "It's for the best." Looking directly at the doctor with his saucer-shaped dark eyes welled up with tears, Mike mouths, "Thanks, Dr. Sacks."

In a state of shock, Mike slaps his thigh and groans, "What do we do next? Call the funeral director?" Calmly the doctor adds, "Since you are Catholics I assume you should call your parish priest. Ettie would like that." Years of administering to the dying and the people left behind and knowing Mike's family history, Dr. Sacks reaffirms, "Before you make those calls, it would be appropriate to allow your sister a few more moments privately with her husband." The seasoned doctor warily looks at Mike and suggests, "You should call Rosaria."

Still in a state of shock and dismayed but being the head of the family Mike nods affirmatively at the doctor. He laboriously walks over to the phone. Noticing Rosaria's work phone number on a pad near it, Mike picks up the receiver, quickly dials the number and anxiously awaits for someone to pick up. He hears a firm female voice announce, "Margaret Hague Maternity Hospital, Fourth Floor, Nurse Megan Healy speaking." Mike, says, "Get my niece Rosaria Cortino on the phone immediately."

Without thinking, he screams, "Her father just died!" He hears the phone placed down loudly, feet running, and someone calling Rosaria's name.

In less than a minute, Rosaria picks up the phone. In a panic she cries out, "Who is this? What happened?" Mike calms down momentarily and with a composed voice explains to Rosaria, "You must come home now. Your father passed away a short while ago." No response, a few seconds later Rosaria, with a contrived, calm voice asks, "Is my Mother okay?" Mike assures his niece that her mother is coping. Rosaria cries out, "Who is with her? Does Blaise know?" Mike regains his composure and tells her that he and Dr. Sacks are with her mother. He commands her, "Get home now! We'll get in touch with Blaise when you get here." Voice quivering Rosaria inquires, "Uncle Mike, how was Dad before he. . ." Mike does not answer; he rushes his niece off the phone by assuring her, "We'll talk later." With kindness yet authority he says, "Rosaria, I have to go. I want to be with your mother now, also I must contract the proper authorities." He places the receiver down before Rosaria can ask any further questions.

While Mike was on the phone with his niece, Dr. Saul Sacks went back to the bedroom after giving Ettie a few precious moments with her newly deceased husband. He quietly enters and stands next to Ettie placing his arm lightly on her as she is laying across her late husband. The doctor convinces her to remove herself from Carlo's body so he can cover him properly. Ettie reluctantly gets up, stands stoic with rosary beads held tightly in her quivering hands. Desperately trying to keep her composure this devastated new widow rocks back and forth moaning under her labored breath, "My Carlo; my poor, poor Carlo!"

Mike quietly enters the bedroom. Ettie stops moaning when she sees her brother. Mike lets his sister know that Rosaria will be coming as soon as possible. Seeing his sister going deeper into despair, he insists, "Ettie please come into the kitchen and rest." In a hypnotic state, Ettie complies. Like a lost sheep who follows unquestioningly a shepherd she follows her adored brother. *At this moment she is a lost sheep.*

The kitchen is where Ettie feels the most comfortable and at home. It is her safe haven. Mike insists she sit. He again assures her that Rosaria will be here as soon as she is able. With Ettie sitting quietly saying her comforting rosary Mike lets his weary sister know that he is going upstairs to call Monsignor Kelly and to contact the family-run funeral parlor. This devoted brother intends to spare his bereaved sister of hearing him making the necessary arrangements for Carlo's last rites and to have his remains picked up. As the male head of the family, this has been the burden and duty Mike has had to take on for far too many times. Over the years he has performed this reverently for his and Ettie's beloved deceased, immediate family members.

An hour later Rosaria comes rushing into the house. She goes right up to her mother who is still in the kitchen praying. She hugs her mother tightly. The two women, with tears pouring down their distressed faces, attempt to comfort one another. Selfless Ettie does not want to upset her pregnant daughter so she calms down and assures Rosaria that she is fine. Mike comes down from upstairs after making the necessary arrangements. He embraces Rosaria and expresses his sympathy to his grieving niece. Rosaria acknowledges her Uncle and heads into the bedroom where her father is. She is taken back for a second when she sees Dr. Sacks alone in the room. He is writing the death certificate. When he hears her, the doctor immediately expresses his condolences to Rosaria, "I will leave you alone for a few minutes to be with your father," he says. Rosaria stands in disbelief. Solemnly she looks at her dad's lifeless form.

The respectful doctor leaves Rosaria and goes into the kitchen. Eileen is standing there trying to figure out what to do next. She is in shock! Dr. Sacks motions for her to go into the living room for now. She leaves the room and looks over at Ettie hoping to offer her condolences to her but Ettie is now busy making coffee. Her duties as woman of the house never ceases even in time of death. Recognizing it would be better to leave Ettie be, Eileen goes into the living room.

Seeing his sister making coffee Mike insists she sit down. He reminds her that he will take care of things. Ettie ignores him. He asks where Eileen is? She behaves as if Mike isn't in the room. Like a body shield, with her well-worn apron on, Ettie proceeds to set the table with coffee cups and places her homemade cookies out. "Guests must be fed!" she calls out to Mike as he gives her an angry stare. Coming to terms with what is to be, Ettie looks over at Mike. She insists, "We must not let Tess and Elena know!" She pauses for a moment and comments, "You should not burden them Mike. Let them get safely to California." Mike makes a grim face. Ettie firmly adds, "You can contact them after the services!"

Mike is enraged, "Burden! Why spare Tess?" With disdain he rages on, "Why should Tess be spared? She's my wife. There is no excuse for her." He slams his trembling hand on the table and remarks, "It's her duty as a member of this family to grieve with us!" He turns and heads to Ettie's kitchen cabinet; pulls it open; reaches way back and takes out a bottle of grappa. Mike pours himself a huge glass full. He holds up the glass and says, "No coffee for me Ettie. I need a real drink! Salute." He quickly slugs this hard liquor down his throat in one gulp making it feel like it is on fire. *If Mike breathed out, it would be like a dragon throwing out wild flaring flames.*

Upset, Ettie looks over at her brother and cries out in despair, "What am I going to do with you men?" She stops and adds, "Oh my goodness where is Blaise and the priest? Father Kelly must bless my Carlo before they take him away." Embarrassed about his dreadful behavior Mike walks over to Ettie. He holds his sister tightly. He reassures her that the priest will be here shortly.

Mike calms Ettie down by also telling her, "I got in touch with Blaise." Excitedly Ettie asks, "What did he say? Is he alright? When is he coming?" Mike grabs his sister's trembling hands and informs her, "He's making arrangements to come as soon as he can. As a Marine Ettie, there is certain protocol he must adhere to." Ettie is temporarily relieved and further inquires, "When can he be here?" Mike answers her, "As soon as he knows, he'll contact us and will give us his time frame." Ettie begins to groan, "My poor Blaise!" Continuing to comfort his sister Mike shares with her, "He knew his dad was very ill. Blaise prepared himself Ettie."

This wife and now widow is crying uncontrollably, "My Carlo worked all those many hard years in that polluted chemical factory. Dr. Sacks thinks that's what poisoned his lungs." "Along with those cigarettes," under his breath Mike comments. Attempting to appease his hysterical sister he pleads, "Ettie stop! Carlo was a man who lived the way he wanted to and your son is a military guy he can handle it!" He quietly adds, "Rosaria is a grown woman and a nurse she'll be fine too." Feeling powerless, Mike pours himself another grappa.

Alone in the bedroom, Rosaria gently kisses her father's now cooling forehead and whispers into his ear, "Dad, I love you. I promise I will make sure Mom is taken care of." She sits down on the chair next to the bed, rubs her soon to be very swollen belly and quietly speaks to her unborn child, "If you are a boy, your name will be Carlo." Rosaria sways getting up. She quickly steadies herself, leans over and for the last time kisses her father's forehead. This dutiful daughter softly says, "Dad, you're going to be a Grandpa."

Unbeknownst to Rosaria, the door opens to the bedroom. Dr. Sacks enters. He politely tells Rosaria that the priest and the funeral director will be here shortly to take her father. Emotional Dr. Sacks ponders a moment. Getting his courage up he asks, "Rosaria, do you want me to let my son David know about your Dad?" She looks down at her deceased father, her future child's deceased grandfather, turns slightly and gazes at her future child's paternal grandfather, Dr. Sacks. She boldly relays, "David already knows!" She unflinchingly walks out leaving Dr. Sacks standing there mortified. *Death and birth go hand in hand.*

The doorbell rings breaking the morbid mood in the house. Mike rushes to answer it. Father Arthur Schultz is standing at the door with Juan Flores the church's young janitor. Noticing Mike's perplexed look, the priest explains, "Unfortunately, Monsignor Kelly is away at a church conference." "Oh," Mike responds in a negative manner. "When I called to tell him about Carlo, he was deeply saddened and terribly sorry that he is unable to be with you today," the priest explains. Mike questions, "But my brother-in-law has to have the last rites?" Father Schultz immediately says, "Monsignor asked me to perform the last rites." Mike stands there perplexed. Father Schultz sensing Mike's hesitation adds, "Monsignor sends his sincerest condolences and told me to inform you that he will be available to say the funeral mass and conduct the burial services."

Hearing this temporarily appeases Mike. He leads the priest to the bedroom. Carrying the anointed holy oil, Juan follows them. Knowing his sister and niece want to be there for the anointing, Mike goes to the kitchen and informs Ettie and Rosaria that the priest is here to anoint Carlo. Immediately, Ettie jumps up and rushes into the bedroom followed by her daughter Rosaria.

Seeing the priest and the immediate family enter the bedroom for their final goodbye and blessing, Dr. Saul Sacks recognizes it is the proper time for him to take leave. He expresses his loyalty to the family and assures them, "Call me if you need anything." He looks at Mike and in a hush tone says, "If Ettie needs a sedative I will be happy to write a prescription." Mike thanks the doctor and asks him to let himself out. The good doctor, preparing to leave, stops a moment.

Noticing the despondent, exhausted Rosaria's expanded waist, Dr. Sacks gazes woefully at her. She is bravely standing next to her grieving mother holding her up. Dr. Sacks quietly mouths, "I am here for you also Rosaria." She looks unflinchingly at the doctor and stubbornly does not respond. Ettie, Rosaria, Mike, Father Schultz and his assistant Juan are now alone in the bedroom. There is momentary silence until the sound of the front door closes. Dr. Saul Sacks is gone leaving Carlo's bereaved immediately family and the clergy hovering over his recently deceased body.

Carlo Cortino's immediate family, minus his son Blaise, are now alone in Ettie and Carlo's conjugal bedroom with Father Arthur Schultz and Juan Flores. Ettie's family is all Carlo has left. He lost his parents at a young age. His only bachelor brother Pedro died over ten years ago suddenly leaving Carlo void of his biological family. Father Schultz performs the last rites on Carlo while his devoted wife, dutiful daughter, and distressed brother-in-law solemnly look on. On cue, they pray along with the priest and Juan. When this pious sacrament is completed, the mournful and dazed Ettie, still doing her wifely duty, politely invites the clergy and his assistant Juan into the kitchen for coffee and her homemade cookies. Wiping her moist, swollen, blood-shot eyes, Rosaria follows her brave mother into the kitchen to help her. Father Schultz and Juan respectively follow them. "We can only stay a few minutes," Father Schultz tells Ettie. Juan is mute. The young janitor politely refuses coffee and treats while the priest heartily enjoys the dark-rich coffee and excessively devours at least a half dozen of Ettie's delicious sweet treats.

Eileen sheepishly enters the kitchen where everyone is now congregating. Juan is surprised when he sees Eileen walk into the kitchen. The priest ignores her but scans her up and down like a hungry wolf. Tony's new bride offers to help. At first Ettie resists holding tightly onto the coffee pot. She finally relinquishes her kitchen duties to Eileen since her weary body is betraying her with insufferable fatigue. Eileen takes the coffee pot from Ettie and pours the priest his second cup of dark, steaming coffee. One would get the sense that she wants to spill it on him from the grotesque look on her face while serving him. Rosaria is writing notes on a blank piece of paper near the phone. Hearing her mother cough, a signal to her daughter to stop what she is doing and not to be disrespectful, Rosaria stops writing. She sits down with her mother, the priest, and his assistant. Juan weirdly stares at Eileen. He is anxious to address her. She looks back at him, blinks, and with a stern look on her face Juan realizes that she is signaling him to be silent.

Rosaria informs the priest that as soon as her brother Blaise arrives, she and her mother will sit down with him or Father Kelly to go over the funeral mass and burial services at the parish office. She inquires as to whether Monsignor Kelly will be back to perform the funeral mass. Father Schultz hesitates then mentions, "As I told Mike, Monsignor Kelly said he would." While Father Schultz and Rosaria are conversing, Juan does not take his eyes off of Eileen. The priest turns and notices. He stops talking with Rosaria and questions Eileen as to why she is here. Ettie immediately explains to the priest about her doctor recommending Eileen help her while her husband was ill. She emphasized that her brother Mike insisted. This once more brings tears to this new widow's bloodshot swollen eyes.

Ettie makes a weird, painful, guttural sound and turns to Eileen and moans, "Guess I will no longer need your services now that my Carlo is gone." Observing Ettie's distraught face, Eileen looks lovingly over at the grieving widow. She attempts to comfort her by sharing this, "My kind-pious, widowed mother from the old country Ireland always said, 'Relationships are eternal.'" Ettie wipes her moist eyes with her sleeve. She finally acknowledges Eileen with a sweet smile. Embarrassed and fearful of the attention, Eileen walks over to the sink and begins to wash the coffee pot desperately trying to stay under the radar of the questioning eyes by the others in the somber kitchen.

The priest demonically glares over at Eileen and sarcastically remarks, "You should know what it is like to be a widow." Hearing this Ettie is shocked and cries out to Eileen who is standing there frozen, "Widowed? I thought you and Tony just got married?" Concerned, Ettie asks, "Is Tony alright? Did something happen to him?" Eileen stares down the priest and assures Ettie that Tony is fine, "Ettie, my new husband is fine. He's away on business."

Fearing further confrontation, Juan jumps up, goes to Father Schultz and whispers into his ear causing the priest to immediately rise. He announces, "Yes, Juan, thank you for reminding me. It is time to say our goodbyes." He looks slyly at Juan and says, "We have other parish duties to attend to." The stiff, statue-like priests inform, "Juan and I will leave now!" He looks over at Eileen and tauntingly comments, "If you need my guidance Merry Widow. . ." Smirking he sarcastically adds, "Or should I say Bride of Frankenstein, you know where you can find me." This flaming red-headed Colleen's Irish temper is boiling over. She is fuming mad; steam is blazing out of her ears. With her trembling hands Eileen prepares to throw a dish at the malicious priest. Aiming to hit him, she shouts, "Why you egotistical, overblown thug!"

Rosaria, recognizing an altercation ready to erupt, plays devil's advocate. She reaches for the now amused priest, takes him by his arm and orders, "I'll show you out!" Ettie is perplexed. Eileen looks at Rosaria escorting the hostile priest out, puts the dish down and mouths, "Thank you." The haughty priest and the edgy Juan follow the mystified Rosaria out of the house.

After they leave, and the coast is clear, Eileen goes over to Ettie who is now crying loudly calling Carlo's name, "Carlo, my Carlo how will I live without you?" This widow's heart is torn open and bleeding. [*I love thee with the breath, smiles, tears, of all my life!* ~ Elizabeth Barrett Browning.] Saddened to view this, Eileen goes over to Ettie and gently wipes her weary, tear stained face with a clean dish cloth. She attempts to console her, "Trust me, you will manage." Once arch enemies these two polar-opposite women

bond under unusual yet mutual circumstances. *Love lost and Love found.
Love is all we have, the only way that each can help the other.* ~Euripides

Oblivious to what has occurred in the kitchen, still in Carlo's bedroom, and hearing the priest and Juan leave, Mike heads into the living room. His cousin Nicholas Scat, and his assistants are patiently waiting in there for the word to come to take Carlo's body. Nick Scat's father and Mike's Dad, originally from Salerno, Italy, were brothers and partners in business when they first arrived in America at the turn of the 20th Century. They settled in Jersey City. Mike goes up to his cousin Nicholas. They immediately embrace. The close cousins exchange a few words. Mike, the grieving brother for his sister Ettie, accompanies Nicholas Scat and his assistants into the bedroom where Carlo's body is alone.

As the oldest Italian American male in the family, and since Carlo's son Blaise has not arrived yet, Mike is responsible to make sure the men properly take Carlo away. He is also responsible to make arrangements for a respectable funeral. The professionals do their respective duty. They quietly remove Carlo's body from the house. As Mike observes his once confrontational brother-in-law Carlo leaving his home for the last time, and knowing how religious his sister Ettie is, he is deeply disturbed that Monsignor John Kelly did not perform the last rites. This is particularly disappointing since the Monsignor performed this in the past for Mike's entire deceased family members: Mike and Ettie's beloved mother Antonella, dutiful father Nicholas, and kindhearted, yet feisty younger sister Rose Annette, whom they all adored.

Italian Catholic wakes in the 50s traditionally lasted three full days. Afternoon and nights at the local funeral home. The fourth day a formal funeral mass at the family parish, in this case St. Victor's Roman Catholic church, is offered for the deceased and attended by family and friends. Religious music, special prayers, and chosen bible readings are performed. The priest celebrates the mass. A close family member usually gives sentimental remembrances about the deceased. The funeral mass is normally followed by the burial at the family plot in a local consecrated Catholic cemetery.

Customarily, only the priest, immediate family and intimate friends attend the burial. After the somber service recited by the priest near the burial plot, many tears are shed. Carlo's immediate family, close friends, and clergy will say their final farewell at the burial spot. When the pious ceremony is complete, the head of the family invite guests to share a full-course luncheon with plenty of drinks including libations. There, Carlo Cortino's memory will be respectfully celebrated. The repose luncheon is typically held either at the deceased party's home or at a local restaurant. In this case, Carlo's repose luncheon will be held at their local favorite Italian restaurant, Cafe Amore. Clearly, Ettie, Rosaria, Blaise, and Mike have a lot of planning to do in the next few sorrowful days to honor the life of Carlo Cortino.

While Ettie and Eileen remain in the kitchen, Mike reassures his cousin Nick Scat, the funeral director, that the wishes regarding the funeral and burial arrangements will be discussed with Ettie, Rosaria, and son Blaise. They must first wait for his nephew Corporal Blaise Cortino to arrive home. Knowing time is of the essence, Mike assures Nick that they will come to see him with their decisions by tomorrow after noon; assuming Blaise will be home by then. With great respect, Mike's cousin, the funeral director, shakes Mike's hands and once more offers his sincerest condolences. Nicholas Scat profusely assures Mike he will do a respectable and fine job especially since they are 'familia.' With dignity and reverence Nick's assistants remove Carlo from his home.

In the kitchen Rosaria is pensive and Ettie is mournful. Temporarily putting aside the vicious and cruel comments by Father Schultz, Eileen is compassionate and supportive to the lost women in this grief-stricken household. The Irish lass, once an adversary, is now a sturdy crutch for these fragile women, Ettie and Rosaria, to lean on.

Mike is pensively standing unaccompanied on the snow-covered red brick porch of 391 Armstrong Avenue sorrowfully observing the men place his brother-in-law in the stately, long, shiny black hearse. Wiping the moisture on his shirt sleeve from his soulful eyes, Mike regretfully reflects on how he and Carlo had their negative issues and multiple differences for so many *wasted* years. More so Mike is overwhelmed with grief for his sister and her two adult children. This retrospective man knows how devastating it is to lose a parent at any age. When he sees and hears the highly polished, sleek black, stately hearse slowly drive away from 391 Armstrong Avenue, Mike comes out of his reflective state. He smiles as he thinks how Carlo would have preferred his last ride on this earth to be on his trusty shinny motorcycle or in his beat up but faithful old car with its infamous missing front windowpane.

No longer able to see the hearse, Mike makes the Sign of the Cross, turns and heads upstairs to his empty house. This sensitive but able man is anxious to get in touch with his wife Tess Adeline to share the sad news. He assumes she and Elena should be in Chicago waiting to take the next train to the Los Angeles, California. He hopes he can reach her; if not in Chicago, he will contact Tess's mother in Los Angeles. *Mike misses Tess and Elena terribly.* Reflecting back on the last few disturbing weeks and how his life has become unraveled and uncertain especially with his wife, Tess, Mike hears echoes of Brendan quoting Shakespeare: "The course of true love never did run smooth." He questions, *"How and when did Tess's and his love go wrong? What happened to his happy go-lucky- little girl, Elena Rose?"*

In the kitchen, Ettie, Rosaria, and Eileen stop talking when they hear the front doorbell ring. Rosaria jolts up. "Mom stay put with Eileen. I'll go see who it is." Ettie shouts, "Oh, I hope it's my boy, Blaise!" Rosaria responds, "I doubt it Mom. Blaise should be here by tomorrow." Reaching the front door and opening it, Rosaria is surprised to see standing there Robbie Savini. He is Blaise's childhood and best friend who lives up the street. He immediately grabs Rosaria and gives her a huge bear hug. A little taken back, she gently moves him aside. Robbie murmurs, "I can't tell you how sorry I am to hear about your father's passing Rosaria." Confused, she asks, "How did you know?" "Your brother contacted me as soon as he heard. He asked me to come by and see if there is anything I can do until he can arrange to get home," he informs her.

Wiping a tear from her eye Rosaria questions, "How is my brother Blaise doing?" "He's as well as can be expected," with compassion Robbie assures her. "Good," Rosaria grimaced. "Now that he is the man of the house, your brother wants to make sure you and your Mom are okay," Robbie continues. "Thank you for coming by Robbie," Rosaria says. She adds, "We are also doing as well as can be expected." She pauses and reveals, "Although, I fear my mother is keeping a strong front and will break soon." The two long-time neighbors and friends stand frozen in time for a moment and at a loss for words. Realizing the uncomfortable silence, Rosaria suggests, "Please come in Robbie. I know Mom would love to see you." Ettie hollers from the kitchen, "Rosaria, who is it? Is everything alright?" "Yes, Mom," she answers. Robbie courteously follows Rosaria into the kitchen. When Ettie sees him, she begins to cry. Robbie runs over to her and puts his long arms around her gently. She is like a second mother to him. Robbie recalls all the great meals he ate in Ettie's welcoming kitchen with Blaise while they were growing up and watching TV in their welcoming living room.

Eileen quietly observes this touching scene. Rosaria asks Robbie if he would like some coffee or something stronger like grappa. For a moment she casts aside her sorrow and teases Robbie, "Are you old enough to drink the hard liquor now?" He looks at her and laughs then immediately gets serious and defensively snaps, "Sure I am. I'm older than Blaise." Eileen wants to keep things in a serious note so Ettie doesn't get upset. She extends her hand and introduces herself to Robbie while Rosaria goes for the grappa. Like old times, Ettie immediately begins to fill a plate of cookies for him.

Robbie thanks Ettie while keeping a sharp eye on Rosaria. He observes what a confident, capable and beautiful woman she turned out to be. Rosaria is his best friend Blaise's older sister who always was annoyed by them. Especially every Saturday afternoon when he and Blaise lounged in the Cortino family living room watching sports for hours. Ettie kept bringing them grilled cheese sandwiches, unlimited drinks, and her homemade sweets all afternoon long. Carlo was always in his bedroom reading the encyclopedia in his favorite worn-out lounge chair. Blaise and Robbie continually taunted Rosaria during those carefree days. They teased her constantly and called her the Gestapo, Iron Woman, and other derogatory names. Rosaria was constantly on their case. It annoyed her that they totally ignored her and that they referred to her as a cold fish and an old maid. "Wicked Witch of the West," they hollered at her when she told them to get off the couch and get a job.

Mike enters and is pleased to see Robbie. Having another man around is reinforcing. As soon as he sees Uncle Mike, Robbie jumps up and offers his heartfelt condolences to him. Mike pats Blaise's friend and good neighbor on his back. He immediately brags, "Eileen, this bright young man graduated with a B.S. in physics with honors from St. Peter's College located here in Jersey City." Robbie is red faced. Mike smiles at him and proceeds, "This ambitious young stud went on to earn a M.S. in physics from Fordham University." Blushing Robbie pleads, "Uncle Mike, enough about me." "Don't be so modest," Mike calls back. He resumes, "After earning his Master's in physics he attended Adelphi University where he earned an MBA in aerospace." Mike halts a moment, again slaps Robbie's slouched shoulder and adds, "Robbie currently has an esteemed position in the aerospace field."

In the background Rosaria is listening intently. Ettie and Eileen uniformly shout out, "How wonderful!" Seeing Robbie uncomfortable Mike teases further, "Making the big bucks now, hey Big Shot." Mike continues his banter, "I bet all the good-looking girls are hovering around you these days. You must be a real lady killer." Uncomfortable with this attention yet Robbie boasts, "I've had my share of woman but none I want to take home to my mother." Rosaria looks up at Robbie in a new light. Ettie chimes in, "How's your dear mother?" Immediately Robbie responds, "Mom's fine. She has her share of aches and pains but manages at her age." "Well," adds Ettie, "She raised a fine young man." To take the spotlight off of him, Robbie quickly changes the subject. He shares that he spoke with Blaise and assures them that Blaise is handling the sad news as well as he can. "No worries, he should be home late tomorrow," Robbie informs.

Recognizing the family needs time to discuss the next phase of this mourning process, Robbie and Eileen decide to take leave. Eileen offers to come by tomorrow as a friend and not an employee to help Ettie. Robbie gallantly offers his assistance to Ettie, Rosaria, and Mike, "Please know I am here for you in any capacity." Robbie assures Rosaria that he will pick Blaise up at the train station and bring him straight home. He hesitates a moment, looks over at Rosaria who is busy writing down something on the pad near the phone. He offers, "Rosaria, if you or your mother need anything, please call me." Robbie walks over to Rosaria, takes the pencil from her and a piece of paper and writes down his phone number. He hands it to Rosaria. "Here's my phone number; make sure you put it in a safe place," he emphasizes. Rosaria looks at Robbie with new respect. She takes the paper with his phone number on it from him; folds it; turns away from him; and slips securely inside her black silk blouse. He turns and requests, "I'm a grown man now Rosaria; please call me Rob. I've outgrown Robbie." She nods, affirmatively; pauses and says, "Robert, I think I'll call you Robert." Pleased, he looks at her and says, "Fine with me!"

Ettie and Mike are both intensely observing the two of them. Rosaria sits down and takes the folded paper out and looks at the telephone number Robert wrote down for her. Mike glances over at his bereaved sister and insists that she let Eileen come and help her. Eileen and Robert are preparing to leave. Mike calls out to Eileen, "Eileen, make sure you come tomorrow when you can." He adds, "Ettie will leave a key for you if we aren't here." Always cautious, he whispers, "Under the front door mat." Eileen nods her head gesturing she understands. She proceeds to follow Robert out. Once more the door to Ettie's front exit in this two-family house closes but not for long.

As Eileen and Robert are walking down the outside brick porch steps, Sister Margaret Mary is walking quickly toward the house. She hurriedly nods at both of them and proceeds to go to the front door. Robert remembers her from St. Victor's Parish and knows well enough to let her be. Eileen says goodbye to Robert as he heads up Armstrong Avenue to his family home. At the top step of the stoop Sister Margaret Mary is impatiently ringing the doorbell with a vengeance. She is clearly upset no one has opened the door yet. The anxious sister looks up and down the street as if someone is following her. Finally, she hears footsteps coming toward the door.

Hearing the endless bagging on the door and the consistent ringing of the doorbell, annoyed, Mike rushes to the front door. He is surprised to see Sister Margaret Mary standing there in a huff. She blurts out, "Finally!" "Oh, Sister, I hope Father Schultz didn't insist you come. Juan and the priest left already." Seeing Sister act indifferent, he explains, "The funeral director was here. They took Carlo to the funeral parlor." She blurts out, "Mike I came to see you! I have something urgent I must tell you and I fear it is critical." Baffled and taken aback Mike questions, "Sister you're not here because my sister Ettie's husband Carlo Cortino died?" The stately and stern nun looks straight at the bewildered Mike. Fluttering she announces, "No!" Stops a second to compose herself. Reverently Sister Margaret Mary says, "I am terribly sorry to hear this and will pray for Carlo and the family." With that said she blurts out, "Mike, I rushed over here about something totally different and it is extremely important!"

Perplexed, Mike insists, "Please calm down, Sister Margaret Mary." Sister catches her breath. Mike says, "Good, now explain why you are here?" In a hushed voice she informs Mike, "I have an urgent message for you from Monsignor Kelly." Baffled, Mike repeats, "Father Kelly?" "Yes!" emphatically she calls out. "Monsignor begged me to come here to warn you." Perplexed Mike echoes, "Warn me?" In her stark black, full- nun's habit, Sister Margaret Mary, with an eagle's eyes, looks around to see if anyone else is in the vicinity. She grabs Mike's arm. Like the 'cries of the damned' holding tightly onto Mike's arm, she reiterates, "Yes, Mike, I am here to WARN you!" With a sneer on his face, Mike releases his arm. The determined, frustrated nun grabs Mike again. She shakes him screaming, "Damn it! Listen to me son!" *This saintly but insistent nun tries to shake some sense in Mike or the hell out of him.*

CHAPTER THIRTY-ONE

Birth, Death, Rebirth
Walpole, New Hampshire
1857

ANXIOUS ANNA LEE is patiently waiting for Zeke to return home to inform her that her husband Austin made his connections safely. Hoping for his sake that he will be on time for his pressing business trip to Australia. Sitting in her rocking chair in the parlor next to the fireplace knitting she is fervently listening for Zeke's arrival. Upstairs she hears her daughter Theresa Edith laughing with Nannette. Comfortable near the cozy fireplace she ponders over her life at her husband Austin's family estate. Now her home. Anna Lee reflects back on the few years when she first came to Walpole, New Hampshire as a young bride from Virginia. This proud mother fondly recalls giving birth to her precious daughter Theresa Edith. Sadly, she remembers her great fear while her husband was fighting for the Union Army in the Civil War. Looking down at her swollen belly Anna Lee is pleasantly reminded that their second child is to be born in a few months. This sensitive, compassionate young woman earnestly ponders over the future.

Anna Lee's determined husband Austin is a strong, confident and motivated man and she admires him for all of it. Yet, many times, she is painfully lonely. With each passing day Anna Lee longs for her husband to share his deepest thoughts and concerns with her. In her husband's strikingly mystifying eyes this astute wife notices an apprehension. Is he suppressing angst over something from his past? She wonders. Subconsciously she feels something terrible happened to him during the war or, she ponders, perhaps his lonesome childhood has affected him more than he reveals. *This questionable melancholy engulfs both Anna Lee and Austin.*

Knocking on her kitchen door startles Anna Lee out of her concerns. She hears Nannette calling, "I'm coming Zeke." Before Anna Lee can get into the kitchen, Nannette opens the door. A tired looking Zeke enters. He asks Nannette to seek out Anna Lee. He is anxious to inform her that Austin met his connection in a timely manner. Nannette goes to the entrance of the parlor. She tells Anna Lee that Zeke is here and he would like to speak with her. Before Nannette can get a response, Anna Lee calls out, "Zeke, please come in here." She motions for Nannette to leave and says, "I am sure Theresa Edith is waiting for you." Nannette does not move. Anna Lee stresses, "Go to her now!" Nannette reluctantly leaves.

Zeke walks in slowly. Anna Lee asks him to sit by the fire. "You must be cold. Sit by the fire; it will warm you quickly." He ignores her and sits across from her away from the roaring fireplace. "Well," Anna Lee asks, "Did my husband's arrangements for his travel go according to his desired plan?" "Yes, all went as planned so far," Zeke interjects before she can ask any more questions. A broad smile crosses her face. She calls out, "I am pleased." Standing up abruptly Zeke asks, "If that will be all Ma'am I'll head out to the barn and finish my chores." Anna Lee stops him, "Please stay I have a few more pertinent questions I would like to ask you."

Zeke is exhausted but out of respect he stays. "Zeke," Anna Lee begins, "You have known my husband for more years than I have." Zeke nods his head in agreement. "I notice at times his mind seems to be far away and I see an agonizing look on his face which comes out-of-the-blue," Anna Lee reveals. Zeke is uncomfortable; he is not used to having a personal conversation with a woman especially one of her stature and his boss's wife. "Well, I'm not entirely sure what you're getting at?" he cautiously questions. "I will try to be clearer." She motions for him and politely requests, "Please sit down." Recognizing Anna Lee is dead serious Zeke dutifully but reluctantly sits across the room again away from the fire.

Anna Lee resumes her query, "I know very little about my husband's childhood. Only that his mother and father died when he was a young child and his grandfather raised him." Not one to have such an intimate conversation but knowing that Anna Lee is not one to let him leave without a valid response, he answers. "Yes, that's true, Ma'am," Zeke responds. Anna Lee stands up and walks closer to Zeke. With a hushed voice she asks, "How did his parents die?" Zeke is at a loss for words but with Anna Lee's persistence, he answers. "Austin has never told me nor have I felt I had the right to inquire." Feeling as if he is walking on thin ice, Zeke tries to explain the best he can. "Well," wiping his sweaty forehead with a calico handkerchief, he responds, "Not sure if it's my place to tell." Anna Lee is determined. She boldly calls out, "I am his wife, the mother of his child and future child." In a calm voice she whispers, "I love Austin dearly." She pleads, "I only want to know so I can understand and perhaps help ease his pain."

Trapped and flustered but having compassion for this lonesome wife and future mother to another child, Zeke halfheartedly complies, "All I know is that they died in a mysterious fire on this very property." Anna Lee sighs. "My poor, poor Austin!" Nervous, Zeke wipes his sweating brow with the cuff of his sleeve. Noticing Zeke upset she employs, "Forgive me for my outburst. Please continue." Zeke continues, "I hear it was a fierce barn fire and no one knows how it happened." "Oh, dear!" Anna Lee cries out in anguish. She inquires, "Where was Austin?" "Word has it he was with his grandpa on a fishing outing," Zeke nervously answers. Even though she is sad to hear this Anna Lee is desperate to learn more. She asks, "They never found out how it ignited?" "Some say the fire was started by a disgruntled unknown person who harbored a long-time feud with the O'Brien-Stevens family both here and abroad." "Arson?" She places her trembling hand on her heart and prays, "Oh my Lord! How awful for my darling Austin and his dear, dear parents!" Fearful he has said too much, Zeke jolts up to leave. This loner is not good at consoling people especially the female gender. No longer engaged with Zeke, Anna Lee murmurs to herself, "How devastating and abandoned my husband must have felt especially since he was an only child." This sweet, caring wife's soulful, violet-blue eyes cloud over with tears. Anna Lee's usually soft voice is suddenly filled with mournful moans.

Zeke is beyond uncomfortable. He attempts to console his mistress, "Mrs. Stevens I'm sorry this has upset you so." Putting his shaking hands in his pocket he insists. "Ma'am, shall I call Nannette to make you some tea to settle you down?" He compassionately adds, "You gots [sic] to think of your future baby." The distressed young wife and mother sits crying with her hands covering her face as tears are streaming down her anxious, sweet face.

Upstairs Nannette and Theresa Edith hear the crying. They rush down and enter the parlor. "Can I be of any help?" Nannette frantically asks. Theresa Edith, who is upset hearing her mother's cries, runs over to her and hugs her tightly. Not to upset her daughter, Anna Lee quiets herself and says, "I will be fine Nannette." She reaches for her daughter; places her on her lap. She gently strokes Theresa Edith's long blonde hair to soothe her. Noticing Nannette is concerned, Anna Lee requests, "Thank you! A cup of tea would be lovely for me and some warm milk for Theresa Edith." She squeezes her daughter tightly and politely says, "Zeke, you may leave now." Kindly she adds, "Thank you." She kisses her frightened daughter on the forehead and whispers in her ear to console her, "Sweetheart, all is fine."

Anxious to leave, Zeke follows Nannette into the kitchen only to be shocked by hearing violent pounding on the kitchen door. In fear, Nannette stops in her track. Zeke instinctively reaches for a broom near the stove. He cautiously proceeds to the kitchen side door; peeks out and is disturbed to see and hear Dr. Jeremiah Holden beating on the door screaming, "Let me in now!" Zeke hesitates. Dr. Holden, adds, "My wife is dead, and it is all that bastard Austin's fault!" Zeke orders the frightened Nannette to go into the parlor to comfort Anna Lee and Theresa Edith who are alone in the parlor. "Go to the others in the parlor. I will handle this," he orders. Nannette hesitates, but Zeke vigorously motions for her to go.

Hearing Dr. Holden's persistent banging on the door and his fury, before she leaves Nannette tells Zeke, "I promised to take Theresa Edith ice skating on the pond." She hesitates and adds, "Perhaps I should leave by the front door and take her out of here?" Zeke ignores her. She informs, "Theresa Edith is so easily frightened!" Realizing this is no place for a child to be right now Zeke consents, "Good idea but first ask Mrs. Stevens if it is okay to take Theresa Edith ice skating." Zeke adds, "If Ma'am gives her permission then go!" Restless Nannette leaves immediately. After Nannette gets Mrs. Stevens permission to go ice skating with Theresa Edith she prepares to leave. Theresa Edith calms down when she sees her mother. She is excited to go ice skating. Before Nannette leaves with Theresa Edith, she once more looks into the kitchen. With sincere concern she asks Zeke, who is near the kitchen door keeping the manic veterinarian at bay, "Will you be okay?" With manly confidence Zeke shouts out, "Sure will be! Now go!"

Hearing the commotion in the kitchen Anna Lee wants her young daughter out of immediate danger. She calls out to Nannette and tells her, "Before you go outside put on your warm hat, gloves and coat, be safe and have fun skating." Thankfully they had their winter clothing in the parlor. Nannette and Theresa Edith hurriedly dress for the winter freeze. "Be careful," Anna Lee calls out as Nannette and Theresa Edith go out the front door. Theresa Edith turns and with an angelic strange look on her face calls out, "Momma, I love you." With their winter gear on, and sure Zeke is okay, Nannette leads Theresa Edith out to the barn where the ice skates are hanging. At the barn Theresa Edith and Nannette retrieve their ice skates. Theresa Edith suddenly stops. She walks over to Buck and pets him gently. "Love you too Buck," she whispers. Nannette strokes Splash Dancer the new American Paint Horse recently acquired by Zeke to keep Buck company. The two innocent young females head down to the pond excited to be going ice skating.

Waiting patiently to make certain that the young women folks are safely out of the house, and Anna Lee is calm, Zeke hollers out to Dr. Holden who has settled down,

"What do you want?" "Please let me in," Dr. Holden begs. Standing firmly behind the kitchen door holding onto the broom stick, Zeke lectures, "How dare you come here and scare the women folk in this fine household and slur my boss's good name!" Distressed, Dr. Holden calms down and pleads, "Please, I need help! I am at a loss for what to do." Zeke opens the door slightly. In a firm voice demands, "Act like a man and I will come out and talk to you privately."

The desperate Dr. Holden is ready to pounce on Zeke again. Zeke threatens him, "You will not come here in a rage and upset the lady of the house." He demands, "Calmly tell me what's wrong and then maybe I will help you." The enraged veterinarian cries out, "My wife is dead! I need assistance." Zeke stands there unaffected. Dr. Holden screams, "If only your selfish boss Austin would have let Nannette come and help me with my ailing wife when I begged him, she might be alive today." Zeke is ready to punch him in the mouth when Anna Lee comes into the kitchen where the door is wide opened. She overhears what Dr. Holden said about his wife dying. "Let him in Zeke! The poor man just lost his dear wife." With tears in her eyes Anna Lee walks over to the door and gently guides the enraged Zeke away. With sincere pity, she invites the despondent widower in, "Please come in Dr. Holden. I am truly sorry to hear about the loss of sweet Mrs. Holden." She looks at his trembling body and compassionately comments, "You are freezing cold. Go in by the parlor fire. I will make you tea to warm you."

Anna Lee turns and looks directly at Zeke. With authority orders, "Zeke, show the good doctor into the parlor and seat him by the fire." She glares at Zeke who refuses to move. She insists, "Make him comfortable while I will prepare the tea." Dr. Holden looks out the window and observes Nannette and Theresa Edith walking toward the pond carrying ice skates. He stares at them strangely. Noticing this, it further angers Zeke. With sarcasm Zeke orders Dr. Holden, "You heard the too gracious lady of the house, go sit near the fire." Under his breath he curses, "You belong in the fires of hell."

Deeply upset by hearing the death of her sweet neighbor Rebecca, Anna Lee calls out from the kitchen to Dr. Holden "I beg of you doctor try to find some comfort here. I will be joining you shortly with some soothing tea." She adds, "Zeke, go and get a bottle of brandy to add to our distraught neighbor's tea." Zeke is fuming mad but does as Anna Lee requests. He does not move immediately; he is carefully watching Dr. Holden looking at the window. Both men observe the two young ladies putting on ice skates at the edge of the frozen pond. Zeke and Dr. Holden watch them as they cautiously place their skated feet on the ice.

Anna Lee enters the parlor carefully carrying the hot fresh brewed tea. She also looks out the window and notices the girls outside. "Zeke, did you shovel the snow off the pond so the girls can glide on the ice easily?" She then questions, "Is it solid?" "Yes, I did both; but I wish they hadn't gone out without me there." Dr. Holden chimes in, "I'm sure they will be fine." Zeke grudgingly heads downstairs to retrieve a bottle of brandy. He brings it up and resentfully hands it to Anna Lee.

Pouring the tea and adding the brandy, Anna Lee caringly questions, "I don't mean to upset you but may I inquire as to what happened?" Not responding to her question, Dr. Holden gulps the tea down. To engage him she adds, "I knew your sweet, young wife was very ill but not at death's door?" Dr. Holden cries, "I am also shocked." Wiping his eyes with a fine white linen handkerchief he removes from his black wool waist coat explains, "As you know, my dear Mrs. Stevens, my wife has no family left." Anna Lee reaches over to hold his hand. Zeke rudely interjects, "You left your deceased wife alone on her death bed to come here?" he is itching to punch Dr. Holden. He blurts out, "Where I come from that 's disrespectful." Embarrassed, Anna Lee reprimands, "Zeke, please have reverence for a grieving husband."

Giving Zeke a skeptical grimace Dr. Holden mutters, "I was all alone when it happened. If only I had a helper such as Nannette perhaps she would have lived longer." Sympathetically, Anna Lee inquires, "What can we do for you?" She glances over at the annoyed Zeke, "Perhaps Zeke can contact the proper people to help with this dreadful, mournful chore." Zeke responds immediately, "Sorry Mrs. Anna Lee Stevens but that's not my job." He slaps his knee and adds, "Taking care of you women here, the animals etcetera. that's my sole responsibility." Before she can reply Zeke says emphatically, "As Mr. Austin instructed me!" Anna Lee is taken back. She glances over at Dr. Holden with empathy. She kindly offers, "I will contact Minister Jacob Smiley. Along with the fine compassionate women from his congregation, we will take care of all the necessary arrangements."

Dr. Holden smiles at Anna Lee and staring at Zeke with scorn he pronounces, "You are truly a saint my good lady." Dr. Holden praises, "How lucky your husband is to have you." She shyly smiles when he adds, "I hope he appreciates you." Looking glaringly at Zeke he comments, "And all those fortunate ones around you." Fuming mad Zeke responds, "Mr. Stevens and myself included know what an honorable woman Mrs. Stevens is. We just don't want her associating with the wrong kind, if you know what I mean!" He jolts up to leave and announces, "I don't intend to get involved with you even at the expense of your poor deceased wife." Before Mrs. Stevens or Dr. Holden can comment Zeke blurts out, "As far as I am concerned that sweet fragile lady didn't stand a chance with your type."

Anna Lee is appalled by Zeke's insolent comment, "Zeke, how uncharitable! I will not have such impertinence in my home." She kindly looks over at Dr. Holden and offers, "Since Zeke refuses to assist you, and you are unable to find anyone else, it will be my Christian, neighborly duty and honor to come back with you to properly prepare your angel-of-a wife's body." With a lingering southern accent she reminisces, "I saw my dear mother do it for my lovable grandmother when she passed away a few years back in my home state of Virginia."

Anna Lee rises up. With sincere humility she suggests, "We will go as soon as you finish your brandied tea." Dr. Holden looks over at an enraged Zeke and responds, "How good of you dear woman but you are with child and have your little girl to attend to. I am sure Nannette can assist me." Anna Lee responds, "Yes, of course. I will ask her as soon as Zeke goes out and tells her to come in and prepare herself to go with you." Upset yet feeling powerless, Zeke stands there speechless. Mrs. Stevens assures Dr. Holden, "I will explain to Nannette exactly what to do." Before another word is spoken, Anna Lee, Zeke and Dr. Holden sitting in the parlor are startled and distressed by earth shattering screams coming from the pond, "Help! Help! Help!!!!"

CHAPTER THIRTY-TWO

Hello to Hollywood
Chicago to Los Angeles
January 1956

ELENA AND TESS are enjoying their pithy time in Chicago experiencing an elegant lunch at Marshall Fields Department Store. Also, visiting the famous Art Institute of Chicago. Mother and daughter are in awe viewing the magnificent paintings of their favorite artists the cubist Georges Braque, impressionists Vincent Van Gogh, Georges Seurat and American realist Edward Hopper. Elena purchased a copy of a Braque cubist painting. For some reason, it fascinated her. It was a cultural highlight for both mother and daughter. In the Windy City Chicago, arm-in-arm, Tess and Elena are happily strolling through the bitter-cold, snow-covered streets. This frigid, hustling town, not only of culture but of political and mobster intrigue, cleared mother and daughter's cluttered heads of what they left behind in Jersey City and what they might encounter in Los Angeles. Their limited but special time together in Chicago goes by quickly. Feeling more positive, Tess is ready to depart on the next train taking them to their final destination Los Angeles where Grandma Hollywood is waiting for them.

On the El Capitan Super train, the last leg of their final destination, Tess is determined not to contemplate thoughts of Jersey City. Tess calls home from Chicago. Surprisingly no one answers not even at Ettie and Carlo's house. Since Tess does not receive an answer on either phone, she decides to call again when they arrive at her mother's house in Hollywood. Having mailed a post card to her friend Ginny, Elena is momentarily content. The monstrous revelation learned from the newly acquainted Monsignor James Cooney on the first leg of their journey west is temporarily stored away for now. Both mother and daughter put all unpleasant thoughts aside for the time being.

Tess and Elena's brief enjoyable time in Chicago will forever be a happy and memorable experience.

Independently of Rodney Sheridan, Tess and Elena went sightseeing together. He was at The University of Chicago. One of the exemplary higher education institutions his family generously donates money to. His paternal grandfather insists that his grandson Rodney seriously consider this prestigious institution for his future college education. It is not Rodney's first choice but always wanting to please his grandfather, he agrees to have an interview with the head of the admissions committee while he is in Chicago. This appealing young man would have preferred to spend the few hours in the Windy City with his new friends, Tess and Elena, showing them around this fascinating town. Rodney appreciates and frequents fine dining and the arts. Sharing all of this town's abundant wealth of dining, sights and culture would have given him immense pleasure. While sitting in the waiting room of the Admissions Office at The University of Chicago, reflecting on this, Rodney confidently calls out, "There will be many other times!"

While Tess, Elena and Rodney are sightseeing or attending to personal matters around Chicago, Monsignor James Cooney is back at Notre Dame University in South Bend, Indiana. This pious priest is desperately attempting to unravel and get to the bottom of the mysterious disappearance of his respected colleague and fellow clergyman, Father Arthur Schultz. The new acquaintances, Tess, Elena, and the dignified, reverent Monsignor James Cooney, happened by fate or chance to meet on the train from New York to Chicago.

Unfortunately, these innocents are enmeshed in a bizarre, absurd, and mystifying drama which commenced in El Paso, Texas and Juarez, Mexico. Surprisingly resurfacing in St. Victor's Roman Catholic Church in Jersey City, New Jersey. This baffling state of affairs is bonding these unlikely, unsuspecting people together more than they are currently aware of. Temporarily putting this unknown aside, Tess, Elena and Rodney intend to enjoy their journey to Los Angles on the Super Chief-El Capitan streamline passenger train.

At Notre Dame University, Monsignor James Cooney is ardently and passionately researching and further investigating Father Arthur Schultz's unfathomable disappearance and his so-called strange reappearance in Jersey City, New Jersey. The unwavering priest fervently prays he will find the true Father Arthur Schulz alive or, if necessary, to expose and punish by law a cunning-deceitful imposter. Monsignor James Cooney passionately believes this is his human and divine duty as a religious representative of man and God.

Though Tess and Elena spent a short time in Chicago, it left a permanent and fulfilling mark on mother and daughter. Yet they are anxious to move on. Tess and Elena are safely and comfortably aboard the El Capitan train preparing to journey to their final destination, Los Angeles, California to be with Grandma Elena or, as her namesake Elena coined her, "Grandma Hollywood." The gargantuan train slowly crawls out of Union Station in Chicago but soon will be roaring full throttle ahead to the West Coast. Excited mother and daughter are settled in their reserved space on the train.

Elena is preparing to indulge her thirst for knowledge by reading from the infamous book Sister Margaret Mary lent her. Tess is secretly pondering over her disturbing discussion with Monsignor James Cooney about the questionable Father Arthur Schultz. Rodney is in another area of the train alone feverishly writing on a huge note pad the first phase of his inaugural film he titled, "The Bizarre Mystery of the Missing Priest."

Sitting in her assigned seat in their coach car, Elena pulls the huge book from her carryon and commences to read. Tess noticing how intense her daughter is into the infamous book questions her, "Is that the history book Sister Margaret Mary gave you? The one her family's personal story is in?" Elena raises her head, halfheartedly glances at her mother but does not respond. Not wanting to upset her daughter after having such a fantastic bonding time in Chicago, Tess does not further question Elena. Sadly, it makes her feel alienated and renews her concerns.

The El Capitan is racing along at full capacity. Expecting the first call for dinner will be announced shortly Tess bolts up and heads to the lavatory to refresh herself. She informs Elena, "Sweetheart, I'm going to wash up and put on some fresh makeup. The first call for dinner will be announced any moment now." Elena is so engrossed in the book, she does not respond to her mother. Frustrated, Tess leaves! As soon as she departs, Elena slams the book shut and instantly experiences a sudden anxiety attack. "Oh, no, please god no!" she cries out as she feels herself rising up. *'Absence disembodies-so does Death, Hiding individuals from the Earth, Superstitions helps, as well as love. . .'* ~ Emily Dickinson

In a special private car, at the farther end of the train, Rodney is deeply engrossed writing the first scene for his introductory movie script. He decides to change the title to, "Clergy: Risen from the Dead." This free-spirited, inspired young man frantically plans on finishing it before they reach Los Angeles. Along the journey, he intends to entice Elena to read it. Rodney's active imagination is vivid and at times bizarre.

Unfortunately and naively, he does not heed Monsignor James Cooney's warnings about keeping it a secret. This is not a primary concern for this budding yet immature hopeful artist. He is frivolous yet not deliberately evil. The wicked gossip about the missing priest on the train between Tess, Elena, Monsignor James Cooney, and Rodney is not taken seriously by this adolescent. He secretly justifies his writing about it by convincing himself that what he heard has no real validity. To him it is only a mere coincidence. Rodney has persuaded himself of this so he can release himself of any wrong doing. His motive is only to create his initial 'triumphant film script.' "I will be famous and the world will finally notice me," he cries out as he completes the first act.

Stately in an impeccable black suit and tie and with great pose, walking through the train car, a porter rings the bell announcing 'first call for dinner' on the elegant El Capitan. He arrives at Tess and Elena's train car. Looking refreshed and pretty, Tess returns from the lavatory. She is more than ready to eat a hearty meal. Tess goes to Elena's seat. She becomes extremely alarmed when she sees her daughter's head fallen on her lap with the huge opened book sprawled over her feet. "Elena," she cries out lifting her daughter's slackened head, "What's wrong?" With her motionless daughter in Tess's quivering arms, Elena's eyes roll back into her head. Tess screams. The porter, who is announcing dinner, quickly hands the bell over to a puzzled passenger and rushes over to assist with the unconscious Elena. "What's wrong Madam?" he inquires. "She needs water and bring something cool to wipe her brow," Tess franticly instructs him. The anxious but dutiful porter runs to obtain both. Soon after he arrives with the water and moist washcloth. Semi awake now, Elena sips the water as Tess wipes her sweaty forehead with the cool, moist washcloth. Tess thanks the helpful porter and assures him she will take care of her daughter. Before he leaves he offers, "Please Madam if you need anything at all, let me know." She nods. He adds, "We have a doctor on board if need be." "Thank you, but she will be fine," Tess reassures the kind porter.

Alert now, Elena stares at her worried-to-death mother. In a low, weak voice she pleads, "Mom, please don't make a fuss. I'm better." Tess kisses her daughter. Elena attempts to make her mother feel better. She explains, "I had a bad dream." Relieved, Tess smiles at the other concerned passengers and calls out, "She is fine! She just needs to eat." As the other alarmed passengers go back to their seats feeling pleased that the young girl is okay now, Elena, in despair, under her breath sighs, "I hope I am not too late." With fear she soberly calls out, "She must not . . .!" "What?" In a panic Tess questions her mournful daughter, "Did you say die?" "No, Mother," Elena Rose consoles Tess, "I did not!" To divert the situation, Elena cautiously rises up, grabs her mother's hand and quickly calls out, "Let's go eat. I am starving."

CHAPTER THIRTY-THREE

Grief is an Expression of Love
Walpole, New Hampshire
January 1867
*Moral Suffering Sicken of the soul is worse
than bodily pain.* ~ St. Augustine

HEARING THE HEART-WRENCHING, blood curdling screams coming from the frozen pond, Zeke dashes out the front door while calling for Dr. Holden to come and assist him. Frightened half to death, Anna Lee is crying out hysterically, "What is going on?" Falling to her knees she pleads, "My God, please don't let it be." Down at the pond Nannette is still screaming, "Help, help please somebody!" while desperately holding onto the outstretched tiny, frozen hand of Theresa Edith to no avail. The lower extremities of her petite body are submerging further down into the frigid water.

Bewildered Zeke gallops down the hill to the pond followed by the frantic Dr. Holden. When they reach the spot, out-of-control Nannette cries out, "Theresa Edith fell through the hole in the cracked ice into the freezing water." In agony she apologies, "I tried to hold on to her. I couldn't hold on any longer!" Like a howling deranged banshee Nannette screams out, "She disappeared!" In a flash, Zeke further cracks open the hole in the ice where Theresa Edith is, praying to have a better advantage to reach further down to raise her up. He desperately reaches down to grab onto the submerged Theresa Edith's frigid hand. With all his might Zeke finally pulls her up. Dr. Holden is comforting the bewildered and insanely hysterical Nannette. "Get over here now!" Zeke screams to Dr. Holden, "I need your help!"

Slipping on the ice, the panicked veterinarian rushes over. When he gets there both shocked men try to aid and save the blue, frozen little angel as she lays motionless on the solid ice area. Taking off Theresa Edith's soaking wet jacket, Zeke tears off his heavy wool shirt and wraps the almost lifeless body of Theresa Edith desperately attempting to warm her frozen-stiff body. Dr. Holden instinctively bends over, turns her and bangs on her fragile back attempting to have her vomit out the water trapped in her weak compromised lungs. Dr. Holden continues to bang on Theresa Edith's fragile back as Zeke shouts for Nannette to go and comfort Mrs. Stevens.

Standing like a frozen statue, Nannette hesitates until Zeke screams, "Do as I say. Now!" His booming voice shocks her into action. Nannette runs with great difficulty toward the house in the snow with her ice skates still on. Zeke is hovering over Theresa Edith trying to release the water out of her lungs. She is still motionless. Hopelessly, Dr. Holden stands there feeling powerless. Zeke holds up Theresa Edith's head cradling her in his arms while pleading into her ear, "Please stay with me little angel."

Standing like a stone statue by the window overlooking the frozen pond, the frantic mother and mother-to-be, Anna Lee, is in a state of panic and disbelief. The tormented Nannette runs to her. The two women embrace while an avalanche of tears pour down their bewildered faces. Stunned herself, Nannette has no words to comfort this out of her mind mother. Anna Lee screams out, "What's happening?" She further questions, "Where is my precious baby girl?"

Trembling, Nannette holds Anna Lee tightly in her arms. With a pathetic angst voice, she answers, "I don't know what happened?" Under her labored breath Nannette recalls, "We were happily skating near the edge of the pond. I was holding onto her hand tightly." This frightened young woman sighs and then shouts, "Something attracted Theresa Edith." In a state of disbelief Nannette continues, "Theresa Edith let go of my hand and quickly skated away from me." "What?" the bereft mother sobs. "In a flash she was in the middle of the pond." Nannette screams, "It cracked open!" Losing all control she cries out in excruciating pain, "She fell in!" Pounding Nannette's chest screaming Anna Lee cries out, "How could you let her go?" In defense, the flustered frightened Nannette sobs, "I immediately skated over to her but I couldn't pull her out." "Dear God! Please don't tell me. . ." the frantic mother hysterically screams.

In a somber tone Nannette moans under her breath, "She fell in and went under." Weak and sobbing, Nannette falls to her knees. At that moment, the helpless mother Anna Lee collapses down to the floor clutching her swollen stomach. An earth-shattering scream comes from her, "Help me!" In terror Nannette turns, looks at Anna Lee as water, mixed with traces of blood flows from under her long skirt. Frantically, Nannette reaches over to help her but Anna Lee screams out, "Leave me be! Go and find out how my precious little girl is." In extreme, unbearable agony this distressed mother begs and pleads, "She must not die!"

Zeke is frantically running from the pond up the hill toward the main house carrying the listless body of Theresa Edith followed by the deeply shaken Dr. Holden. It is a surreal and unfathomed moment in time. Nannette runs out of the house screaming out to the two stunned men, "Come quickly there is something terribly wrong with Mrs. Stevens!" She shouts, "She fainted and is bleeding." Hearing this Dr. Holden runs ahead of Zeke who is holding onto Theresa Edith for dear life. The perplexed veterinarian rushes toward the house to the frantic Nannette. Zeke is following in full force with listless Theresa Edith in his arms.

While poor, pathetic Anna Lee is curled in a fetal position on the floor clinging to her stomach, Zeke is fretfully holding onto the listless body of Theresa Edith. Meanwhile, on her hands and knees shaken, the guilt-ridden Nannette is crying uncontrollably. The perplexed, newly widowed Dr. Holden is preparing to administer to the pregnant Anna Lee; the gloomy house is morbidly still.

To dispel the eerie mood, prayers are heard coming from Zeke, "You up There, please don't let this innocent child die." Nannette is sulking and moaning, "Please God, I ask for very little, I beg of YOU - save little Theresa Edith." Dr. Holden is shouting, "This cannot be, my dear wife and now this innocent child!" The heavily distressed winter clouds above are covering over the weakening winter sun. Out of nowhere, darkness soon spreads over the entire property and structures. Nannette looks up out the panoramic window. She is silenced when she sees a miraculous bright light peering through the gloomy ink-dark clouds. Staring at the bright light she pleadingly begs, "Whoever is up there, please answer our prayers."

Dr. Jeremiah Holden, unable to mourn his own wife, is now desperately trying to save the life of a young, pregnant mother and her unborn child. Zeke is doing everything in his humanly power to save Austin and Anna Lee's precious, innocent little girl's life. Jeremiah Holden hovers over the weakened Anna Lee and orders, "Hold on Mrs. Stevens. Your soon-to-be-born child is coming now." He tries to comfort her and himself, "I have delivered many calves and foals but never a baby before you." He wipes his profusely sweating brow and promises, "I will do my very best to deliver this soon-to-be born babe." Crushed Anna Lee weakly stares up at him and pleads, "Leave me. Save my Theresa Edith."

Mesmerized by the glorious golden light Nannette is outside on her knees staring at the miraculous sky praying in French. Realizing the baby is ready to come, in a panic Dr. Holden cries out to Nannette, "Nannette come in here now! I need boiling water, clean cloths, and brandy immediately!" Nannette pulls off her ice skates and in her stocking feet runs like a banshee into the house while buckets of tears stream out of her red swollen eyes. She is praying for a miracle. Inside the house the petrified Zeke is painfully hovering over the motionless, beautiful, lethargic Theresa Edith. He throws his trembling body over her fragile frame and like the haunting sound of a howling wolf cries out, "Hold on little Miss Stevens!" He kisses her cold, clay-white face and screams out, "No, no, no! You must not go!"

Outside, the rolling black clouds are parting showcasing the brightest beam of light piercing through the heavens. It streams all over Austin Stevens New England ancestral property. The mystifying light illuminates the earth and sky beyond any one's imagination. Sounding like St. Gabriel blowing his horn, a fierce wind is blasting while a choir of winter birds sing to console the mourning heavenly angels. Like honor guards saluting a lost hero or soul, the mammoth ancient trees surrounding the naked winter landscape around the pond stand solemnly in a military manner. A monstrous, immense and magnificent golden hawk majestically flies over the frozen pond and regally lingers over the cracked hole in the middle of the ice pond where the innocent, princess angel Theresa Edith Stevens took her final, sweet breath. With blinding brightness, the celestial heaven's open up. A melodious, ethereal resonance is echoing, *"I have enjoyed the happiness of the world; I have lived and loved."* ~ Johann von Schiller

CHAPTER THIRTY-FOUR

What we have once enjoyed we can never lose. . . ~ Helen Keller
Jersey City, New Jersey
January 1956

MIKE SLIDES OUT the front seat of the long-black, funeral car which just pulled up at 391 Armstrong Avenue. It is a dreary, frigid-late January afternoon. He walks around to the other side of the long black sedan and opens the back door where Ettie, Rosaria and Blaise are seated. "Ettie, give me your hand," Mike instructs his sister. She reaches for her brother's hand. He cautions his shaken, weary sister, "Be very careful; it's extremely icy." Mike holds his heartbreaking sister's arm tightly. Ettie is dressed in widow weeds; mourning frocks. She is dressed in black from head to toe. While Mike gently assists his bereaved sister out, from the other side of the limousine, Blaise helps his sister Rosaria out. All are suitably dress in bereavement black as they slowly saunter up the brick stoop to go inside Ettie's first floor abode.

Seeing his bereaved but brave sister safely in her house with her children, Mike heads back to talk with the funeral car driver, Rocco. Thanking him, he hands the driver an envelope with cash which he pulls out of the inside pocket of his long black formal coat. Rocco immediately puts the envelope away in his pants pocket. Mike asks him to tell his cousin Nick Scat, Rocco's boss, that he will contact him first thing in the morning to thank him formally for the fine job he did with the funeral and burial services for his brother-in-law Carlo. Rocco nods affirmatively and rolls up the car window as he leaves. As the long black stretch limousine slowly goes down the street and turns the corner, Mike looks around, wipes his sweating brow with his black leathered gloves and heads into the house where the others are waiting.

When Mike enters Ettie's house he immediately smells the familiar fresh coffee brewing. He is not surprised to hear his sister running around the kitchen getting her infamous cookies. Still wearing her black hat with face veil, Blaise hollers at his mother, "We just finished a huge meal at the repose Mom. We can't possibly eat anymore!" In frustration he runs over to his mother ordering, "Take off the hat! It gives me the creeps and forget the damn cookies!" While removing the hat and veil, Ettie ignores her son. She pushes him aside and heads into the pantry to get the cookies. With a choked voice she hollers back, "You never know who might come by." Ettie shares, "I invited Monsignor Kelly to stop by." With a quivering voice she says, "The mass for my Carlo he officiated was breathtaking." Rosaria agrees, "His homily with such touching words about Dad was truly inspiring and charitable." Nodding, Blaise agrees; although he is frustrated with his mother entertaining as if it were a birthday party. "I agree about the mass and burial services that Father Kelly performed. But, did you have to invite him over here?" Sarcastically, Blaise says, "For goodness sake Ettie this is not a celebration."

Annoyed, Rosaria glares at Blaise. She snaps, "Leave her be, little brother!" She explains, "Mom needs to do this to keep her mind off of things." He sneers at his bossy older sister. She defends, "This is what makes Mom feel as if nothing has happened." Exhausted, Blaise plops down on a kitchen chair, takes off his blue-black jacket, and black and white checkered tie. Rosaria loosens the leather belt from her stately black wool dress. She proceeds to get the coffee cups from the kitchen cabinet. Mike, not wanting to get involved with a sister/brother confrontation, calmly removes his jet-black suit jacket, solid black tie and unfastens the top buttons from his starched white shirt. He and Blaise are wearing black mourning arm bands out of respect for Carlo. The arm band is a symbolic male show-of-respect to the deceased. Finally, there is total silence in Ettie's kitchen. Exhaustion and sorrow make them all completely at a loss for words.

After a brief silence, in military fashion, Blaise stands tall; he marches right up to Mike. In a business-like tone, inquires, "Uncle Mike, what do we owe for the funeral and burial expenses?" Mike ignores him. Blaise persists, "When I asked Nick Scat about the bill he said it was all taken care of." The proud nephew stares straight into his Uncle Mike's dark piercing eyes and firmly insists, "My Dad would never want anyone but us to pay for his burial." Rosaria looks at her brother affirming, "I rarely agree with my little brother but this time Uncle Mike, Blaise is right." Mike looks at both of them and responds, "No need to concern yourself with the cost of the funeral and burial. Your mother's cousin Nick Scat did it gratis." He pulls off his tie and adds, "Nick Scat's father and your grandfather were brothers." He looks straight at his niece and nephew proclaiming, "Family never takes money from family; it is disrespectful."

"But . . ." Blaise cries out. Before he finishes, Mike interjects, "Never question the family!" As Blaise protests, Mike puts up his hand, "Finito. It's done and that's that!" He pats his nephew's strong shoulder muttering, "I don't want to hear another word." Rosaria adds, "But Uncle Mike, my Dad . . ." "Did you hear me Rosaria? It's taken care of!" Mike repeats loudly, "Finito!" He looks over at his niece and nephew professing, "We are family. We take care of one another." Emphasizing, "It would be insulting to my cousin if I offered him money." Brother and sister glance at one another. Noticing their Uncle Mike's stern grin, in unison they acquiesce, "Finito!"

Ettie walks in with a plate of cookies. Mike glares sternly over at Rosaria and Blaise putting his finger to his lip symbol of mum's the word. "What's going on in here?" Ettie inquires. "I hear babbling. A disagreement?" Rosaria rushes over to her mother. She puts her arms around Ettie and reassures her, "Mom, everything is fine. Let me get you a nice cup of coffee." Mike shouts, "It smells good; I'll have one too." Before Rosaria can retrieve the coffee pot, the phone rings. She reaches over to answer it. "Hello! Oh, hi Mrs. Rapp! So nice to hear your voice." There is a pause. Rosaria responds, "Yes, Mike is here. I'll put him right on." Mike immediately grabs the phone out of Rosaria's hands. "Hi Mom! How are Tess and Elena? Did they arrive safely? Let me talk to my wife now!" Mike asks. He listens to his mother-in-law then yells out, "What? What do you mean the train was delayed?" There is silence as Mike continues to listen to his mother-in-law's response. "Yeah, yeah, I understand but I am not happy about any of this," he moans into the receiver. "I know you don't want to get involved but my sister Ettie's husband Carlo died the day Tess and my Elena left," Mike informs his mother-in-law. Everyone in the kitchen is quiet while Mike is on the phone. "Thank you. I will let my sister and her children know," they hear Mike say to Tess's mother.

Ettie, Rosaria, and Blaise are listening attentively. Losing his cool, Mike shouts into the receiver, "You tell my wife to call me as soon as she arrives and that it's an emergency!" Ettie tries to grab the phone from Mike to calm him down. He moves his sister away shouting into the receiver, "You hear me Mom? I'm damn pissed off Tess left and took Elena!" Screaming into the receiver, Mike reiterates, "I demand she get in touch with me sooner rather than later!" Before his mother-in-law can respond, Mike slams down the receiver knocking the phone down. In a rage, this frustrated man excuses himself. Mike runs out the front door leaving Ettie, Rosaria, and Blaise standing there perplexed. Rosaria and Blaise look at their mother for answers. Ettie does not say a word; she proceeds to pour coffee into the cups.

Running down the porch steps, Mike knocks into Robbie, Blaise's good friend, as he is walking up the steps carrying a box in his hands. The baffled Robbie looks back at Mike as he keeps running down the steps. Mike hollers after Robbie, "Let yourself in; my sister just made coffee." Puzzled, Robbie calls after Mike, "Thanks." Hearing noise outside, Rosaria goes to the front door, peers out and sees Robbie standing there holding a cake box.

Rosaria opens the door. Robbie hands Rosaria the box apologizing, "Hope I am not intruding. My Mom wanted me to drop off this cake." Rosaria takes the cake. "My Mom made it for your family," Robbie says. Rosaria does not respond she is gazing down the street at her uncle hurrying away. To get Rosaria's attention, Robbie coughs loudly and reports, "My Mom asked me to tell you how sorry she is that she was too ill to come to your father's mass and funeral services." Tears welling in her eyes, Rosaria is not responding. In a low voice Robbie adds, "My mother sends her deepest sympathies to all, as do I."

In deep thought, Rosaria holding the cake Robbie brought, is looking down the street at her Uncle Mike running toward Walsh's Tavern. Freezing and realizing that Rosaria is not aware of him standing there, Robbie coughs again to gain her attention. Finally hearing his cough,

Rosaria realizes Robbie is still standing there. Halfheartedly she says, "Come on in." Nervous, Robbie questions, "Do you think it is okay with your Mom?" Finally coming to her senses, Rosaria grabs his arm and apologizes, "Please forgive me. It has been a very trying day on so many levels." She leads Robbie into the warm house. As the door to Ettie's house closes behind Rosaria and Robbie, the door to Walsh's Tavern opens. Furious, Mike enters. *When one door closes another door opens???*

CHAPTER THIRTY-FIVE

In Los Angeles, Everyone is a Star. ~ Denzel Washington
California
January 1956

THE ILLUSTRIOUS IRON horse, El Capitan Train, is slowing down its incredible speed as Tess and Elena are finishing up their last breakfast in the dining car with their newly acquired friend Rodney. This confident and sophisticated young man wipes his firm mouth with the once fine white, now soiled, linen napkin. He properly folds it, placing it next to his empty plate where shortly before flaky- sweet pancakes, covered with real maple syrup and spicy thick sausages enhanced it. Pushing his chair back, Rodney hoists himself up. Standing tall and stately he cheerfully announces, "Well lovely ladies looks like we are ready to disembark from our fascinating rail journey across the good old USA." Bowing he adds, "Soon to commence in the thrilling City of Angels." With pomp and circumstance he adds, "And the fantasy of unashamedly glamorous Hollywood." With a curt smirk on her face, Elena glares at him. With sarcasm she asks, "Why do you always have to be so dramatic and pompous?" Under her breath she comments, "You remind me of someone in my family."

Bemused, Rodney attempts to defend himself when Tess, staring at her daughter with daggers in her eyes, reprimands her moody daughter, "Elena, how rude! You owe Rodney an apology." Adding more fuel to fiery Tess's fury, defiantly Elena ignores her mother. "Elena this fine young man has been nothing but a gentleman; a knowledgeable traveling companion and hopefully, a future friend to us in California," Tess lectures. In a huff Elena bolts out of her seat, almost knocking her chair over. She throws her crumpled napkin over her half-finished poached eggs. Sarcastically

Elena blurts out, "Sorry!" Rodney reaches to clutch her hand. He defends, "No need to apologize Elena." Looking over at frustrated Tess, Rodney comments, "I should thank both of you for befriending me on this very enlightening journey."

The aggravated teenager Elena pulls her hand away from Rodney. Dismayed, Tess glares at her daughter as she storms out echoing Rodney, "Enlightening!" Frustrated Tess is deeply puzzled over her daughter. She thought things were getting so much better for Elena. Rodney, attempting to hide his wounded feelings and to comfort Tess, exclaims, "Clearly she is exhausted." Rodney further suggests, "With all that has evolved these last few days, I can certainly appreciate Elena's erratic mood." Mortified, Tess says, "There are no excuses for her rude behavior!" She offers her apologies, "Rodney, I am extremely sorry over the ill manners of my daughter." Again, Rodney insists, "It's perfectly understandable!" Smiling he calls out, "Enlightening!"

Embarrassed, Tess explains, "Since last night when I heard Elena talking in her sleep she has not been herself." Pondering Tess adds, "Elena seems to be elsewhere." "Certainly understandable," Rodney tries to soften things. "Ever since we heard that story about the missing priest and perhaps the fraudulent one in your church parish it is no wonder she is upset," he defends Elena. Tess reaches over and hugs Rodney and whispers, "I believe you are right." Not ever remembering being hugged Rodney is greatly pleased. Tess praises him, "Young man you are so righteous and understanding." Taking hold of Rodney's smooth, white delicate hands Tess reinforces, "Remember, Monsignor James Cooney does not want us to mention this!" With compassion, Tess says, "We are so fortunate our paths have crossed." "Must be fate," Rodney whispers. Tess comments, "Your parents must be so proud of you." Rodney does not respond. With a forlorn look on his face he suggests, "We should leave." Tess and Rodney go their separate ways ready to engage in sunny, funny Los Angeles. *Grandma Hollywood awaits.*

As the El Capitan slows down to turtle speed, restless Tess and Elena are preparing to disembark. Neither one acknowledges what happened previously in the dining car. Both mother and daughter are anxious to get off the train and greet Tess's mother, Elena's Grandma Hollywood. Arriving at the door where they will disembark, Elena searches around to see if Rodney is anywhere. He is nowhere to be found. The train is now stationary. The porter slides the door open, thanks them for coming, and announces, "Hope you had a pleasant trip. Please come again." Tess hands him an envelope in gratitude for his courteous service. The worthy porter thanks her profusely. Tess and Elena carefully step down off the train onto the station platform. *Hopefully into a new pleasant adventure.*

Safely and securely on the platform both mother and daughter search around for familiar faces. Not seeing her mother, Tess tells Elena, "I am going to retrieve our luggage. You keep a sharp eye out for your grandmother, if not. . ." Pointing to an empty bench she instructs, "Go over and sit on the bench and wait for me." Seeing that Elena is not paying any attention she shouts, "Do you hear me?" Startling other passengers who are rushing around. Elena pays no mind to her mother. In a daze, she is completely ignoring her mother, holding tightly onto her large book. Finally, Elena slowly walks to the available bench. Relieved seeing her daughter at the bench, Tess calls out, "If you happen to see Grandma please tell her to wait here with you." Elena nods half-heartedly. Worried her daughter will not heed her Tess stresses, "Don't move Elena. If you see Rodney tell him we will call him in a few days." This comment further annoys Elena. She stamps her foot and shouts back, "You tell him!"

Speed walking ahead of a porter who is pulling a lorry stacked high with Louis Vuitton luggage, Rodney is frantically scanning the station. He hears the shouts of a familiar voice and immediately swivels around. Spotting Elena sitting on a bench looking upset and preoccupied, he calls out, "Stop!" to the person who is pulling his luggage. Excited, Rodney hurries over to Elena shouting, "I finally found you!" He plops down next to her and bursts out, "I looked all over for you and your Mom on the platform but to no avail." Elena stares at Rodney barely acknowledging his presence. Not to be rude she responds, "Mom was in a hurry to get off the train so we can make sure my grandmother came to pick us up." Searching around Rodney inquires, "Where is your mother now?" Just then they hear Tess calling, "Elena, I got our luggage." Pointing she adds, "It's with a porter." She motions for her to follow her. Tess orders, "Hurry and follow me. Grandmother is waiting in the front of the station with a driver." Anxious to connect with her mother, Tess does not notice Rodney sitting next to Elena who has his back to her.

Observing closer at the bench, Tess recognizes who is sitting with Elena. She hustles over, "Oh, my goodness, Rodney, so glad we connected." Rodney jumps up and clutches Tess's hand. Tess holds on tightly to his pulsing hands. With a huge smile Rodney suggestively comments, "Why I would have been terribly upset if I didn't say goodbye for now to my two favorite-gorgeous, Jersey women." Smiling broadly Tess politely insists, "I'd love to chat dear Rodney but Elena and I must hurry." Motioning for Elena to get up she explains, "My mother and the driver are patiently waiting for us." He nods in agreement. Tess comments, "Rodney, I'm so happy we shared contact information." Running to the exit Tess turns promising, "In a few days we'll make definite arrangements to meet." Annoyed, Elena, cries out, "Mom, please. . ."

Beaming ear to ear, Rodney shouts out emphatically, "Absolutely! I will contact you in a day or two. I am eager to show you around the fabulous City of Angels where everyone is a star." Looking directly at Elena Rodney winks; teasingly remarks, "We might even find a devil or two for the fun of it." Sulking, under her breath, Elena murmurs, "I think we already found a devil among us." Speed walking, Tess and Elena, with the tolerant porter heatedly following, head toward the exit where Grandma Hollywood is patiently standing next to a pink Cadillac convertible with a dramatic looking, handsome young male alongside her.

CHAPTER THIRTY-SIX

The Beauty and Mystery of Life and Death
Walpole, New Hampshire
February 1858

DRESSED ALL IN black in her mourning weeds, Anna Lee is sitting in her rocker in the parlor. She is holding on tightly to her month-old baby boy, Austin Hamish. With her petite foot Anna Lee gently rocks the new wooden baby cradle back and forth where beautiful little infant Rachel Melanie is sleeping soundly. As much as Anna Lee adores and loves her recently born twins, her heart is permanently shattered over the tragic death of her dearest, sweetheart daughter Theresa Edith. Life will never be the same for her. The devastating loss overshadows the joy of giving birth to twins - a healthy boy and girl. Her nurturing, motherly instinct and her spiritual upbringing gives Anna Lee the will and strength to carry on for these two innocent babies and her equally devastated husband.

Regrettably, her husband Austin, who recently received the horrific news of the tragic death of his beloved daughter Theresa Edith, was still in Australia on business when he got word of this shocking, unfathomable tragic news. It makes the bliss of becoming a father of two hearty, beautiful babies pale. The guilt of not being there to protect and save his first-born beloved daughter Theresa Edith is overwhelming and is permanently life altering for this once confident, proud, husband, father, and Civil War survivor.

Austin desperately wanted a son to carry on the Stevens illustrious name and to someday inherit and run his magnificent estate. This dream is now shattered and clouded over with unimaginable pain from the unbearable loss of Theresa Edith. He is filled with excoriating pain and endless guilt. To make it more insufferable, to think the man he questioned, Dr. Jeremiah Holden, was present for the unspeakable accident and birth of his innocent twins. For Austin it is agonizing to imagine that he will be obliged to thank this unsavory man for saving his wife's life and delivering their newborn twins. To add to this, Austin's complexity over Zeke's inability to avoid this unthinkable disaster is unpalatable and dreadfully calamitous. Nannette, the young girl he championed, is the one person who truly knows what happened and how it happened. To comprehend that he engaged this young unknown woman to care for his precious Theresa Edith is unbelievable.

This devoted husband and father entrusted Zeke to take care and watch over his fragile pregnant wife and vulnerable young daughter. It is implausible for Austin to accept how this trusted person, who he respected and grew to love, was unable to save his defenseless daughter; henceforth, to spare his grieving wife from this unbearable loss. For Austin this is beyond understanding and exceedingly agonizing. Visibly the bereaved father Austin, is filled with uncontrollable rage along with debilitating guilt.

To add to this insufferable wound, Austin confidently believed that the sweet, capable Nannette would be the perfect companion for his wife and a reliable nanny for his young daughter. It is beyond comprehension for him to grasp that she was the person with his helpless daughter Theresa Edith at the time of this fatal catastrophe. Austin questions over and over again, "Why did she not caution my daughter not to go off on the ice alone and where was Zeke?" These questions haunt him. How it occurred and why it occurred are the unanswerable questions that will stay with him forever.

To add insult to injury, Austin is enraged to think that Nannette is now living in the house with the newly widowed Dr. Jeremiah Holden as his housekeeper and perhaps more, he assumes. He questions, "How did Zeke, who distrusted this man, allow his ward to go and live with him?" Even the birth of his twins, and finally having, a healthy son, an heir, does not comfort him. Too many unanswered questions agonize and torture this once confident, in control husband, father, boss, military, and well-respected New England gentleman.

After the tragic loss of the much loved, young Theresa Edith and the premature birth of the twins, Anna Lee's zealot religious mother Sarah Campbell traveled from Virginia to New Hampshire to stay with her grieving daughter and to assist in the care of the newborn twins. Thankfully, the twin babies are doing well and growing stronger each day. Understandably, yet unfortunately, Anna Lee is still not faring well both physically and emotionally. When Austin finally returns from Australia his wife rallies somewhat; therefore, Anna Lee's mother felt it was time to return to her elderly, ailing husband and allow her daughter, her husband, and the twin babies to settle into a new life.

Anna Lee and Austin are trying desperately to create some semblance of a family life together with their new babies without their beloved deceased daughter. Sitting alone with the twins, Anna Lee calls out to Austin, "Dear, please come and help me with the babies." He does not answer. Distraught, Austin is heading to the barn to have a confrontation with Zeke. He temporarily put it aside for the sake of his wife and visiting mother-in-law. Anna Lee calls out loudly but still no response. She gently places her sleeping son, Austin Hamish in the second new cradle next to his slumbering sister the delicate, Rachel Melanie. Rachel Melanie is sleeping in the original cradle that Zeke made for Theresa Edith when she was born. Anna Lee rises. Comfortable knowing the twins are asleep and safe, she quietly heads to the kitchen.

In the kitchen Anna Lee peeks out through the door window observing her husband heading to the barn in a huff. Knowing things have been bitter between him and Zeke, her heart pounds loudly fearing that he and Zeke will get into an altercation. This is not only due to the tragic death of their daughter but also the fact that Zeke is now defending Dr. Holden. To add to his anger is the fact that Zeke permitted Nannette to go and live with 'that scoundrel'. Actually, Anna Lee is no longer at odds with Zeke or Dr. Holden. She believes they both did their best under the dreadful circumstances. This gentle southern lady developed a soft spot for Dr. Holden since he lost his young wife and delivered her twins safely all on the same day. Whenever Anna Lee sees Nannette it painfully reminds her of her deceased daughter Theresa Edith therefore she is relieved she is no longer living with them. Austin has his own reasons and issues regarding this matter. He is determined to fire Zeke and send him on his way. If it weren't for his wife pleading with him to keep and forgive Zeke, he would be gone by now. *This obstinate, angry man will not let it go easily.*

With her forgiving Christian heart Anna Lee comes to the realization that God had a special plan for her 'angel of a daughter.' She is determined to concentrate on her twins, Rachel Melanie and Austin Hamish and to restore her shaky marriage. Still gazing out the window, this spiritual and compassionate woman whispers her pious mother's biblical words of wisdom, 'The Lord Taketh and the Lord Giveth.'" Even though her heart is torn she prays her husband will forgive and thereby heal his broken heart. She prays, "If Austin will accept these words of comfort and acceptance, then hopefully he can move on to a place of forgiveness and love."

CHAPTER THIRTY-SEVEN

Guys and Dolls
Los Angeles, California
Early January 1956

TESS RUNS OVER to her mother who is standing next to the pink Cadillac convertible in a striking white pant suit, with a large straw sunhat with pink flowers around the brim. She is wearing sparkling silver high heel sandals and has on large round pink sunglasses framing her youthful looking, wrinkle-free, powered white skin. Grandma Hollywood's full lips are perfectly shaped in a bright pink shade, her favorite color, *Pink Lady*. Tess and her mother embrace. Elena stands back. She has her eye fixed on the young man standing near the impressive car. He is dressed in black tight pants, a red and black shirt opened up almost to his navel and a thick gold chain with a gold shaped horn hanging from it. He is wearing black aviator sunglasses and has a head full of black curly hair which falls below his ears. Clearly, he is full of himself.

Grandma Hollywood pushes her daughter Tess away and in a husky voice orders, "Enough hugging and kissing; you will wrinkle my new suit and mess my makeup." She looks over at Elena and asks, "Is that my name-sake granddaughter Elena?" No response from Elena. Tess calls over to her daughter, "Go over to your grandmother and give her a hug." Elena walks slowly over to her grandmother who has her tanned arms opened wide towards her. With her pink polished fingernails which are covered with numerous gem stoned mammoth rings Grandma Hollywood reaches out to her. Hesitantly Elena walks up to her grandmother and stands there. She is afraid to hug her or kiss her Grandma Hollywood least she soil her fancy suit and smear her heavily applied makeup. Grandma Hollywood takes hold of her granddaughter and gives her a hug and a tiny peck on both

Elena's cheek. She then moves back looks her granddaughter up and down and comments, "Why you are a chubby little cherub." She pinches Elena's blushing check and adds, "Darling, you must lose those extra pounds, and you definitely need a new hairdo." Elena turns back and looks angrily at her mother. "Mom," Annoyed Tess shouts to her mother, "We've been on a long trip. We are tired…let's go."

Grandma Hollywood responds, "Fine, but first I want you to meet Mateo, my driver and assistant. Mateo saunters over, puts out his well-tanned hand to Tess. Tess refuses and says, "Hi! Can we go now?" He walks over to Elena and takes the book she is carrying. "Here, pretty young thing, let me put that in the car with the other bags." He winks at her as he saunters back to the car. Tess can't believe what she sees. Elena doesn't even let her mother hold the infamous book and here she gives it over so freely to Mateo. Loudly Tess says, "This is going to be one interesting time." Grandma Hollywood is already seated in the back of the car. Tess goes over and let's herself in. Mateo takes Elena's hand and tells her to sit up front with him. Elena feels she is in another world. She has temporarily forgotten all about Jersey City, the mystery of the priest, and her friend Ginny and the horrible dream she had on the train. She gets in the car and whispers, "Only wish my Dad was here."

"Ready to take off Bella Signorinas," Mateo shouts. As if in a drag race or the famous Monte Carlo Grand Prix, sexy Mateo slams his Ferragamo sandaled foot down on the gas pedal and takes off. He races out onto the Los Angeles Thruway. Grandma Hollywood holds onto her huge hat laughing, "Mateo, you are showing off for my granddaughter." Tess asks her mother, "I thought Uncle Albert would be with you to pick us up." Grandma Hollywood immediately responds, "Sorry dear, my brother Albert, your only uncle, had to head up to Fresno, California on family business." She smiles boasting, "Your Uncle Albert is the one who introduced me to Mateo." Tess is disappointed about the absence of her Uncle Albert and extremely upset about this pompous Mateo's questionable relationship with her mother.

With a serious look on her face, Grandma Hollywood turns toward her daughter Tess. In a hush voice she informs, "Tess, your husband Mike called me yesterday. He insists that you call him the minute you get to my house." Tess ignores her mother's comment. "He seemed very upset and to be honest, furious at you," she mouths to Tess. Because the convertible is going full speed it is almost impossible to talk or hear one another. Grandma Hollywood, Tess, Elena, and Mateo sit listening to Frank Sinatra song on the radio. Carefree, Mateo is flinging his arms out the car singly loudly along with Old Blue Eyes, *"I've got the World on a String Sittin'on a Rainbow."* Tess whispers to herself, "A short while ago Elena was pouting and seemed far away." Seeing the smile on her daughter's face she murmurs, "Look at her now; singing a Frank Sinatra song and having her first real crush on an Italian gigolo." Tess's mother hears this; laughing she comments, "Like her mother did!"

About forty-five minutes later, after enduring the heavy traffic on the Los Angeles Thruway, they pull up to Grandma Hollywood's house. Mateo springs out of the car. With flair he opens the door for Grandma Elena. When she is safely out, Mateo heads over to help Tess out. She adamantly refuses to give him her hand. Smirking, he moves on to Elena who is still sitting in the front seat. The Italian gigolo takes hold of Elena's hand, kisses it then sing songs, "Bella Signorina, Elena, at your service." She is overwhelmed with this whole trip. In a cloud, Elena responds, "Grazie." Once out of the car Mateo makes Elena stand there. He bows requesting, 'May I escort you, bella Elena, tomorrow night to the Hollywood Bowl to hear the famous Italian Maestro Arturo Toscanini." Grandma overhears and calls out, "Why of course she is going. I bought the tickets. You must go! Rumor has it this will be the Maestro's last concert." Mateo smiles and blows a kiss at Grandma Hollywood. She stresses, "First we have to get my granddaughter new clothes, hairdo, and makeup at Max Factors." Tess is drained, "Enough, let's go in the house, clean up, eat, and we will discuss it further."

Turning and seeing the Italian Stallion still standing there with daggers in her tired eyes, Tess stares straight at him. She sarcastically calls out, "Arrividelci, Mateo!" "Of course, Bella Signora." He bows, blows a kiss and hollers out, "Chow." He sings, "I will see you beautiful ladies' tomorrow." He jumps in the car and takes off with the radio blasting singing loudly in his sexy Italian accent, "Hello to Hollywood." "What a phony!" Tess snaps as the women are left carrying the luggage in. "Whose car is it Mom?" Huffing and puffing Tess questions. Grandma Hollywood proudly responds, "Why mine of course!" "Why is he driving off with it," annoyed Tess asks. Grandma Hollywood replies, "I let him use it." "As I surmised Mom, he's using you." In a hushed voice she adds, "A real gigolo." In defense Grandma Hollywood explains, "Mateo has an Italian Vespa." Laughing she further informs, "I might feel and look young darling but I am a bit too advanced in age to ride on the back of a Vespa with him." Pouting Tess finds no humor in this. She yells, "Enough, Mom!"

Lugging the suitcases up the porch steps Tess is taken back when the door suddenly opens and her sister Mary Grace and her daughter Regina Helen are standing there. "What the hell!" Tess shouts out. Mary Grace takes hold of her surprised sister, gives her a tight squeeze. Regina runs past them down to her surprised cousin Elena. Not believing her sister is standing in front of her, Tess is speechless. Mary Grace orders, "Come in Sis and I will explain it to you." They proceed to go in. Cleo, Grandma's spoiled and precious Cocker Spaniel is barking at the strangers. Mary Grace hands him a treat; the dog moves happily away.

Outside Elena is also confused seeing her cousin Regina Helen standing boldly in front of her. "Here let me help you with the luggage, Cuz," Regina offers. Curious about the book Elena is holding onto for dear life, Regina insists, "Give me that book!" "No!" holding on tightly to it she yells. Elena asks, "What are you doing here Regina?" With a huge smile on her milky-white face Regina orders, "Come in. My Mom and I will tell you all about it." Elena refuses to move. Regina stays with her cousin. "I don't blame you for wanting to stay outdoors." She smiles and adds, "What beautiful weather in California! No snow, sleet or freezing weather here." Boldly she reveals, "That's why I want to make it big in the movie industry in Hollywood." She sings, *"There's No Business Like Show Business. . ."*

Grandma Hollywood is outside observing everything. Talking to herself she mutters, "This will be very interesting when Mary Grace and Regina explain everything to Tess and Elena." She pauses. Whispering she says, "First things first. Tess better call Jersey City." Walking toward the house Grandma Hollywood says to her two granddaughters, "Okay, my Fair Ladies, in the house for some treats or you'll wind up with unwanted tricks."

When they are all in Grandmother Hollywood's house, they go directly to the kitchen. The hostess with the mostess, Mary Grace decorated the table beautifully with lovely fresh flowers, an array of fresh fruit, artesian cheeses, and her special homemade Sangria. For the young girls' lemonade. Grandma Hollywood looks at it remarking, "Lovely presentation Mary Grace. You always entertain beautifully." Tess, staring at her sister Mary Grace, comments, "All well and good but what I want to know is how you got here so fast?" Grandma Hollywood goes up to Tess and whispers in her ear, "There is time enough for Mary Grace to explain. Let's go to my bedroom. You must call your husband Mike." The two young cousins are nibbling. Mary Grace pours Elena and Regina lemonade. They drink it with gusto. Before Tess goes to her mother's bedroom, Mary Grace hands Tess a tall glass of Sangria. Wisely, she had it ready for Tess before she set foot in their mother's house.

Grandma Hollywood escorts her reluctant daughter Tess to her bedroom. Tess quickly takes a gulp of the Sangria. In her bedroom Grandma Hollywood immediately takes the receiver off the hook of her pink princess telephone, she hands it to her baffled daughter Tess ordering, "Put that drink down. Call Mike now!" Grandma Hollywood heads out of the bedroom. Considerately she closes the door to give her daughter privacy. Tess, with receiver in her hand, and a disdained look on her face, tentatively dials the phone. In a minute or so she hears a frantic voice on the other end yelling, "Who is this?" "It's Tess. Is this Ettie?" confused Tess asks. "Oh dear god, finally, we have been waiting for you to call," Ettie cries out. Hearing Ettie's frantic voice Tess immediately inquires, "What's wrong?" Ettie is sobbing over the phone. "Let me speak to Mike. My mother said he was anxious to talk with me." Ettie shouts, "I can't put him on!" "What? Why?" Tess questions her hysterical sister-in-law. Ettie blurts out, "Mike is missing Tess." "Calm down Ettie, I am not sure I 'm hearing you right." Ettie attempts to settle down to explain, "My Carlo died and after the funeral," Tess mutters, "Carlo died?" Ettie pays no attention she continues, "After the funeral, Mike left the house alone. My Rosaria saw him rushing toward Walsh's tavern. She thought he was going there for a drink with his buddies." Ettie pauses to catch her breath. In a state of confusion Tess insists, "Go on Ettie!" "Mike never came home! His car is still out front and no one has seen or heard from him since," Mike's distraught sister cries out.

Trying to remain calm so she can process all of this, Tess downs the Sangria, and breathes in deeply. With guarded composure she asks, "Did you check with Ray or the men at Walsh's tavern?" "Yes! They said Mike opened the door to the bar that night. Something distracted him, he turned suddenly and ran." Tess questions, "Then what?" "As I told you, none of them saw him after that or to this day," weeping Ettie responds. Truly frightened Tess moans, "Ray hasn't heard from him!?" "No! He said the last time he saw or talked with Mike was at Carlo's funeral." Ettie pauses. "Go on Ettie." She cries, "Ray said Mike never showed up the next day to play handball with him." Tess pleads, "Did you call the police?" "Of course!" Ettie responds. She resumes, "Rosaria made sure before Blaise left to return to his military post that he go to the police station in person and alert them about Mike missing." Upset, Tess sarcastically comments, "I hope the police, who take bribes from the political and other savory characters, will follow up." Angry at Tess now, Ettie defends them, "Tess, you are wrong! The police in this city would do anything for my brother Mike." "Okay, settle down Ettie." Truly angry, Tess remarks mockingly, "What did Jersey City's finest say?" Ettie, in a lower tone, sadly responds, "They have no leads." Bewildered and alarmed, Tess is temporarily silent. Not for long. Enraged, she shouts, "What else is new in that god damn corrupt city!"

Ettie, a devoted religious woman, sighs, "I put my trust in God now Tess." She lectures, "That's what I do and you should too." Tess does not respond. Mike's pious sister adds, "In fact, Monsignor Kelly is having prayers said for Mike daily." Ettie stops to blow her nose and wipe her eyes. After she adds, "Also, Father Schultz, along with Juan his young assistant, are both doing everything to help find him."

Frightened and shocked Tess immediately interjects, "What? Father Arthur Schultz? Has Mike been with him lately?" Calming down, Mike's disturbed sister answers, "Not that I know of." "What about Sister Margaret Mary, has she offered any suggestions?" Tess inquires. "Oh dear, I totally forgot to tell you. No one has heard or seen Sister Margaret Mary since she came the night of Carlo's funeral at my house." "Go on Ettie." She continues, "My son's friend Robbie saw Sister Margaret Mary talking with Mike on the stoop that night but she never came in the house." "Oh, dear god!" Tess blurts out. "Why do you ask Tess?" No response from her sister-in-law so Ettie explains, "We assumed Sister Margaret Mary went away for a few days to a Catholic retreat." Ettie pauses and recalls, "Although, Robbie said she seemed very upset when he saw her talking with Mike." "Strange, to say the least," Tess mutters under her labored breath.

Tess decides to go another route hoping not to upset herself. She asks Ettie, "What about Eileen? Could her racketeer husband Marty Goldstein be involved?" Ettie cries out, "Oh heavens no; he's dead!" "What!" Tess screams. "The police found his body in the garbage dump." Ettie further shares, "Eileen is now married to Big Tony." Tess, needing time to figure everything out alone, and wanting to end this conversation with Ettie, inquires, "Ettie, are Rosaria and Blaise with you?" Weeping Ettie moans, "Blaise had to go back to his post. Rosaria is with me but she is not home right now." "Try to relax Ettie. Make yourself a cup of strong coffee." No answer. Tess attempts to reassure her, "Ettie, it will be all right. I promise you." She says, "I'll call you back later

Tess is unable to totally fathom all she just heard. Mystified, she pauses a second. With sincerity she offers, "Ettie, I am deeply sorry over the loss of your Carlo. I know he meant the world to you." Her distraught sister-in-law is silent. Tess comments, "Elena will be very sad too. She loves you so much Ettie and I know she will feel your pain when I tell her." Under her breath Tess pontificates, "My poor Elena, her father missing, uncle dying, and perhaps even faithful Sister Margaret Mary not to be found." Settling down, in a hushed voice Ettie responds, "Thank you for condolences about Carlo." Before Elena can reply Ettie begs, "Listen to me Tess, please spare my little sweetheart. Don't tell Elena about Carlo. Definitely not about Mike!" "Okay," Tess agrees. Barely audible Ettie comments, "My darling niece Elena is too fragile right now." Ettie prayerfully cries out, "God Bless you and all of us. And my dearest Mike." Sobbing she hangs up.

Tears welling in her puzzled eyes, deeply distressed, Tess places the receiver down on the pink princess phone. In a state of shock and disbelief, she throws herself across her mother's king size bed covered over with an elegant pink satin quilted bed spread. With a blinding headache and a fiercely beating heart Tess moans, "What do I tell Elena?" Hearing her mother, daughter, sister and niece chattering and laughing in the kitchen Tess attempts to compose herself. Quivering, Tess sits up. She wipes her red-rimmed, moist eyes with the satin bedspread moaning, "My poor Elena. Oh dear God, please let them find Mike safe and sound."

In the kitchen, unbeknownst to the others about Mike missing, a lively conversation is going on. "Yes, Elena," Regina, with a huge smile on her face, tells her baffled cousin, "I have an audition for a part in a movie here in Hollywood!" She further informs, "Grandma heard about it from her friends at Max Factor Studio. She contacted my mother and here we are!" She pauses. Perking up, Regina shouts, "And yes, my parents are most likely getting a divorce." Sad, Elena questions, "What about your brother Timothy?" "No worries about him," Regina announces. "He's joining the Army as soon as he graduates this June. Tim wants to be like my loony Uncle Danny."

Shocked and annoyed Elena further questions, "How come you never told us any of this when we saw you and your mother in front of our house the day we were leaving?" Before Regina can respond Elena blurts out, "You never explained how you got here before us?" Right away her Aunt Mary Grace interjects, "We flew here on an airplane the next day." Grandma Hollywood quickly adds, "Mary Grace called me after she made the plane reservations." Looking apologetic she explains, "Your Aunt begged me not to tell anyone."

Elena, looks at her Aunt sheepishly inquires, "You and Uncle Geoff are getting a divorce?" Before Mary Grace can respond, white-as-a-ghost, Tess drags herself into the kitchen. "Who's getting divorced?" she asks. Before anyone responds, Tess starts groaning, "What else is going to happen!?" The women stand there staring at one another in silence. Grandma Hollywood whispers to Mary Grace, "Mike must have told her that Ettie's husband Carlo died." Elena does not hear what her grandmother whispered to her Aunt Mary Grace nor did Regina.

The doorbell rings. Regina runs toward the door and shouts back, "I'll get it." Elena goes over to her mother to comfort her still not understanding why her mother is so upset. With vigor Regina Helen opens the front door. Standing with a magnificent bouquet of fresh-cut, exotic flowers in hand, with a pompous attitude is this young unfamiliar man. Glaring Regina up and down he exhorts, "Why, hello pretty young thing!" She stares him down. Not one to give up easily he announces, "My name is Rodney Sheridan. What is yours?" Flirtatiously Rodney hands Regina the flowers and enters.

CHAPTER THIRTY-EIGHT

War and Peace
Walpole, New Hampshire
February 1867

FRAGILE ANNA LEE is extremely concerned looking out the kitchen-door window observing her husband Austin limping toward the barn. He is carrying his favorite Henry Rifle. This anxious young wife immediately opens the door. The blustery winter air hits her in the face. It stuns her but she is determined to get her husband's attention. "Austin, come back. I need your help!" Near the barn enraged, Austin does not hear his desperate wife's call. Almost blown down by the door from the wind pushing against it Anna Lee screams out louder, "Austin, please come back!" No response. Smacked with fury, Austin enters the barn. Disturbed, Anna Lee heads back to the parlor to check on the twins. They are sound asleep, therefore she goes back to the kitchen. Anna Lee proceeds to grab a wrap from a hook on the back of the kitchen door. She hastily throws it over her frail shoulders, pulls on a wool hat and runs out the door toward the barn.

Carrots in hand Zeke feeds horses Buck and the Paint Gelding, Splash Dancer. He is shocked seeing Austin with a manic look on his face barging into the barn pointing a rifle at him. With fury Austin commands, "Stand right there Zeke! I want you to answer some questions for me before I give you your walking papers." Zeke drops the carrots to the ground, puts up his hands in defense and attempts to walk forward. Austin screams, "Did you hear me? Don't move or I'll use this rifle on you." The shouting causes Buck and Splash Dancer to bound up. Zeke instinctively directs the anxious horses to their stalls. Hoping the carrots he gave them earlier will calm them down.

Austin wipes the sweat pouring down his distraught face and cries out, "I've tried to make sense of what happened that horrific day that my darling daughter died in an unfathomable, senseless tragedy." Sleeping on the other side of the barn Brutus the dog is woken by the loud commotion. He rises on all fours, barks and glares his teeth at Austin. "Shut that brut up," Austin orders. Zeke shushes Brutus who obeys Zeke immediately.

Austin resumes his tirade at Zeke, "I can't believe you were present and you did not protect my helpless innocent daughter." Whimpering he looks over at his beloved Buck. "You took better care of my horse than my daughter." Austin mutters, "Other than my wife, I entrusted my two most prized possessions with you Theresa Edith and Buck." The anxious dog is barking louder frustrating Austin. Zeke calls over to Brutus to calm the dog down. Hearing Zeke, Brutus again stops barking. Zeke attempts to clear things up, "Mr. Stevens, I am still trying to figure out what happened." Moaning he pounds on his chest, "I haven't slept a night since. I punish myself every day. I feel her loss as much as you and Mrs. Stevens do." The barn door squeaks. It is slightly ajar. The men do not notice out of the shadows the trembling Anna Lee silently standing there.

Austin pays no heed to Zeke's painful lamentation. He resumes his verbal rampage on him, "I've held in this hatred for you only to appease my wife and to be sure the twins will be well." He stammers, "Now I must release this poison in me." Brutus rushes over to Austin. He growls at him with sharp teeth showing. Zeke pulls the dog away and immediately responds, "Mr. Stevens, please calm down. I know how agonizing this is for you. Let me express my deepest sympathies and clear matters up for you." Austin ignores Zeke. He spurts out, "To add to my revulsion you betrayed me! Your disloyalty enrages me!" "Betrayed, disloyal?" Zeke shouts back. "Yes, Zeke," Austin answers. "You allowed Nannette to go and live with that scoundrel Dr. Holden. That monster!" Weakening Austin lowers the rifle to the ground. Buck and Splash Dancer are restless; wise Brutus goes up to them to calm them. The horses nuzzle the canine. Deeply pained to see his boss so distraught and fearful, Zeke stands motionless trying to gage what his boss will do next.

Seeing Austin dropping the rifle and with immense humiliation for hurting his devoted boss, Zeke bows his head in shame. In plain words, he defends himself, "When Jeremiah came that sad day screaming, alarmed

Mrs. Stevens told me to let him in." Filled with so much uncontrollable rage and fury Austin is hardly listening to Zeke. Zeke resumes, "Believe me, I tried to get him to leave. When he cried out that his wife just died, your wife heard him. In her goodness she felt sorry for him." Without empathy Austin rises his head. He screams, "He probably killed his wife too!" Resuming his explanation, Zeke defends, "Your kind wife ordered me to let Dr. Holden in!"

Listening to their confrontation greatly disturbs Anna Lee. She gently enters the barn and walks over to Austin. Putting her arms around her hysterical husband she reaffirms, "Yes dear blame me. I insisted that Zeke let Dr. Holden in." She strokes her husband's quivering hand pleading, "Darling, a good Christian woman and caring neighbor would do the same hearing that a neighbor's sweet, young wife just died." In anger Austin pushes his wife aside. He picks up the rifle and points it back at Zeke. The dog rushes over to Zeke and bares his teeth at Austin. Zeke grabs the dog.

Shouting at his wife and Zeke Austin demands, "Explain to me why three grown adults would let an innocent child and a frivolous young lady go ice skating alone?" Furious, Austin stamps his lame foot. He points his razor-sharp finger at both his trembling wife and fretful Zeke. He vehemently accuses, "You two incompetents were too busy feeling sorry for that fool Holden to attend to your responsible duties." He pounds his throbbing chest and cries out, "Because of your blatant negligence my innocent daughter is dead!" The screaming and shouting in the barn not only upsets Anna Lee and Zeke but makes the animals extremely restless and highly agitated. Adding to the tension in this once quiet barn, the wailing from the horses and incessant barking of the defensive dog is deafening.

Lamenting, Austin pathetically moans, "You were supposed to protect her!" Zeke tries to further clarify and defend Anna Lee who stands there mournfully, "Mrs. Stevens didn't want the girls to be upset hearing about the death of Mrs. Holden. She wisely thought she would distract Theresa Edith by letting her go outside with Nannette to occupy her." Austin does not reply. Zeke further explains, "That's why Mrs. Stevens gave Nannette permission to take Theresa Edith ice skating." Zeke puts his right hand over his woeful heart, "I swear to god I heard your wife tell Nannette and Theresa Edith to be careful." In defense of Anna Lee he exhorts, "Your dear wife insisted they make sure the ice was safe." Meekly Anna Lee nods her head in agreement. Not accepting this, Austin harshly infers, "Didn't you Zeke have the common sense to check out the ice first?" Torn and deeply distressed, Austin's head hangs low as he half-heartedly listens to Zeke. With tears in his eyes Zeke informs, "Mr. Stevens, I tested the pond earlier that morning." Pleading he reveals, "I swear, it was totally solid even in the middle." In anguish Austin screams, "Well, it wasn't! Was it Zeke!?" He turns and stares Zeke down who is wiping his moist eyes with his soiled work shirt. "Wipe those crocodile tears from your devious eyes," Austin shouts throwing down the rifle. Sobbing he collapses down on to his knees. In defense, his once trusted worker responds, "I walked across the ice myself and I weigh a lot more than those two innocent young girls put together." Seeing his boss in such a state, shaking his head back and forth Zeke moans, "I ask myself daily why and how the ice cracked making sweet little Theresa Edith fall in."

Taking hold of his rifle, Austin gradually rises. With vengeance, he glares straight at Zeke pronouncing, "I took you in; a complete stranger, when no one would!" Again he raises the rifle and points it at Zeke. "I trusted you," Austin shouts. "I even took in Nannette an unknown person." Zeke cries out, "And we are forever grateful, Boss." "I treated you like family and this is the thanks I get!" he cries out. Austin's verbal tirade is endless. "Even when my wife felt uncomfortable with you and she didn't want Nannette, I stood up for both of you." Ashamed with guilt Zeke breathlessly mutters, "I thanks my lucky stars every day." He despondently shares, "I would have left but after Mrs. Stevens mother departed to return to Virginia, I vowed I stay to help you and Mrs. Stevens with the twins, the barn duties and care for the animals." Zeke wipes his wet eyes with his torn sleeve and declares, "I owes you!"

Zeke's desperate explanation does not appease or comfort Austin. This inconsolable, sorrowful husband, father, and boss turns his back on Zeke. He stands soulfully, emotionally paralyzed followed by a rush of uncontrollable rage pouring out of him. He bends over howling in unbearable pain. *Letting go of his destructive emotions does not alleviate Austin of his excruciating grief. Grief is a sign of love.* Greatly alarmed, Anna Lee reaches to comfort her husband. He pushes her aside; calms down and in an eerie manner he rises and shuffles over to Buck. He gently strokes his beloved Buck's long, silky mane. *Only this devoted horse is able to give some semblance of peace to this angry bitter soul.*

Rejected by her husband tears spring back to Anna Lee. Walking over to Zeke she places her dainty hand on his slouching shoulder to console him. Softly she assures, "Zeke, please excuse my husband; he is not himself of late." Under her breath she moans, "Nor I fear of sound mind." She pauses, groans, "And rightfully so." She attempts to lessen her husband's vicious accusation towards Zeke, "If it weren't for you Zeke, Dr. Holden and Nannette my innocent twins would not be here to comfort me. Nor I be here to take care of them." Taking a cotton handkerchief out of her sleeve she wipes her moist eyes pontificating, "My only consolation is that my sweet, innocent angel Theresa Edith is up there watching over us."

Normally unable to express his sentimental nature, Zeke is now visibly emotional. Anna Lee assures him, "My precious Theresa Edith loved you Zeke." "And I loved her," with a wretched look on his aged, rawhide face, Zeke moans. Anna Lee shares, "My dearest Theresa Edith took the special Nutcracker you made for her to bed every night." Wiping her teary eyes she reveals, "We buried it with her." Tears are freely dripping down Zeke's taunt humiliated face. Noticing his embarrassment, and respecting Zeke's privacy, she leaves. Solemnly Anna Lee walks over to her weary husband. Austin is still stroking Buck. This young woman desperately needs her husband's strong arms to console and comfort her. *Sorrowfully this will not happen yet.*

Earlier, while listening to his wife and Zeke conversing, Austin turns and glares at his fragile wife with disgust. He vomits out, "All that nonsense about a Nutcracker and taking care of my twins will not bring my daughter back!" He hostilely sneers over at Zeke and accuses, "Nor will it explain why that turncoat Nannette is not here taking care of our twins." "It is my fault Nannette left. I didn't want her here!" cries out Anna Lee. With compassion for Anna Lee, Zeke shouts over, "If it weren't for Jeremiah. . ." "Oh, Jeremiah, calling that turn coat by his first name," Austin harshly interjects. "Interesting Zeke, your once arch enemy is now your intimate friend." Austin mocks, "How pathetic!"

In defense Anna Lee pleads, "Be kind Austin. Dr. Holden saved my life." She continues to try and appease her husband, "The twins wouldn't be here if it weren't for Dr. Holden." "Traitor! Don't you dare defend that man or Zeke. Those Benedict Arnolds," Austin screams at his wife. Staring at Zeke with hatred he spurts out, "And as for Nannette, she has a lot of explaining to do." He pours out his distorted reasoning, "Going to live with that scoundrel." With venom he accuses, "That orphan turned whore with that devil in disguise veterinarian!" Shocked and ashamed, Anna Lee reprimands, "How horrible, Austin, your blasphemy is unforgiveable!"

With a strained face, Zeke defends, "Dr. Holden did save your wife and the twins lives." Zeke further adds, "As far as Nannette is concerned, blame me." He pauses and adds, "After the horrible accident, I knew her being here would be very distressing for you and your mourning wife." Gaining confidence and strength, Zeke looks straight at Austin and boldly says, "I ordered Nannette to go and take care of Jeremiah." He stops to correct himself, "I mean Dr. Holden." Austin ponders, "I always surmised there was a lot more you did not tell me about your relationship with Nannette." He accuses, "Or your past life for that matter, Zeke!" Lowering his head, Zeke murmurs, "Let old dogs die."

Not hearing him, Austin continues to voice his immense anger, "I should have questioned and investigated your strange relationship with Nannette." He stops, catches his breath and blurts out, "Especially YOU." With dignity Austin claims, "Being a gentleman and respecting your privacy, I never interrogated you." Condescending Austin proclaims, "I am a man of my word." He looks at his beloved horse Buck and announces, "You may stay Zeke just to take care of the barn and Buck. I know you love him and he in turn loves you." He glances at Splash Dancer and adds, "And his faithful companion Splash Dancer."

Looking disdainful at the dog Brutus Austin demands, "As far as that yapping Brut is concerned, he is your dog now! I want no part of him either." With resentment, staring demonically at Zeke, Austin orders, "Do your job but stay out of MY way!" Placing the rifle over his broad shoulder with a stern military voice Austin calls out, "And that is a direct order!"

Sulking, holding onto it tightly Austin hoists the rifle further up resuming his tirade at Zeke, "You should kneel down on the ground before me on broken glass and kiss my feet after I opened my home to you and Nannette with no questions asked." Silently Zeke hangs his head. Turning around and staring at Zeke, Austin growls, "This is the thanks I get!" Limping out of the barn holding the infamous Henry Rifle over his taunt shoulder, he suddenly halts. Austin reaffirms, "Remember Zeke, take good care of my Buck." With agony in his piercing moist eyes Austin cries out glaring at Ann Lee, "He is the only thing I have left that I truly care about." He stops, stares back at Zeke and shouts, "Or can trust!" Bitterly depressed Austin resumes his verbal rampage, "I would have gotten rid of you Zeke as soon as I got home from Australia but, as I stated, I had no one to take care of Buck and his buddy Splash Dancer." He swings around and proceeds to exit the barn. Deeply wounded by her husband's comments about the only thing he cares about is Buck, but being a dutiful wife and pious woman, Anna Lee suppresses her deep hurt. Crying, Anna Lee begs, "Austin, for you own good, please make peace before you leave." She looks over at the despondent Zeke who is grieving the loss of his admired boss's respect. She offers, "Zeke, please ignore my husband's insolent comments, he knows not what he is saying."

Taken aback and embarrassed, and not hearing Anna Lee's remarks, Zeke murmurs, "I've done it again! I've committed treason and to a man who was only good to me." Mortified, yet with pity, questioningly Anna Lee stares over at the dazed Zeke and mimics, "Treason?" Greatly distressed she excuses herself, "I must leave Zeke. Forgive my husband." Gravely, Anna Lee reveals, "Independently of the heart wrenching tragedy of what happened to our precious Theresa Edith, my troubled husband has not been the same for some time." Pondering Anna Lee echoes, "I believe long before he left for Australia." Lifting his head, Zeke whirls around, gazes at Anna Lee questioningly. She whispers, "I fear something in Australia has gone terribly wrong also."

Closing the shawl tightly around her, Anna Lee soberly moans, "Sadly, Austin has not shared it with me." Zeke is mute. Preparing to go after her grieving husband, Anna Lee gazes directly into Zeke's grey, murky eyes. She laments pleading, "Forgive him Zeke; his immense pain is clouding his reality." He looks at this kind woman with great pity. She adds, "It is

I Zeke my husband is truly angry with." She pauses and whispers, "And whatever else is going on in his private life." Similar to when he first came to Austin Stevens estate, Zeke is speechless; mute. He lowers his head in grave sorrow.

Shocked and mortified that she shared personal issues to a none family member, Anna Lee sheepishly announces, "I must go check on the twins. I've left them too long." With faithful Brutus quietly following uncomfortable Zeke, he walks over to calm Buck and Splash Dancer. The horses are agitated by the relentless commotion. Finding his voice, Zeke, with compassion and concern, calls over to Anna Lee as she is leaving the barn, "Don't worry about me! Take good care of those twins and yourself Mrs. Stevens." Whimpering as she is leaving the barn Anna Lee agonizingly reminisces, "Last time I left my child alone. . ." Catching her breath she mournfully weeps, "She died!" *The Good Lord Taketh and the Good Lord Giveth* ~ The Book of Job

CHAPTER THIRTY-NINE

There's No Business Like Show Business
Hollywood, California
January 1956

TESS DETERMINEDLY DECIDES she will not discuss anything about her husband Mike missing, Carlo's death, and Sister Margaret Mary's unknown whereabouts. Grandma Hollywood and Tess's sister Mary Grace wisely agree with her. Their main concern is to protect innocent, fragile Elena Rose and inquisitive, demonstrative Regina from knowing about it for now.

Grandma Hollywood encourages her adult daughters to clean up the kitchen quickly. Immediately after, she surprises her daughters Tess and Mary Grace by informing them she has very *special* outfits for them to wear tonight. Grandma Hollywood's dear friend, physician-nutritionist, the infamous Dr. Rudolpho Della Porta, a vigilant vegetarian, is graciously hosting in his palatial estate in Beverly Hills, a welcoming party for Grandma Hollywood's New Jersey daughters and her teenage granddaughters to Hollywood. This grand man came to Hollywood years ago from Venosa, Italy after graduating from the University of Bologna Medical School.

While the mothers are cleaning the kitchen and Grandma Hollywood is in her bedroom getting ready for the party, Elena Rose and Regina Helen are in the living room with Rodney. Regina is preoccupied placing the beautiful flowers Rodney bought in a magnificent Waterford crystal vase. Annoyed, Elena questions Rodney, "How come you came here unannounced and so quickly?" Smirking, she adds, "I thought you were going to contact us in a few days." Responding, Rodney informs her, "I couldn't wait to let you know about the script I am writing." He gazes at her in appreciation announcing, "You are the only one I can trust to read it and give me honest feedback." Elena calls out, "Script!?" "Hush," Rodney whispers. One who never misses a trick, nor ever wants to be left out, Regina calls out. "A Script! What script?" She glides over to the pink satin loveseat where Elena is sitting and Rodney is standing next to. They both remain totally silent deliberately ignoring Regina. "What? No one answers?" She adds, "Are you both deaf?" No response. Regina mockingly questions, "What is this some big, dark mystery?" Rodney turns reassuring Regina, "When the right time comes, Greta Garbo, you'll be one of the first to know." In anger, Regina stamps her foot. "If you know of a script I should know about, I want to hear about it now!" She goes up to Rodney, putting her face right up to his, she brags, "I am going to be a famous actress, as I told you when you first entered this house, when you asked who I was." "Yes," Rodney responds, "You said you were an up-and-coming actress." He lectures, "You must also respect that I am an up-and-coming script writer." Scanning to see if anyone else is near, in a low tone, he says, "There are certain things in this town that must be kept private." Merely audible, Rodney cautions, "There are producer pirates in this town who steal scripts at any cost."

"You are so dramatic!" laughing loudly Regina accuses. She pushes Rodney. He falls right onto Elena's lap. Elena screams, "Rodney, get off of me!" He jumps up, smoothes his tight Levi jeans. Settling down, Rodney comments, "You certainly will make a good actress; you are one hell of a drama queen, Regina!" Staring at her sternly he states, "And I am King and Lord of my script! A true wordsmith."

Regina looks over at Elena who is ignoring the two of them. To draw her cousin in Regina asks, "By the way Elena, why so quiet?" She ponders then shouts, "You are in love!" "What!" screams back Elena. "Well, you did go to that surprise New Year's Eve birthday party for a boy with those fancy-schmancy velvet slippers." Laughing, Regina mockingly inquires, "Why Cinderella, did you lose your magical glass slippers?" Incensed, Elena is preparing to pounce on her cousin. Before she can, Regina's sarcasm escalates. "You look flushed, Cuz." She further infuriates Elena by insinuating, "You two hooked up at that party?!" In defense of his friend Elena, Rodney attacks Regina. Pointing at Regina he singsongs, "My, my the Ugly Stepsister rears her ghastly head." Everyone glares at one another after hearing the matriarch's booming voice. Calling from her boudoir, Grandma Hollywood says, "My Fair Ladies, say your polite goodbyes to your charming friend." Determined, she hollers louder, "We must get ready for my dear friend Dr. Rudolpho Della Porta's special soirée. He is graciously hosting this party for you." The cousins look at one another blurting out, "A party?" Flustered, Rodney repeats, "Dr. Rudolpho Della Porta?" While preparing to leave he winks at the girls and coyly remarks, "You two femme fatales are only in town a day or so and you are already invited to a party at one of the most illustrious, esteemed personalities in this crazy pretentious town." He bows deeply announcing, "I will see you two there, My Fair Ladies." Leaving, Rodney educates, "Dr. Della Porta is known to have invested millions in films." Glaring at one another, Elena and Regina stand there speechless.

Grandma Hollywood, Tess, Mary Grace, and Regina are sitting in the back of the pink Cadillac with the top up not to ruin the women' hairdos. Elena is sitting up front next to Mateo in the driver seat. Looking in the mirror Mateo calls back, "Why you lovely ladies look incredible. You all are so glamorous." Ecstatically, Grandma Hollywood responds, "Why thank you Mateo." She notices her two daughters' soar faces. "It took a lot of convincing on my part to let them wear the gowns I designed for an up-and-coming movie." Noticing Tess and Mary Grace, Mateo whistles, "My, my you two glamour queens make Marilyn Monroe and Rita Hayward look like the ugly stepsisters." Silence from the sisters. Regina responds, "One in gold lame and the other in silver sparkles. They look like they just escaped from Fort Knox."

"The green-eyed monster is alive and well," Mateo calls back to Regina. She is dressed in an Audrey Hepburn type A-line, white and black dress. Stunning patent leather open-toe high heels encase her delicate feet. "I think it takes one to know one," Regina says to Mateo. Laughing he retorts, "I like my women feisty!" "Enough!" Grandma Hollywood calls out. Grinning, Mateo gazes over at Elena who is silently sitting next to him in a flowing, tea-length burgundy skirt with a satin pink halter top splashed with a large pink flower design." Mateo flirts with Elena, "Bella Signorina, Sophia Loren has nothing on you." The flirting and bantering ceases when they pull up to a huge, highly decorated wrought iron gate. Mateo puts his hand out and pushes a button near the gate. Over an intercom a man asks for their names. Mateo announces their arrival. The gate swings open automatically. The pink Cadillac, filled with the glamorous women and the handsome young gigolo driver, slowly meanders through the heavily tree-lined canopy driveway. At the end of the road they reach a circular drive in front of a magnificent mansion. It is magnificently surrounded by massive impressive flora verdant grounds.

Grandly standing on a beautifully lit terrace is a reed-thin, distinguished looking aged man in an elegant tuxedo. He has a lioness, luxurious head of silver gray hair and a matching fine trimmed mustache. This debonair gentleman is waving wildly as he calls down, "Marvelous! Hear, Hear, my honored guests have arrived!" He requests an attractive young waitress in a very short, ruffled uniform to, "Bring my honored guests' my special mock cocktails immediately." Dr. Rudolpho Della Porta notices Mateo. The host instructs, "Mateo, make sure you escort these beautiful ladies up here safely." From the background a full orchestra is playing. *There is no business-like show business.*

An abundance of famous and wanna-a-be stars, starlets, producers, directors and scriptwriters in the movie industry are attending this envious party. The honored guests are finally safely upstairs. Dr. Della Porta hugs Grandma Hollywood and kisses both her cheeks European style. This distinguished, elderly gentleman turns admiring Grandma Hollywood's adult daughters and teenage granddaughters. He enchantingly remarks, "Charmed to meet you." He looks over at Grandma Hollywood and gloweringly comments, "Elena, you have such beautiful women in your family." The coy charismatic Dr. Della Porta adds, "They take after you, darling Signora Elena." Blushing but pleased, Grandma Hollywood comments, "Why Rudy, you are too, too kind!"

Holding on to her drink, Tess shares, "Dr. Della Porta, thank you for having us. As for the cocktails, I must inform you my daughter and niece are too young to drink." He laughs heartily with elucidation, "My dear woman, I do not serve hard liquor. Didn't your mother inform you I am an ardent herbal tea enthusiast and staunch vegetarian?" The doctor navigates his delicate hand to his stomach proclaiming, "No poison ever enters my temple-of-a body nor will it enter any of my guests." He gazes at Tess clutching her mock cocktail and reassures her, "My dear young lady, only fresh, organic watermelon, peach, and cranberry juice, tinged with fresh mint, are in my renowned mock cocktails." He raises her chin ordering, "Now drink up my beauty." Livid, he dare touch her, Tess instantly moves away from the 'ardent vegetarian.' "What an egotistical Quack!" under her breath she utters.

Unaware of the negative effect he has on Tess, Rudolpho glances around. He questions Grandma Hollywood, "Where is Mateo and your delightful brother Alberto? Why have they not joined us?" Grandma Hollywood explains, "Dear, dear Rudy, my brother Albert has not even seen my daughters or granddaughters yet. He left a few days ago for Fresno on business." She grasps Dr. Della Porta's delicate hand and informs, "Albert sends his regrets." Curtly Rudolpho responds, "Be sure you give Alberto my best and assure him we must get together soon."

Dr. Della Porto gazes around and mentions, "I saw Mateo earlier. Where is he? I want to ask him to come by and trim my hair and mustache." He touches his precious mane of hair and squeals, "Mateo is the only one who cuts and trims it the way I like it." Grandma Hollywood assures him, "I will tell him." She further explains, "Dear Rudy, Mateo has been busy hairstyling and wig making at the movie studio." Acting like a peacock she brags, "You know darling, I met Mateo at the Arthur Murray Dance Studio." She twirls around and sings out, "He was my first instructor." Proudly Grandma Hollywood further informs, "We did a mean Samba together." Boasting, she shares, "We won a gold medal at a competition for our legendary Samba." Continuing to boast, "I was the person who got him the prestigious position at Max Factor Studio making wigs for the movies." Before the doctor can respond, someone calls for him. He kisses Grandma Elena's hand and politely announces, "Excuse me for now bella Signora, I must attend to an important matter."

With that said, a different, striking young waitress carrying a large silver tray of luscious ruby red edibles, offers Grandma Hollywood and her family fancy watermelon balls covered with an array of assorted huge fresh berries. Regina and Elena look at one another and begin to chuckle. Grandma Hollywood whispers a reprimand, "Don't judge." Pointing at the watermelon, she says, "This is why Dr. Della Porta looks so youthful, trim, and fit at ninety-two." "A few face lifts help too," giggling Regina mocks. Grandma Hollywood lectures, "Regina, mind your manners." She glances up and down at Elena and mentions, "You will soon be trim, my dearest granddaughter, once Dr. Della Porta gets you started on his world renowned, healthy-diet regime."

❧

Before Elena and Regina speak another word they hear a familiar voice, "Hello, my Fair Ladies. I see you arrived here before me." Standing there grinning widely in a cream linen double breasted suite and pink silk bowtie is Rodney Sheridan. "How the hell did you get invited here?" Regina blurts out. "Why my family and Dr. Della Porta have been friends for years." He adjusts his pink polka dotted silk bowtie and proudly adds, "He is like my other grandfather."

On the other side of the elaborate marble terrace, wanting to move away from the pretentious Dr. Della Porta and her pompous mother, Tess is relieved and surprised to see Rodney. She quickly grabs onto her sister Mary Grace's arm as she heads over to him calling out, "Rodney, so happy to see you here!"

❧

Rodney is anxious to speak with Tess. He politely takes hold of Tess's arm offering, "May I show you around the property?" Mary Grace is anxious to introduce herself to some important people in the movie industry therefore she encourages her sister, "Go Tess, I'm going to mingle." She notices Tess's hesitation. She adds, "I'm a big girl now Sis. Go!" Tess is taken aback. Rodney instructs, "Follow me! I want to show you the magnificent Venus statue water fountain around back. "You seem to know your way around here, Rodney," Tess comments. "I've been here numerous times with my grandfather," he boasts. Leading Tess, Rodney repeats, "Follow me!"

At the back of the mansion there are elegant formal gardens and a magnificent illuminated Venus flowing water fountain. An elaborate marble bench is strategically placed near it. Rodney escorts Tess to the marble bench. "Please sit down." He whispers, "I have an urgent message for you from Monsignor Cooney." Rodney shares the message. Bewildered,

301

Tess pleadingly begs, "What does the Monsignor suggest I do with this information?" Rodney clasps her quivering hands. He responds, "Nothing!" he pauses … "at the moment." He adds, "Monsignor James Cooney wants you to call him when you have a private moment."

Without a care in the world Rodney suggests, "In the meantime enjoy your visit with your Mom." Frowning she employs, "How can I enjoy my visit knowing that the Father Schultz in Jersey City might be an imposter?" Tess wiggles her foot losing her backless, gold high heel shoe. Shuddering, this fiery redhead bemoans, "Even dangerous!"

Observing Tess's distress Rodney tries his best to comfort her by making light of it. Grinning, he offers, "Well it sure is exciting!" Puffing his chest out he offers, "Just think, like Sherlock Holmes we might be the heroes that solve a great mystery Watson!" Shivering with fear, Tess glares at him, "No way!" Regaining her strength Tess demands, "You will not share this with Elena, Regina or anyone!" She grabs his arm, placing his right hand near his heart. She insists, "Swear to me that you will not tell a soul." Recognizing her seriousness, Rodney complies, "I understand totally!" The two conspirators settle down. Like the handsome prince in Cinderella, Rodney places the golden slipper back on Tess's smooth-white quivering foot. A majestic dragonfly glides past them and lands on the beautiful fountain. Bewildered Tess and excited Rodney head back to the party. Tess is determined to behave as if nothing unusual conspired between them.

Dr. Rudolpho Della Porta's honored guests Grandma Hollywood, Tess, Elena, Mary Grace and Regina, along with Rodney desperately attempt to make the best of this remarkable evening. Unfortunately, their muddled minds are elsewhere. Tess is deeply distraught over Rodney's message from Monsignor James Cooney; worried sick about her lost husband Mike; and the alleged imposter clergyman at St. Victor's parish. Most aggrieved of all, Elena's recent dreadful dream is silently torturing this young, impressionable teenager. Naive, self-absorbed Rodney is restless about getting his script written and produced. Determined Mary Grace is anxious about her daughter Regina's audition tomorrow, as is the alias ugly stepsister.

Not a care in the world, Mateo is comfortably slouching with his legs hanging out of the pink Cadillac convertible parked in Dr. Della

Porta's Cypress lined driveway. He is behaving as he does best, flirting with bleached-blond, willowy waitresses in their short sexy uniforms. This young Italian stallion is not indulging in mock cocktails or fancy watermelon treats. Munching on salted, oily peanuts, the Italian gigolo is indulging long swigs of hard liquor from a bottle of whiskey he hides in Grandma Elena's convertible.

On the terrace, the successful, wealthy movie producer and nutritionist-physician, Dr. Rudolpho Della Porta, along with costume designer Grandma Hollywood are having a marvelous time on this beautiful night listening to the golden voice of singer, movie/opera star, Mario Lanza.

In a formal tuxedo a divinely handsome Mario Lanza is crooning his latest hit: "It's the Loveliest Night of the Year." Listening to this new young opera star Grandma Hollywood whispers in the doctor's ear; "Mario Lanza is truly gifted but he is no Enrico Caruso." The doctor proclaims, "And never will be!" With a huge smile on his face Rudolpho adds, "But he is far more handsome."

CHAPTER FORTY

The Housewife Blues/The Godfather Returns
Jersey City, New Jersey
January 1956

IT HAS BEEN days since Carlo Cortino's funeral and the mysterious missing of Mike Policino. His devoted sister Ettie has been sitting by the phone, not eating or sleeping desperately waiting to hear news about her dear missing brother Mike. Her recent friend and caregiver Eileen is in the basement doing the laundry. As soon as she heard about Mike missing, this new bride and Irish lassie insisted on staying with Ettie. Also learning that Ettie's daughter Rosaria left and went to New England to stay with an ill friend and her son Blaise is back on duty at the Marine camp it encouraged Eileen to move in with Ettie. Having her new husband Big Tony out of the country for a while made it even more feasible for her to stay with Ettie. These two lonely, tense women have bonded under unpleasant circumstances. They fill one another's need for comfort and companionship. Ettie is mourning the loss of her husband along with the mystery of her missing brother Mike. Eileen is longing for Big Tony to return to the states to resume their young marriage and be parents to Tony's young daughter Angela Maria. Being with Ettie lessens the pain and vice versa.

Her deep faith and church family have always been Ettie's spiritual salvation. She no longer finds solace from either. Monsignor Jack Kelly is engulfed with solving the ambiguity surrounding Sister Margaret Mary who mysteriously has not returned to the rectory. This once loyal priest and family friend does not have a moment to visit Ettie. Nor has he inquired about Mike; hurting Ettie immensely. Monsignor Jack Kelly is deeply troubled and preoccupied by the recent disturbing call from Monsignor

James Cooney from Notre Dame. If not from her immediate family or parish priest, where will Ettie find peace, she questions. Currently Eileen is her only source regrettably, she has her own concerns.

Eileen keeps in touch with the barkeeper and the cronies who frequent Walsh's Tavern. The barkeeper Walsh, the Professor Brendan and Mike's best friend Ray go there daily hoping the door to the tavern will open and Mike will walk in good as new with a great heroic tale to share. Ray has contacted Ettie a few times eager to hear if she has information about Mike or if Tess has heard anything. Ray also checks in with the police daily. So far they have no leads. Walsh has his theory, as does Brendan, but neither share their fears. For once in his life, Brendan is at a loss for words. Walsh secretly says his rosary in the back of the bar. Collectively, in their own way, they miss and pray for Mike's safe return. They are counting on Big Tony to return soon knowing his determination and admiration for Mike, his boss, he'll get to the bottom of it pronto!

Sitting alone in the kitchen waiting for the phone to ring is all Ettie has been doing these days. The fatal day of Carlo's funeral and her brother Mike's mysterious disappearance turned Ettie's once routine life upside down. This proud, active homemaker no longer cooks, bakes nor listens to her soap operas or classical opera on the radio due to the current tragic situation. Missing her family terribly, Ettie has no will to go on fearing no one needs her any longer. Agonizing, day after day, Ettie waits to hear news about the safe return of Mike. She is also anxious to hear from her daughter Rosaria who is due to give birth to an illegitimate child any day now. Along with these pressing concerns, Ettie fears her son Blaise will be deployed to unknown dangerous lands and die in a war. The horrific memory of World War II is permanently etched in her mind. Her precious niece Elena Rose is way across the country with her mother Tess, making her feel truly abandoned and alone. All this leaves Ettie with a broken heart. Having no one to take care for, she is withering away emotionally and physically. Having Eileen is a comfort but since she does most of the work around the house now, Ettie feels useless and unneeded. Hopelessness and powerlessness surround this sorrowful woman.

Carrying a laundry basket filled with dried clothes up from the basement Eileen hears Ettie's house phone ringing. Rushing to get to the phone, Ettie trips over the chair. She falls down hitting her head hard on the kitchen counter. The loud bang causes Eileen to drop the basket of clothes and run into the kitchen. Seeing Ettie on the floor frightens her. Her first instinct is to go to her but Ettie screams, "Leave me be; answer the phone!" Eileen throws a clean dish cloth to Ettie motioning her to wipe her bleeding head.

As Ettie insists, Eileen answers the phone. "Hello," Eileen yells into it. "No, this is not Tess Policano, Mike Policino's wife, she's out of state. Ettie Cortino, Mike's sister is here." She quickly hands Ettie the phone. In a hushed but firm tone Eileen instructs, "Ettie, tell the police you're Mike's sister." Holding the receiver to her ear, frantic Ettie calls out, "Is my brother Mike okay?" On the other end of the line a strong male voice announces, "This is Captain Francis Burn of the Jersey City Police Department." He clear's his hoarse voice, "Mrs. Cortino please verify that you are Mike Policino's sister." "Yes, I'm his sister!" Ettie reaffirms. Captain Burn, pauses, Ettie demands, "Where is my brother? Is he okay?" With an authoritative voice, the Chief of Police announces, "We have Mike Policano at the downtown precinct; your brother is alive but . . ." Eileen is hovering over Ettie listening to the phone conversation. With her head bleeding profusely, Ettie cries, "Thank God!" Eileen takes the phone from Ettie. She cautiously informs, "Mrs. Cortino is not well at the moment. I 'm her caregiver. I'll take the rest of the message for her." "What is your name?" the Captain asks, "Eileen Rivera." He pauses then responds, "Please let Mrs. Cortino know that we are waiting for an ambulance to take her brother to the Jersey City Medical Center." Frantic, Eileen asks, "How is he?" "He's in bad shape," Captain Burn answers. "Alive?" Eileen urgently inquires. "He is but incoherent. I suggest you take his Sister to the hospital immediately," the Captain insists. "She must bring proof that she is his biological sister," he informs.

Panicking, Eileen quickly cleans Ettie's head hastily putting a butterfly bandage on it. She explains to Ettie they must go to the hospital to see Mike. Eileen reaches for Ettie; making sure she is steady; then grabs their coats. She removes the keys to her car from her purse. Suddenly Eileen stops a moment, rushes to the phone and dials Walsh's Tavern. Walsh answers. He can hardly make out what Eileen is screaming into the phone. "Is this Eileen? Slow down; I can't understand you." "Is Ray Sinnotti there?" "Yes, he is," Walsh responds. "Please tell him to meet me at the Jersey City Medical Center as fast as he can." "What the hell is going on?" the tavern owner brusquely asks. "They found Mike!" "Alive?" Walsh hollers. "Yes, but barely," she cries out. Eileen slams the phone down.

The tavern owner Walsh runs over to Ray pulling at his shirt collar. Blaring, he gives Ray Eileen's message, "Faith and Be Golly, they found our Mike!" Ray sits there in a daze. "Get your butt down to the Medical Center in a flash!" the tavern owner screams. Walsh pushes the confused Ray off the bar stool and shoves him out the door. "Better get there lickety-split before the goons find out and beat you to it." Keenly observing and hearing from the end of the bar, Brendan stands up, raises his glass and calls out, "The Godfather rises again." Upset, Walsh says, "Me hopes so!"

Driving as fast as her second-hand car is capable of, and trying to stay calm, Eileen is desperately trying to keep Ettie from fainting. Her bruised head is pretty serious. The shock of hearing her brother being rushed to the hospital is compromising Ettie's shaky emotions and health. In a panic, Mike's sister cries out, "Eileen, we must call Tess, Rosaria, and Blaise." Making the Sign of the Cross Ettie pleads, "Monsignor Kelly must go to the hospital." Weeping she groans, "Mike might need his blessings." "Ettie relax; you're making me nervous." Eileen attempts to soothe Ettie, "As soon as we get to the hospital and see Mike, we'll make all the calls you wish." They arrive at the Medical Center, hastily park the car on the street and rush toward the hospital's main entrance. As woozy as Ettie feels, she moves quickly. Even in her weakness, her maternal love for her brother gives her the necessary strength she needs.

There is a patrolman standing at the hospital entrance. Infuriated, standing next to him is Ray. The men are in a heated conversation. Talking loudly Ray insists, "But I 'm his best friend. His wife and daughter are in California and his sister is mourning the recent loss of her husband."

Agitated, Ray yells louder, "His sister asked me to meet her here!" The policeman informs, "This is a police matter. The missing man we located today is still in serious danger." Ray takes out his driver's license, his photo ID as a licensed pharmacist and a photo of him and Mike. The cold-as-ice cop is not impressed. "You'll have to talk to my superior Captain Francis Burn when he arrives." With his paddy stick raised he vigorously waves it ordering Ray, "Now stay back!"

In a fluster Ray sees Ettie and Eileen walking fast toward the hospital entrance. He is desperately trying to stand away from the determined cop. Mike's best buddy, Ray, runs up to them, grabs Ettie's arm and escorts her up the numerous hospital steps. Following behind holding onto Ettie's pocketbook is anxious Eileen. Determined, Ray brings Ettie up to the stoic policeman announcing, "This is Mike Policano's sister, Ettie Cortino." Eileen pulls out Ettie's wallet and shows the policeman Ettie's St. Victor's parishioner identification card. Her only identification since she does not have a driver's license. The annoyed patrolman inspects it; stares at the distraught, head bandaged Ettie with authority orders, "You may go in; but these two have to stay behind." Eileen looks at him coldly shouting, "Just a minute; I'm her caregiver; she just got hurt and needs me to assist her." Noticing her aggressive manner is not working, Eileen smiles and sweetly coos, "Officer, please let me go with her." Patrolman Pharrell longingly gazes at Eileen with her long red hair and blazing green eyes. He proudly says, "An Irish Lassie! You may certainly go with her." He glares at Ray and sarcastically orders, "You stay back! You Italian wops have caused enough trouble in this city." Enraged, Ray is about to punch him in the face. Eileen intercepts. She hands Ray a piece of paper. Defuses him begging, "Don't be a fool; take this phone number and call Tess in California. She must know about Mike." Turning back, Eileen shouts to Ray, "If you can, call St. Victor's and get a priest here, it will make Ettie very happy." *Saint and Sinner!?*

Giving the Irish patrolman Pharrell a vile look, Ray runs down the hospital steps. Noticing a local coffee shop across the street, Ray enters shouting, "Where's the phone booth?" He takes out a five dollar bill asking the proprietor for change. The nonchalant owner hands him loose change. Ray rushes over to the phone booth holding onto the paper Eileen handed him with a phone number to reach Tess. In the phone booth, Ray closes the door; putting change in he asks the operator for long distance. He anxiously gives the phone number. He impatiently waits. His fidgety fingers are tapping the glass door of the smelly, tight booth. The long-distance line is ringing. It rings for a very long time. No one answers. Frustrated, Ray hangs up and dials Walsh's Tavern. Walsh, hearing Ray's urgent voice hollers, "How's our Mike?" "Not sure yet." Ray explains about the Irish policeman and his derogatory comments about Italians. Walsh laughs and says, "About time you Italians get the blunt of the insults. I've been called a dirty *mick* many a times. Get over it!"

Annoyed and anxious Ray requests, "Walsh, do you know any Irish cops you can call who will sneak me in the hospital to check on Mike?" No response from Walsh. Ray cries out, "I fear Mike is still in danger?" Walsh responds, "In that case, I'm good friends with Captain Francis Burn. I'll give him a call at the precinct." Walsh orders, "Wait there Ray and call me back in about ten minutes." Ray leaves the phone booth, buys a cup of coffee there. He stands impatiently waiting. After ten minutes, nervous Ray enters the phone booth and calls the tavern. Walsh answers, "Okay Ray, my Italian Pisano, go to the main hospital entrance again. Captain Francis Burn is waiting for you. He'll escort you in." Walsh adds, "You're now going to make a huge donation to the Police Benevolent Association." Relieved, Ray screams, "Anything. You're one hell of a guy Walsh. I owe you one. You old Mick!" Before hanging up Ray asks Walsh to do one more thing for him. Soon after, he leaves the phone booth and races out of the store. Running full speed like the half back he was at St. Peter's Prep back to the hospital, Ray bolts up the large marble steps two by two. At the top he is greeted by Captain Francis Burn. Coldly Patrolman Pharrell glares at Ray.

On the Fourth Floor of the Jersey City Medical Center, another Jersey City policeman is standing guard by a private room. The door is closed. Alongside of him, pacing back and forth, is nervous Eileen. Solemn Ettie is sitting on a chair while an elderly nurse Marie Linfante is administering to her head wound. Frustrated, Ettie pleads, "Please leave me alone. I'm fine. I'm here to see my brother." Nurse Marie kindly informs, "Be patient; after I clean this, and the proper authorities say it is okay, then you might be able to see your brother." Looking at the frazzled, woozy, wounded woman the nurse suggests, "I highly recommend Ettie that you see your doctor soon. You might have a mild concussion." Ettie explodes, "I don't care about me! I only care about my brother Mike!" Trying to calm Ettie, Eileen goes over to her and gently strokes Ettie's quivering, withered, rough hardworking hands.

The Fourth-Floor elevator door opens. Speedily walking out side by side are Captain Burn and Ray Sinnotti. Seeing the Captain, the slouching guard stands straight as an arrow. Captain Burn approaches him questioning, "Sergeant Pearsal has it been quiet here?" Stammering, he answers, "Yes sir!" "In that case, open the door, check inside. Let me know if all is in order," Captain Burn instructs. "Yes sir, Captain Burn," the sergeant dutifully responds. "After you report to me all is clear, I'm accompanying Mrs. Cortino in to see her brother." Eileen interjects, "Can I go in with her? She's unsteady from her fall." "No, I cannot allow you in. Only the immediate family!" Attempting to console her he assures Eileen, "No worries. I'll be there with her." The Captain looks over at Ray, ordering Eileen, "Mrs. Rivera stay with Mr. Sinnotti." He adds, "When I deem it's safe and wise, I'll decide whether to let you two in." Sergeant Walter Pearsall comes out of Mike's hospital room. He informs Captain Burn all is in order inside. Securely holding Mike's fretful sister Ettie's trembling hands, the high ranking official, Captain Burn escorts her into the hospital room. Sergeant Pearsall resumes his station guarding the hospital door to Mike's room. Anxiously waiting outside near the aloof sergeant are Ray and Eileen. The Irish lassie is pacing the floor furiously rubbing her sweaty hands. Fists tight, wiping a bead of sweat from his forehead, Ray is ready to punch the arrogant sergeant smack in the face.

Restless to find out what is going on, Ray sneaks up to the sergeant. He cunningly attempts to befriend him. Sergeant Pearsall is unduly twitchy. Ray hands him a stick of Wrigley's Spearmint gum with a ten dollar bill wrapped around it. With a hush voice Ray says, "Keep the pack." The sergeant looks at it showing no reaction. To further get in the guard's good graces, Ray brags, "Sergeant you know the guy in that hospital bed is my best friend since we were thirteen years old?" "Oh, really," unimpressed the sergeant shoves the gum and cash in his shirt pocket. Not one to give up, Ray continues to try to get in good with him. "You look like an informed cop. What happened to my best buddy in there?" Receiving no response Ray persists, "How did he get hurt and who is responsible?" The sergeant takes out the ten-dollar bill Ray gave him. With an authoritative manner he sarcastically asks, "You got any more of these, best buddy?" Looking around so no one observes, Ray pulls out a fifty-dollar bill from his wallet. He hands it to the sergeant. Grabbing it quickly, the cop scans the area; no one is around. He sneakily shoves it in his shirt pocket along with the ten-dollar bill in it. Pulling Ray closer to him, with a hushed voice the cop reveals, "They found your best buddy brutally beaten up under a bridge near the burnt-down garbage company." "What garbage company?" stunned, Ray echoes. "I heard them say it was the one the victim owned," replies the sergeant. Hearing this devastates Ray. Rubbing his face and moaning like a wounded animal Ray almost collapses. Enjoying seeing Ray falling apart, the bizarre questionable sergeant further reveals, "All the garbage trucks were burnt too!" With a menacing glare, the sleazy cop pulls Ray's arm warning him, "Remember wop, you didn't hear any of this from me." Observing this unsavory behavior from Jersey City's finest enrages Eileen. With shallow breath the fiery Irish lassie stammers, "He's worse than the goons that worked for my ex-husband." Sighing, Eileen adds, "Nothing worse than a corrupt cop'er."

Out-of-the blue Ray, along with frantic Eileen, are startled hearing earth shattering screams coming from Mike's hospital room where Captain Burn and Ettie entered a short time ago. In a flash, Captain Francis Burn storms out of the hospital room shouting for back up pushing Sergeant Pearsall, "Get in there armed and vigilant!" The sergeant draws his revolver and dashes into the room where Mike and Ettie are. Heading back in there, the Captain warns Ray and Eileen, "Stand back and take cover." Trembling, Eileen gathers all the strength she has trying to hold Ray from running in the room with the Captain. Gun shots are heard!!!!

CHAPTER FORTY-ONE

Friends, Foes, Foibles
Walpole, New Hampshire
February 1867

IN THE BARN, despondent Zeke is tending to Buck and Splash Dancer with his faithful canine Brutus right alongside him. Deeply troubled, Anna Lee mournfully exits the barn. Both are gravely pained and thwarted over what occurred between them with anguished, gravely malcontent Austin. Neither one feels exonerated even after pleading and genuinely attempting to elucidate to Austin as to what occurred the dreadful day Anna Lee and Austin's beautiful little girl Theresa Edith died in a hideous drowning accident.

With unbearable grief, along with Nannette and Dr. Jeremiah Holden, Anna Lee and Zeke endeavor to shield themselves from Austin's cruel and unfounded accusations. Austin violently blames them for his daughter's untimely, shocking death. Their genuine, and heartfelt plea fell on deaf ears. Austin is their judge and jury and they were, to him, all indisputably guilty.

After this disturbing encounter with his boss, trying to distract himself, Zeke half-heartedly brushes Buck. Brokenhearted, Anna Lee leaves the barn. Suddenly they are startled by the sound of an earth shattering gunshot shocking Anna Lee and Zeke. The blast from the gunshot agitates Buck, Splash Dancer and Brutus, the retired, military canine. Extremely fearful Anna Lee and Zeke are paralyzed not knowing what happened. Secretly Anna Lee fears her husband might have used the gun on himself.

Prior to the gunshot, with the infamous Henry Rifle on his burdened shoulder, frantic Austin hustles away from the barn. His devastating confrontation with his once loyal barn hand and trusted friend Zeke shook this once confident man to the core. As a husband, he is also enraged that his wife Anna Lee had the audacity and insolence to defend Zeke, Nannette and Dr. Jeremiah Holden. Austin convinces himself that through their lethal neglect they caused the death of his innocent Theresa Edith. As he is about to reach the main house, Austin notices a horse-drawn sleigh pulling up on his property. To his utter shock and rage, it is Dr. Holden and Nannette. When the horse is at a dead stop, the veterinarian and Nannette prepare to disembark from the sleigh.

Rising from the sleigh Dr. Holden addresses Austin. A shrieking gunshot silences the unsuspecting veterinarian. Dr. Holden is thrown down to the ground holding onto his chest. Unemotional, Austin stands there holding the pointed, smoking rifle at the fallen veterinarian. Traumatized Nannette screams. She jumps down from the sleigh. Whimpering, she hovers over the injured man pleading, "Jeremiah are you alright?" Austin throws down the rifle; sneering, he stammers, "Move away from that coward Nannette. If you don't, I'll shoot you too." He shouts, "This is war and you are my enemies." After hearing the shot, Zeke and Anna Lee are alert. They run like banshees toward Austin, the fallen Jeremiah, and hysterical Nannette.

Nannette throws herself over the wounded Dr. Holden. Seeing blood seeping out of his chest, nausea comes over her. She vomits. Seeing Austin standing there with pointed rifle, Anna Lee shouts, "Austin put that rifle down!" He points it at her. Racing toward them Zeke explodes, "Mr. Stevens put that gun down! If you hurt a hair on those women's heads, I'll kill you with my bare hands." Weary, Austin throws down the rifle. His knees buckle. He falls to the ground howling in pain as if he were the person shot. In terror, but with unbridle strength, Anna Lee goes to Nannette. Hands her a handkerchief to wipe the vomit from her face. Seeing she is calmer, Anna Lee orders Nannette, "Get up. Go into the house and take care of my babies." She reassures the terrified Nannette, "I will tend to Dr. Holden." Fearful, Nannette stares over at Austin who is on the ground. Like a hawk, Zeke is watching him.

Seeing that Austin is quieting down and heading toward the house with the rifle pointed at the ground, Anna Lee requests, "Hurry Zeke, go in the house. Bring me bandages and solutions for me to address Dr. Holden's wound." Anxious, Zeke observes Austin heading to the house. Austin's wife infers, "Zeke, my husband will be fine. He needed to get his unbearable festering pain out." Gazing on this horror scene, Anna Lee apologizes, "Sadly it had to be this way." She insists, "Go get the bandages. I must address Dr. Holden's wound now!" Hesitantly, Zeke obeys her.

Quickly returning from the main house, Zeke hands Anna Lee the items she requested. To contain the bleeding, she is pressing down hard on Dr. Holden's wound. "Zeke, we must carry him into the barn. I fear what might happen if we bring Dr. Holden into the house!" With tear-stained eyes Anna Lee exhorts, "It will truly disturb my tortured husband." "Sure Mrs. Stevens. I'll hurry and get a blanket and wheel barrel to bring him in."

Fretfully, Anna Lee inquires, "Are the twins good and Nannette?" She pauses, breathlessly adding, "How is Austin?" "You need not worry Ma'am; all okay in there!" He cautions, "First things first; let's take care of Jeremiah." He pauses warning, "We must be sure that the neighbors or officials don't find out about this *accident*." Hearing their conversation, the wounded Jeremiah moans an apology, "Sorry to cause you this trouble. I only came to bring you news." "No talking, Dr. Holden. You must save your energy!" Anna Lee lectures him. Covering Jeremiah with a blanket, Zeke carefully places him in the wheel barrel.

As Zeke is preparing to bring Dr. Holden to the barn, a pious woman of steel, Anna Lee gallantly preaches, "Heal the wounds of the body first, then the soul." Zeke and Dr. Holden stare at her in awe. They are deeply impressed by the calm wisdom of this refined, petite southern lady. *Love, loss, and strength transform Anna Lee Stevens into a Wise, Warrior Woman!*

CHAPTER FORTY-TWO

Transformation, Traditions, and Toads
Hollywood California
February 1956

IT IS THE morning after the infamous Dr. Rudolpho Della Porta's celebrity party welcoming Grandma Hollywood's daughters and granddaughters. Mary Grace and her daughter are up bright and early ready to leave for Regina Helen's audition. Mateo offered to drive them. Not one to look for favors, but unsure about driving around this overpopulated area, Mary Grace hesitantly accepts Mateo's offer. Annoyed, Regina questions her mother's decision, "Why do we need him to drive us?" Irritated she suggests, "Mom, you can drive the pink Cadillac. Besides that's your favorite color and we'll look like confident women when we pull up to the studio." Before Mary Grace can respond, singing, Mateo struts in. He kisses Mary Grace's well-polished, long nails on her slim hand, "Why you look beautiful day and night, Sunshine Mary," Mateo quips. He sultry gazes over at the sullen Regina and remarks, "You'll be famous pretty girl after this audition." Teasingly he suggests, "You might be too popular to accompany me and Elena to the Hollywood Bowl tonight." Regina shoots him a loathing glare. Not one bit phased, Mateo pompously announces, "My handsome friend Nunzio will be your escort pretty young thing."

Scowling, Regina shouts, "Shut that phony trap! You are nothing but a misfit. I 'm not going tonight or any time with you or your cohort Nunzio." Amused, Mateo laughs heartily. Regina retorts, "When I am famous, you'll be dead as a doorknob to me." To calm them down and in a hurry to leave, Mary Grace teases, "They say when two people fight with one another, it really means they are attracted to each other." "You are a very wise woman, Mary Grace," Mateo coos. He looks over at Regina. "I am attracted to woman who have fight in them," Mateo says. Looking at his Rolex watch he announces, "We must leave this minute before you miss your audition." Bowing Mateo says, "Your chariot awaits you!" These three strong-willed, confident, egocentric people strut out to the chariot. The pink Cadillac convertible awaits them.

Not aware of what was transpiring this morning between Mateo, Regina and Mary Grace, Grandma Hollywood is sound asleep in her flouncy pink boudoir. Getting beauty sleep is top priority to this expectant, ageless woman. Granddaughter Elena is in the bedroom she shares with Regina reading. She heard the bantering between Mateo and Regina; not wanting to get involved, Elena deliberately stays sequestered in the room. Whereas Tess, in the third bedroom which she is sharing with her sister Mary Grace, hears the chatter in the other room. She has more important issues to address than deal with their egotistical behavior. While Grandma Hollywood, Tess, and Elena are addressing their personal needs, they are suddenly startled by Grandma Hollywood's dog, Cleo the Cocker Spaniel barking at the ringing doorbell.

Not wanting to deal with Cleo, Tess calls for her mother, "Mom there is someone at the door and Cleo is getting frisky." In a deep sleep, Tess's mother does not respond. Not wanting to bother her daughter, Tess quickly throws on a bathrobe and heads to the door. Cleo is standing there showing teeth to Tess. Scared, but trying to be brave, Tess grabs hold of the want-to-be watch dog in her shaking arms. Holding tightly onto squirming Cleo, Tess peers through the peek hole. Seeing Rodney, she quickly opens the door. Tess thrushes the wiggling Cleo into Rodney's hands, turns and gestures for him to follow her as she heads to the kitchen.

Preparing to make coffee, Tess calls out to Rodney who dropped Cleo in the living room with a squeak rubber toad toy he found on the floor. He rushes into the kitchen. Tess offers, "Elena is still in the bedroom. Regina and her mother left for the audition." Getting herself a coffee cup, she asks, "Why are you here so early in the morning?" Apologizing, Rodney replies, "I have something I want Elena to read." He pulls a folder from his canvas pack on his back. He jokes, "I fancy Regina will want to read it also." "Regina will not be back until late afternoon and I don't want to disturb Elena." Bringing her coffee to the table Tess remarks, "My daughter must be exhausted."

Bored with his squeaky rubber toad, Cleo scampers over to Grandma Hollywood's bedroom. He flops down near the door. He is trained not to wake her up too early in the morning. In the kitchen, Tess retrieves cream from the refrigerator. She mentions, "As you know, we only arrived yesterday and my mother insisted we go to that bizarre party last night." Rodney is half listening; he is fussing with the folder. Tess blurts out, "I fear all this excitement with little rest will tax Elena and make her ill." Compassionately, but insistent, Rodney states, "I will leave the folder here for you to give to Elena." Adamantly he states, "Make sure she gets it! I left a note explaining why I want her to read it ASAP."

Actually, not interested in what Rodney is saying about some folder, yet baffled, Tess, scanning to be sure her mother and daughter are not around, offers, "Personally, I thought you came here to remind me to get in touch with Monsignor James Cooney." Whispering, Rodney says, "I was hoping you already contacted him and had information for me." "Rodney!" Tess raises her voice, "It is only eight thirty in the morning!" Slamming down her coffee cup she exclaims, "I'm fatigued and need time to prepare myself for this delicate conversation." Rodney stands there startled by her aggressive reaction.

The phone rings. Both stare at the phone. Tess ponders whether to pick it up. She waits; on the fourth ring she hesitantly raises the receiver. "Hello? Yes, this is Tess Policino." Hearing what the person on the other end informs, Tess lets out a high shrill, "Oh my god!" Staggering she grabs onto the kitchen chair to balance herself. Rodney takes the phone from her. Tess pulls it out of his hand instructing him, "Please, let yourself out; this urgent call is personal!" Rodney swivels around inquiring, "Is it Monsignor James Cooney?" Shaking, Tess vehemently screams, "No! Please leave." Preparing to depart, Rodney instructs, "I'll leave this folder on the kitchen table." He plops it down insisting, "Make sure Elena gets it!" Holding her hand over the phone she shouts, "Go!"

Leaving, Rodney disturbs Cleo. His barking wakes up Grandma Hollywood and alerts Elena. Simultaneously Grandmother Hollywood and Elena exit their bedrooms. Followed by Cleo, they head to the kitchen. With downcast eyes; head low on her pulsing chest; tears rolling down her fearful face; Tess is shaking uncontrollably. Elena runs to her mother. Taking hold of Tess's head she raises it; looks at her mother's red-rimmed eyes; frantically questions, "What's wrong Mom?" Still sleepy, Grandma Hollywood walks over to perplexed Elena. She takes her by the shoulder moving her away from Tess. "Elena go to your bedroom. Your Mom's exhausted," explaining this to her confused granddaughter. Compassionately Grandma Hollywood infers, "Your Mom needs substance. I'll make her a nice cup of tea and she'll be fine."

Tears streaming down her face, Tess glares at her mother. Scornfully announcing, "This time Mom, tea will not solve this unspeakable issue." Elena stops in her tracks hearing her distraught Mother's forewarning. Reluctantly leaving the kitchen, Elena notices the folder on the kitchen table with her name on it. Quizzically, Elena takes hold of it. Keeping the folder close to her pulsing heart; a stark awareness comes over her. Dismayed, Elena cries out, "Oh, No! Did my worst nightmare come true!?"

CHAPTER FORTY-THREE

Gangsters, Gambling, Drugs, Corruption

Jersey City Medical Center
February 1956

SHRIEKING GUNSHOTS ARE heard coming from hospital Room 408 where unconscious Mike and compromised Ettie are in. Captain Burn races out of the room calling for backup. Chaos infiltrates this once quiet hospital. With revolver in hand the Captain runs back in. As ordered, the sergeant who was guarding the room is already in there. More shots are heard. Petrified, Ray and Eileen huddle together. Deafening sirens are heard throughout the hospital along with the sound of police squad cars outside. Ray can no longer stand idly by. He orders Eileen to stay under cover. Fearless, Ray grabs the chair Ettie was sitting on. Holding it like a shield or weapon he crashes into the chaotic hospital Room 408. Shots, banging, screams, and moans are heard from Room 408.

Police are pouring out of the elevator onto the Fourth Floor of the Jersey Medical Center. They spread out. A handful are checking every room. Others vigilantly enter Room 408. Piercing noises and weeping are heard from there. Exiting the elevator after the cops, nurse Marie Linfante runs over to shivering, hysterical Eileen. The devoted, competent nurse covers her over with her strong arms inquiring, "Where is Ettie?" Eileen points to Room 408 screaming. "She's in there!" She further inquires, "Is the priest in there too?" "What priest?" confused Eileen questions. Nurse Marie explains, "A young priest came into the hospital a short while ago. He said he received a call from Ettie requesting he come to the hospital to give a blessing to her brother." "I guess Ray did get to call St. Victor's?" Eileen responds.

Fearing something is not right, Eileen further questions the nurse, "Would the priest only have access to the room through the door of the one guarded by the cop?" "Yes," Marie Linfante quickly replies. Puzzled she further questions, "Why?" Eileen explains, "Ray and I never left this area. We never saw a priest enter or anyone for that matter other than police." Worried, Eileen interrogates further, "Marie, is there any other way in there?" Awareness stuns Marie. She calls out, "There's a fire escape in the back." Distressed she recalls, "Oh my goodness, it goes up to the window in that room!" Nurse Marie orders Eileen, "We must get out of here immediately and notify the officials."

Policemen are surrounding the entire fourth floor. A cop approaches them. "We have to escort you out of here now," the patrolman orders Eileen and nurse Marie. He informs, "We'll cover you till you get to the elevator." Attempting to keep their anxiety low he assures them, "A policeman will accompany you down to safety." Nurse Marie heads to the elevator, imploring the policeman, "I have something important to tell you!" Not heeding her, he orders, "Move on!"

Not trusting the cop, Eileen refuses to go. The cop loses his patience. With anger he warns, "Move before I arrest you." With the cop dragging her out, Eileen moans, "Tony, where are you when I need you!" As the elevator door is closing on obstinate Eileen and nurse Marie Linfante, who is desperately trying to alert the cop, multiple shots, followed by terrifying screams, are heard from room 408.

CHAPTER FORTY-FOUR

Regrets, Revelations, and Remembrances
Walpole, New Hampshire
February 1857

RACING TO THE barn with the wounded Dr. Holden in a wheel barrel, Zeke flings open the heavy barn door then rolls the injured vet over to an empty stall. Heatedly Anna Lee follows carrying bandages and solutions in her sweaty, shaking hands. In the barn, she immediately goes over to the wounded veterinarian. As Anna Lee is cleaning the wound, she instructs Zeke to tear a piece of the white bandage. "Farm hand to nurse," he murmurs as he hands her the bandage folded properly. Anna Lee interrogates, "Zeke you seem to know what you are doing." "Well, Ma'am I learned during the war." They stop talking hearing Jeremiah moan. Anna Lee calms him by informing, "Thank goodness Dr. Holden it is only a superficial wound." Wiping the bloody area, pleased she says, "The bleeding is stopping." Sighs of relief are heard from Jeremiah. Zeke automatically hands her another clean bandage and tape. He is also impressed with Anna Lee's nursing ability. "Do you think he needs stitches?" Zeke inquires. "He might," Anna Lee answers. "Let's see if this bandage keeps it from opening," she comments. Knowledgeably Zeke includes, "We'll have to watch for infection."

Dr. Jeremiah Holden stammers, "Is Nannette alright?" "Yes. She is in the house with my twins," wiping his moist brow, Anna Lee assures him. With bulging eyes, Dr. Holden stares up at Anna Lee recollecting, "I saved your life and your twins; now you saved my life." "Fate," he calls out. Closing his eyes, the injured vet murmurs, "My sweet Nannette." He dozes off. Zeke comments, "Fate or pay back?" Noticing Anna Lee not responding he asks, "Should I go and check on Mr. Stevens?" Suddenly, the barn door swings open. Austin stands there looking dreadful and pitiful. In a bitter yet conciliatory voice he cries out, "What have I done?" He stumbles over to Dr. Holden who is covered over with a clean horse blanket sleeping on soft hay. Hearing Austin's voice, Buck whines. Smelling liquor on Austin's breath, Zeke grabs hold of Austin before he falls on top of Dr. Holden. "Come on Boss, let's go over to Buck he wants you to stroke him," insists Zeke.

With hands twitching, Austin awkwardly shuffles along with Zeke. Observing her husband in this condition and loathing what he did to Dr. Holden, Anna Lee turns her head away from him. She moves from Dr. Holden calling over to Zeke, "As soon as you are able and confident he will heal, I want you to bring Dr. Holden to his sleigh." Zeke looks at her in disbelieve. Anna Lee reiterates, "You can take him and Nannette back to his house where he will be safe." Seeing Zeke bewildered, she adds, "Nannette is more than capable to nurse him back to good health."

Revived yet dejected, Austin turns and pleads with his wife, "Take Jeremiah into the house. I will behave." He shudders, "We need to resolve this dreadful situation now!" Zeke and Anna Lee look at him questionably. They are not sure whether he is sincere or has other sinister thoughts. Noticing their scornful look and terror, Austin retorts belligerently, "You gave the vet lying there a pardon, I believe I deserve the same in kind." Austin crouches down near Buck who nozzles him calming him. Having an epiphany, Anna Lee's husband rises up. In a contrite voice Austin announces, "I wish to make reparations for my loathsome behavior."

In the parlor by the dwindling fire Nannette is holding tightly the sleeping twins in each of her arms. Gently rocking them back and forth soothing them gives her comfort. Nannette is waiting patiently to find out how Dr. Holden is. Hearing Austin leaving the house she is extremely concerned. Shortly after, voices are heard as the kitchen door opens. Zeke is conversing with Anna Lee. Nannette is relieved hearing Jeremiah call out her name. She is surprised hearing Austin's contrite tone politely saying, "Dr. Holden, Zeke will place you on the sofa near the fire to warm you. It is too cold in the barn." After Zeke brings Jeremiah to the sofa, Austin requests, "Zeke, please go to the cellar and bring up a bottle of my finest brandy." Under his breath Zeke murmurs, "Hope it's not for you; you had enough already."

Anna Lee runs over to Nannette, thanks her, carefully taking the twins from her. She kisses both of them murmuring, "My dear Austin Hamish and sweet Rachel Melanie; your mean mother abandoned you." Tears streaming down her face, Anna Lee swears, "I promise you I will never let you be harmed or leave you alone ever!" Hearing his wife's torturous plea, Austin lowers his head in shame. His grieving wife's touching words move him deeply. "How selfish of me. My dear Anna Lee has been enduring this grief alone," Austin moans.

Dr. Jeremiah Holden overhears what Austin says. With shallow breath he comments, "Don't be so hard on yourself Mr. Stevens, we all have secrets and past infractions." Interrupting Dr. Holden, Zeke enters the room carrying a bottle of age-old brandy. Austin thanks Zeke; takes it from him; opens it and pours a glass full. He carries it over to Dr. Holden. "Here, sip it slowly; this is the best medicine ever." Stunned by Austin's kind attention to Dr. Holden, Anna Lee, Zeke, and Nannette are in disbelief. Surprisingly, Austin hovers over Dr. Holden with intense consideration.

The twins' sudden crying startle the unique group of people back to reality. Anna Lee excuses herself, "I must go nurse the babies." Nannette offers to carry one of them upstairs. The three men gaze at the women leaving the room carrying the twins. Their piercing cries consume the atmosphere. "Good lungs on those two," Zeke remarks. "Of course," Austin proudly interjects, "They are Stevens!" He immediately apologizes, "Please excuse me; there I go again being an arrogant bastard." Dr. Holden and Zeke are amused that Austin let his hair down. With the women and babies out of the room, Austin requests, "Zeke, would you mind if I ask you to leave? Dr. Holden and I have much to discuss and absolve." In a friendly jester, patting Zeke on his shoulder, Austin stammers, "We will have our man to man talk later Zeke."

Austin pauses, looks over at Jeremiah. He is alert. Austin requests, "If you are up to it, my good man, we have much to resolve." Dr. Holden glances at him perplexed. With down cast eyes Austin pleads, "I must make proper atonement for shooting you without a valid cause." Jeremiah weakly retorts, "There is much I must share with you also."

Before he and Jeremiah have their heart-to-heart discussion, something stirs Austin. He tells Dr. Holden, "I'll be with you in a moment." He heads over to Zeke. Austin whispers in his ear, "Zeke, I left the rifle in the kitchen behind the closet door. Take it back to the barn and lock it up." "Sure enough, Mr. Stevens," relieved he answers. Tapping Zeke on his back, Austin adds, "My apologies to you too." With sincerity in his voice Austin offers, "No excuses for my bad behavior. Hope you have it in you to forgive me; if not, I totally understand." Mute, Zeke nods affirmatively adding a thumbs up. Zeke stares at Austin beseeching, "Mr. Stevens, no need to apologize to me." He wipes the moisture from his eye and adds, "It's that fine woman you married, Mrs. Anna Lee, the mother of those beautiful twins, that's the *one* who deserves your apology!" Pausing Zeke adds, "Your wife and love." Austin bows his head in disgrace. In a hush voice he responds, "You are a wise man Zeke." *As different as these two men are, their commonalities are greater.*

Dutifully carrying the rifle to the barn Zeke wonders what transpired in a short time to alter Austin's previous bitter almost fatal action. Just a few hours ago, Zeke recalls, his boss Austin, was violently accusing his wife and him for the death of his daughter along with spitting hate and disgust over Nannette and Dr. Jeremiah Holden's current situation. Zeke, before he enters the barn, stops short, stares at the rifle and reflects back to another time and another place. Memories sweep through him. "Everyone has skeletons in their closet," shuddering he reminisces.

Upstairs in the twin's bedroom, Anna Lee is nursing famished Austin Hamish while Nannette is holding and quietly singing to content Rachel Melanie. Believing she does not have the right to talk to Mrs. Stevens on a personal level, Nannette remains silent. Yet, she is bursting to clear up with Anna Lee what transpired the terrible day of Theresa Edith's unbearable death; the birth of the twins; and her going to live with Dr. Holden as his homemaker. There is much to be discussed and resolved between these two worthy women. *Their female gender bonds them together more than they currently recognize.*

CHAPTER FORTY-FIVE

Strange Awakenings, Startling Revelations, Stark Epiphanies
Hollywood, California
January 1956

RODNEY IS LEAVING. Terrified Tess is on the phone. After placing a folder on kitchen table for Elena, Rodney departs slamming the front door shut. Spirited Cleo's earsplitting barking wakes Grandma Hollywood and disturbs Elena. The two get up and leave their bedrooms followed by demanding Cleo. Grandmother and granddaughter enter the kitchen. Sitting on a kitchen chair bent over, with her head in her hands Tess is moaning. "What is wrong with you Tess?" her concerned mother cries out. Elena winces, "Mom, what's the matter?" Hearing her daughter's alarmed voice makes Tess put on a good front; she does not want to upset Elena. "Nothing, sweetheart. I'm just tired from last night." To distract her daughter, Tess points to the kitchen table whispering, "Rodney left a folder for you on the table." "I see it Mom." Elena says with agitation. Silence in the room is deafening. No one wants to upset the apple cart. They are all hoping to get their strength back after last night's party.

Not one to have a day go by without something exciting to do or celebrate, Grandma Hollywood announces, "Well my dears today I have plans to take you both to Max Factor's Studio to get makeovers and hairdos." She smiles broadly revealing, "I have a surprise too. Elena will be modeling some of my costumes." Infuriated, Elena screams, "Absolutely not!" Shaken up by the recent phone call, Tess throws her arms up in the air and shouts, "Please; enough you two." Taking a sip of her now cold coffee, Tess murmurs, "I have an urgent matter to attend to." Pouring herself a cup of fresh hot coffee Grandma Hollywood, along with Elena, who is holding onto the folder Rodney left, stand there waiting for Tess to calm down.

Standing up, Tess apologizes to Elena, "Sorry to upset you dear. I'm fine." Forcing a smile, she suggests, "Take the folder into the bedroom. Rodney was persistent that you look at it ASAP." Noticing Elena hesitating, Tess offers, "I'll make you some tea and toast and bring it into the bedroom." Avoiding more drama Elena concedes. Clutching the folder from Rodney she leaves. Panting along, Cleo follows her. As soon as Elena is out of the kitchen and they hear her bedroom door close, Grandma Hollywood interrogates, "Tess, what's going on? You look like you've seen a ghost?" Putting the tea kettle on the stove and placing slices of oatmeal bread in the toaster, in a hush tone Tess reveals, "Mom, I received a call from the Jersey City Police Department early this morning." With shallow breath, Tess squeaks, "They found Mike. He's been missing for days." "Oh my dear," blurts out Grandma Hollywood. "Shush!" Tess requests. "This is not for Elena's ears or anyone else," she cautions her mother. Fearful, Grandma Hollywood plops down on a chair. "What the..." Grandma says. "Don't interject, Mom. I'll explain further the best I can without getting too emotional," adamant Tess says to her puzzled mother. Choked up, Tess attempts to clarify, "A few days ago they found Mike under a railroad trestle viciously beaten and in a coma. It was near his now burnt down garbage company." "Oh, my god!" holding onto her pulsating heart Grandma Hollywood calls out. "Quiet, Mom or I'll say no more." "I promise," Grandma Hollywood whispers prompting Tess to go on. "Mike is in the hospital semiconscious, but the police told me the doctor's say he should be okay!" Tess wipes the tears rolling down her morbid face. "I told the police I will take a plane and fly home as soon as possible." Grandma Hollywood bolts up ready to dispute this when Tess reveals, "The police were adamant that I stay here; they warned me that..." Tess chokes up, "I would be in grave danger as Mike still is."

With Neiman Marcus potholders in hand, Tess takes the tea kettle, pours the boiling water in a cup which has a green tea bag in it. She hastily butters the toast. "Wait here, I'll bring these to Elena." Tess is back shortly. "Tess, my heart is pounding, I think you should . . ." Angry, Tess warns, "If you say another word Mom, I'll end this conversation right now!" "Forgive me. I'm an old woman. After your father died suddenly, I'm always fearful of hearing bad news." Grandma Hollywood glances at her distressed daughter and confirms, "For you my dear Tess, I'm ready to hear all without interruption." Flustered Grandma Hollywood places her trembling hand over her pulsing heart and professes, "I promise you Tess, I will keep it safely locked up in my fragile heart."

Surprised by her mother's vulnerability, and warmed by her mother's sensitive side, in a low voice, Tess reiterates, "As I mentioned, Mike was brought to Jersey City Medical Center alive but in very bad shape." "This is terrible," Tess's mother mouths. "His hospital room is heavily guarded," Tess informs. "Why?" Grandma Hollywood asks. "Word on the street is there is a vendetta against Mike's family as far back as the turn of the century beginning in Salerno, Italy." After taking a sip of her cold coffee, Tess resumes, "For years, I heard whispers between Mike and his sister Ettie, saying Mike's grandfather and their Uncle Nick Scat were involved in a murder in the old country."

Tess pauses, reflecting on her sister-in-law Ettie's fear of the Malocchio, the Italian Evil Eye. "Oh my gosh, Ettie always warned Mike about the dreadful Evil Eye." "What?" her mother asks. Upset, Tess further explains, "The old Italians believe that if someone is jealous of you or out to get you for a past vendetta, they put the Malocchio or Evil Eye on you." Grandma Hollywood echoes, "Evil Eye? Like Voodoo?" Tess reiterates, "Yes Mom, they believe it will even cause a terrible death. Murder!" In disbelief, Grandma Hollywood places her shaking hand to her mouth. To quell her mother from further scrutiny Tess pleads, "Mother, don't say another word, until I finish!" Tess admonishes her shocked mother. "This is serious business; we are talking about the Mafia," Tess alerts. "Oh, my god! This is awful!" Grandma Hollywood dramatically cries out.

Opening the door Elena calls out, "Mom, what time are we going with Grandma? I must get in touch with Rodney before we go!" "Elena, not now. I am busy with Grandma. We'll discuss it after I finish here." Annoyed, Elena slams the door on Cleo's paw. The bruised dog howls. Hearing his painful growls, Elena opens the door. Cleo limps in. Back in her bedroom Elena resumes reading the notorious script Rodney left her. A stunned look etches across her face. She can't believe Rodney wrote this after he was warned by Monsignor Cooney and her mother not to discuss a thing about this to a soul; never mind write about it in hopes of having it produced. She recalls Rodney swearing 'never to reveal a word.' "When I reach him, I will give him hell," she utters under her breath. Fear of the repercussions it may cause, Elena groans, "He is risking the lives of people I care about. Rodney's blabbering mouth is a loose cannon and perhaps even dangerous." She slams the script on the floor. "He must be stopped!" she explodes. Cleo places his paws over his floppy ears. Hostile, Elena glares down at the script admonishing, "My god, Rodney's wicked written words about this undisclosed mystery is a death sentence for innocent people." In a child-like manner Elena mockingly makes fun, "Not only like the devil's, Rodney's ears are huge like his fat ugly mouth!" "Dear me," fearful, she cries out, "His pen's a deadly sword; a weapon of destruction!"

In the kitchen Tess is desperately trying to figure out the horrors that went on in Jersey City while she and Elena were traveling to California. She reveals to her mother Grandma Hollywood, "I've noticed for a long time that Mike has not been himself but I did nothing about it. I've been preoccupied with Elena's mood swings these last few months." Wiping her moist eyes with her sleeve Tess moans, "Elena is my priority!" "I realize your daughter is the most vulnerable and your number one concern, but what about your husband's needs?" Grandma Hollywood tenderly lectures her frazzled daughter. "I don't know what to do Mom?" Tess moans. Pausing and pondering, Tess shouts out, "I'm going to fly back to New Jersey. I will leave Elena here with you and Mary Grace." "As the police warned you Tess it is not safe for you to go back there," fearful Grandma Hollywood alerts her determined daughter.

Grandma Hollywood further cautions, "This so-called mafia vendetta most likely will apply to you as Mike's wife and I fear for Elena too." She is seriously frightened for her daughter and granddaughter. Tess strikes back, "I know Mom, but he is my husband!" She informs, "I intend to contact Ettie or Mike's friend Ray and feel them out."

Tess and her mother cease talking when they hear the door to Elena's room open. Quickly, Grandma Hollywood suggests, "You stay here Tess and make your calls. I'll take Elena with me." Relieved, Tess responds, "Thank you Mom. I must take care of this immediately and I don't want Elena aware of any of it." Grandma Hollywood rises, hugs her troubled daughter. "Elena will be fine in my hands." She stops, lovingly looks at her daughter and with compassion remarks, "I know you will make the right decision. I am proud of you Tess." Grandma Hollywood hugs her daughter tightly.

Elena walks in. She is surprised to see her mother and Grandma Hollywood in a warm embrace. "What's going on in here?" she shyly calls out. The mother and grown daughter separate. Tess goes up to her daughter. She gives Elena a kiss on both her cheeks, "Elena, you and your grandmother will be going alone to Max Factor Studio this morning." Smoothing down Elena's curly hair, she mentions, "I forgot I have to arrange for you to start high school classes here." Handing Elena the tea and toasts she says, "Today is the deadline."

Elena is ready to interject when Tess orders, "Contact Rodney then get ready to go with Grandma." Before Elena can say a word, Tess heads to her bedroom to make her calls to Jersey City. Grandma Hollywood grandly announces, "Dear, dear Elena, you and I will have a grand time today." She reminds Elena, "Remember, you and Regina are going to the Hollywood Bowl tonight with Mateo and Nunzio." Moving Elena toward the bedroom she gloats, "I promise you, you'll talk about it for years after." Noticing Elena ready to refute her, Grandma Hollywood points her ringed finger at Elena, "Don't say another word! Never forget, my word is the law here." She looks at her frustrated granddaughter. Teasingly she demands, "Finish your toast and tea. Then go get dressed. We leave in an hour!" Trying to lighten things up Grandma Hollywood sings out, "As they say in Hollywood, 'The Show Must Go On.'"

In the bedroom, nervous but determined, Tess, through the long-distance operator, places her call to Jersey City. She decides to bypass Ettie and Ray for now. She is determined to go directly to the authorities. This distraught wife murmurs a short prayer while holding on line waiting for a response. Tess is relieved when she hears the operator announce, "Your long-distance call is connected. You may proceed with it now." "Hello, hello," Tess, calls out. A moment of deadly silence. Finally Tess is relieved when she finally hears a voice inquiring, "Is this Tess Policino? Mike Policano's wife?" "Yes, this is she. Who am I speaking with?" she asks. "This is Captain Burn of the Jersey City Police Department; we spoke earlier." "How is my husband?" Tess blurts out, "He's doing somewhat better. Although, I must inform you he is still being guarded in a secret location and still under medical care." "Why under guard?" Tess bursts out. The Captain takes a deep breath and reveals, "This might be difficult for you to hear but someone attempted to shoot him dead in the hospital room." He hesitates then continues, "His sister Ettie Cortino saved his life." "Ettie? My god, how?" Tess screams. "That brave little woman threw herself on top of him." Panicking Tess asks, "Is she alright?" The Captain immediately explains, "She is! Someone up there was watching over her." He further relays, "The perpetrator, or shooter in lay terms, missed her by a hair." He pauses and adds, "We believe he was shocked to see a woman of her age do that. The shooter dropped his arm, the gun fell to the ground and went off and hit another innocent by stander." Tess is in disbelief. She immediately asks, "Did they get the shooter?" He corrects her, "Shooters. Yes, Mrs. Policino, we did but we are not at liberty to release any further information." "Why not, I have a right to know! They were trying to kill my husband." He explains, "Mrs. Policino I understand your reasoning, but it is still under investigation." Tess concedes, "I am not pleased but I hear you."

Pondering Tess reveals, "I will fly home soon. I must see my husband!" She further inquires, "Why are they after my husband?" Tess experiences total silence on the other end of the phone after asking this question. After a few noiseless moments, the Captain with sincerity and concern responds, "This question cannot be answered at the present time. As I warned you before, it is not wise Mrs. Policino for you to come home under these precarious circumstances." After taking a long deep breath the Captain with a stern voice informs, "We discussed this with your family here in Jersey City along with the police authorities, including the FBI." "FBI!" shouts Tess. "Yes, Mrs. Policino they had to be brought in since your husband was missing for a few days. It is considered a kidnapping after two days." "Really?" Tess questions. "The FBI must be notified," he reiterates.

"Back to my original recommendation Mrs. Policino I cannot stress enough, you must not attempt to come back to Jersey City at the present time." Vehemently Tess disagrees, "I think I have the right to make that decision for myself. For her safety, I will leave my daughter here with my mother." In a harsh voice the Captain demands, "Mrs. Policino you will be making a grave mistake if you come back here." Tess does not respond. The Captain tries to convince her by informing, "Even your husband insists we warn you. Mike demanded we officially order you to stay where you are." The Captain delineates and underlines the real danger Tess will be encountering, "We are dealing with illegal drugs and gambling, deadly revenge, mass corruption and gangsters who are ruthless murderers." He takes a deep breath and shouts, "The Mob!" "You mean the Mafia, don't you Captain?" Tess responds. The Captain is silent. Recognizing that he has her best interests in mind she concedes, "I hear you but my gut tells me my place belongs with my husband." Still silence from the Captain.

Tess again inquires, "Why are they after my husband?" "Mrs. Policino, while I appreciate your concern, I must once again inform you, this is an ongoing, active investigation. We cannot reveal any information." He further cautions, "First and foremost, my duty is to alert you. You, your immediate and extended family, and perhaps friends, are in great danger." "My extended family and friends too? Oh, dear!" Tess blurts out. "Now do you understand Mrs. Policino why you are safer staying right where you are? We don't want you in harm's way!" the Captain robustly reiterates. After a second, he boldly insists, "Must end this call now. I have a lot to do ma'am. Stay put and safe!" Tess hears a click on the phone. The Captain hangs up.

Solemnly standing there, Tess is desperately trying to absorb and digest all she just heard. This cautionary phone call has the makings of a scandalous revelation, a rude awaking, and a frantic warning for Tess and her family. This heart-wrenching, informative phone conversation is overwhelmingly inconceivable for Tess to totally process. Inhaling deeply, a past remembrance enlightens her. Tess experiences an alarming epiphany as she cries out, "Father Arthur Schwartz and Juan!"

CHAPTER FORTY-SIX

Gangsters are Breaking Up that Old Gang of Mine
Walsh's Tavern, Jersey City, NJ
January 1956

WALSH'S TAVERN IS a buzz with all the drama that has recently occurred with buddies Michael Policino and Ray Sinnotti. Stoic Walsh stands behind the bar preaching about the horrific shenanigans that occurred these last few days in his fair but corrupt Jersey City. Inebriated Brendan, the Professor, is back at his old bar stool pontificating about the *Fall of Man*. He is still mourning and grieving the loss of his dear, sweet, pious Irish-born mother. Deep down both of these fine old Irishmen, who have seen and heard a lot in their many years, are feeling the strains of life. Walsh and Brendan are suffering a longing of the good old days.

Suddenly the heavy-wooded door to the bar swings wide open blowing in a huge commanding figure. To Walsh's surprise and joy it is his hero and savior, the Big Guy, Tony Rivera. Brendan lifts his fallen head from off the bar, looks over at the Big Guy and shouts, "Well, well, well, look what the wayward winds have blown in; Hercules." The Professor further pontificates gazing at Tony, "Have you returned from Crete where you sent the Cretan Bull back to Eurystheus, who released it into the streets of Marathon?" Big Tony stares at him without remarking.

Walsh immediately places a Boiler Maker in front of the Big Guy. Tony stands in front of the bar facing the bar owner. "Thanks, Walsh." Tony slugs down the bourbon followed by the ice-cold lager beer. "Welcome back, Amigo," Walsh calls out. "We've missed you." Tony looks around. He remarks, "Heard a lot happened after I left!" "You can say that again," Walsh calls out. "Before we discuss it; did you bring your daughter, Angela Maria home with you from your hometown in Columbia?" Walsh asks.

With a broad smile on his bearded face, the Big Guy brags, "Sure did and she is prettier than ever." Brendan shouts from the end of the bar, "Where is she?" Big Tony looks hesitantly at Brendan and responds, "Safe and sound; and don't ask any more questions." Noticing that Tony means business, Walsh fills his glass up again and remarks, "Tony, guess you heard about Mike and Ray?" He slugs down his bourbon and beer then slams the glass down on the bar. In a booming voice the Big Guy hollers, "Sure the hell did and I ain't happy about any of it!"

Soon after, two Jersey City police officers enter the bar laughing and talking loudly. "We finally got those damn Italian wops," the older cop brags. He turns and orders, "Hey Walsh pour this rookie Sal a short one and me a tall one." The tavern owner brings it over to them. The two cops continue to talk loudly. The arrogant and older one says, "They still can't figure out how that Kraut and that Gringo got in Mike's guarded hospital room." "The brainless cop guarding it is now under investigation," in a lower voice, he says. Patrolman Sal reveals, "Word around the precinct is that he was on the take." Looking around at Big Tony, Brendan and Walsh, the older cop shoves the rookie ordering, "Keep quiet numskull this is police business." Sneering at the others at the bar, the older cop warns, "There are big ears around here."

Fuming, the older cop saunters up to Walsh, throws some money on the bar, and calls over his shoulder, "Hey big mouth; we're out of here. Get a move on!" In a huff, the seasoned, racist cop and raw rookie leave slamming the door behind them. Sarcastically Walsh hollers back, "Thanks. See you later than sooner Flatfoot!" Brendan calls after, "Another one bites the dust." He adds insult to injury, "Soon that naive rookie, alias numskull, will be dust if he doesn't sew his trap shut." Walsh sneers, "That older Flatfoot gives the Jersey City Police Department a bad name." Raising his head from the bar, Brendan echoes, "Dark as the devil's soul. Corruption at its finest."

Scanning the bar and room and seeing it is empty other than Walsh, Brendan and himself, Tony further questions, "Okay, now that we are alone; what in hells name is the real story about Mike? Damn it, how did Ray get involved?" Walsh informs, "First, Mike was missing for a day or so. The night of his brother-in-law Carlo's funeral, Mike opens the door to my bar. He was about to enter when he turns around and poof, he disappears into thin air. From that moment on Mike was missing." "Yeah, yeah, I heard that from Eileen and he was found a day or so later beaten up under the railroad trestle." "Right you are Big Guy! I'm sure you also know those evil bastards burnt down Mike's garbage company." Stamping his feet, in a fury Walsh shouts, "Even all of those expensive garbage trucks; every last one of them!" "Yeah, yeah I heard it!" Tony bangs his fits on the bar shouting, "Those rotten sons of bitches. If I get my hands on them." Raising his head again, Brendan warns, "You might think your Hercules Big Guy, but you are no match for those evil mobsters. You better shut your trap or you'll be swimming with the sharks like Eileen's ex, Marty Goldstein." After saying this, Brendan's head flops back on the bar. "Ignore him Big Guy nothing can shut that trap up," Walsh warns. Tony is shaken up; but not his out-of-control rage.

To calm him down, Walsh changes the subject asking, "Is your little angel happy to be with her daddy, her new mommy, and that squawking parrot Flaubert?" "Yeah, yeah, Angela Maria is and we're happy she's with us. But that's not why I'm here," Tony shouts. "Tell me how Mike is and what happened to Ray." "First let me pour you another. You're gonna need it," Walsh lectures. He gives Tony another Boiler Maker and begins his tall sad tale. When he finishes, Tony stands there stunned and overwhelmed. He repeats the story Walsh just told him, "You mean to tell me those bastards got into the guarded hospital room and almost killed Ettie that frail little lady? So Mike's sister saved his life?" Tony gulps his drink and reiterates, "Then those lousy no good goon turns around and shoot Ray in the arm. Eileen told me she tried to stop Ray but he ran in the hospital room with only a metal chair as protection." "You got it, Big Guy!"

Walsh says adding, "Can you believe that sleazy cop'er, that no-good son of a bitch policeman, the one guarding Mike's room, was on the take?" "I'm not shocked, half the police are on the take in this corrupt city," Tony says. Brendan calls out, "Leave those good policemen alone. Most risk their lives every day." "Rumor has it that one of Mike's cousin's employees told them goons how to get into the hospital room via the fire escape," Tony mentions. Concerned, the Big Guy asks, "How's Ray?" "He'll live," Walsh assures Tony. "Good to hear," banging the bar, Tony calls out. "But, it'll be a hell of a long time before Mike will be in here for a drink and arm wrestling with Ray," mournfully Walsh murmurs. With a weird smirk on his face, Brendan calls out, "No need to concern yourself Tony your boss Mike is in good hands. The best!" Holding up his empty whiskey glass the Professor hollers over to Walsh, "Pour me another one, Sherlock Holmes." "Okay, Watson," the clever tavern owner retaliates.

Tony and Walsh turn hearing Brendan shout out, "You two fools forgot the mafia! The murderous gangsters. They were the ones who had it in for Mike and his family." "What?" questions Tony. Brendan continues, "The vendetta against Mike's father and uncle. Those murderous guys never forget!" Brendan informs them, "They finally got their pay back; their revenge, their vendetta fulfilled." "What pay back?" exasperated Tony asks. "The garbage company; they burned it down!" The Professor laughs mockingly, "You call yourself smart Big Guy; no one ever gets away with crossing those rotten goons. Vile Gangsters!" Frustrated, Brendan hollers over to Walsh directing it at Tony, "Finish the story! I am tired of trying to teach this slow learner." Insulting, Brendan adds, "His body may be big but his brain is undersized."

Ignoring Professor Brendan, Tony insists, "Go ahead, Walsh, I'm all ears!" "Word has it that Mike's father and his Uncle refused to get involved with illegal drugs and brothels." Walsh further informs, "They paid no mind to the illegal numbers racket and under the table money for special favors the Policino family participated in. So I hear, people say the police, clergy, and housewives where all on the take." Tony is listening intently, "Continue, Walsh." "Well, when Mike took over the garbage business the bosses, the Godfathers or the heads of local mafia approached Mike thinking he'd be willing to participate in illegal drugs, prostitution, murder for hire and all of the above. They were shocked and enraged when Mike, like his father and uncle before him, also refused." Tony asks, "They really were upset with Mike refusing them?" Walsh looks at him and hollers, "They sure were angry, dead angry! They warned and threatened him but Mike thought in time they would bypass him and move on to the Connecticut and New York mobs." Wiping his sweaty brow, Tony swears, "Those rotten no good bastards; if I had known, I would of . . ." "What!" shouts Brendan. "You could have done nothing!" The Professor educates, "Those goons would have gotten you too!"

"Yeah, yeah, yeah," annoyed Tony hollers. "How the hell will Mike ever be safe?" upset Tony questions the tavern owner. Walsh reveals, "Word has it, all Mike has to do is stay out of the garbage business forever and do whatever they tell him. The local mob brings in their own workers and trucks and take over the county contracts." Walsh adds, "Mike will have to give them lots of money too; *payolla*." "Mike better have deep pockets, to keep them off his back," Professor warns. "Then and only then, will they leave him alone!" Brendan shouts. Wiping his dripping wet brow, Walsh cries out, "Our Mike can never have anything to do with garbage ever again; anywhere in this county or anywhere for that matter." Slamming his hand on the bar, "Finito!" cries out Brendan.

"The only thing Mike has going for him is that he is a full-blooded Italian with close ties to "The Camorra Family" in Naples, Italy. That should protect him as long as he stays out of the vicious Sicilian Cosa Nostra's territory." "Keep his nose clean. That's what you mean?" Tony questions. "Blood is blood that's the Italian code. Once your family is involved you are in it for life; but stay out of the 'Other Families Territories' if you don't want trouble." "Trouble?" questions Tony. "Boy, oh boy, you are so naive and dumb for such a Big Guy." Professor Brendan instructs, "Death! Is the real meaning of 'Trouble' in 'The Family's language' it's their final warning; their code; a death sentence!"

Walsh chimes in, "He's right Big Guy but there's more to this." Choking up he reiterates, "Mike will have to start a new business; leave the mob alone or they will kill him once and for all." Silence. Walsh hesitantly offers, "There is a hidden story too." Walsh pour himself a shot, drinks it down in one gulp and resumes his tall tale, "The guy that tried to kill Mike and shot our Ray was someone no one would have ever suspected or guessed." "Who?" Tony screams. "If I get my big paws on him, I'll break him in half; he'll never walk, talk, or live," the Big Guy threatens. "Wait, do you know Sister Margaret Mary from St. Victor's parish?" Walsh asks

Tony. "Yeah, I know of her. The nun. She helped Eileen get her brother Sean into AA. Why? What does she have to do with all this?" Before Walsh can answer Tony, the door to the bar flings open. Eileen rushes into the bar. This time she is not bringing her homemade Irish Soda Bread.

CHAPTER FORTY-SEVEN

Surprises, Suspense, Submission
Walpole, New Hampshire
Winter, 1857

THE WOUNDED DR. JEREMIAH HOLDEN is sitting near the fire sipping fine-aged brandy Austin Stevens gave him as token of apology for shooting him. Anna Lee is relieved her infant twins are fed and sleeping soundly upstairs where Nannette is watching over them. Seated across from the roaring fire, Zeke is remorseful over the happenings of this past month and years past. Austin, aware of Zeke's withdrawing mute behavior, decides to lighten up the tenseness by making honest compensation for the unwarranted damages he has caused.

Offering his deepest and sincerest apologies Austin lovingly and remorsefully goes over to his wife, takes hold of her delicate hand, pleading, "My dear Anna Lee, I must make amends to you in front of these men. Jurors if you may, for my unfounded, cruel and heartless accusations regarding the accidental death of our, daughter Theresa Edith; our angel." Brushing away tears streaming down her face and typical of a forgiving dutiful wife, Anna Lee insists, "Austin please, no need to beg my pardon." She sighs, "I know your pain is unbearable." She reaches up, gently kisses him, smiles and affirms, "There is no need for forgiveness. Just love me and our twins that is all I ask." Pausing, Anna Lee pleads, "First, my dear husband, you must forgive yourself." "Never!" he cries out. "I should have been here with you when it happened. I am the guilty party." "We all are," Anna Lee whispers.

Seeing this private encounter between husband and wife, embarrassed, Zeke rises up requesting, "May I go now? I must attend to my duties at the barn." "Sit down, Zeke!" Austin demands. "I have not finished. You are a major component in my healing and clemency journey." Wishing he could leave, reluctantly Zeke sits down. With close eye contact on Zeke and Jeremiah, Austin recites, "I want you all to hear. I know now, from my heart and soul, Zeke and Dr. Holden, you did all you humanly could to save my Theresa Edith." Blotting tears streaming down his distraught face, contrite Austin offers, "You saved my wife and my twins and for that I will be eternally grateful." Sighing he asks, "For my vicious, unwarranted accusations, please accept my sincerest and genuine apology." With earnestness Austin relays, "If you choose not to, I truly understand!"

"Your apology accepted Mr. Stevens but there is no need for it!" Zeke jolts out of his seat announcing. Quivering, Zeke begs, "I should apologize to you and Mrs. Stevens." Hesitating, Zeke murmurs, "I have been deceitful. You see, innocent Nannette is not my ward." He pauses, takes a deep breath. "I need some of that brandy." Perplexed, Austin immediately pours him some. With shaking hands Zeke gulps the brandy down.

Resuming his confession Zeke shockingly reveals, "Nannette is my biological daughter." Sighs and moans from Anna Lee, Austin, and Jeremiah are heard. Speechless they stare at Zeke. After a moment, Dr. Holden calls out, "How can that be? I came here also to share with you something about Nannette." Raising his hand to quiet him Austin suggests, "Hold that thought Jeremiah; we must let Zeke finish what he started." Confused, Anna Lee precariously sits at the edge of the love seat. White as a ghost, Austin pours himself another brandy. Holding onto his throbbing wound, Dr. Jeremiah Holden is stunned.

Innocently Anna Lee requests, "Zeke, should I leave the room? Might this not be for a lady to hear?" "No!" Austin lectures, "If Zeke wanted you to leave my dear he would have said so." Flushed, Anne Lee dutifully sits back. Clearing his parched throat Zeke continues, "I lived in New Orleans where I was a volunteer medic in the Confederate Army. I met Nannette's young, innocent mother Louisa Anouilh at a local Army camp." Pausing to reflect, he continues, "Beautiful, selfless Louisa volunteered her nursing services also. She compassionately attended to the multiple, young wounded and dying soldiers." Reminiscing Zeke heartfelt reveals, "From the very first day I saw Louisa, I fell madly in love with her." Smiling he adds, "Shortly after, to my surprise and joy, Louisa did also. We loved each other deeply."

Revealing more details about Louisa, Zeke recalls, "Louisa's mother died giving birth to her." "Oh, dear me, how sad," Anna Lee murmurs. "Go on Zeke," Austin interjects. "Her father Pierre, a strict-cold Frenchman, raised Louisa alone the best he could." Sighing Zeke utters, "Louisa received no love from him." Anna Lee moans, "Poor child!" "Yes, she was, Mrs. Stevens." Anxious to learn more, Austin insists, "Let him finish dear." Shedding light on his young life, Zeke shares. "I was an orphan and never knew my parents. The war gave me a purpose." Zeke stops talking. Hesitating, he looks over at Anna Lee, "Ma'am perhaps now you should close your ears." Respecting Zeke's request, Anna Lee places her petite hands over her sensitive ears. Vacillating, Austin takes a deep breath; after, he encourages, "Please continue." Zeke resumes, "Louisa and I loved each other deeply but her father was against our relationship. He threatened to have me jailed." "Jailed?" Dr. Holden echoes. Reflectively, Zeke murmurs, "Perhaps I deserved jail. Our secretive, undying love made Louisa pregnant." The room is silent. "Needless to say, we were both terrified and rightfully so. When her father found out, he hid her from me." Groaning, Zeke continues, "Exactly where and when Louisa had the baby was unknown to me. Her father Pierre, a cold-hearted man, without telling my sweet Louisa gave the baby girl to an adoption agency." Interested, Austin questions, "Where did you get your information?" Zeke responds, "A trustworthy source." Choking up, Zeke utters, "My beautiful Louisa contracted Tuberculosis and.. ." He cries out, "The love of my life died!" Over hearing "TB and died," Anna Lee removes her shaking hands from her ears. Mournfully she gazes at distressed Zeke. Deeply moved and seeing how devastated Zeke is, sensitive Anna Lee, moans, "Dreadfully sad."

Streams of tears are pouring down Zeke's blood-shot eyes. Collecting himself, Zeke further explains, "I had nothing left to live for. I insisted they assign me to go into the heat of a battle." Austin inquires, "I always had my suspicions that you experienced the horrors of the war." Somberly reflecting, Zeke responds, "During one of the worst battles, a raging, untamable fire spread for miles. I witnessed hundreds of young, innocent soldiers burn to death right in front of me." Zeke closes his eyes and moans, "I was one of the lucky ones, or unlucky ones. I decided then and there that no war was worth this senseless, dreadful slaughter of innocent young lives." Hanging his head in shame Zeke utters, "I deserted, not only because of that atrocious slaughter but also because I was warned that Pierre, Louisa's spiteful father, hired henchmen to kill me." He cries out, "Even though I had nothing to live for and wanted to die, I always hoped I would find my long-lost daughter. This gave me my only reason to live."

Considering Zeke deeply anguished, Austin attempts to change the subject, asking "What did you do before you came here?" Relieved to change the subject, Zeke responds, "I traveled across the south doing odd jobs heading eastward. I was a drifter with no purpose in life until I heard my baby girl was alive living in an orphanage." He moans, "I had nothing to offer her. So, I sent money monthly." Offering further clarification Zeke informs, "As Nannette mentioned, the kind lady at the orphanage, Miss Elizabeth, surmised Nannette was my biological daughter." "Thankfully," he whispers, "Never telling Nannette that she thought I might be her father." Choking up, Zeke praises, "The intuitive, caring Miss Elizabeth guided my daughter Nannette to me." Rising, sternly staring at the others Zeke orders, "Nannette should never know!" Wanting no sympathy, further questions, or comments, walking out Zeke announces, "I'll pack my bags and leave immediately!"

"No," screams Dr. Holden. "You must stay. Zeke, I believe you will change your mind after you hear my story." Zeke, Anna Lee, and Austin stare at Jeremiah in utter shock. Austin blurts out, "My good man, Dr. Holden, what possibly more can you offer?" Curious, Zeke stops short. He moves over to Dr. Holden. Glaring smack in his face, Zeke warns, "I am all ears, Dr. Holden. It better be worth my staying here one minute more." Adamantly Dr. Jeremiah Holden replies, "I promise you Zeke, it will be!"

Wounded and weak Jeremiah Holden commences with his personal disclosure, "No beating around, I will expose my hidden secret immediately." He calls out, "Nannette is a close relative of mine." Sighs from those listening. Jeremiah further explains, "She is my biological, younger first cousin!" *Complete silence.* This disclosure shakes Zeke to the core. At first Anna Lee and Austin are unable to fully comprehend especially after just hearing Zeke's shocking revelation that Nannette is his daughter. "My good man, I know I wounded you, perhaps the shock affected your mind," craftily Austin suggests. "No, absolutely not! I am of sound mind. Please allow me to clarify," Jeremiah Holden pleads. Coming to his senses, Zeke encourages, "Go on Jeremiah, I'm waiting to hear how this could be!" Dr. Holden begins, "I was born in New Orleans also. My mother died when I was around two. After she died, I was told that my father was not interested in raising me. Henceforth, he placed me in a Catholic convent in the area." Jeremiah politely states, "I was blessed to be raised by pious but tough nuns."

Intrigued, Austin fills Jeremiah's glass with more brandy. He encourages Jeremiah, "Continue!" Puzzled, Zeke questions, "Where are you going with this?" Anna Lee is overwhelmed. Curious she respectfully sits and listens intently to Jeremiah's further explanation. "Nannette's mother had a brother, also named Jeremiah. That Jeremiah is my father!" Sighs from Anna Lee. "Quiet, Anna Lee! Go on Jeremiah," firmly Austin requests. "Yes, making Nannette's mother's brother, Jeremiah, my father, Nannette's uncle. Making Nannette and I, first cousins." Trying to absorb this, Austin demands, "How and when did you figure this connection?" "Miss Elizabeth had all of Nannette's records. As Nannette was approaching her sixteenth year and would be released from the orphanage, she kindly helped Nannette find her living relatives."

"Where do I fit into this picture?" all ears Zeke questions. Dr. Holden immediately explains, "Your name Zeke came up along with my father Jeremiah; he is Nannette's uncle." Dr. Holden sips his brandy then reaffirms, "The only Jeremiah Holden Miss Elizabeth could locate was me. Ironically, miraculously, as the nuns would pray, Zeke, you and I were both living in Walpole, NH." Baffled, Zeke, questions, "I thought all records are kept a secret in orphanages." "Yes, you are absolutely right but Miss Elizabeth, a truly altruistic woman felt great compassion for sweet, innocent Nannette. She was determined to make sure your daughter and my cousin had someone of significance and hopefully safe to go to."

Listening intently with a passionate nature, Anna Lee murmurs, "Zeke, how painful it must have been for you to be around Nannette and not be able to share or acknowledge her as your daughter." Turning toward Dr. Holden, Anna Lee, with wisdom offers, "Dr. Holden, your obsessive interest in Nannette was not for romantic reasons. I believe for you, it was to have a close relative to bond with and eventually to love." Zeke, Austin and Dr. Holden pause, they are amazed and impressed by this perceptive, compassionate woman's insight. *Passionately Anna Lee beautifully sums up these complex disclosures.*

Attempting to sort out all this information, Austin inquires, "Jeremiah, how did you wind up in Walpole New Hampshire?" "My father had a trust fund set up for me. The nuns at the convent encouraged me to get an education. I always loved animals henceforth being a veterinarian was the wisest and easiest choice." He pauses. "Continue," Austin encourages. "Through sources in New England, the nuns heard about an opening for a veterinarian in this area. I pursued it." "Ah," moans Austin. Dr. Holden further clarifies, "The old veterinarian Dr. Joshua Goldsmith from Walpole, also a dear friend of your grandfather's Austin was planning on retiring. Joshua was also a good friend of my late wife's family; the infamous Watkins family. It was through them it was arranged my taking over Dr. Goldsmith's practice. Also, my prearranged marriage to Rebecca." Anna Lee murmurs, "Incredible." Defending this action Dr. Holden mentions, "My late wife Rebecca and I very much wanted to have children."

"Interesting? That's the reason you married," Austin chimes in. Motioning for Austin to be silent Anna Lee encourages, "Please, continue Dr. Holden." "As you know now, but unbeknownst to me at the time, my sweet, young wife Rebecca was chronically ill nor could she ever bear children." "Heartbreaking," Anna Lee murmurs. Dr. Holden reveals, "You are aware, the Watkin's family did not have a male heir. As a woman, my wife Rebecca could not take over or inherit the Watkin's Hill estate unless she married." Strained from the wound and the subject matter, Dr. Holden is tired and breathless. "Take a deep breath my good man," Austin encourages. Once he does, intrigued Austin encourages, "Please resume." Stronger, Jeremiah continues, "Legally, Rebecca Watkin's husband could take over the estate. The family trust stated we could remain on the estate since Rebecca was a full-blooded relative until she died." Mournfully, Jeremiah Holden gutters, "If Rebecca and I had a male child, when he was of legal age, he would inherit and run the entire estate."

Hearing this, remorseful Austin apologies, "My good man, I falsely accused you of selfishly and greedily wanting innocent Rebecca's money and property." Dr. Holden defends, "Not at all. In fact, in my wife's last will and testament it officially states: 'If she dies before me, I can legally remain on the property for as long as I like but no monies of my wife's will I ever receive.' Although, when I die, or if I decide to leave, the property and her entire estate will be sold." It also states: 'All of the proceeds will go to charity," Holden adds. Emphatically Jeremiah Holden reiterates, "I did not receive anything when we married or after she died; nor did I ever intend to or desire too." He reminisces, "The Sisters of Charity taught me well: 'Poverty is a virtue.'"

Concerned for his long-lost daughter, Zeke chimes in, "All well and good about your late wife and the Watkin's estate, but have you, or do you intend to tell Nannette all this?" He pauses and also asks Jeremiah, "Are you planning on staying in Walpole?" Jeremiah Holden offers, "This is something I must think about Zeke." Pondering for a moment, Jeremiah Holden agonizingly mutters, "Too much has happened lately. I will figure it out soon." He glances over at Zeke and preaches, "As I'm sure you also must do Zeke."

Listening intently, Anna Lee and Austin are absorbing all this unfathomable information. The room becomes disturbingly quiet. Rising, Austin commends, "I applaud you Zeke and Dr. Holden for sharing your personal, private-family secrets." Standing straight in military manner Austin announces, "My good men, you have given me the courage to share my story also." As Austin is preparing to share, a noise is heard coming from the kitchen. Anna Lee, Austin, Zeke, and Dr. Holden hold their breath as Nannette enters.

CHAPTER FORTY-EIGHT

Concertos, Costumes, Confusion
Hollywood, California
1956

THE DOORBELL SOUNDS at Grandma Hollywood's house. Mary Grace eagerly rushes to the door. When she opens it, two dramatic looking young men bow to her. Both kiss her hand. Mateo and his friend Nunzio enter following flattered Mary Grace in. These Italian men are finely dressed in black silk shirts, open almost to their navels, linen-cream tight slacks, and coal black, blinding shinny shoes with raised heels. "My two handsome Italians are here to escort my two beautiful granddaughters to the Hollywood Bowl." Grandma Hollywood calls from the living room. "Absolutely, Bella Signora," Mateo responds.

In the bathroom Elena and Regina are fussing with their new hairdos which they had done at Max Factor's studio by Mateo. "I hate the way I look. This hairdo makes me look like Grandma Mosses," moans Elena. Regina ignores her cousin. Elena has been complaining the entire day. She has not been herself. The only reason she agrees to go is because Regina begged her. "You look pretty cool Elena. I'm sure Nunzio will like you," Regina comments while fussing with her long blond hair. "Nunzio? I didn't know we were pairing off?" cryptically Elena says. "I know you are nervous and anxious about your audition. I thought if we went out tonight, it would take your mind off of it," Elena explains. "This is the only reason I agreed to go," she calls out. "You will make any excuse to blame me!" Regina accuses. Elena defends, "Grandma insists we go since she bought 'expensive, front row tickets.'"

Glaring at her cousin, Elena reiterates, "It is not a date night!" "Well for me it is," coos Regina. "Guess you left your heart in Jersey City."

Regina teases Elena. Elena is ready to bounce on her cousin but hearing Grandma Hollywood calling out, the cousins stop their bantering. "Elena and Regina, your handsome dates are here!" Regina pats her cousin on the arm reaffirming, "Dates! I rest my case!" Rushing out of the bathroom Regina insists, "Now let's make this a night to remember Cuz." Pulling infuriated Elena out of the bathroom, Regina boasts, "Come on slowpoke; how many girls from New Jersey can say they went to the Hollywood Bowl with two Italian hunks and a half!?"

Grandma Hollywood, Mary Grace and Tess say their goodbyes as the four young guys and gals are leaving. Thrilled seeing them going to the Hollywood Bowl and looking so glamorous, Grandma Hollywood calls out, "Have a great time Elena, Regina, Mateo and Nunzio; you all look fantastic!" When the door slams shut, Tess swiftly heads to her bedroom. Grandma Hollywood and Mary Grace follow her. Choking up, Tess's sister squeaks, "Our daughters look so grown up and stunning tonight." Turning to her mother Mary Grace praises, "Mom, your granddaughters look fabulous in the outfits you made for them to wear just for tonight." A huge, proud smile spreads across Grandma Hollywood's face. "Imagine," Mary Grace sighs, "Elena and Regina going to the Hollywood Bowl with two sexy Italian guys." In the bedroom, Tess murmurs, "You mean gigolos!"

Grandma Hollywood and Mary Grace enter Tess's bedroom. "I'm not so sure I like the whole idea of Elena going especially with those unknown guys," Tess shares her concern. Defending, "With Elena not acting right, and Regina worried about not getting the part in the movie, I think it will be good for both of them," Grandma Hollywood interjects. Mary Grace says, "Wish it were me!" Crooning she adds, "Nunzio is so handsome and charming." Winking, Mary Grace singsongs, "He's totally my type!" Shouting, Tess demands, "Enough about the Hollywood Bowl and those Italian Stallions." Forthrightly staring at her mother and sister, straight away Tess says, "There is something important I must tell you!"

Perplexed, Grandma Hollywood and Mary Grace gaze at one another, "We're all ears, darling," her mother says. "What is it now Tess?" frustrated Mary Grace squawks. "Let her talk, Mary Grace," Grandma Hollywood reprimands her younger feisty daughter. "I booked a flight on TWA leaving tomorrow for New York," promptly Tess reports. "What? You just got here!" annoyed Mary Grace calls out. "You were told by that Jersey City Police Captain not to go back now!" pleads Tess's forlorn mother. "They warned you Sis that it will be too dangerous for you to go at this time!" expresses Mary Grace. "Well, I am going and that's that!" Tess shouts back. "What about Elena?" disturbed Mary Grace questions. Taking out her luggage to pack, Tess says, "Elena will stay here with you and Mom." Taken aback, Grandma Hollywood and Mary Grace are at a loss for words. To break the silence, Tess mutters, "I have no doubt creative Regina will keep my daughter busy."

In disbelief, Grandma Hollywood and Mary Grace stare at one another. Tess apologizes, "I know I'm imposing on you two." Looking at her mother and sister pleading, "You must trust me. I have to go!" "No worries Sis," reconciled, Mary Grace assures. She takes hold of her sister and hugs Tess tightly. Seeing her two daughters bonding makes Grandma Hollywood extremely happy. "Mary Grace and I will take good care of Elena," Tess's mother reassures her. Emotional, Tess affirms, "Mike is my husband. If anything happens to him, not only will I not forgive myself, but Elena will hate me forever." Grandma Hollywood agrees, "Yes, dear, you must go!" In hopes of making Tess feel good about leaving Elena in California with them, elatedly, Grandma Hollywood announces, "Mary Grace and I will take Elena and Regina to marvelous Catalina Island for a weekend!" *They don't call Grandma Hollywood adventurous and fabulous for nothing.*

It is one a.m. in the morning. Sitting in the living room, Tess and Mary Grace are patiently waiting for their daughters to return from the Hollywood Bowl. In bed by ten p.m., Grandma Hollywood is in her plush bedroom getting her beauty sleep. Cleo, her faithful dog, nightly stands guard by her room. The front door springs open, Cleo jumps up and barks. Regina comes flying in, followed by unenthusiastic Elena. Mateo and Nunzio are chatting away as they saunter into the living room. "Well young ladies how did you enjoy the concert?" staring at Nunzio, Mary Grace questions. "It was fantastic!" Regina shouts. "Did you enjoy yourself also, Elena?" hoping, Tess asks. Elena is silent. Huffing, she scampers away toward her bedroom.

Observing the edgy women, Mateo sings out, "We had a delightful time." Putting his two fingers together to his lips he throws a kiss into the air. "The music was magnifico! The Maestro, beyond words," Mateo gallantly announces. Quietly, Nunzio stands there observing his dramatic friend. "How did you like it Nunzio?" flirting, Mary Grace coos. Unassumingly he answers, "As Mateo stated, it was a night to remember!" Looking around Nunzio questions, "Where did Elena go? I'm disappointed. I don't think she enjoyed herself." Mary Grace responds, "I'm sure she did." Moving closer to him, touching Nunzio's long, strong arm, Mary Grace whispers in his ear, "I know I would have." Not pleased seeing Mary Grace acting this way, Grandma Hollywood gives her a warning look. Hoping not to upset Grandma Hollywood further, bowing to Regina and Mary Grace, Mateo politely says, "Buono Notte." The two Italian stallions depart.

Unaware as to what went on in the living room, passing by her bedroom, Elena goes into her mother's. Tess is packing. Elena notices. Puzzled, she inquires, "What are you doing Mother?" Tess skirts around her daughter's query by asking, "Did you enjoy the concert?" "Mother, I'd rather not go there." Staring at her mother's open luggage, Elena mutters, "Let's just say I am glad the night is over." Tess motions her daughter to sit next to her on the bed. "You look exhausted dear." "Mom, can you believe that Rodney showed up at the Hollywood Bowl too?" Elena groans. "It's as if he is stalking me," she cries out. "I'm sure he's not. Rodney just wants to be your good friend," Tess suggests. "Friend or foe?" Elena calls out.

"Mom, you're not going to believe or be happy with what I'm about to tell you. Rodney is going to squeal on Monsignor James Cooney." "Say that again?" confused Tess inquires. "Rodney is going to make it known about the questionable Father Schultz from St. Victor's in Jersey City," Elena reveals. More concerned about Mike, Tess makes light of it, "Nothing for you to do about it now Elena. You should go and get some sleep." Noticing

Elena still glaring at her luggage, nonchalantly Tess curtly mentions, "I'm going back home tomorrow." Bolting off the bed, Elena screams, "What did you say Mom?" Grasping what her mother said, Elena excitedly calls out, "Great! I'm coming too!"

CHAPTER FORTY-NINE

Omerta, Goons, Guys, Gals
Jersey City, New Jersey
1956

A YELLOW TAXI cab pulls up to 391 Armstrong Avenue. Opening the back door, Tess swings her legs over and gets out. Standing on the curb she takes money out of her purse. The elderly cab driver walks over to the trunk and takes out her luggage. Immediately Tess hands him a wad of money. "Do you want me to bring your bag up the steps?" seeing her generous tip the cab driver asks. Before Tess can respond the front door flies opens. Ray Sinnotti runs down the steps. Reaching Tess, he gives her a welcoming bear hug. He takes hold of her luggage teasing, "You look absolutely fabulous darling. Hollywood agrees with you, Rita, excuse me, Tess." Observing and hearing this, the cab driver looks at Tess and smiles at her. Like a happy camper the old geezer driver gets back in the cab. He drives off singing, "'There Ain't Nothing like a Dame.'" Calling out, "A true redhead; Rita Hayward type; my kind of woman!"

Since Tess was informed that Ray was injured in Mike's hospital room, she is surprised and perplexed seeing Ray walking and talking. "Are you alright, Ray?" Tess questions. "Do I look bad?" making light of it, he remarks. "Well, I was told you were shot!" Tess comments. Avoiding the remark, Ray suggests, "It's cold out here. Let's go inside." Grabbing her hand, he adds, "It's not a good idea to expose yourself openly around here." Noticing Tess is wondering what he is suggesting, Ray murmurs, "Too many unfriendly eyes might be watching a gal like you." "Why, Ray, because I'm Mike Policino's wife?" Tess inquires. Nervously scanning the neighborhood, with a bandaged shoulder Ray holding Tess's arm and her only piece of luggage with his good arm, he hustles his best-buddy Mike's wife along. Rushing up the porch steps to Ettie's warm, hopefully safe home.

Entering Ettie's place, Ray hollers, "Is the coffee ready?" As Tess and Ray enter the kitchen, Ray jokingly calls out, "Look who I found hanging around the old neighborhood?" Coming out of the pantry and seeing Tess standing next to Ray, Ettie screams, "Thank you God! My prayers are answered." She runs over to Tess, hugs and kisses her. "Okay ladies enough of that stuff; we have business to take care of," Ray reprimands. Ettie moves away from her sister-in-law heading over to the stove she questions, "Is Elena with you?" "No, Ettie, she didn't come. She's with my mother, sister and Regina." Recognizing her sister-in-law's concern, Tess reassures Ettie, "Elena is fine." Relieved, Ettie mutters, "Good. My little sweetheart will be safe there."

Noticing Ettie is alone, Tess inquires, "I know as a Marine Blaise must be at his post, but where is Rosaria?" Ettie hesitates. Tess resumes her questioning, "Wasn't your daughter supposed to stay here with you after Carlo died?" Instantly, Ettie responds, "She stayed with me for a while but a friend of hers in New England needed her help." Wiping her sweaty forehead with her apron Ettie continues, "My good Samaritan daughter went to help her and I encouraged Rosaria." Having more important issues to deal with, Tess accepts Ettie's explanation.

One day Tess is in Hollywood at her mother's house, next she is back in Jersey City in Ettie's kitchen; she is overwhelmed. Taking off her jacket, placing it over a chair in the kitchen, Tess slips down on the chair. With a stern voice she questions, "How is Mike?" No response. Tess is more aggressive. "When can I see my husband?" she asks firmly. Standing at the stove with her well-worn Sears potholders carrying the hot coffee pot Ettie freezes, looking over at Ray praying he will answer Tess.

Ray does not disappoint he offers, "As Mike's wife Tess, you have every right to see him, but under the precarious, dangerous circumstances, trust me, it's safer for you not to." "What!?" bolting off the chair, Tess hollers.

"I'm his wife; if you and Ettie know where he is, then I should know!" "Drink some coffee Tess," Ray begs. Adding, "You're absolutely right; you should know Tess." He further explains, "Mike's kidnapping; vicious brutal beating; and his long-time family run company burnt to the ground; with these criminal acts the police and FBI are dealing with dangerous, deadly mobsters." Tess is listening attentively. "For your protection and Mike's, the police highly recommend that you be anonymous for now." "Anonymous?" Tess questions. "In other words Tess; stay away from Mike." "I don't understand?" Tess cries out. "What's for you to understand?! It's for your own safety Tess!" Enraged Ray screams back.

In her own simple way, Ettie attempts to explain to Tess. "Like the ancient fig bushes out back, planted by my deceased father and his father before him, they must be covered every winter or there will be no figs on the bush the next year." "Figs?" questions Tess. "Yes," Ettie resumes, "Like covering the figs one must always protect the family. As Ray said, it's for your safety," Ettie prophecies and pleads. "Please Ettie, no disrespect but I don't need a lecture about damn figs right now!" frustrated, Tess responds. Seeing her sister-in-law upset, Ettie moans, "Ray, if I were Tess, even though you and the police are trying to protect her, I would want to know how my husband was and would like to see him." Recognizing that she is being unfair and unkind to Ettie, whom she should be thanking for throwing herself over Mike's body in the hospital and saving his life, Tess smiles at Ettie and murmurs, "Thank you for saving Mike's life."

Perplexed and pondering, Ray concedes, "I give up! You women win; but I am not supposed to know any of this either. Whatever I tell you must not leave this room." The women glance at one another pleased but fearful of what they are going to hear. Ray motions for the Ettie to sit down at the kitchen table next to Tess. "Ettie, you are a religious woman, and Tess you are a trustworthy friend, whatever I tell you must stay here!" Searching around, Ray cautions, "You know walls have ears too." Whispering Ray, Mike's best buddy, commences.

As Ray begins to explain, Ettie's doorbell rings. Startled, Ray jumps up from his seat, "Stay here ladies. I'll see who it is and get rid of them." At a loss for words, Tess and Ettie nod their heads affirmatively. At the door Ray is relieved to see Eileen standing outside holding something. He immediately opens it. "Thank god you're here. Tess just arrived. I was just beginning to fill them both in about Mike." "Tess is here?" shocked, Eileen murmurs. "Yes," Ray answers. He motions her to follow him to the kitchen. As they enter, Ray further explains, "I knew Tess was coming; we've been in contact since the horrific events." Looking over at Tess for confirmation, he adds, "She made me promise not to tell anyone." Tess nods in agreement. Nervous, Eileen whispers in Ray's ear, "I fear Tess is not happy to see me." "No worries Eileen," he whispers back, "After she hears what I have to tell her, you and Tony will be Tess's heroes," Ray reassures frightened Eileen Moriarty Goldstein Rivera.

Fidgety while sitting at the kitchen table and anxious to hear what Ray has to say, Tess is dazed seeing an unfamiliar woman come in. Eileen hands Ettie the box. "They're empanadas. Angela Maria and her dad Tony made them for you," she tells Ettie. "Thank you," while bringing them to the counter Ettie says. Ettie is anxious to make Eileen feel comfortable around Tess and vice versa. She questions "Eileen how is your parrot Flaubert? Does Angela Maria like him?" Eileen grins and murmurs, "There's a bit of jealousy on both their parts but I am sure it will work out soon." Attempting to get back on track, Ray introduces, "Tess, I'm not sure if you met Eileen before. She's been a great help for Ettie." Like a stone-cold statue, Tess maintains her composure. To lighten the mood, Ray further informs, "Eileen was originally hired to be a caregiver for Carlo during his illness. After he died, Eileen became Ettie's helper."

Nodding her head affirmatively Ettie retrieves the coffee pot and pours Eileen a cup of coffee. Ettie questions, "Eileen I know you were going to see Father Kelly." Hearing the priest's name interests Tess, she immediately interjects, "What about Father Kelly?" "Enough!" stamping his foot, Ray screams. Realizing it's upsetting Ray, Ettie whispers, "We'll talk about this later, Tess." Noticing things are getting testy, wisely Eileen says, "Call me if you need me Ettie. I'll be in the living room dusting."

"Forget about the priest for now; let's clarify things. Again, do you know Eileen?" Ray asks Tess. Smirking, Tess curtly responds, "Yes, I know of her." Upset for Eileen, Ettie shares, "Eileen and her husband Tony have been a godsent to me and my brother. A blessing." "A blessing!" Tess mocks ready to pounce on them. "Yes, Tess, a blessing. Let me explain," Ray interjects. Deliberately no response from Tess. "Are you ready to listen Tess and not judge until I'm finished?" Ray interrogates. "Do I have a choice?" Tess murmurs. "As far as Eileen is concerned, I have nothing good or bad to say about Mrs. Rivera," Tess coyly infers. "Does that settle it, Ray?" sarcastically Tess remarks. She hastily requests, "With that resolved, please tell me how Mike is. Where is he; and when can I see my husband!?" "Of course Tess, I realize that's the reason you left California and came back to New Jersey," respectfully Ray responds.

Recognizing how upsetting this must be for Tess, with renewed compassion, Ray commences. "It is critically important Tess, first I explain what happened and why it happened to Mike," Ray tells Tess. "Before you start Ray, please tell me if Mike is alright?" misty-eyed Tess pleads. "Forgive me Tess for being so selfish. Mike is going to be alright. I promise you." "Praise God," Tess cries out. With a serious look on his face, Ray begs, "Let me start!" He explains, "As the Italians believe and honor, family comes first no matter what! It was imbedded into Mike's head since the time he could walk and talk. The motto: 'If a mere drop of Policino-Scat blood is in your veins there is nothing the family will not do for you, even die!' It was an unspoken oath all Italian men know deep inside and must respect. It is firmly imprinted in the makeup and etched in their bones." Looking over at Mike's sister, Ray further explains, "As Ettie can attest, Mike, being the oldest male in his family, he was destined to continue the legacy with no questions asked."

Antsy, Tess takes a sip of her coffee. Ray resumes, "Tess that's why Mike had to take over the garbage business after his father and uncle died. They willed it to Mike and he made an eternal promise to them." Ettie shakes her head in agreement. "Mike had to take over the sanitation company and his cousin Nick Scat the funeral parlor," Ray adds. Seeing a questionable smirk on Tess's face, firmly, Ray reiterates, "Tess, Mike must defend and protect the *family* at any cost! He is obligated to fulfill ancient promises and honor the reputation of his family's name. That's the Italian code!" staunchly Ray emphasizes.

Impatient, "I understand!" Tess shouts, "What does that have to do with Mike being kidnapped, beaten almost to death, and the burning down of the garbage company?" Trying to process all of this, questioning Tess moans. "Who are his enemies, and why didn't the Salerno family in Italy help him?" shuddering Tess vehemently questions. Ray rubs his sore arm as he proceeds to inform her, "There's an old Sicilian Mafia vendetta against Mike's Camorra Mafia family, as far back as a killing in Salerno, Italy." "Yes, yes, I know; but that was years ago; what does that have to do with us here in America now?" distraught Tess inquires. Ray attempts to explain, "An Italian vendetta never dies unless a compromise is made between the families who are at odds." Weeping Ettie shakes her head in agreement. "Omerta is a Southern Italian code of silence, reflecting the deeply rooted Sicilian belief that no person should go to authorities to seek justice for a crime and never ever under pain of death cooperate with authorities." Further clearing up his best buddy's role in this, Ray explains, "As a full-blooded member and head of his Italian family, Mike has no other option but to protect his family without involving other official authorities; in other words, outsiders." He calls out, "The Police! Capeesh?"

Ray attempts to further explain the complex dynamics of this, "The sons of the affronted, aggrieved criminal family who, like Mike, were born in America took over the Sicilian crime family here on the East coast. They have been after Mike's family ever since there was an Omerta on Mike's great-grandfather." Throat dry, Ray asks Ettie, "Please pour me more coffee?" "Go on, Ray," Ettie encourages as she rushes to get the coffee pot. "To protect his family from the opposing family, Mike's great-grandfather had to murder the head or the Godfather of the opposing family or they would have killed his entire family," Ray informs. Ettie moans, "There's a curse on our family. I believe God has not forgiven the Policino family for this murder."

Learning about this for the first time, devastated, Tess becomes abnormally silent. "Tess," to get her full attention, Ray cries out, "Listen up Tess." Seeing he finally has her full attention, Ray continues, "For some time now, these goons have been threatening Mike that they would destroy his business or worse, to fulfill the Omerta on Mike's great-grandfather for killing their great-grandfather in Italy." Finally putting all of this together, "What next?" Tess cries out. Seeing her sister-in-law upset, Ettie insists, "Ray, tell Tess all of it." "Unless Mike did exactly what they told him to do," Ray further informs, "Mike, his entire family and his business would be put on their hit list." Under his breath Ray sighs, "Even innocent Elena." The threat from a crime mob usually proves deadly if not heeded." "What did they want Mike to do?!" shuddering Tess screams. "This is top secret only the mob families know," sighing Ray concedes. Ray murmurs, "I 'm going to break the code and tell you Tess." He takes hold of Tess's shivering hands pleading, "I beg you! No one is ever to know that you know or who told you." Ray bangs the table. "If the wrong people find out, were all as good as dead," Ray vehemently warns. In agreement with Ray, Ettie passionately shakes her head in agreement. *Mums the word!*

Hearing this shakes Tess to the core prompting her to beg, "Ettie, get me the grappa!" "Ray, wait until I get liquid courage before you say another word," Tess pleads. Ettie retrieves the bottle and quickly pours a huge water-size glass full of grappa for Tess, Ray, and herself. They each immediately drink half a glass full. Deeply concerned, Tess inquires, "Is Eileen still here? Can she hear?" "No worries about Eileen or her husband Tony, they have been Mike's savior." Anxious, Ray demands, "Let's get this over with Tess, we have important decisions to make."

Moving close to Tess, in a hushed voice, Ray resumes, "The opposing Sicilian Mafiosa family demanded Mike be a part of their nationwide, illegal drug, prostitution, gambling, and hit-man organization." "Why Ray?" Tess questions. "There's more money in it than you can even imagine. You see Tess, Mike has great connections," Ray educates her. Ray defends his best buddy, "Mike adamantly refused even after they offered a huge share in the total take. When Mike vehemently told them 'No, and back off,' those loathsome henchmen placed a death sentence on Mike." "I don't know if I can hear anymore," Ettie cries out. "I know this is hard for you to hear Ettie but I must continue." "Please Ray, continue I must know it all," Tess insists. "I can't impress this on you enough, those vile creeps also threatened to harm Mike's family and destroy his business." Swallowing more grappa, wiping his mouth, sneering Ray reveals, "Mike thought they were bluffing! He basically told them he would not interfere with their illegal operations. He assured them he would turn a blind eye and deaf ear to what they do." Ray pauses and emphasizes, "Mike wanted no blood money on his hands."

Listening, Ettie cries, "The sins of the father." Wiping her face with the end of her apron, she praises, "My brother is a good man. Mike never wanted any part of this; all he ever wanted to do was become an honest lawyer." Mike's devoted sister, who saved his life, is inconsolable. Hearing Ettie upset, Eileen is ready to go in the kitchen but hesitates; she wants to respect Tess.

"So, this is why they kidnapped Mike, beat him, and burned down the business?" trying to comprehend it all, remorsefully Tess remarks. "Yes Tess, that's exactly right." Puzzled, Tess continues to question, "Ray, how do you know all this?" "Mike told me a few days before Christmas. Even Tony his foreman knew; they threatened the Big Guy too." Choked up Ettie reveals, "Eileen secretly told me, her evil ex-husband Marty Goldstein, the head of the illegal numbers racket in Hudson County, privately bragged to her that the Sicilian mob hired him to kill Mike after he refused their offer." After listening to all this, in a daze, unmoored Tess is grief stricken, shaken, and fearfully vulnerable.

After downing all his grappa, gaining courage, Ray resumes, "There's more Tess that will unsettle you further." "What possibly more can you tell me Ray that would shock me?" Tess cries out. "The Jersey City police, Nick Scat's Funeral parlor, and St. Victor's parish are all involved." "Oh no!" screams Tess taking her half-empty glass of grappa and swallowing it in one gulp. Standing up to stretch and catch his breath, Ray moans loudly. Mike's best buddy is beyond devastated about all this. He is now second guessing himself about revealing all of this to Tess. Ray feels he broke Mike's eternal brotherhood code. Observing Ray and Tess upset, nervous Ettie runs into the living room. She begs reluctant Eileen to come into the kitchen. Sobbing Ettie pleads, "Eileen, please I need you to help Ray explain to Tess what Tony and you know."

While Ray and Tess are conversing quietly, Ettie sneaks back into the kitchen followed by Eileen. "Ray, I think Eileen might be able to explain to Tess, the police, politicians and church's part in all of this," shyly Ettie offers. Relieved, Ray wholehearted agrees but recommends, "I believe first we must explain to Tess where the police have hidden Mike for his safety and the role Tony, Eileen, and Walsh's tavern play in all of this." Jumping up, Tess shouts, "Oh my god, Walsh's tavern? What the hell next!"

CHAPTER FIFTY

Angels in Disguise
Walpole, New Hampshire
Winter 1857
Cast a cold Eye on Life, on death, Horseman, pass ~ William Butler Yeats

IN UTTER DESPAIR and fear, Anna Lee, Austin, Zeke, and Jeremiah Holden remain stoic as stone as ashen faced Nannette shuffles into the parlor. Austin jumps up offering her a seat, "Nannette, please sit down; you don't look well." Ghost-like, she slowly sinks into the love seat next to Anna Lee. "May I pour you some brandy, Nannette?" at a loss for what to say, Austin asks. Looking over at Zeke with glazed misty eyes, Nannette responds, "Yes, I believe I might need a sip for medicinal purposes." Anna Lee is sitting near Jeremiah whispering, "I believe that poor young girl heard our entire conversation."

Limping over with the glass of brandy, Zeke stops Austin requesting permission, "Mr. Austin, if you don't mind, I'd like to take the brandy to Nannette." Grim face, Austin hands Zeke the brandy sniffer. Zeke's shaking hand makes the golden brandy swirl around the fine cut crystal sniffer. Carrying the liquor, Zeke walks cautiously over to Nannette. Not taking her eyes off of Zeke, when he gets near Nannette and hands her the brandy, she takes it in her quivering hand. Everyone is silent. With cloudy eyes downcast Nannette sips the smooth brandy. As a caring mother, Anna Lee inquires, "Nannette, are the twins sleeping?" Lifting her head up and looking directly at Anna Lee Nannette reassures her, "Yes, they are sleeping soundly." When Zeke hears the two women conversing, he proceeds to walk away from Nannette.

"Zeke," Nannette calls out to him as he turns to go to the other end of the room. "Please come back; I want to look at you." Momentarily stalling in his tracks, Zeke moves back over to Nannette who is staring at Zeke. The room is silent, only the roaring fire is heard crackling. When Zeke goes up to Nannette, she takes hold of Zeke's sweating hands. Squeezes them tightly, she cries out, "I always wanted to know what it feels like to hold my father's hands." Hearing her words, Zeke falls to his knees in front of Nannette. As in the past, Zeke is mute. With deep compassion, Nannette whispers, "No need to say a word. I heard everything you said, I understand why you did what you did, Father."

Wiping his moist eyes with his shirt sleeve, Zeke looks directly at his daughter. With his voice returned, he apologizes and explains, "I am so sorry Nannette. I didn't mean to abandon you!" With her soft tender hands, Nannette gently takes hold of Zeke's mournful face to comfort him. He looks up at her revealing, "After I heard you were alive, I only did what I thought was best for you." She wipes the one lone tear slowly dripping down Zeke's face. "There hasn't been a moment since the day I heard you were born that I didn't pine for you; love you; and want to protect you." Zeke's heart-wrenching cries move all in the room.

Nannette places a kiss on his rough, red cheeks. She takes her hand and pulls a gold heart-shaped locket which she wears around her neck and shows it to Zeke. "Father, Miss Elizabeth gave this to me the day I left the orphanage. She said it was my mother's, "What do you know about it?" Stunned, Zeke looks at it; he opens the locket and there is a miniature photo of a young woman. Emotional Zeke cries out, "Wow! It is a picture of my Louisa; your mother Nannette. I gave it to her just before her father separated us." Nannette takes his quivering hand, "Father, it is fine; I wear it proudly." Zeke moans, "I don't deserve you and I didn't deserve your mother."

Slowly rising up on shaking knees, Zeke stares over at the others saying, "I owe all of you an apology." Denouncing his past behavior, he infers, "I've been nothing but a scoundrel! I lied and was deceitful to you all." With shoulders bent low, Zeke broods, "You must think of me as an untrustworthy person for abandoning my own flesh and blood." Feeling Zeke's pain, Austin goes over to him, puts his arms around him saying, "You do not have to apologize to any of us. God only knows we all have skeletons in our closet." Looking over at Nannette, Austin remarks, "Only

Nannette has to forgive you and from what we just viewed here, she has forgiven you!"

Walking over to Nannette, in a kindly manner, Austin instructs, "Zeke, come back here and kiss your daughter. You must make up for lost time." "Yes," Nannette calls out. She pontificates, "Father, from the first day I met you here, I knew we had some sort of connection. Secretly, I prayed you were my father." She praises, "Thank God, my prayers have been answered." Not feeling worthy of her forgiveness, remorseful, Zeke remains quiet. Rising from the love seat Nannette heads over to him. She places her arms around Zeke hugging him as if never wanting to let him go. Finally, Zeke releases his inhibitions. He kisses Nannette all over her beautiful face. When he ceases, looking at her lovingly, he proudly calls out, "My daughter. My flesh and blood!" He stops to wipe the tears from his eyes and moans, "My beautiful Louisa's baby. Our baby!" Mournfully he whispers to Nannette, "I only wish your mother was here to see what a fine young lady you turned out to be."

Instinctively, Zeke turns and gazes at Austin groaning, "When I thought I lost Nannette forever, I knew how unbearably painful it was for you and Mrs. Stevens to lose your precious child." Austin is mournfully silent. With contriteness, Zeke reveals, "For me, Theresa Edith was like the child I lost." He resumes while blaming, "I found my daughter, but because of me, you lost yours!" Virtuous Anna Lee directs this to Zeke, "Please, let's not dwell on the past. We must focus on the blessed new life we now have." Zeke is ready to denounce her. Before he has the opportunity Anna Lee pontificates, "My faith has given me the strength and comfort to bear the tremendous loss of my angel of a daughter." Positive, she adds, "I now appreciate and thank God for the gift of my twins." Austin is at a loss for words. Only pathetic moaning is heard from this grieving father.

On the second floor from the nursery, the twins cry loudly. Jumping up, Nannette offers, "I will go and check on the baby twins." She gazes over at Zeke pleading, "Please don't leave Father! I will return." "No Nannette," Anna Lee orders, "You stay here. I will go and take care of my babies." "Yes, stay!" Dr. Holden blurts out. "You see Nannette, we have much to discuss." Aware, Nannette responds, "I know all about our family connection,

Jeremiah. If I hadn't, I never would have gone to live with you." "What?" in unison Jeremiah and Austin respond. "Yes, you see, before I left the kind Miss Elizabeth at the orphanage she told me about Jeremiah and my family connection." She adds, "Sweet Miss Elizabeth has great compassion for all her wards." Noticing her impressed captive audience Nannette further praises, "Dear Miss Elizabeth is so kind and caring, she even adopted an orphan boy slightly older than I." Smiling, she fondly recalls, "He was such a nice boy; his name is James. I often think about him."

Pondering Nannette sips her brandy, stares at her cousin Jeremiah and returns to their original story, "You, Jeremiah, was the reason I headed to Walpole, New Hampshire." Interjecting, "Did Miss Elizabeth know about me too?" inquisitive Zeke questions Nannette. "No, not exactly; but in my heart of hearts Father, I truly believe she had a strong inkling," meditatively Nannette responds. Hearing this, in his weakened state, Jeremiah moans, "Zeke you and I have a lot to thank Miss Elizabeth for." Amazed, Zeke calls out, "Miss Elizabeth is surely one special woman!" The vet sighs, "A rare breed; an angel in disguise!"

Absorbing all that has been revealed in the Stevens parlor, Austin walks over to Jeremiah. He carefully inspects Jeremiah Holden's recent wound he inflicted on him. With remorse, Austin solemnly remarks, "Jeremiah, I truly hope the physical wound I inflicted on you today heals quickly." Body shaking, Austin cries out, "I was out of control; the vile demons inside of me took over." Austin pauses, with shallow breath he moans, "I fear, unlike the physical wound, the emotional wounds I also inflicted on you Jeremiah will sadly take time to heal." Sighing, Austin repents, "For that my good man, I am deeply and truly remorseful."

Staring at penitent Austin with newfound pity, Dr. Jeremiah Holden offers, "As your dear wife so valiantly said, we must put all of this behind us." Taking hold of Austin's trembling hands, Jeremiah mournfully states, "The shocking loss of your young daughter Theresa Edith is far greater than anything I have ever had to endure; even the loss of my young wife." Sighing he says, "She was always ailing. I was well aware she was ill; therefore, as sad as it was, I was prepared." Humbly, Austin murmurs, "I'm so sorry. I have been so self-absorbed. I totally dismissed your recent loss and that you are a widower." Bowing his head in shame, Austin moans, "I am not worthy of your forgiveness."

Silently Nannette is sitting on the love seat, patiently listening to these two once intense enemies resolve their major aversion and distrust of one another. More than anything, Nannette wished Jeremiah and Austin would make amends; seeing them construct atonement with one another, pleases her greatly. Along with Nannette, observing and listening intently, Zeke is moved by his boss's contrite behavior and Jeremiah's generous forgiveness. At last the room is peaceful. The stillness is broken by the sound of Austin dragging his damaged leg as he limps away from Jeremiah. Now sitting by the roaring fireplace with his bent head in his shaking hands Austin cries out, "I truly need an angel to watch over me." Softly entering the room Anna Lee is mystified hearing her husband's pleading comment. *The Truth will Set you Free* ~ Jesus, Book of John

CHAPTER FIFTY-ONE

Hooray for Hollywood
Hollywood, California
Winter 1956

GRANDMA HOLLYWOOD'S FRONT door swings open. Grandma Hollywood, Mary Grace, Elena, and Regina with overnight bags in hand, drag themselves into the house. "Thank you so much Grandma. Catalina Island was fantastic!" Regina gushes. Beaming, Grandma Hollywood responds, "Why thank you my darling." The dog Cleo is overly excited having them return. Looking at Elena petting Cleo, trying to engage her, Grandma asks, "How did you like Catalina Island Elena?" Retrieving her overnight bag which she placed near Cleo, Elena politely with lack of emotion responds, "It was very nice Grandma; thank you for taking us."

"Very nice! Is that all you have to say, Elena?" annoyed Aunt Mary Grace remarks. Irritated with her moody niece Mary Grace calls out, "Why it was marvelous!" Mary Grace questions, "Weren't you impressed with those magnificent yachts owned by famous movie stars moored on the gorgeous, azure blue-green water?" Going up to Elena, her aunt reminds and asks, "Didn't you enjoy the delightful tourist train that drove us around this enchanted Island? What about the lush foliage and beautiful, golden bronze gorgeous people?" She adds, "And it is only 26 miles from Los Angeles' mainland." "The ride over on the tourist boat was so much fun," Regina gushes. Staring at stone-faced Elena, Mary Grace proclaims, "You just experienced the dream of every young girl." Regina interjects, "It was absolutely amazing!" Brushing aside her blond hair from her eyes, Regina mentions, "Although, I was disappointed. I thought for sure we were going to see Rodney Sheridan sunbathing nude on one of those fabulous yachts." Hearing Rodney's name associated with nude, Elena glares at her cousin with aversion. Ignoring moody Elena, excitedly Regina singsongs, "The Wrigley Mansion on top of Mt. Ada is a fairytale castle." Sighing she murmurs, "I thought I was dreaming."

Peering directly at her niece and daughter Mary Grace emphasizes, "And for you two, Elena and Regina, that dream came true this weekend!" Regina calls out, "Yes, yes, Mom we know." Mockingly Regina comments, "I noticed you liked all those young muscle men in those teeny weenie Speedo bathing suits, Mother!!" To defuse the tension, exhausted, Grandma Hollywood suggests, "We're all tired. Let's clean up and have a light dinner." Cleo happily pitter patters after Grandma Hollywood to her plush pink bedroom. The rest head to their respective rooms.

After taking long hot bubble baths, and putting on comfortable clothes, the four women are sitting out back on the patio eating cottage cheese and peaches along with sipping homemade lemonade. *Grandma Hollywood is determined her girls stay in shape.* Since moving to California, her motto is, "You can never be too thin or too rich." After finishing her peaches and cottage cheese, Elena rises and proceeds to head back into the house with Cleo following. "Where are you going darling? You must stay outdoors for a while, the night is young and beautiful," Grandma Hollywood attempts to entice Elena. "I'm going to call my mother and tell her I want to go home!" Elena informs. Mary Grace interjects, "Before you call your Mom, perhaps you would like to hear what I have to tell you." Stopping in her tracks, Elena quickly turns and walks over to her Aunt. "Unless this has to do with my mother, father or Aunt Ettie, I don't want to hear anything." Aunt Mary Grace grasps Elena's hand tenderly leads her back to the patio table. Politely she asks her niece to sit. Reassuring her, "Yes Elena, it's about all of them!" Wide eyed, Elena plops down on the wicker chair, calling out, "I'm all ears!"

Pushing away from the patio table, Grandma Hollywood slowly rises up; she motions for Regina to follow her offering, "Mary Grace, Regina and I will bring the plates inside and wash the dishes." Hearing the dishes being removed, Regina makes a frown noticing her mother's serious tone, she follows her insistent grandmother into the kitchen. Aware of what Mary Grace plans on telling Elena, privacy is a must, wisely Grandma Hollywood recognizes.

Elena pleads, "Aunt Mary Grace, hurry I'm at my wits end! What is it that you have to tell me?" Mary Grace states, "I won't beat around the bush. You are old enough and deserve to know, Elena." "Then go on!" Elena demands. "First, your Aunt Ettie's husband, your Uncle Carlo, passed away the day you and your Mom left for California." "Oh dear, I knew there was something wrong with him. Uncle Carlo coughed all the time," eyes misty, Elena cries out. Anxious, she asks, "Is my Aunt Ettie okay? Is that why my Mom went back to Jersey City?"

Holding Elena's quivering hands, she assures, "Your Aunt Ettie is fine. Rosaria, Blaise, and the priest were there for her." Mary Grace further explains, "Your Aunt Ettie hired your Dad's foreman Tony's wife Eileen to help her." "Eileen? Not the woman my Mom and I saw on Christmas night near my Dad?" annoyed Elena calls out. Mary Grace responds, "Yes, she's the one." Looking directly at her niece, to defuse her anger she further enlightens, "Elena, Eileen is a good woman; it was not what you and your Mom thought you saw that night. Tony and Eileen are married. Everything is fine with everyone now."

Not convinced, Elena further inquires, "What about my Dad? You've not said a word about him." "For one thing, your Father was the best man at Tony and Eileen's wedding." "That's what was so important that you had to tell me about my Dad?" frustrated Elena calls out. Uneasy, Mary Grace, inhales and proceeds to further explain, "No, not exactly. You see Elena, your Father had some enemies in Jersey City. After your Uncle Carlo's funeral, your Dad . . ." Elena listens intently to her Aunt Mary Grace as she shares the situation at home regarding her Father. Wisely, Mary Grace edits the truth to fit what is proper for a young daughter to hear. Tactfully, Mary Grace reveals, "Your Father was hurt; your father is getting better; your mother needed to go home to take care of your Dad and to handle important business matters." Hearing all this, Elena settles down, conceding, "As long as my Dad is fine and Mom is taking care of him, I'm good!"

Elena's unexpected mature response appeases her nervous Aunt Mary Grace. "You are certainly a mature young lady Elena. I am so proud of how well you are handling this." Prudently, Mary Grace did not share the mafia connection; the burning down of her father's business; the FBI's involvement; and the underlying, continuing threat. "I appreciate your telling me this Aunt Grace, but I still want to go home!" "No! Elena, you cannot go home!" Mary Grace screams. Seeing Elena alarmed, Mary Grace calms down then offers, "Not now, Elena. Your mother, especially your father, insist you stay here until they feel it is wise for you to return!" "But why?" groaning, Elena questions. "Please, trust us Elena," Mary Grace begs.

❧

It was a restless night for Elena. She is deeply concerned about her parents back home in New Jersey. For their sake, Elena acquiesces. She will remain in California until her parents feel it is the right time for her to return. Right now, Elena must get ready to go with her grandmother and the others to visit with her great Uncle Albert, Grandma Hollywood's only sibling bachelor brother. Elena always heard that he is very distinguished and a notable man. He is also a wonderful brother to Grandma Hollywood. Out of respect, Elena will go; her Father's motto of 'Family First' is deeply ingrained in Elena's psyche.

Cleo's incessant barking at the doorbell ringing causes Regina to see who it is. Flustered, moving back and forth at the door is Rodney. "Where is Tess and Elena? I must speak with them immediately!" eerily looking around he insists. "Calm down! You look like you saw a ghost; besides my Aunt Tess is not here. She's back in New Jersey," Regina tells him. "When is she due back?" in a state of panic Rodney questions. Not aware of why her Aunt Tess left for New Jersey, Regina responds, "Your guess is as good as mine."

Noticing how upset Rodney is, soothingly Regina murmurs, "Relax, Elena's here." Paying no heed, Rodney runs into the house. "Stop Rodney, my Mom threatened me under the pain of death not to disturb Elena; Mom said Elena needs her rest!" "I must speak with Elena immediately," Rodney pleads. Glaring at him, Regina warns, "Trust me Rodney you don't want to get my Mother mad." Hearing Regina's warning Rodney stops. "My Mom is very upset." In her bedroom primping herself Grandma Hollywood is waiting for Mateo to come by to return her pink convertible so they can drive to Fresno later to visit with her brother Albert. Hearing the noise outside, she calls out, "Regina, is that Mateo?"

As Regina goes to attend to her grandmother, Rodney takes the opportunity to run to Elena's bedroom; he knocks loudly. "Elena, I just heard from Monsignor James Cooney." Huffing and puffing he insists, "It is urgent we talk now!" Hearing this, Elena answers from behind the door, "I am not dressed yet; give me a minute. Wait out back in the patio." Aunt Mary Grace comes from the kitchen carrying a Brown Derby restaurant mug filled with coffee. She notices Rodney standing near Elena's bedroom door. Walking up to him and pointing at the logo on the mug she proudly informs, "Rodney, this is where my mother took us for lunch the day we arrived." She sighs, "So many famous people were there." Noticing Rodney is not paying her any mind and standing near Elena's door, Mary Grace inquires, "What's so urgent that you have to disturb my niece?"

Listening from behind the door her aunt's distress with Rodney, Elena assures her, "Aunt Mary Grace, it's fine." Elena infers, "I'm assuming it's about a movie script Rodney is writing. I told him I will look at it for him." "You better not be pulling my leg Elena! If that's all it is, I'll let you be," Mary Grace warns and concedes. She further cautions, "If I find out you are lying, you'll both regret it." "Pinky promise," Elena swears as she comes out of the bedroom. Stiff as a rod, standing nervously by listening to them, Rodney reassures, "That's correct I came here to talk to Elena about my script." He proudly adds, "I have an important producer who wants to discuss it with me this afternoon." "Well then . . ." Mary Grace hesitates, turns and glares at her niece, "Are you alright Elena? I mean about what we discussed last night?" Intending to have her aunt leave, Elena reassures, "As I said, I'll stay here until my parents tell me it is okay to go back home." With this said, relieved Mary Grace leaves Elena and Rodney alone.

Still anxious about what she has learned about her father, and now Rodney rushing in informing her he has something urgent to discuss, Elena is at her wits end. "This better be important Rodney. I'm not in the mood for any of your fool hearted nonsense," she cautions him. They walk back to the patio where they can be alone. "Sit down Elena. Since your Mom is not here; I have to relay it to you." Very seriously Rodney informs, "Elena, you must get in touch with your Mom and tell her everything I'm going to tell you." Impatient, Elena blurts out, "Let's hear it." "I received a call from Monsignor Cooney from Notre Dame last night about the mysterious priest Father Schultz from your parish back home," he nervously tells Elena. "Oh," startled, Elena cries out. "Listen and don't interrupt until I finish," Rodney pleads. "Evidently, there's a weird, perhaps even dangerous connection between the priest missing in El Paso, Texas and the so-called Father Arthur Schultz from your Jersey City parish."

Rodney stops to catch his breath. "Go on Rodney, you got my attention," Elena insists. "Do you know a Sister Margaret Mary?" Rodney asks. Elena bolts out of her chair and hollers, "Yes! Why?" "It seems as if she is also involved." Both pause a moment to breathe. Rodney continues, "Elena, it's urgent that Monsignor Cooney talk with your Mother and the head clergy at your parish as soon as possible." "Father Kelly?" questions Elena. "Yes! Father John Kelly!" Rodney repeats. Suddenly Regina strolls in with Grandma Hollywood followed by shy Nunzio.

Seeing them come in Rodney and Elena stare at one another and clam up. "You two look like you've seen a ghost! It's only Nunzio," Regina chimes in. Beaming from ear to ear, she screams out, "Guess what Elena? I have great news. I'm going to be a stand-in for the young actress Nathalie Wood." Regina takes a bow bragging. Nunzio and Grandma Hollywood clap giving her a standing ovation. For a second, Rodney forgets the urgency of his visit. He calls out, "Bravo!" After the applause and the announcement, with Brown Derby mug in hand, Mary Grace walks in. She proudly informs, "Isn't this exciting for my Regina." "Although," she further informs, "Being a stand-in is not a speaking part." Regina is annoyed, "Mom!" Mary Grace explains, "I am happy for you darling; although, Regina as a stand in, you only stand in front of the camera which is not rolling. You're not in the movie. What happens is that Nathalie Wood comes in for the final take. She is the star!"

Nunzio further explains, "Stand-ins are the people who double for a cast member during rehearsals. Regina will stand there while Nathalie Wood is off camera and prepares to do the scene." "Still not sure what stand in means," questions Elena. "Regina's purpose is to remain there under the bright camera lights until the camera crew have the right settings," Nunzio further explains. "See, I will be a very important person on the movie lot," thrilled Regina calls out. She takes another deep bow. Nunzio teases in a flirtatious way, "Not so glamorous Regina." Politely he cautions, "There will be times you will have to endure water thrown at you, harsh dusty wind, hot lights, and take it all like a champ." He adds, "After all that, and you are hot and messy, cool, calm Nathalie Wood comes in for the final take." Regina chimes in, "Who cares! I'm willing to go through a tornado just to be on the set with all those famous movie stars." Thrilled, she cries out, "Never know, it might be my big break!"

Searching around, Grandma Hollywood asks, "Nunzio, where' s Mateo?" "I'm sorry I should have told you sooner, he went to Dr. Della Porta's house to cut his hair," he responds. Seeing Grandma Hollywood perplexed, Nunzio informs, "Mateo asked me to bring your car back here." Being a neat freak and considerate, he adds, "I believe it needs to be washed." Grandma looks flustered. "I would be happy to take it for you," Nunzio suggests. Regina immediately offers, "I'll take a ride with you Nunzio. I'd like to pick your brain; you know a lot about the movie business." "Yes," Grandma Hollywood says, "Nunzio works there as a script reader and writer." Smiling at him Grandma Hollywood brags, "I predict that someday he will be a director, if he plays his cards right." Blushing Nunzio responds, "You are too kind Signora."

Hastily, Regina grabs Nunzio's hands and calls out, "Avanti, let's get this car primped up!" "Wait," Mary Grace calls out, "How old are you Nunzio? Regina is not even sixteen; she can't drive." He stops, turns to answer Mary Grace, "I will be twenty this coming August 4th." Pulling Nunzio away, Regina cries out, "Age means nothing to me Mother. As you always said, I came out of your womb at forty." Grandma Hollywood assures Mary Grace, "She'll be fine. Nunzio is a real gentleman." Smirking at Mary Grace who would have loved to go with Nunzio, Grandma Hollywood lectures, "My darling married daughter, he's much too young for you." In a grand manner grandma reiterates, "Let's get ready to go visit my brother Albert. We must leave as soon as Nunzio returns with my pink

Cadillac convertible all spruced up." Under her breath, Mary Grace groans, "Dad would never be seen dead in a fancy car like that!"

While everyone gets ready to head to Fresno, Rodney glares at Elena. He orders, "Call your mom now!" "I'll call her when I am good and ready!" annoyed she rebukes. "Why hasn't Monsignor James Cooney contacted Father Kelly himself? My Mom has enough on her plate right now," frustrated Elena questions. Temporarily Rodney is speechless. As Elena prepares to leave, Rodney brags, "My script is coming along nicely; if things go my way, I will be another F. Scott Fitzgerald." He informs, "Did you know Elena that Fitzgerald started writing his first novel, *This Side of Paradise*, at the age of sixteen?" Mocking, Elena sighs, "You and my cousin Regina would make a great couple. You, arrogant Fitzgerald and Regina, Zelda, Fitzgerald's kooky wife." She rushes away from Rodney, calling out, "Let yourself out F. Scott. I have to go!"

When Elena hears the front door slam shut, and confident Rodney left, she sits on the bed pondering whether or not she should call her mother informing her to contact Monsignor James Cooney. Mystified, she reaches under the bed and pulls out the huge book she has faithfully carried with her this entire trip. Teary eyed Elena opens it to the inside front cover reading the inscription: "To my O'Brien-Stevens family." Below the inscription is a handwritten notification: *This book is the private property of Sister Margaret Mary O'Brien*. Sad, Elena slams the book shut as she shoves it under her bed moaning, "Poor Sister Margaret Mary." Making the Sign of the Cross, she pleads, "I pray to God she's okay?" Impatient, Grandma Hollywood calls, "Is everybody ready? Nunzio and Regina returned." No response, therefore, Grandma Hollywood screeches, "Avanti!" The sparkling clean pink Cadillac convertible is ready." Dressed to the nines, Mary Grace is ready, echoing, "Let's roll." Smoothly Mary Grace coos, "I'm so excited to see Uncle Albert." She sighs, "Paradise is what people call Uncle Albert's extravagant home!"

CHAPTER FIFTY-TWO

The Surprise Safe House
Jersey City, New Jersey
Late Winter 1956

DRIVEN IN A counterfeit ambulance, escorted by two undercover police, Tess is disguised in a short black and grey wig; padding to make her look hefty; dressed like a homeless woman; and wearing dark sunglasses. Tess and Ray are being taken to an undisclosed house where Mike is concealed. For the safety of his life Mike is guarded in an undisclosed house with assigned police agents.

Before the authorities agreed to allow Tess to visit Mike, she was harshly warned that her going there, even closely shielded, is a dangerous risk not only for herself but her husband. This same warning was given to Ray Sinnotti. Paying no heed, Tess absolutely insists, as does Ray. *Tess had to see her husband and Ray his best buddy.* Thankfully Mike was not told; if he had been, he would have been enraged and vehemently demanded Tess and Ray not be given permission.

Still recovering from his wound, Ray bravely accompanies Tess. Ray is also disguised. Slow moving, Tess drags along outside. To maintain the cover up, an EMT assists Tess with the walker and helps her into the house. Mainly, to be sure she doesn't blow her cover or the safe house. Desperately wanting to see Mike, Ray is transformed into an old man, supposedly the elderly woman's invalid husband who was just released from a nursing home. This scheme was plotted and executed by plain clothesmen. Tess and Ray were instructed to go to a designated nursing home, where outfits would be there to disguise them. After, with their eyes covered, they will be transported in an ambulance to the secret place where Mike is being heavily guarded and concealed.

The officers were also disguised as EMTs. As they escorted Tess and Ray in the ambulance one of them commented, "What a motley looking couple." After a short ride, they arrived at the designated place. Before exiting the ambulance, the fake EMT cops search the house inside and out and canvass the neighborhood thoroughly. When certain all is safe, they carry disguised Ray in on a stretcher, followed by limping disguised Tess holding onto a walker. Peeking through her mask, Tess is surprised to see the house is located in a pristine middle-class neighborhood. It is a small, impeccable looking one-family cottage-like dwelling.

An American flag, along with an Irish flag are on a flagpole in front of the single dwelling house. Tess is surprised to see a holly Christmas wreath still hanging on the front door. While Tess is inspecting the exterior of the house, an EMT readjusts her eye mask, and hurries Tess into the white clapboard house. His main interest is that Tess doesn't blow the cover, risking everyone's safety.

Shortly after Tess is safely in the house, Ray is brought in on a stretcher. Hidden surveillance cameras are placed all around the house's interior and exterior. So far, all is going as planned. Tess's eye covering is removed once she is in the safe house. She is surprised to notice the house is neat as a pin. Her eyes focus on a large wooden Crucifix hanging over a desk in the corner. There is a large silver frame with a photo of an elderly woman with a younger man at her side. A statue of the Blessed Mother Mary is displayed on an upright piano near the cozy flowered sofa. On the wall near the Crucifix hangs Regis High School and Fordham College diplomas. The interior shades are pulled down and interior lights are low. Nervously, Ray looks around. All is eerily quiet. Within a minute, an officer wheels Mike into the living room where the others are waiting.

Gasping when she realizes who has just entered, with knots in her stomach, Tess is shocked to see her husband Mike frail sitting in a wheelchair. Noticing Tess traumatized, mortified, Mike moans, "Tess I hate for you to see me like this." Tess murmurs, "Mike, you're as handsome as ever." Pulling off her wig, Tess runs over to him. Weeping she bends down near Mike and hugs her apologetic husband. "Mike, I'm so sorry. Please forgive me." She glances over at Ray and assures Mike, "Your best buddy explained everything to me." Mike is silent. He is overwhelmed seeing Tess, and fears for her safety.

Best buddy Ray stands back giving husband and wife a chance to be alone. A few minutes later, after Tess and Mike finish hugging, kissing, and crying, Ray goes over to them. Joking he orders, "Move over Tess, give me a chance with my old Prep buddy." Misty eyed, Mike stares at Ray. Teasing, Ray adds, "Hey you big lug, give me a hug. After all, I took a bullet for you." Seeing his wife and best buddy, Mike mutters, "Sorry I put you all through this. I'm not worthy of your attention." Pondering, Mike cries out, "How's my baby; my Elena Rose?" Clutching his hand tightly, Tess assures him, "She's fine; Elena is safe in California with my mother." "Thankfully!" Mike says.

Pausing to catch his breath, Mike moans, "Ettie? How's my sister?" He hesitates and adds, "Last thing I remember in the hospital was she threw herself on top of me and then I heard shots." Compassionately, Tess assures him, "Mike, your sister is fine. Eileen is with her." Ray interjects immediately, "Your sister is a real hero. Brave and strong like an ox." Seeing Mike talking and conscious, Ray is relieved. To distract him from becoming melancholy, sniffing, Ray says, "Do I smell coffee? I can sure use a cup." With that said, an elderly woman calls out from the kitchen, "I'm making it for all of you; be patient!" The counterfeit EMT cop calls out, "Thanks; you're terrific."

Carrying a tray with a coffee pot, milk in a ceramic creamer, sugar cubes and blue china cups, a gray-haired woman mentions, "Mike, I already put a little sugar and milk in your coffee. You need the calories." She looks him up and down and boldly announces, "Faith and Be Golly, you got too thin." Handing him the Fordham coffee mug and placing the tray on the highly polished mahogany oval coffee table with Waterford crystal bowl filled with age old mints, she says, "Ettie will be angry with me if I don't feed you well." Ready to fall over, Tess screams, "What the hell? Sister Margaret Mary!" "I hope you said heaven and not hell," Sister Margaret Mary jokingly responds. Shocked, Tess stands frozen, turns and glares at Ray and Mike. She chastises, "Okay you guys, you have more explaining to do." With a quivering finger pointing at Sister Margaret Mary, Tess demands, "Where exactly are we and what is Sister doing here?" The undercover cops' smirk but remain quiet as church mice. "For everyone's safety Tess, I left a few things out," mumbling Ray excuses.

Sister Margaret Mary clutches Tess's shaking hands compassionately whispers, "Sit down Tess; you're lucky to be here." Looking over at Ray, Sister answers, "Ray will fill you in Tess." Mike's best buddy remains quiet; therefore, reverently Sister Margaret Mary makes the Sign of the Cross praising God. Pontificating she educates Tess, "Faith and be Golly, your hunted down, wounded husband is safe under the roof of the kindly, pious, deceased Irish born mother of Professor Brendan O'Connor." Sternly, Sister explains, "This house is where Mike has been and where you are right now." Gazing over at Ray, she remarks, "As to why? I'll leave that up to Ray and Mike." Sister pours coffee for the stone-faced policeman Quinn. Rookie cop Sal shakes his head no to the coffee.

Tess is still trying to process all of this. Mute, Ray and Mike leave it all up to Sister Margaret Mary. The nun, realizing Ray and Mike refuse to explain further, she reveals, "It was Tom Walsh, the Irish tavern owner's brilliant suggestion to Captain Burn, his close friend, to hide Mike here at Brendan's deceased mother Peggy's quaint house." "Touchdown!" Ray adds, "After Brendan's house was checked out thoroughly, the police went along with the idea. Professor Brendan O'Connor wholehearted gave them permission to use his and his sweet dear deceased mother's humble abode. The neighbors were told through a contrived, planted gossipy grapevine, that Brendan's deceased mother's older brother Aloysius had hip surgery and after rehab he and his elderly wife Noreen will stay here with Brendan until he fully recuperates."

Gazing over at Sister, Ray adds, "It was Father Kelly's idea to send Sister Margaret Mary to be Mike's caregiver here at the official safe house." Not wanting to take all the credit, Sister Margaret Mary mentions, "A kind elderly doctor, the one who cared for Ettie's husband . . ." She stops mid-sentence to recall, "I believe his name was Dr. Spats; he came here undercover to check on Mike." "Dr. Saul Sacks?" Tess calls out. Sister Margaret Mary resumes, "Yes, Sacks that's the name, he secretly administered to Mike's wounds." Enough said, tired Sister Margaret Mary sits down on the nearby rocking chair where a crochet blanket covered with shamrocks graces it. She closes her blurry worn out eyes. Not thinking, Ray slips, "I hear Father Jack Kelly is deeply concerned for Sister Margaret Mary's safety too."

No longer listening, the elderly nun yawns. Ray gazes sympathetically over at the fatigued, aged nun. Her eyes closed and snoring. The elderly nun has been diligently nursing Mike day and night at Brendan's alias safe house where for months prior she also tended to Brendan's mother during her illness. With Sister Margaret Mary sleeping, noticing Tess is perplexed, Ray whispers, "For her safety, Father Kelly's intention is that the good Sister be hidden here from her predators." "Excuse me? Why does Sister Margaret Mary need to be protected?" apprehensive, Tess inquires. "Unfortunately, Sister is somehow involved with this horrific situation," secretly Ray sneaks out.

In a panic Tess bolts up waking the sleeping Nun hollering, "What? Why?" Staring at the Nun who is now wide awake, shuddering, Tess cautiously asks, "Sister Margaret Mary what do you know about Father Arthur Schultz and Juan?" Sister Margaret Mary murmurs, "Oh dear how do you know about the conversation between Monsignor James Cooney and our Monsignor John Kelly?" Before Tess can further interrogate Sister Margaret Mary, angered with the bantering and ruckus, Officer Quinn, the aggravated policeman, heatedly orders, "All of you quiet down!" They stare at the fuming cop as he demands, "No more talk until Captain Burn arrives!" Ray attempts to speak, the older rough cop Quinn, rushes over to him, grabs Ray by the collar screaming, "Are you deaf? Shut that mouth or I'll shut it for you." Hearing the disgruntled cop Quinn explode, they all settle down only to be spooked by a loud noise outside. Fearful, Tess mimics Monsignor James Cooney's mantra, *"God Protect the Innocents."*

CHAPTER FIFTY-THREE

Secrets Down Under Uncovered; Innocent Lambs, The Shady Caper
Walpole, New Hampshire
1857

HOLDING TIGHTLY ONTO the twins in her tender arms, Anna Lee enters the O'Brien Stevens parlor. Austin, Zeke, Nannette, and Dr. Jeremiah Holden are sitting there sipping their brandy anticipating Austin to speak. Pleased to see his wife entering with his babies, Austin limps over to Anna Lee, kisses her, and gently pecks the cheeks of their twin babies. Taking hold of the male infant Austin Hamish in his arms, Austin suggests, "Anna Lee, I'll hold my robust, namesake son Austin, you cuddle our tiny, sweet daughter, Rachel Melanie." Guiding his wife over to the love seat, he requests, "Sit Anna Lee." Pleased his wife is comfortably sitting holding their baby daughter, and gazing over at Zeke, Nannette, and Jeremiah, Austin commences, "May I have your attention please. After intently listening and absorbing all these fine, brave soul's life's stories, secrets, and future, I recognize it is my turn to share mine too." Austin is requesting Anna Lee's approval, "As long as you don't mind dear." Thrilled, Anna Lee freely and warmly agrees, "Why darling my prayers are answered. I beg of you to share." She looks lovingly at her husband pleading, "My dearest, you must in order to release all your inner turmoil in hopes of finding peace."

The baby Austin Hamish, in his father Austin's strong arms, is fussy. Nannette goes over and takes him from Austin, "Let me have him so you can speak freely with no distractions." Relinquishing his son, Austin begins to share his personal history; his trials and errors. Anna Lee, Zeke,

Nannette, and Jeremiah silently and patiently sit waiting. Austin sips his brandy, clears his throat, and rises. He begins, "Please bear with me. I have been harboring this for a year or so now." Hands shaking, he questions himself, "I am not sure where to begin." "Start from the beginning," Anna Lee anxiously encourages her timid husband while holding her daughter Rachel Melanie who is sleeping soundly.

With his wife's heartening support, Austin gains the courage to speak. "As some of you know, I inherited a huge and prosperous sheep farm in Australia from my dear grandfather. It produces the finest wool which is exported to England." Zeke murmurs, "England? My Irish ancestor enemies." Austin is so consumed he does not hear Zeke. He resumes, "The sheep farm has been extremely lucrative for years and has greatly sustained the Stevens family financially." Dr. Jeremiah Holden is impressed, "How fortunate; but I am sure at times it can be burdensome. Sheep can have many medical issues if not taken care of properly."

Austin immediately responds, "You are absolutely right Jeremiah; in fact, about a year ago, our sheep came down with a deadly unknown disease. We lost over half of our stock." "Dear me, you never said a word to me," sorrowfully, Anna Lee cries out. "Diagnosed at first as lice. We treated the poor animals accordingly assuming we had it under control," Austin resumes. "Lice spreads wildly and can be deadly. Although, if caught early it is treatable," with authority Dr. Holden explains. Austin interjects, "You are right Jeremiah; but not so in my situation. After a few months, the infected sheep were dying from it; in fact, almost our entire herd." Rocking the baby boy in her arms, Nannette murmurs, "How sad for the sheep." Watching Austin wiping his sweaty forehead with a linen handkerchief, Nannette adds, "Of course, for you also Mr. Stevens."

Listening intently, Zeke fretfully moans, "How difficult this must have been for you boss and to lose your precious daughter too." "My poor, poor darling I am so sorry I was not aware; hence, I was unable to support you through this terrible crisis," Anna Lee chastises herself. Raising his hand to hush everyone, Austin begs, "Please let me continue." All heed. Austin resumes, "It turns out the lice and other deadly diseases were deliberately planted on my sheep by unsavory, jealous competitors, pros who set out to destroy my sheep, therefore, our wool production." Sneering Austin pauses to wipe his sweaty hands. In anger he calls out, "Forcing me out of the lucrative wool producing industry forever."

Austin takes a sip of his fine aged brandy. His captive audience patiently waits for him to continue. Dr. Holden asks, "There was nothing you could have done? Isn't there a organization to back you?" Immediately Austin explains, "There was absolutely nothing I could do or no one I could turn to. I was given a ruthless-harsh warning to get out of the business or else." Austin defends, "At first, I did not heed their bullying." "Damn it Mr. Stevens, if I'd had known this, I would of went there and gave those rotten no good bullies a piece of my fist and then some," growls Zeke. "Unfortunately Zeke, you could not have helped. Unbeknownst to me, they were professional criminals who used deadly force on anyone who does not heed their warning." "What did you do?" interested, Jeremiah questions. Head lowered in shame, Austin murmurs, "I gave in. They took my farm; what sheep was left, and all the land." Distraught, Austin places his head in his hands in disgrace.

Hearing about Austin's horrific loss, the others are painfully moved but powerless to comfort him. Complete silence; a pin could drop and no one would hear it until Austin moans, "My grandfather is turning in his grave!" Staring at his captive audience, Austin apologizes, "You see, I had no choice. These criminals have people here in America." He sighs, "My dear wife and innocent babies' lives were at stake."

Mournfully gazing directly at Anna Lee, fretful, Austin mutters, "My biggest and most unbearable regret is, I went to Australia and left my vulnerable young daughter Theresa Edith and my pregnant wife helpless and alone." Wiping the tears cascading down his distressed face, Austin cries out, "Because of those scoundrels, I was not here to protect my daughter, my wife, and to be here for the birth of our twins." "Please don't torture yourself my darling," Anna Lee begs. Austin cries out, "I should have been here! If I was, my Theresa Edith might still be alive."

Remorseful, and trying to comfort her devastated husband, Anna Lee hands her slumbering baby girl to Zeke. She slowly walks over to her mournful husband. Placing her tender hand on his shoulder, Anna Lee mourns, "How much more can one person take?" Austin looks deeply into his wife's moist, beautiful violet eyes and cautions, "Sadly, my dear, there is more." Anna Lee pulls back and glares at her fretful husband, "More?" Hearing this, the others are astonished. Austin takes hold of the half empty brandy bottle raising it high for all to see. "This here, my good people, was once my number one friend but now it is my deadly foe." Austin's captive audience stares skeptically at the brandy glasses near them; then at the brandy bottle raised in Austin's shuddering hand. Dr. Jeremiah Holden is the first to question, "Austin, after learning your shocking story about you being forced to relinquish your sheep farm under deadly duress, how do we duly process *brandy* as your worst enemy?" "Thank you for your undivided attention," he sighs. With sincerity, Austin further remarks, "I earnestly apologize for bringing so much sadness to you but as you all so bravely proved, sharing is a warranted catharsis for me as it was for you." With undivided attention from the rest, Austin resumes, "It took me a while to acknowledge that deep seeded secrets are more damaging than honest sincere truth." Anxious to hear more, Anna Lee encourages, "Please dear enlighten us regarding the questionable *brandy* issue." Austin wife's advice gives him the daring to speak. "Years ago, my grandfather met an English gentleman while he was on a business trip in London regarding the wool industry." Grinning Austin resumes, "Unbeknownst to my grandfather, this so-called gentleman, was a phony who dealt with illegal, rare and exceedingly expensive spirits." "You mean alcohol? That's why you have stored so much brandy in your cellar?" Zeke calls out. "Yes! You see, I always thought my grandfather paid for it and had it legally shipped here but . . ." Austin abruptly stops talking.

"Darling, why do you hesitate?" innocently Anna Lee questions. "You see, Anna Lee, this unsavory Englishman, my naive grandfather met and trusted in London, stole and distributed illegally rare, aged, fine expensive brandy from the innocent monks in France. The sleazy so-called gentleman sold it to unsavory con men who engaged and entrapped blameless people, including my grandfather, to have the illegal brandy shipped to their homes here is America." Austin sighs, "Unfortunately, my inexperienced grandfather was one of their unsuspecting victims." "Where I come from Mr. Austin, we call them low-down, no good, bootlegging crooks," ornery, Zeke blurts out.

Austin motions for Zeke to calm down. Hoping to exonerate himself, Austin justifies, "As for myself, I swear I was not aware of this illegal, covert arrangement. My grandfather was under the erroneous assumption it was legal brandy which he paid for handsomely." Pausing and reflecting, white as a ghost, Austin cries out, "Like the innocent lambs in Australia, my parents where sacrificial lambs." Enraged, he further reveals, "The barn fire that killed my parents, I now know who the arsonists were and why." Gulping down the last of this illegal culprit, mockingly Austin cries out, "May they burn in hell for all eternity while my poor parents look down on them from the heavenly gate!" With that said, relieved, Austin shouts out, "Cheers!" Sneering at the bottle of brandy, Austin moans, "My grandfather savored and indulged this culprit, as I did." Looking at their empty brandy glasses in front of the others, Austin calls out, "As you all did!" With levity, mockingly Austin calls out, "Down the hatch." Zeke mocks, "More ways than one."

Suddenly Zeke quickly hands baby Rachel Melanie back to Anna Lee. He shouts out, "Oh my gosh!" Startling the others even the twins. Zeke recalls, "Mr. Stevens, I remember the night you went down the cellar to retrieve a bottle of brandy and you mysteriously fell." Austin shakes his head in agreement. "You called me to come down and help you. While there, you whispered to me in confidence and swore that someone pushed you." Zeke apologizes, "At the time I thought you were dizzy from the fall and paid you no mind." Remembering, Zeke further mentions, "You even ordered me, Mr. Stevens, to check the cellar the next day to see if I could find anything suspicious." Frustrated, Zeke cries out, "As you asked, I searched all over, but didn't notice anything out of order." Pounding his foot, Zeke hollers, "Damn it to hell, one of those bootlegging monstrous creeps must have been there." "Yes, Zeke, I am sure there was a sinister person down there." Painfully, Austin shares, "Most likely to steal the brandy and harm me and perhaps my family."

Listening intently, Jeremiah interjects, "Have you had any contact with these insalubrious people since?" "Sadly, yes. When I arrived home from Australia and learned about the unbearable death of my Theresa Edith, a few days later I received a threatening letter saying they wanted all the brandy I have in my cellar. They demanded I pay for the bottles I've used and then some." Sighing, Austin adds, "The amount of money they demanded was inconceivable." Innocent, Nannette suggests, "You should have notified the authorities and had these men put in jail." "Heaven's no, Nannette, they were illegally shipped here. I am culpable." Wiping his forehead, Austin screams, "I can go to jail!" "Jail?" Anna Lee moans. Coming to her senses, Austin's wise wife adds, "As horrific as all this is, I praise the good Lord you were able to share this with us; you have been so depressed even before our angel Theresa Edith passed." Weeping and ashamed, Anna Lee apologizes, "Here I thought you no longer loved me Austin. I convinced myself you had another woman in Australia." Pulling her closer to him, Austin kisses his wife's tearful cheeks. "My darling you are the only woman I have ever loved or ever will love."

Pleased to observe this previous forlorn couple finding comfort and love again, still anxious to hear what Austin must do, Jeremiah questions, "Austin what do you plan to do about the illegal brandy situation?" "Happy you asked, my good man. I have reliable sources who will contact the monastery that produces this rare brandy in France. This same source will assist me in shipping it back to the monks." They promise me they will also inform the proper authorities about the illegitimate brandy caper and clear the good name of O'Brien-Stevens." Primping his chest out, he proudly says, "This will exonerate my grandfather and myself." Anna Lee cries out, "Thank you Lord." Patting her moist eyes with a lace hanky, she exclaims, "My dearest Austin, I am beyond relieved and pleased for you." The rest are elated to hear this. The physically wounded Dr. Jeremiah Holden, although pleased, is silent for the moment.

The veterinarian Dr. Jeremiah Holden, now friend of Austin, sorrowfully pontificates, "I only wish I could have advised you Austin about the diseased sheep. Perhaps I could have helped you save your Australian family sheep farm." Before Austin can respond, Jeremiah Holden questions, "After hearing all the horrific events that have happened to you, especially the shocking death of your child, I can truly understand your being hostile to everyone around you; including me." Quizzically, Jeremiah requests, "Austin, may I ask, what made you have such a sudden turn in acceptance and forgiveness with us?" Anna Lee, Zeke, and Nannette listen intently for Austin's response. Pausing to absorb Jeremiah's question, Austin somberly responds, "Observing how beautifully my compassionate wife has accepted my unforgiveable treatment of her and all of you, also recognizing my violent, riotous behavior and severe hatred that has caused her so much pain, I suddenly had a rude awakening!" He looks over at Anna Lee and moans, "The dreadful fear that I would lose my beautiful wife and my innocent twins was excruciating." Sobbing, Austin cries out, "I could not bear it!" Distraught, this newly contrite husband drags himself over to tearful Anna Lee and takes her tender hand. "My dearest wife, we are truly blessed. Not only do we have a special angel in heaven watching over us, we have two angels here on earth to bring us a life-time of joy." Clutching her hand tightly, Austin expresses his appreciation, "Ann Lee, your altruistic nature and unwavering faith in God guided me in recognizing my true blessings and taught me what is important in life." Holding tightly onto his wife's tender hand, Austin gazes fondly and lovingly at their twins, his faithful main man Zeke, kind Nannette, and out of the ordinary Jeremiah Holden. *The Truth will Set You Free.*

CHAPTER FIFTY-FOUR

Last Piece of the Puzzle
Jersey City, New Jersey
1956

THE JERSEY CITY policemen are not pleased about watching two extra people, Tess and Ray, in the safe house especially when they hear a loud noise outside. Thankfully, after inspecting it, it was the backfiring of a delivery truck. Sister Margaret Mary, Mike, Tess, and Ray were relieved to learn the loud noise was nothing for them to be alarmed about. The older, rougher cop, Quinn peeks out the window, turns and asks the younger rookie cop Sal, "What time did Captain Burn say he was due here?" Officer Sal, answers, "He should have been here an hour ago." "We get off duty soon and I am not sure when these," sneering over at Tess and Ray, "are supposed to be out of here," caustically Quinn remarks. Mike overhears the policemen's chatter. He also observes Tess and Ray restless. Mike motions for the younger, compliant cop to come over to him. "Yes Mike, what is it?" the rookie cop Sal asks. "I heard Policeman Quinn ask you what time Captain Burn is due; my wife and friend should get the hell out of here now; it isn't safe." "No worries," answers Sal, the rookie cop. "The Captain will be here any minute." With that said, a key is heard at the back door. Captain Francis Burn boldly enters.

All are relieved to see him other than Tess. She is the only one who never saw him nor is she fully aware of his connection with Mike's situation. Patrolman Quinn goes up to the Captain who hands him his long winter coat and woolen cap that he wears to disguise himself as Professor Brendan O'Connor. "Captain, the guys to relieve us aren't here yet; any word from then?" "No, but they'll be here soon." Captain Burn goes up to Mike, whispers in his ear; turns and gives a hug to Sister Margaret Mary. Ray walks over to Captain Burn questioning, "You remember me don't you Captain? I'm a good friend of your buddy Walsh." The Captain seems confused, Ray adds, "Because of Walsh and your connections with him I was able to get into the hospital to see Mike." Realizing the association, the enlightened Captain slaps Ray hard on the back, making Ray groan. "Sorry Ray, I forgot you took a bullet for our guy Mike; are you okay now?" "Sure enough Captain. As long as my best buddy is good, I'm good," Ray says. Standing near the piano Tess is observing this. Sister Margaret Mary takes Tess's hand and brings her over to the Captain. "This here is Mike's lovely wife, Tess Policino." The Captain puts his hand out to shake Tess's hand. Hesitantly, Tess gives him her sweaty hand as she says, "Now that we've been properly introduced, let's get down to business." Impressed and smiling, Captain Burn remarks, "Clever young woman; I always said red heads are smarter than they appear."

The pleasantries are over as the Captain calls over to Patrolman Quinn, "You can go." Looking over at the younger cop he orders, "Officer Sal, you stay here until the others come to relieve you." Anxious to get the hell out of there, Officer Quinn is out the back door in two shakes of a leg. "Officer Sal, go in the kitchen and wait there. I want to be alone with this motley crew," Captain Burn sarcastically teases. Mike sits up in the wheelchair almost ready to jump out. "What's up Captain?" anxious Mike asks. "Sit down all of you; I have good news and not such good news." Sister Margaret Mary, who dislikes hesitation and nonsense calls out, "Good Lord; no dilly tallying. Speak your piece; I'm not getting any younger!"

Gazing at Mike, Captain Burn shouts out, "We got your assailants!" "Thank god!" Tess cries out. Mike defiantly glares at his wife and reprimands, "Tess, please don't interrupt, let Captain Burn finish." Ray goes over to Tess and puts his arm on her shoulder to relax her. "Sister Margaret Mary, you are a wise sleuth; as you knew all along, Father Arthur Schultz was an imposter hired by the despicable New Jersey mob bosses to get rid of Mike after he refused to play ball with them as a lesson and warning to anyone who refuses them." Everyone is shocked to hear this. "I thought the phony priest was from El Paso, Texas; what does he have to do with Jersey City?" Tess looks over at Sister Margaret Mary. "Sister, I believe you knew Father Schultz was an imposter all along?" Tess blurts out. "Yeah," Ray interjects, "I'm confused; how does the El Paso priest fit in with St. Victor's and our Sister Margaret Mary? Where's the connection?"

Infuriated, Mike screams, "Quiet! Let the Captain speak or I'll ask him to send you all home!" Fuming Mike adds, "I'm the one they're after! I'm the one they tried to kill and permanently ruined my family business." Sister Margaret Mary attempts to calm Mike down, "Please Mike relax, you'll never recuperate if you don't." Quieting down, Mike sighs, "I didn't want my wife or Ray here." "Sorry," Ray calls out. Putting her head into her hands, Tess bows her head in shame and sorrow. Sister Margaret Mary prays, "My dear people, all of you have suffered greatly; let's not let these evil people, whom the devil placed here, destroy your peace or your love for one another."

Hearing the noise, Sal comes out of the kitchen. Sister Margaret Mary quickly calmed the atmosphere in the living room. Captain Burn walks to the other end of the room with the policeman Sal. In a low voice, he reveals, "If all goes well Sal, which I anticipate will be soon, we'll close up this so-called safe house and give it back to Professor Brendan O'Connor." Wiping his sweaty brow with his large paw of a hand, the Captain offers, "Sal you can go back to your normal beat and Mike back home healed and safe." Sal is surprised, "Gee Captain I never thought we would get this case solved so quickly." Standing tall, Sal the young cop remarks, "It's been a honor to work with you on this case Captain Burn even though I had a minor role." "Look Sal, as the saying goes, 'it's not over till it's over.' There are a lot of issues to settle first."

Captain Burn checks to see the others are not listening. Captain Burn informs, "As I am sure you heard, the police guard at Mike's hospital room door was a crooked cop." "Yeah, Captain, word gets around fast at the precinct," officer Sal remarks. "He sold his badge, his uniform and soul for the all mighty dollar!" infuriated Captain mocks. Adding, "He was the mob's other mole. They paid the scoundrel well." "What a mistake," Sal comments. "The fool will be wearing stripes now," Captain Burn responds. The Captain motions for rookie Sal to be quiet and informs, "We had our suspicions about him but we wanted to be sure. We're no fools, we had our own mole." "Wow, great police work Captain," Sal calls out. The Captain continues, "I knew and admired your dad Police Captain Philipo Fermo very well Sal. He was a fine police officer for 25 years. I feel it's only right

I be a role model for you." Captain pats shy rookie Sal on the back and says, "I plan on being there for you to make sure you follow in your father's illustrious footsteps as an upstanding, loyal cop." "Thanks Captain Burn, I truly appreciate it. I won't disappoint." Red faced, Captain Burn continues, "We got the bad guys Sal. Only regret is Mike's family business is gone and the repercussions will linger for a long time for him and his family."

Wanting to move, Mike calls out, "Sal, come get me." Hearing Mike, Sal excuses himself, "I better go see what he needs Captain." "Sure Sal, that's why you're here to assist Mike and to relieve the good nun." Proudly Sal calls out, "My duty and pleasure Captain." "Sister Margaret Mary has done more than enough for us beyond the call of duty," winking, Captain Burn mutters. As Sal heads over to Mike, the Captain warns, "Hey Sal, all said here just now is not for publication; it's official business. That's an order!" Sal nods his head affirmatively. Sister Margaret Mary is pushing Mike's wheelchair. "I've got it Sister," Sal offers grabbing the wheelchair from Sister Margaret Mary. Sister hesitates, she is used to helping others and does not appreciate others to take over.

As Sal is moving Mike in the wheelchair to the other side of the living room to rest, Captain Burn struts over to Sister Margaret Mary praising, "You've done more than your share Sister; let Sal take over now." Talking to Mike, Captain Burn says, "I've got more good news for you Mike." Looking over at Tess, the Captain teases, "Also for you, Mike's feisty red-headed wife." Hearing this, Mike orders, "Don't mince words Captain give it to me straight." Boldly the Captain states, "You're going back home Mike to your wife and daughter whenever she returns." "What?" Mike calls out. "Yes, it's safe for all of you. We apprehended the person who attempted to shoot you and accidently got Ray; also the arsonists who burned down your business; and the low-down mole who lead them to your hospital room."

Perplexed, Tess is speechless. Stunned, Ray questions, "Who were the rotten bastards?" "That's not for you to know now; but they are all incarcerated." Captain Burn further informs, "There's a special person to thank for helping us solve this so quickly." "Who?" Tess shouts out. "You both sound like owls," Sister Margaret Mary quips. Calm as can be, nonchalantly Sister offers smiling, "Who wants fresh coffee before we go and pack our bags to go home?" Sister Margaret Mary heads into the kitchen calling out, "My coffee might not be as good as Ettie's but, Praise the Good Lord, I'm getting better." Mike, Tess, Ray, and Sal look over at the Captain questioningly. Grinning, the Captain comments, "She's one hell of a good woman!" He apologizes, "I mean nun." He laughs heartily. Joking, Captain Burn mutters, "I hate to get on the wrong side of that Nun of this and Nun of that!"

Puzzled, Tess excuses herself calling out as she heads to the kitchen, "Let me help." While Sister Margaret Mary is preparing a fresh pot of coffee, Tess walks right up to her and boldly inquires, "What's going on Sister? Ettie told me you saw Mike the night he disappeared outside our house and you were extremely upset." Quiet as a church mouse, Sister continues to pour water into the coffee pot ignoring Tess's question. Not accepting her innocent behavior, Tess demands, "Don't play dumb Sister Margaret Mary; you can't fool me. I have a right to know." Not responding, Sister takes cream from the refrigerator. Disturbed, Tess goes behind her, slams shut the refrigerator door and blocks Sister Margaret Mary from moving, pleading, "No disrespect Sister but my daughter's life was in danger too." Sister Margaret Mary sternly stares Tess in the eye but remains quiet.

Beyond frustrated, Tess informs, "Elena has not been herself for a while. She's very attached to you; she guards that infamous book you gave her like it was the holy grail or the Holy Bible." Tess demands, "I'm begging you Sister Margaret Mary help me understand all this." The stern nun stands firm, unmovable, solid as a rock. Tess shouts, "Please tell me! What really happened and who are you protecting?" Calmly, Sister Margaret Mary asks, "Do you want sugar and cream in your coffee?"

Beseeching, Tess insists, "What did Monsignor James Cooney from Notre Dame and our Father Jack Kelly have to do with all this?" Contrite, respectfully Sister Margret Mary whispers, "Sit down Tess. Yes, you have every right to know." Putting the coffee pot back on the stove the elderly nun reveals, "Now that the evil devil and his fallen angels will soon be out of here and safe behind bars, I'll share with you what I know and sadly witnessed." Her back turned from Tess, before she shares, Sister Margaret

Mary makes the Sign of the Cross and whispers, "Faith and Be Golly, I hope Juan is exonerated and my wee sweetheart Elena finds peace." Wishing it was grappa, pouring herself coffee, Tess does not hear the Nuns comment about Juan or her sweetheart Elena.

"Hey, ladies, where's that coffee? I could have made it myself," teasing Ray shouts. "You better not push your luck Ray. Tess is not one to be ordered around," Mike warns his best buddy. "Or Sister Margaret Mary," interjecting, Captain Burn mimics. Sleepy, Mike closes his eyes. He is still recuperating and desperately needs rest.

The others are still anxious to learn more. The rookie cop Sal, walks up to the Captain whispering, "Hope you don't mind my asking but I think I can learn a lot from you if I am to advance my police career." "Shoot," Captain Burn says. "I noticed when you told Mike who were incarcerated, you never mentioned the phony priest or his cohort." In a low voice Captain Burn explains, "It was not easy to get evidence to incriminate them."

Wiping his now sweaty red face with his large hand, Captain sighs, "Secretly, the good Monsignor Kelly took the phony priest's finger prints off the wine chalice after Schultz said mass." "Fantastic," Sal says. "The fingerprints were immediately sent to El Paso police headquarters to see if it was a match for the real Father Arthur Schultz who is missing." Proudly, he boasts, "Bingo! We lucked out. Not so for the evil phony Father Schultz. His luck ran out!" With a broad smile across his Irish mug, Captain Burn adds, "That phony priest's corrupt fingerprints were not a match for the missing real Father Schultz finally proving he was a bonafide fake." Police officer Sal further inquires," "What happens next to him?" "Good question. Not up to our department; it's out of our jurisdiction." Taking officer Sal by the shoulder Burn whispers, "The no good phony priest will be extradited to El Paso, Texas for further investigation and hopefully sent to jail for a very long time."

"And the young Mexican kid?" officer Sal asks. "Juan was the phony priest's victim. The innocent kid should be exonerated." "Oh, I get it," officer Sal says. "Juan was his pawn; he was forced to be a mule hiding drugs on his body for that shyster, phony priest." Patting him on his back

Captain Burn praises, "You got it, Sal! Impostor Father Arthur Schultz was a big-time, illegal drug dealer, and heavily involved in child prostitution in Juarez, Mexico. Evidently the fake Schultz was part of the Juarez mob." Happily, officer Sal slaps his knees. Captain Burn says, "That greedy imposter priest is in deep shit trouble. I hate to see or will delight in what will happen to him if the Mexican drug cartel gets to him first." Captain Burn blurts out, "In my book, that no good low-down bum is already a dead man." "Wow, this is way out of my league; you have a lot to deal with Captain," rookie Sal nervously comments.

Grinning, Captain Burn declares, "Not my worry. Once we ship phony Schultz the hell out of here, we'll have our own problems to resolve." Fascinated, Sal asks, "How the hell did he get to Jersey City?" "That miserable, vile crook had the real innocent pious Father Arthur Schultz from El Paso kidnapped by the Mexican cartel. They threw him in a hell hole of a Mexican jail. The poor holy man was rotting in that jail while this no good scum bag bum was strutting around acting like a holier than thou priest." Infuriated, Captain Burn continues, "The mob in our area, along with the Mexican cartel, paid the phony priest plenty to intimidate and force Mike Policino to agree to distribute their drugs in our area for the mob here. If not?! Need I say more."

"The Catholic Church higher ups had a huge role in solving this too; a Monsignor James Cooney from Notre Dame, a close friend of the real Father Schultz, along with St. Victor's Monsignor Jack Kelly, who also knew the real Father Schultz, were instrumental in assisting us in solving this bizarre mystery." "So," suggests Sal, "The trick was to weed out the phony and the treat was to catch him red handed. How the hell did they do that?" amazed Sal asks. "It took a lot of people and thankfully in a short amount of time," Burn remarks. "Makes me have hope there are good people in this crazy mixed up world, Sal," saying this as a lone tear slowly rolls down the Captain's ruddy round face.

"Unbelievable!" Sal sighs. He reiterates, "The mob both south of the border and here in Jersey infiltrated and used the church to enhance their illegal deadly operations." "Don't forget Mike didn't play ball that's why they were out to kill him," the Captain reports. Sal enumerates, "This is better than a crime movie." "Sal, this is not a movie, it's real life and Mike was almost the deadly victim." "All the pieces of the missing puzzle of this crime are coming together; proud to be a part of it," boldly Sal says. Captain Burn pats Sal on the back humoring yet praising, "You're wiser than I thought Sal my man; keep this up and you'll be a sergeant before you know it."

Still trying to put the last pieces of this mystery puzzle together, Sal quizzically inquires, "Who was our mole?" Captain Burn mutters, "You're not as quick as I thought you were Sal." Smirking, Burn teases, "Our mole has been right under your nose these last few days." "Oh!, you mean. . .?" "Don't say it Sal, I'm warning you," Captain Burn orders. To change the direction of the conversation Captain Burn hollers, "Where the hell is that coffee!" "Coffee?" officer Sal has an immediate epiphany. He adds, "This is more complicated than I thought but I'm learning more today than I did at the police academy." Under his breath, excited, Sal murmurs, "Now I've got it! Sister Margret Mary was not here just to nurse Mike; she was here under our witness protection program." *Last piece of the puzzle?*

Still hovering and whispering in a quiet corner in the living room, Captain gives Sal a look to warn him, "The Father Schultz caper is taboo for now." "One more question Captain. When Mike was in the hospital, who told the hit man where he was?" asks Sal. Looking around, Captain Burn informs, "Sad to say Sal, it was Mike's cousin Nick Scat's funeral driver, Rocco. That turn coat was another mole placed there by the bad guys."

Straight as an arrow, Burn informs, "Happy to report Sal, Mike's cousin Nick had no idea. The gangsters hired and paid the phony priest a pretty penny knowing he would take it since he was under the control of the Mexican cartel and that shit head Rocco." "Holy hell!" Sal shouts. The scream from Sal brings Tess and Sister Margaret Mary out of the kitchen in a frenzy. On the other side of the living room, startled, Ray turns in a panic. Captain Burn reassures them calling out, "No worries; the rookie officer Sal just got a little excited when I told him I might promote him." Unbeknownst to Captain Burn and rookie cop Sal, who thought Mike was sleeping, Mike overheard every single word the Captain revealed to Sal.

CHAPTER FIFTY-FIVE

Life Moves On and On and On
Walsh's Tavern, Jersey City, New Jersey
Spring 1956

THE IRISH TAVERN owner Tom Walsh is behind the bar half-heartedly wiping the bar. He is preoccupied in his thoughts. The door to the bar swings open, Professor Brendan O'Conner walks in followed by Big Tony and Ray Sinnotti. "Well, well, well, look what the cat dragged in," Walsh call out. Brendan goes to the end of the bar to his special bar stool while Tony and Ray go and sit down at the bar in front of Walsh. "My man Walsh, drinks are on me; we have a lot to discuss regarding what we talked about last week," Tony says. Hearing this, Brendan's ears perk up as does Ray's. "What are you two hooligans talking about?" Brendan hollers over. "Listen Brendan, now that you got your infamous safe house back, our Mike is recuperating, and the goons are behind bars or hope to be soon, settle down; your role is over," teasing Walsh comments. "Yeah, I hear Mike is going to law school. What are you up to Professor?" Tony inquires.

"For your information, my good man, I decided to sell the house. Perhaps it will be a museum piece for the Jersey City Police Department," cleverly the Professor shares. "What?" Tony shouts. "Where the hell do you think you're going to live behind this bar?" Walsh shouts back. "Not a bad idea; he lives here most of the time," Ray chimes in. Tony remains silent. Changing the subject, Ray says, "I'm happy for Mike. It will be hard to go back to law school especially at his age, but he'll do it." He adds, "Tess will support him in more ways than one." Tony and Walsh nod in agreement.

As Walsh is pouring the drinks, he mentions, "Hey Big Guy, maybe this is the time we tell these two what we've been discussing of late." He hands Tony his usually Boiler Maker and pours Ray a tall cold beer. Tony grabs his drinks, a shot of bourbon, followed by a nice cold beer. In two big gulps Tony finishes it; wiping his mouth with his sleeve, he slams down the empty glasses on the bar. Ray turns to Tony inquiring, "Spill the beans Tony. What are you and Walsh up to?"

Tony looks over at Walsh. He orders, "Pour me another Walsh." Rising from the bar stool Tony begins, "Now that Mike will not be able to start up his garbage business and is going to law school with the money the insurance company gave him, I realized I better look for a job." Ray looks over at Brendan and prompts, "You know everything Professor Big Mouth; what are these two characters referring to?" Brendan puts his hands to his ears and says, "I see no evil; I hear no evil!" and swallows down his whiskey and says, "I speak no evil."

Wiping the bar with much vigor, Walsh commences, "Well, as you know I'm getting older. I've always wanted to go back to the old country; the land of my birth; the Emerald Isle." Sighs, "Beautiful Ireland." Pausing, Walsh breathes deeply and adds, "First I had to get my name cleared there, then sell this tavern. When I mention selling the tavern, Tony asked me how much . . ." Ray interjects, "Oh I think I know where this is going." Ray looks at Tony and says, "You're going to buy this place?" "You bet I am! I will also make changes." Beaming, Tony informs, "We're planning to serve light food and spruce up this dull looking joint." Tony laughs, he adds, "My wife Eileen has some great ideas." Ray shouts out, "Good idea, Tony. Now that you are a married man and have Angela Maria, you should be thinking of your future." Agreeing, Tony adds, "Walsh offered to stay awhile to help me settle in and learn the trade." Tony and Walsh clap hands.

Professor Big Mouth is at a loss for words. Tony inquires, "Why are you looking so sad Brendan?" Staring at Brendan, Walsh encourages, "Tell the Big Guy and Ray what you're planning on doing?" Mournfully, Brendan comments, "After my sweet mother passed, I retired from the university and sold the house." "Sold the house!" Tony and Ray shout out. "Yes, sold it!" Brendan mimics. "Go on Professor, tell them the rest," Walsh instructs. "When I learned Walsh was going to Ireland, I decided it might be time for me to go there too."

In disbelief, Ray hollers out, "What the hell! You two old Irishmen are going to hook up; what next?" "Well, if you really want to know," Walsh continues, "I'm going back to hopefully get hooked." "What about your criminal record there?" Ray shouts almost falling off the bar stool. "Faith and be Golly, I've been exonerated; story too long to tell." "Help him out Walsh, this is confusing," Tony insists. "Alright, blushing he shares, "See, there's this woman I knew years ago in Ireland who works at the lawyer's office the one I have been dealing with to clear my name." Tony pats Walsh on the back teasing, "Don't be shy, tell the rest." Walsh mutters, "I am going to ask her to marry me when I get there." Baffled, Ray hollers over, "Married! What about you Professor? You getting married too?" Blushing, Brendan explains, "No my good man; I intend to do research at Trinity College in Dublin on the history of the blight of the poor Irish people from the tragic 1845-1852 Great Irish Famine." He looks over at the others with a serious gaze and shares, "I always wanted to write a book about it." Brendan piously makes the Sign of the Cross and proudly calls out, "In memory of my dear sweet mother."

"Drinks on the house!" Walsh calls out. After all of these intriguing revelations, the three "wise" men settle down and partake of their celebratory drinks. Gulping down his whiskey, holding his empty shot glass up high, Professor Brendan rises from his bar stool commenting, "Since we all shared our true confessions, I am adding one more." Pounding his empty glass on the bar, breaking and shattering it, Professor Brendan announces, "I am giving my holy mother her dying wish. I am giving up drinking permanently." He looks at the shattered glass in front of him professing, "This was my final libation." Sighs are heard in the tavern. The others stare at Brendan stunned and speechless. Further explaining Brendan shares, "I have Eileen's brother Sean, who attends AA-Alcoholics Anonymous meetings religiously." Sitting back on his bar stool while Walsh sweeps up the broken glass, Professor Brendan praises, "That brave young man has been sober now for many months. Sean gave me the courage to lead a sober life." "Celibacy, too!" with mockery Walsh teases. Flushed, Ray wipes his sweaty face and shouts, "Where the hell is Mike when I need him; this is all too much for me to hear in one day."

After hearing Brendan's extraordinary pronouncement, the others are in a paralyzing daze until the tavern door swings opens. Eileen walks in holding her homemade Irish Soda bread followed by Tony's young daughter, timid Angela Maria carefully carrying her homemade empanadas and tacos made by Juan. Ray is preparing to leave. He sits down quickly seeing Juan walking in with Father Jack Kelly behind Eileen and Angela Maria. Strutting in Father Kelly pronounces, "We have blessed news." Smiling knowingly, Tony requests, "Juan, why don't you tell them." "I'm going to be living with Eileen, Tony, and Angela Maria as soon as my name is cleared and my immigration papers are finalized." Gazing over at Tony with pride Juan calls out, "I'm also excited; I will be working with Tony in this tavern."

Smiling ear to ear, Eileen adds, "We are so happy to have you Juan. Our Angela Maria is thrilled to have a big brother to look up to." Proudly Tony adds, "Also, hopefully Angela Maria will someday have a baby brother or baby sister." He glances lovingly at his wife teasing, "Right Eileen?" Embarrassed, Eileen grins at Tony murmuring, "Yes Tony, you're right on the money; you're going to be a father again!" Surprised, Tony is absolutely floored. He grabs Eileen and hugs her so tight she is breathless. "You mean, you're pregnant?" babbling Tony further inquires. "Yes, Antonio," softly Eileen responds. Hearing this, Angela Maria and Juan rush up to Eileen and Tony and put their arms around them.

Pleased to hear this good news, Walsh, Brendan and Ray rise cheering loudly. Shyly, Juan sits down next to exhilarated Big Tony who plops down on a chair overwhelmed by all this excitement in one day. On the side, Walsh, Brendan, and Father Kelly are discussing Ireland. Enough surprises for Ray he is about to leave when Eileen sneaks up to him. She whispers in his ear. Ray listens intently. "What the hell?" Ray shouts. Adding, "How are Mike and Ettie taking this?" "They're fine. In fact, Ettie is elated."

Noticing Eileen and Ray secretly chatting, Walsh is curious, "Hey you two! Why so hush hush?" Happily Eileen reveals, "Mike Policino is an uncle and Ettie Cortino is a grandmother." "Faith and Be Golly - another baby? You guys should open a nursery," Walsh shouts. "Who had a baby?" Brendan inquires. Eileen humbly responds, "Ettie's daughter Rosaria just had a baby girl. She named her Carla Antonella after her late father Carlo, Ettie and Mike's deceased mother, her maternal grandmother, Antonella." "Immaculate Conception," Brendan mutters. "Another round for everyone!" Walsh calls out. Resolved, Brendan requests, "Ginger ale please." Piously observing his joyful flock, Father Jack Kelly pronounces, "I am going to Christen the young child when Rosaria returns from New England." *"The Lord Giveth. . ."*

CHAPTER FIFTY-SIX

Mother Daughter Discussions; Sleuths and Nuisances
Hollywood, California
Early Spring 1956

GRANDMA HOLLYWOOD AND Aunt Mary Grace are alone in the house with Cleo the almost human Cocker Spaniel. They are waiting for Elena and Regina to return from Hollywood Arts High School where they are sophomores and Rodney a senior. The two cousins have been attending classes there soon after they arrived in California. Regina is thrilled and thriving whereas Elena is surviving only to please her parents knowing it is only temporary. Rodney is beyond delighted having them at the school and has been mentoring them. *Annoyingly so for Elena*

In hopes of getting the early spring sun, in Grandma Hollywood's kitchen, Mary Grace is preparing a fresh batch of iced tea with mint to bring out to the patio. Grandma Hollywood is anxiously waiting there. She has multiple and significant questions to ask her daughter Mary Grace. Calling out to her daughter, Grandma Hollywood -says, "We have to talk before the girls come home from school." Finally, mother and daughter are comfortably sitting in white wicker chairs next to the round glass patio table. A large red and white stripped umbrella covers them. Sipping iced tea and nibbling Social Tea cookies Mary Grace puts down her glass, swallows her cookie and says, "Okay Mom, I know you want to talk with me. I'm ready for your inquisition!"

Not one to mince words, Grandma Hollywood blurts out, "Are you and Geoff getting a divorce and if so, why?" "Wow Mom, you mean business," Mary Grace remarks. "You never talk about it, Mary Grace.

You're living here in California with me while your husband Geoff and son Tim are in New Jersey." Flustered Mary Grace recognizes she owes her mother an explanation. Wiping her moist eyes with the linen napkin she explains, "First, yes, Geoff and I will start divorce proceedings soon." "Why?" her anxious mother asks. "Geoff has had a girlfriend for a while now. A younger woman from his office." Pausing to take a sip of ice tea, Mary Grace continues, "I turned a blind eye Mom thinking Geoff was going through a middle age crisis. Not so! Geoff insists he loves her." Mary Grace bursts out crying. Grandma Hollywood reaches over to hold her daughter's shaking hands. "Sorry to hear this. Trust me Mary Grace, you are a strong, beautiful woman; you'll move on and be happy one day," to comfort her distraught daughter Grandma Hollywood assures her.

"Thanks Mom," Mary Grace mutters. With gratitude, she adds, "I appreciate your encouragement and for having Regina and I staying with you these last months." "How is Regina with all this?" a concerned grandmother inquires. Mary Grace squeezes her mother's quivering hand. She responds, "Regina is smart for her age. Sadly, she knows about everything and is resigned to it." Sighing, Mary Grace reveals, "My poor son Tim knew long before I did. I fear that's why he was acting out so miserably."

"Tim is living with his father in your house in New Jersey; how is he managing with Geoff?" vexed Grandma Hollywood inquires. "My Tim is managing. Geoff is gone most of the time; he only comes home to get more clothes." Grandma Hollywood listens intently wisely allowing her daughter to vent. Mary Grace adds, "Dan, Geoff's brother, is living at the house with Tim; they always got along." She further shares, "Like his Uncle Danny, Tim is going to join the Army as soon as he graduates high school." Hearing this, apprehensive Grandma Hollywood inquires, "Is Dan alright, Mary Grace? I always thought he was strange." "Yes Mom. With Tim's insistence, Geoff found an excellent Veterans Mental Health program sponsored by the VA for Dan." Mary Grace adds, "Tim assures me, since going there, Dan is better than ever." To relieve the tension, Mary Grace jokes, "Tim says his Uncle Danny is a better cook than me." Mother and daughter laugh.

Like a typical mother, Grandma Hollywood further inquires, "You and Regina seem to be adjusting here in California; are you planning on staying permanently? If so, you better get a job Mary Grace." Mary Grace does not respond. "I'm not worried about Regina; she's adjusting beautifully but you need to start a new life for yourself, Mary Grace," Grandma Hollywood lectures.

Barking loudly Cleo startles mother and daughter. From Grandma Hollywood's driveway, Mateo hollers, "Anyone home?" "Back in the patio!" Grandma Hollywood calls out. Mateo struts in with Nunzio quietly following. "Ciao! We're here because we want to ask Mary Grace something," Mateo announces. "Yes," Nunzio echoes. "Now that Regina is doing stand-in at the movie studio and Mary Grace accompanies her, we thought you'd like to work there too," winking Mateo mentions. Mary Grace is confused. "Doing what?" Grandma inquires. "I can use a script girl," Nunzio shares. Bolting out of her chair, "Oh my goodness, someone up there likes me. Yes, yes, yes, I accept!" screams out Mary Grace. "Well, with that being said, we'll make the arrangements and get back to you in a day or so," Mateo says. "Si, Si. We'll get back to you very soon," Nunzio mimics. "Ciao. We must be going. Rudolpho is waiting for me to trim his infamous mustache," flamboyantly waving Mateo calls out followed by Nunzio who politely murmurs, "Arrividerci."

Hearing the car zooming out of the driveway and confident Mateo and Nunzio are gone, Grandma Hollywood continues her inquiry, "That sounds exciting, Mary Grace. You will do well as a script reader." Keyed up, Mary Grace smiles broadly. With angst, Grandma Hollywood asks, "Now that I know your plans Mary Grace, please fill me in on your sister Tess's current situation. I'm worried sick over her and Mike." Staring directly at her mother Mary Grace shares what she knows. "Thank god, things are looking good for both Mom." Grandma Hollywood sighs in relief. "Mike is almost healed from his wound and the police have captured and incarcerated the monsters that burned down his company and tried to kill him."

Happily, Mary Grace adds, "Tess finally convinced Mike to go to law school; he was planning on going after he graduated from Villanova University but he was obligated to take over the family sanitation company." "Law school? How will they support themselves?" Grandma interjects.

"Thankfully the garbage company had excellent insurance. Tess convinced Mike to use the insurance money to pay the tuition." Reaching for her mother's cold, quivering hand, Mary Grace adds, "Also, Mike's cousin Nick Scat offered him work in the funeral parlor to make amends for his underhanded worker Rocco, the moron who snitched on Mike."

"Mobs, snitches? This is too much for me to take in," Grandma moans. Mary Grace kisses her mother on the top of her head to calm her down. "How does Mike know he'll get into law school?" fretful Grandma asks. "It was Mike's high LSAT scores. Thanks to Tess's diligent, demanding tutoring, along with his excellent Villanova transcript. This insured Mike getting accepted," proudly Mary Grace announces. Grandma interjects, "Mike was always smart!" She further infers, "I'm sure Ettie is thrilled for her brother." Agreeing, Mary Grace offers, "I have no doubt Ettie is happy for her precious brother. For years, altruistically, Mike put aside his personal interests for his Policino family." Somberly Mary Grace mentions, "Sadly for Ettie, recently losing her husband and Mike's horrific events have taken a toll on this, selfless woman." Hearing Elena, Regina and Rodney entering the house, the informative conversation between Grandma Hollywood and Mary Grace ends abruptly. *Typically they only hear Regina and Rodney's vibrant voices; Elena is usually silent.*

"Let's go inside and see how the girls are Mom," Mary Grace suggests. "Yes, I 'm exhausted hearing all this information. I'm going to my bedroom to take a nap," Grandma moans. Carrying a tray with a half empty iced tea pitcher, the empty glasses, and the left-over tea biscuits Mary Grace heads into the kitchen. With the refrigerator opened, Elena is taking out her cottage cheese and peaches for a snack. Regina retrieves a box of Oreo cookies which she and Rodney will share with milk. "Hi Mother dear," Regina mumbles while chewing on a cookie. "Why are you eating cookies? Eat something healthy like your cousin," annoyed Mary Grace suggests. "Because I'm skinny and Elena needs to lose weight," she jokes. "I heard that Regina," Elena mutters. "For your information, I've lost fifteen pounds since I arrived here," gleefully Elena informs.

To ease the tension between the cousins, Rodney responds, "Both of you are fantastic looking. Each one of you have your own unique style and manner; glamorous Regina and enigmatic Elena." "Rodney, you are so clever and level headed," Mary Grace interjects. "I have good news for you Regina. Come into the living room, there's something I can't wait to tell you," Mary Grace takes Regina's hand leading her into the living room while chatting, "Nunzio was just here. He offered me a position at the studio where you work." Instantly, Regina stops and stares eerily at her enthusiastic mother.

Since Regina and Mary Grace are no longer in ear shot, Rodney heads over to Elena insisting, "Let's go on the patio. I have more news for you about the mysterious priest." Hesitantly, Elena heads to the patio munching on a diet Melba toast cracker. Following right behind her is Rodney devouring fattening Oreos. Observing him devouring the cookies by the fist full, Elena teases, "Thank goodness you have a great metabolism or you'll be a Fatty Arbuckle soon." "Just because your grandmother and Rudolpho put you on a low calorie diet, and you're getting slim and trim, no need to call me insulting names," Rodney strikes back. "Sorry Rodney! That was mean of me." In the patio, Elena sits down on a chair demanding, "Let's get down to business. What's the update on the mysterious priest?" Nervous Elena implores.

"I spoke with Monsignor James Cooney at Notre Dame University last night," with a low tone Rodney mutters. "You did? What did he say?" jumpy Elena asks. Unmistakably the so-called Father Arthur Schultz at your St. Victor's Parish in Jersey City is a down-right fraud. An imposter!" dramatically Rodney shares. "I could have told you that," remorseful Elena sighs. "Let me finish, there is more," Rodney insists. "For a while now, the El Paso, Texas police department, along with the church higher ups, have been closely following the fraudulent Father Schultz. Even the Juarez authorities in Mexico are on it," spectacularly Rodney reveals. "Does Father Kelly and Sister Margaret Mary know about this?" fearful Elena blurts out. "According to Monsignor James Cooney, yes!" he replies. "Why didn't they stop him? They should have sent the police to get him out of St. Victor's before he could do all that damage," beyond angry Elena implies. Before Rodney can respond, with fear in her eyes, Elena cries out, "What about Juan!?" "Juan? Not sure who he is or where he fits in," baffled

Rodney questions. Immediately adding, "Good news is that your father and mother are safe. The Jersey City police extradited the pathetic, phony Father Schultz back to El Paso." "Hope he rots in a Mexican, hell-hole jail," Elena screams. "He should Elena. He has a long police record of illegal drug dealings, kidnapping, child trafficking/pornography and intimate connections with the Mexican drug cartel." Hesitating, Rodney adds, "Along with the cartel he's been part of questionable gangs and mobster rings here in the United States."

Slouching in the chair mortified, Elena has an epiphany, "Something just struck me. Awhile ago I overheard my father on the phone screaming to some creeps, 'Over my dead body; never will I get involved with that lethal, poisonous crap!'" Wiping her moist eyes Elena mutters, "Someone was strong arming my Dad to do things he didn't want to do." Sympathetically she adds, "To think he endured all that trauma for standing up for what he believed in; almost dying."

Sniffling, Elena calls out, "Oh my god, I feel horrible I didn't help him." Under her breath she moans, "I could have but I was too frightened." "What did you just say?" confused Rodney asks. "Nothing," Elena answers. She further questions, "Is there anything else you know?" No response from Rodney. Pondering for a moment Elena questions, "How is it that Monsignor James Cooney is able to confide in you all this private police and higher-up church information?" "Monsignor James Cooney has been a mentor and my confidant since I was a young boy. My father and I have a poor relationship; Monsignor James Cooney filled in." A dragonfly flies over their heads causing them to pause and look at it. It flies off. "Are you saying he was a father image for you?" Elena inquires. "He was my mentor and he always treated me as a son," Rodney shares. Talking with authority and firmly Elena infers, "I still feel that Monsignor James Cooney telling you this is unprofessional and unwise." For once Rodney is at a loss for words. "Rodney, you better be telling me the truth that you heard all of this from Monsignor James Cooney?" anxious Elena warns.

Defiantly and defending himself, hostile Rodney reveals, "For your information Princess Elena, the Catholic Church, Monsignor James Cooney, and your so-called confidant Sister Margaret Mary have been secretly conspiring with the Rio Grande border patrol in Juarez Mexico helping the poor Mexican orphans who are physically forced into illegal drug dealings and child prostitution. Enraging the cartel." Elena hollers, "You're lying! Sweet Sister Margaret Mary has been my family's close friend for years. She would have alerted my parents!" Standing up and placing her red-hot face up to Rodney's she shouts, "For your information Mr. Know-It-All Sister Margaret Mary teaches history and piano lessons at St. Victor's and is a scholar on the American Civil War. That's it! She is not an undercover agent!" Pausing to catch her breath, Elena murmurs, "I would have known if she was involved with orphans from Mexico."

Rodney is relieved to see Mary Grace and Regina walking toward the patio with Cleo following close behind. "Why do I hear all this shouting going on out here?" inquires Mary Grace. "Mom, these two always scream. That's how they normally talk with one another," Regina says adding much needed humor to the disturbance between Elena and Rodney.

CHAPTER FIFTY-SEVEN

When One Door Closes Another Door Opens
Jersey City, New Jersey
Late Spring 1956

THE CROCUS AND daffodils are bursting through the hard winter earth. The trees lined along Armstrong Avenue in Jersey City are sprouting green buds a sure sign of spring's arrival. The sparrows are chirping early in the morning and a lone robin or two are seen. As usual, Ettie is in her kitchen making a fresh pot of coffee while listening to her morning news broadcast on the radio. The coffee is perking vigorously; the rich fragrance of the potent beans fills the house. In her usual apron Ettie opens her side door, stands in the hallway hollering up to Tess and Mike, "Coffee's almost ready! Come down when you can. I also have Stella Dora breakfast biscuits." Going back in and closing the side door Ettie hears the front door opening.

Still having a key, Eileen opens the front door and enters Ettie's house. Five months pregnant with her and Tony's future baby, elated Eileen struts in. Seeing Eileen, Ettie notices she is filling out her maternity dress. "What are you doing here Eileen? I told you to take the day off and keep off your feet," motherly Ettie preaches. "No worries. Tony dropped me off; he's driving Angela Maria to St. Victor School," smiling Eileen explains. "Okay," resigned, Ettie says. "Besides, I need to keep busy," Eileen comments while walking toward the kitchen. "How is the tavern business going?" Ettie inquires. "It's going well. Although, there's so much to learn and do yet," smirking Eileen responds as she grabs a Stella Dora biscuit. "Big hearted Walsh has been a huge help to Tony," munching Eileen informs. Turning off the radio, thrilled Ettie shares, "Rosaria called to confirm she is coming back from New England with my granddaughter any day now." Noticing Ettie has not been herself lately, Eileen responds "Yes Ettie, I know that's why I'm here to help you get everything ready for them," reminding Ettie.

The side door swings open. Dressed and ready for the day, Mike bursts in. He gives a nod to the women and immediately pours coffee into his favorite New York Yankee mug. Gulping down the coffee almost burning his tongue, he blows on it to cool. Teasing he asks, "Hi, Eileen. What's up? Besides your belly growing!? "All's going great Mike. Tony is very busy at the tavern; Angela Maria is happy with school; and I'm pleased to be here helping Ettie get the house ready for Rosaria's arrival with Ettie's baby granddaughter, Carla Antonella." Seeing Ettie beaming ear to ear, Mike goes up to his sister and gives her a squeeze.

"How's school? Law school must be very challenging," Eileen sincerely inquires. "It's going," Mike sighs adding, "You have to be disciplined with your schedule but I'm one lucky guy. Tess is a huge help." He cautiously sips his now cooled coffee offering, "I hope to be a good role model for my daughter Elena." Hearing her niece's name, Ettie says, "I'm so excited, as soon as Elena finishes her sophomore year at that fancy school in Hollywood, she'll be coming back home." Looking at Eileen and beaming at her brother Mike, Ettie brags, "Elena will be so proud of her Dad when she hears he's going to law school." Mike smiles, "Wait until I finish Ettie before you boast." "Mike, rumor in the district is that many are hoping you will run for mayor here in Jersey City some day. If so, you're a shoe in to win!" proudly Ettie adds. Giving Ettie a murky look Mike puts his empty New York Yankee mug in the sink announcing, "Enough about city politics! I better be going. First to the library then over to the funeral parlor to work." He pats Ettie on the top of her head, swivels around grinning at Eileen. He winks saying, "Gotta make money the honest way." Mike flies out the door.

As Mike closes the front door, the back side door opens. Tess enters. She is neatly and professionally dressed to go to work at the Jersey City school system. Tess brings her Rider College mug down, heads over to the stove, grabs the coffee pot, and pours herself a cup of Ettie's coffee. She acknowledges Eileen with a nod. "Thanks for making us coffee every morning Ettie. It helps Mike and I get out on time." Tess smiles at Ettie, "Besides, I never make coffee as good as you and never will."

Pleasantly, Tess glances at Eileen. Noticing her pregnancy is showing, she gives a half smile to Eileen. Tess swings around, looks at Ettie, who seems a little frail. "Ettie I hear Rosaria and little Carla will be coming home any day now. Are you ready for them?" excitedly Tess asks. Happily, Eileen interjects, "Yes! Ettie 's ready. I've been helping her." Recognizing Tess and Ettie need time alone, Eileen heads to the spare bedroom where Rosaria and baby Carla will be staying until they are settled elsewhere. "I'll be in the future nursery. I have a few more things to do," rushing out of the kitchen Eileen calls out.

Assured Eileen is in the spare bedroom and future nursery, Tess inquires, "Is Rosaria driving with the baby alone all the way from New England?" "Thank the Good Lord she isn't," Ettie responds. Pouring herself some coffee and adding lots of milk and sugar Ettie mentions, "You know Blaise's friend Robbie, he offered to pick Rosaria and baby Carla up since my son couldn't get leave from the Marine Corp." Relieved, Tess responds, "Glad to hear she has someone to travel with her and the baby."

Boldly with sarcasm, Tess further inquires, "Has Rosaria heard from Dr. Sacks or his infamous son Dr. David Sacks?" Not looking at Tess, walking over to the kitchen sink to wash the cups, Ettie mutters, "Dr. Saul Sacks has been good." She adds, "Sadly, the poor man is in the middle of this misfortune between his married son and my unwed daughter." "And his new granddaughter!" brazenly Tess remarks. "Dr. Saul Sacks will be a good grandfather to our Carla," in his defense Ettie responds.

Wiping away her tears on the dish towel, Ettie adds, "Evidently, Dr. Sacks' son, Dr. David Sack and his estranged wife reconciled." Soberly Ettie mutters, "You know Dr. David has two small children with his wife." Noticing Ettie getting upset, Tess is speechless. Sobbing, Ettie moans, "Leaving my poor daughter Rosaria a single mother and her innocent baby without an available father." "Does Blaise know who the father is?" worried

Tess inquires. "No!" screams Ettie. "Blaise must never know! He would go crazy and do something terrible," heatedly Ettie warns.

Suddenly, holding her stomach, Ettie slides down to her knees moaning out in pain. Eileen hears her. She runs into the kitchen, grabs a dishtowel pouring cold water on it. Frightened, Tess is hovering over weary Ettie crying, "What's wrong Ettie?" "She's been having these stomach pains for a while now," while placing a cool cloth on Ettie's forehead Eileen informs Tess. "Stubborn as she is, Ettie absolutely refuses to tell Dr. Sacks or go to any doctor," alarmed Eileen informs Tess. "Does Mike, Blaise or Rosaria know?" distressed Tess inquires. Eileen responds, "Absolutely not! Only I know." Gently wiping Ettie's face, Eileen whispers, "Ettie made me swear not to say anything to anyone." "She never takes care of herself," annoyed Tess says. Eileen hesitantly mentions, "She assured me it was just her nerves."

Troubled, Tess asks, "You've been her so-called caregiver, do you think it's more serious?" "Helping her these last few months, I've noticed Ettie's appetite greatly decreased, her sudden weight loss, her sweating profusely and in constant pain. Yes, I am concerned. I believe it's more than nerves," despondently Eileen shares. Greatly worried, Tess insists, "We must do something. I'm going to let Mike know right away." Carefully lifting Ettie onto a kitchen chair and giving her water to drink, Eileen murmurs "Being so religious, Ettie insists that God knows what's best for her." Angered, Tess calls out, "We'll see about that!"

After placing a cool compress on Ettie's forehead, and swallowing an entire glass of water, Ettie is slightly better. Laboriously rising up off the kitchen chair Ettie announces, "I've got to change my clothes. I forgot Father Jack Kelly is coming by to talk with me about Carla's Christening." Stunned, "Christening? Is this what Rosaria wants?" Tess asks. With rage Ettie demands, "She has no say in this matter. Rosaria gave birth to this innocent baby without a husband. It's my Christian duty and responsibility as Carla's grandmother to make sure her little soul is pure and atone for her mother and father's indiscretion." Extremely emotional and physically exhausted, Ettie plops down again on the chair, placing her drooping head in her hands weeping. Shaking her head in disbelief and truly upset, Tess turns to Eileen requesting, "Please take care of Ettie. I hate to leave but I must get to work." Eileen nods affirmatively. As she leaves, Tess closes the back door. Hearing the front doorbell ring, Eileen goes to open it. Standing there is faithful friend and pastor of St. Victor's Parish Father Jack Kelly. *Death is easy, life is hard.*

CHAPTER FIFTY-EIGHT

I Will Raise you Up on Eagles Wings
Walpole, New Hampshire
Thanksgiving 1899

THE KITCHEN IN Anna Lee's farmhouse is cozy and warm. The intense heat is penetrating out from the cast iron oven where a fresh-killed turkey is sizzling and has been cooking for a few hours. The wonderful aromas from homemade pumpkin and apple pies made earlier swirl around the house. This will be Anna Lee's first Thanksgiving dinner without her devoted husband Austin O'Brien-Stevens. Although missing him dearly, Anna Lee is determined to make this a blessed Thanksgiving. She is anxiously waiting for her adult twins, daughter Rachel Melanie and son Austin Hamish, to arrive with their respective families. Bending over the open oven, basting the mammoth turkey, Anna Lee hears the familiar sound of boots heading toward her kitchen door. Slowly standing up, closing the heavy oven door, she hobbles over and peeks out the moist-pane glass window.

Shivering, old-faithful handyman and friend Zeke stands there holding on tightly to a large brown and white clay jug. Quickly Anna Lee opens the door. The harsh late-fall howling wind fiercely blows in almost knocking this frail woman down. Swiftly, Anna Lee orders, "Hurry in Zeke. You're letting all the leaves in and whatever else nature has to offer." Looking at him closely she adds, "Dear me, you will catch your death of a cold with that flimsy, worn-out jacket of yours." Zeke holding the jug of cider, enters the kitchen; pushes the door shut, and securely latches it. In a snail's pace Zeke walks over and places the heavy jug of hard apple cider on the side table. With that done, Zeke hangs his old faithful jacket on a hook on the back of the kitchen door.

"When are you expecting the young ones to come?" old man Zeke inquires. Smiling, fragile Anna Lee corrects, "They're not so young any more Zeke. The twins are in their thirties and have children of their own." Wiping his forehead Zeke grins. "Making me a delighted grandmother," beaming Anna Lee proudly adds. "Guess you're right Ma'am. My Nannette is near fifty. She could be a grand maw someday too," Zeke mentions. "Yes Zeke you are so right. Nannette is a full grown woman." Peeling potatoes and placing them in a large blue ceramic bowl, Anna Lee continues inquiring, "How old is Nannette's son and daughter now?" Due to his diminished hearing, Zeke does not respond, hence, Anna Lee speaks louder, "Your grandson's name is Louis Ezekiel and granddaughter Elizabeth Amanda. How old are they?" Pausing a second Anna Lee comments, "Oh dear me, I'm getting so forgetful these days Zeke." Smirking, Zeke pointing to himself, calls out, "Not as forgetful as this old goat. If I was a horse, they'd shoot me." He thinks a moment then answers, "Not sure; maybe my grandson is fourteen or so? Any ways, Louis, or Lou Zeke, as I call him, is old enough to come here this summer and help with the sheep once school ends for the summer," proudly Zeke responds. "What age is Elizabeth Amanda?" Anna Lee further inquires. "Not sure but like her mother, she's going to nursing school," proudly Zeke reports.

Suddenly and eerily the kitchen door swings wide open. The fiercest howling wind blows in causing the blue ceramic bowl filled with peeled potatoes to fall off the table onto the floor. Throwing himself on the door Zeke attempts to close it with his feeble body but to no avail. Like a roaring train the sinister wind storms through the kitchen. Anna Lee screams, "What happened! I thought you closed and latched the door Zeke?" She falls to her knees; hands holding her intense face, Anna Lee calls out, "Oh My Lord, it is my dear angel Theresa Edith and her Dad, my darling deceased Austin, coming to wish us a Happy Thanksgiving." With authority she pronounces, "Dear me Zeke, since we were so engrossed with one another, we ignored their spirits who were desperately attempting to get our attention." Perplexed Zeke looks at her questioningly. Confounded, Zeke questioning asks, "You mean the howling wind?" Anna Lee responds, "Like in the bible proverb 'He that troubles his own house shall inherit the wind.'" "Yes! Austin and Theresa Edith's spirits came in like a tornado to shake us up," prophetically Anna Lee preaches.

With the kitchen door securely closed, Zeke weirdly gazes over at Anna Lee offering, "Normally Ma'am I would have said you were loony but experiencing this, I might have to agree." He brushes the dry leaves the unsuspecting wind blew in off his shirt murmuring, "Voodoo or no voodoo, I must admit that was spooky." Staring at him dazed, Anna Lee further offers, "Perhaps it was your late wife Louisa with my Austin and Theresa Edith too, Zeke?" Picking up the potatoes, Zeke glares back at ethereal Anna Lee. "I'm not a religious man. Nature is what I believe in. For me that creepy, forceful wind felt like a flock of determined eagles flying in here." Wiping his sweaty, wrinkled face with the plaid, triangle scarf he wears around his neck, reflective Zeke offers, "When I was a boy Ma'am I remember someone singing, 'And I will Raise You Up on Eagles Wings.'"

Carefully rising from the floor, impressionable Anna Lee saunters over to the jug of hard apple cider. She opens it and pours herself a cup full and one for Zeke. She hands it to him. Elderly Zeke takes it, and like a true gentleman, he waits for Anna Lee to drink her cider first. After Anna Lee takes a sip, Zeke swigs his down in one fast gulp. Wiping his mouth with his worn-out favorite red and white shirt sleeve he shares, "Ma'am, I never told you this, but after our sweet Theresa Edith went up to the great beyond, in confidence Nannette told me that after that innocent child took her last breath, my Nannette witnessed the brightest light ever piercing through the dark clouds." Pausing to catch his breath, Zeke resumes, "Choking with emotion, my Nannette said, 'When the clouds burst opened and the light flooded the pond, a magnificent eagle flew in circles over the area where the ice cracked . . .'" With misty eyes, whimpering Zeke finishes, "Where our little angel Theresa Edith fell in." Sighing he adds, "I believe those eagles came to take her home."

Standing up and moping over to slumped shouldered Zeke, Ann Lee places her frail, petite arms around him and praises, "Thank you Zeke for sharing this with me; especially on this auspicious day of Thanksgiving." "I didn't mean to make you sad, Ma'am," Zeke moans. "No, not at all. You made me joyful," Anna Lee assures him. Adding, "That sign from above and that spirited wind assured me that my darling husband and my precious Theresa Edith are finally together."

Abruptly Anna Lee stops and recalls, "My goodness, all those years back, I believe it was 1865, the night my husband Austin, little Theresa Edith and I returned home on Thanksgiving after having dinner with our neighbors, young Theresa Edith mentioned the special angel that watched over her. Beaming she pointed at a bright star in the sky that night. She insisted it was her 'Princess Angel'. Sighing, Anna Lee reminisces, "Zeke you were there too. At the time I thought it was her vivid, infantile imagination. Now I believe her!" Anna Lee cries out. Speechless Anna Lee and Zeke stand there reflectively. Hearing bells from a horse drawn sleigh pulling into the front driveway, they are jolted back to this time and place.

Excitedly Anna Lee rushes to the front door followed by Zeke. Peering through the windowpane, Anna Lee announces, "It's my son Austin Hamish and his family." Another sleigh pulls up behind carrying her daughter Rachel Melanie and her family. Zeke opens the door and heads out to help and escort them in.

Cold and anxious to go into the house, the twins smile at their eager mother as they rush into the warm home where they grew up. Anna Lee's twins and family are now hovering near the parlor where earlier in the day Zeke prepared the fire in the stone fireplace. His fear of fires now resolved, Zeke lights it with confidence. The Austin O'Brien-Stevens stone fireplace is a glow with a comforting blazing fire. "My dear family, welcome!" Anna Lee calls out. "Hope your journey from Hanover, New Hampshire to Walpole was pleasant," Anna Lee says. "It was tedious yet fine Mother," her son Austin Hamish reassures Anna Lee. "Yes, 'mother dear,' ours was fine also," her daughter Rachel Melanie offers.

Inside Anna Lee's children and family remove their outer garments and hand Anna Lee their contributions to the Thanksgiving meal. Finally, they settle in sitting near the fire to warm their frigid bodies. Looking lovingly over at her adult twins, their loyal spouses, Eleanor Stevens and Thomas Pharrell, and her grandchildren, Anna Lee gently pats away her tears of joy. "Zeke, please bring a bottle of brandy from the cellar. The one my husband Austin kept. We must have a toast before dinner," Anna Lee cheerily requests. "What about the cider Ma'am?" Zeke asks. "Not now. Having my children and their family here calls for a real toast." Nodding his head affirmatively, Zeke understands. "My husband Austin would insist," beaming Anna Lee jests as she lovingly gazes over at her twins. Enthusiastically, Zeke goes to retrieve a bottle from the dark, cold cellar. Pleased, knowing that years back his boss Austin was able to keep the infamous brandy after arduously and legally resolving the issue of it being questionable contraband.

As done traditionally, the pouring and distributing of the brandy, are in Waterford crystal brandy sniffers. It is performed by Austin Hamish, now the oldest male Stevens. The adults raise their brandy sniffers high. "Wait, before you drink," Anna Lee calls out. "Austin Hamish, please make a toast," gazing fondly at her son Anna Lee requests. Upright and stately like his Dad, Austin professes, "To an honorable, brave Civil War military Captain; a devoted husband, I offer this toast to a man I am proud to call father, Austin O'Brien-Stevens!" "Hear, hear!" they all respond. "Well said!" Zeke exclaims. Solemnly Zeke murmurs, "To think Mr. Stevens was badly wounded in the war; almost killed many times and survived." Looking over at Anna Lee he adds, "Thankfully he died peacefully in the arms of his devoted wife." The adults shout again, "Hear, hear!" then drink the brandy. With lovely, blue misty eyes, daughter, Rachel Melanie, glances over at her teary-eyed 'mother dear' including, "I must add, to a wonderful 'mother dear' who kept this family together after one tragedy after another." Rachel Melanie recalls, "My sister Theresa Edith's sudden death the day my brother and I were miraculously born, and years ago, when her beloved husband, our dear father, died suddenly of a stroke right here in this very room as they were quietly sitting together near this very fireplace." *With a multitude of respect and love surrounding them, the somber memories are palatable.*

Moving on, smiling Austin Hamish glances over at Zeke and inquires, "How are you doing, Zeke?" In good faith, Zeke nods his head affirmatively. "Zeke, we can never thank you enough. After my father decided to raise sheep here in the states due to the horrific loss in Australia and he dying suddenly leaving my helpless mother at a loss as what to do, you came to her and the farms' rescue," Austin Hamish acknowledged Zeke. "My mother could never have stayed here alone without your presence," Rachel

Melanie appreciates. Anna Lee quickly adds, "As in the bible: 'Like sheep in the midst of wolves,' you saved our family Zeke. You stayed to help raise the sheep and remarkably kept the farm financially profitable." Zeke is humbled, "Please, I did nothing compared to what your husband and father did for me years back. Mr. Stevens saved me from poverty and loneliness." Pausing, Zeke murmurs, "He even took in my daughter Nannette; a complete stranger." Zeke blurts out, "I owe him my life!" Anna Lee murmurs, "As the bible preaches: 'Be shrewd as serpents and simple as doves' that's our Zeke." Gazing fondly over the entire Stevens' family, shyly Zeke praises, "I thank you all!"

Sweet and compassionate, like her mother, Rachel Melanie politely inquires, "How are Nannette and her children doing?" "Good! I was just telling your mother earlier today how well they all are," as Zeke gazes over at Anna Lee with a grin. "Any news about Jeremiah, Mom?" Austin asks. "You mean Dr. Holden?" Austin Hamish's wife Eleanor questions. "Yes," he responds smiling at his usually quiet as a mouse wife. "Zeke knows more about him than I do lately, please fill us in." Anna Lee requests. "As you know, Jeremiah left Walpole years back when Nannette and her cousin Dr. Holden also left for New Orleans, Louisiana," shares Zeke. "Jeremiah never took a dime from his late wife's estate; it all went to charity." Anna Lee adds, "Thankfully, Dr. Holden inherited a small trust fund from his late father." Zeke jumps in adding, "The good veterinarian invested it in a farm where to this day he tends to and care's for old abandoned and sick horses." "That is extremely impressive!" Austin Hamish remarks. "Sure is, Master Stevens. Those poor helpless horses would have been shot and used for food," boldly Zeke praises Dr. Holden.

Noticing the time, the women excuse themselves. They head to the kitchen to attend to the Thanksgiving feast. Rachel Melanie's husband Dr. Thomas Pharrell stays with the men and children who are seen and not heard. "As a physician, I admire and appreciate what the good Dr. Holden is doing. As a healer, whether for man or beast, it is laborious and only altruistic people should be doing it," Anna Lee's son-in-law Dr. Thomas Pharrell proclaims. Pouring more brandy in the men's sniffers, Austin Hamish shouts out, "Hear! Hear!" The men, Austin Hamish, Zeke, and Thomas Pharrell drink their brandy down quickly. "Where are the cigars

Zeke? My father must have hidden them somewhere around here?" Austin Hamish inquires.

Within an hour, the women carry the plentiful Thanksgiving dinner into the dining room and place it on the large oval-wooden dining room table. Candles are lit, a center piece of natural pumpkins garnished with vibrant leaves grace the table. The fabulous aroma from the turkey and other homemade fare fills the room stimulating the waiting family's taste buds. Seated, everyone is ready to bow their heads and listen to son Austin Hamish offer a prayer of Thanksgiving. As he rises, a knock on the backdoor startles everyone.

Zeke gets up and heads to the kitchen door. He is flabbergasted and overjoyed to see his daughter Nannette, her husband George Mann, and their son Louis standing there shivering. "Oh, my, my! My sweet Nannette, George, and Lou Zeke, my grandson, it does my heart good to see you," Zeke cries out. "This is truly one of the best Thanksgivings ever," Zeke shouts out overwhelmed and feeling no pain from the brandy.

Looking back outside, Zeke inquires, "Where's my granddaughter Elizabeth Amanda?" "Dad she is in nursing school and unfortunately unable to join us." Pecking her disappointed father's check Nannette banteringly comments, "Ezekiel, hopefully you will see her Christmas, if you ever decide to come visit us in New Orleans." "Ezekiel? No one has called me that in years except for your mother Louisa. We'll discuss Christmas later; now follow me," hurriedly Zeke orders. Changing the delicate subject, Zeke comments, "Anna Lee and her family will be so pleased to see you all."

Zeke leads Nannette and her family to the dining room. The others are surprised and thrilled to see them. "I am overly delighted you came," Anna Lee comments. Glancing behind them, she questions, "Where is Jeremiah?" Son, Austin Hamish interjects, "Mother, first things first; let's welcome them properly." Head of the family, Austin Hamish turns to the surprised guests cordially requesting, "Let me take your outer garments." When Nannette takes off her magenta wrap, Zeke notices the gold heart locket she is wearing around her neck. He recalls, it was the one he gave Nannette's mother Louisa years ago. It holds a miniature photo of Louisa in it. Miss Elizabeth from the orphanage found the locket with the items young Nannette came with years ago. She put it away for safe keeping and gave it to Nannette along with the magenta shawl when she left the orphanage.

Putting the clothing items away, Austin Hamish returns and warmly remarks, "Please be seated at the table. There is an over abundance of good food." At first shocked seeing them, Anna Lee is remote. Recognizing her rudeness, Anna Lee rises from the table, goes to Nannette, hugs her apologizing, "I must ask for your forgiveness for my being dismissive. I am taken back by your coming but overly delighted you did." Glancing at Zeke, she adds, "I didn't tell your father that I invited you." Smiling, Zeke nods at Anna Lee. Finally settled Austin Hamish offers a pithy, pleasant blessing. He carves the turkey, places slices on plates and passes them to the guests. Rachel Melanie, taking on the role of her mother, passes the various side dishes to the famished family and guests. When the meal is completed, Rachel Melanie and Eleanor insist that Anna Lee stay at the table while they remove the dishes and food and take them into the kitchen.

Not one to sit idle or interested in hearing the men talk business and politics, Anna Lee excuses herself from the dining room table. She slowly walks to the kitchen. Inquisitive Anna Lee is anxious to question Nannette about Jeremiah who lives and runs a horse farm outside New Orleans. Regrettably Anna Lee has had no correspondence with him for a while. Fortunately, she was able to get a message to Jeremiah about the sudden death of her husband Austin.

Austin Hamish, Zeke, Thomas and George, excluding young Louis, are now comfortably sitting in the parlor near the fire smoking fine Cuban cigars. Where, unbeknownst to Anna Lee, Zeke knew where Austin, Sr. hid them. They were in the harpsichord bench, the one Anna Lee's parents sent her as a gift years back. While Nannette and Eleanor are putting dishes away and retrieving small dessert plates for the homemade apple and pumpkin pies to be served shortly, Anna Lee interrogates Nannette. "Now that you are settled in and your hunger abided Nannette, please explain to me why Jeremiah chose not to come with you today?" concerned Anna Lee questions. "Sit down Anna Lee," calmly, Nannette suggests.

Eleanor, Austin Hamish's wife brings her mother-in-law over and places Anna Lee on a kitchen chair. Nannette, having Anna Lee's full attention, is ready to respond. "Like my father Zeke, I am not much for words," Nannette comments. "Therefore, I will cull my response to your question." "You have my undivided attention," Anna Lee says. Nannette responds, "Aging has not been kind to Jeremiah. His doctor originally thought he had the gout; but not so. Rheumatoid Arthritis, the final diagnosis, is extremely painful and crippling." Putting her hands to her face, "I am deeply distressed hearing this," Anna Lee sighs adding, "It must be difficult for Jeremiah since he never married and lives alone." Teary eyed, Ann Lee questions, "Who cares for him?" Clasping Anna Lee's tender hand Nannette responds, "My husband George and son Louis frequently assists him with the horse farm. I send over food and visit him whenever I can." "How very kind of you Nannette, your husband, and son." "Jeremiah is family and we are more than pleased to do it," Nannette interjects. "Is Jeremiah happy?" Anna Lee asks. "Please do not fret, Anna Lee, my cousin Jeremiah is handling it well. The horses he saved and cared for are his family and his salvation." Nannette is laughing uncontrollably. She chokes out, "He does enjoy his life. One Halloween years back he dressed as the Headless Horseman and rode around his farm petrifying the little children who came to see the horses." The women laugh. "Underneath that dark mood persona, my cousin Jeremiah has a humorous side too," Nannette offers.

Something awakens in Anna Lee. She recalls, "Years back I remember when we hardly knew Jeremiah and sorry to say had a faulty opinion of him, he was leaving our farm on his sleigh down extremely icy Watkins Hill Road. Jeremiah's sleigh was pulled by his magnificent black horse Diablo. Sadly the horse skidded, fell, and broke his leg." Moaning, Anna Lee informs, "Jeremiah had to shoot poor Diablo." Looking directly at Nannette she adds, "Your dad Zeke, along with my late husband, blamed Jeremiah for his horse's deadly accident. When I hear now how caring and loving he is to damaged, abandoned horses and devoted his life is to them; poor Jeremiah was gravely misunderstood." Nannette interjects, "Perhaps his undying devotion to sick horses is how he is making amends for what happened to his beloved Diablo." "I pray, in his old age and alone, Jeremiah is properly taken care of," Anna Lee expresses her desire.

Pecking Anna Lee's drained compassionate face, Nannette reveals, "For years now I have been corresponding with Miss Elizabeth, as has my daughter Elizabeth Amanda whose name is Elizabeth in honor of that remarkable woman." "Wonderful!" Anna Lee interjects. "Miss Elizabeth is old now and has no one to care for her. Her adopted son James moved to Texas and has a café there. My husband George and I have offered to have her come live with us. We also offered this opportunity to my cousin Jeremiah." "How very kind and generous of you," Anna Lee reiterates. "Elizabeth accepted. I know her presence will not only comfort us but also Jeremiah." Nannette shares. "This news comforts and pleases me," contentedly Anna Lee remarks. Smiling Nannette announces, "Jeremiah sends his heartfelt love to you." Hearing this, Anna Lee beams brightly. Listening to the women chatting, Rachel Melanie, who was in the dining room putting items away, enters the kitchen. "Mother dear, are you alright?" she inquires. "Yes, perfectly fine," Anna Lee assures her daughter.

Nannette is sitting next to Anna Lee. Noticing something shiny around Nannette's neck, Anna Lee takes hold of it. It is the gold heart shaped locket. "Is this the locket with your mother's picture in it? The one your Dad gave her years back?" inquisitive Anna Lee asks Nannette. "Yes it is. I never take it off. The only time I will is when I present it to my daughter Elizabeth Amanda the day she gets married," emotionally Nannette responds. Quiet-as-a-mouse, observing and listening to the two women, Ann Lee's daughter-in-law Eleanor is deeply moved. Shyly she comments, "I am so blessed to be a part of this fine family where loyalty and love are abundant in the O'Brien-Stevens family." Jumping up, Nannette blurts out, "O'Brien!" Glancing over at Anna Lee, she cries out, "Oh my, I never knew Miss Elizabeth's last name until recently. It is Elizabeth Margaret O'Brien!"

CHAPTER FIFTY-NINE

Whose That Pretty Lady?
Jersey City, New Jersey
July 1956

HAVING JUST RETURNED from California a few days ago, Elena is walking down Armstrong Avenue heading back to her home. She was visiting her best friend Ginny. As she is strolling down the street, a car pulls over and the fellow driver whistles and calls out, "Who's that Pretty Lady." He drives away. Although Elena is excited to be back home with her mother and father and seeing her Aunt Ettie, she is missing California. Grandma Hollywood turned out to be a true and caring mentor for Elena. As much as she hated eating peaches and watermelon with cottage cheese every day, and having her clothes handpicked for her, for once in her life she felt pretty, confident and had a vision of what she hoped her future would be.

Arriving at 391 Armstrong Avenue Elena rushes up the front stoop, opens the door to be greeted by her older cousin Rosaria. She is clutching her baby daughter Carla tightly in her arms. "My goodness, if it isn't Elena," she calls out. Rosaria looks Elena up and down adding, "I hardly recognized you. You changed so much since I last saw you." "You look different also Rosaria holding a baby," surprised, Elena comments. Rosaria is not sure how to explain the baby to Elena. "I guess with all that has been going on here with your Dad, and you being away, I assume no one told you I had a baby," Elena's older cousin Rosaria remarks. "My Aunt Mary Grace, who now lives and works in Hollywood, mentioned something to me while I was there," peeking at the baby Carla tactfully Elena responds. "She's cute," smiling Elena says. "Thank you Elena. Are you going upstairs to be with your parents? Your mom and dad are downstairs with my Mom." Rosaria opens the door for Elena. "Go on in. As sick as my Mom is, she made homemade cookies," annoyed Rosaria mocks. With the door open, Robbie Savini walks out carrying a diaper bag and a baby bottle. Staring at Elena, Robbie comments, "Who do we have here? You're pretty as a picture." "Robert!" "That's Elena; my cousin. Mike's daughter," cries out Rosaria. "Wow, Elena. I didn't recognize you. You look like a movie star. I heard you were in Hollywood. You sure had a makeover," winking at Elena he murmurs. "Robert, we must get going. I want to be back to help my mother. She's not doing well today," Rosaria murmurs. "Not well? My Dad and Mom said she's better!" upset Elena moans. Baby Carla Antonella is fussing. Rosaria and Robbie say their goodbyes and head down the porch. "She sure lost a lot of weight and her long silky hair is no longer short and frizzy," kindly Robert comments to Rosaria. Soon after, Elena enters her Aunt Ettie's place. "Mom, Dad, Aunt Ettie. Guess who?" Elena is trying to lighten the mood in Ettie's somber place.

Hearing Elena call out, a full-blown pregnant Eileen rushes up to her whispering, "Please be quiet. We just gave your Aunt Ettie another pain killer so she can rest. We waited to give it to her since she wanted to be alert so she could hold her granddaughter Carla," Eileen informs. "My parents are here?" Elena inquires. "Yes, they're in the kitchen. They've been waiting for you," Eileen says. "Elena, I want to say how happy I am that you are home. You've grown up so much in a few months and look gorgeous. I'm sure Tony and Juan will be surprised to see how much you have changed," Eileen says while leading Elena into the kitchen.

Seeing her parents, feeling enraged, Elena questions, "I thought you told me Aunt Ettie was better? Rosaria told me that she is not well today. I'm not a child; please tell me the truth!" Shushing her, Mike instructs, "When we're upstairs Elena, I promise you we'll share all we know." Agreeing, Tess admonishes, "Your father's right Elena. This is not the time or place to discuss this." Understanding, Elena nods agreeably.

The doorbell rings. Eileen rushes to answers it. Standing there is Dr. Saul Sacks. Tess contacted him earlier urgently requesting he come to check on Ettie. She informed him, "Even with the increased pain killers, Ettie is still writhing in pain." Mike is devastated by his sister's unsuspected illness. He instructs Tess and Eileen to be with Dr. Sacks since he is angry Dr. Sacks' son David has not made good with his niece Rosaria and fears he might lose his temper. Mike and Elena go upstairs and leave Tess and Eileen with Dr. Saul Sacks.

Upstairs, Mike's law books are spread all across the dining room table. Elena walks over and opens a large book, glances at it commenting, "This looks like Greek to me Dad. I don't know how you can study at your age especially with Mom hovering over you?" "No worries, I have my studying and your mother under control." They both go into the kitchen. Mike opens a bottle of grappa and pours himself a glass. "You don't mind do you Elena? I need this for medicinal purposes," he winks at her. Under his breath he says, "It's been a tough couple of months." Leaving the kitchen, Elena saunters over to the piano in the living room. She sits on the bench. After drinking his grappa, Mike goes into the living room. Walking over to Elena where she is sitting on the piano bench he says, "Okay kid what is it you want to know? I owe it to you."

Weeping, Elena questions, "Dad, are you sure all those bad guys are no longer able to hurt you or anyone?" Putting his strong arms around Elena, Mike moans, "Oh, my poor, poor daughter, what have I put you and your mom through?" He glances directly into Elena's dark brown eyes, mirrors of his own, Mike assures, "Have no fear daughter of mine, blood of my blood, those rotten no good bums are permanently where they belong." He kisses the top of Elena's head sharing, "I've changed my life Elena. I'm walking the straight and narrow." Elena hugs her dad as he further promises, "I swear to you Elena Rose, I will make you, your Mom and my sister Ettie proud of me."

Doubtful and fearful Elena pleads for reassurance, "Are you sure Dad all of those sinister creeps are put away forever?" "Yes! The police extradited them back to Mexico. They are safely locked in jail for life. What makes you doubt me?" concerned Mike asks. Looking straight at Elena's perplexed face, suspecting she knows more he further questions, "Do you know something I don't know?" Nervous Elena answers, "No Dad! I just want to be certain you will be safe." Not wishing her father to hear, Elena whispers, "I pray so!" The father-daughter tense conversation is disrupted hearing Tess calling them, "Mike come down; we need you!" Insisting, Tess says, "Make sure Elena stays up there and answers the letter

Rodney wrote her." Grinning at his daughter Mike jokes, "Rodney? You heard your mother Elena, get your pen and paper and snap to it." Elena makes a silly face at her dad. Smirking back, Mike assures Elena, "I'll be up as soon as possible. I have studying to do!" He kisses Elena's slim face and heads down to Ettie's.

When Mike enters Ettie's place, Tess and Eileen observe the tension between him and Dr. Saul Sacks. An old-time respectable professional physician, Dr. Sacks politely asks Mike to come in the living room to discuss Ettie's prognosis. Reluctantly, but anxious to hear about his sister, Mike follows the aging solemn doctor. "I will not mince words with you Mike, your sister Ettie is very ill," Dr. Sacks immediately says. Mike is shocked. "It pains me more than you know to tell you this," Dr. Sacks informs Mike. "Then don't mince words, give it to me straight!" Mike demands. "The tests came back. Your sister has pancreatic cancer. It spread all over and is inoperable." Distraught and speechless, Mike slumps over. "I pray God takes her quickly," the devoted family doctor and now grandfather to Ettie's granddaughter sighs. Placing his face in his shaking hands Mike moans, "To think Ettie saved my life and now she's losing hers." He stands up, stamps his foot shouting, "That saint of a woman never catches a damn break." Distraught himself, Dr. Sacks pats Mike on his slumped shoulders. "What I put that selfless, pious woman through these last few months is unforgiveable," moaning Mike cries. "Don't punish yourself Mike; this horrendous cancer has been violating and spreading inside her for a while." Dr. Sacks decrees, "I truly believe Ettie knew all along."

Attempting to console Mike, Dr. Sacks illuminates, "There is an old Jewish saying 'Days are long but the years are short.'" Reflecting Mike exclaims, "The years are certainly short in this family!" The flustered doctor expresses his grief, "I am sad that our mutual granddaughter Carla Antonella will never get to know Ettie, her wonderful maternal grandmother. Hearing this, Mike raises his head. He offers Dr. Sacks his conciliatory hand to shake commenting, "I totally forgot about that innocent child Carla Antonella." With sudden awareness, Mike looks into Dr. Sacks' soulful eyes saying, "We are truly family now!" Silently Tess walks into the living room. She is relieved seeing Mike and Dr. Sacks shaking hands and then patting each other's back. With joy there is also sorrow. Sadly, Tess and Eileen will soon learn about Ettie's devastating, fatal prognosis. *Bless the Innocents.*

Bored, antsy, and anxious to show her mother the letter she wrote in response to the one Rodney sent her, Elena runs down the stairs. Carefree she bursts into her Aunt Ettie's place. Eileen is in the kitchen washing dishes. "Oh, Eileen. Where's my Mom and Dad?" Elena questions. "They're in the living room with Dr. Sacks," wiping her moist eyes with a dish towel, Eileen responds. "Why is Dr. Sacks here?" puzzled Elena asks. "You'll have to ask your parents," weeping Eileen responds. Hearing her daughter, Tess goes to the kitchen and places her arms around Elena. "What do you have here?" noticing the letter in Elena's hands Tess asks. "Forget the letter Mom; what's going on with Aunt Ettie?" Elena asks with a firm demanding voice. Followed by Dr. Sacks, Mike comes in the kitchen. Eileen offers, "I'll make a quick pot of coffee Dr. Sacks." "No, please don't bother. I will check on Ettie and then I must leave," the good doctor responds. "Make a pot for me Eileen." Mike requests.

The front door opens and closes signaling Dr. Saul Sacks has left. "Dad, Mom, what's going on with Aunt Ettie?" Elena demands. Hearing Elena's voice, weakly Ettie whispers from the bedroom, "My sweet beautiful Elena Rose come." Tess, Mike, and Eileen look at one another with concern. Not waiting to hear her parent's response to her question and hearing her aunt calling, Elena quickly heads to her Aunt Ettie's bedroom. As Elena enters her aunt's bedroom, emotional Ettie cries out, "Seeing you my precious niece, Elena Rose, makes my heart leap for joy." Hearing Ettie's tender words to Elena Mike comments, "For my Sister, there is no better medicine than Elena." Walking over to her husband Mike and kissing him, Tess echoes, "That's what Ettie always preached..." *Blood is thicker than water.*

CHAPTER SIXTY

That's Amore
Hollywood, California
Spring 1956

CLEO, THE SPOILED Cocker Spaniel, hearing the door open, springs to his feet and clip claps over to see who is coming. Walking in Mary Grace, Regina, and Rodney are chattering away. "Thought you'd never come home; look what time it is?" annoyed Grandma Hollywood hollers from the bedroom. "Mom, we had to stay at the studio late; there were a lot of retakes," Mary Grace calls back. Regina and Rodney rush into the kitchen and pour themselves a glass of ice tea. "Do you want Oreo's?" Regina asks Rodney as she grabs carrots out of the refrigerator. "Do you even have to ask?" he teases her. Smiling Grandma Hollywood, in a long silk Chinese robe, her coarse gray hair piled up with bobby pins, hollers, "Rodney, Rudolpho and Mateo have tried in vain to get you to eat healthy," attempting to grab the cookie out of his hand. He swallows it down whole. With the mail in her hands, upset, Mary Grace rushes in admonishing, "Mom, these have been in the mailbox for days now! What's wrong with you?" "I'm not sure what you mean? It's Sunday; we never get mail delivered on Sundays," mixed up her mother responds. Since it is Wednesday, the others look at Grandma Hollywood with apprehension.

Temporarily ignoring her mother, Mary Grace hands a large envelope to Rodney teasing, "This is from Elena." Rodney reaches to take it from her hand. Mary Grace pulls back clutching it to her chest. "Stop playing games with me Mary Grace or I'll have you fired as script reader from my movie set," Rodney jokes back. "Stop you two!" dramatically Regina orders. Staring at Rodney, Regina warns, "You'll never fire or replace me. Don't ever threaten me, Regal Regina the star of your film or you'll be sorry!" She bows low. Smirking Rodney mocks her, "Greta Garbo at her finest!"

"Open your letter, Rodney," Mary Grace insists. He rips the large envelope; takes out the multiple pages; reads a few lines; and shouts, "Wow!" "Wow, what?" in unison, Mary Grace and Regina call out. Shoving another Oreo cookie in his mouth as Grandma Hollywood takes one too, Rodney ignores them. Mary Grace pulls the sheets of paper out of Rodney's hands and sits down at the table. Quietly she reads it in total. Wiping her teary eyes, Mary Grace gazes over at patient but anxious Grandma Hollywood, Regina, and Rodney. "Sit down all of you," Mary Grace orders. All three do so in kind. "This letter has a lot in it. I'll sum it up as quickly and as best I can," Mary Grace alerts the three. "After reading this, I appreciate your 'Wow' Rodney." He grins at her. Mary Grace shares, "Elena immediately opens her written letter with:"

> *My dear Aunt Ettie passed away last week after a brave battle with pancreatic cancer. Rosaria, my Aunt Ettie's daughter, along with her baby Carla Antonella, named after my late Uncle Carlo and Aunt Ettie, lived and cared for her mother during her illness. My dad Mike is in his last year of law school. My mother Tess is teaching creative writing at Jersey City State College where I will also apply. Eileen and Tony, my father's foreman of the burnt down garbage company and his Irish wife have a new baby, a son named Antonio Miguel Sean, Miguel, Michael, named for my Dad. Eileen and Tony, who purchased my Dad's friend Mr. Walsh bar and turned it into a cafe/tavern. It is doing extremely well. Tony's daughter Angela Maria serves her empanadas to the delight of the expanding cafe/tavern customers. Juan who works there makes his famous tacos to be served as well.*

Sitting there in a daze, Grandma Hollywood interrupts, "Dear me, Mary Grace, I'm mixed up; who are you talking about? Are these friends of Rodney's and yours?" "No need to get upset Mom. I'll explain it all to you later. Go to your bedroom and get dressed." As Grandma Hollywood rises, Mary Grace informs, "Nunzio and Uncle Albert will be stopping by for a late dinner. I picked up a large vegetarian salad and a nice bottle of white wine." Grandma Hollywood shuffles toward her bedroom. Relieved she is gone but sad to see how she has been declining these last few months, Rodney and Regina encourage Mary Grace to finish her summation of Elena's informative letter.

Culling the lengthy, wordy letter, Mary Grace comes to an interesting paragraph. "How wonderful!" she calls out. "Wonderful! Don't pause; spit it out Mother," Regina insists. Mary Grace continues to read, "Rosaria finally got married. Unfortunately, a day or two before her wedding her mother, my dear Aunt Ettie died. My cousin married the love of her life." "Married! Ugh! I thought you said wonderful?" Regina blurts out. "For once, I agree with you Regal Regina," smirking Rodney comments. Mary Grace admonishes, "You two think you are so cool. For Rosaria, her little girl, and especially now, for deceased Ettie, this is wonderful news." "You have a short memory Mom; where did marriage get you?" Regina lectures her mother. Noticing she upset her mother, Regina attempts to smooth things over, "Didn't mean to bring that up Mom; forgive me." "It's okay Regina; we all suffered. Not only me but you and Tim also." She smiles at her daughter. Picking up the letter Mary Grace resumes reading Elena's revealing narrative, *"I'll close with this happy note, I have a huge crush on an older boy."* "Who?" surprised, Regina inquires. "She does not name him but I can feel her pulsing heart through the letter," romantic Mary Grace sighs. "Ugh," Regina cries out rushing out of the room remarking, "Maybe her infamous velvet slippers finally performed magic for my cousin Elena Rose." Mary Grace orders, "Go change your clothes sweetheart. Nunzio is coming soon."

Alone now, Rodney politely requests, "Since Elena wrote the letter for me Mary Grace, may I have it." Folding it neatly she hands it to him. "I fear you didn't finish or share all of it with us," confidently Rodney suggests. "Right you are! You're a very clever young man Rodney." She looks directly at him and comments, "After reading and editing your movie script, I'm convinced the story line did not come exclusively from your creative imagination." Rodney stares at her accountable. "Am I correct in assuming Elena and you are coconspirators or co-victims?" smirking Mary Grace inquires.

Rodney stops dead in his tracks. He courageously but coyly responds, "You are correct in your theory. I will leave it at that!" "You're an intelligent young man. I'm certain you got my niece's permission. If not, her father, Mike Policino, who will be a shrewd lawyer soon, will send you an official letter you might not want to receive about plagiarism," brilliantly Mary Grace cautions. Disturbing Rodney further, she adds, "Did you miss the class on copyright law in that exclusive New York film school you hope to attend?" Not waiting for his response, confidently Mary Grace rises announcing, "I have to arrange the light dinner ready for our guests." Swaying her hips, grinning ear to ear, Mary Grace makes a grand proud exit. Not one to get ruffled, Rodney gives Mary Grace a standing ovation calling out, "Bravo, Bette Davis. A great performance. You should be the star in *MY* movie."

Settling down, Rodney skims through Elena's letter. He comes across a section Mary Grace missed or deliberately ignored. He silently reads the rest of Elena's letter,

> *Please do not tell my Grandmother, my aunt or, cousin Regina this. Geoff, Aunt Mary Grace's estranged husband and Regina's father, has been accused of insurance fraud. If found guilty, he can face jail time. Ironically his so-called girlfriend or mistress, as Grandma Hollywood calls her, left him high and dry. Thankfully, his brother Army vet Danny, who everyone thought was crazy, has been staying with my cousin Timothy, the one who always aggravated me.*

> *Happy to report, Tim graduated from high school and is doing fantastic. Like his Uncle Dan, Tim is joining the Army any day now. Rumor has it, Tim is interested in a new girl; goodbye Nancy! I am still upset about Sister Margaret Mary and the past situation with Juan. Sadly and with much guilt there is nothing I can do about it now. Hopefully, someday I will be brave enough to let the truth come out. I will close now. I must get dressed.*

I am going out with my best girlfriend Ginny. We have a lot to talk about. Sometimes secrets between friends are the best. Good luck with the movie. I enjoyed reading the script even though I have my reservations. You sure have a bizarre, creepy, weird view on things, but I applaud you. Break a leg exceptional creature.

Rodney puts down Elena's letter, taking a deep breath he then resumes reading it: *Oh, by the way, Monsignor Jack Kelly and Monsignor James Cooney are retiring from their perspective parish and university duties-St. Victor's and Notre Dame. They are on their way to Juarez, Mexico to minister and help the abused, orphan children. No worries, a new young priest, Father Gerard Scarpetta, has been assigned to replace Monsignor Kelly and I am sure some young impressionable priest maybe a true "Fighting Irishman," will soon replace Monsignor James Cooney. I'll end this letter with these profound words, 'God Bless the Innocents!' Sound familiar? You'll always be my imaginative, craziest, dearest traveling, Hollywood conspirator and friend forever! Ciao, Elena Rose Policino.*

Ghost-white, Rodney carefully folds the letter saying, "I think I have to make adjustments to my script. I need a new ending." Rising, he pauses hearing a car pull up. He peeks out to the driveway. Nunzio is standing there. In a flowing white summer dress, Regina runs toward him with arms wide open. "Wish I had my camera," smirking Rodney comments.

Hand-in-hand Nunzio and Regina stroll slowly towards the patio. Rodney welcomes them and announces, "I must leave I have a heavy date with someone very special!" Before they respond, Rodney runs into Uncle Albert, Grandma Hollywood's bachelor sibling. "What is your hurry young man?" Uncle Albert calls out as he walks to the patio where Regina and Nunzio are now sitting side by side, hip to hip. Looking directly at Regina, Albert inquires, "Where is my sister Elena and your mother Mary Grace my niece?" "I'm right here Uncle Albert; Mother will be out shortly," Mary Grace says as she walks over and pecks his cheek. "How is my sister doing?" Albert inquires. "Sit down Uncle Albert. I would like to discuss something with you about her," Mary Grace comments. Albert looks over at Regina and Nunzio ordering, "Please take a walk you young lovers, my niece and I need our privacy." Regina grabs hold of Nunzio and coos,

"Come Nunzio, Cleo can use a walk." Like a lap dog, Nunzio follows her. Watching Regina and Nunzio strolling along hand in hand, Albert sings out, "*That's Amore!*"

"Before Mother comes out Uncle Albert, I need to share with you some concerns I have about her." Albert immediately requests, "I need a glass of wine my dear before you resume. I fear I know what you are going to tell me," he says. Having a bottle of Pinot Grigio icing on the sidebar on the patio, Mary Grace heads over, opens it and pours Uncle Albert and herself a full glass. "Prego," Albert singsongs while she hands him his vino. They both take a sip. "I will save you time, my dear niece. Your mother, my sister, has become forgetful, confused, and careless for a while now. I've noticed it long before you arrived here, causing me to discuss this with Dr. Rudolpho Della Porta. He claims that he also noticed the change in her," Uncle Albert shares. "What does the doctor and you think?" alarmed Mary Grace inquires. "Senility! Aging of the brain. She might do well seeing a neurologist before she harms herself or someone else," agonizingly Albert suggests.

"Well, well, well, look who the cats dragged in," still dressed in the kimono she wore all day, Grandma Hollywood shuffles in with no shoes shouting. Albert rises and clutches his sister's hand accompanying her to a chair. Grandma Elena sits. Her brother Albert sits next to her. "If you weren't my fiancé, I'll have my brother Albert punch you for touching me like that," Grandma blurts out. "Mom, this is your brother Albert. He is the reason you came to California to live near him. Remember he helped you acquire your position at the studio?" Perplexed Grandma asks, "He's not my fiancé?" "You have no fiancé, Mom!" Mary Grace admonishes. Lecturing Mary Grace, Grandma Hollywood says, "Mateo is my fiancé. We are getting married today. My brother Albert is coming shortly to give me away." "What?" shouts Albert. Seeing his sister confused, calming down, patiently he attempts to explain, "My dear sister Elena, Dr. Rudolpho Della Porta would be very unhappy hearing you say this. As you well know, Rudolpho and Mateo are exclusively committed to one another." Albert looks her straight in the eye reinforcing, "You and everyone in this special community already know this." Shocked, Mary Grace stares over at her Uncle. "What next?" she murmurs.

At this point, Grandma Hollywood is not sure what's going on. Noticing her mother's extreme confusion Mary Grace mutters to her Uncle Albert, "Absolutely. She needs to see a neurologist!" Feeling remorseful, Albert takes hold of his sister's arthritic hand kissing it gently. Entering the patio after their walk with Cleo, Regina and Nunzio observe Albert kissing Grandma Hollywood's hand. Regina giggles and pecks Nunzio's cheek. Seeing Regina kissing Nunzio, Albert sings out, "That's Amore!" Falsely believing this is her wedding day, Grandma Hollywood beams her infectious smile at them all as she boldly calls out, "Ah! Amore!"

CHAPTER SIXTY-ONE

*There is no Greater Agony than Bearing an Untold
Story Inside You* ~ Maya Angelou
Walpole, New Hampshire
Halloween 2007

"THERE'S NO MORE trick or treat candy left," Elena's husband hollers up to her. "Please honey, I have no time for this. The book signing is in less than an hour," calling from their upstairs bedroom, frazzled Elena answers. "Sorry dear. I'll shut the lights off outside. Hopefully none of those scary, adorable children ring the bell asking for treats," joking, he calls back to his wife. "As I warned you, you should not have picked Halloween to host a book signing," frustrated he remarks. "It's done now! Honey, I hope you're dressed appropriately and not wearing a costume," Elena hollers down.

The front doorbell rings. Elena's husband hobbles over to the door calling out, "Sorry, no more trick or treats here. A grouchy old witch lives here and didn't buy enough candy." "Excuse me sir, the book signing is tonight?" a woman with an accent from behind the door asks. Opening the door, he immediately apologizes, "I'm terribly sorry. Please come in." An attractive woman puts out her hand. As they shake hands she remarks, "I assume you are Elena's husband. It's a pleasure to meet you. I am Ventrice." "You have a lyrical accent. Where are you from?" Angelo asks. "I'm originally from the Caribbean island of Jamaica." "You're a little early. Happy to have you; come in the living room. Can I get you something to drink?" "No, thank you. I'm fine," Ventrice replies. "Let me take your coat. Make yourself comfortable. I'll go and hurry my wife," Elena's husband politely requests.

Elena's husband rushes into their bedroom. Elena is wearing a lovely orange sheath dress. "Was that Ventrice, honey?" she asks. He nods affirmatively. "She's always on time!" "Ventrice seems to be a nice woman," looking at his graying hair in the mirror Angelo remarks. Touching Elena's hand lovingly he questions, "You never mentioned Ventrice to me before." Smoothing her dress Elena informs, "Shortly before I retired, Ventrice was hired at Keene State. She's teaching Women's Studies and a new program African American Studies." "Interesting," he responds. Further explaining their relationship, Elena adds, "We're also in the same book club together with Sue Buffton and my Lit Loonies." Bending over, Elena slips on a pair of black velvet dress slippers studded with multicolored stones. "I can't believe they still fit," she whispers. The doorbell is ringing. "Honey, please hurry down and answer the door. I want to spray a little perfume on me. Then I'll be right down." "Arpege by Lanvin, your Mom's favorite perfume," winking Angelo says.

At the door, a middle age woman and man stand anxiously waiting to enter. Flabbergasted Elena's husband shouts out, "My gosh, I can't believe my eyes. Come on in. Elena will be so surprised!" Looking directly at Elena's husband the woman says, "Well, since we never got to go Trick-or-Treating as Jersey City kids, I thought I'd come here and go with my brother and best friend Elena." Angelo hugs and kisses his sister Ginny. Turning to her husband, he teases, "Tim, you old military badass, good to see you. It's been too long." Hugging like old buddies, Tim hollers out, "Where the hell is my cousin Elena; the one who I drove crazy with Regina?" Ventrice enters the room and introduces herself. Beautifully dressed Elena walks down the stairs. Seeing her best friend Ginny and cousin Tim, she screams, "Is this a trick or am I dreaming? Are you really here?" excited Elena cries out.

Rushing over to Elena, Ginny grabs her long-time best friend, squeezes her tightly saying, "No more begging for Thanksgiving or tricks kid. I'm your Halloween treat." "What's this I hear you wrote a tell-all book?" mocking Tim says. "Yes, Mr. Jokester, Elena's first novel and it's going to be a best seller," Ginny admonishes her husband. "You, my dear wife, might have come for the infamous book signing but I'm here for the food and booze," Tim jokes with Ginny. Looking over at Elena she points at her husband. "You have to excuse him; fighting in the jungles in Viet Nam touched him," embarrassed Ginny apologizes.

Patting Tim on the back, Elena's husband counter attacks, "Leave your husband alone Ginny; he's a hero in my eyes. Any person who fought in that ghastly war and came back alive in one piece deserves to be given the utmost respect." Looking directly at his sister, Angelo admonishes. Ginny adds, "I am proud of Tim. He went to Officer's Candidate Training School at Fort Bennington. He made a career out of the Army. After he retired from the Army as a major, he worked at the VA helping wounded soldiers." Elena adds, "My cousin Blaise was a Marine. He also fought in Vietnam. He is retired from the Marine Corps and is living near the Marine Corps Base Camp Pendleton, in San Diego, California." "Your cousin Blaise never married. Right Elena?" Ginny asks. Elena nods affirmatively. "I honor anyone who fought for this country," seriously Tim remarks. Mournfully Tim adds, "My late Uncle Danny was a true hero. As a young guy in Korea, he fought in the deadly battle of Pork Chop Hill and came home in one piece. Only his mental state was affected." Pointing at Elena's husband, Tim praises, "You're an upstanding guy, Angelo Cimino, and a great contractor." Joking Tim adds, "Must admit Angelo, I had my doubts when my younger cousin Elena told me she was going to marry you. Now I whole heartedly approve!"

"Those good old days in Jersey City are long behind us but never leave us," Ginny comments. Looking over at Elena she reminisces, "My best friend Elena marries my annoying brother Angelo and I, Ginny from up the block, marries your equally annoying cousin Tim." "Elena, who'd a thought?" grinning Ginny comments. "Amen," echoes Elena. "Let's have a drink and get this book signing party started," Elena's proud husband Angelo calls out.

The fabulous four, the two cousins, and sister and brother, married to each other enter the living room. Content, Ventrice is peeking at the books to be signed while enjoying the background music of Frank Sinatra singing: *The Way You Look Tonight*. Hearing the lyrics of this song, Angelo lovingly glances over at his sweetheart of many years. Seeing Elena bubbly and happier than ever, beaming ear to ear, he echoes, "When we are really old and gray, I'll think of you . . ." He sings, "And the way you look tonight." Sneaking up behind Elena, Angelo kisses his wife's blushing cheek. "Angelo, stop; you'll mess my makeup! Go offer our guests drinks," amusingly she reprimands.

A ringing doorbell prompts Angelo to rush and see who it is. Opening the front door wide, Angelo encounters five middle-aged women, wearing Halloween masks, mockingly hollering, "Trick or Treat! Is this where the book signing is being held?" Giggling one says, "Forget the book, how about some spicy, spiked hot apple cider." Still holding the door open, amazed Angelo stands there observing the Lit Loonies chatting away while heading into the living room where Elena is. Angelo is not aware of an older woman and gentleman standing there. "It's freezing out here Angelo; aren't you going to welcome your family in your house?" boldly Rosaria says. "Oh my goodness! You received Elena's invite? I never thought you'd come all the way up here from New Jersey," stunned Angelo calls out. Robert, Rosaria's husband, shakes Angelo's hand saying, "Long drive but my Rosaria wouldn't miss this for the world. She couldn't wait to surprise her little cousin." "Robbie, so good to see you. Wait till you see who's inside; some of the old Armstrong Avenue gang," excited Angelo announces. "You know Angelo, my wife Rosaria and I still live on Armstrong Avenue. Ettie left the house to Rosaria and Blaise. Blaise generously willed his share back to us," Robert explains. "Good old 391 Armstrong Avenue is still alive and well! I bet Ettie's good cooking aroma still surrounds the house," Angelo remarks. "Sure does and some!" smirking Robert remarks.

"What's all the noise out here?" rushing to the foyer Elena questions. Taking one look at Rosaria and Robbie, she literally screams, "Thank God! My prayers are answered." Standing back to get a good look at Rosaria, Elena sighing says, "I never dreamed in a million years you would make it." Glancing behind her she asks, "Your brother Blaise, did he come too?" "Blaise never leaves California. He's too busy playing golf," frustrated Rosaria answers. "And chasing young girls. He's a real Casanova. Nice to be a bachelor," teasing Robert remarks. "Robbie, do I hear a touch of jealousy in your voice?" Angelo jokes. "Come in I want you to meet my friends," proudly Elena says. Leading her cousin Rosaria to the living room she further questions, "How's your daughter Carla and son Robert doing?" "They're doing well. Both college graduates and working in New York. The

Big Apple, as they say," proudly Rosaria informs. "Carlo's grandfather Dr. Saul Sacks passed away a few years ago. As he promised, he left a sizable trust for my daughter, his granddaughter. Carla used most of it to go to New York University where her biological father David graduated from," Rosaria shares. "Does Carla have any contact with her biological father?" Elena whispers. No, not yet, but in time, I believe they will work out their differences. At least I hope so," Rosaria mutters.

Noticing unfamiliar people talking and drinking, Rosaria questions, "Who are all these people?" Pointing, "Those cackling women over there are from my literature group. Angelo coined them the Gang of Five," laughing Elena explains. "The attractive woman in that gorgeous vivid long ethical skirt is Ventrice, a Jamaican colleague of mine from Keen State," Elena informs. "Come with me, I'll introduce you before I formally greet people, read from, and sign books," excitedly saying while leading her cousin Rosaria over to Ventrice, the Gang of Five women, and Ginny and Tim, whom Rosaria already knows. Her Walpole friend, Elena's riding instructor, Sue Buffton is among them. Seeing Rosaria, joking Tim says, "Can you believe our mutual little cousin Elena married that skinny pimple faced Angelo?" Placing her hand over her husband's mouth, Ginny yells out, "Tim, leave my handsome brother alone. Remember what Mom always said, 'if you keep your mouth shut, you'll catch no flies.' Shut it!"

In the foyer, glancing around at the lovely surroundings Robbie remarks, "Nice place you have here Angelo. As a hot-shot teen riding your old bike up and down Armstrong Avenue in Jersey City and me in my broken-down hunk-a-junk car, I never thought you'd be living here and married to Blaise's sweet younger cousin, Elena." Grinning ear to ear, Robbie brags, "Now, she's a soon to be famous novelist from New England." Eyes moist Robbie adds, "The deceased good folks at 391 Armstrong Avenue, Ettie, Tess and Mike, would be so pleased and proud." Grabbing his arm, Angelo jokes, "Come on you old sentimentalist, let me get you a drink." Patting Robbie's back Angelo mutters, "No tears, only sweet treats tonight."

On a long large wooden table, near the mammoth stone-fire place with the large black A and S wooden initials hanging over the roaring hearth,

Elena's hardcover books are neatly stacked. There is a decorated table with beautiful autumn flowers, carved pumpkins, multi- colored gourds strategically placed around vivid autumn leaves and pinecones, all taken from Maple Ridge Farm. Placed around are a variety of tasty finger foods: Aged Vermont cheese and crackers, bowls of green and purple grapes, Angelo's favorite, miniature hot dogs wrapped in flakey dough and a tray of homemade cookies Rosario brought. Bridge chairs are scattered about since the sofa and chairs in the living room are not sufficient enough for seating.

Elena's plan for the evening is to first formally welcome her guests; read a passage or two from her book; answer questions; and sign books at the antique table. A classic Waterman pen is placed there for Elena to sign her book. The special pen is a surprise gift from her honey, Angelo. Holding a sniffer of brandy, realizing it is getting late, Angelo clinks the glass sniffer and politely requests, "Can I have your attention please; refresh your drinks and quickly find a seat." Quieting down the guests adhere to Angelo's request. Feeling no pain after a few drinks, smiling Angelo hollers loudly, "Let's get this party started! My wife, sexy sweetheart Elena, is ready to do her thing." Hearing Angelo's blunt remark, aghast, Elena shoots Angelo a monstrous look.

Beaming, Angelo escorts Elena over to the book signing table. Her family and friends eagerly await. Winking, Angelo hands his wife a glass of champagne saying, "Sip this Elena, it will calm your nerves." Accepting the champagne flute and smiling, she requests, "Thanks, Honey, now please sit down before I ask you to leave." The others laugh releasing Elena's frazzled nerves. Looking stunning in her orange sheath dress and special velvet shoes, Elena takes a deep breath then addresses her intimate audience, "As I look over at all of you, my heart leaps for joy. I am deeply touched, overwhelmed and extremely happy you all came tonight, Halloween, to support me as a first-time novelist." Her captive, warm audience smile back at her.

Raising up the book, Elena continues, "The book I am holding, which I will soon read a short excerpt from, was written with heartfelt tears, raw emotions, and ghastly, yet, healing revelations." She pauses and happily adds, "And many laughs." As Elena opens the book and is about to read, loud banging is heard from the front door. Annoyed, "Oh, no," Angelo jumps from his seat, shouting, "Hold on everyone; it must be those little monsters, trick-or-treating. I'll spook them and get rid of them in a flash."

Walking as fast as he can, arriving at the door, Angelo screams, "Go away! We have no candy!" The person outside behind the door shouts back, "Let me in. I brought my own candy." Peeking through the glass pane, Angelo sees a strange person standing there holding a box of chocolates and flowers. He opens the door ready to tell the intruder to leave. The stranger questions, "What took you so long Angelo? That's how you greet family?" Handing Angelo the candy and flowers he admonishes, "I almost froze to death out here." "Blaise Cortino!?" Angelo shouts. He immediately opens the door to let Blaise in, "All these surprises. I'm not sure my heart can take it," Angelo groans. Blaise asks, "Where's my little cousin Elena? Is she too famous now that she can't come and greet her favorite male cousin?" Shocked, yet excited for his wife, Angelo grabs his arm leading Blaise into the living room saying, "Welcome to Maple Ridge Farm. The home of the famous novelist, Elena Policino Cimino."

Angelo, followed by anxious Blaise, enter the living room. The guests look aghast. Shocked seeing his brother-in-law, Robert calls out, "Casanova arrived." Seeing her brother, Rosaria runs over to him followed by thrilled Elena. Sister and cousin hug and kiss him. "Enough you two; go sit down you can talk later," Angelo admonishes. Looking fondly at Elena, Blaise says, "I'm sorry I'm late; go do your thing cousin." While Angelo escorts Elena back to the book table, Casanova Blaise cases the group. He sits down next to beautiful Ventrice. "Is this seat taken?" flirting Blaise asks. Patting the seat next to her, Ventrice nods for him to sit. Observing this, Robert whispers to his wife Rosaria, "Your brother is a real ladies man." In defense Rosaria mutters back, "My brother, your best friend, treats our children like royalty. He's a terrific uncle!" "Agree!" hen pecked Robert murmurs.

Back at the special table, Elena politely apologies for the sudden disturbance. "Sorry for the interruption. He is someone very special to me and a huge surprise. My cousin Blaise, is the youngest child and only son of the dearest and kindest woman in the world." Looking over at Rosaria and Blaise, she resumes, "My wonderful Aunt Ettie. Sadly she is no longer here on earth. She is an angel in heaven now." Throwing kisses to Elena, "Thank you," Rosaria mutters. Angelo interrupts, "Aunt Ettie was the older sister of Elena's dad, Mike Policino, the best immigration lawyer and father-in-law anyone could ask for. He's in heaven with Saint Ettie and his feisty but fantastic wife Tess too." Pleased, Elena continues, "Okay, Angelo, I got this! Sit down and as you said earlier, "Let me do my thing!" Hearing about Ettie, Ventrice gently touches Blaise's hand. Smiling she whispers, "Aunt Ettie, the heavenly angel, is your mom? Good genes!"

Clapping and chanting, the guests call out, "Elena, Elena! Let's get this party started." Taking a sip of her now warm champagne, inhaling deeply, Elena commences, *After many torturous years of secrets hidden deep down inside my soul, my fears needed to be exhumed. Writing this book has been an essential catharsis for me.* Holding up the Waterman pen Angelo gave her, Elena pronounces, *"This pen is my sword. The written word is my strength. The aphorism, 'The Truth will Set you Free,' became my motto which carried me through this long arduous journey of revealing the unbearable truth."* Sighs and moans are heard from the audience.

Looking out at her guests with love, Elena continues, *"There are many remarkable people I must acknowledge for making this book a reality. People who gave me the courage to write it, to internalize, and finally release it."* Emotional, Elena wipes her eyes. Continuing she mentions, *My redheaded, fiery mother Tess Rapp Policino and my handsome, dark-eyed and haired, father Michael Nicholas Policino, who right up to the day he died, believed in 'family first' they were my role models.* The jokester Angelo calls out, "What about your handsome, dark haired husband, Angelo Anthony Cimino?" The audience boos him; then bursts out laughing. Teasing, Sue Buffton calls out, "Stop making a horses ass out of yourself Angelo." Bantering back Ginny yells out, "Can't take the Jersey City out of the boy!" Tim answers, "Give your brother a break dear." Angelo gives Tim a high five sign.

From the back of the living room another voice calls out, "Elena, what about the sexy blond bombshell, Mary Grace Rapp, your colorful aunt? My crazy brother Tim's mother!!" a stunning looking woman, standing next to an older, handsome golden skinned man shouts out. Shocked and shaking, Elena holds onto the table, almost falling to her knees. Everyone turns around. Getting her bearings Elena shouts out, "Regina! Nunzio!"

"How soon they forget when they become famous," standing in the back of the room, the attractive woman calls out to Elena. It is Regal Regina.

"You forgot me too? Your forever friend and loyal traveler on your journey in life?" Flamboyantly throwing Elena a kiss he adds, "Who will make a movie out of your book, if you allow me," a slim, blonde haired dramatic looking gentleman, with a rainbow-colored bow tie, holding the hand of a striking African American man proclaims. Finally recognizing them, Elena excuses herself to her guests, she rushes over to her cousin Regina and her life-time partner Nunzio. Quickly she hugs them.

Elena turns to Rodney calling out, "I can't believe you came?" "I wouldn't have missed it for the world," he says. Rodney takes Elena's quivering hand introducing her to his friend, "Meet Reggie, short for Reginald, my long-time, forever companion." Shyly Elena shakes handsome young Reggie's hands. Proudly Rodney shares, "Reginald Kola is an award-winning documentary photographer." Winking at Reggie, Rodney brags, "We just returned from Nigeria. We filmed a magnificent documentary on the abuses of women and sex trafficking around the world."

After greeting Regina, Nunzio, Rodney and Reggie, Elena turns and profusely apologizes to her guests. She pleads, "Please forgive me; this is not a Halloween trick but they are truly special people in my life. Ghosts of the past. Treats to savor." Calling out to the confused guests, Angelo points to the table filled with finger food announcing, "Looks like my wife Elena will be a while. Help yourself to our table of plenty and more drinks." Happily, the guests nibble and refresh their drinks while chatting about Elena's surprise family and friends. The unique and complex Halloween book signing party is going well. In a corner of the room, standing near one another, Ventrice and Blaise are enjoying a lively conversation with one another. Blaise says, "So, you're from Jamaica. I've vacationed there and love it." Looking deeply into her entrancing black eyes, Blaise whispers, "Perhaps someday we can go together." "You move fast, Blaise Cortino! I like that in a man," boldly Ventrice responds. Ventrice turns and looks at Blaise and asks, "What did you do when you retired from the Marines?" Blaise responds, "Moved to Los Angeles and went into real estate." Ventrice questions, "Sold houses?" He replies, "No, I bought strip malls and laundromats." "Interesting!" Ventrice comments.

After catching up with her California family and friends, Elena excuses herself and hurries back to the antique table. "Again, I am truly sorry for the interruptions. I promise I'll make my welcoming speech short," sweating Elena apologizes. Going back to their seats, the guests start clapping loudly cheering on Elena. Standing erect, Elena proudly announces, "I dedicated this book to my three sons." Sitting next to Angelo whispering, Rosaria inquires, "Are your sons and their families here?" Putting his fingers to his mouth to shush Rosaria, Angelo murmurs, "Sadly, no!" "Why not? They should be. Elena dedicated the book to them." "Long story. Let's give Elena our undivided attention for now."

Stately and confidently, Elena begins, *There are so many people, some worthy and some not so worthy, who have influenced me to write this book.* Stopping to gather her courage, she resumes, *After I retired from Keene State, I felt unmoored and felt I had no purpose in life. My sons grew up and moved on. Retiring, along with the loss and pain of the empty nest syndrome, I went into a deep and paralyzing depression.* You could hear a pin drop in the room. Elena had the audience in the palm of her hands. *After much coaching by my dear husband Angelo, I conceded and agreed to see a therapist.* Elena throws a kiss to Angelo and calls out to him, *It was one of the best decisions I ever made.* She resumes, *By unearthing my deep seeded fears, I discovered my depression was not from retirement or my sons' independence from me. It was deeply rooted in my past!* Hearing this, uncomfortable, the guests move around in their chairs. As Elena further delves into her reasons for writing this book, she captivates her audience.

An unbearable, unspeakable childhood memory was buried deep down inside of me it was the source of my latent depression. Glancing over at her honey smiling, Elena repeats, *Again, I must give credit to my persistent husband Angelo for encouraging me to sit down, pound on my laptop and as he profoundly said, 'Go ahead sweetheart, spill the beans.'* This humorous comment released the tension in the room. On a roll, Elena shares, *I instructed my honey, instead of the beans, I prefer to open my heart fully and face the truth.* Not a sound is heard from her audience. The warmth, genuineness and sincerity of Elena's words touched and moved everyone.

Standing up to defend himself, in a joking manner, Angelo exclaims, "Sweetheart I'm not an English teacher like you; I'm a down-to-earth Jersey City guy. A laborer who built houses." Taking a bow he says, "Spilling the beans is my truth." The female Gang of Five, Jill, Noreen, Ellen, Peggy and Helena, the infamous Lit Loonies, and friend Sue Buffton with humor, "boo" Angelo. The minority male guests laugh heartily.

With love in her heart, Elena winks at her husband and proceeds to read a segment from her book: *It's a bright, frosty Thanksgiving morning in 1955 in Jersey City, NJ. The young girl's mother and father inquire as to why she is not going begging for Thanksgiving; before her parents can question her further, she abruptly leaves the kitchen, in a flash, like a Time Traveler, she transports herself back to 1899 to Walpole, New Hampshire.* Stopping abruptly, Elena closes the book. Gazing over at her captive audience, Elena emotionally offers, "I'll end here in hopes I stimulated your interest, enticing you to purchase the book." Sipping the rest of her now warm champagne Elena nervously adds, "If you are so inclined, I promise you, you'll find out why this intriguing young girl harbors a devastating secret." Similar to a circus barker, Angelo rises up calling out, "Hurry, hurry, step right up to the table and buy a book or two." Glancing over at red-faced Elena, Angelo adds, "My Sweetheart will gladly sign it for you with a very expensive fountain pen!"

After signing a number of books and chatting with her guests; Elena places the gifted Waterman pen down; rises from the chair; and walks over to the piano where Regina, Nunzio, Rodney and Reggie are conversing with Ventrice and Blaise. "Well? How did I do?" taking hold of Rodney's arm Elena inquires. He pecks her cheek. Elena whispers, "Thank you so much for coming; I thought you were still in Africa?" "Your husband Angelo called us. He insisted we come. Angelo even offered to pay our airfare," Rodney explains. "We politely declined your husband's generous offer for the tickets. Reggie and I flew first class with Regal Regina and Italian, now gray haired, Stallion Nunzio," he further explains.

Before Rodney can talk further with Elena, Regina with a champagne flute in hand comments, "Nice place you have here cousin. Although, a little too puritan New England for me." "Well it's not Hollywood. I love it here!" Elena shouts back. "Do you have any ghosts in this haunted house?" joking Regina inquires. "Yes, oddly enough, we do! Read the book," sarcastically Elena lectures. Ignoring Elena and Regina, Rodney, Nunzio, and Reggie huddle near Ventrice asking her many questions. Blaise listens intently. He is clearly smitten by this stately, smart Jamaican beauty.

Pulling Elena aside, Regina sarcastically reprimands, "You beautifully acknowledged your father's family. What about Grandma Hollywood and my mother, your Aunt Mary Grace and me!?" Elena retorts back, "You know how much I love and miss them and you Regina but the book is mostly about Jersey City and Walpole, New Hampshire. Hollywood was an important part of my life but it is not the heart and soul of this book." Gently stroking Regina's hand Elena pleads, "Dearest cousin, you and your dear Mom are doing well. After Grandma Hollywood died from ovarian cancer, she generously left the house in Hollywood and her full membership to Author Murray Dance Studio to your Mom. Deservingly so since she devotedly cared for Grandma during her tortuous illness." Regina is not convinced. Trying to appease Regina, Elena mentions, "After your Dad came to Hollywood begging for your Mom's forgiveness they got back together. That's your and Tim's happy ending!" Elena tells her cousin. Tim, Regina's brother, overhears their conversation. He sneaks up behind them teasing, "Hey, Pick and Peck, let's leave the past behind." Regina moves away from her brother Tim, "Don't get involved, big brother, go back to Ginny. To this day I can't image why she ever married you," she lectures.

The cousins' bantering is abruptly halted as Rodney, sitting at the piano, calls out, "Can I have everyone's attention please; even the friendly ghosts who roam this place." Pointing at Elena he singsongs, "Will my talented, beautiful, Jersey City, Chicago, Hollywood, and Walpole New Hampshire traveling gal come here." Teasing, Angelo says, "Sorry Rodney,

Mrs. Eleanor Margaret O'Brien, the so-called in-house ghost left the premises." Heading over to Rodney smirking, Elena leaves Angelo's side.

Elena sits on the piano bench next to Rodney. "I have great news for you Elena. My handsome, cleaver Reggie was able to contact your publishing house and obtain a pre-copy of your novel." "What, why?" Elena questions. "We both read it. With your full permission Elena Policino Cimino; we are asking you to give us the rights to make a movie out of it." Everyone claps, shouting, "Hear, Hear!" "A published book and now, my little, chubby, cousin from Jersey City is going to have a movie made of it," Tim shouts. Embarrassed, to shut him up, Ginny places her hand over her husband's mouth.

Shocking everyone, Elena politely responds, "Thank you Rodney, but I'm not sure I want to give you the rights." Looking at his disappointed face, she shares, "There is someone else who deserves the credit. I might have written it; but there is another person more worthy who deserves the honor; one who lived it." Total silence in the room; even Angelo is speechless. To break the somber mood, Elena announces, "I neglected to mention, all the proceeds from the sale of the book will go to a special charity." "What charity? I hope it is the Retired Actors Guild," Regina chimes in. Embarrassed, Nunzio blurts out, "Silenzio; stai zitto."

Rising from the piano bench, Elena proudly announces, "All proceeds will go to a home for deserted, abused, violated, and deserving children from El Paso, Texas and nearby Juarez, Mexico." With this announcement, the Walpole folk are confused; the Jersey City friends and family are questioning it; the Hollywood snobs are aloof. "What is the name of this so-called special charity?" suspicious Rodney inquires. "The Sister Margaret Mary O'Brien School and Home for Children." The brandy sniffer falls from Rodney's hand. The large letters, A and S, hanging over the roaring fireplace representing Austin O'Brien Steven falls shocking the guests. "Spooky," Blaise shouts. "Voodoo?" Ventrice mimics. Angelo calls out, "Mrs. O'Brien rises."

Staring strangely at Elena, Rodney whispers, "I'm relieved. I thought you'd say, 'The Imposter Father Arthur Schultz School for Criminals.'" Noticing Elena is offended by Rodney's comment, he apologies, "I didn't mean to offend you or the memory of Sister Margaret Mary. I know how much she meant to you and how you both shared a horrible experience and secret together. Please forgive me." Wiping a small tear flowing down her now aged cheek, Elena responds, "Thank you Rodney; apology accepted."

Directing Rodney to a private corner in the room, Elena shares with him, "After all these many long years and writing this book as a catharsis, the horrible, painful sight of that wicked, evil imposter, beating and violating poor innocent Juan in front of Sister Margaret Mary while hidden behind the piano at St. Victor's, I still need to block it from my unbelieving eyes and wounded heart." Rodney takes her shaking body into his arms to comfort her. "After I read this part in your book, I wanted to find that immoral, rotten monster and murder him," he moans. Taking hold of Rodney's long, slim white, heavily veined hand, Elena strokes it gently.

Reaching for Elena's hand, Rodney gently kisses it. With extreme compassion he says, "Reading further about how you protected your innocent, hurting young self by taking flight to another time and place, I painfully realized it was your only means for mental survival." "Yes Rodney, it took me years to realize this too. It was the diary, photo album, and history book Sister Margaret Mary gave me about her family who lived in Walpole, New Hampshire in the nineteen hundreds from the Civil War up to the early twentieth century that saved me." Hearing her guests preparing to leave, Elena whispers to Rodney, "I must go and say goodbye to my guests." Rising, pleading she insists, "Please stay Rodney; we must continue this conversation."

With signed books under their arms, and a gifted Halloween Trick or Treat Bag from Elena in the other, the guests say their goodbyes. The devoted family and friends who traveled from New Jersey and California assure Elena they reserved rooms in the Watkins Hill Bed and Breakfast down the road. Professor Ventrice Jackson invites Blaise to accompany her to her apartment in Keene for a drink. He happily accepts.

With the front door open a bright spectacular harvest moon shines above. Elena and Angelo wave goodbye to their guests. Closing the door, Angelo grabs Elena around her expanding waist. He kisses her, then murmurs, "Sweetheart, you were fantastic. You spoke your truth from the heart; you had your audience in the palm of your hands. But most of all, you look fantastic in that orange sheath dress. Still sexy as ever you wicked witch." She smiles at him and prepares to go back to Rodney and Reggie. Winking at Elena, Angelo says, "We'll clean up later; let's go to bed so I can give you your Halloween Treat." Rodney, followed by Reggie, calls out, "Treats? Where's the candy?" Angelo, surmises his wife wants time alone with Rodney, graciously calls out, "Goodnight, Elena; I need my beauty sleep. Enjoy your Hollywood contingency."

Appreciating the closeness between Elena and Rodney and their past history, Reggie recognizes these two friends need time alone. He selflessly says, "I'll walk down the road to Watkins Bed and Breakfast now. I need the air and want to relish the brilliant starry winter sky out there. Hopefully, I might see that special Princess Angel star you wrote about in your book Elena." Lovingly, Rodney blows Reggie a kiss. "When you're ready to leave, take the rental car since you're a lot older than I am dear," teasing Reggie calls out to Rodney. Taking Elena's hand, Rodney leads her to the living room where the fire is diminishing slowly. While pouring brandy into fine crystal sniffers for herself and Rodney, Rodney asks Elena, "Is this Austin's finest brandy?" Glancing over at the corner smiling Rodney further inquires, "Is that the harpsichord Anna Lee's family gifted her with?" Pointing at a frame hung over the desk, Rodney calls out, "Oh dear me, there's the copy of the Braque painting you bought in Chicago." Beaming Elena gives Rodney the brandy. Elena raises her brandy sniffer. Rodney does the same; in unison the two long-time friends and conspirators call out, "Salute."

CHAPTER SIXTY-TWO

What do We do when Our Hearts Hurt?
Thanksgiving Day
Walpole, New Hampshire
2006

IT IS THANKSGIVING Day a few weeks after Elena Policino Cimino's book signing. A turkey is cooking in the large stove in the kitchen at Maple Ridge Farm. With apron on, Elena is bending over basting the freshly killed turkey. Hearing cars pulling up her driveway Elena anxiously rises. Knocks heard on the door puts a smile on Elena's face. She rushes to the door and flings it open. Piling in with heavily loaded handfuls of goodies are her oldest son Christian, followed by his wife Nathalie and daughters Tess Elena and Geraldine. As they are entering, a Porsche arrives with her youngest son Anthony Joseph and his wife Jenny and their daughters. Turning to her son Chris, Elena asks, "Where's your middle brother Nicholas?" Putting his arms around his mother, he reassures her, "No worries Mom, he'll be here." Anthony Joseph followed by wife and daughters Geralyn and Sophia Jane come rushing up to Elena. Lots of hugs and kisses are exchanged. Chris teases youngest brother Anthony patting his stomach, "Putting on a little weight, eh little brother." Retaliating back, Anthony rubs Chris's head saying, "I can see your balding scalp through your meager hair."

The women are in the house. The grandchildren rush into the living room and play the piano. Daughter-in-laws, Jenny and Nathalie, are putting food in the refrigerator with Elena's help. "Mom, how are you doing?" Nat asks. Jenny interjects, "I don't know why you insisted on having Thanksgiving especially since. . ." "Please Jen and Nat, let's not say another word," Elena blurts out. Wiping her eyes with the bottom of the apron, Elena explains, "Cooking keeps me busy and prevents me from thinking about the unbearable."

Outside, admiring the new black Porsche Anthony recently purchased, Chris remarks, "Nice wheels little brother. Best of luck with it." Solemnly Anthony turns, glares at his older brother muttering, "Only wish Dad was here to see it. I told him about it just before. . ." Patting his brother on the back Chris whispers, "I know. I'm still in shock." A roaring sound is heard coming up Watkins Hill Road. A blue Harley Davidson motorcycle pulls up. Their middle brother shuts off the motor, takes the helmet off his head and helps his wife Cynthia off the back. "Holey Moley, Nick, when Mom sees you on this she's going to go ballistic!" "Guess the women are in the kitchen?" handing her helmet to her husband Cynthia questions and heads into the house. "Where are your girls?" Anthony inquires. "Melody, my oldest, has rehearsals this entire weekend. She'll be performing in Handel's *Messiah* for the Christmas Holidays. My youngest daughter Madison is with her other grandmother visiting family in Cape Cod," while wiping his bike down, Nick responds. Teasing and taunting one another the three brothers suddenly stop and soberly gaze around Maple Ridge Farm.

Everyone is comfortably settled in the house. Drinks and nibbles are served near the fireplace in the living room. All are patiently waiting for the traditional big bird to be served. Finally, the huge holiday meal is ready. Elena asks everyone to come into the dining room. Prayers of thanksgiving and remembrance are said. The plentiful meal is served; the delicious food is eaten; the laughter; teasing, along with tearful memories are shared. When dinner is over, Elena's daughter-in-laws insist she go into the living room with her sons- their husbands. "You cooked this fantastic dinner. We'll clean up. Go relax," Jenny insists. "You must have a lot to discuss with your sons," serious Nathalie says. Older granddaughters, Tess Elena and Geraldine go upstairs to the guest bedrooms. With coats, hats, and gloves on, younger granddaughters, Sophia Jane and Geralyn, head out to the barn to visit the horse Buck III, dog Atlas, and cat Raven. "Be careful out there, girls. We'll call you to come in when dessert is ready," Jenny tells her daughters.

Near the fireplace, in the living room, Elena's sons drill their mother. Looking directly at his mother, Anthony says, "Sadly, we were not here for you Mom when you needed us the most. If it isn't too painful for you, please . . ." Wiping his sweating face, Chris interjects, "What actually happened to Dad!?" Mournful, Elena sinks deep down into the love seat and sighs, "It's still a blur in my mind. I fear my broken heart will never heal." To support her, Nicholas Michael goes over to his bereaved mother and takes her fragile hand. In a low tone, Elena shares, "As you know, it was Halloween, the night of my book signing. Dad and I were having a marvelous time; so many surprise friends and guests showed up. At the end, everyone left except my friend Rodney; his partner Reggie left to go to the Bed and Breakfast alone." "You mean the Hollywood duo Dad coined the Two Roaring Rs, Rough and Ready?" trying to lighten the mood up, joking Nicholas Michael questions. "Yes, they're the ones," Elena answers.

Anxious to hear more, Anthony hands his mother a tissue insisting, "Let's get back to what happened!" With tissue twisting in her hand, Elena somberly looks over at her distraught sons and resumes, "At the end of the book signing, Dad said he was tired. He excused himself and went up to bed leaving me alone with Rodney." Looking directly at her sons Elena continues, "The entire night Dad was in great Halloween spirits. He seemed perfectly fine," she says this while stopping to pat her misty eyes with the tissue. "I know this is hard for you Mom, but please go on," Anthony encourages. "About an hour later, Rodney and I hear this god forsaken loud crash upstairs. We immediately ran up." Elena stops to regain her control then continues, "My honey, your Dad, was sprawled out on the floor in our bathroom." Sobbing Elena places her hands over her face. Distressed and sad, Chris, Nicholas and Anthony comfort their grieving mother. Calming herself, Elena continues, "The EMT's came soon after Rodney called. The doctor at the hospital pronounced him DOA, dead on arrival." Wiping her flowing tears Elena cries out, "It was a brain embolism!" Her sons attempt to comfort their mother. Quietly the daughter-in-laws' enter the room. Cynthia hands Elena a cup of tea while

Jenny and Nathalie bring water to their distressed husbands. Sitting up straight, wiping her face, Elena puts on a brave front for her family's sake.

Lovingly gazing over at her sons and their wives, Elena requests, "While my granddaughters are occupied, I have something important to tell you." They all look at Elena with interest and concern. "Your Dad and I have been planning this for a while now. We put Maple Ridge Farm on the market early this fall." "You did what?" questions Chris. Ignoring him, Elena continues, "We received a great offer, more than we were asking. We signed the deal two days before Halloween." "You never told us?" shocked her three sons call out. "Please hear me out. I know this is a complete surprise to you. You have your lives and Dad and I had ours," courageously Elena remarks. "Who bought the house?" Chris asks. "Remember Mr. and Mrs. Ebenizer Johnson's son Daniel, the physician?" Elena questions. "Sure we do Mom. He bought the house?" Nicholas asks. "Yes!" Elena adamantly calls out. "But," Anthony exclaims. "Let Mom finish," Nicholas reprimands. "Yes," Nathalie and Cynthia agree. "Go on," Jenny encourages. "The closing is a week before Christmas. Dad and I planned to go on a holiday trip right after," Elena informs. "You were planning on being away for Christmas?" upset Anthony questions. "Yes, I will be away this Christmas!" Elena responds. "You're not going to spend Christmas with us?" Nathalie asks. Immediately Elena emphatically calls out, "No! I will not be with you Christmas. I'm going on a very special mission." "A mission? Does this have anything to do with your book, Mom?" Chris questions. Hesitating, Elena murmurs, "Sort of!" "You're not going alone. I'll go with you," Nicholas shouts. "No Nicholas I have to do this by myself." Hearing Tess Elena and Geraldine racing down the stairs shouting something, the conversation abruptly ends.

"What are you two girls so excited about?" Jenny inquires. Noticing items in their hands. "You girls had better not have gone up to the third-floor attic," Anthony reprimands. Red in the face both girls look guilty. Elena requests, "Come here. Let me see what you have?" Geraldine hands her grandmother a blue decorated jacket and a worn-out beaten up work jacket. Looking at it closely, Elena sighs, "My goodness, we were warned never to go up to the attic because of the ghost, Mrs. O'Brien who haunted up there." Chris, Nicholas, and Anthony take a close look at the clothing items. "Wow, this is an old Civil War Union officer's jacket," Nicholas calls out. Checking out the other jacket, Anthony says, "There's a name written in ink inside it. I think, Zak?" "Zeke?" Elena calls out. "It must be Zeke's," emphatically she reiterates. "You're right, Mom. Zeke it is!" Looking over at Geraldine questioning, Nathalie asks, "What's that behind you young lady?" Sighing she hands it to her mother Nathalie. "Oh my gosh, this is beautiful! It looks like a wedding gown," excitedly Nathalie says. "Please let me see it," Elena requests. In her hands Elena clutches an ivory silk, petite gown. Stroking it, Elena sighs, "Ann Lee's." "Did you say something Mom?" Jenny asks. Elena gently hugs the dress; she is elsewhere.

"Girls let's go and get the lemon meringue pie out of the refrigerator; we could all use some dessert," Nathalie comments. Going up to their mother, Elena's sons, individually assure their mother they will help her settle wherever she decides to go. "First things first," Elena insists. "I am leaving early Christmas Eve morning for my trip." Defiantly, staring at her sons, she pleads, "Don't try to stop me. I know exactly what I am doing. I'll be home for New Year's Eve." "You'll be with us for the New Year," her sons say in unison. "No, my cousin Regina and I have plans," smiling Elena informs her confused sons. "Okay Elena Rose, as Dad called you whenever he wanted to get back in your good graces, what ever you say!" Nicholas Michael promises. "As Dad always said, 'Can't keep a good woman down,'" Anthony remarks. The three sons smile knowingly at one another. "Where's the brandy or grappa? We can use it!" Chris questions. "Now you're talking!" Nicholas calls out. "Tomorrow is Dad's memorial service; we need to get our strength," mournfully Anthony remarks. The three sons hauntingly are silent; but only for a moment. Shouting is heard from the kitchen, "Come and get it! Dessert is waiting; especially Grandma Hollywood's infamous lemon meringue pie and Aunt Ettie's delicious cookies, Grandpa Mike's favorite," Cynthia calls out. "Taken from the recipe book Grandma Tess published," the giggling granddaughter's say, "Family traditions live on," Elena whispers. "Family First!" Anthony adds.

EPILOGUE

Hark the Herald Angels Sing
El Paso, Texas
Christmas Eve
2005

ON A WARM Christmas Eve morning, with suitcase next to her, Elena is ringing the doorbell of an old adobe building. "I'm coming!" a male voice is heard. The heavy solid pine door swings open. A dark skinned, dark haired older man looking stunned stands there. "Well, aren't you going to invite me in Juan?" smiling Elena questions. Grabbing and hugging her, Juan profusely apologizes, "I didn't think you were going to arrive this early." Lifting Elena's small suitcase Juan also reaches to take the large folder in her hand. "No, please; I want to keep this with me," she insists. "Come in; you must be hungry. Before the children come down to eat, I'll see if the women in the kitchen have coffee and rolls ready," Juan mentions while leading Elena into the large guest room. Looking around impressed, Elena comments, "You've done a marvelous job converting this old adobe mission into a wonderful residential school for the children."

A bell rings. The rustling sound of young people chatting and rushing around is heard upstairs. Elena stops to look up, seeing the well-fed, well-clothed once homeless children brings a huge smile to her face. Noticing Elena observing them, compassionately Juan mentions, "Elena, we're so happy you came; especially after just losing your husband Angelo. We pray for him daily." "I am happy to be here. Angelo would have come. God had other plans for him," she offers. Looking at him Elena implores, "Juan, while I'm anxious for you to give me a tour of this wonderful home and school, the main reason I came was . . ." Juan immediately responds, "Yes,

I know." Juan takes Elena into the kitchen and asks one of the ladies to give her coffee. "Wait here, I'll be back in a minute," Juan exclaims.

Elena just finished her coffee when Juan enters, "If you follow me Elena, I'll bring you there." Jumping up, taking hold of her large folder, Elena follows Juan. At an arched entrance, Juan leads Elena to a darkly lit small chapel. Holding rosary beads, a person is sitting in front of a statue of the Blessed Virgin Mary. "Go ahead Elena, I'll leave you two alone." Excited, but nervous, Elena quietly, slowly walks over to the wheelchair. Elena coughs, an elderly woman all in black raises her covered head. "Who is there?" with a low voice she questions. Taking her fragile hand, Elena whispers, "Sister Margaret Mary, it is the little girl who many years ago took piano lessons from you at St. Victor's parish in Jersey City." Straining to look at Elena closely she murmurs, "Dear Lord, if it isn't little Elena, Tess and Mike's daughter; the one who moved to Walpole, New Hampshire." "Yes," speaking loudly so Sister can hear, Elena responds.

Well into her late nineties, Sister Margaret Mary motions for Elena to sit in a straight wooden chair next to her. "Now tell me child, why did you come all this way from New Hampshire?" Sister asks. "I came here to return something to you; to gift you with something; and most of all to thank you," lovingly Elena answers. Opening the large folder she has with her, Elena takes out a worn-out book and a brand new book. First she places the older book on Sister's lap. "What is this?" grasping onto the item Elena placed on her. "It's your New England ancestors-family diary about the Civil War and other historical information about the O'Brien Stevens family. Remember, you lent it to me hoping it would help improve my history grade?" Stroking the book with her aged-veined shaking hand, Sister Margaret Mary murmurs, "My, my, how things come back to haunt you."

Taking out the new book, Elena says, "There's something else I want you to have." "No, my child." Holding onto the family album tightly, Sister offers, "This is all I need." Looking at the diary album, Elena continues, "It was the best gift I ever received Sister. It saved my life! It got me through the horrors we both experienced in the basement of St. Victor's with Juan." "Where is Juan? Every morning he takes me to the students before their classes begin. We pray together," Sister implores. "It is Christmas Eve Sister I don't think there are classes today," Elena attempts to explain. "We pray every day!" raising her voice Sister harshly comments. "Please let me give you this book first," Elena begs as she shows it to Sister. Gazing at it, Elena explains, "I wrote this book for me to heal from the trauma I experienced with you." Recognizing she might be too old to remember or not wanting to bring up past horrible memories, Elena closes the book and places it back in her folder. "Give me that!" orders Sister Margaret Mary. "My child, I might be old and senile but there are some things that are etched permanently in my heart and soul."

Tears are streaming down Elena's face. "Child, I never knew you were observing that fraud of a priest attacking Juan and then attempting to abuse me. My heart breaks thinking about it," Sister Margaret Mary moans. "How did you know I saw?" Elena asks. "When your Dad became a lawyer and made sure Juan's immigration papers were firm and he could live in America legally, Juan told me he wanted to come back to El Paso and help other poor abused children and protect them from people like that devil-in-disguise priest Arthur Schultz." Elena is shocked. "Juan told me he saw you hiding behind the piano and you saw everything," Sister reveals to Elena. She takes hold of Elena's hand and pleads, "Please forgive me for not being aware." "No Sister, thank you. After reading your family book and living my life through them, I thank you for being a shining star in my life." Sister Margaret Mary gently takes hold of Elena's hand murmuring, "Often the hardest person to forgive is yourself." *They have a spiritual kinship.*

Entering, Juan overhears this, he whispers, "Amen." Standing tall he reminds, "I hate to disturb you, but the children are waiting to pray with you Sister Margaret Mary." "I'll wheel her back; may I pray with you also?" Elena requests. Sister hands the infamous family-historical album for Juan to put away for safe keeping. Sister Margaret Mary holds tightly onto Elena's book. Relieved and happy Elena wheels Sister. The three, who experienced the unbearable together, all proceed happily outside to pray around the statue of Our Lady of Guadalupe. Outside Elena looks up smiling at the huge sign hanging over the entrance **Sister Margaret Mary O'Brien School and Home for Children.** Below is a smaller sign with the proverb: *The Truth Will Set You Free. Protect the Innocents.*

It is Christmas Eve. People are arriving to attend midnight mass. In the front of the chapel, the students in red and white choir gowns, with tongues of angels, are singing *Hark the Herald Angels Sing*. The altar is beautifully decorated with glorious red and white live Poinsettias and blooming Christmas Cacti. Sister Margaret Mary and Elena are sitting in front row seats. "Where is Juan?" Elena whispers in Sister's ear. She does not respond to Elena's question. In the back of the chapel, dressed in white and black are altar boys. One is holding a large Crucifix. Elena notices two figures standing behind the two altar boys. The Priests are regally dressed in traditional white and gold Christmas vestments. Three people sit down next to Sister and Elena; an elderly huge man, a petite older woman and a much younger, attractive dark-haired young lady. The man turns and looks at Elena wishing, "Feliz Navidad Elena Rose Policino." To Elena's surprise it is Tony, Eileen, and adult daughter Angela Maria Rivera. Ready to say something, in a hushed voice, Tony says to Elena, "Shush. We'll talk after mass." Eileen reaches over and proudly brags, "Our son Antonio Miguel, is carrying the Crucifix." Elena smiles.

The organ plays the entrance hymn. All rise; clergy, students, family and friends. Proudly holding the gold Crucifix high, Antonio Miguel marches in first. Followed by an elderly Anglo Saxon priest, after him, by a younger priest. Straining to make out who they are, Elena's knees shake as they get closer. "Is that Juan?" amazed, Elena questions. "Yes, the real Father Arthur Schultz ordained Juan a few years back," filled with pride, Sister Margaret Mary responds. "The authentic Father Arthur Schultz came to concelebrate Christmas Eve Mass with Father Juan tonight," Tony informs. As Father Juan Flores walks near Elena, he humbly bows his head. Sister Margaret Mary, Tony, and Eileen look at Elena lovingly.

The beautiful, memorable Christmas Eve Mass is over but it is just the beginning for many young, once homeless abused children, at this humble, charitable and compassionate place. Sister Margaret Mary goes up to her long-time friend, the original Father Arthur Schultz. She mournfully mutters, "It's a pity Monsignor John Kelly and Monsignor James Cooney couldn't be here to witness this special night." "Yes, Bless and Praise their souls, they truly deserve to be here to see Father Juan and I." Holding Sister Margaret Mary's delicate hand, the real Father Schultz praises, "They were instrumental, along with you dear Sister, saving my life and Father Juan's."

Elena recalls, "I fondly remember and cherish Monsignor James Cooney preaching, 'Protect the Innocents,' his blessed motto and 'The truth will set you free.'" These profound words were healing for me also Elena," Father Juan adds with much appreciation.

The joyful congregation is outside wishing one another, "Feliz Navidad." It is a glorious night. Gazing up at the brilliant spectacle of stars filling the dramatic night sky, Elena reflects back to Christmases past in Jersey City with her parents and Aunt Ettie; and in Walpole, New Hampshire with her honey Angelo and her three dear sons and their wonderful families.

Awed this Holy Night, a holy spectacle in the heavenly sky, the brightest star Elena has ever seen, beams down on her. This mysterious magical star mesmerizes and fills Elena with indescribable harmony. Staring up at the sky, Elena Rose Policino Cimino makes a wish: *My special princess angel, Theresa Edith, please watch over my Angelo, precious family, and devoted friends.* Elena Rose's heart is overflowing with joy. No Trick or Treats. No begging for Thanksgiving. "I received the best treat ever today. Praise God!" elated, Elena notes. On this Holiest of Nights, as the angels watch over her, Elena Rose finally finds eternal peace.

Everything you love will probably be lost, but in the end, love will return in another way. -Franz Kafka